French Tales of
Alien Encounters

FROM THE SAME PUBLISHER

Jean-Marc & Randy Lofficier. *The French Fantasy Treasury* (3 volumes)
Jean-Marc & Randy Lofficier. *French Tales of Cataclysm*
Jean-Marc & Randy Lofficier. *Shadowmen: Heroes & Villains of French Pulp Fiction*
Jean-Marc & Randy Lofficier. *Shadowmen 2: Heroes & Villains of French Comics*
Brian Stableford. *Automata: The Imaginative Legacy of Jacques de Vaucanson*
Brian Stableford. *The Plurality of Imaginary Worlds: The Evolution of French* Roman Scientifique
Brian Stableford. *Tales of Enchantment and Disenchantment: A History of Faerie, with an Exemplary Anthology of Tales*
Brian Stableford. *Weird Fiction in France: A Showcase Anthology of its Origins and Development*

French Tales of Alien Encounters

by
**Charles Cros, Paul Gsell,
Maurice Leblanc, Guy de Maupassant,
José Moselli, C. Paulon,
Maurice Renard, J. H. Rosny *Aîné*,
Edmé Rousseau** and **Paul Vibert**

translated, annotated and introduced by
Brian Stableford
(with the exception of *The Three Eyes*)

edited by
Jean-Marc & Randy Lofficier

A Black Coat Press Book

ISBN 978-1-64932-109-1. First Printing. February 2022. Published by Black Coat Press, an imprint of Hollywood Comics.com, LLC, P.O. Box 17270, Encino, CA 91416. All rights reserved. Except for review purposes, no part of this book may be reproduced or transmitted in any form or by any means, electronic or mechanical, including photocopying, recording, or by any information storage and retrieval system, without permission in writing from the publisher. The stories and characters depicted in this novel are entirely fictional. Printed in the United States of America.

TABLE OF CONTENTS

LES NAVIGATEURS DE L'INFINI

PAR

ROSNY Aîné
DE L'ACADÉMIE GONCOURT

LE RAYON
FANTASTIQUE

FOREST

Introduction

The theme of alien encounters runs throughout the history of the French *roman scientifique*—a genre that some might call proto-sf—from the 18th century to today.

We have gathered in this thematic collection nine remarkable short stories published between 1859 and 1939, plus a full-length novel by Maurice Leblanc—the father of Arsène Lupin. But there are other, equally remarkable, but longer works which deserve to be mentioned in this introduction for the benefit of those wishing to further study the amazing range of ideas and variety of styles in which this theme was handled by French writers in past centuries.

A number of these works have already been translated and published by Black Coat Press (as indicated in **bold**) and are available on paper or as ebooks on our site, *www.blackcoatpress.com*, on Amazon, Barnes & Noble, or wherever books are sold online.

The first alien encounter in French fiction is featured in Voltaire's classic *Micromegas* (1752), in which the title character, a giant alien from Sirius, accompanied by an equally gigantic Saturnian, comes to visit Earth. Even though Voltaire's primary purpose was satire, he nevertheless relied on well-researched scientific foundations for his story.

Micromegas was roughly contemporary with the Chevalier de Béthune's *Relation du Monde de Mercure* [**The World of Mercury**] (1750) (Black Coat Press, ISBN 978-1-61227-410-2), one of the few fantasies of the time unaffected by religious dogma. In this novel, which anticipates E. R. Eddison's Zimiamvian trilogy, Béthune describes in great detail a colorful utopia of immortal, winged beings inhabiting the planet Mercury. His alien world shines with originality, adventure and bizarrerie. The description of the aerial conflict between the defenders of Mercury and the monstrous invaders expelled from the "crust" of the Sun is eccentric, matching in its colorful extravagance any 20th century space opera. However, since Béthune watches the Mercurians from afar with a super-telescope, there is no actual alien encounter in the story.

During the rest of the 18th century, the theme of alien encounters, following in Voltaire's footsteps, was often a pretext for social satire. Two notable works fall into that category:

Le Voyageur Philosophe dans un Pays Inconnu aux Habitants de la Terre [**The Philosophical Voyager In A Land Unknown To The Inhabitants Of The Earth**] (1761) (Black Coat Press, ISBN 978-1-61227-367-9) by Monsieur de Listonai (the pseudonym of Daniel Jost Villeneuve) describes an Earthman's journey to the dark side of the Moon, which is reached via a flying galley, complete with pilot, navigator and crew. There, our hero meets a Selenite who takes him to the city of Selenopolis, built according to universal philosophical principles.

Fourteen years later, Louis-Guillaume de La Follie, a scientist and industrial chemist, penned *Le Philosophe sans Prétention* [**The Unpretentious Philosopher**] (1775) (Black Coat Press, ISBN 978-1-61227-136-1), in which an inhabitant of Mercury uses an electric-powered spaceship to visit Earth, but becomes stranded on our world when his ship crashes. This forces him to embark on a long search for the exotic materials required to repair it, giving him an opportunity to communicate his advanced understanding of science to an inquisitive Earthling. La Follie was the first writer to put the "hard" sciences of physics and chemistry at the heart of his work. His ambitious purpose was to communicate new scientific ideas by using what he saw as an entertaining fictional device.

Marie-Anne de Roumier-Robert's *Voyage de Milord Céton dans les Sept Planètes* [**The Voyages of Lord Seaton to the Seven Planets**] (1765) (Black Coat Press, ISBN 978-1-61227-446-1) leans more towards fantasy and fairy tales. In it, the eponymous hero and his sister travel to the seven planets of the Solar System on the wings of a genie. They discover that the inhabitants of each world represent a human character trait—Selenites (i.e. Lunatics) are capricious, Martians bellicose, Venusians lovers, etc.

A century later, Charles-Ischir Defontenay MD outdid the Chevalier de Béthune with his *Star, ou Psi de Cassiopée* [**Star (Psi Cassiopeia)**] (1854) (Black Coat Press, ISBN 978-1-932983-99-9). This astonishing novel describes in amazing detail the long history of an alien civilization from a far-off system with three stars and five planets. However, the only contact with our world is a treasure trove of documents hidden inside an asteroid that fell to Earth.

Les Aventures d'un Aéronaute Parisien dans les Mondes Inconnus [**The Adventures Of A Parisian Aeronaut**] (1856) by Alfred Driou (Black Coat Press, ISBN 978-1-61227-067-8) is a social satire in which the eponymous hero travels to the Moon in a hot air balloon and encounters an advanced civilization of Selenites. The book stands out as an anomalous item of its times, not merely for its imaginative extravagance, but also for its keen interest in technological progress. Predating Jules Verne by several years, Driou might be reckoned a pioneer in the popularization of science in France.

Henri de Parville's *Un Habitant de la Planète Mars* [**An Inhabitant Of The Planet Mars**] (1865) (Black Coat Press, ISBN 978-1-934543-45-0) describes how the calcified body of an ancient Martian, taken away from the red planet by a comet long ago, is dug up in America. Parville achieved a striking combination of quasi-non-fiction and speculative fiction, developing a theory of life in the universe that was ahead of its time.

Jules Verne, perhaps wisely, chose to avoid the theme of alien encounters; however, some of his successors were bolder.

The most ambitious were Georges Le Faure & Henry de Graffigny with *Les Aventures Extraordinaires d'un Savant Russe* [**The Extraordinary Adventures Of A Russian Scientist Across The Solar System**] (1888-96) (Black Coat Press, two volumes, ISBNs 978-1-934543-81-8 and -82-5). There, the eponymous Russian Professor Mikhail Ossipoff launches a spaceship from a canon built inside a volcano with a crew consisting of himself, his daughter Selena, her fiancé, a French polymath and an American tycoon. They reach the Moon where they encounter an ancient civilization. When Selena is taken prisoner by their evil rival, Fedor Sharp, the heroes pursue him in a jet-propelled craft to Venus, then in a solar-powered ship to Mercury. After many adventures, they embark on a comet and reach Mars, where they face new dangers. They pursue Sharp through the storms of Jupiter and the rings of Saturn. Then, chancing upon a means of faster-than-light propulsion, after a tour of Uranus and Neptune, they embark on the first-ever journey out of the Solar System, to Alpha Centauri and beyond!

J.-H. Rosny Aîné's short story *Les Xipehuz* (1887) (included in the Black Coat Press' **The Navigators of Space & Other Alien Encounters**, ISBN 978-1-935558-35-4) tell how primitive humans from a thousand years before Babylon encounter inorganic aliens, with whom all forms of communication prove impossible. Men eventually drive away the invaders, but the hero mourns the loss of another form of life. This was the first time that French science fiction abandoned the anthropomorphic approach in its description of aliens.

In 1896, Pierre de Sélènes penned *Un Monde Inconnu* [**An Unknown World**] (Black Coat Press, ISBN 978-1-61227-302-0), an unauthorized sequel to Verne's classic *From The Earth To The Moon*, in which the very same cannon was used to send a new crew of explorers to the Moon. There, they encounter the advanced civilization of the Meolicenes who live inside our satellite.

With a new century, and the brilliant example of H. G. Wells in England, French authors kicked it up a notch when it came to describing aliens, many of them turning their attention to the planet Mars.

Arnould Galopin's *Le Docteur Oméga* [**Doctor Omega**] (1906) (Black Coat Press, ISBN 978-1-0-9740711-1-4) features a mysterious scientist who uses a projectile-shaped spacecraft powered by a gravity-repelling substance called "stellite" to travel to the Red Planet. Mars turned out to be a primitive world inhabited by savage reptilian warriors and macrocephalic gnomes who attempt to seize the ship.

In Gustave Le Rouge's *Le Prisonnier de la Planète Mars* and its sequel, *La Guerre des Vampires* (1908-09) [collected in one volume as **The War Of The Vampires**, Black Coat Press, ISBN 978-1-934543-30-6), Robert Darvel, a young American engineer, builds a psychic-powered spaceship to travel to Mars. The Red Planet is elaborately described, with its fauna, flora and various races, not unlike in C. S. Lewis's *Out of the Silent Planet* (1938). Darvel runs afoul of Mars' hostile, bat-winged, blood-sucking natives, a once-powerful civilization now ruled by the Great Brain. (Perhaps the first time a giant living brain was used in SF!) The Great Brain eventually sends Darvel back to Earth with some of his vampires. The second volume deals with Earth's war on Earth against the alien vampires. Le Rouge's novel is unique in that it blends the two genres of planetary romance with Lovecraftian horror as the characters switch from swashbuckling he-men to helpless bundles of gibbering terror.

That same year, Henri Gayar wrote *Les Aventures Merveilleuses de Serge Myrandhal sur la Planète Mars* [**The Marvelous Adventures Of Serge Myrandhal On Mars**] (1908) (Black Coat Press, ISBN 978-1-61227-265-8). Gayar's Mars was inhabited by the Houas, small, red-furred anthropoids who live underground, and by the Zoas, beautiful winged humanoids, also referred to as Elohim.

Lastly, that same year, Jean de La Hire (the creator of the pulp hero The Nyctalope) penned *La Roue Fulgurante* [**The Fiery Wheel**] (1908) (Black Coat Press, ISBN 978-1-61227-217-7), in which five Earthmen are abducted in the eponymous spacecraft by aliens from Saturn, and taken to Venus and Mercury where they encounter strange lifeforms, before returning to Earth through mind transfer. The book is the first work to feature the theme of alien abduction, all the more remarkable because such abductions are achieved by means of a vehicle resembling the flying saucers we came to know many years later.

Jean de La Hire returned to Mars in *Le Mystère des XV* [**The Nyctalope on Mars**] (1911) (Black Coat Press, ISBN 978-1-934543-46-7), in which his hero, Leo Saint-Clair, a.k.a. The Nyctalope, fights the megalomaniacal Oxus, master of a secret society plotting to conquer Earth from a secret base located on Mars. After defeating them, the Nyctalope must then face native Martians remarkably similar to H. G. Wells' before embarking on the French colonization of Mars!

Maurice Renard's *Le Péril Bleu* [**The Blue Peril**] (1912) (Black Coat Press, ISBN 978-1-935558-17-0), which many consider to be his masterpiece, postulated the existence of unimaginable, invisible creatures who live in the upper strata of the atmosphere and fish for humans the way earthmen capture fish. These aliens, dubbed "Sarvants" by the scientists who discovered them, feel threatened by our incursions into space, the way people would feel threatened by an invasion of crabs from the sea, and retaliate by capturing men, keeping them in a space zoo and studying them. Eventually, when the Sarvants come to the realization that humans are intelligent, they release their captives. The book expresses a humanistic and tolerant philosophy, rather than a fearful xenophobic one. By comparison, in the United States, Hugo Gernsback had just published *Ralph 124C41+* in *Modern Electrics* (1911) and *Amazing Stories* was still fifteen years in the future.

In 1919, Maurice Leblanc wrote *Les Trois Yeux* [**The Three Eyes**], included and reviewed in this volume.

Two years later, Théo Varlet & Octave Jonquel wrote a two-volume epic, *Les Titans du Ciel* (1921) and *L'Agonie de la Terre* (1922), [collected in one volume as **The Martian Epic**, Black Coat Press, ISBN 978-1-934543-41-2), which was influenced by Wells' *War of the Worlds*. In it, the Jovians intervene after another Martian attack on Earth. They then destroy Mars, using focused solar energy. But the Martians migrate to Earth en masse. Our planet is then revealed as the place where Martian souls go to reincarnate. Souls are alleged to travel inward from Mars, to Earth, to Venus, to Mercury, before ending up as one with the Sun. Varlet & Jonquel's Martians are not at all like Wells' but more like Le Rouge's.

In *Les Navigateurs de l'Infini* [**The Navigators Of Space**] (1925) (q.v.), J.-H. Rosny Aîné's heroes travel to Mars in a spaceship powered by artificial gravity and made of an indestructible, transparent material. On the Red Planet, they encounter the gentle, peaceful, six-eyed, three-legged Tripeds, a dying race slowly being replaced by the Zoomorphs. A young Martian female, capable of bearing children parthenogetically by merely wishing it, eventually gives birth to a child after falling in love with one of the human explorers, undoubtedly the first interspecies romance. The book is a colorful, poetic ode to the powers of love and science, a plea for understanding between races, and the view that all living creatures—men as well as aliens—are somehow connected; a sharp departure from the usually more xenophobic approach shaped by Wells with *War of the Worlds*.

Later works, including recent ones, deserve to be mentioned here, but we chose to stop in 1930 because afterward, and especially after World War II, French science fiction began to reflect the growing influence of American science fiction. We are pleased to refer readers who would like to have a more detailed study of the field to Brian Stableford's **The Plurality of Imaginary Worlds** (Black Coat Press, ISBN 978-1-61227-503-1) and our own *French Science Fiction, Fantasy, Horror & Pulp Fiction* (McFarland, 2000, ISBN 0-7864-0596-1), now out of print but still available online.

Jean-Marc & Randy Lofficier

Illustration by E. Bouard for Doctor Omega *(1906)*

Edmé Rousseau: *The Aerial Journey*
(1859)

The text translated here as "The Aerial Journey" by Edmé Rousseau was originally published in Limoges by Barbou et Cie.—the publisher of all the author's works—in two small volumes, as Le Songe, ou voyage aérien [The Dream; or, Aerial Journey] (1864) and Le Rêve, ou Promenades dans les espaces imaginaires [The Dream; or, Excursions in Imaginary Spaces] (1876). The Bibliothèque Nationale refuses to identify their author with the artist Edmé Rousseau (1815-1868), who was best known as a miniaturist, presumably because the publication dates of the editions it possesses of the works credited in its catalogue to "Edmé Rousseau, romancier" are mostly later than that of the artist's death, but their publication pattern is strongly suggestive of some posthumous publication, and the two individuals might well be one and the same; if not, nothing at all is known about the writer—and, indeed, very little is known about the artist, except that he worked for a while in America, although his works are nowadays very collectible.

The composition of the two texts, the first of which indicates that it was written in 1859, predates the boom in the popularization of science and its extension into works of fiction—including the first significant flowering of interplanetary fiction in France—that occurred in the 1860s. It is, therefore, not entirely surprising that it is primarily remarkable for its eccentricity. In fact, the episodic story told in the two texts fully justifies the original titles describing them as dreams; the visits to the various major and minor planets, especially the exceedingly strange "imaginary" planets featured in the latter half of the narrative, do indeed have something of the texture of dreams, and Freudians will have no difficulty finding material there for interpretation in accordance with Freud's theory of dreams as wish-fulfillments laden with sexual symbolism. Although the final section of the narrative clearly reflects the modifications to the city of Paris then being carried out under the aegis of Baron Haussmann, the translation of a similar project to an exotic other world and its concentration on the erection of a colossal symbolic column make it far stranger than any of the other utopian fantasies provoked by that endeavor.

Rousseau's story must have seemed to contemporary eyes to be monumentally silly, without the saving grace of the silliness being entirely deliberate, but the passage of time has lent it a slightly different gloss, and it can now be viewed as an exotic exercise in proto-surrealism. It is deliberately old-fashioned in using "génies" [genii, or perhaps genies in the sense of djinn] as a method of interplanetary travel, after the fashion of Voltaire and Tiphaigne de la Roche a hundred years earlier, in addition to the second layer of apology provided by dreaming, but that does help to license a certain flamboyance which is interesting, and perhaps admirable in itself.

Rousseau's story remains highly original, in presenting an image of the solar system far more bizarre and complex than any other work of interplanetary fiction, refusing to be fettered by the inconvenient detail of astronomical observation. It is unique, albeit within the framework provided by the rich tradition of fantastic voyages, and provides a striking illustration the broadness of that spectrum.

B.S.

THE AERIAL JOURNEY

Part One

I

I am delivering this new work to print because I consider it as a sequel to my work on the grandeur of the works of God,[1] the beauties and marvels of nature, in which I only speak, as it were, about the globe that we inhabit, and did not say very much about those we see traveling so distantly, rotating and circling in the zodiac. I thought that a description of other worlds might serve to complete the work on the grandeur of God's works.

The idea made me smile at first; then I was frightened by the great difficulties that I would have to vanquish; but the great difficulties did not stop me; there was an idiopathy in me, an inclination that brought me back incessantly to the desire to know all the heavenly bodies, great and small, that I saw in the immensity; scientific astronomers have given us descriptions of them, of course, but many of those descriptions are only based on appearances, and I desired ardently to know the reality. But how could I succeed in discovering that reality?

There my embarrassment was augmented to such a point that I was almost discouraged. However, my idiopathy did not weaken; I thought, day and night, about how I could attain that reality. I thought that there was no other means to employ than that of balloons I have invented and with which one can navigate in the air without running any risk. However, I thought, when I arrive on a planet, how will I be received, if it is true, as it is said, that they are all inhabited and that even the sun has its inhabitants?

---

[1] *Grandeur des oeuvres de dieu, ou L'Ouvrage des six jours.* The Bibliothèque Nationale catalogue gives its initial publication date as 1867, three years after the first publication of the present text; Barbou might have published the works out of sequence, but the phrasing of the sentence suggests that there was an earlier first edition.

All these reflections occupied my mind continually; and then another very important difficulty presented itself: how would I live on an unknown world? I am not a geophage. I thought then of filling the nacelle of one of those little transport aerostats with food, water and everything that I thought necessary for a voyage of several million leagues. One travels quickly by way of the air, and that reflection encouraged me a little.

But another difficulty presented itself: that of going to visit globes or worlds of whose inhabitants I knew no more than they knew of me. How would they receive a being of which they doubtless had no idea? If it was as an enemy, my situation would become very embarrassing; how could I defend myself, alone against a crowd whose members might be led to insult or maltreat me by the curiosity of such a novel spectacle?

By precaution and prudence, two things essential to voyagers, I thought of filing one of the nacelles of the transport aerostat with weapons and ammunition, in order to prepare for defense when I approached the planets I wanted to visit.

This is the itinerary had had the intention of following: the Moon, Venus, Mercury, Iris, Flora, Parthenope and the Sun.

I was very preoccupied with the voyage I was planning, and in which I had already glimpsed many difficulties that seemed to me to be insurmountable, but which did not take long to disappear completely, as you shall see; a benevolent genius was watching over me.

On a beautiful day in the month of June, the atmosphere was warm, the air was embalmed with the perfumes of odorous flowers coming from a long way away. Flora had triumphed over cold winter, and appeared in our gardens. Zephyr had succeeded the Aquilonian frosts; everyone was breathing a mild, warm air. The body abandoned itself to a lazy nonchalance, and thought drifted, abandoned to a gentle reverie. One could taste a wellbeing that made one love life.

After my dinner, the air was refreshed, and the sunset reminded me of those I had admired so much in America. I went down to take a stroll in the little wood that is twenty paces from the house in which I live, and, as the heat of the day had fatigued me slightly, I sat down on a couch of grass and stretched myself out delightedly. I did not take long to fall into a reverie while contemplating the firmament, which was soon strewn with stars that I had long desired to know at closer range. But what could I do to visit them? I saw the impossibility of it, but I was dreaming of it at that moment more than ever.

My reverie caused me to fall into a torpor that numbed my senses, and I went to sleep. I had a dream that is still present in my memory, and this is it.

I felt myself being lifted into the air; how and by what I did not know, and I was not overly anxious about it, for I felt quite well; it was as if I were cradled in an invisible hand. I fell into a somnolence, from which I as soon extracted by the cold I felt; I have learned since that I was then in the high regions of the atmosphere, which are cold and damp. I made a few movements, and felt that I was covered by a warm and light fabric.

A soft voice said to me: "Have no fear; you're in my care. I am your good genius, and I am charged with taking you wherever you want to go and protecting you there; such is the order I have received from Zadir, our chief.[2]

"Ah!" I said to him. "You fill me with joy. How will I be able to thank you for your care and devotion?"

"You do not owe me anything," he replied. "Zadir has an affection for you, even a tenderness, and everything that I shall do for you is only owed to Zadir. As for me, I am only carrying out his orders, which I fulfill with pleasure."

"But at least permit me to shake your hand as a sign of gratitude," I said to him. "Hold it out to me, for I can hear you but I cannot see you; you're invisible to my eyes."

"I always will be," he replied. "But if you have need of me, pronounced three times, aloud: *Za, Za, Za*, and I will immediately be beside you. Now, where do you want to go?"

"I'd like to commence my voyage with the Moon," I replied.

"Very well," he said. "You'll be there in a few minutes, for it's no more than ninety-three thousand leagues distant from the Earth."

I was amazed to hear him say that, but I thought that his speed was probably as rapid as that of light, which travels seventy-seven thousand leagues in a second. We set off, and a few seconds after our departure we arrived on the Moon, a planet that is sixty times smaller than the Earth.

My arrival on that planet produced an extraordinary effect on its inhabitants. I say *my* arrival because Za—that was the name of my genius—could not be seen, since he was invisible. The news of what was for them a phenomenon spread rapidly, and a numerous crowd of inhabitants soon gathered in order to see me. I saw nothing hostile in their attitude, however; they doubtless saw me as a being of their species who only differed from them in the matter of costume.

I thought that, and made no reparation for defense, since I was not being attacked, and, on the contrary, I hoped for a favorable welcome. I had judged well; son I saw an innumerable host of curious people coming from all directions, in the midst of which I could distinguish individuals of high rank, to judge by their brilliant escort. Several of those individuals were mounted on small horses, others were being carried in palanquins of a sort.

When they arrived nearby, one of the important individuals approached me and asked me who I was, where I came from and what brought me to their coun-

---

[2] The interplanetary fantasies of Tiphaigne de La Roche and Madame Roumier-Robert both feature genii with names beginning with Za—as do several other fantasies of that period, so Rousseau is following an established tradition, albeit a trifle belatedly.

try. Za, on quitting me, had left me the gift of understanding all the languages spoken on the planets that I wanted to visit, which he did in accordance with the order that his chief, Zadir, had given him. I was therefore able to reply to the important individual, who appeared to be satisfied with my responses and withdrew, followed by his escort.

About an hour after that visit I received another of greater importance; it was that of an ambassador or minister of King Dirzali, who addressed himself to me in order to invite me to accept an apartment in his palace. I accepted his offer with alacrity, because I saw it as a good means of being respected in the country of which King Dirzali was the sovereign, and obtaining more easily all the information that I desired to collect.

I therefore departed with the minister, and in less than an hour we arrived at the King's palace, situated in the center of the city of Enul, the capital of the realm. During the short journey I had made with the minister I had asked him to instruct me regarding the ceremony that it was necessary to observe when he introduced me to the King.

"On entering the Throne Room," he told me, "You must make three genuflections; then you approach the king, who will be waiting for you, sitting on his throne; you should prostate yourself at his feet, and remain in that posture until I say to you: 'Alazati.' Then you get up, and the King will offer you his hand, which you should place on your head, and then kiss respectfully.

"When that ceremony is complete, the King will invite you to dine at his table, around which are couches of a sort with cushions, on which you stretch yourself out and support yourself. Then, after the meal, you will be taken into a neighboring room, which is the desert room, where Queen Dirzali will be present, and the queen's mother, whose name is Douri. The presentation is made in that fashion, and then you will be recognized as one of the palace guests, because the horses and litters of the court will be at your disposal."

I thanked him for his kindness, and he told me that he was glad to have been useful to me.

The beginning of my voyage commenced under good auspices, for, on the very day of my arrival, I acquired powerful friends. The generosity of the King, and the sympathy that the Ministers seemed to have for me, assured me of tranquility during my sojourn on the planet, where the inhabitants are generally good. Their stature is slightly less than ours; the women there are similar, although a trifle plump in the face and too gross in a certain part of the body, which probably comes from their being inhabitants of the Moon, for in certain regards they had a hint of the Hottentot Venus about them What would be a deformity among us is a beauty in the inhabitants of the moon; everything is for the best.

I took advantage of the privileges that my title as a guest of the palace gave me, and asked that I might be given some kind of vehicle and a guide in order to

17

visit the realm. I was given a kind of litter carried by two small horses and I set out.

II

The landscape of the Moon is very hilly and mountainous. I saw mountains there of a considerable height, very steep and terminating in a peak. Crags of enormous size can be seen there, and precipices of great depth, which is doubtless why people think they can see eyes, a nose and a mouth on the Moon. The effect that it produces on our eyes when one gazes at it from Earth only comes from the parts of it that are illuminated by the sun, and those which, being are deprived of it, form shadows, and those shadows might come from profound cavities that do not receive any light. In addition to those cavities there are also seas, gulfs, lakes and rivers, which cannot transmit any light; they can, in consequence, be placed at the rank of shadows; and by a bizarrerie of nature, those different parts give the Moon, seen from our Earth, the appearance of a human face.

Seeing nothing very remarkable in the part of the realm that I visited, I climbed into my litter again and continued my journey on a less rugged road. The country was quite pleasant, but monotonous for me; I only saw things similar, or nearly so, to those of Earth. The vegetation and trees were beautiful; some were covered in flowers, others with fruits that were still green. A few birds animated the landscape somewhat; a few inhabitants were occupied in rustic labor, others were grazing flocks of small animals with some analogy to our sheep, and other, larger animals that had no resemblance to any of ours.

I therefore saw nothing that could interest me, or distract me from the ennui that I was beginning to experience, and I resolved to continue my great voyage. I asked my guide to take me back to Enul, from which I would depart to visit the planet Venus, where I hoped to find agreeable distractions

We set out, and that night I slept in my apartment in Enul. Before going to bed I received a visit from the Minister and announced my imminent departure to him. It was still daylight, whereas it was night in my homeland. I asked the Minister whether it would be possible to take my leave of the King; he replied affirmatively. And I followed him to the King, employing the same ceremony as I had on my arrival. I added my thanks for the royal welcome that he had made me, and told him that I was leaving penetrated by his generosity toward me.

When the ceremony was concluded I went back to my apartment and made my preparations. Night had fallen and, in a hurry to depart, I called out "Za, Za, Za."

My good genius did not make me wait, for a soft voice said to me: "I know what you want of me. You want to leave."

"Yes, I replied, and as soon as possible."

"This very instant," he replied. "Where do you want to go?"

"To Venus."

"That's easy, but it's rather late, and to enjoy the beauty of that planet, it would be better to wait for daylight. Rest tonight, and tomorrow morning, before sunrise, I'll deposit you near Venere, which is the capital city of that planet."

"I'll follow your advice," I said. "I abandon myself entirely to you."

I went to bed, but fully dressed, and slept so profoundly that I did not feel my good genius lift me up when, responding to my request, he carried me through the air, whose freshness woke me up.

"We'll arrive momentarily in Venere," my good genius said to me. "The Sun is about to appear and illuminate the monuments of that charming city, the most beautiful capital in all the planets. The Sun is rising and lighting it up; look and judge."

I looked, and remained ecstatic in contemplating all the beautiful things offered to my gaze. I was enchanted.

When Za thought that my admiration and curiosity were satisfied, he said: "I shall now deposit you in the pretty summer-house that you can see from here, near to which are groups of young women lightly dressed in white; some are singing, others playing various instruments and others dancing. Those charming young women are the maids of honor of Queen Vénusté,[3] thus named because of her grace, her beauty and the generosity of her mind. The Queen's maids are quite curious; they won't take long to see you in the summer-house and hasten to inform the Queen, who will come to visit you. All that will happen as I predict, and soon. I won't leave you, although I shall still be invisible. Have no fear of anything; whatever happens, I shall always be nearby to protect you, and to defend you if necessary."

In fact, I soon heard soft music full of harmony, which filled my heart with a keen emotion. I ran to the window of the summer-house and saw a numerous cortege approaching, preceded by richly-dressed individuals. They were followed by young women whose physiognomy respired pleasure and sensuality. They surrounded a palanquin in which a woman of great beauty was seated. She had a young child next to her, who was entirely naked; he was crowned with various flowers, which were in perfect harmony with the curls of his blond hair. He had wings attached to his shoulders and was carrying a quiver full of arrows; he was holding a bow in his left hand. He was the son of Queen Vénusté.

The cortege stopped at the door of the summer-house where I was stationed. One of the important individuals then approached, and I ran out to meet him. He came in and sat on the sofa. He told me that he had come on the Queen's order to ask who I was and for what reason I had come to her estates. I answered all his questions and he left to make his report to the Queen, who descended from her palanquin shortly thereafter, at the door of my summer-house.

---

[3] "*Vénusté*" means charm, in the sense of sex-appeal, in French.

I went to meet her and received her with all the marks of respect due to her rank. She took her place on the sofa and did me the honor of asking me to sit next to her. I was delighted by admiration next to that Queen, so beautiful, so benevolent and so full of graces. She perceived my delight, and capped it by inviting me to go and live in her palace—and offer that I accepted gladly, for I would have at my disposal all the means of visiting the planet and discovering the customs and mores of its inhabitants.

However, a thought crossed my mind and darkened that brilliant dream of happiness slightly. Honored as I would be by the generosity of the Queen, would I not become an object of jealousy and envy for the important people she had with her? Would I not be the target of hatred, calumny and the dangers that might result therefrom?

Those thoughts were darkening my mind when a soft voice said to me: "Don't worry; have no fear of hatred. As for calumny, a good man ought not to dread it; the testimony of his conscience ought to suffice for him. Don't torment yourself; Zadir has put you under my protection, and I shall fulfill my mission."

I therefore departed with Za, who transported me, without my being able to say how, to the door of the Palace, into which I entered. A man suddenly appeared, who excited my curiosity, and several people approached me. Among those people I recognized the man who had come to the summer-house. I asked him to present me to the Queen, which he did with pleasure.

I approached Vénusté with all the external signs of a profound respect. She greeted me graciously, without any other ceremony. We were alone, and she said to me with her characteristic bounty:

"I was waiting for you, and I have prepared an apartment for you in my palace, where you will find everything necessary, and everything that might be agreeable to you, I hope. You meals will be served in your apartment until further notice. My apartment communicates with yours by means of a secret passage and I shall come to see you in order to learn from you many things that I do not know, but which you ought to, for you must have as much science as courage to have succeeded in penetrating into this land, where no stranger has ever appeared before."

I thanked her for the confidence that she was testifying and told her that I would be glad to be able to give her proofs of my gratitude and devotion. She held out her white hand to me, which I pressed lightly in mine, and I was bold enough to raise it to my lips. She was not offended, and from then on, a sentiment of amity reigned between us.

When I saw the Queen, she said to me: "I have thought that, in order to put an end to the conspiracy that is being woven, you would do well to visit my realm, which you desire to know. An officer will accompany you and provide everything that you might need during your journey. When you return, all the fuss will have died down, and you can remain tranquil next to me."

I accepted the proposal the Queen had made and left.

III

The country was beautiful. The trees were laden with fruit, for it is hot on that planet, and everything feels that influence. I admired the beauty of meadows enameled with flowers, tall trees in the shade of which handsome young men were lying beside pretty young women, who were laughing as they listened to their affectionate words. I judged that they were affectionate because the couples seemed very animated, and their faces bore the imprint of joy.

All is amour and sensuality on that planet. At the commencement of the journey everything appeared to me to be very reminiscent of Tuscany; afterwards I saw locations that bore a strong resemblance to those one sees between Rome and Naples As much by virtue of the landscape as the heat, there is a good deal of analogy between the planet Venus and the southern part of Italy and Sicily.

Further away, the scene changed, but it lost none of its beauty. Mountains presented a magnificent aspect of waterfalls, cascades and torrents, which reminded me of those of Terni and Tivoli. Those waters alimented a beautiful lake in which pretty young women were bathing: beautiful women with contours as pure as statues by Phidias and Praxiteles. Some were shining whitely in the sunlight by virtue of the beauty of their skin; others were sheltering from the Sun, protected by large rocks and the huge braches of trees that grew among their fissures. They enjoyed an agreeable freshness there. They frolicked in the water like swans; their laughter and great hilarity testified to their happiness.

Further on, I saw beautiful hills covered with trees and bushes, among which I glimpsed a few pretty fabrications formed like little temples. I assumed that they were dedicated to some local deity.

From a bend on one of the hillside I perceived a certain number of buildings, including a few large edifices. I judged that it was a town, and asked my guide. He told me that it was Cyprine, the second city of the realm, and more beautiful than the capital. I wanted to see it and my guide took my carriage into it, which attracted a great deal of curiosity. When they perceived me, that intensified greatly. The news promptly spread through the entire town, and a large crowd surrounded my litter.

They found out from my guide who I was, and the distinction with which the Queen honored me; that was enough for me to obtain the highest regard, so it was not long before I saw the governor of the town arrive; he invited me to dinner and offered me an apartment in the palace where he lived. I thanked him for his courtesy, and accepted.

While waiting for dinner time, I continued my visit to the town and the port, which was known as Porto Venere. I was singularly surprised by that name, which is that of a small Italian town on the shore of the Gulf of Spezia, between Genoa and Livorno. How had that name reached the planet Venus? I don't know. My genius Za might have known, but I did not want to disturb him merely to satisfy my curiosity.

A short distance from the port I noticed a little island, the sight of which charmed me, and I experienced a desire to visit it. I said so to my guide and he summoned a kind of launch. In very little time we arrived at the island of Cythera—not the ancient isle of Cythera, nowadays known as Cerigo. The interior of the little island was charming; myrtles that were still green, and rose-bushes covered with roses surrounded a little temple of elegant form, which I assumed to have been constructed and educated to the goddess whose name the planet bore.

I was confounded by astonishment. How had all those names reached that planet? How had they been able to construct a little temple in conformity with Greek architecture? I could not get over my surprise—or, rather, my amazement. I had therefore delivered myself profoundly to my reflections when my guide came to inform me that it was time to return to the town in order to respond to the governor's invitation.

We left, and as soon as we arrived in Cyprine he took me to the governor's palace, where he received me with distinction. He led me into the dining room, where I found everything prepared for dinner. Around the room there was a sort of vast sofa on which several women of distinction were sitting, all of ravishing beauty. The one who occupied the principal place was the governor's wife. He introduced me to her.

I saluted by bowing deeply and placing my hands on my head. She replied to my salutation by placing two fingers of her right hand on her forehead and extending her left hand, which was very beautiful, toward me. I took it and bore it to my forehead, in accordance with the instructions I had received from my guide.

When the presentation was complete, a whistle-blast was heard, and all the ladies took their places at the table, each placed in accordance with her rank. The seats were three-legged stools; those which had a back were occupied by women of superior rank.

Dinner was served; it comprised several kinds of meat, principally that of large birds similar to pigeons, which are very numerous in that country, and a few fish, which includes a cyprian fish whose flesh is highly esteemed in the realm, which is very similar to our carp. Afterwards came vegetables, some cooked and others raw, which were seasoned with a kind of cream or piquant juice; that was the salad. It was cleared away, and a kind of dais that seemed to be part of the ceiling descended on to the table, and by that means brought a well-ordered dessert composed of various fruits, compotes and preserves.

During the dinner there were no other beverages than water, but during dessert jars were brought full of a spirituous but sweet liqueur, which I drank with pleasure. The cup that I had before me was filled with it. Because glass is unknown in that country, all liquids are drunk from vessels of fine clay, a sort of kaolin, which, when baked, takes on a transparency equal to our porcelain.

After dinner we went into the garden to an arbor covered in verdure, through which the sun's rays could not penetrate; one enjoyed a mild coolness there, and breathed the air pleasurably, gently agitated by light breeze. A lady sang; her voice was soft and harmonious. Another lady accompanied her on an instrument similar to a mandolin , and another on a kind of harp, which she plucked with fingers as slender and delicate as those of the Medici Venus.

The agreeable evening was terminated by a few refreshments, brought to us by pretty young women with the gracious and delicate figures with which almost all the women of the planet Venus are endowed; then everyone retired.

When I woke up the next day, I thought that it was time to return to the capital and to Queen Vénusté. I hoped that the absence would have calmed jealous minds. A vain hope. I arrived in the presence of Queen Vénusté, and I read in her eyes that she was glad to see me; when we were alone she told me that the greatest tranquility had reigned since my departure and that she had taken the measures necessary to maintain order, but among the important people of the realm I noticed many somber faces. I pretended not to notice them and made polite advances, to which they responded coldly.

In sum, I read on many faces that they were not pleased to see me again. I had been convinced of that in advance and was not disconcerted. I had no fear of those people but I feared their secret plots, either to have me murdered or to irritate the people and excite them against me. I recalled what my good genius had said on that subject and was no longer anxious, but I expected to see some conspiracy burst forth.

Three days later a crowd of the people presented themselves in large square of the palace, loudly demanding the expulsion of the foreigner, and the leaders of the insurrection demanded to speak to the queen, who permitted the three principal chiefs to be admitted.

The Queen received them in the throne room, sitting on the throne. She was full of grace and majesty. Her throne was surrounded by guards, some of whom were guarding the entrance to the room in order to subdue the noise and ensure that there was no disorder. The three principal leaders of the insurrection were brought in, and the Queen, standing up, asked them what they wanted.

The men, however, dazzled by the Queen's majesty, the splendor of the throne and everything surrounding them, were nonplused, and were only able to stammer that they had come to beg their gracious sovereign to send the foreigner away.

"Those who sent you," the Queen said to them, "do not know this stranger. I know him, and I am informed as to the motives that brought him to my realm. What I can tell you, in order to testify to the confidence that I have in you, is that he only came here to ensure your wellbeing. Go tell those you have brought to lack the respect and confidence that you owe your Queen that I shall not send the foreigner away, and that I know how to make myself respected. You are the dupes of schemers who have abused your good faith. Go inform them of my reply. I know those who have prompted you to take this offensive step. Go; I forgive you and think only of making you happy."

The three leaders withdrew after having sworn devotion and respect to the Queen.

Shortly after their departure, cries of joy were heard in the palace square, provoked by the report of the three envoys, who told the people about the fine and noble reception that the Queen had given them. But the nobles were not content and were already weaving a new plot.

They decided to accuse the foreigner of seeking to take possession of the throne and become their king; to that effect they hired a number of commoners to affirm, as witnesses in the lawsuit they intended to bring, that the foreigner had promised them large rewards if they would associate themselves with his project, which was to overthrow the Queen's government, and recognize him as their King. The men who had woven the plot denounced me to the Chief Justice, and I was summoned to appear in three days at the Supreme Court. All the hired witnesses were obliged to appear before the judges at the same time as me.

When the Queen learned that I was to be brought before the judges of the criminal court she came to me and said: "Is the news that I have just heard really true, my friend? You have been accused of being the author of a plot against me? Can that be possible? I can't believe it."

"You're right, my friend; I'm incapable of it, and you have judged me correctly—but let them do it. I'm tranquil on the subject that obliges me to appear before the judges. Be present at my trial on the appointed day, and you will see my calumniators confounded."

IV

The day of my judgment arrived. There was a great stir in the town; people were coming and going in all directions and there was a confused murmur of voices. The sun's rays only illuminated the day lugubriously; large clouds announced an impending storm; everything was somber and sad.

The Queen had come to my apartment at an early hour; anxiety had kept her awake all night. "Well, my friend," she said, when she came in, weeping. "It is today that you will be tried and perhaps convicted unjustly; I will not permit that. My guards will be at the tribunal, ready to act at my first signal."

"Thank you, my Queen, my good friend, but, as I've already told you, let them do it. I shall be convicted, without a doubt, but promise me that you will remain a tranquil spectator of everything that happens, for it is then that you will know me better and will be assured of my perfect innocence."

"I promise," she said. "I see you so full of confidence that my fears die down and you reanimate my courage."

"I shall be convicted, as you say, but don't worry, I implore you."

"You will be content with me, my friend."

"And come to see me this evening, my noble friend, so that I can thank you."

"I will come," she said.

The palace square was covered by the people, curious to see me pass on my way to the tribunal. I went there alone; I had not wanted an escort. The crowd opened a passage for me, and I went through the middle of it without having heard the slightest murmur. For her part, the Queen went there carried on a palanquin by her servants; she was followed by her maids of honor and escorted by guards.

I went into the tribunal hall; an usher indicated the seat that was reserved for me on a platform facing the judges. The Queen was on a platform surmounted by an awning. On the opposite side were the dignitaries of the State and the commoners called as witnesses. Some of the Queen's guards were placed beneath the sovereign's platform, while others were posted at various points in the hall and others at the entrance door—for the room was vast. The air circulated freely, for glazed windows are unknown in the realm; people are only protected from the insults of the weather and the sun's rays by means of large curtains opened and closed at will; on cloudy days all of them are open.

The greatest silence reigned in the hall. At a sign given by the Great Judge the usher told me to stand up, and the interrogation commenced.

"Who are you?"

"I'm a foreigner."

"Where do you come from?"

"The Earth."

"What is your name?"

"Pcer."

"Why did you come here?"

"To educate myself."

"You have no other designs?"

"No."

"You are accused of wanting to take possession of the throne."

"It is a false accusation."

"However, there are witnesses that you have tried to suborn."

"They are false witnesses."

"How can you prove that?"

"By confounding them."

"How will you confound them?"

"By putting them in my presence and making them identify the true suborners, for I know who they are."

Then there was a murmur among the noblemen of the realm; several of them approached the Great Judge and spoke to him in a low voice. The Great

Judge said to me: "Accused, your defense is inadmissible, and in any case, we are enlightened by witnesses worthy of faith. We shall return to the deliberation room, and I shall return to inform you of the result."

The judges retired, and reappeared a short time afterwards. The Great Judge read the result of their deliberation and said to me: "Accused, you are convicted and judged guilty of the crime of lèse-majesté, and as such, condemned to the penalty of death by the torture of scatole."[4]

A stifled exclamation departed from the Queen's platform. I was standing up; I looked at her, and my calmness reassured her.

"Jailer," said the Judge, "take possession of the guilty party, take him to the tower and guard him there until the time of his execution."

The jailer approached and made as if to take possession of me, but at that moment, the collision of the electrified clouds produced a flash of lightning. Thunder crashed, and already the jailer had fallen at my feet, struck dead.

Great was the astonishment and consternation that reigned in the hall; terror was painted on the faces of a few highly-placed individuals. The thunder was still rumbling. The crowd was prostrated, fearful of great misfortunes. The Queen was calm.

The Great Judge, at the instigation of my enemies, had a turnkey summoned from the tower, and ordered him to take possession of me, to take me away and guard me until further notice. The turnkey approached me, but, at the moment when he was about to take hold of me, I disappeared from all eyes. My good genius Za had rendered me invisible like him and had transported me to the apartment I occupied at the palace, where I thanked him sincerely for the further service that he had just rendered me.

"It will always be the same, every time you are in danger," he told me, in his soft voice. "You were accused unjustly, and I must protect your innocence; I would not have done it if you had been guilty. Such are the orders I have received from Zadir. If you do not deviate from the conduct you have maintained thus far, your good genius will not cease to protect you—but if you were weak enough to cede to the insinuation of the few evil genii who are our enemies, Zadir would abandon you and forbid me to be useful to you. I cannot give you advice—that is forbidden to me—but the one thing I am permitted to advise you to do is always take your honor as the guide of your conduct."

I assured him that my conduct would always be exempt from evil actions.

"If that is so," he said, "and I believe you to be sincere, you can always count on my protection, wherever you are; you know the three words that you must pronounce to summon me to your aid. Pronounce them in case of need and

---

[4] The word *scatole* usually signifies a product of putrefaction that has the odor of feces. Its employment here is a trifle enigmatic, as is the protagonist naming himself as Pcer. It is possible that both are the result of typesetting errors, but if so, it is not obvious what the intended formulations might have been.

I shall be with you immediately. Now, when do you want to continue your voyage, and what planet do you have the intention of visiting?"

"Mercury," I told him.

"It isn't far from here," he said, "and you can be there in a few moments. Inform me when you are ready."

I thanked him and he vanished. Left alone, I ate some food that was on my table, and then lay down on the sofa to reflect on the events of that terrible day, which had terminated so well for me.

Suddenly, the Queen appeared in my apartment, and said to me: "You can be tranquil now."

"It's necessary to hope so, at least," I replied.

"What!" she said to me. "Don't you believe that the sedition is appeased?"

"I think it has relented," I replied, "but in suspense, for the same ferments exist. It will not take much to excite the people again, and believe that they are working on that at this moment. It's me that they want and it's on me that the hatred and jealous of the nobles will pour. For myself, I have no fear—you've had the proof of that—but I fear the annoyances and torments that my presence here will cause you. It's necessary, for your tranquility, that I go away for a time."

Scarcely had I finished speaking that we heard a roar similar to that of waves violently agitated by a tempest and breaking into surf against reefs.

"What's that noise?" she asked me.

"It's the voice of the people," I replied.

Immediately, a horrible cracking sound was heard.

"What's that?" she asked.

"It's the doors of your palace being broken down. Go back to your apartment; they won't abuse you and no harm will come to you; it's only me they want. You can see that I'm an obstacle to your tranquility."

And as the mob had invaded the palace, and was approaching my apartment, I urged the Queen to return to her own. Scarcely had she gone than I summoned Za. He appeared immediately. I asked him to render me invisible to the crowd that was about to irrupt into my apartment and, once it had gone and I had made sure that the Queen was safe, that we should depart for the planet Mercury.

"Very well," he said.

The crowd precipitated into my apartment, and remained mute with astonishment at not seeing me there. A powerful voice made these words heard: "The one you seek is not here; he has gone. Go away, or fear the effects of my wrath."

Consternated by that superhuman voice, the crowd withdrew in silence. Then I asked my genius to let me go to the Queen's apartment to make sure that she was tranquil and in no anger.

"Very well," he said. "Go; I'll wait."

I went to the Queen's apartment, still invisible to all eyes. Everything was calm. I went in without being seen; I found her sad and pensive, and said to her: "Have courage and hope; adieu, my noble friend."

That adieu pierced my heart, but I had a sacred duty to fulfill: a duty and sacrifice that honor ordered me to fulfill.

V

I returned to my good genius Za, and we departed immediately for Mercury, where we arrived in a few moments. The heat is excessive on that planet, where it is seven times stronger than in our hottest summers, to the extent that it liquefies metals. The inhabitants are extremely lively and frolicsome; one might think that they were afflicted by calenture, a species of delirium to which Europeans are subject in the tropics.

It was on that planet that Za set me down, and as soon as the inhabitants perceived me they ran to look at me, some on their hands instead of making use of their feet, others turning cartwheels and other uttering fearful cries.

I thought that they were all afflicted by madness, and said so to my good genius, who had not quit me.

"You've judged them accurately," he told me, "And I doubt that you'll like it here—or that you'll obtain any pleasure from visiting the planet, which is covered with saltpeter, and where the excessive heat might make you uncomfortable. I think it might be better for you to leave."

"You've divined my desire and anticipated the request that I was about to make for you to transport me to another, more habitable, planet."

"I'm entirely ready to do so," he replied. "Where would you like to go?"

"First, to Iris," because I believe it's not far from here."

"That's true," he said. "You'll be there in five minutes."

Indeed. Five minutes later he deposited me on the planet Iris, beside an elegant summer-house in the garden of the Queen of that planet.

The Queen's maids of honor perceived me and hastened to inform her that there was a stranger in the garden near the summer-house, and that they could not understand how the man in question had been introduced.

The Queen sent one of the ladies of the palace with her maids of honor to find out who I was. They soon arrived in my presence, and after having examined me for a few minutes the lady of the palace told me that the Queen had sent her to find out who I was, where I came from and why I had come to her realm.

I answered all her questions, and she seemed to be satisfied with my replies.

"I shall go report the extraordinary things you've told me to our Queen," she said, "and she will doubtless want to see you."

"I am at Her Majesty's disposal," I told her.

She returned to the palace, and a short time later, I saw a person arriving whose clothes were gaudily adorned. He came toward me placing the back of his hand on his forehead, told me that the Queen desired to see me and invited me to follow him. During the journey I asked him what ceremony I ought to observe.

"On entering the throne room, you bow, crossing our arms over your chest; then you advance toward her, put one knee on the ground and say to her: 'Great Queen, dispose of your servant,' And when she says to you: '*Ben venuto*,' you get up and bow profoundly.

"That ceremony concluded, she will doubtless invite you to dine at her table, and then you will become a commensal or guest of the palace, for the queen likes to learn, and as you appear to me to be very knowledgeable about things that are unknown here, it's probable that she will want to you to be close to her, in order to profit from your instruction."

At that moment, another officer came to inform me that the Queen was waiting for me, and that he had been instructed to take me to her. I got up and followed him. On entering the room, I saw Queen Irisa on her throne. She was clad in a long white dress of a very light fabric, striped in various places with the colors of the rainbow.

I approached her, observing the ceremonial custom of which I had been informed. She observed me with great curiosity. She was young and very beautiful, but unlike Vénusté, who had blue eyes and blonde hair, Queen Irisa had brown eyes and chestnut-colored hair. Her face was both noble and piquant; she respired bounty.

"According to what I've been told, it appears that you come from a long way away and have come here to learn—but I'm also told that you appear to be very learned."

"I am, in fact, educated, but Your Majesty knows that there are no limits to science; the more one possess, the more one can acquire."

"I like to hear you talk thus," she told me. "I think exactly the same. But what learning do you think you can acquire in this land, where it is non-existent?"

"Forgive me, Madame; I wanted to acquire the knowledge of your planet and judge the reality of something that I had only seen at a distance of thirty-three million leagues, with the aid of our binoculars and telescopes."

"You are talking about things that are entirely strange to me, which excite my curiosity to the highest degree, and the desire to satisfy it. Would you like to instruct me regarding the marvelous things you have just mentioned?"

"I will do that with great pleasure, Madame, and to facilitate that instruction, I will draw you a plan of the planetary system, which will help you to understand easily what the heavenly bodies are, the place that they occupy in the firmament, and how they circulate there."

"You throw me into an astonishment that I've never felt before. And you have the ability to teach me all these beautiful things, which seem so marvelous?"

"Yes, Madame."

"And when will you commence my instruction?"

"Whenever it pleases Your Majesty."

"Tomorrow," she said, swiftly. "The apartment will be prepared that I invite you to occupy in my palace, in which you will be perfectly free. Your meals will be served at the times you indicated, and all the things necessary to you. One of the rooms in your apartment will be your study; it is far away from noise and perfectly suitable for study and meditation. You will find everything there that might be useful to you in your scientific studies. It is in your study that I shall receive your precious lessons. That study communicates with my apartment, which is above yours, by a secret stairway constructed between two walls, and it's by means of that stairway that I shall come to your rooms to collect the knowledge that I lack and that I have a great desire to possess."

That secret stairway reminded me of Vénusté's passage, and I sighed profoundly.

Queen Irisa did indeed, come down to me apartment the following day, to examine the various rooms, especially the one intended as my study.

"How do you like this room?" she asked. "Do you think it will be suitable? What objects do you need for your work?"

"What is indispensable," I replied, "is paper, ink and a pen."

"But I don't know what paper and ink are. Tell me."

"Paper is a composition made of old linen, which is allowed to soak in water for a long time and reduced to paste; one then lays that paste very thinly over frames in the shape of the paper, and when it has dried out one peels it away, and the sheet of paper is made. If the paper is to be used for ink drawing or painting with water colors, it is soaked in gummed water in order to prevent it from being absorbent, and then laid out to dry. You have here a tree-bark that is analogous to the papyrus whose internal bark once served as paper, but that papyrus was only used by the ancient Egyptians to write in hieroglyphs on subjects of religion, the scientists and the arts."

"But I've never heard mention of any of what you've just told me. Will you be kind enough to teach me about all these things, for the more I hear the more my desire to learn increases?"

"I have the honor of telling you, Madame, that I will do so with great pleasure, for I am entirely devoted to your orders."

"My orders?" she said. "But you have none to receive from me, for I consider you as a friend."

With those words she extended her hand to me, which I pressed in mine.

"Where shall we commence with my instruction?" she asked.

"With the planetary system," I replied. "But I shall precede that with the knowledge of God, who is the author of nature—which is to say, of all created things. God alone is uncreated. God exists by virtue of himself. God is a pure spirit, a divine essence that extends in everything and penetrates everywhere. That is why God is the immensity—which is to say that he is present everywhere, that he sees everything and can do anything. God is eternal wisdom. God is all of eternity. God is prescience. God alone is infinite—which is to say that his power is limitless."

VI

Irisa stared at me with an indescribable astonishment.

"Oh, my friend," she said. "What emotions, what hitherto unknown sentiments your instruction causes me to experience! Continue, I beg you."

"When God created the world, chaos existed—which is to say that everything was in confusion. At his omnipotent voice, light succeeded darkness; chaos disappeared. In six days God, created the universe—which is to say, the entire world, al the celestial bodies, the Earth and its inhabitants. Now I will give you an idea of the position of the celestial bodies, comprising the sun and all the planets that God has placed in the firmament, in the zodiac, which is divided into two equal parts by a line known as the ecliptic, which the sun seems to travel.

"Now, Madame, with this planetary system, which I have drawn as best I can, you will understand with greater facility all that I have told you about the celestial bodies, and these planets, which are all the works of God."

"So, my friend, the sun is not a God?"

"No, Madame, it is only a creature of God, which has been formed in order to fecundate the Earth by the heat of its rays and to ripen the fruits that produce the vegetables that serve as our nourishment and that of animals. But let us leave that subject and go back, if you are agreeable, to our conversation about the things you desire to know."

"You could not give me a greater pleasure, my friend, for since you have talked to me about God and creation my mind has been working hard, and it seems to me that the subject is not exhausted, and that you have many interesting things to teach me."

"You have thought correctly, my friend, because we have to talk about the celestial spirits."

"What do you mean by celestial spirits? Are they other gods?"

"No, Madame, for there is only one God. The other celestial spirits are spiritual creatures, created by God to announce and carry out his orders; they inhabit heaven and surround the throne of God, all resplendent with glory, from which he dictates his laws to the entire universe.

"But what is heaven, my friend, and what are the names of these celestial spirits?"

"Heaven is the empyrean: that is the highest sky, in which God has placed paradise. Under the empyrean is the firmament, which appears to us to be a beautiful azure blue; that color is apparently produced by the ether, a very subtle fluid that is assumed to fill the space above the atmosphere, and which is not breathable. The ether is the firmament; it is what is known poetically as the azure vault; it is there that the stars circulate sand accomplish their rotation or revolution. The celestial spirits are called Angels. God created them entirely out of divine substance; each one is an entirely spiritual creation, a spirit with which the immortal soul that God has given them is united, whereas the immortal soul that God has given to humans is united with a material body—that is the only difference. The number of angels is several million."

"Thank you, my friend. But tell me what Paradise is, and what an immortal soul is. I've never heard mention of either of those things."

"Paradise is in heaven; it is the city of the blessed, where they enjoy an eternal felicity, if they have merited it. God formed humans out of clay. When humans had been formed from that material substance, God gave them an immortal soul, which is the divine breath; it is principally by means of the soul that God gave us that humans are created in the image of their Creator. It is thus that God, the Supreme Being, has rendered humans masters of the animals, and made them monarchs of the Earth. Our soul is spiritual, since it emanates from God; it is of the same nature as that of the angels, who are created like us, except that their soul is united, as I said, with a spiritual nature, while in humans the soul is united with a material nature. An angel is the noblest of creatures. Our soul possesses admirable faculties, at the head of which it is necessary to place thought, which is an operation of the intelligent substance and free will, which is the operation, or rather the faculty, that the soul possesses in making a decision.

"A human being contains one thing that is certainly not material, and that is a spirit, the soul, the image of God, as the matter that forms humans is the image of earth. Animals have a soul that is nothing but intellect, and at death it returns to oblivion, while ours, much more perfect, has a higher, eternal destiny. Humans are intermediate between animal and intellectual nature."

The Queen seemed to be plunged in a profound reverie. She came round and said: "Everything that you have just told me has thrown my mind into a strange agitation. I need to meditate in order to conceive and analyze the elevated things that you have told me—too elevated for me, who had no idea of them. I hope that you will help me to draw my mind out of the obscurity in which it is still enveloped."

"I am entirely at your discretion, my good friend. Tell me what the matters are that you would like clarified, and I will write you notes that will help you to interpret what you have found obscure in all that I have just told you."

"That is an excellent idea, my friend, for I can study your notes in my hours of solitude and we can continue in your study my instruction on the celestial bodies, in accordance with the planetary system that you have drawn for me."

VII

The next day, the Queen came to my study and I began my lessons in astronomy.

"Astronomy is the knowledge of the celestial bodies and the sky. Physical astronomy explains its phenomena.

"Uranography is the description of the sky.

"Uranometry is the art of measuring the heavenly bodies.

"The Sun, the torch of the world, occupies the center of the universe, where it is motionless. Mercury rotates around the Sun, in such a way that the Sun is at the center of the circle described by Mercury. Above Mercury is Venus, which similarly rotates around the Sun. The Moon is sometimes close to the sun and sometimes further away, and it is the same with the other planets, which all rotate around the Sun. Only the Moon rotates around the Earth and illuminates it by night. After Venus come the Moon and the Earth, which, being higher than Mercury and Venus, describe a larger circle than those plants. Finally, Mars, Jupiter and Saturn, describe even greater circles around the sun than all the others. That is why the other planets take longer to complete their revolution.

"The Sun is luminous by itself, by reason of the substance that composes it, and whose continual incandescence is the cause of the luminosity. English astronomers claim that the center of the Sun, which they call "the stone" and we call the nucleus, does not produce the heat. That opinion already existed among French astronomers, who have compared the heat of the nucleus with the most brilliant part of the solar disk, which they call the photosphere, and from which the sun's rays depart. In addition to the five hundred planets discovered by Herschel in 1802,[5] other planets exist around the sun: Iris and Flora, discovered in 1847; Metis in 1848. Hygiea in 1849, Parthenope and Victoria in 1850, Irene and Eunomia in 1851.[6]

---

[5] 1802 was the year when William Herschel suggested the name "asteroid" for the minor planets, following his observations of Ceres and Pallas, but the figure of five hundred must refer to the additional items he added in that year to his catalogue of "nebulae" and other stellar objects, far outside the solar system.

[6] The minor planets Iris and Flora—the seventh and eighth to be named—were discovered by J. R. Hind in 1847; Hind also discovered Victoria in 1850 and Irene in 1851. Metis was discovered by Andrew Graham in 1848, Hygieia, Parthenope and Eunomia by Annibale de Gasparis in 1849, 1850 and 1851 respectively. All the bodies in question orbit between Mars and Jupiter, and none goes anywhere near Mercury, as is alleged when this list is repeated a little further on.

"The Sun takes more than twenty-five days to rotate on its axis; the Earth takes twenty-four hours. The days of Mercury are twenty-four hours three minutes, the days of Venus twenty-three hours twenty-one minutes. On Mercury the heat is seven times more intense than in our hottest summers; it is so strong there that it even liquefies metals. On Saturn, by contrast, it is twenty-four times colder than in our most rigorous winters; everything there is frozen. Saturn is a very long way from the Sun, which seems very small there, only appearing as a small pale star of very feeble heat. The cold there is excessive, as I said, which renders the inhabitants unsociable by their phlegmatic humor and the absence of all gaiety. The distance of Saturn from the Sun is three hundred million leagues.

"The Sun is one million four hundred thousand nine hundred and twenty times larger than the Earth, from which it is thirty-eight million leagues distant—some say thirty-three, other thirty-five; once it was thirty-six million. On Mercury, the character is opposite to that of Saturn.

"The stars are, in general, celestial bodies that shine by night. The stars are fixed in relation to the Sun; wandering stars are planets; falling stars are luminous meteors.

"A constellation is an assemblage of neighboring stars designated by a single name; one says, for example, the constellation of Canis Major, Taurus or Virgo.

"Sirius is a star in the constellation Canis Major, the brightest in the firmament.

"The distance of the stars from the Earth is about two hundred and six thousand times the distance that separates the Sun from the Earth, about thirty billon leagues.

"Light travels seventy-seven thousand leagues per second. With the most powerful telescope one can discover more than forty million fixed stars of fourteen different magnitudes. Three thousand stars are visible to the naked eye in a single hemisphere.

"The light of the star nearest to the Earth, which arrives in the evening, departed three years ago from the start that sent it. The light of the most distant stars needs three or four thousand years to reach us, traveling, as I said at seventy-seven leagues a second, and beyond those stars one assumes that there are others more distant, which could only be seen with more powerful instruments than the ones we possess.

"A comet is a kind of planet that rotates around the Sun in a greatly elongated circle. As they get closer to the sun their tail extends further, and when they draw away, their tails gradually shorten, and end up disappearing. The tail of a comet is its atmosphere, which becomes luminous and visible in separating from the opaque body of the planet. Heat is produced by the interaction of solar rays with the atmosphere.

"The center of the Earth is the center of gravity of the objects on its surface. But as the Earth rotates around the Sun with all that it contains, it follows that the Earth's center of gravity or point of support is in the Sun.

"Vortices are masses of matter whose parts, separate from one another, all move in the same direction. A whirlwind is an infinity of particles of air which spin around together and envelop those that they encounter.

"The planets are borne in the celestial matter, which is prodigiously subtle and agitated; that entire great mass of celestial matter, which extends from the Sun to the fixed stars, spins around, carrying the planets with it, causing them to rotate in the same direction around the Sun, which occupies the center. Our great vortex is composed of sixteen planets, of which we can only see seven. Uranus and Neptune are in the same category as Saturn with regard to cold; everything there is frozen.

"The Chariot is composed of the Sun, the Moon, and five planets, Mercury, Venus, Mars, Jupiter and Saturn. The planet Jupiter is situated between Mars and Saturn. Jupiter is a thousand times larger than the Earth; that planet is a hundred and sixty-five million leagues distant from the Sun; it is illuminated by four moons, little inhabited planets; seen from the closest of those little planets, Jupiter is six hundred times larger than our Moon appears to be to us. Saturn has five moons.

"The air that surrounds the Earth only extends to a certain height, about twenty leagues. That air follows the Earth and rotates with it, both in its rotation and its revolution.

"The Earth is sixty times larger than the Moon, which has neither dawn nor dusk, nor does it have rainbows.

"In addition to five hundred planets discovered by Herschel in 1802, Iris and Flora were discovered in 1847, Metis in 1848, Hygiea in 1849, Parthenope and Victoria in 1850 and Eunomia in 1851. These latter planets are all situated around the circle described by Mercury.

"Thus you see, Madame, that the planet Iris, of which you are the Queen, has been known to us for twelve years."[7]

"I can see that, my friend; but I would like to know by what means it was discovered at such a great distance from your Earth."

"As I have told you, it was with the aid of our telescopes."

"But I do not know what they are; will you explain them to me?"

"A telescope or long-view, is a tube fitted at each of its two extremities with a glass lens, which magnifies distant objects. There are also large reflecting telescopes, which enlarge objects and make them seem closer. An astrolabe is an instrument for calculating the height of stars. A heliometer is an instrument for measuring the diameter of the Sun and of planets. A helioscope in an instrument for looking at the Sun."

---

[7] Thus indicating a date of composition of 1859.

"But tell me, I beg you, what glass is, for I have no idea."

"Glass is a fragile transparent substance that is obtained by the fusion of a mixture of sand and an alkali salt, caustic soda, extracted from the ashes of ferns, a kind of plant that grows in the woods."

"I understand that, but I don't understand how it magnifies objects."

"To magnify or make objects seem smaller on makes use of concave lenses—which is to say, hollowed out roundly, and it is by that means that the lenses placed in telescopes obtain the approach or distancing of objects.

"In order to measure the diameter of stars, astronomers employ a reticule, which consists of wire placed in the focal plane of the telescope in the form of a network or lattice, and it is by the distance between the wires that one can judge by calculation the distance of objects."

"In truth, my friend, you augment from day to day not only my astonishment but also my admiration, by means of all the marvels that you relate to me. But tell me: this glass to which you attribute so many marvels; is it only used by astronomers for their telescopes?"

"It serves several other purposes. When the glass is molten, and can be blown, one makes it into vessels from which liquids are drunk, carafes and bottles to contain liquids, panes to garnish frames that are fitted into windows to provide protection from bad weather. Mirrors are made from it—looking glasses that reproduce the resemblance of objects presented to them, which appear behind the mirror. The ancients did not know glass, they used oiled paper, or obsidian stone—a translucent stone—to replace widow-panes. Oiled paper is translucent, but one cannot see through it."

"But my friend, that discovery would be of great utility here. If the plant you mentioned exists on this planet we might, perhaps, with the precious information that you can give, succeed in making glass. If you are agreeable, we can go to explore my realm together and visit its woods, to try to discover fern there and other plants whose ashes we might use to make glass."

"I consent to that willingly, my noble friend; you know that I'm entirely devoted to you. But do you have in our capital, or elsewhere, a man who has some knowledge of Phytology?"

"I don't know that science."

"It's that of knowing and describing plants."

"I don't know, my friend, but I will have enquiries made, and if I discover a capable man, he will be brought here, and if he can give us satisfactory information, that will spare us a good deal of perhaps futile research."

VIII

The next day, a man was brought who was said to know plants. The Queen summoned me, and I questioned the man in her presence. It was difficult for me to refer to ferns in his language, because I did not know the word; I therefore made the decision to draw one, and he told the Queen that he had seen them in a wood near the village of Baleno.

Furnished with that information we hoped that our journey would not be fruitless, and the Queen decided that we would leave when the heat was less intense, for we were close to Mercury and we know how hot that planet is.

In the meantime, I continued giving the Queen lessons, and sometimes went to walk in her gardens, which were vast and well planted with flowers; that was a great attraction for me, because I had the intention of drawing a flower.

One day, when I was very occupied in examining the flowers, I heard the cries of several women, shouting: "Elpo, Elpo!"—which is a cry of distress, appealing for help. The cries were coming from a nearby grove of trees. I ran in that direction—or, rather, flew, because the cries were getting louder—and launched myself into the little wood, and in a few seconds I reached the edge of a pool where I saw the Queen's ladies, frightened and sobbing, only able to express the subject of their desperation to me by signs.

Finally, I understood that the Queen had disappeared in the middle of the pond. Throwing myself into the water and diving was the affair of an eye-blink, and I reappeared almost immediately on the surface, holding the Queen in my left arm while using the right and my feet to swim.

Cries of joy were uttered by the maids of honor, and when found my forting I hasted as much as possible to reach the bank, carrying my precious burden.

I laid the Queen down on the grass. She had lost consciousness, but her heard was beating quite regularly, and the cares that I lavished on her brought her round. She opened her eyes, and a sweet smile was my recompense.

I advised the ladies-in-waiting to change the Queen's garments quickly, and when everything was ready for the change I left the grove, but I stayed nearby in case I was needed. I informed the maids of honor of that, and allowed my clothes to dry on my body. I was not in any danger; the heat dried them out rapidly.

I was fortunate, glad to have saved the lady's life; I experienced all the happiness one feels on accomplishing a good deed.

I had asked the ladies-in-waiting to send me news of the Queen, and, indeed, they did so twice during the night. The Queen was feeling quite well, experiencing no distress except for a slight lassitude, and she was generous enough to ask for news of me.

The next day, the Queen came into my apartment by the door to the secret stairway; she was a little pale, but not in pain.

"I have come, my dear friend," she said, "to assure you of my gratitude for the service you rendered me. You have saved me from an imminent peril by which I was threatened; without you I would no longer exist."

"I give thanks to God, my good friend, for having been good enough to choose me to extract you from danger. He deigned to grant my prayer, and it's to him that you owe thanks, not to me; I am only the instrument of which he made use."

"And you believe," the Queen said to me, "that it is to God that I ought to be grateful? But I'm not of your religion, and I have no right to the protection of your God, whom I only know imperfectly and who does not know me."

"Forgive me, Madame, but my God is yours as he is mine; his bounty and his divine providence extend over everything that breathes; he protects all human equally, whatever their religion might be, for he considers them all to be his children. Doubtless he must have a certain predilection for those attached to his worship, but the God I adore is not a jealous God; he excuses those who worship imaginary gods, idols that are the image of a false divinity, fetishes, which are the idols of negroes, various beliefs such as those that still exist in the Oriental Indies, and the Egyptians, who adore the sacred bull Apis, animals and even reptiles.

"The savages of America adore the Great Spirit; they are more reasonable, living in tribes in their age-old forests, always in the presence of nature, their thoughts fermented, and they understood that that beautiful nature, and the resplendent stars, must have been created by a superior being. They were unable to conceive of an invisible God, Bossuet has said, and they called him the Great Spirit, but since that time, the majority have been enlightened by our missionaries."

"But my friend," said the Queen, excitedly, "can you not enlighten me as well as these missionaries have done for the savages? For all that you tell me ignites within me a keen desire to know the beauties and verities of your religion."

"I will do gladly, my noble friend. I will do more; I will give you the knowledge of God, the definition of the divinity, by means of convincing proofs that only I can give. Others before me have sought to resolve that great problem, but in vain. Even Simonides, the celebrated poet of antiquity, who lived five hundred years before Jesus Christ, failed in that definition, which was demanded of him by Hieron, King of Syracuse,[8] but I will give you proofs, and verbally, because I do not want to offend the opinions of others, which might give birth to controversies, and I am opposed to all contestation, either verbally or in writing."

"I approve, my worthy friend."

"When you're disposed to listen to me, we'll take a walk to the most remote corner of your gardens, where I can speak to you without fear of being

---

[8] The lyric poet Simonides (c556–468 B.C.) did spend some time at the court of King Hieron of Syracuse. This anecdote, originally related by Xenophon, appears—among many other places—in Pierre Bayle's *Dictionnaire historique et critique*, where Rousseau might well have found it.

overheard, and there we shall be in view of a part of the marvels of creation whose divine author I will make known to you."

The next day, the queen said to me: "My friend. I'm awaiting a great service from you. I cannot put off asking you for it any longer."

"Whatever it is, great Queen, I agree to it in advance."

"My friend, I desire ardently to know, to possess, what you promised me: the knowledge of the true God, the one that you adore."

"Today, my Queen, you shall be satisfied. When the ardor of the sun is less fierce, we shall go, as I said, into a solitary place in your gardens, and I will unveil the great mystery, the immensity of God. Your mind will be suddenly enlightened; you will understand then how God can be present at the same time throughout the universe, how he sees everything, and knows everything."

"How grateful I shall be to you, my worthy friend. Come to dinner with me today, and after dinner we shall go into the most isolated garden, where, without any other witness than God, you will make me know him and we shall adore him together. My heart enjoys in advance the happiness that awaits it. Oh, my friend, how dear you have become to me!"

I went to dine with the Queen, and did not perceive any sign of jealousy in the physiognomy of those present; everyone knew that the Queen's conversations with me were merely concerned with instruction. I had the reputation of being a scholar and I did not excite envy.

After dinner, I accompanied the Queen into the isolated garden, and after we had made sure that we would not have any indiscreet witnesses, I communicated to the Queen all my science regarding the knowledge of God, in his immensity and his infinite power. I explained how God was manifest in his works; I invited her to admire the beautiful vegetation that was around us; I told her how that vegetation was made, how the fruits succeeded the flowers, how the nucleus was formed inside them, enclosing the nut or the pips that served for reproduction.

Our conversation went on for a long time, and I perceived that the Queen was absorbed in her thoughts.

"I think, my noble friend," I said to her, "that that's enough for today with regard to vegetables. You would be too tired if this first lesson were prolonged, for there still remains a great deal for me to tell you about the marvels of nature; it's an inexhaustible subject."

"So much the better, my friend; I would have liked to listen to you for longer and to enjoy the pleasure that your precious lessons procure me; I'm delighted by today's, for it promises me a series of others that will be no less interesting and instructive."

""We're getting close to dusk," I said. "The sun is about to disappear in the Occident; we'll enjoy the beauty of a sunset."

"What do you mean, my friend, by the Occident?"

"The Occident is one of the four cardinal points, with are the north, the south, the Orient and the Occident. I shall mark them on the planetary system, that I drew for you."

"My friend," she said, "I would like to know one thing, but it might be a great indiscretion that would abuse your generosity."

"Have I not told you, my noble friend, that I'm entirely devoted to you."

"Yes, and you've given me proof of it, but I dare not demand this new thing of you."

"Dare, my noble friend, for it would offend me and cause me a good deal of pan if you doubted my willingness to satisfy you. Oh, I beg you tell me what you desire."

"What I desire, my worthy friend, is something that you possess and that I would like to possess too."

"Speak, my noble friend; everything that I have belongs to you—do you not know that in friendship, all property is common?"

"Oh, I know that. Well, what I desire is to know the language that you speak."

"But what you are asking me, my noble friend, would give me the greatest pleasure. We can commence right away, with the worlds and short familiar phrases that the most commonly used. That the way to learn a language quickly: first the practice and then the theory. Begin right away by asking me the names of things. Have no fear of questioning me, for it's by asking questions that one learns promptly. You have a great deal of perspicacity and a vivid conception; in very little time you'll understand everything that I tell you in my language."

IX

The Queen did, in fact, follow my advice, and a few days later, she knew a quantity of words and we already pronouncing a few short sentences that I had taught her very competently.

I was delighted with my royal pupil's progress; rapid success was certain.

I was fortunate enough to find, in a remote part of the gardens, a block of marl, or calcareous earth, which had doubtless been thrown there by a gardener who had found it while digging in the garden. The marl was quite soft and beautifully white; I thought that I might make sticks of chalk out of it, so I summoned one of the gardeners and asked him to carry the block to the palace for me.

I departed with my discovery and had it deposited in a cellar with the intention of going down there the next day in order to break the block into fragments similar to our sticks of chalk. In order to have a black marker I might be able to burn some wood, which I could extinguish in time to produce charcoal. I thought that during my expedition to Baleno with the Queen I might perhaps find charcoal, or some substance with which I could make black pencils, and perhaps find galls on oaks or other trees produces on the leaves and stems of certain trees by the injections of certain hemipterous insects; then I would be able to make ink. Quill pens were not difficult to find, and in any case, I would be able to make more.

The next day, when the Queen came to my study, I told her about the block that I had discovered and what I hoped to get out of it while hoping to find something better, but I needed an intelligent man to cut the block for me. She told me that she would send me a skillful man who could do the work. I also told the Queen that when we went to the wood at Baleno I hoped to find a substance with which to make ink, after which we would be able to write.

"So much the better!!" she said, enthusiastically. "I am longing to know how to write, because I believe that my progress in your language would be more rapid."

"I agree with you, my noble friend, and it's also to help you with that task that I shall try to make paper."

"In truth, my friend, I admire you, but I recall that you need old linen for that, and I shall give the order to find some. Then, whenever you want, we'll go to the wood at Baleno to look for the plants for the glass. The man who has seen the plant will go with us to show us the place. The weather is less hot, and will be favorable to our expedition. If nothing prevents us, we'll leave tomorrow."

We did, indeed, leave the following day. We passed through Arco, which is the planet's capital, without pausing, because the Queen wanted to remain incognito. Baleno is very close to the city, and we soon arrived at the wood where the man who was to go with us joined us.

We went into the wood and found the ferns, and other analogous plants. The Queen instructed him to cut all the plants and send them to her residence, taking care to separate the species, especially the fern.

I asked the men whether he knew of any place in the wood or its surroundings where there were minerals. He replied affirmatively that there were granite rocks and stones the color of lead. I asked to see them and he guided me to them. I examined the stones and put some of them aside in order to be sent to the royal residence along with the plants. He promised that he would do so, and kept his word.

I rejoined the Queen, who was sitting at the foot of a tree waiting for me, and told her about my discovery, and the hope I had, by cutting up the stones, of obtaining pencils like those of plumbago.

We returned to the residence, where, when we arrived, the Queen went up to her apartment—but as she was turning a corner on a stairway her foot slipped. She uttered a loud plaintive cry, followed by groans; her women ran to help her, but the Queen's dolorous plaints, which augmented when they touched her, threw them into a quandary. Alarm and consternation were general; they did not know how to soothe the Queen or what to do in order to transport her to her bed.

Couriers were sent on horseback to Arco and Baleno to bring back physicians and surgeons, with orders to go and come back at a gallop.

The wait for assistance was an overwhelming anxiety for all the palace personnel. The queen was still lying on the stairs, and no one could touch her without her uttering frightful cries. After some two hours, two physicians arrived; they went to the Queen, but she was in such great pain and prostration that they could not get any information out of her as to the pain she was experiencing. They consulted with one another and decided to have her carried to her bed in order to palpate her and discover where the seat of the trouble was.

It was a terrible moment when the Queen as transported to her bed; it was a heart-rending spectacle, and all the witnesses were penetrated by a sharp distress. The Queen's screams were frightful, and yet she could not have been left any longer where she was. The greatest pains were taken to minimize her suffering, and they finally succeeded in moving her to her bed, where she lay completely inert for some time. The physicians made her breathe in different odors, which calmed her somewhat, and started searching for the source of the trouble.

The queen had broken her thigh and the great trochanter at the head of the femur. It was incurable! The thigh was already swelling up and the swelling was getting worse; all hope was lost. The heat was intense and gangrene was to be feared; the condition was visibly deteriorating.

The Queen was endowed with a great strength of mind; she understood her situation and wanted to be instructed positively by the physicians. She summoned them and asked them to tell her frankly what they thought of her prospects.

The physicians were nonplussed, and stammered a few words, but the Queen said to them: "Have no hesitation in replying to me, Gentlemen. I need to know where I stand, and how long I still have to live."

"Your Majesty might live until tomorrow, but if she has dispositions to make, she had better make them today."

"That you, Gentlemen, That's sufficient."

The doctors withdrew, and she had one of her ladies-in-waiting summon me. I immediately went to her. She smiled at me and held out her hand.

"Come closer, my friend; I need to talk to you. I have to thank you for your kindness toward me, your devotion and the great and useful instruction that I received from you, of the knowledge of God, and the great truths and maxims of your holy religion. You have not sown in barren ground; those seeds have borne fruit, and I want to die a Christian, but I lack one thing for that, which I desire ardently, and that is to receive baptism. But who can confer that sacrament on me, my friend."

"Me, my noble friend."

"What! You have the authority to do that?"

"Yes, every Christian has the right to baptize by pronouncing the sacramental words."

"And when can you baptize me?"

"Right now, if that is your desire."

"Yes, my friend, right now."

"Yes, my sister—for we are about to be brother and sister in Jesus Christ. You are thoroughly penetrated, my sister, with all the verities that I have revealed to you?"

"Yes, my brother."

Then I took a little water, which I poured over her head, saying: "Angélique, I baptize you in the name of the Father, the Son and the Holy Spirit. So be it."

The Queen was admirable in that solemn moment, which rendered her a Christian. I made the sign of the cross and said to her: "Angélique, my sister, you are now a Christian."

"What joy! And it's to you that I owe it!"

The Queen died during the night. I watched over her with her women, and toward midnight she was able to recognize me. She said to me, in a very faint voice: "Adieu, my friend, adieu." She held out her hand, which went cold in mine. Her soul returned to God.

Unable to bear the sight of that abode, I resolved to leave as soon as possible.

X

I summoned Za; he arrived beside me almost immediately.

"You're grief-stricken," he said, "and I understand why you want to leave this place. Where would you like to go?"

"To the planet Flora," I replied.

"Very well; you'll be there in a moment, for it isn't far away."

We did, in fact, arrive a few minutes later.

As we approached the planet, Za said to me: "That edifice you perceive in the residence of Queen Flora, sovereign of this planet. Look closely at her palace; you will see an arbor covered with large leaves decorated with flowers; at this moment. At this moment the queen is sitting in that arbor, where her nymphs are presenting her with baskets and flowers; others are singing their sovereign's praises; their charming chords are accompanied by instruments that produce a soft and agreeable melody.

"It's in the presence of the sovereign that I'll deposit you. Your appearance will surprise her, without a doubt, but don't worry about it and have no fear; I shall be nearby."

These words had scarcely been pronounced when I was already at the feet of Queen Flora, who uttered a cry of fright on seeing me.

"Have no fear, great Queen; I mean you no harm—on the contrary. I am a man who has come thirty million leagues to visit your planet, and who hopes to obtain a favorable welcome from Your Majesty."

"You see me disposed," he Queen said to me, "but where do you come from? Who are you? Why have you come to my estates?"

"Great Queen, I come from the Earth, which is a planet like yours; I am a man always occupied in scientific research. I thought that your planet ought to produce flowers unfamiliar to us; my design is therefore to acquire a knowledge of the flowers you possess here, to draw and to paint them, if I can procure colors."

"What! You know how to draw and paint?" she said to me. "If you could teach me your talents, it would give me the greatest pleasure. Can you instruct me in those arts?"

"Undoubtedly, Madame, if Your Majesty has the desire."

"If I have the desire, you say! But it would be a joy! We have tried in vain to draw our flowers, but have been unable to succeed. That is probably because there are means to employ of which we are unaware."

"Your remark is very just, Madame. Those means consist of a knowledge of rules and principle."

"And you know these rules and principles?"

"Perfectly, Madame."

"And you will be kind enough to teach them to me?"

"I shall make it a duty."

"What expression are you using there? I would have preferred it to be out of amity."

"You Majesty does me much honor, and I shall be able to recognize her bounty toward me with my entire devotion."

"That's very good, my friend. I see in you a man endowed with distinguished sentiments, and from this moment you are a guest of the palace. I will have an apartment prepared for you, where you will be served everything that you require. You shall indicate the times for your meals, and choose in our apartment the most convenient room to make into your study and work-room. You will dine with me today, in order that everyone will know how I regard you, and that you possess my esteem."

"Thank you, Madame. My conduct will prove to you that I merit it."

"I'm convinced of it, my friend. Now, what shall we do about the lessons in drawing and painting?"

"We'll begin with drawing, which it is necessary to know before painting. From the very first lesson Your Majesty will understand how important it is to know how to draw before commencing painting; a painter, no matter how careful he is, is always detestable if his drawing is poor; a good drawing, made simply in black pencil, is a thousand times preferable to a bad painting."

"Good! I shall follow your instructions exactly, my friend."

"It will be to your benefit, for Your Majesty will understand promptly how important drawing is to the rapid progress she will make when she commences painting."

I went to dinner with the Queen. Her reception was very gracious, and simultaneously testified to her deference for me. People gazed at me curiously, some in a kindly fashion, others with a jealous eye.

The Queen gave each of her nymphs the name of a flower, which it is necessary to translate as Primrose, Pansy, Clematis, Violet, Daisy, Marguerite, Wallflower, Hyacinth, Eglantine, Rose, Hortensia, Convolvulus, Tulip, Lily, Heliotrope, Jasmine, Camellia and Dahlia.

The number of her nymphs was not fixed. She had three for whom she had more affection; they were her confidantes; she therefore confided to them that I knew how to draw and paint, and that I was going to give her lessons to teach her that art. Their joy was great, and they testified to the Queen the desire they had also to receive my lessons.

"I don't know, my dear friends, whether he will agree to give them to you, but I will ask him, and will tell you what he replies."

Soon, the whole troop of pretty nymphs had the same desire, when they knew that I would soon begin giving my lessons to the Queen, who came to visit me in my apartment to see whether there were any changes I wanted to make.

I asked for a curtain, in order that I could obtain the level of light that was necessary to me.

"One will be put up for you," she told me. "When would you like to commence my lessons?"

"When it pleases Your Majesty—but what we lack is pencils."

"I have some, and I think that you will be able to make use of them."

The Queen came the next day and had all the objects of which she made use for drawing brought to me. You will understand in advance that none of it was of much use to me. There was a kind of paper in use in the country that, strictly speaking, might serve for drawing, and soft stones of various colors to serve as pencils. I carved some of the latter, giving them the form of pencils, and the lesson commenced.

I asked the Queen to draw a vase that I placed in front of her on the table, in which I put a flower. It was a lily.

She began with the lily; I made her begin with the vase. She began with the mouth of the vase; I made her draw a line perpendicular to the horizontal, and then divide up the vase into sections—which is to say, to indicate the planes of the neck, body and foot of the vase, and then to indicate the contours of the vase on the indicated planes, commencing on the left.

She did as I said, and understood immediately the great advantage of the facility that one finds in following the rules of an art. She trembled with joy at having been able to draw a vase so rapidly and so accurately.

"How content I am, my friend. You have just made me understand instantly the importance there is in knowing and following the principles of an art. I also understand why one must not start painting until one understands drawing perfectly. Thank you, my friend, for that good lesson, which is of great importance for me. Now I have something to ask of you which might perhaps be indiscreet on my part."

"Speak, Madame, and if what you have to ask me is within my power, you will find me disposed to satisfy your desire."

"How good you are, my worthy friend. Well, if you are agreeable, we will go to visit Florina, which is the capital city of my realm. That will enable to you get to know a small part of my realm, and during the journey I shall tell you what I have to ask of you."

"I accept your offer with great pleasure," I told the Queen, "for I desire to know the interior of your planet."

"If this journey interests you we can, if you wish, go to Floresca the day after, which is the second city of my realm."

"Very gladly, Madame. I shall go with you wherever you wish."

What the Queen might have to ask my worried me; it was a vague anxiety, to be sure, but it troubled my mind nevertheless.

I departed, therefore the following day, with the Queen in her litter, carried by two small horses.

XI

I did not see anything remarkable on the route that we followed, except that almost all of the countryside was covered with flowers that embalmed the air; there were few picturesque locations, nothing but the flowers. I like flowers a great deal, but seeing nothing else everywhere became tedious.

We arrived in Florina, through which the Queen wanted to pass incognito. The city is quite pretty but has nothing worthy of remark.

We came back that same evening to the residence. During the journey the Queen did not speak to me about the request she had to maker of me, and I did not prompt her. I thought that it would do as well the flowing day.

The next day, we went to Floresca. The landscape was almost identical to the one I had seen the previous day; always flowers.

The Queen was pensive. Finally, she said to me: "My friend, this is what I have to say to you. You know that among my nymphs there are three for whom I have a marked predilection; I have confided to them that I am receiving lessons in drawing from you. They have mentioned it to their companions, and several of them desire to receive our precious lessons. What do you say?"

I received that confidence rather coldly, and I replied: "I'll think about it, Madame, and let you know my answer tomorrow."

As I was not enthusiastic to give lessons to anyone but the Queen, I made the most prudent decision, that of going away. I summoned Za, who arrived immediately.

He said to me: "I know what's worrying you and the decision you've made; I can but approve. Where do you want to go?"

"To the planet Parthenope," I told him.

"Very well; we'll leave tomorrow morning. Prepare yourself: go to bed fully dressed and at sunrise, I'll wake you up within sight of Parthenope.

I thanked my good genius, and he disappeared. I made my preparations, ate a little and went to bed fully dressed, as my good genius had told me to do.

He woke me up at sunrise within sight of Parthenope.

"Look," he said.

I looked, and was astonished to see a planet whose topography was not unknown to me; the more I gazed the more locations I recognized that I had seen before: the city that I perceived recalled memories; I recognized a few monuments—if, at least, thought I recognized them, because it could only be an illusion, since I had never come to this planet. Perhaps it was a kind if mirage, like the one that exists in deserts, and even at sea; I did not know which conjecture was the most probable. Finally, weary of conjecturing, I decided to wait.

My good genius undoubtedly saw what was happening within me, for a voice said to me: "Everything you see is agitating your mind, but don't worry; you'll soon know the reality. Can you see a great cortege accompanying a woman dressed in rich garments?"

"Yes," I replied.

"That's Queen Partha, who is going to take a stroll on the shore of a bay that you ought to be able to see; it is there, in her presence, that I shall set you down. Respond to the questions that she asks you. She's a little hard of hearing, but that comes from the language of the planet, for the Queen is good and I hope that she'll give you a good welcome. In any case, as always, don't worry about anything; I shall be nearby."

At that moment, a delightful music became audible; it was coming from the cortege, and my good genius set me on the ground directly in front of the Queen. My sudden appearance caused her a certain alarm, and stopped the progress of the cortege.

"What do you want with me? Who are you?"

"Great Queen," I replied, "I have come to your realm to learn and to assure myself of the reality of things that I have only seen thirty million leagues from your planet."

"What is he saying?" the important individuals who were with her asked her. "He's mad, I believe."

"No, great Queen, I'm not mad; I'm telling you the truth."

"But how is that possible?"

"An individual approached the Queen, and by this gestures—which are frequently employed in that country—I was able to determine that he was talking about me. He often looked at me, and with interest. Perhaps he took me for an astronomer, or at least for a man knowledgeable about astronomy.

The Queen said to me: "*Siete il ben venuto, Signore.* You will be lodged in my palace, and I shall come to see you in order to obtain an explanation of the things that you have said to me, which pique my curiosity."

The Queen seemed benevolent. I thought that my sojourn with her would be pleasant and useful.

The Queen came to see me the following day, asked me how I found my apartment, whether I was well cared for, and if I lacked anything.

"I'm perfectly comfortable here, great Queen, and I have only to thank Your Majesty for her kindness toward me."

"But tell me, Sire, how you have been able to discover my realm at a distance of thirty million leagues? That seems impossible to me, and it excites my curiosity as well as that of the other people who heard you."

Then I told the Queen about the means of telescopes, of which I gave her an explanation. The Queen manifested great surprise as she listened to me, and only expressed herself in exclamations of astonishment."

"*O che cosa bella, o che maraviglia!* Tell me, *caro mio*, is it possible for you to procure such instruments? I would be charmed to see things so far away. One of the people who heard you when you arrived told me that you appeared to have knowledge of astronomy. What is that science?"

"It's the knowledge of the stars."

"And you possess it?"

"Yes, Madame."

"*Va bene.* Come to dine with me today, and after dinner I shall take great pleasure in hearing you talk to those people. Perhaps the knowledge you possess will be useful to them."

"I desire to be, Madame, and I shall be very glad to have been agreeable to you in something."

"*Benissimo mio caro.* Someone will come to fetch you at dinner time, *sitate pronto. Si maestro io lo saro.*"

One of the Queen's officers came to notify me, and I went down immediately. The Queen received me with distinction, and had me seated next to her. Although flattered by that preference, I feared that it might excite the jealousy of the nobles present at the dinner. At dessert, however, the frowns cleared.

The Queen was uniformly cheerful and showed a great deal of natural wit. Behind her there were two of her maids of honor to serve her; one of them gazed at me with sustained attention and seemed to be examining all the guests. She found an opportunity to say to me: "*Ho da parlavi, do poprenzo.*"

What could she have to say to me?

48

After diner, as everyone withdrew, and the Queen was accompanied by the nobles, she seized a moment when she was not observed and said to me: "*Badate.*"

I looked at her in surprise. What had I to fear?

She indicated a passage to me with a gesture and said: "*Siguitemi.*"

I followed her, and when she saw that she could talk to me without being overheard by the nobles, she said to me: "The marks of distinction that you have received from the Queen have awakened the jealousy of the noblemen. Be prudent, and never go out without being armed with a stiletto, which is the offensive and defensive weapon of this country—for it's to be feared that someone might seek to murder you."

I thanked the charming young woman, and she disappeared rapidly.

What I had just learned gave me pause for thought, and I resolved to procure a stiletto—but to whom should I address myself in order to obtain that weapon?

The domestic who served me and who appeared to be attached to me seemed to be appropriate to fulfill that task, and I decided to talk to him about it that same evening. To buy anything, however, I needed local money, and I only had French. I emptied my purse, and to my great surprise, several small gold coins fell out whose value I did not know.

I summoned my domestic. "Gennaro," I said. "I desire to have a stiletto."

"That will be easy, *Excellenza.*"

"How much does a stiletto cost?"

"*Se condo la grandezza at la bellazza.*"

"I'd like a simple one to carry inside my coat."

"*Un buone stiletto, costera due ducati con lo stucio.*"

I took out my purse and asked him what the little gold coins were.

"*Sono ducati,*" he replied.

I took two of them, which I gave him to buy the stiletto, and gave him one to keep the secret. He brought me a stiletto without a sheath, which suited me perfectly, and I put it inside my jacket, with the intention of always carrying it on my person, because I saw in the young woman's warning and the gold coins that I had found in my purse another precaution of my good genius, who doubtless approved of that prudent measure.

XII

That existence of always being on the alert became intolerable to me, however, and I resolved to continue my voyage and conclude it with the Sun. I was not tempted to go to Jupiter, Saturn, Uranus and Neptune; those cold regions made me tremble in advance.

Before quitting the planet Parthenope, however, I desired to see the capital city and its surroundings. One morning, therefore, I set out toward the capital.

On the road I encountered a vehicle that was going in that direction—a kind of cabriolet called a *coricoli*.

I soon arrived in the great city, the sight of which caused me a great astonishment, because it seemed to me that I knew it. Its monuments, which I could see from a distance, I had certainly seen before—but where? I could not succeed in remembering.

Having arrived at the city I asked my driver to take me to a good hotel, and he took me to the hotel *del Sole, sulla piazza del Sole*. It was then that my astonishment reached its peak; I was in a city exactly similar to Naples, in the same hotel, and in the same room, that I had occupied twenty years before. I was in the city that I loved so much, and whose surroundings had so many attractions for me.

I did not waste a moment. I went out armed with my stiletto and headed toward *Chiaja*, going past the beautiful San Carlo theater, and did not take long to arrive *al giardino reale*, at the end of which is the grotto of Posillipo. I stopped at the entrance to the grotto, next to the tomb of Virgil, nicknamed the Swan of Mantua, where he was born. He was, it is said, a pupil of Parthenius.

Parthenope was a siren whose body was found on the sea shore. A Greek colony was established on that shore, known today as the Bay of Naples. They founded a city there, which they named Neopolis or Neapolis, which means "new city." It received the name Napoli in Italian, doubtless borrowed from Napoli, city of Greece. The French call it Naples.

Sitting next to Virgil's tomb—or, at least, the place that it really occupies in Naples—I had before me the whole extent of the bay, the beautiful bat identical to the Bay of Naples, and for a horizon Vesuvius, and the Somma, at the foot of Vesuvius. I admired a pretty town similar to Portici, to my left, Castel Sant Elmo, and to my right, an island similar to Capri, celebrated for the shameful debauches of Tiberius, which he called his delights.

I took a coricoli to visit the environs of the capital of Parthenope. I collected a few souvenirs of my youth there, by virtue of the resemblance of a few locations to those in the environs of Naples, or, at least, I took pleasure in imagining that the resemblance existed. Satisfied with the excursion, I asked my driver to take me back to the Queen's palace.

There I thought about all the annoyances and torments that awaited me occasioned by the jealousy of the nobles, and I took the firm resolution to leave. I summoned Za, and told him that I intended to quit Parthenope in order to visit the Sun.

"Very well," he said to me. "We'll leave tomorrow at daybreak. Go to bed fully dressed, as usual, and we'll arrive at the Sun in no time at all—but you won't be able to stay there for long, for although the Sun has its inhabitants, you won't be able to live with them. Content yourself with visiting them for your instruction, and we'll leave the same day to go wherever you please."

"That will be to France," I told him, "my dear fatherland, where I left a beloved sister that I'm in a hurry to see again, and who is doubtless anxious, awaiting my return impatiently, for he has no idea where I am."

I went to bed fully dressed, and the next morning, Za deposited me on the edge of the center of the Sun, before the immense ocean of fire, which I consider to be an igneous substance whose heat rises to the photosphere, from which the Sun's rays depart.

It was on the edge of that sea of fire that my good genius set me down, and I stayed there without being inconvenienced by the heat, because I was protected from it by the Sunspots, some of which are of very great extent.

I was sitting down and contemplating the immense hearth that I had before my eyes, which wearied them slightly. I turned to look in another direction and perceived two men, who could see me but who did not pay any attention to me. The men were enormously corpulent and had muscular limbs; they were naked, and their skin was red. The sight of them reminded me of the Patagonians that I had seen in America, and were very nearly the same height, which is said to be seven feet, although it is necessary to remark that their feet only measure eleven inches.

The two men drew away from me; left alone, and experiencing the need to take a little nourishment, I was wondering how to appease my hunger when I perceived a basket some distance away, which I hastened to visit.

What joy! It was filled with provisions. It was an attention that I doubtless owed to my god genius, and I shouted "Thank you, Za."

Having nothing more to see on the Sun I summed him, and told him that I desired to return to France, to the very spot where he had raised me up on my departure.

"And when do you want to leave?"

"Whenever you like," I relied.

"At this very moment—and you'll sleep at home tonight."

I did, indeed—and without anyone having noticed my absence.

Part Two

Introduction

I had just concluded my voyage to the Moon, the other planets and the Sun when my good genius Za transported me from that star to the Earth, to the very spot from which he had lifted me up.

"Before you go," I said to him, "I have a request to make of you."

"What?"

"I desire to go to visit the space beyond the fixed stars, where I suppose there are others much more distant, which our astronomers have not yet discovered; it is that space, which I shall call *imaginary*, that I desire to visit, in order to know the truth."

"What you are asking might be difficult for me to obtain, for it's very far away, and it will take many years to get there. But other imaginary spaces exist, of which your scientists are perhaps unaware, although they are much closer at hand, to which it would be possible for me to transport you.

"I'll go talk to our chief Zadir about it, and I'll accompany you, if he permits it. If not, I'll have you accompanied by two genii of the air who are subordinate to me: a sylph and a sylphide, his sister. They'll be very useful to you, without a doubt, in those spaces, where everything is so different from the planets you have visited, where many events probably await you; but I'll give them the order and the power to protect you throughout your voyage, and when it ends, they'll bring you back here. When do you want to go?"

"Whenever you think it appropriate."

"I'll go warn them to collect provisions sufficient for the journey."

My good genius informed me when everything was ready for the voyage, and we left the following day.

Three days after our departure we arrived in the imaginary spaces.

I

The imaginary spaces are situated in different parts of the immensity; they are unknown to scientists. They are not planets that rotate on their axes and circle the zodiac; their only movement is oscillation, like that of a pendulum. They are islands, flat on the upper surface and round underneath, which gives them the form of the drums known as kettledrums, used by the cavalry. The inferior part, being higher than the Sun, receives the light of the star, and the upper part receives that of the fixed stars, which are as many suns.

In nebulous times, those islands are illuminated, in part, by birds like those in America which are called Firebirds. These birds are very abundant around the islands, where they find their nourishment. The islands are numerous; the majority are nameless, because they are small and uninhabited; they form Cyclades, and atolls in archipelagos.

The best known of these islands are those of Reveries, Fictions, Illusions, Tricks, Prodigies and Marvels. In addition to those there is a gathering of islands in the form of a delta, of which the three principal ones, which occupy the angles, are the Isles of Chimeras, Metamorphoses and Visions. Other islands also exist in a nearby space—I say nearby because it is only five thousand leagues distant from the one where we are now. I learned that from my sylph, but as a veridical voyager, I shall only speak about those islands when I have visited them.

On our arrival in the imaginary spaces we descended on the Isle of Reveries, where we saw beings of human form that were marching or strolling in silence. They could probably see us, but they did not appear to be astonished; their thoughts, if they had any, were doubtless wandering in the waves of the air. Their taciturnity did not make them very amiable hosts. The men and women appeared to be of the same humor; only the children seemed more alert. The men, woman and children were all naked; only the women had, for a girdle around the midriff, a liana bearing a few leaves. The people did not seem very hospitable.

I made those remarks aloud; my sylph heard them, and, as the brother and sister thought as I did, they transported me to the Isle of Fictions in a matter of minutes

There were saw beings of human form, to be sure, but with elongated heads, and double eyes on each side, like the fish called *Anablepsis*. Others had bird-like beaks instead of jaws, like the animals of that name which exist in New Holland.[9] Others had only one eye in the middle of the forehead, like certain crustaceans called *Polyphemus*. Others had a mouth so small that one could scarcely see it, like the animals knows as *Anostomes*. Others, in large numbers, resembled monkeys, with the exception that they had no tails. Others had heads like horses. Others, finally, had muzzles like lions, like the leprosy of Arabs known as *Leontiasis*. All these beings were frightening in their appearance, all the more so because they had the cries of monkeys, the whinnies of horses and the roar of lions.

I regretted having undertaken the voyage, but I was *en route*, and I hoped to find people less ugly on the other islands. Then I asked my sylph to transport me to the Isle of Illusions.

When we arrived on that island, I found that everything had a very agreeable appearance; the men were good enough, at least in appearance; the women seemed to me to be pretty. We were given a good welcome by the islanders, who received us in their huts, which were constructed of branches and mud, but I found the interior very neat.

The atmosphere was thick; the air was laden with large clouds, which the light of the stars could not traverse entirely; one only received at intervals the fugitive light of firebirds and that of glow-worms, which were in the grass and in the bushes by which the hut I was in was surrounded. Those glow-worms emitted as much light as a candle, and the multitude of those insects produced a considerable clarity, at least sufficient for us not to be in complete obscurity. When dawn appears,[10] however, all that lighting is soon replaced by daylight, in which one can judge things better.

---

[9] i.e. "duckbills"—the Platypus.

[10] It is not obvious how dawn can appear on the imaginary worlds, given the configuration previously indicated, but there appears to be a cycle of day and night on all of them.

I had thrown myself down on a kind of bed on the floor in the corner of the hut. When I awoke I found myself lying on a coarse mat, with my head placed on a bundle of dried plants. In spite of the hardness of that couch, I had slept very well. An agreeable dream had transported me to my own bed, with its flexible mattress and mahogany frame, surrounded by curtains suspended from a crown attached to the ceiling and ornamented with elegant drapes.

I no longer saw anything in their place but a host of insects and little animals, all stirring, running, agitating crazily, jumping and capering; and in order that everything should be in keeping, I heard on the floor below the hiss of reptiles and the croaking of frogs and toads. There was a complete cacophony, when, suddenly, all those discordant sounds gave way to a gentle harmony, a delightful symphony that ravished my senses and drew me out of my torpor.

I awoke entirely, therefore, and no longer saw anything of what I had seen, or heard anything of what I had heard, and was convinced that I had been the victim of an illusion.

I got up from my bed, already dressed, and I went out to breathe in the morning air and stroll around the island, where I hoped to encounter my sylph or my sylphide in some form—for I did not know them; they were invisible to me, as my good genius Za had been. It was probable, however, that my sylph would speak to me in order to ask whether I had anything to ask of him. I could not summon him, because I did not know his name, or that of his sister; I had forgotten to ask.

I went out, therefore, and at the door of my hut I found myself face to face with my host and hostess, who saluted me by putting their hands on their head and saying: "*Salamicadi!*" I replied to their politeness, and recommenced my stroll.

About half an hour after my departure from the hut, I sat down at the foot of a tree. The subtle air of the island was stimulating my appetite when I saw a charming woman suddenly appear, with gracious manners and gestures, who reminded me of Fanny Elssler in her role as *La Sylphide*.[11]

"Is that you, Fanny, that I can see once more?"

"No," she replied. "I'm the sylphide who is the sister of the sylph accompanying you. My brother has asked me to bring you this basket, in which you'll find your morning meal."

"I'm very grateful to you, but I beg you to tell me your brother's name."

"My brother's name is Zico. That is the name that you should pronounce three times when you have need of him."

"And may I ask yours?"

---

[11] Fanny Elssler (1810-1884) was an Austrian ballerina who first came to France in 1834. She danced *La Sylphide* in 1838, apparently in an attempt to outdo her great rival Marie Taglioni, for whom the role had been created, but she failed.

"Mine is Zica. My brother has a sympathy for you, and will acquit with pleasure the orders he has received from his chief, the genius Za."

"By what title should I address you when you give me the pleasure of coming to visit me?"

"None," she said. "Simply Zica. When you have need of my services you call me by pronouncing it three times: *Zica! Zica! Zica!*—and I shall be with you immediately. But it's late and you must need to eat. I'll leave you in order to return to my brother, but before leaving you, tell me how you spent the night."

"I sleep well, although rather poorly couched."

"Would you like to change island? I'll notify my brother."

"I'd like that, but will you accompany us?"

"We've received orders to accompany you wherever you desire to go."

"In that case, I desire to go to the Isle of Tricks."

"Very well. I'll go tell my brother, and it probably won't take us long to get there. While awaiting our departure, rest in order to repair the fatigue caused by a sleepless night."

With those words, she disappeared. I ate, and after the meal, which I needed, I leaned back against the tree at the foot of which I was sitting and went to sleep.

II

I do not know how long my sleep lasted, but I was wrenched out of it by a sudden brightness that struck my heavy eyelids. I woke up with a start, and my eyes were dazzled by the glare of a bright light coming from a flock of firebirds that were passing beneath us.

Then Zico said to me: "We'll be on the Isle of Tricks shortly, the capital of which is Lutèce."

"Lutèce!" I exclaimed. "How has that name reached all the way here? That ancient village composed of huts? Those huts, it's true, have mostly become sumptuous town houses and palaces: the Tuileries, the Louvre and Notre Dame have been built in the place once occupied by those miserable huts!"

"Look, here's the Isle of Tricks. Can you see its capital?"

I looked, and was stuck motionless by surprise on seeing before my eyes all the admirable monuments that embellish the modern Lutèce, Paris, admired by all strangers, where the science and arts flourish and appear to have arranged a rendezvous. I could not get enough of the pleasure that I experienced in contemplating that city, over which I love to run my eyes.

But is it an illusion, then? For I no longer recognize the majority of its streets; in their place I see, either spacious squares or new streets lined with magnificent houses, and they are all sculpted, ornamented with balconies; all those streets are broad and magnificent; I can no longer see the labyrinth of narrow and dirty little streets lateral to the Rue Saint-Martin; that entire miry quarter has disappeared, to give way to beautiful and airy streets. The Rue Saint-Martin itself has disappeared; in its place I see a superb boulevard traversing that great quarter of Paris; everywhere I see nothing but embellishments. The Louvre, which was already so beautiful, is now admirably sumptuous, where the great and the beautiful are combined in exquisite taste. It needed a genius to complete that beautiful work, worthy of the Parthenon of the new Athens.

If the beautiful garden of the Tuileries, the Champs-Élysées and the beautiful palace that I see there, the Hôtel-de-Ville, the Bibliothèque and so many other monuments that I perceive are only a trick, an illusion, I cannot complain—I owe them a few moments of joy!

Shortly afterwards, Zico deposited me in Lutèce, at a house in the Chaussée d'Antin, where I lived with my family for several years. He set me down in the garden—the garden that I had embellished so much, having an excellent gardener care for it. Night had fallen, and I hastened to go into the house, where I found many dear objects of my tenderness, and my amour.

When I went into the drawing room, there was a unanimous cry of joy. I was surrounded by cherished individuals, who lavished their caresses upon me. The sweet and intense emotion that we all experienced prevented us from expressing ourselves other then in abrupt, inconsequential remarks, but the tears of joy and happiness that we shed spoke for us. It was the eloquence of the heart, easily understood by any sensitive soul.

We dined *en famille*—what a joy for us, who had not savored it for a long time! The dinner was long and peaceful; we did not say much, having too many things to say, but our eyes expressed all our thoughts better than words could have done.

Finally, the time arrived to go to bed, and everyone retired, regretfully to their bedrooms; but none of us savored the pleasures of sleep. How could we sleep after so much emotion? So we got up early.

I was unaware of all the disasters, all the changes that had overtaken the house. After our ruination, it had been sold to entrepreneurs; all the lovely things that I had had constructed had been taken out or demolished. I experienced a constriction in the heat, but I did not allow it to depress me; my courage did not abandon me, and that of my wife and sister did not weaken. We had embarked on a new enterprise, which prospered to begin with, but was destroyed by a revolution in Paris.

I spent the day with my family, but the next morning, when I woke up, I saw none of the members of my family around. I thought, and was convinced, that everything pleasant that had happened to me was a dream, an illusion that had vanished; only the misfortune was real, and had remained. That house, that place of joy for me, was no longer anything to the eye but a skeleton that reminded me at every step, at every moment, of the happy times, so regrettable, that I had spent there. I could no longer bear it there, and I decided to leave.

I summoned my sylph and told him that I desired to go to the Isle of Prodigies.

"Very well," he said. "We'll leave tomorrow before sunrise. Make your preparations go to bed fully dressed, and we'll transport you to the Isle of Prodigies."

III

The next day, at sunrise, we were within sight of the Isle of Prodigies. I was profoundly asleep. Zica woke me up, and my sylph said: "There's the Isle of Prodigies, whose capital city, which you can see from here, is called Prodigium.

I contemplated the island, which appeared to me to be very singular, in that all the houses, all the monuments and all the edifices were inclined, but my astonishment did not last long. I remembered the leaning tower of Pisa, opposite the Baptistry, and the leaning tower of Bologna, known as the Asinelli, and then I found nothing surprising in it, although it was singular, fantastic and capricious, because for me it was not a phenomenon, something extraordinary. I expected, however to find bizarre and eccentric inhabitants.

Zico, as he had been instructed to do by my genius Za, had given me the faculty of understanding and speaking the languages of the islanders of the imaginary spaces. He set me down at the portal of a house of grandiose appearance, which was not inclined. When they perceived me, the servants of the house approached me. Some were black, others a very pale white, like the albinos that are regarded in India as degenerate beings and only go out at night; they are called *kakerlak*,[12] and also known as white negroes. Others were of different hues. Night was falling; I was surrounded by all those people coming to see me; for them I was an object of curiosity.

The noise they were making was overheard by the mistress of the house, who wanted to know the cause of it. She was told that it was a man such as had never been seen, that he was a stranger and seemed to be expecting to be offered hospitality. The lady, whose name was Belladone, belonged to a great family of the city of Prodigium. She wanted to see me and gave orders that I was to be taken up to a small room adjacent to the one she occupied.

Her order was carried out, and someone came to invite me to go to see the lady. I went up a magnificent staircase, very similar to ours. I was shown into the small room indicated by the lady, and soon afterwards, I saw a woman come in whose beauty dazzled me.

She doubtless perceived my disturbance, for she said: "Don't worry; you're in my house; you'll receive all the assistance and cares of hospitality; but may I, without offending you, ask who you are? For you're a stranger, from a

---

[12] Literally, cockroaches.

land that I doubtless do not know. By your distinguished manners, I judge that you're of a good family."

"You're not mistaken in our judgment, Madame; I am, In fact, of a very good family; the education I received gave birth in me to the desire to know everything that exists in the immensity. I was born on a planet that is in that immensity, and which is some thirty million leagues distant from your island."

"What!" she exclaimed. "You have been able to come from so far away?"

"Yes, Madame."

"But how did you do it?—you have no wings."

"No, Madame, but I was transported to your island by a superhuman power, which protects me and has given me the means of visiting several planets, and even the Sun."

"The Sun!" she exclaimed. "What, you have been to the sun, and you were not burned there?"

"No, Madame."

"But you are saying things that are marvelous."

"I agree, Madame, and, before having visited that immense globe of fire, I would have thought like you; but the observations made by astronomers have taught me that the center of the Sun is not burning, since it is inhabited, and that the heat that comes to us from its disk, where the heat of that sea of fire rises to what astronomers cal the photosphere—that is the most luminous part of the Sun, from which its rays depart, which illuminate, fecundate and heat everything that exists in the universe, and bring about the maturity of the fruits that vegetables give us.

"On your island, you do not enjoy all the benefits of the sun in their entirety, because it is situated beyond its elevation, and it only illuminates it from underneath, but that underside is not far away, and receives its rays almost horizontally—principally its vertical rays, which give the center of your island a heat almost equal to the volcanoes that we have in the center of our planet. You thus enjoy the same advantages that we possess in that regard, but it is not the same for the upper surface of your island; it is scarcely lit by the sun, but it receives from below the warmth necessary to the vegetation, which must be very beautiful. The upper part of your island receives the light of the fixed stars that are around the Sun. You have, in addition, the multitude of firebirds that surround your island and illuminate it by night, and the other multitude of glowworms, which illuminate the countryside. Those advantages are not, without a doubt, comparable to those we possess on our planets, which all rotate on their axes and around the sun, which alone remains motionless at the center of the universe."

Belladone, whom I shall call *Belladonna*, paid the closest attention to what I was saying. She did not take her eyes off me, and seemed astonished by the things I said—which she was doubtless hearing for the first time, for she uttered a profound sigh and said to me:

"Everything that you have just told me interests me a great deal and gives me the greatest pleasure. I can see that you possess a great deal of learning; perhaps it would be agreeable for you to augment it with a knowledge of the island that I inhabit."

"That is my intention, Madame, and I propose to explore it."

"If such is your intention," said Belladonna, "I offer to accompany you in your research; that will give you the means to examine everything without fatigue, because we can make the little excursion in a barouche, and you will be free to stop at all the places you would like to examine. If you wish, we can go to visit Prodigium, the capital city of the island."

"I accept your offer with great pleasure, Madame, and even with gratitude."

We set out the following morning in a little caleche drawn by two animals of the deer genre, a kind of reindeer, very light in running.

The landscape of that island is charming; the vegetation is prodigious in the beauty, the variety and the freshness of its plants, which were all unknown to me, but nevertheless attracted my admiration. I asked Belladonna their names but she did not know them. The trees were surprising in their beauty, their fruits admirable.

We arrived at a little wood, which it was necessary to traverse. We found ourselves at a crossroads, where Belladonna proposed that we stop in order to rest our animals. We got down from the barouche, and sat down at the feet of two of the large and beautiful trees by which the crossroads was surrounded. We savored the pleasure that the soul experiences in contemplating the marvels of creation.

"Don't you think," I said to Belladonna, "that thoughts are sweetest when one is confronted by the works of God?"

"What do you mean by God?" he asked.

"I mean by God," I replied, "the Sovereign Being who created everything that exists in nature: the beautiful sky that we are contemplating, the earth we inhabit, all the plants with which it is ornamented, all the animals, and these charming birds whose delightful songs sing the praises of their Creator!"

At that moment we had the harmonious concert of numerous birds that were in the trees at the feet of which we were sitting.

Belladonna took my arm and squeezed it, saying: "What you have just told me, my friend, causes me an impression that I have never felt before. And you believe that it is God, whose name you have just pronounced, that created all these beautiful things?"

"I am convinced of it, Madame, and in the 5864 years[13] since he created it, everything has remained in the same state. After having created the heavens,

---

[13] Indicating a date of composition of 1860, if the author is employing James Ussher's calculation of the creation having occurred in 4004 B.C.

God created the angels to announce and execute his orders; then God created the Firmament, in which he placed the Sun, and created the planets and stars in the same way. Then he created the fish and the birds. On the sixth day he created the animals and man, and concluded with the masterpiece of nature, by creating woman!

"The wisdom of God is so profound that everything he has created is subject to his supreme law. The sun is motionless at the center of the universe where God has placed it; the planets rotates around it and receive light from it, which some of them, called moons, transmit to other planets by reflection during the night.

"For humans and for animals his divine providence had foreseen and provided for their needs; for God, by his immensity, is present at all times in all the parts of the universe. That is why God sees everything, knows everything and provides everything; that is what is called Providence.

"All the animals find on land the nourishment appropriate to them. Who gives them that nourishment, if not the one that created them? The fish find their nourishment in the waters; the birds find theirs on land and in the air; the insects find it everywhere.

"The quadrupeds find it in vegetables and in animals.

"The humans who inhabit lands where agriculture is unknown receive their nourishment from flocks of birds of passage that pause over their territory, but their principal nourishment is that of synagelotic fish—which is to say, fish that swim on shoals, especially herrings, whose fecundity is prodigious.

"The peoples who take their nourishment from fish are called icthyophages; others are acridophages; they eat grasshoppers. Carnivores nourish themselves on flesh.

"The inhabitants of the kingdom of Siam, in India, nourish themselves on the flesh of raw fish. The inhabitants of the Bavis Strait, in North America, which separates Greenland from New Brittany, nourish themselves in the same way.

"Geophages are a few savage peoples whom hunger reduces to eating earth. Anthropophages are savages who eat human flesh.

"The peoples that I have just mentioned are part of the peoples known as barbaric—which is to say, uncivilized: idle, devoid of industry, sagacity and intelligence.

"Humans are born without industry, it's true, but they have to profit from the ideas of God, the type of which are seen throughout nature; they can also profit from the instincts of animas, which gives them at birth an industry appropriate to them. Only humans are born without instinct and without industry; they are obliged to acquire that industry, but always by imitation; it is only after a great deal of time, toil and reflection that they have succeeded in surpassing the animals. Aerostatic inventions, hydraulic machine team engines, astronomical instruments, ships with propellers, railways, clocks, watches, the fabrication of cloths, machinery, etc., the science and the arts, prove that humans possess a portion of divine essence, the immortal soul."

Belladonna listened to me with the greatest attention, and said: "Everything that you have told me transports me with admiration and astonishment. I admire the bounty of God, his divine Providence—but I'm astonished that he does not protect all humans equally."

"Your remark is just, Madame, but your astonishment will cease when you know that humans, whom God created good, went astray and became wicked and ingrate toward their creator. Their iniquity became intolerable, and God resolved to annihilate them by means of the universal deluge, in the year of the world 1536 or 1606. A single man was saved with his wife and children, three of whom were sons: Shem, Japhet and Ham. The last of them was cursed by his father, along with his posterity.

"The peoples that I have mentioned to you—the barbarians, the savages— are the posterity of Ham, and were abandoned by God. However, among those men soiled with crime and iniquity, there are good ones whom God protects, for God is just and good."

"I can easily understand what you have just told me, but I will need to be instructed and to be able to meditate profoundly on the beings and things that you have mentioned, which I only understand imperfectly. Will you be generous enough to instruct me in the knowledge that I lack?"

"Have no doubt of it, Madame; I shall do so with pleasure."

"Thank you, my friend. Now, would you like to go to Prodigium?"

"Willingly, Madame."

We climbed back into the little caleche and set off. I admired all the plants over which the luxury of the vegetation extended. I noticed a few animals that were unknown to me, but which were extraordinary. I decided to visit the island alone and on foot, in order to be able to draw the plants and animals.

IV

The city of Prodigium had a very bizarre, incongruous appearance, owed equally to all its aspects. All the inclined buildings were eccentric in appearance, caprice having played a greater part in their construction than taste, but that was certainly not a prodigy of art. We went into the city, where I was extremely astonished to see that all its inhabitants were lame, all having one leg shorter that the other, with the consequence that couples walking arm in arm, if they were not lame in the same leg, bruised their shoulders and their heads by virtue of their proximity. It was truly bizarre to see that unsteady movement, which often degenerated into grotesquerie, everywhere.

Belladonna stopped the caleche at the door of a beautiful house inhabited by one of her relatives, who received us cordially. We stayed there the next day and the day after that, and then we returned to Belladonna's house.

On the way, I told her that I had the intention of traveling the island alone and on foot; what had fortified that resolution was that I had discovered in Prodigium a kind of paper and stones that I could carve into the form of crayons. But Belladonna did not want to let me depart alone, because very singular events sometimes occurred on the island.

"But I have nothing to fear, my good friend—and besides, I still have my stiletto, which I habitually carry on my person to defend myself in case of need."

"Nonetheless," she said, "I shall accompany you everywhere. We'll travel the island together in the barouche; I'll have it stop in any place you indicate; the barouche will be furnished with provisions, and in the evening we'll come back here, to recommence the following day, if you wish. All the time that you're occupied with your drawings, I'll wait for you in the barouche, or remain beside you. What do you say?"

"I say that you're as good as you're beautiful!"

The following day we put the plan into execution; Belladonna no longer left me; we ate in the barouche, where the servant prepared everything; then I went to draw, and Belladonna remained sitting next to me watching me work. Such was our plan of campaign.

I began by drawing a few plants and small animals. Then a larger quadruped, a kind of kangaroo, arrived in front of us. I was about to sketch it when it hurled itself upon Belladonna. To draw my stiletto and strike it was the work of an eye-blink; it fell dead. Belladonna whistled for her domestic, who came running, and she ordered him to put the animal in the barouche, in order to take it away as a trophy of my victory. Belladonna was excited by the scene that had just unfolded; she squeezed my hand and kissed me. That was the first time, and for the first time, I reciprocated. The kisses were those of gratitude and the purest amity.

"You see," I said to Belladonna, "that my precaution was not futile."

"No," she said, "I probably owe it to you that I was not disfigured by that vile animal."

The next day I did not want her to get down from the barouche. I went on my own to the place where I had killed the kangaroo. Then I went a little further on, where I saw some enormous fruits similar to pumpkins. I was examining those products when I noticed that they were moving. What could be causing that movement?

In accordance with my habit of seeking the causes of effects, I wanted to know. I took out my stiletto and struck the fruit with it, making an opening, from which a thick smoke emerged. I kicked it forcefully with my foot, and it split; a hideous animal came out of it, which fixed sparkling eyes upon me and opened a menacing maw. I was still holding my stiletto, and I struck at it so effectively that black blood escaped from the wound, and soon afterwards it died in convulsions.

I put off until the next day visiting other products. I went back to Belladonna, to whom I made a tribute of the new trophy. She was frightened by the sight of the hideous animal, and told me that she did not want me to expose myself to danger again, or else she would accompany me.

Even so, I went back the following day, and she remained in the barouche. I went to the same place and cut into another fruit, from which emerged, in the mist of blue-tinted smoke, a multitude of butterflies, with variegated wings in the most beautiful colors.

A burst of laugher that I heard behind me caused me to turn me head, and I saw Belladonna, followed by her domestic, armed with a stout staff.

"Luckily," she said to me, "today's hunt is more agreeable and less dangerous that yesterday's."

That adventure amused Belladonna and made her want to attempt another. The following day we returned to the same place, but I went alone to the location of the big fruits. I noticed one of them whose form was different from the others and I thought that it might contain different things. Its shape was an elongated cube, the top of which was slightly curved. With my stiletto I traced two fairly deep lines in a cross on the top, extended slightly along the sides.

Immediately, the surface of the fruits split into flaps of a sort, which rose up about a meter and a half, and formed a kind of aviary filled with birds, resembling canaries, warblers, linnets, nightingales, colingas with rich plumage and hummingbirds, the smallest and prettiest of all birds, with found themselves enclosed in that improvised cage.

I heard a cry of joy, and saw Belladonna a few paces away, marveling at what she saw. Her domestic was following her at a distance, still armed with his staff, in order to help me in case of need. I offered my new conquest to Belladonna, who accepted it with great pleasure. Aided by the domestic, I carried the aviary to the barouche, and we left.

Belladonna was ravishingly beautiful; the pleasure that she experienced gave her a new shine. The evening was cheerful, and we planned to return to the same place, but I begged Belladonna not to come, because it was not certain that we would have butterflies or birds to deal with.

"Nevertheless," she said, "I'll go, and if there's danger, I'll share it with you."

It was necessary for me to consent, and the following morning, we set forth as usual. I got down alone and advised Belladonna to stay in the barouche, telling the domestic not to leave her for a moment.

I went further than usual in the area where the fruits were. I soon found myself between two banks, in the middle of which, at the bottom, a little stream was running, which gave the plants bordering it a prodigious exuberance of vegetation. Among the plants I discovered a few large fruits like those I have already mentioned. One of them attracted my attention by virtue of its enormous size. I approached it and examined it attentively; its color was a very pale yellowish green, but its stalk was surrounded by a beautiful black areola.

I experienced something singular as I contemplated that extraordinary vegetable. Finally, I wanted to know what it contained. I made a circular cut with my stiletto around the areola, which made it into a kind of lid, which separated noisily from the spherical body of the vegetable and the opening. First of all the head of a man emerged, and then the entire body, which was very tall. Then he said to me:

"Who permitted you to trouble my repose and destroy the dwelling I had chosen? Have I done you any harm? Why did you do that to me?"

"Sire," I replied, utterly nonplussed, "My intention was not to do you any harm, but to learn all the knowledge that I might be able to acquire in these spaces."

"I know what the motive is for your voyage in the imaginary spaces; if it were to do harm I would already have pulverized you. Zadir, whose friend I am, as well as that of Za and Zico, give you the best of recommendations. You can, therefore, count on my good offices in case of need. My name is Dizzaca."

With those words, he disappeared. For my part, I was about to rejoin Belladonna in the barouche when I met her, coming to look for me, tormented as she was by my long absence.

I reflected during the night on the day's events, and thought it might be prudent to abstain from all curiosity, and especially of seeking to delve into extraordinary things, for that curiosity, although innocent in itself, since it had no other motive than my instruction, was nevertheless indiscreet and blameworthy, as had been seen. To avoid any recidivism that might be unpardonable, I judged it necessary and prudent to leave the Isle of Prodigies.

Having made that decision I summoned Zico and told him that I wanted to visit the Isle of Marvels.

"That's easy," he said. "When do you want to leave?"

"Whenever you like."

"Then we'll leave tomorrow morning before sunrise, in order that you can enjoy the admirable effect that its rise produces over the old capital of the island, which is called Mirabilis.

V

The next day, my sylph and his sister having transported me to within sight of the Isle of Marvels, Zico said to me: "Look at Mirabilis, the marvelous city with which no other in the entire world can be comparable."

I looked, and thought once again that I was the victim of an illusion; I could not believe my eyes. I rubbed them in vain; it was not an illusion; what I was seeing really was real. My astonishment as I saw, and was able to contemplate, that vast and beautiful city is comprehensible; instead of being built on the ground, all of its houses, all of its monuments and all of its edifices were suspended in mid air, sustained and supported by an atmosphere that was probably particular to them.

All those constructions formed streets or surrounded squares, but that surprising city was subject to considerable movements caused by the wind, which often changed the location of constructions and made Mirabilis, in consequence, a city that was always new.

Zico set me down at the gate of that marvelous city. I went into it with the intention of exploring it and getting to know its inhabitants; the men were handsome ad well-built; the women were marvelously beautiful, as much for their facial features as for the perfection of their bodily figures, which attained excellence in the majority.

I was marveling at everything I saw and so absorbed in my contemplation and my thoughts that I did not notice the effect that I was having on the inhabitants, some of whom were following me while others were observing me curiously.

I arrived in a place in the city where I saw several benches placed in front of the entrance to a house. I sat down on one of them, because I was tired, and a few minutes later an exceedingly pretty woman came to invite me to go into her house. At that invitation, made so cordially, I got up and followed her.

She took me into a room where I saw a large table covered with different foodstuffs that were unfamiliar to me, but which simultaneously flattered sight, the sense of smell and the stomach. Benches were placed around the table and several people were already sitting there. The lady of the house offered me her hand and led me to the top of the table, where she sat me down beside her, which I did with pleasure. Immediately, she covered my plate with morsels of food, which I ate with a hearty appetite, because they were good and I was hungry.

The lady seemed benevolent and showed considerable interest in me. She asked me who I was, where I came from and what was the motive for my voyage to their country, where no man like me had ever been seen before. I answered all her questions; she seemed amazed by my replies.

The astonishment they caused her was noticed by the other guests, who did not take long to enquire as to the cause of her astonishment, and it was supposable that I would soon be known throughout the city—a supposition that was promptly verified. The news of the presence of an extraordinary man in Mirabilis reached the governor, who came to see me and invited me to be his guest, which invitation I accepted.

I thanked the lady who had given me hospitality and went with the governor, who took me to his palace, where I was splendidly lodged and served perfectly, with regard to my meals and everything else that I needed.

On the first day the governor invited me to dine with him, but before dinner he introduced me to his wife, who welcomed me graciously. She was in a sumptuously decorated drawing room, sitting on a sofa of which she occupied one end; she was marvelously beautiful. All the ladies who were sitting with her did not cede anything to her in that regard. I bowed respectfully, to which she responded with a nod of her head, and offered me her hand.

The governor then took me into a large hall, where several seats were arranged in a circle in the middle. The ladies I had seen in the drawing room came into the hall, preceded by the governor's wife, and took their places in the circle of seats. At a sign from the governor, a domestic blew into a stout pipe that passed through the floor, and the part around which the ladies were gathered sank, soon to be replaced by a table covered with the most appetizing dishes. Then the governor's wife drew her chair closer to the table that had risen up through the opening in the floor; everyone else followed her example.

The carver fulfilled his function, and when everyone had eaten, the table sank down and was almost immediately replaced by another, laden with the dessert. Then everyone returned to the drawing room, where some of the ladies sang, in a delightful manner. Then we went for a stroll in the gardens, which were admirable. The evening was very beautiful, although the air was slightly agitated, and finally, as the wind increased, everyone went back indoors.

Toward the middle of the night, however, a storm broke out; we were tossed around in the palace as if we had been on a ship at sea, rolling and pitching. There were gusts of wind that caused considerable damage in the palace, and caused almost all its residents to pass a sleepless night, because beds were thrown in various directions, and items of furniture followed the same movement. There was an upheaval, and general turmoil.

The next morning, I went out in order to go and see the hospitable lady, but I could no longer find her house; all of them had changed places. I no longer recognized the streets along which I had passed the day before, new streets having been formed by the upsets of the night. However, I was not tempted to explore that new city, because I feared that if I got lost in the labyrinth I might not be able to find my way back to the governor's palace. That is why I retraced my steps and succeeded, although not without difficulty, in finding it again.

I saw the governor, who was coming back after going to see the King, in order to give him an account of all the changes occasioned in the city by the hurricane, and to receive his orders. He had spoken to him about me, and had depicted me as a man endowed with extraordinary knowledge.

"I would be very glad to see this man," the King had said to him. "He might be able to indicate to us means of repairing, if not everything, at least a part of the disasters and upheavals that occurred last night. Tell him that I desire to see him, and bring him to me."

"You Majesty will be obeyed. When does he want me to have the honor of introducing this stranger to him?"

"As soon as possible and without ceremony; I desire to judge in advance my fashion of introducing myself to him."

The governor asked me if I was ready to yield to the King's desire.

"Your expression is very just, for a King's desire is an order, a summons. I can't refuse, and we'll leave whenever it pleases Your Excellency."

"That's good," he said. "We'll have lunch and then set off."

We ate, and immediately afterwards we went to see the King, who gave me a very generous welcome. Then he asked me a great many questions about matters concerning me personally, about my homeland, and, principally, the knowledge I had acquired—which occasioned his astonishment, manifested by exclamations of enthusiasm. Then he spoke to me about the night's events, the disturbance of his capital, which had been so beautiful and had now lost its beauty in the confusion—a misfortune that caused him a great deal of chagrin.

"Your Majesty can be reassured," I told him. "The evil is not without remedy."

"What!" said the King, excitedly. "You believe that the damage is not irreparable?"

"I do believe that, Sire, and if Your Majesty will give me the means, I hope to be able to return his capital to him, not merely as beautiful, but more beautiful than it was before."

"More beautiful!" cried the King, at the peak of astonishment. "You have the power to do that, my friend?"

"Yes, Sire; but my power is nothing but the intelligence and the experience I have acquired by my studies, my observations and my imagination."

The King appeared to be enchanted; his handsome features expressed the happiness that he was experiencing internally. He took my hands, shook them, and lavished the most affectionate names and expressions upon me.

"But how will you achieve this miracle, my friend?" he asked me.

"There will be no miracle, Sire, for the power to work miracles is the attribute of the Divinity. I shall only employ my intelligence, which I owe to God and to profound studies. I shall begin by drawing a plan of the new Mirabilis, which I shall submit to Your Majesty's examination. If he accepts it, then I shall put my best foot forward to carry it out. To accomplish that task, Your Majesty must put at my disposal the men who will be necessary to the operation, such as carpenters, locksmiths, blacksmiths, rope-makers and ditch-diggers—in sum, all the workmen I need—with the injunction of obey my orders."

"That is just and indispensable," the King said, "and I beg you to accept the title of Director General of Works in Mirabilis."

"I accept it, Sire, because I hope to merit it to your entire satisfaction."

"I don't doubt it, my good friend. You've rendered me very happy, and as I want everyone to know the high esteem in which I hold you, and the amity that you have inspired in me, come to dinner with me today."

I accepted his invitation; I was announced by the usher under the title that the King had given me, which surprised all the people who were present. The King received me with distinction and introduced me to the Queen, who gave me the most gracious welcome. All eyes were fixed upon me. Even the governor, who was present, seemed astonished by the great favor that I enjoyed with the King, because he did not know the reason for it. At dessert, however, the King addressed his guests and made the following speech:

"Sires, the extraordinary man that you know by the title of Director General of Works in Mirabilis seems to us to have been sent by the heavens in order to repair the upheavals that occurred last night in our beautiful city. I therefore call upon your collaboration to procure him everything that he will need to cry out this vast and useful enterprise, which is for the good and the wellbeing of all."

The dignitaries stood up and held out their hands as a sign of acquiescence. After dinner they came to congratulate me, shake my hand and offer me their services and their amity.

The next day I made the plan of the new Mirabilis, which I went to present to the King the day after. I left it with him so that he could examine it at his leisure. I had made a duplicate of the plan, which I kept for myself. I was busy studying it when the governor came to see me, in the apartment that I occupied in his palace.

"My friend," he said to me, "the King has asked to tell you that he is impatient to see you to give him an explanation of the plan you handed to him, which he does not understand very well. He desires to know the significance of all the lines you have traced."

"Excellency, I am under the King's orders, and we shall go to see him whenever you think it appropriate."

"The let's go right away. The King will dine more cheerfully, and will be glad to understand your projects, which interest him so keenly."

We immediately went to the King's residence. He seemed delighted to see me. He took me into his study, where I saw the plan that I had drawn displayed on his table.

"I thank you," the King said, "for having come to my aid; for without you, it would have been impossible for me to understand what all these lines signify."

"Your Majesty will understand it very soon. I beg him to follow me in the explanation that I shall have the honor of giving him. The circle that you see in the center of these lines is the location where Your Majesty's palace will be; the double circle represents the space left free between the palace and the city. All the lines that end at the circle that surrounds the palace are the streets of the city; the small circles in the lines of the streets are for squares or for monuments that Your Majesty might like to erect there. In accordance with his plan, Your Majesty will be able, without leaving his palace, to see all the principal streets of the city."

"Oh, what an excellent idea you have had, my friend! Will you consent to my showing your plan to my engineers? I believe that kind of deference will dispose them to assist you in all your operations, and I think their collaboration will be useful to you, in furnishing you with all that you will need to carry out your great and noble design."

"Your Majesty thinks wisely, for there will be no offended self-esteem, and I gladly renounce the title of author of the project in order to avoid any species of jealousy. The most difficult thing now if the execution of the gigantic project; that is my concern, but the cooperation of engineers will be very useful to me and accelerate my execution, in that they will furnish me, more easily than I could achieve, with all the necessary and indispensable things that I have already listed for Your Majesty; they can procure me the carpenters, smiths, rope-makers and ditch-diggers they know, and I can have the machines that I need for the execution built by those artisans. When the operation is finished, I plan to make all the houses safe from a further upheaval."

"What?" said the King. "You can neutralize the terrible effects of the wind, and storms?"

"Yes, Sire."

"But, my friend, you are acquiring new rights to my gratitude every day."

"You do not owe me any, Sire; I am acquitting, as best I can, the generosity that Your Majesty has shown to me, and which I hope to retain."

"It is acquired in advance; you have my royal word on that."

The King summoned the engineers to a room in the palace, and presented my plan to them. They thought it perfect, but did not understand the means of execution. Then the King proposed to put them in communication with me, which they accepted unanimously and promptly. The King arranged our meeting for the following day, in the hall of public sessions, in order that no one would be unaware that I was the author of the plan and the project of execution. I thus found myself at that session, presided over by the king, the next day.

The hall was filled with the notable people of the city; the engineers were gathered around the King. When I entered the hall they came to meet me, and we went to the King together. He was seated at a table on which my plan was displayed. After having examined it, the engineers complimented me, but they did not understand the means that I would employ in its execution.

"It is for that execution, Gentlemen," I replied, "that I need your cooperation, to give me the workers that I need to construct the machines whose designs I shall supply to them, and of which, if necessary, I shall make a small model. When all the machines are ready, I shall indicate their employment to each of you, and in a matter of days, Mirabilis will be rebuilt on unshakeable bases."

Unanimous applause greeted my last words.

The next day, the engineers brought me the artisans that I needed to build my machines and carry out other tasks. From the carpenters I ordered horizontal and vertical capstans, all with their hand-spikes. From the blacksmiths I ordered large iron rings and pitons, hooks of different shapes and strong chains of different lengths. From the rope-makers I ordered ropes and cords, from the mechanics, jacks.

I explained to all the artisans, not only in words but also by drawings and small models in wood and clay, all the machines that I needed, and gave them the dimensions that they had to have. I supervised their work, and four days afterwards, I was able to bring together the large fraction of my machinery. Only the mechanics did not succeed, but I had the means of substituting for the jacks by means of a scaffold that I set up, pulleys that I had attached to it, ropes, capstans and levers.

On the sixth day I assembled the engineers to trace the double circle for the placement of the royal palace, and the points at which all the city streets were to terminate. That work was completed in a day.

On the seventh day, all the artisans succeeded in bring the machines that I had ordered into the double circle, and I had them placed at the locations they were to occupy, facing and by the sides of the palace.

On the eighth day, I asked the engineers to furnish me with two hundred men and fifty horses.

On the ninth day, everything I needed was ready. I went to inform the king, and told him that my operation would commence the following morning. The King, intoxicated by joy, shook my hands and embraced me, lavishing the most flattering and affectionate expressions upon me.

On the morning of the tenth day, an unusual stir reigned all over the city; the news that I had conveyed to the King was soon known to all the inhabitants, whose joy reached a peak. They were all mounted on their houses—if I might be forgiven the wordplay—impatient to enjoy the success of my operations.

It was a curious spectacle to see all those houses, covered by their inhabitants, who were manifesting their joy with animated gestures, songs and the sounds of various musical instruments; it was a general joy caused by the imminent re-edification of their city, once so lovely, which they would soon see more beautiful still, by virtue of its regularity. Soon, the labyrinth would disappear; chaos would give way to a new creation.

I was at the palace at the hour that I had indicated; I saw the engineers arrive; we shook hands. We were all in perfect accord, all animated by the finest spirit; they were all ready to carry out my orders. We went into the enclosure traced by the double circle, where I had had the artisans place my machines. I explained the properties of each one to the engineers. I had the iron rings attached to the facades and the sides of the palace. I put ten men in service at each capstan, explaining to them the use of the hand-spikes, and five men at each of the iron rings on the façade and sides of the palace; the horses were placed behind the capstans, in order to have them all to hand in case of need.

Everything was ready, and I sent one of the engineers to inform the King that I was about to commence my operation.

The King appeared on his balcony with the Queen, and we saluted them with cries of "Long live the King!" and "Long live the Queen!" They waved their hands.

Then I shouted, loudly: "Pay attention!" I checked that everyone was at his post and shouted to the engineer I had placed at the capstans: "Start up the facing capstans!"

The palace advanced majestically as far as the line, and I shouted: "Halt!"

The same maneuver was carried out at the sides of the palace, which was positioned regularly on the base that I had had the diggers and the masons prepare for it.

The King and the Queen seemed very emotional, and testified to their joy and happiness with the salutes and hand-kisses that they sent to us. The same testimonies and acclamations came to us from the ladies and the dignitaries who were occupying all the windows of the palace. But my work was not finished; it still remained for me to anchor the palace to the position that it now occupied. Everything was prepared for that operation. I had chains fixed to the iron rings that I had attached to the framework of the underside of the palace, and the other ends of the chains were sealed in massive blocks of stone that I had prepared. The masons and the blacksmiths did their work, and the palace was secured against the blasts of the wind.

The engineers and I then occupied ourselves with the task of future days, with would consist of organizing the streets of the city. That was now the engineers' affair; they had my plan and the machines that I had set up, and they could operate them as they had seen me do for the palace. However, I did not abandon my post as Director General, and on the eleventh day I was one of the first there; I intended the most beautiful houses to be placed on the circle, facing the palace or at the ends of the city streets, and the other house to be relegated to more distant positions. The important thing, for the moment, was to clear the quarter neighboring the palace, in order to be able to begin tracing out the streets.

After having given my orders, I went to visit the governor. As soon as I came in he said: "You've arrived at a good time. Here is a package that King instructed me to hand to you personally. I'm glad for you, for it must be something very important. Read the message, and you'll be as impatient as I am to know what it contains.

I opened the package, which contained two documents. One was a handwritten letter from the King, which complimented me on the success of my operations and expressed his satisfaction with them; the other was a kind of parchment, at the head of which was written:

Title of nobility and property given by us, Mirabilo Premiero, King of the Isle of Marvels, to out Director General of Works in Mirabilis, whom we name Duke of Maraviglia and owner of the land that we establish as his Duchy.
Made at our palace in Mirabilis, on the, etc.

The governor congratulated me on my success and I left him in order to go to my post. I saw with pleasure that all my orders were being executed perfectly, and testified my satisfaction to the engineers, whose zeal was augmented to such a degree that, on that same day, everything was ready for the streets to be traced, along with the squares, public gardens, fountains, columns and so on.

On the twelfth day, the tracing of the streets, squares and gardens was executed, and the thirteenth, fourteenth and fifteenth days were employed in placing the houses along the lines.

The sixteenth, seventeenth, eighteenth and nineteenth days were employed in preparing and surrounding with temporary wooden fences the public gardens, squares and areas that were to be occupied by the fountains.

I went to see the King to tell him that we were approaching the end of the essential work, and that His Majesty could visit the new city the following day if he so desired.

"It's my most ardent desire," the King said to me. "I'll go to admire your work tomorrow."

"However, Sire, it's not yet perfected; the essential work is done, but I'll need a few more days to complete the embellishment of Mirabilis. I shall have the honor of acquainting Your Majesty with all the ornaments with which I have the intention of decorating his capital."

"In that regard, my good friend, as in everything that I judge you capable of doing, I leave you complete liberty."

"Thank you, Sire. Your Majesty will be satisfied."

"The following day, the twentieth, the King and the Queen, carried in a litter by two horses, came to visit the new Mirabilis, which they entered by the Royal Road that terminated in front of the royal palace. Their Majesties were followed by a numerous cavalcade composed of dignitaries and the King's guards. Their Majesties were received by the inhabitants with shouts of "Long live the King!" and "Long live the Queen!" The long Royal Road resounded with the acclamations of the multitude.

Their Majesties seemed happy and manifested their joy by means of gracious salutes, which they addressed to the people, to the engineers, to the artisans and to the laborers, among which cries of "Long live the Director General!" were uttered. When Their Majesties arrived at the locations destined for the gardens, squares, fountains, etc., they could not dissimulate their joy and admiration in imagining what they would look like when they were finished.

The King and the Queen, wanting to testify their satisfaction with my endeavors immediately, summoned me; I was not far away, for I was desirous of judging for myself the effect that the execution of my plan produced on Their Majesties. I was easily found and I went to them.

On seeing me, the King said: "Come my good friend, come and enjoy the pleasure that you are procuring us by the admirable success of your operations.

Come to dine with us today, and explain to us your intentions for the perfection and embellishment of the locations that you have prepared.

At dinner time I went to the royal palace. The usher announced me, presumably in accordance with the King's order, under the title of "His Lordship, the Duke of Maraviglia, Director General of Works in Mirabilis." Those titles did not appear to cause any surprise to the people present, because they had been witnesses to the success of my operations and shared the general enthusiasm.

After dinner, I made the King and Queen party to the embellishments that I intended to execute on the plans that I had prepared, and on which I would established gardens, squares and fountains, explaining that the wooden fences, being only temporary, would be replaced by others in iron; that I was about to occupy myself with the ornaments and designs, and that everything would be finished in eight or ten days.

The King and Queen were delighted, and manifested their happiness in their gazes and affectionate words.

The next day, I designed my fountains and their ornaments, which I had already composed, as well as those of the fences.

On the twenty-second day I had the gardens and squares traced out, in the middle of which I traced the plans for the fountains.

I charged an engineer with having the stone carved for the fountains in accordance with the drawings and sections that I gave him, and also for the bases that were to support the iron railings. I indicated the places where the gates were to be placed, and provided the design of the railings, each of which would be surmounted by a gilded spike; the metal was not very rare on the Isle of Marvels, but its use in gilding was unknown. I instructed artisans in gold-beating and the technique of applying it to the objects to be gilded. The engineers seconded me so well that a week later, the fountains were constructed and the railings placed.

I had the gardens and squares dug, and the paths traced in accordance with the designs that I gave the engineers, whose zeal and activity rivaled that of the artisans and laborers.

On the twenty-third day, I had the trees, ornamental bushes and clumps of flowers brought; they were planted in the placed I had marked, while the gilders applied their gold leaf to the spikes of the railings. I had had two large temporary reservoirs set up near the fountains, and had them filled with water, in order that they would be able to flow at the moment when the King and Queen came to visit my works the following day. Then I went to see the King in order to announce to him that my works were concluded and that Their Majesties would do me the greatest honor by visiting them.

"We cannot render you too much honor, my dear Duke. Come to lunch with us tomorrow, and then we shall go to admire your new works."

After that lunch, I went in all haste to the square that I had completed in order to make sure that everything was in order for the arrival of the august visitors. Everything was as I had instructed. I placed a man next to each reservoir with orders to open the taps when the King and Queen arrived. Everyone was at his post, and I waited impatiently for the royal cortege.

Soon, the acclamations of the multitude announced it, and I saw Their Majesties' litter coming into the square. They made a tour of it. I was in the garden, near one of the gates, from where I was able to judge the effect that my work produced on the King and Queen. They seemed surprised, astonished and wonderstruck by all that they saw.

The King perceived me, stopped his litter and beckoned to me. I opened the gate near which I was standing and approached Their Majesties.

"Enjoy your work, my good friend," said the King. "You are making our tears flow, but they are tears of joy and happiness. I am too emotional to express to you all that I am experiencing; I will do that later; give me the pleasure for the moment, of accepting this slight testimony of my gratitude and the title of Excellency, Minister of Public Works."

With those words, he detached his gold chain, which he placed around my neck, and the Queen offered me her hand to kiss.

At that moment, applause burst forth from all the windows of the beautiful houses with which I had had the square surrounded. Women waved their handkerchiefs and the men cried: "Long live the King! Long live the Queen!"

"You hear that," said the King. "*Vox populi.* They are sharing all the happiness that you have given us."

I could not find words to reply to the King; the emotion I was experiencing had taken away the faculty of speech. The King perceived that and held out his hand; a silence followed, and the King and Queen invited me to dine with them.

At that royal banquet, I found a gathering of all the high dignitaries of the State, of which I was now a part. All those gentlemen gave me a very gracious welcome. Was it sincere or was it simulated? That did not worry me very much. I possessed the amity of the King; that was all I desired.

The next day, I went to visit the King, who received me with open arms.

"I'm delighted to see you, my good friend, for I have to renew my thanks for the happiness I'm achieving. I've never been as happy as I am now; that's why I have the intention of establishing an annual celebration of the re-edification of Mirabilis."

"To that effect, Sire, I also have another project."

"What is it, my friend? It must be good."

"It would be, Sire to erect a column in the square at the end of the Royal Road; it would be an agreeable viewpoint, and a beautiful perspective, seen from the royal palace, of the long convergent lines."

"Your idea is superb, my friend."

"But sire, the column would be a rather long endeavor, because of the ornaments with which I want to decorate it, the principal one of which can perhaps only be sculpted by me. It would eternalize Your Majesty's reign, and the epoch of the re-edification of Mirabilis, which its inhabitants, and those of the Isle of Marvels, owe to you."

"And also to you, my dear friend," said the King, swiftly. "But tell me, my friend, what will be the ornaments of this column? Excuse my curiosity, but I can't resist."

"The shaft of the column will be placed on a pedestal whose four sides will be ornamented with sculptures related to the subject, and the summit of the column will be crowned with a statue of Your Majesty."

"What!" said the King, trembling with emotion. "We can accomplish such a fine project?"

"Yes, Sire, and tomorrow I hope to be able to give you designs of the column and its ornaments. If our Majesty approves of them, I shall have the stones carved, as well as the cladding of white marble, which I shall sculpt. For the statue of Your Majesty, I shall have a block of white marble taken from a quarry, which I shall also sculpt myself, and I shall execute that work in Maraviglia, because it will not be seen by anyone before being placed on the column. Your Majesty alone shall see it in my studio; he will be able to judge better than anyone else the difference that exists when it is put in the place that it is to occupy. When I have deposited by block of marble, Your Majesty might be kind enough to come to Maraviglia to grant me the sittings that I shall need to make his resemblance—or, in order not to disturb him, I shall model the head in Mirabilis in clay, which I shall copy in the marble."

"I will do as you wish, my good friend; dispose of me in complete liberty."

"Thank you, Sire, for this final work will complete the beauty of the splendid Mirabilis."

"Oh, my good friend, you will put the crown on my happiness!"

The King shook my hands, and tears of joy inundated his noble face.

Shortly afterwards, I took my leave of His Majesty in order to go and sketch my column, so that I would be able to present a final version to him the following day. My project was so well imprinted in my imagination that it was terminated the following morning. I went to take it to the King, who thought it marvelous, and asked the Queen to come to his study in order to show it to her. The Queen was delighted on examining my project, which she thought admirable. I took my leave of Their Majesties, and announced to the King that I would leave the following day for Maraviglia in order to prepare all the marbles of which I had need.

VI

I therefore left for Maraviglia the following day, with three domestics. It was a charming property, which was unfamiliar to me, but of which I took possession with great pleasure.

The building comprised a principal residential block, with two wings in the form of pavilions. Behind were the supplementary buildings: garage, stables, poultry-yard, etc. I was astonished to see that these constructions were not sustained by the air, like those in Mirabilis, and was content with that—but that contentment did not last long.

The next morning, when I woke up, I went to open the window of my room, and I saw that all the buildings had risen into the air to a height of ten or twelve feet, which annoyed me a great deal. A short time afterwards, however, I noticed that they were drawing closer to the ground. That observation caused me to reflect, and I thought that the Sun, which illuminated and warmed the underside of the islands, must produce vapors that elevated the houses, and that when those vapors expanded in the air, the houses descended toward the ground again.

I had remarked from my window a hillock that I wanted to visit. Desiring to get to know my property, I descended to the ground and set forth into my terrain. I arrived at the foot of the hillock, which I climbed. It was covered in ash and bituminous volcanic material, lava, pumice stone, etc.

I arrived at the summit of the hillock; the ground was dry and hard; it seemed to me that I could hear it resonating beneath my feet. I stamped my foot hard, and there was a frightful cracking sound; that was the dry cap of the hillock splitting, cracks running in all directions. The crust gave way at the place where I was standing and I fell into the precipice that it was covering.

My fall was not rapid; it seemed to me that I was sustained by an invisible force. A voice said to me: "Have no fear; I'm watching over you."

It was the voice of my sylphide, Zica.

I descended thus to the bottom of the precipice, where I was greeted by my sylph, Zico, who said to me: "You've fallen here into the midst of our enemies, the gnomes, who want to dispute with us the treasures that this precipice contains, and which belong to us. Look at everything and have no fear. Your good genius Za has confided you to my protection and has given me the power to defend you—power and orders that he has received from Zadir, the chief of us all. So, act without any dread."

Then I got up from the stone on which I was sitting in order to explore the subterrain, where I received no other light that what reached me through the hole into which I had fallen. That light was very faint and diminished as I advanced into the subterrain. Eventually, it suddenly disappeared. I found myself in obscurity.

I was continuing to march when my eyes were struck by a dazzling light coming from a large fissure. I was approaching it in order to go into it when the passage was disputed by a monstrous animal. It was an enormous dragon, whose eyes were like two carbuncles, and whose frightful mouth was vomiting flames.

I was trying to continue going forward when the furious animal launched itself upon me to devour me; even more promptly, however, I drew my stiletto and drove it forcefully into its skull. It collapsed, uttering a long roar, which, repeated by all the echoes of the subterrain, resembled a rumble of thunder. It deployed the long coils of its tail, which was terminated by two darts, in order to pierce me, but the blow that I had struck was mortal; it fell in convulsions, executing frightful somersaults, but I was still on my guard.

Finally, exhausted by that terrible agony, it died, vomiting thick black blood with a fetid odor, which spread through the subterrain.

Meanwhile, I entered resolutely into the grotto that had suddenly illuminated with bright light. I was dazzled by the glare of the radiance that was departing from all the sides of the grotto, which was filled with precious stones and numerous vases in gold or silver, of incalculable value.

I summoned Zico, who arrived immediately, and said to me, in a soft voice: "I congratulate you on your victory, and you've now become the richest man in the universe."

"No," I replied, "this treasure belongs to the corps of good genii, and I'm glad to be able to return it to its legitimate owners."

"Very good, my friend. Za and Zadir will be informed of your brave and noble conduct."

With those words, he left me, but a short while afterwards I received a visit from Zica, who appeared to me as she had done on the Isle of Fictions.

"I've been sent to you by my brother," she said, "in order to get you out of this precipice, so that you can return home and devote yourself to your affairs."

She remained with me for some time, and in spite of the pleasure that her presence gave me, I was unable to resist an imperious need for sleep, which she had doubtless provoked—for when I awoke, I found myself transported on to the hillock, from which I perceived my house. I immediately returned to it, and was astonished to see it decorated with a staircase in order to go up and down when the house was sustained and supported in mid-air.

My domestics had been worried by my long absence, and had searched for me in vain; they testified their joy on seeing me again.

I went up to my apartment, and was very surprised to find it richly decorated and filled with magnificent furniture of a refined taste. I understood that my good genius Za was the author of the metamorphosis, and was glad.

I then started work on the Column of Mirabilis. I summoned the owners of marble quarries from the small town of which I was the seigneur, and they furnished me with the marbles I needed. I designated the most suitable of the outbuildings to be converted into a studio. Fortunately, those buildings remained on the ground and were not, like the others, lifted up into the air during the night. That made it much easier for the miners to bring in the marbles and stones that I needed in order to sculpt them. Afterwards, I sent for a locksmith, to make me tools of which I provided him with models, and a carpenter to build me a scaffold, a step-ladder, a stool and a pedestal.

While waiting for all these things to be brought, I visited my habitation in detail, inside and out, examining it minutely and very attentively. I especially admired the exquisite taste of the ornaments and the beauty of the furniture in my apartment. I sat down in an exceedingly beautiful armchair, the soft cushions of which, along with the silence and the feeling of wellbeing I was experiencing made me drowsy, and I eventually fell asleep.

I dreamed that I was in the grotto in the precipice, and, although profoundly asleep, I sensed that my eyes were struck by the glare of the radiance emitted by all the precious stones that it contained. All those stones were, however, in the state of cabochons—which is to say, polished—so why were they gleaming as if they had been cut into facets? The eyes would have been unable to sustain it for long without being wounded. It was a very seductive sight, but I did not regret the sacrifice I had made. On the contrary, I was glad to have done my duty. I slept peacefully, like a just man whose conscience is pure.

When I awoke, I experienced the pleasure of contemplating my apartment. Were all those furnishings, so beautiful, really mine? I noticed, for the first time, that the keys were in the doors and drawers of each item of furniture. The desire gripped me to see inside. I began with the one that was closest to me; it was a beautiful writing-desk. I opened it and saw a set of drawers to either side, all garnished with golden rods; the handle of each drawer was formed by a large diamond cut into facets. The square section between the two sets of drawers was occupied by a box of precious wood incrusted with arabesques in gold thread, which had emeralds for leaves ad diamonds rubies, topazes, amethysts and aquamarines for flowers. I opened the drawers first, and was surprised to see that they were filled with gold coins, with were stamped with my head seen in profile, with the legend: *Russo, Duce Maraviglia et civita bellina*, and, for a exergue: *Mirabilis annus MVIIILX*.

Then I opened a chest of drawers; I pulled out the drawers. The top drawer was filed with precious gems, and the other three with silver coins bearing the same date *MVIIILX*.

Then I opened the cupboards; the upper shelves were garnished with linen of the highest quality, in shirts, sheets, etc. The bottom of each cupboard was filled with boxes containing silver coins of various values, struck with the same image, the same legend and the same date as the gold coins. The undersides of the wardrobes were occupied by boxes containing small change.

Then I opened two larger cupboards or wardrobes, furnished with a considerable number of garments, as many for my everyday use as for social occasions; the latter were ornamented with rich embroideries and with court mantles, which were of great magnificence. In a richly ornamented box I found my ducal crown.

A few days later I received my marbles, which I had deposited in my workplace. I charged the men with bringing me, as soon as possible, potter's clay or marl, in quantities that I indicated, and to be careful to wrap it up in large damp cloths.

While I was waiting for the clay, I bought two horses and a litter.

I went to visit Civita Bellina, of which I was the seigneur, and had the satisfaction of being given a very good welcome by the inhabitants.

When I returned to Maraviglia, I saw with pleasure that the miners had brought the clay, and the next morning, I left for Mirabilis with two of my domestics. I stayed with the governor, who received me as a friend. I occupied the same apartment, and asked him for a ground floor room in his palace, which I needed for a work of sculpture and in which I could receive the King, who would sometimes come to visit me there.

"You know, my friend," he said, "that my palace is at your disposal. Choose the room that suits you."

I visited the palace, and chose a room appropriate to my work.

I sent for one of the engineers, whom I charged with making me a step-ladder, a pedestal and a stool. He promised them to me for the next day. Then I went to visit the King, who received me as usual, with the same generosity. I told His Majesty that everything was ready for the commencement of his statue, the head of which I would make in Mirabilis, although it would be better, for the body of the statue, to model it in the studio I had established in Maraviglia.

"Very well, my good friend; I shall come to your residence, and for me it will be a pleasure trip."

"And for me, Sire a day of joy."

The head was modeled the same day, but I asked the King to give me a second sitting the following day in order to apply the finishing touches. The King consented with pleasure. The next day, the head was finished, and the King decided that he would come to Maraviglia a week later.

"But Sire, if the sitting is prolonged, will Your Majesty deign to grant me the favor of accepting the hospitality of his humble subject's abode?"

"Say the abode of a friend," replied the King. "But my dear Duke, the hospitality of a friend's abode is too pleasant and too agreeable to be refused. I therefore accept your invitation with great pleasure."

Having no assistant, I was obliged to carve out my block of marble myself and to sketch the head in accordance with the clay model that I had made of it. That work, although laborious, was completed in six days; on the seventh, I rested and went to stroll by a small lake that I had on my property.

The atmosphere was warm; the limpidity of the water gave me a desire to bathe in it. I took off my clothes and jumped into the beautiful lake, surrounded by trees and bushes that were reflected on the surface of its waters. I was swimming back and forth in all directions when I encountered a whirlpool that I had noticed from the bank and had been imprudent enough not to avoid.

The rule in such circumstances is to go with the movement until one is two or three feet below the surface and then, with a mariner's kick, to cleave through the whirlpool and emerge from it. I neglected that movement and was drawn into a subterranean tunnel where, very fortunately, I collided with a rock on to whose cracks I was able to cling. I climbed swiftly up its ledges, and was fortunate enough to arrive in a hole into which the air penetrated. I was just in time; that moment of respiration reanimated my strength. I succeeded in entering the hole, which broadened out as I went further; soon I was able to stand up.

I continued advancing, but instead of rising toward the surface of the earth, as I had hoped, I sensed that I was heading in the opposite direction. I was in profound darkness, when my eyes were dazzled by a bright light, toward which I headed, and I entered into a space where the bright glare of luminous rays blinded me and forced mine to close my eyes for a few moments.

I was in a crystal enclosure, through which sunlight penetrated. In fact, I was above the sun, and hence beneath the superior surface of the Isle of Marvels, from which I could perceive the recently discovered planets that I would visit later.

VII

I found myself in a very embarrassing situation inside my crystal rock. How could I get out? I could not climb up to swim through the subterranean channel because of its rapidity and the weakness I was experiencing because of lack of nourishment. I therefore had recourse to Zico, to whom I appealed, and almost immediately heard his soft voice, which nevertheless scolded me slightly for my imprudence.

An instant later, I found myself transported to the shore of the lake, where I found my clothes, which I put on. After having thanked Zico, I went home, where I put everything in order to receive the King, who was due to arrive the following day.

I sent to Civita Bellina to buy the provisions that we needed for the King's sojourn. Apartments were prepared to receive him and his entourage. My studio was carefully cleaned, and I had a beautiful armchair placed where the King would need to sit. Everything was ready for his reception.

The next day the King arrived, without an escort and only accompanied by three domestics. I went to meet him as he got down from his litter. He shook my hand affectionately, and I took him to the drawing room, which he examined attentively, seemingly marveling at the beauty of the ornaments, all the merit of which he attributed to me. He did not permit me to dissuade him; it was necessary for me, reluctantly, to remain silent.

The same day, the King gave me a sitting for the head, and I showed him a drawing of the statue, of which he approved.

The next day, I prepared the last phase of the marble head, which was concluded the day after.

The King departed for Mirabilis, and I promised him that the statue and the white marble plaques would be transported in a fortnight's time. I asked His Majesty to have the engineers set up a tent near the area that I had marked out for the column to occupy, in order to deposit therein all the objects that I was fabricating. He promised to do so.

Left alone, I carved out the body of the statue, prepared the ornaments for the cladding, and occupied myself with means of transporting all those objects. Those means were supplied by the kind inhabitants of Civita Bellina, who hastened to respond to my appeal, which was for the service of the King and my own.

On the designated day, twenty-five men arrived at Maraviglia, leading twelve horses and three sleighs, on to which they loaded the statue and the marble plaques, which I had covered with stout cloth.

The convoy set out for Mirabilis; I followed it in my litter, and everything arrived at its destination in perfect condition. The engineers had prepared the tent, in which the statues and the cladding were deposited, after which I went to visit the King, who welcomed me generously and invited me to stay for diner. He seemed delighted to learn that all the things I had made had arrived in Mirabilis intact and had been deposited in the tent, where no one would see them before the erection of the column. After dinner, I went to visit the governor, who informed me that my apartment had been prepared to receive me, and that he begged me to treat his home as if it were my own.

I spent a very good night, and the next day, I went to the placement of the column, where I found the engineers gathered, in accordance with the orders they had received from the governor. They all came to shake my hand and seemed to be pleased to see me again. I asked them to send me stone-carvers and masons as soon as possible to establish the stone block for the foundations of the column, the pedestal of which would rest on that block. I traced out the dimensions of the hole that they were to dig in order to establish solid foundations.

They were diligent, for when I arrived at the work site the following morning, I found all the workers occupied, each with his own concerns. I had the hole for the foundations dug out to a depth of about twenty feet; the stone-carvers worked ardently, and I lavished words of encouragement on them. The next day, the hole was dug and the masons were ready to commence the block. Then I gave the engineers the diameters of each rounded block for the shaft of the column, and the breadth of the stones for the square pedestal.

In sum, everything proceeded at such a rapid pace that, for days later, the pedestal could be placed on the foundations. Every evening, I reported to the governor on the progress of my work, perfectly understood and seconded by the engineers, the artisans and the laborers, and asked him to keep the King informed.

"I shall do so with pleasure, my friend, because it is just that the King testifies his satisfaction to them, in order that they will attribute it to the report that you have made, and they will assist you with greater ardor."

That is what happened a few days later; I had the base of the column put in place, on which the engineers would superimpose the other stones of the shaft, the diameter of which I had specified.

Finally, a fortnight later, the column had reached the height that I had designated for its crown; the pedestal of the statue was placed upon it, lined with marble at the base, on the faces and the cornice. Then I employed carpenters to build the scaffolding around the column in order to lift the statue. I employed the same means that I had seen employed in Paris for the column in the Place Vendôme.

Everything succeeded perfectly. I went to inform the King that everything was ready for the inauguration of his statue on the column, and asked him to designate the day that suited him for that inauguration.

Transported by joy, the King said: "As soon as possible, my friend."

"In that case, Sire, it will be tomorrow."

All the inhabitants were notified in no time. Delight spread throughout the city.

The next day, the square and the Royal Road were covered by inhabitants, all palpitating with trepidation and pleasure. The moment was solemn. Everyone was experiencing a certain anxiety, but when they saw the statue of the King elevated above the top of the column and it was posed majestically on its pedestal, rid of the cloth by which it had been covered until then, the deathly silence that had reigned during the operation gave way to the acclamations of the crowd, which manifested its joy and its happiness with shouts of "Long live our good King!" and "Honor to the Director General!"

The enthusiasm was at its peak.

The next day, I had twelve boundary-stones set up, surmounted by balls of gilded copper; I placed three of them on each side of the column's pedestal. Those boundary-markers were linked together by chains with oblong rings, whose ends, attached at will to the copper balls, formed a kind of garland hanging between them. The ground was flattened and smoothed, and covered with a fine gravel.

The King and Queen came to visit and examine my work, which they had only seen imperfectly the day before because of the vast crowds of citizens and the emotion they experienced. They congratulated me on the beauty of my work and invited me to dine with them. I accepted their invitation. I received the congratulations of the King, the Queen, and all the dignitaries.

Then I addressed the King and Queen.

"I receive your Majesties' felicitations with thanks; that is my sweetest recompense. But it remains for me to complete the ornamentation of the pedestal of the column, which have only been sketched out. When that work is terminated, I shall have another project."

"What is it, my good friend?" exclaimed the King.

"Sire, my project will be to establish fountains in the square that I have made, and by that means, to supply water to all the quarters of your capital, for the needs of its inhabitants. For public health and hygiene I shall establish public baths and wash-houses, in order to maintain the cleanliness no useful to health."

"Excellent!" exclaimed the King. "But my good friend, how will you do it? We have no water here."

"I shall bring it, Sire."

"Sublime!" the King exclaimed.

And my project was welcomed by all the guests at the royal banquet with the sound of their applause, to which that of the King and Queen was joined.

The next day I gave orders to an engineer to have mobile scaffolds placed, decked with cloth, around the pedestal of the column, in order to be able to finish the ornaments.

I returned to the governor's palace, but as I passed along one of the new streets I saw a pretty woman, on the doorstep of a house, who saluted me with her hand, smiling. I recognized her immediately; it was the hospitable lady who had welcomed me when I had arrived in Mirabilis. I expressed the joy I felt at that encounter, after having searched for her in vain.

"But I've seen you several times during our great works as Director General of Works in Mirabilis," she told me. "I didn't dare speak to you, for the King has made you a great lord, and you certainly merit it."

"But you were wrong," I said, "for if I had been able to be agreeable to you, I would have seized the opportunity gladly to recognize the hospitable welcome you gave me without knowing me. If you ever have need of my services, address yourself to me, either at the residence of the governor of Mirabilis, under the title of His Excellency to Minister of Public Works, or at Maraviglia, under the title of the Duke of Maraviglia, and be sure that I shall employ all my credit to be useful to you. Have no fear of importuning me, for you would be giving me the greatest pleasure by accepting my offer. You know my titles and my residence; would you care to give me your name and address?"

"With great pleasure. My name is Kissa, Via Grande."

Having returned to the governor's palace, I asked him to summon the engineers, in order to communicate my plans to them and my instructions for the machinery to manufacture and the works to be carried out in order to bring water to Mirabilis and establish fountains, baths and public wash-houses. I had already drawn up the plans.

The engineers assembled the following morning in the apartment I occupied in the governor's house. I explained my plans and the means of their execution. They understood them all, with the exception of the fire-pumps, which they could not comprehend. I explained to them that it was by means of the motive force of steam that the pump was activated; they were amazed, and told me that they did not think that their mechanicians were capable of fabricating such an extraordinary machine.

"That's unfortunate," I told them, "but we'll substitute windmills of which I'll give you the design. They'll understand that better."

The engineers came back to see me the following day. I have made drawings of the fountains, baths, wash-houses and the windmill, which was to be constructed on the shoe of my lake, the beautiful water of which would aliment the fountains, baths and wash-houses of Mirabilis. I had designed the windmill on the model of those I had seen in Holland, which serve the same purpose. Then I made a second plan, which was similarly aimed at my objective, which was to fill the large elevated reservoir that I intended to construct with water. The means employed for that would be the Archimedean screw.

The engineers ended up understanding me perfectly.

Then I ordered them to excavate a small canal between Maraviglia and Mirabilis for the passage of the waters. I went to Maraviglia with two engineers to map out the placement of the windmill, the reservoir and he canal. I told them to employ the kind of heavy plow that they employed to work the land in order to give more depth to the trace, and then have it excavated by the number of men they judged necessary for the accomplishment of our works.

I had almost finished the ornaments on the pedestal of the column.

After a month, the fountains, baths and wash-houses were terminated, as well as the windmills, the reservoirs and the canal. I went to inform the King, and told him that the waters would arrive in Mirabilis the following day.

The King experienced such emotion that he could not articulate any words to express his satisfaction. He hugged me in his arms and invited me to come to the morning meal the next day, so that we could go together afterwards to admire my new marvels. Those were his words.

Early the next day, all the inhabitants of Mirabilis were up and about; they know that the water was due to arrive in the city that day; they joy was inexpressible.

I went to the morning meal with the King and afterwards, I climbed into his great litter, where he made me sit next to him. The Queen followed in another litter accompanied by her first maid of honor. The entire Royal Guard and all the dignitaries of the kingdom were on horseback, escorting the two royal litters. The cortege was brilliant. Joy appeared to be animating all the faces. The people were enthused. Cries of "Long live the King!" "Long live the Queen!" and "Long live the Director General!" burst forth from all directions.

All the fountains that I had had constructed functioned very well; the baths and the public wash-houses were filled with water. In sum, everything succeeded in accordance with my desire.

When we returned to the palace the King stopped the litter in front of the column, which was now clear of all the mobile scaffolding and cloth that had masked the ornaments. He admired them, and shook my hand as a sign of satisfaction. Then he told me that, in order to conclude such a fine day, he was giving a feast for the important people of his Court, and he invited me to take part in it.

I thanked him for the signal honor that he had deigned to give me, and went to the royal feast. I was welcomed there with distinction. All my works were concluded. I had abandoned, for the moment, the project of going to visit the three isles of the Delta; I would do that later.

Deciding to return to my family, I took my leave of the King, who dissolved in tears in bidding me farewell.

Charles Cros: *An Interastral Drama*
(1872)

Despite the thinness of his output, Charles Cros (1842-1888) is one of the most interesting pioneers of French scientific romance, by virtue of having attempted to follow a scientific career as well as a literary one.

Charles' father, Henri Cros (1803-1876) had shown excellent prospects as a scholar and had obtained a doctorate in law, but had scorned the bar in order to devote his attention to literature and philosophy, settling in the south of France, where he made a modest living running a small boarding-school. Charles was the youngest of four children; his siblings were Antoine (1835-1903), Henriette (1838-1924) and Henry (1840-1907). By the time Charles was born, his father had published two editions of his ostensible philosophical masterpiece, Théorie de l'Homme intellectuel et moral, *in 1836 and 1838, but its lack of appreciation had extended so far as his being condemned as an unfit educator by virtue of his ardent republicanism and outspoken agnosticism, and he had been forced to abandon his boarding-school in 1839. The family was in dire straits by the time Henri Cros moved it to Paris in 1844 and tried unsuccessfully to obtain academic post.*

At the age of 18, Charles obtained a job at the Institution des Sourd-Muets; Henry joined him there in 1861, but was expelled in 1863 for dueling with one of his colleagues and Charles was suspended soon thereafter for chronic absenteeism. He began medical studies, following in Antoine's footsteps—the latter had established a medical practice in 1857—but did not finish them, although he acted as his brother's auxiliary during the cholera epidemic of 1865. By that time, Henry was ardently pursuing a career as sculptor, having exhibited work in the famous Salon des Refusés *in 1863. Charles lived an unsettled Bohemian existence, but thought that he might make a career as an inventor, and began work on an "autographic" telegraph system—a primitive fax machine—for which he applied for a patent in 1866.*

Antoine hosted a literary salon in addition to his booming medical practice, and frequented several others, along with his younger brothers, including the one hosted by Camille Flammarion, who was then in the process of writing his Récits de l'infini, *the most important of which was* Lumen *(1866-69). The other regular attendees included Paul Verlaine as well as Victorien Sardou. Charles had become interested in the problem of color photography—he sent a paper on the topic to the Académie des Sciences in 1867—and Flammarion took him under his wing. The friends he made at Flammarion's salon introduced him to another, hosted by Nina de Villard, which was a very different kettle of fish.*

Nina's lavish salon was ostentatiously avant-garde, and she delighted in hosting performances of various kinds; the star of her private shows was the Comte Auguste Villiers de l'Isle-Adam, with whom Charles became fast friends. Other writers Charles encountered there who were later to make important contributions to speculative fiction included Louis Boussenard and Anatole France, but he quarreled violently with the latter over Nina's affections and tried to strangle him in the climax of a violent quarrel. Nina's salon was not to everyone's taste—the Goncourt brothers described it as "l'atelier de détraquage cérébral" (the mental breakdown factory)—but that only added to its fame, and Charles was glad to become a central figure therein when he and Nina became lovers.

Camille Flammarion, who put on a staid lecture series at his own salon, invited Charles to talk about another of his hobby-horses, the possibility of interplanetary communication using light signals, in May 1869. Charles submitted the text to the Académie des Science in July, and it was published in Victor Meunier's Cosmos *in August before being reissued as pamphlet. He began publishing poetry in the same year; he and Nina were both admitted to second showcase anthology of the Parnasse contemporain, although it did not appear until 1871, the delay in its publication being caused by the Franco-Prussian War and the Paris Commune.*

In December 1870, the house in which Charles was still living with his parents was hit by a shell and destroyed. Henri took the rest of the family south, to stay with his wife's family, while Charles was taken in by Madame Mauté, Paul Verlaine's mother-in-law. Cros and Verlaine were good friends by then, but the invitation owed more to the fact that Antoine Cros had nursed both Mathilde Verlaine and Madame Mauté through bouts of smallpox. Charles busied himself with experiments in "modern alchemy," attempting to synthesize gemstones, but acted again as his brother's medical auxiliary during the chaos precipitated by the Commune. Once the Commune had fallen, Antoine and Charles were both denounced as Communards, but the charge failed to stick, because Antoine was held in great esteem by his prosperous clients in the Faubourg Saint-Germain. Nina, however, had entertained many of the leading Communards in her salon and thought it politic to flee to Geneva.

In 1871, Verlaine showed Charles the poems he had received from Arthur Rimbaud and they went to meet the poet at the railway station when Verlaine invited him to Paris (although they missed him). Charles was now becoming interested in theoretical science, and submitted the outline of treatise on Mécanique cérébrale *[Cerebral Mechanics] to the Académie des Sciences in May—effectively a prospectus for neuropsychology, which was handed for consideration and evaluation to Claude Bernard, the great pioneer of experimental physiology. At the same time, however, he associated himself with an avant-garde literary group centered on Rimbaud, known as the* Vilains Bonhommes. *He began to publish poems in* La Renaissance littéraire et artistique, *where he also published his first scientific romance, "Un drame interastral" in the July 6 and August 24, 1872 issues.*

In July 1872, Verlaine and Rimbaud ran away together, causing a great scandal; Charles, unsurprisingly, sided with Mathilde in the ensuing long-distance quarrel, but left Paris shortly afterwards to meet up with Nina, who eventually thought it safe to return in the following April, shortly after the publication of Charles's first poetry collection, Le Coffret de Santal *[The Sandal-wood Box]. He also struck up a correspondence at this time with the Comte de Chousy, who was subsequently to publish the satirical scientific romance* Ignis *(1883)[14]; it might have been Charles who introduced Chousy to Villiers de l'Isle-Adam, who sent him a complimentary copy of his own satirical scientific romance* L'Ève future *(1887).*

In March 1874, Charles launched a periodical of his own, the Revue du Monde Nouveau, *in collaboration with Henri Mercier, which published his latest scientific romance in its second issue; unfortunately, its third issue was its last. Charles wrote a comedy drama in the vein of Beaumarchais, "La Machine à changer le caractère des femmes" [The Machine for Changing the Character of Women], but it only saw had two performances, both enacted privately at Nina's salon; Villiers served as his co-star. He also wrote another play in collaboration with Nina, "Le Moine bleu" [The Blue Monk], which suffered the same fate. In 1876, Charles and Nina were both blackballed from the third Parnasse contemporain showcase by Anatole France—never a man to forgive and forget—but that setback was countered by the success of a series of monologues that Charles wrote for the actor Ernest Coquelin, more familiarly known as Coquelin cadet [the younger]. The first and most famous was "L'Hareng saur" [The Salted Herring], in honor of which Nina decorated her salon with salted herrings hung from the ceiling. There were, however, more disappointments to come.*

In March 1877, Charles found a financial backer for his work on color photography in the Duc de Chaulnes, and also began work on a device he called the paléophone; he sent a sealed description of the latter device to the Académie in April, and built a prototype, but the Duc would not provide funds to develop it. Eight months later, Thomas Edison applied for a French patent on a near-identical device called the phonograph, and it was granted.

Charles' monologues continued to be successfully performed, but Coquelin cadet pocketed the money they earned him, only paying the writer a small flat fee for each one. In 1878, Charles married Mary Hjardermaal; their son Guy-Charles was born the following year, during which he published a second, much-expanded edition of Le Coffret de Santal. *Charles was now attempting to develop an acid-free battery without metal electrodes, and published the early chapters of his* Principes de Mécanique cérébrale *in* Synthèse Médicale, *a jour-*

---

[14] Available from Black Coat Press, ISBN 9781935543887.

nal edited by his brother Antoine, but the journal folded with the text incomplete, and it is doubtful that he ever wrote any more.

While continuing his increasingly desperate quest to make a living as an inventor, Charles jointed Emile Goudeau's literary club, the Hydropathes, through which he met and became friends with Alphonse Allais. The club became too popular for its own good and its meetings became unmanageable; it was suspended in 1880, when its journal, L'Hydropathe, was revamped as Tout-Paris; the latter only lasted five issues, but one of them included Charles's third scientific romance.

Charles continued his work on color photography in collaboration with an engineer named Jules Carpentier, but could not devise a marketable method. At the end of 1881, however, Rodolphe Salis founded a café called Le Chat Noir, with the ambition of making it Paris's leading literary café and Charles became one of its earliest regulars, along with other Hydropathes—Salis had requested Goudeau to revive the club with Le Chat Noir as its base. It was there that his friendship with Allais matured, Villiers having fallen on hard times, and Nina de Villard's salon being defunct. Charles missed the "double act" that he and Villiers had put on chez Nina, and started a new one with Allais; Gabriel Astruc's Le Pavillon des fantômes (1929) recalls Cros and Allais exchanging "des passes d'armes contradictoires où la fantaisie se mêlait au document. Tous deux fabriquaient du Jules Verne ou du Robida avec une profusion et un cachet d'authenticité stupéfiants" [argumentative duels in which fantasy mingled with the documentary. Both fabricated work in the manner of Jules Verne of Robida with an amazing profusion and stamp of authenticity].

It is possible that Charles' finest work in the field of scientific romance was done, and essentially frittered away, in these performance pieces—but it seems probable that some of the humorous scientific and pseudoscientific speculations that Allais subsequently put into the squibs he wrote for various humorous papers originated from these flights of fancy. Unfortunately, the pieces in question were randomly scattered through Allais' various collections, obscuring the extent of his contribution to the rich tradition of French satirical scientific romance. Several of the other writers who hung out at the Chat Noir also went on to write scientific romance, including Edmond Haraucourt, Henri Rivière and Charles Laumann (a.k.a. E. M. Laumann).

Charles, however, made little or no further attempt to publish any literary work connected to his scientific endeavors. His principal literary effort in the context of Le Chat Noir was the founding of a group he called the Zutistes (a calculated echo of Rimbaud) in 1883. It went nowhere, but the eventual publication of the contents of a manuscript intended to be its showcase, L'Album Zutique, gave it a certain belated notoriety. He did do some published work in collaboration with Allais, including a series of "contes sens dessus dessous" (upside-down tales) issued under the pseudonym Carlemyll, for the periodical

Gil Blas, *but it only included two works of marginal speculative relevance before being cut short.*

Charles was not initially involved in the editorship of the café's journal, Le Chat Noir, *founded in 1882, but he did take a hand in it after April 1883. He subsequently involved himself with* Le Scapin *and* La Décadence, *both founded in 1885, but he was in poor health by then—presumably due to the heavy drinking he had begun in Nina de Villard's salon and continued in* Le Chat Noir— *and both aspects of his languishing career suffered from his increasing incapacity. In 1884, Joris-Karl Huysmans published his "Decadent handbook"* À rebours, *in which he included a remarkably harsh criticism of Charles. There was no mention at all of him in the second foundation-stone of the Decadent Movement, Verlaine's non-fictional account of* Poètes maudits. *Perhaps the omission was coincidental, given that the book was a hastily-compiled collection of essays, but Verlaine probably had not forgotten that Charles had sided with his wife when his marriage had disintegrated.*

It might have been the sting of Huysmans' dismissal that led Charles to reprint his scientific romances in Le Chat Noir *in 1886—a sequence that might have formed a basis to the continuation of a series and the birth of a genre had he not been so prematurely weary and seriously ill by then. He accomplished little more before dying, a broken man, on August 9, 1888, leaving his family nothing but debts.*

An Interastral Drama *is, inevitably, primitive by modern standards, but its interest is not confined to its anticipation of developments in media, or its blithe assumption that space travel will never become practicable. Its greatest fascination lies in what it refuses to say, most conspicuously about the particular charms of Venusian women (which obviously exceed those of Earthly women, in the eyes of Earthly men) and other "Mysteries of the Cupola," but also about the other speculative elements contained in the story, all of which are deliberately consigned to a vagueness aptly symbolized by the moving images of the hero's inamorata, lovingly reproduced in swirling smoke.*

B.S.

AN INTERASTRAL DRAMA

La Esperanza, August 24, 2872

Ordinance CXVII of the 32nd Grand-Master of Terrestrial Astronomy has provoked whining from the entire Satirist party. Let us say right away that this party, although it denies it vehemently, is strongly reminiscent of that of the Freethinkers of a few centuries ago. It is so strongly reminiscent that one might fear seeing it go to the same negative extremes, which would consequently necessitate the same repressions.

The Satirists have been talking about a return to the onions of Egypt,[15] to the darkness of the 19th and 20th century; they have proclaimed it a restoration of the clergies of yesteryear, a superstitious measure, a mythological fantasy introduced into that which is most essential to the smooth progress of modern human society.

It will be easy for me to nullify these vain claims. Firstly, it is necessary to observe that the ordinance establishes nothing that has not been actual practice for many years. It does nothing but formalize what already exists in the particular regulations of all terrestrial observatories, and also the results of numerous decisions of the Supreme Court.

Indeed, it requires an ignorance of the most elementary study of administrative law to be unfamiliar with the formalities demanded by all the Observatory councils for admission into the Grand Cupola and the Correspondence Terrace. It is necessary not to have read any of the astronomical publications of this century not to know that the term "Mysteries of the Cupola and the Terrace," so critical in the ordinance at issue, is in common usage, and that certain official documents, already ancient, employ it explicitly. It is part and parcel of the special regime, of the obligatory celibacy of astronomers who desire to surpass the fourth grade, of the oath demanded of them and the particular penalties to which they are subject—penalties that become more severe as the grade of the offender becomes more elevated.

It has been the case for a long time that in requests for admission to superior grades, aspirants mention first and foremost their celibate status and the austerity of their morals, with supporting evidence. Now, these things have been compulsory in reality for a long time, and ordinance CXVII is simply a regularization of a custom recognized as necessary from a moral and political point of view. In this respect, the action of the ordinance, rather than further restricting the custom, has rendered it more equitable and broader in scope, by anticipating the abuse of certain excessively severe restrictions that were beginning to be introduced into several courses in Astronomy.

I know, however, that the Satirists will not be satisfied by these explanations. Custom it may be, they will say, but an unjust and evil custom: an abuse of power, and so on.

---

[15] I have translated "*aux oignons d'Égypte*" literally, although the phrase in question (from *Exodus* 16:3) only appears in French Bibles, not English ones. The Hebrews, while wandering in the desert with Moses, are said to have regretted leaving Egypt, where they had had enough to eat: the French version of the phrase was adopted metaphorically for reference to nostalgia. The King James version has "flesh pots" instead of onions, reflecting a marked cultural difference in patterns of regret.

With respect to this objection—which, moreover, immediately proves the ignorance and thoughtlessness of those who raise it—I do not want to enter into a debate in the strict sense of the term. I shall limit myself to telling a story that will demonstrate, even to the simplest minds, the necessity of strong regulation of the sort that has naturally prevailed, and which has now been defined by ordinance CXVII.

Perhaps you will recall the sudden and unexplained retirement of a director of the Observatory of the Southern Andes, and the rumors surrounding that retirement. There as mention of culpable negligence and the violation of the Mysteries of the Cupola. The word *mysteries* can even be found in the newspapers of the period. The government wisely hushed up the affair, and the director, although missed by virtue of his remarkable work—especially his work on the equatorial flora of Venus—took early retirement on health grounds. He has now been dead for a long time, as are the majority of those involved. Here, therefore, are the facts as they happened. I shall not give any names.

The director in question—exceptionally, even in that era, as I have said—was married. To be strictly accurate, he was a widower at the time of his appointment—but he had a son of 22 or 23.

The young man, endowed with a vivid, almost undisciplined, imagination, had no taste for astronomical studies, and did not want to do anything but paint and compose verses. He has, in fact, left behind poems highly rated by specialists, although they have a characteristic strangeness scarcely tolerable to those who, like me, only like the normal and uncontestable masterpieces of the 25th century. Let us return to our story.

Studies of the Venusian flora were carried out by exchange, in accordance with normal practice—which is to say that it was necessary to transmit as many specimens of terrestrial flora as were received from Venus. Use was made to this effect of the great battery of 3000 50-centimeter objectives and the adjoining reflectors. It is common knowledge that this battery, which resembles an immense insectile eye, and which cost the constructors 29 years of work and the government 95 millions, is still one of the finest batteries on Earth. Images are reproduced at 1/400th of their diameter by the distance between Earth and Venus, with the consequence that it suffices for Venusian astronomers to magnify the images 400 times on the transmission surface to enable us to receive them at their actual size.

An exchange of Venusian and terrestrial botanical specimens was therefore under way, and the battery was constantly aimed at a Venusian peak, which it is unnecessary to identify. The director, absorbed by the powerful interest of his research, had the idea—more unfortunate than culpable—of making use of his son's help in the fixation and classification of the photographs transmitted to him. Later, he went so far as to confide the direct observation-post at the ocular to the young man. This can only be explained by a sort of senile folly, for, in order to explain such a grave neglect of metaplanetary convention during the inquiry, the unfortunate director simply alleged that he had been suffering *eye-strain* at the time. But let us continue.

The great botanical research project occupied half of the transmission time; the other half was dedicated to current correspondence. The young man was therefore acquainted with the entire procedural operation of that correspondence, without any preparatory studies, regulation, grade or taking any oath!

The subordinate astronomers, perhaps more concerned with protecting their salaries than looking out for the interests of society, or perhaps because of their otherwise-praiseworthy habit of absolute obedience and respect with regard to their director, let things be. At any rate, as they told the enquiry, the correspondence service was conducted, in these irregular conditions, in a very active and fecund manner.

Simply for the sake of the story's convenience, I shall call the young man by the banal and commonplace name of Glaux. Glaux, therefore, seemed suddenly to have taken his ocular functions very much to heart, He asked everyone about possible improvements relating to the transmission process. He even became the first person to put into practice many means previously neglected as purely theoretical and inapplicable. Indeed, it is only since these events that we have been able to transmit and receive sonorous phenomena. The utility of that has been denied; it is argued that we do not have much understanding of Venusian music, and that, with respect to spoken languages, we can only have them pronounced by mechanical articulators. Speaking them ourselves, it is added, would be a waste of time, except in the evidently absurd supposition of an interplanetary voyage. This is, in my opinion, an excessively hasty and ill-tempered conclusion—but I shall move on.

Whence came this sudden astronomical zeal? Its cause would have been easy to anticipate, if the old routine did not bring the majority of men to consider the most natural things in the world as strange or impossible. In truth, science has progressed more rapidly than reason and common sense.

This is what had happened.

Glaux, having concluded the current transmissions one day, was about to quit his post when he saw a creature advancing across the terrace of the Venusian observatory that he did not recognize as belonging to its personnel.

Positing in advance that I am taking account of the distinctions and restrictions of science, I shall say, in order to speak briefly, that it was a *woman*.

Here my task as a narrator becomes difficult. It would be impossible if ordinance CXVII itself had not exactly defined the offences of expression. I shall therefore keep strictly within legal limits and I shall be very sparing with details.

It was, therefore, a woman. Glaux, piqued by curiosity, observed her movements. She went idly back and forth, I cannot say anything about her *extraterrestrial* beauty, or of her attire, of which our most sumptuous flowers give only a dull and monotonous idea. Only sworn astronomers of the 11th grade can be precisely informed in these matters, and that by other means than a description formulated in words.

But here *She* is, arriving at the terrestrial correspondence apparatus, and pausing there. Glaux then makes the greeting customary at the beginning of correspondence. *She* replies very pertinently, repressing what might be called, by virtue of a legitimate analogy, *a burst of laughter*. These details come from a journal in prose and verse that Glaux left behind.

By means of a few exchanged signs, Glaux sees with surprise that *She* is familiar—perhaps more so than him—with the interplanetary language, and the dialogue continues. But Earth and Venus rotate; atmospheric refractions blue the images and soon permit no more than the several-times-repeated signs: Until tomorrow! It is from that day onwards that Glaux is seen to put so much zeal and ingenious activity into his job of correspondent.

Did he imagine for himself those marvelous methods, which one no longer thinks of admiring, now that their usage is continual, or were they communicated to him? Perhaps they were the indiscretions, very advantageous to us, of the young Venusian woman, careless—as women generally are—of keeping the scientific secrets of her planet.

You have guessed, of course, that the two young people were smitten with one another. What folly! What a deplorable consequence of a failure to observe the rules!

They thought they could vanquish the distance that separated them by exchanging the most complete accounts of themselves. They sent one another their photographs in series sufficient for the reproduction of three-dimensionality and movements.[16] In the hours when observation had finished, Glaux shut himself up in a room and reproduced the moving image of his beloved in smoke or dust: an impalpable image made of light alone. He also realized her motionless form in plastic substances.

It is then that they thought of sending the sound of their voices, their words, their songs. All of that was recorded in curves and reproduced by an electrical tuning-fork apparatus.[17] I cannot say anything about the words and songs (?) that came from so far away.

---

[16] This anticipation of cinema—though not its holographic aspect—might have been inspired by a scientist Cros met at Camille Flammarion's salon, Étienne-Jules Marey, who shared his interest in photographic technology; Marey developed a "chronophotographic gun" in 1882 for analyzing movement by means of multiple exposures, and might have mentioned the possibility to Cros some time before bringing the project to fruition.

[17] This was written five years before Cros submitted his design for such an apparatus to the Académie des Sciences. It is interesting that Cros subsequently refers to *phonographies* [phonographs] although he called his own apparatus a *paléophone*.

Everything that I have just stated so briefly—for good reason—lasted three years.

The third year was terrible, a mixture of ecstasy and despair. Would it have been possible to save the two lunatics at that point, by forceful measures? It is doubtful. The harm was done, irreparable. One evening, when our dusk corresponded with dusk in the Venusian country in question, and all the preparations had been made on both sides. Glaux and the young woman exchanged one last kiss across implacable space and killed themselves.

This catastrophe nearly compromised the good relationship between two planets, for the young Venusian woman was the daughter of one of the most powerful astronomers of that world. Everything was settled by precise metaplanetary conventions, which were then put in place. Ordinance CXVII has implemented these conventions of Earth. The unfortunate consequences that were momentarily dreaded will thus be avoided.

All Glaux's papers, photographs, photosculptures and phonographs are filed in the central archives. It is necessary, as I have said, to have reached the 11th grade to have access to them.

Despite what I have just recounted, by superior authorization, I would not be surprised to see the Satirists continue to deny the expediency of ordinance CXVII.

Guy de Maupassant: *Martian Mankind*
(1887)

Guy de Maupassant (1850-1893), the foremost French short story writer of his admittedly-brief era, became famous as a naturalist by virtue of pioneering the development of anecdotal slice-of-life stories and calculatedly low-key contes cruels, *which helped define the narrative method of the modern short story, but the range of his work extended much further.*

His most famous alliance with speculative motifs was the classic and much reprinted Le Horla *(1887), an ambiguous story whose distressed narrator becomes convinced that he is being tormented by an invisible creature, which must have come from Brazil on a passing ship, and that its species may be in the process of displacing humankind on Earth.*

In the same year, he produced L'Homme de Mars*[Martian Mankind], which complemented Flammarion's speculations—most elaborately fictionalized in* Uranie *(1889)—regarding the forms that Martian life might have taken in adapting to the physical conditions of the planet's surface.*

Although it still retains an echo of the apologetic formula used by Louis-Sébastien Mercier and Eugène Mouton—which Maupassant had brought to a kind of perfection in Le Horla—Martian Mankind *is a fundamentally earnest story, which is prepared to take its central hypothesis seriously, and the scientific data it quotes were all deemed accurate at the time. Its suggestion that Mars might be a warm world despite its distance from the Sun, by virtue of the influence of the greenhouse effect, proved dead wrong, but its underlying logic deserves some credit. Its account of a brief glimpse of alien life—remarkably similar to modern day UFO reports—strikes a subtle note of exotic poignancy that was to become one of the keynotes of 20th-century science fiction.*

B.S.

MARTIAN MANKIND

I was busy working when my servant announced: "Monsieur, there is a Monsieur asking to speak to Monsieur."

"Show him in."

I perceived a small man, who bowed. He had the appearance of a puny and bespectacled assistant schoolmaster. His clothing was too large, hanging loosely from his thin body at every point.

"I beg your pardon, Monsieur," he stammered. "Forgive me for disturbing you."

"Sit down, Monsieur," I said.

He sat down, and continued: "*Mon Dieu*, Monsieur, I am deeply troubled by the step that I am about to take, but it is absolutely necessary that I fix upon someone, and there is no one but you, only you... Finally, I have plucked up the courage, but to tell the truth... I no longer dare."

"Then be bold, Monsieur."

"You see, Monsieur, the problem is that as soon as I begin to speak, you will take me for a madman."

"*Mon Dieu*, Monsieur, that depends on what it is you have to say to me."

"Exactly, Monsieur. What I have come to tell you is bizarre. But I beg you to consider the possibility that I am not mad, for the very reason that I admit the strangeness of my story."

"Well then, Monsieur, get on with it."

"No, Monsieur, I am not mad, but I have the distracted appearance of men who are more thoughtful than others and who have gone a little–so little–beyond the limits of the average mind. Just imagine, Monsieur, how few people in this world ever think about anything. Everyone is occupied with his own affairs, his own fortunes, his own pleasures–with his own life, in sum–or with petty and trifling amusements like the theater, painting, music, politics–the greatest nonsense of all–or matters of trade. So who really thinks? Who, exactly? No one! Oh, pardon me... I'm getting carried away! I'll get back to the point.

"It was five years ago that I came here, Monsieur. You don't know me, but I know you very well... I never mingle with the crowds at your beach or your casino. I live on the cliffs. I positively adore the cliffs of Etretat. I know none more beautiful or healthier–I mean healthy in a spiritual sense. There's an excellent pathway between the sky and the sea, a verdant route that runs along the great wall of white rock, which takes you along the rim of the world, the rim of the land, above the Ocean. My best days are those I have spent stretched out on a grassy slope, in broad daylight, a hundred meters above the waves, dreaming. Do you understand what I'm saying?"

"Yes, Monsieur, perfectly."

"Now, would you be kind enough to let me ask you a question?"

"Ask, Monsieur."

"Do you believe that the other planets are inhabited?"

"Certainly I believe it," I replied, without hesitation or any evident surprise.

He got up, moved by vehement joy and seized by a manifest desire to clasp me in his arms, then sat down again. "Oh, what luck!" he exclaimed. "What a blessing! I can breathe! But how could I ever have doubted you? A man would not be intelligent if he did not believe other worlds inhabited. He would have to be a fool, a cretin, an idiot, a brute to suppose that the myriads of the universe shine and spin solely to amuse and astonish that imbecile insect man, to fail to understand that the earth is nothing but an invisible mote in the dust of worlds... that our entire solar system is naught but a handful of molecules of sidereal life, which will perish soon enough.

"Look at the Milky Way, that river of stars, and realize that it is nothing but a smear on the expanse that is infinity. Only think about that for ten minutes and you will understand why we know nothing, we divine nothing, we understand nothing. We know only one place, nothing of anything beyond or outside it, of anywhere else–but we believe and we have faith. Oh! If it were suddenly revealed to us, the secret of the vast extent of extraterrestrial life, how astonished we would be!

"But no... no... it's my turn to be stupid. We don't understand it, because our mentality is crafted to understand none but earthly things. It cannot extend much further; it is limited, like human life, trapped on this little globe that carries us, and it judges everything by that standard. So you see, Monsieur, that the whole world is stupid, narrow-minded, and fully persuaded of the power of our intelligence, which scarcely surpasses that of animal instinct. We do not even have the capacity to perceive our infirmity; we are shaped to know the price of butter and corn, and–at the most–to haggle over the value of a couple of horses, a couple of boats, a couple of ministers or a couple of artists. That's all.

"We are just about fit for tilling the land and clumsily making use of that which lies upon it. Having only just begun to construct working machinery, we are childishly amazed by every discovery that we ought to have made centuries ago, had we been superior beings. We are still surrounded by the unknown, even at the moment when, after thousands of years of intelligent life, electricity has been discovered. Are you and I of the same opinion?"

"Yes, Monsieur," I replied, laughing.

"Very well, then. Well, Monsieur, do you ever pay any attention to Mars?"

"To Mars?"

"Yes, to the planet Mars?"

"No, Monsieur."

"You know nothing at all about it?"

"No, Monsieur."

"Will you permit me to tell you a little about it?"

"Yes, Monsieur, with great pleasure."

"You know, presumably, that the worlds of our solar system, our little family, have been formed by the condensation into globes of rings of primal gas, detached one after the other from the solar nebula?"

"Yes, Monsieur."

"It follows from this that the most distant planets are the oldest, and in consequence, must be the most civilized. This was the order of their birth: Uranus, Saturn, Jupiter, Mars, the Earth, Venus, Mercury. Will you admit that these planets must be inhabited, like the Earth?"

"Certainly. Why suppose that the Earth is an exception?"

"Very well. The man of Mars will have a longer history than the man of Earth... but I'm going too quickly. First, I want to prove that Mars is inhabited. Mars presents to us something very similar to the aspect that Earth presents to Martian observers. The oceans there take up less space and are more widely scattered. They are identifiable by their dark hue, because water absorbs light, while the continents reflect it. Geographical modifications of the planetary surface are frequent, thus proving that its life is active. It has seasons like ours, snow at the poles that can be seen to grow and diminish with the passage of time. Its year is very long: 687 terrestrial days, which is 668 Martian days. That breaks down as follows: 191 days of spring, 191 of summer, 149 of autumn and 147 of winter. Fewer clouds are seen there than here; there must, in consequence, be greater extremes of cold and heat."

I interrupted him. "I beg your pardon, Monsieur, but as Mars is much further from the Sun than we are, it seems to me that it must always be colder there."

My bizarre visitor exclaimed very vehemently: "Wrong, Monsieur! Wrong, totally wrong! We ourselves are more distant from the Sun in summer than in winter. It is colder on the summit of Mont Blanc than at its foot. I refer you, moreover, to the mechanical theory of heat of Helmholtz and Schiaparelli. The heat of the Sun is principally dependent upon the quantity of water vapor contained in the atmosphere. This is why: the absorbant capacity of a molecule of aqueous vapor is 16,000 times more than that of a molecule of dry air, so water vapor is our storehouse of heat. Mars, having fewer clouds, must be both much warmer and much colder than the Earth."

"I no longer contest the point."

"Very good. Now, Monsieur, listen to me with the utmost attention, I beg you."

"I am all ears, Monsieur."

"You have heard talk of the famous canals discovered in 1884 by Monsieur Schiaparelli?"

"Very little."

"Is that possible? Well then, in 1884, while Mars was in opposition to us, separated by a distance of no more than four million leagues, Monsieur Schiaparelli, one of the most eminent astronomers of the century and one of the most adept observers, suddenly discovered a large number of straight and broken black lines forming constant geometrical patterns, crossing the continents to link the seas of Mars! Yes, yes, Monsieur: rectilinear canals, geometrical canals, of a similar width throughout their course, constructed by living beings! Yes, Monsieur, the proof that Mars is inhabited, that there is life there, that there is intelligence there, that there is industry there... which can see us. Do you understand? Do you understand?

"Twenty-six months later, at the time of the next opposition, these canals were visible again, Monsieur, even more numerous—and they are gigantic, no less than a hundred kilometers wide."

I smiled as I replied: "A hundred kilometers wide! It must have required strong workers to dig them."

"Oh, Monsieur, what are you trying to say? You do not know, then, that such labor is infinitely easier on Mars than on Earth, since the density of its material constituents is only 69% of ours. The intensity of its gravity is scarcely 37% of ours. A kilogram of water only weighs 370 grams."

He threw these figures at me with such assurance, with the confidence of a businessman who knows the value of a number, that I could not prevent myself from breaking into laughter, and I was tempted to ask him how much sugar and butter weighed on Mars.

He shook his head.

"You are laughing, Monsieur; instead of taking me for a madman, you take me for an imbecile—but the figures I have quoted you are those that you will find in every specialist textbook of astronomy. The diameter is nearly half as much less than ours; its surface area is only 26% of ours; its volume is six and a half times smaller than that of the Earth and the velocity of its two satellites proves that its mass is ten times less. Now, Monsieur, the intensity of gravity depends on the mass and the volume, which is to say on the mass and the distance of the surface from the center, so the indubitable result is that on the planet there is a state of lightness that makes life completely different, regulating mechanical actions in a manner unknown to us, which must lead to a predominance there of winged species.

"Yes, Monsieur, the Ruling Being of Mars has wings. He flies, passing from one continent to another like a spirit, all around his world, although he is unable to move beyond the vestiges of its atmosphere...

"To conclude, Monsieur, can you imagine this planet, covered with plants, trees and animals whose forms we cannot even suspect, and inhabited by great winged beings like our artists' images of angels? Personally, I see them flying over the plains and cities, in the gilded atmosphere that they have there—for although it was believed in former times that the Martian sky is red while ours is blue, it is actually yellow: a beautiful, golden yellow.

"Are you still amazed that such creatures as those could hollow out canals a hundred kilometers wide? Then again, just think what science has achieved for us, in a single century... in a hundred years... and remind yourself that the inhabitants of Mars may well be far superior to us..."

He fell abruptly silent, lowered his eyes, then murmured in a very low voice: "Now the time has come that you will take me for a madman... When I tell you that I have glimpsed them myself... The other night. You may or may not know that we are in the season of shooting stars. On the nights of the 18th and 19th, especially, they are seen every year in innumerable quantities; it is probable that we are passing at this very moment through the tail of a comet.

"I was, therefore, sitting on the Mane-Porte, that enormous sheer headland that juts into the sea, watching the rain of little worlds overhead. It's prettier and more entertaining than any artificial fire, Monsieur. All at once, I perceived, directly above me, very close, a luminous transparent globe, surrounded by immense beating wings–at least, I thought I saw wings in the semi-darkness of the night. It was fluttering like a wounded bird, turning on its axis with a loud, peculiar noise, seemingly breathless, dying, lost. It passed in front of me. One might have taken it for a monstrous crystal balloon, full of panic-stricken creatures, scarcely discernible but excited, like the crew of a ship in distress, no longer under control but rolling from wave to wave. And the strange globe, having described an immense curve, came crashing down into the sea some distance away, where I heard it plunge into the depths with a noise like a cannon-shot.

"Everyone for miles around heard that mighty impact, which they took for a thunderbolt. I alone have seen... I have seen... If it had fallen on to the shore beside me, I would have met the inhabitants of Mars.

"Don't say a word, Monsieur. Think it over. Think it over for a long while... Then tell the story, one day, if you wish. Yes, I have seen... I have seen... The first spaceship launched into the infinite by thinking beings... Unless I have merely been present at the death of a shooting star captured by the Earth. For you may not know, Monsieur, that the planets hunt the wandering worlds of space as we pursue vagabonds down here. The light and feeble Earth is only able to intercept the smallest of infinity's passers-by."

He stood up, delirious with excitement, opening his arms wide to describe the march of the stars.

"The comets, Monsieur, which roam the frontiers of the great nebula whose condensates we are; the comets, free and luminous birds, coming towards the Sun from the depths of infinity. They come towards the radiant star, trailing their immense tails of light; they come, accelerating so forcefully in their bewilderment that they are unable to unite with their summoner; after the merest brush with it, they are hurled back into space as rapidly as they fell. But if, in the course of their prodigious journeys, they pass close to a powerful planet, if they feel its attraction and are drawn from their route by its irresistible influence, they return then to their new master, which renders them captive henceforth. Their unlimited parabola is transformed into a closed curve, and it is thus that we can calculate the revisitations of periodic comets. Jupiter has eight slaves, Saturn one, Neptune one also,[18] and its exterior planet one again, plus an army of shoot-

---

[18] Although I have left it as it is, this reference to Neptune must be an error. Maupassant must have meant to name Uranus, Neptune–discovered in 1846–being the "exterior planet" mentioned immediately afterwards. (Pluto was not discovered until 1930.)

ing stars... Then... then, perhaps I only saw the Earth intercept a little wandering world...

"Goodbye, Monsieur, make no reply. Reflect, consider, and tell the whole story one day, if you wish..."

That was all. The lunatic seemed to me less stupid than some mere man of independent means.

J.-H. Rosny *Aîné*: *Another World*
(1895)

The writer who made the most striking contributions to visionary specula-tive fiction, however, was associated with a rather different literary community, centered on Edmond de Goncourt's salon, known as the Grenier [Grain-Loft]. That was J.-H. Rosny Aîné (Joseph-Henri Boëx) (1856-1940).[19]

Les Xipehuz *(1887) is one of the classics of roman scientifique, describes the appearance on Earth in prehistoric times of a population of bizarre alien creatures seemingly displaced from another spatial dimension and not fully ac-commodated to the geometry of ours. The humans of the era battle to oppose and obliterate the invasion, successfully in the end, though not without enor-mous difficulty. In the meantime, attempts made to comprehend something of the language and reproductive "biology" of the Xipéhuz—although they do not ap-pear to be organic beings—produce a few tentative conclusions that only serve to emphasize their utter strangeness.*

In the same vein, and probably written at the same time, is a short story apparently improvised from the stub of what was presumably initially intended as a novel, Un Autre Monde *[Another World], about a young man afflicted with a more powerful kind of sight, who discovers that the human world is also in-habited by a complex host of entities that are normally invisible, whose interac-tions with humans therefore go uncomprehended. Although cut short, and only a fraction of what it must have been originally intended to become, that item too came to be hailed as an important exemplar of post-Vernian* roman scientifique.

The principal import of Camille Flammarion's vision of the universe, as elaborated in Lumen, *was that we should not expect other worlds to be simple replicas of ours, with only cosmetic variations, but that there might be potential receptacles for souls that fill a vast spectrum of dissimilarity, extending all the way to entities so different from human beings as to be hardly imaginable by them. Flammarion's own imagination was not particularly well-equipped to il-lustrate and dramatize that argument, and perhaps no one's is, or ever can be, capable of doing so convincingly—but Rosny was at last willing to try, in these*

---

[19] Between 1891 and 1907 the pseudonym J.-H. Rosny was shared by Joseph Boëx with his young brother Justin, and after the split they signed themselves J.-H. Rosny *aîné* and J.-H. Rosny *jeune* respectively, but Justin had nothing like the imagination of his brother, and all the speculative fiction produced during the years when they used the same signature—they very rarely, if ever, worked in collaboration—was Joseph's work, much of it written, or at least begun, be-fore 1891.

and other stories written at intervals throughout his career, alongside more conventional representations of things as they are and relatively elementary variants thereof. He was always aware that it was likely to be a thankless task, because the closer he came to success in his own eyes, the less comprehensible his work would become, and there is only a very limited reader appeal in calculated incomprehensibility. Nevertheless, he thought it worth doing.

Very few other writers indulged in such extreme exercises at the time, but other writers produced visionary accounts of this world and others—and particularly of the relations between them—which exhibited a related consciousness and produced similarly striking imagery. Nor was the approach limited to writers with as much literary pretention as Rosny; something of his attitude and method filtered through to lower strata of the marketplace, where visions of other worlds, including but not restricted to interplanetary fantasies, often began to take on a phantasmagoric dimension more in tune with the cosmological visions of Flammarion and Restif de la Bretonne than the extensions of geographical romance favored by writers employing Vernian templates.

B.S.

ANOTHER WORLD

To Anatole France

I

I am a native of Gelderland. Our patrimony was reduced to a few acres of heath-land and stagnant water. Pines that made a metallic sound as they quivered were growing on its borders. The farmhouse only had a few habitable rooms, and was falling apart, stone by stone, in isolation. We were an old family of herdsmen, once numerous but now reduced to my parents, my sister and myself.

My destiny, bleak at the outset, has become the finest imaginable; I have met someone who understands me; he will learn that which only I knew before—but I have been suffering for a long time. I was in despair, prey to doubt and loneliness, which ended up eroding everything of which I was once certain.

I came into the world with a unique constitution. From the very beginning, I was an object of astonishment. Not that I seemed deformed; I am told that I was more graceful in body and face than is usual in the newly born—but I had the most extraordinary skin color: a kind of pale violet, very pale but quite distinct. By lamplight, especially that of oil-lamps, that tint paled further, becoming a peculiar off-white, like that of a lily submerged in water. That was, at least, how I appeared to other people—for I saw myself differently, as I saw everything in the world differently. To that first peculiarity others were added, which were revealed in due course.

Although born apparently healthy, my development was difficult. I was thin and cried incessantly; at the age of eight months, I had not yet been seen to smile. My parents despaired of my ever growing up. The doctor in Zwartendam declared that I was suffering from a congenital weakness; he saw no other remedy but rigorous hygiene. I continued nonetheless to grow weaker; I was expected to perish at any moment. My father, I believe had resigned himself to it, somewhat dented in his self-respect—his Dutch pride in order and regularity—by his infant's bizarre appearance. My mother, by contrast, loved me all the more for my strangeness, having ended up finding the color of my skin pleasant.

That was how things stood when a very simple occurrence came to my rescue; as everything concerning me was abnormal, though, the event was a cause of scandal and apprehension.

When one of the servants left, she was replaced by a vigorous Friesian girl, very hard-working and honest but inclined to drink. I was confided to the newcomer. Seeing that I was so weak, she took it into her head to give me, secretly, a little beer and water mixed with *schiedam*—a sovereign remedy, in her opinion, against all ills.

The curious thing is that I was not long delayed in recovering my strength, and showed thereafter an extraordinary predilection for alcohol. The young woman rejoiced secretly, not without taking some pleasure in puzzling my parents and the doctor. Under interrogation, however, she ended up revealing the secret. My father was extremely angry; the doctor railed against superstition and ignorance. Strict orders were given to the servants and I was removed from the Friesian woman's care.

I began to grow thinner and weaker again, until, heedless of everything but her affection, my mother put me back on a diet of beer and *schiedam*. I immediately recovered my vigor and vivacity. The experiment was conclusive; alcohol was revealed to be indispensable to my health. My father felt humiliated; the doctor got himself out it by prescribing tonic wines. Since then, my health has been excellent, although no one hesitated to predict a future of drunkenness and debauchery.

Shortly after this incident, a further anomaly was observed by those around me. My eyes, which had seemed normal to begin with, became strangely opaque, acquiring a horny texture like the wing-cases of certain beetles. The doctor predicted that I would lose my sight, but confessed nevertheless that the ailment seemed absolutely bizarre, and that he had never had an opportunity to study one like it. Soon, the pupil was so confused with the iris that it was impossible to distinguish between them. It was noticed, in addition, that I could look directly at the Sun without any discomfort. In truth, I was not blind at all, and it had to be admitted eventually that I could see perfectly well.

I reached the age of three. According to our neighbors, I was then a little monster. The violet color of my skin had hardly changed; my eyes were completely opaque. I spoke badly, with incredible rapidity. I was clever with my hands and well-adapted for all actions that demanded more agility than strength. No one denied that I would have been graceful and good-looking if I my skin color had been natural and my pupils transparent. I showed intelligence, but with gaps that those around me could not fathom, inasmuch as, save for my mother and the Friesian woman, no one liked me very much. To strangers, I was an object of curiosity, and to my father a constant thorn in his side.

At any rate, if my father had conserved any hope of seeing me revert to normality, time certainly disabused him. I became increasingly strange, in my tastes, my habits and my abilities. At six, I nourished myself almost entirely on alcohol, only rarely eating a few mouthfuls of fruit and vegetables. I grew with prodigious rapidity, but I was incredibly thin and light. I mean "light" in terms of specific gravity, which is the opposite of thinness; thus, I could swim without the slightest difficulty, floating like a plank of poplar-wood. My head was no more inclined to sink than the rest of my body.

I was as nimble as I was light. I could run as fast as a roe deer, easily jumping ditches and obstacles that no other man would even have tried to jump. I could reach the top of a beech-tree in the blink of an eye, or—which was even more surprising—leap on to the roof of our farmhouse. On the other hand, the slightest burden was too much for me.

All these things, in sum, were merely phenomena indicative of a special nature, which, in themselves, would only have served to single me out and make me unwelcome; no one would have classified me as other than human. I was undoubtedly a monster, but certainly not to the extent of people born with horns or animal ears, the head of a calf or a horse, fins, devoid of eyes or with a supplementary eye, four arms, four legs or devoid of arms or legs. My skin, despite its unusual tint, was not so very different from sun-tanned skin; my eyes were not repulsive in spite of their opacity. My extreme agility was a talent. My need for alcohol could pass for a mere vice, a hereditary addiction—the country folk, in any case, like our Friesian housemaid, only saw it as a confirmation of their ideas regarding the "power" of *schiedam*, a slightly exaggerated demonstration of the excellence of their tastes. As for the rapidity and volubility of my speech, which was impossible to follow, that seemed little different from faults of pronunciation—stammering, lisping and stuttering—common to many young children. I did not, therefore, have any marked characteristics of monstrosity, even though the ensemble was extraordinary. The most curious aspect of my nature was invisible to those around me: no one was aware that my vision was strangely different from normal vision.

Although I saw some things less well than other people, I could see a great many that no one else saw. That difference manifested itself most obviously in colors. Everything that other people called red, orange, yellow, green, blue and indigo appeared to me as varying shades of darkness, while I perceived violet, and a series of colors beyond that—colors that were nothing but darkness to normal people. I eventually realized that I am able to distinguish 15 colors as dissimilar as, for instance, yellow and green—with infinite gradations, of course.

Furthermore, transparency does not manifest to my eyes in ordinary conditions. I can only see poorly through a window or through water; glass, for me, is brightly colored; water noticeably so, even when very shallow. Many crystals said to be clear are more or less opaque; by contrast, a large number of substances called opaque do not inhibit my vision. In general, I can see through far more substances than you can, and translucency—modified transparency—is so often present that I can say that, for my eyes, it is the general rule of nature, while complete opacity is the exception. Thus, I can discern objects through wood, foliage, the petals of flowers, magnetized iron, coal and so on. At a variable thickness, however, these substances—such as a stout tree-trunk, water a meter deep, a large lump of coal or quartz—become obstacles.

Gold, platinum and mercury are black and opaque; ice is quite dark. Air and water vapor are transparent, but colored, as are certain kinds of steel and very pure clay. Clouds do not prevent me from seeing the Sun or the stars, although I can clearly distinguish those same clouds suspended in the atmosphere.

This difference between my vision and that of other people, as I have said, went largely unnoticed by those around me; they simply thought that I was color-blind—which is too common an infirmity to attract much attention. It was inconsequential for the meager activities of my everyday life, for I saw the shapes of objects in the same fashion—and perhaps more subtly—as the majority of people. The designation of an object by its color, when it was necessary to distinguish it from another object of the same shape, only caused me difficulty if they were unfamiliar. If someone called the color of one waistcoat *blue*, and that of another *red*, it scarcely mattered what color the waistcoats seemed to me to be; *blue* and *red* became purely mnemonic terms.

Given that, you might think that there was some sort of correspondence between my colors and those of others, and that it amounted to the same thing as my being able to see their colors, but as I have already said, red, green, yellow, blue, and so on, when pure—as the colors of the prism are—I perceived as shades of darkness; they were not colors to me. In nature, where no color is simple, it is not the same; one substance called green, for example, is for me a certain composite color,[20] while another substance called green—which is an identical shade so far as you are concerned—is by no means the same color to me. You can see, therefore, that my scale of colors has no correspondence with

---

[20] Rosny's narrator inserts a footnote: "And that composite color, of course, does not include green, since green is darkness to me."

yours; when I consent to call both brass and gold "yellow," it is rather as if you were consenting to call a cornflower "red" as well as a poppy.

II

If the difference between my vision and normal vision stopped there, it would be extraordinary enough, to be sure. That is very little, however, compared to what I still have to tell you. The different coloration, transparency and opacity of the world; the ability to see through clouds, to see the stars on the most overcast nights, to see through a wooden partition-wall what is happening in the next room or outside a house—what is all that compared with the perception of a *living world*, a world of animate creatures moving alongside and around human beings, without humans being aware of it, without them being alerted by any kind of immediate contact?

What is all that, compared with the revelation that there exists on this Earth a fauna other than our fauna, and a fauna with no resemblance to ours in its form, its organization, its mores, or its manner of growth, birth and death? A fauna that lives alongside and in the midst of ours, influencing and influenced by the elements that surround us, nourished by those elements, without our suspecting its presence. A fauna which—as I have proved—is as ignorant of us as we are of it, as insensible to our movements as we are insensible to its movements. A living world, as varied as ours, as powerful as ours—perhaps more so—in its effects on the planet's surface! A kingdom, in sum, extended over land and sea and in the atmosphere, modifying that land, sea and atmosphere in fashions very different from ours but with a very formidable energy—and, by virtue of that, indirectly influencing us, and our destinies!

This, however, is what I—alone among men and animals—have seen; this is what I have *studied*, ardently, for five years, after having spent my childhood and adolescence merely *observing* it.

III

Observing it! For as long as I can remember, I have been instinctively subject to the seduction of that creation, foreign to our own. At first, I confused it with other living things. Perceiving that no one was troubled by its presence—that everyone, on the contrary, seemed indifferent to it—I scarcely felt any need to point out its peculiarities. At the age of six, I was perfectly conscious of its distinction from the plants in the field, the animals in the farmyard and the stables, but I still confused it slightly with inert phenomena like fire and light, running water and clouds. That was because these creatures were intangible; when they touched me, I did not experience any effect of their contact. Besides, their forms, although very various, had the singularity of being so thin in one of their three dimensions that they were comparable to moving drawings, surfaces and geometric lines. They passed through all organic matter; on the other hand, they sometimes seemed to be halted or hampered by invisible obstacles…but I shall describe them later. For the present, I only want to call attention to them, to affirm their variety in shape and size, their near-absence of thickness and their impalpability, in combination with the autonomy of their movements.

By the time I was eight years old, I was perfectly able to distinguish them from atmospheric phenomena as well as the animals of our kingdom. In the excitement that this discovery gave me, I tried to communicate it, but I was never able to succeed. Apart from the fact that my speech was almost completely incomprehensible, as I have said, the extraordinary nature of my vision rendered it suspect. No one took the trouble to interpret my words and gestures, nor was anyone ready to admit that I could see through wooden partitions, even though I gave proof of it many times over. Between me and other people there was an almost-insurmountable barrier.

I became discouraged and took to daydreaming; I became a sort of young recluse; I provoked unease in the company of children of my own age, and was aware of it. I was not exactly a ready-made victim, for my agility put me out of range of infantile malice and gave me a means of avenging myself easily. At the slightest threat, I was far away, mocking any pursuit. No matter how many of them there were, mischief-makers never succeeded in surrounding me, much less in taking hold of me. There was no point in even trying to catch me by trickery. Although too weak to carry any load, my agility was irresistible, freeing me immediately. I could return unexpectedly, and crush my adversary—adversaries, even—with rapid and well-aimed blows. I was, therefore, left in peace. I was taken for both an innocent and something of a magician—but a magician of an unintimidating sort, who could be treated with scorn. By degrees I cultivated an outdoor life, wild and meditative, but not devoid of gentleness. The only humanizing influence I had was my mother's affection, although, being busy all day long, she found little time for caresses.

I shall try to describe, briefly, a few scenes from my tenth year in order to make the preceding explanations more concrete.

It is morning. Broad daylight illuminates the kitchen—a pale yellow glow for my parents and the servants, very various for me. Breakfast is being served, bread and tea—but I don't drink tea. I've been given a glass of *schiedam* and a boiled egg. My mother is taking care of me, affectionately; my father is asking me questions. I try to answer him, slowing down my speech; he only understands the occasional syllable, and shrugs his shoulders.

"He'll never be able to talk!"

My mother looks at me compassionately, convinced that I am a little simple-minded. The domestics and farmhands are no longer even curious about the little violet monster; the Friesian woman returned to her homeland some time ago. As for my sister, who is two years old, she is playing beside me, and I have a profound affection for her.

When breakfast is over, my father goes off to the fields with the farm-hands, and my mother makes a start on her daily chores. I follow her into the farmyard. The animals come to her. I watch them with interest; I like them. The other Kingdom is, however, moving all around us, and captivates me more; it is a mysterious domain known to me alone.

A few forms are extended over the brown earth; they move, they stop, they vibrate at ground level. There are several sorts, different in shape, in their movement, and especially in the arrangement, design and color of the linear features they display. These features constitute, in fact, the major part of their be-ing; even as a child, I can take account of them very well. While the bulk of their form is dull and dark, the lines are almost always sparkling. They form ex-ceedingly complicated networks, emanating from centers, radiating outwards until they become blurred and fade away. Their hues are innumerable, their cures infinite; those shades vary even in a single line—as, to a lesser extent, does their form.

As a whole, each creature is made up of a somewhat irregular but quite dis-tinct border, by centers of radiation, and by multicolored lines that intersect pro-fusely. When it moves, the lines quiver and oscillate, and the centers contract and dilate, while the outline scarcely varies.

All this I can already see quite well, although I am incapable of defining it; an adorable charm possesses me as I contemplate the Moedigen.[21] One of them, a colossus ten meters long and almost as broad, passes slowly through the farm-yard and disappears. That one, with a few stripes as broad as cables and centers as large as an eagle's wing, interests me greatly, and almost frightens me. I con-sider following it momentarily, but others attract my attention. They are very various in size; some do not exceed the length of our smallest insects, while I have seen others more than 30 meters long. They advance over the surface of the ground, as if solidly attached to it. When a material object—a wall or a house—presents itself, they move over it by molding themselves to its surface, always without any significant modification of their shape—but when the obstacle is living matter, or matter that was once alive, they pass directly through it. Thus, I have seen them a thousand times over emerging from a tree, or beneath the feet of an animal or a man. They can also pass through water, but prefer to remain on its surface.

These terrestrial Moedigen are not the only intangible beings. There is an aerial population of a marvelous splendor, subtlety and variety, incomparably

---

[21] Rosny's narrator inserts a footnote: "This is the name that I gave them, spon-taneously, during my childhood, and which they have retained, although it does not correspond to any attribute or form of the creatures in question." *Moedigen* is the plural of *moedig*, which signifies "brave" in Dutch.

spectacular, compared with which the most beautiful birds are dull, slow and ponderous. Here too, there is an outline and linear features, but the background is not dark; it is strangely luminous, sparkling like sunlight, and the lines stand out as vibrant veins, the centers throbbing violently. The Vuren,[22] as I call them, are more irregular in form than the terrestrial Moedigen, and generally navigate with the aid of rhythmic dispositions, increases and decreases of which, in my ignorance, I cannot keep track, and which confuse my imagination.

Meanwhile, I am making my way through a recently-mown meadow; a conflict between one Moedig and another attracts my attention. These conflicts are frequent; they interest me passionately. Sometimes, there is a battle between equals; more often, a strong individual attacks a weak one—the weaker one is not necessarily the smaller. In the present instance, the weaker, after a brief defense, is put to flight, hotly pursued by the aggressor. In spite of the speed at which they are traveling, I follow them and contrive not to lose sight of them before the moment when the fight is resumed. They hurl themselves at one another, solid to one another—hard, even rigid. As they collide, their lines glow, heading toward the point of impact, their centers fade and shrink.

At first, the struggle is fairly equal, the weaker one deploying the more intense energy, even succeeding in forcing a truce from its enemy. It takes advantage of that to flee again, but is rapidly overtaken, forcefully attacked and finally gripped—which is to say, maintained in an indentation in the other's outline. That is exactly what it was trying to avoid, in responding to the stronger one's thrusts with less forceful but more rapid thrusts of its own. Now, I can see all its lines shivering and its centers throbbing desperately. Gradually, the lines fade and thin out, the centers blurring. After a few minutes, it is set free; it draws away slowly, dull and debilitated. Its antagonist, by contrast, is gleaming more brightly; its lines are more colorful, its centers clearer and more active.

The battle has impressed me profoundly; I think about it, comparing it to the contests I have seen between our animals and their smaller kin; I am vaguely aware that the Moedigen, on the whole, do not kill one another—or very rarely—and that victors are content to *absorb strength* at the expense of the vanquished.

The morning wears on; it is nearly 8 a.m.; the school at Zwartendam is about to open. I run back to the farm to get my books—and here I am among my peers, none of whom is aware of the profound mysteries that are happening around them, and none of whom has the vaguest idea of the living creatures through which all human beings pass, and which pass through human beings, without any indication of that mutual penetration.

I am a very poor student. My handwriting is no more than a hasty scrawl, formless and illegible; my speech remains incomprehensible; my distraction is

---

[22] *Vuren* is the plural of *vuur*, which signifies "fire" in Dutch.

manifest. The master continually shouts: "Karel Ondereet, have you finished watching the airborne flies yet?"

Alas, my dear master, it's true that I watch the airborne flies, but how much more interested I am in the mysterious Vuren passing through the room! And what strange sentiments obsess my childish soul in observing everyone's blindness—especially yours, earnest shepherd of minds!

IV

The most painful phase of my life was between the ages of 12 and 18. Initially, my parents tried to send me to secondary school; I found nothing there but misery and frustration.

At the cost of exhausting labor, I succeeded in expressing the most commonplace things in a vaguely comprehensible fashion. Slowing my speech down considerably, I enunciated the syllables awkwardly and with the intonation of the deaf. As soon as anything complicated came up, though, my speech resumed its fatal speed, and no one could any longer follow what I was saying, so I could not make my progress manifest orally.

On the other hand, my handwriting was atrocious; my letters sprawled over one another and, in my impatience, I omitted syllables and whole words; it was monstrous gibberish. In any case, to me, writing was a torture perhaps even more intolerable than speech, of an asphyxiating ponderousness and slowness. If, sometimes, by dint of effort and much sweat, I succeeded in starting an assignment, I soon ran out of strength and patience and felt faint. Then I preferred my masters' remonstrations and my father's fury, punishments and privations to the horrid labor.

I was, therefore, almost totally deprived of means of expression; already an object of ridicule because of my thinness and bizarre complexion, and my strange eyes, I was also taken for some kind of idiot. It was necessary to take me out of school, and become resigned to making me a farm-laborer.

On the day when my father decided to renounce all hope, he said to me, with an unaccustomed gentleness: "You can see, my poor boy, that I've done my duty—everything I can! Never reproach me for your fate!"

I was profoundly moved; I wept profusely; I had never felt my isolation in the midst of humankind so bitterly. I dared to embrace my father tenderly, and murmured: "It's not true that I'm an imbecile, though!"

In fact, I felt superior to those who had been my fellow pupils. For some time, my intelligence had been developing remarkably. I read, I understood, I deduced, and I had immense subjects of meditation—far more than other human beings—in the universe that was visible to me alone.

My father could not make out what I said, but he was softened by my embrace. "Poor boy!" he said.

I looked at him. I was in frightful distress, knowing only too well that the gulf between us would never be bridged. My mother, thanks to the intuition of love, saw at that time that I was not inferior to other boys of my own age; she looked at me tenderly, and said naïve and sweet things to me from the bottom of her heart, but I was condemned nonetheless to cease my studies.

Because of my weak muscular strength, I was put in charge of the sheep and cattle. I acquitted myself marvelously; I had no need of a dog to look after the flock and the dairy herd, and no colt or stallion was as agile as me.

From 14 to 17, therefore, I lived the solitary life of a herdsman. It suited me better than any other. Free to observe and contemplate, and also to do a certain amount of reading, my brain never ceased to develop. I compared the elements of the double creation I had before my eyes incessantly, extracting therefrom ideas as to the constitution of the universe, vaguely sketching hypotheses and theories. Although it is true that my thoughts were not perfectly ordered at that time, not forming any lucid system—for they were adolescent thoughts, uncoordinated, impatient and enthusiastic—they were nevertheless original and fecund. That their value depended exclusively on my unique constitution I shall certainly not deny, but they did not derive all their force therefrom. Without the slightest vanity, I think I may say that they surpassed considerably, in subtlety as in logic, those of ordinary young people.

They alone brought a certain consolation to my sad life as a semi-pariah, devoid of companions or any real communication with those around me, even my adorable mother.

At 17, life became quite unbearable to me. I was weary of dreaming, weary of vegetating on a mental desert island. I fell into idleness and ennui. I sat motionless for long hours, disinterested in the entire world, inattentive to everything that was happening in my family. What good did it do me to know about things more marvelous than other men knew, since that knowledge was bound to die with me? What was the mystery of living organisms to me, or even the duality of the two vital systems that passed through one another without knowing it? These things might have intoxicated me, filling me with enthusiasm and excitement, if I had some way of communicating them or sharing them—but what could I do? Vain and sterile, absurd and miserable, they contributed instead to my perpetual psychic quarantine.

Several times, I thought of writing down some of my observations, to make a permanent record anyway, even at the cost of continual effort—but since I had left school I had abandoned the pen permanently, and I was already so poor a scrivener that I barely knew how to trace, with difficulty, the 26 letters of the alphabet. If I had still had any hope, perhaps I would have persisted—but who would take my wretched efforts seriously? Where was the reader who would not think me mad? Where was the sage who would not treat me with disdain or irony? What was the point, then, in devoting myself to that vain task, that irritating torture, not so very different from that of an ordinary man obliged to engrave his thoughts on marble tablets with a coarse chisel and a titanic hammer? My writing would have to be a kind of shorthand, so far as I was concerned—and a shorthand even more rapid than usual!

I did not have the courage to write, therefore—and yet, I longed fervently for something to happen, some strange and fortunate eventuality. It seemed to me that there must exist, in some corner of the world, impartial, lucid, inquiring minds capable of studying me, of understanding me, or of extracting my great secret from me and communicating it to others—but where were these men? What hope did I have of ever meeting them?

And I fell back into a vast melancholy, into the desire for immobility and annihilation. For an entire autumn, I despaired of the Universe. I languished in a vegetative state, from which I only emerged to utter long groans, followed by painful protests.

I became even thinner, to the point of becoming fantastic. The people of the village called me, ironically, *Den Heyligen Gheest*—the Holy Ghost. My silhouette was as tremulous as those of young poplars, as slight as a shadow—and I attained, along with that, the stature of a giant.

Slowly, I formulated a plan. Since my life was sacrificed, since none of my days was joyful and everything was darkness and bitterness to me, why stagnate in inaction? Even if no mind did exist that could respond to mine, was it not, at least, worth the effort of making sure? Was it not, at least, worth leaving my bleak homeland to go in search of scientists and philosophers in the big cities? Was I not an object of curiosity in myself? Even before calling attention to my extra-human knowledge, could I not excite a desire to study my person? Were not the physical attributes of my being worthy of analysis in themselves: my sight, and the extreme agility of my movements, and the peculiarity of my nutrition.

The more I thought about it, the more reasonable it seemed to hope, and the firmer my resolve became. When the day arrived that it became unbreakable, I confided in my parents. Neither of them understood it very well, but they both ended up yielding to my repeated insistence; I obtained permission to go to Amsterdam, free to return if things did not work out for me.

I left the next morning.

V

The distance from Zwartendam to Amsterdam is about 100 kilometers. I covered that distance easily in two hours, without any other incident than the extreme surprise of passers-by on seeing me run at such a speed, and a few crowds gathering on the edges of little villages and larger towns that I shorted. To ascertain my route I spoke to solitary old men on two or three occasions; my sense of direction, which is excellent, did the rest.

It was about 9 a.m. when I reached Amsterdam. I went into the city resolutely, going along the beautiful canals where merchant fleets are quietly maintained. I did not attract as much attention as I had feared. I walked quickly, in the midst of busy people, enduring the occasional gibes of a few street-urchins. I decided, however, not to pause. I had gone back and forth through the city in every direction before I finally resolved to go into an inn on one of the quays of the Heerengracht.

It was a pleasant spot; the magnificent canal extended, full of life, between shady rows of trees, and among the Moedigen that I saw circulating along its banks, I thought I perceived a new species. After some indecision, I crossed the threshold of the inn and, addressing the proprietor as slowly as I could, I asked him if he would be so kind as to direct me to a hospital.

The landlord looked at me with amazement, suspicion and curiosity, took his stout pipe out of his mouth and put it back again several times, and eventually said: "You're from the colonies, no doubt?"

As there was no point in contradicting him, I replied: "Indeed!"

He seemed delighted with his perspicacity, and asked me another question. "Perhaps you come from that part of Borneo that no one has ever been able to get into?"

"Exactly."

I had spoken too rapidly; is eyes widened.

"Ex-act-ly!" I repeated, more slowly.

"You're having difficulty speaking Dutch, aren't you? So it's a hospital you want? Presumably, you're ill?"

"Yes."

Customers were drawing nearer. The rumor was already going round that I was a cannibal from Borneo; even so, they looked at me with far more curiosity than antipathy. People were coming in from the street. I became nervous and anxious. Nevertheless, I put on a brave face, coughed, and added: "I'm very ill."

"It's the same with monkeys from that region," said a fat man, benevolently. "The Netherlands kill them!"

"What funny skin!" said another.

"And how does he see?" asked a third, pointing to my eyes.

The circle drew closer, enveloping me with 100 curious stares—and newcomers were still coming into the room.

"How tall he is!"

It was true that I was a head taller than the tallest of them.

"And thin!"

"Cannibalism doesn't seem to be very nutritious!"

Not all the voices were malevolent. A few sympathetic individuals defended me: "Don't crowd him like that—he's ill!"

"Come on, friend, be brave!" said the fat man, observing my nervousness. "I'll take you to a hospital myself!"

He took me by the arm; taking it upon himself to clear a way through the crowd, shouting: "Make way for an invalid!"

Dutch crowds are not very aggressive; they let us pass, but went with us. We went along the canal, followed by a compact multitude, and people called out: "It's a cannibal from Borneo!"

Finally, we reached a hospital. It was visiting time. I was taken to an intern, a young man with blue-tinted spectacles, who greeted me sulkily.

"He's a savage from the colonies," my companion told him.

"What do you mean, a savage?" the intern exclaimed. He took off his spectacles to look at me. Surprise immobilized him momentarily. "Can you see?" he asked me, abruptly.

"I can see quite well."

I had spoken too rapidly. "It's his accent!" said the fat man, proudly. "Again, friend!"

I repeated the words, and made myself understood.

"Those aren't human eyes," the student murmured. "And that skin-color! Is that the color of your race?"

Making a terrible effort to speak slowly, I said: "I've come to be examined by a scientist."

"So you aren't ill?"

"No."

"And you're from Borneo?"

"No."

"Where are you from, then?"

"Zwartendam, near Duisburg."

"Then why does your companion claim that you're from Borneo?"

"I didn't want to contradict him."

"And you want to see a scientist?"

"Yes."

"Why?"

"To be studied."

"To earn money?"

"No, for nothing."

"You're not a pauper? A beggar?"

"No!"

"What makes you want to be studied?"

"My constitution..." But I had spoken too rapidly again, in spite of my efforts. I had to repeat myself.

"Are you sure that you can see me?" he asked again, staring at me. "Your eyes are like horn..."

"I can see quite well..." And, going from right to left, I rapidly picked objects up, put them down again, and threw them up in the air in order to catch them.

"That's extraordinary!" said the young man. His softened voice, almost friendly, gave me hope. "Listen," he said, eventually, "I'm sure that Dr. Van den Heuvel will be interested in your case. I'll go and inform him. You can wait in the next room. And by the way...I've forgotten...you're not actually ill?"

"Not at all."

"Good. Wait in here...the doctor won't be long."

I found myself sitting among monsters preserved in alcohol: fetuses, children in bestial form, colossal batrachians, and vaguely anthropomorphic saurians.

It's an apt waiting-room, I thought. *Am I not a candidate for one of these alcoholic sepulchers?*

VI

When Dr. Van den Heuvel appeared, I was overcome by emotion; I felt the thrill of the Promised Land: the joy of reaching it, the fear of being banished therefrom. The doctor, who had a vast bald forehead, a powerful analytical gaze and a soft but obstinate mouth, examined me silently—and, as with everyone else, my excessive thinness, my lofty stature, my ringed eyes and my violet complexion caused him considerable astonishment.

"You say that you want to be studied?" he asked, eventually.

"Yes!" I replied, forcefully—almost violently.

He smiled approvingly, and asked me the usual question: "Can you see well enough with those eyes?"

"Very well. I can even see through wood and clouds..." I had spoken too rapidly though. He looked at me anxiously. I started again, sweating heavily: "I can even see through wood and clouds..."

"Really! That would be extraordinary. Well, what can you see through that door there?" He pointed to a closed door.

"A big glazed bookcase...a carved table..."

"Really!" he repeated, in amazement.

My chest swelled; a profound contentment descended upon my inner being.

The scientist remained silent for a few seconds, then said: "You speak very awkwardly."

"I speak too rapidly otherwise. I can't speak slowly."

"Well, say something in your natural voice."

I then recounted the tale of my entry into Amsterdam. He listened to me with extreme attention, and an intelligent and observant manner that I had never encountered among my peers. He did not understand any of what I said, but he demonstrated the sagacity of his analytical capability:

"If I'm not mistaken, you're pronouncing 15 to 20 syllables a second—which is to say, three or four times as many as the human ear can perceive. Your voice, moreover, is much sharper than any human voice I've ever heard. Your gestures, excessive in their rapidity, correspond perfectly with that speech. Your entire constitution is probably more rapid than ours."

"I can run faster than a greyhound," I said. "I write..."

"Ah!" he interjected. "Let's see your handwriting..."

I scribbled a few words on a writing-pad that he gave me, the first ones fairly readable, the others increasingly scrambled and abbreviated.

"Perfect!" he said, a certain pleasure mingled with his astonishment. "I believe that I shall be very glad to have met you. It would certainly be very interesting to study you..."

"That's my keenest—my only—desire."

"And mine, of course. Science..." He seemed preoccupied, thoughtful. Eventually, he said: "If we could only find an easy means of communication..."

He started pacing back and forth, frowning. Suddenly, he stopped. "How stupid I am! You'll learn stenography, of course! Eh?" A cheerful expression appeared on his face: "And I'm forgetting the phonograph...the perfect confidant. It'll be sufficient to slow down the playback more than the recording. It's settled: you'll stay with me during your sojourn in Amsterdam!"

The joy of a vocation satisfied, the delight of not spending vain and sterile days! In the presence of the intelligent personality of the doctor, in that scientific environment, I felt a delightful sense of well-being; the melancholy of my spiritual solitude, the regret for my wasted abilities, the long misery of the pariah status that had weighed upon me for so many years, all vanished, evaporating in the sentiment of a new life, a real life, a destiny of salvation!

VII

The doctor made all the necessary arrangements the following day. He wrote to my parents; he provided me with a stenography instructor and obtained phonographs. As he was very wealthy and entirely devoted to science, there was no experiment he did not propose to undertake; my vision, my hearing, my musculature and the color of my skin were subjected to scrupulous investigation, which made him increasingly enthusiastic,

"This is prodigious!" he exclaimed.

"I understood perfectly, after the first few days, how important it was that things be done methodically, proceeding from the simple to the complex, from slight abnormalities to marvelous ones—so I had recourse to a little artifice, which I did not try to hide from the doctor, which was only to reveal my abilities to him gradually.

118

The rapidity of my perceptions and my movements claimed his attention first. He was able to convince himself that the subtlety of my hearing corresponded to the rapidity of my speech. Graduated experiments with the most fugitive sounds, which I imitated with ease, and the speech of ten or 15 individuals talking at once, which I could distinguish perfectly, demonstrated the matter beyond all question. The velocity of my vision was no less proven, and comparative trials of my ability to resolve the gallop of a horse and the flight of an insect, against those of instantaneous photographic apparatus, were entirely to the advantage of my eyes. As for perceptions of ordinary things, the simultaneous movements of a group of people, children at play, the movement of machinery, stones thrown into the air or little balls tossed into an alley in order to be counted in flight—they stupefied the doctor's family and friends.

My runs through the large garden, my 20-meter jumps, the instantaneity of my seizing objects and putting them back again, were even more admired, not by the doctor but by his entourage; and it was a continual pleasure for my host's wife and children, during a walk in the country, to see me outrun a galloping horseman or follow the flight of a swallow. There is in fact, no thoroughbred to which I could not give a start of two-thirds of the distance to be covered, whatever it might be, nor any bird that I cannot easily overtake.

The doctor, increasingly satisfied with the results of his experiments, defined me thus: "A human being endowed, in all his movements, with a speed incomparably superior, not merely to other human beings, but also to that of all known animals. That speed, found in the slightest elements of his organic make-up as well as the whole, has created an individual so distinct from the remainder of creation that he merits a special category in the hierarchy of animals all to himself. As for the curious constitution of his eyes, and the violet hue of his skin, it is necessary to consider them as mere indications of that special status."

Tests having been carried out on my muscular system, he found nothing remarkable therein, except for an excessive thinness. No more were my ears furnished with any unique attributes; nor, save for its color, was my epidermis. As for my hair, which was dark—a violet-tinted black—it was as fine as spider-silk, and the doctor examined it minutely.

"I'd have to be able to dissect you!" he said several times, laughing.

The time passed pleasantly in this fashion. I had learned stenography very quickly, thanks to the ardor of my desire and the natural aptitude I showed for that manner of transcription—into which I introduced, moreover, a few new abbreviations. I began to take notes, which my stenographer translated. Furthermore, we had phonographs manufactured according to a special design made by the doctor, which were perfectly adapted to reproduce my speech, considerably slowed down.

My host's confidence eventually became perfect. In the first weeks, he had been unable to help being suspicious—which was entirely natural—that the uniqueness of my abilities might have given rise to some madness, some cerebral derangement. Once that fear was set aside, our relationship became entirely cordial—and, I think, as captivating for each of us as for the other. We carried out analytical tests of my perception through a large number of substances reckoned opaque, and of the dark coloration that water, glass and quartz acquired for me at a certain thickness. You will remember that I can see quite well through wood, the foliage of trees, clouds and many other substances, that I had difficulty distinguishing the bottom of a body of water half a meter deep, and that a window, although transparent, is less so for me than for ordinary people, and rather dark in color. A thick piece of glass appears almost black to me. The doctor convinced himself of all these singularities at his leisure, being particularly struck by my ability to make out the stars on cloudy nights.

It was only then that I began to tell him that I also perceived colors differently. Experiments established beyond doubt that red, orange, yellow, green, blue and indigo were as invisible to me as infra-red or ultra-violet to normal eyes. On the other hand, I was able to provide evidence that I perceived violet and, beyond violet, a whole series of shades: a spectrum of colors with at least twice the range of the spectrum that extends from red to violet.[23]

This astonished the doctor more than anything else. The investigation was long, scrupulous and, moreover, conducted with infinite artistry. It became, in the hands of that skillful experimenter, the source of subtle discoveries in the order of sciences classified by human beings, giving him the key to arcane phenomena of magnetism, chemical affinity and the power of induction, and guiding him toward new notions in physiology. You can easily imagine what an ingenious scientist might be able to deduce from such data as knowing that some metal manifests a series of unknown hues, variable with pressure, temperature and electrical state, and that the most transparent gas has distinct colors even at low density; learning about the infinite richness of the tones of objects that seem more or less black, and that they present a more magnificent spectrum in the ultra-violet than all the known colors; and, finally, knowing how the unknown hues of an electric circuit, the bark of a tree, or the skin of a human being vary from day to day, hour to hour and minute to minute.

At any rate, these studies plunged the doctor into the delight of scientific novelty, compared with which the products of the imagination are as cold as cinders compared with fire. He repeatedly said to me: "It's obvious! Your extra-luminary perception is, in sum, merely an effect of the speeding-up of your organic constitution."

We worked patiently for an entire year without my making any mention of the Moedigen; I wanted my host to be absolutely convinced, to give him innu-

---

[23] The narrator inserts a footnote: "Quartz gives me a spectrum of about eight colors: extreme violet and the seven colors following in the ultra-violet—but there still remain some eight colors that quartz does not separate, which other substances separate to a greater or lesser degree."

merable proofs of my visual abilities before venturing upon the supreme confidence. Finally, the moment arrived when I thought that I could reveal everything.

VIII

It was the morning of a mild Autumn day, overcast with clouds that had been traveling across the vault of the sky for a week without any rain falling. Van den Heuvel and I were strolling in the garden. The doctor was quiet, fully absorbed by speculations of which I was the principal object. Eventually, he began to speak.

"It's pleasant, mind, to imagine being able to see through these clouds…to penetrate as far as the ether, when we're… blind as we are…"

"If only the sky were all I could see!" I replied.

"Oh, yes—the entire world is so different…"

"Much more different than I've told you!"

"What!" he cried, with avid curiosity. "Have you been hiding something from me?"

"The most important thing of all."

He planted himself in front of me, stared at me with a veritable anguish, in which a certain mysticism seemed to be mixed.

"Yes, the most important thing of all!"

We had arrived beside the house; I rushed in to ask for a phonograph. The instrument that was brought was state of the art, much improved by my friend, capable of recording a long speech. The servant deposited it on the stone table at which the doctor and his family took coffee on fine summer evenings. The fine apparatus, miraculously accurate, lent itself admirably to conversation. We could talk almost as easily as in a normal conversation.

"Yes, I've hidden the most important thing from you, wanting to have your entire confidence first. Even now, after all the discoveries that my constitution has permitted you to make, I fear that you might have difficulty believing me, at least to begin with."

I paused in order that my words might be repeated by the instrument. I saw the doctor go pale: the pallor of a great scientist confronted with a new aspect of matter. His hands were trembling.

"I'll believe you!" he said, with a certain solemnity.

"Even if I claim that our creation—I mean our animal and vegetable world—is not the only life on Earth—that there is another, just as vast, as numerous and as complicated…invisible to your eyes?"

He suspected occultism, and could not help saying: "The world of the fourth dimension: souls, phantoms and spirits."

"No, no—nothing like that. A world of living beings, condemned, as we are, to a brief existence, organic needs, birth, growth and conflict…a world as frail and ephemeral as ours; a world submissive to laws as fixed as ours, if not identical; a world similarly imprisoned by the Earth, similarly vulnerable to contingencies…but also completely different from ours, without any influence upon us, as we have no influence upon it, save for the modifications it makes to our common foundation, the Earth, or the parallel modifications to which we subject that same Earth."

I don't know whether Van den Heuvel believed me, but he was certainly in the grip of a keen excitement. "In brief, they're fluid?" he queried.

"That's something I can't say, for their properties are too contradictory to the idea we've formed of matter. The Earth is as resistant to them as to us, as are the majority of minerals, although they can penetrate some way into humus. They are also quite impermeable—solid—with respect to one another, but they pass through plants, animals and organic tissues, albeit with a certain difficulty, and we pass through them in the same way. If one of them could see us, we would probably appear fluid in relation to them in its eyes, as they appear fluid in relation to us in mine—but it would probably be no more able to *conclude* that than I am; it would be struck by parallel contradictions.

"Their form has the strange quality of having very little thickness. Their size is infinitely variable. I've known some of them to reach a hundred meters in length, and others as small as our tiniest insects. Some of them derive nutrition at the expense of the Earth and weather phenomena, others at the expense of weather phenomena and the individuals of their kingdom—without, however, that being a cause of murder, as among us, since it is sufficient for the stronger to draw energy, that energy presumably being extractable without exhausting the vital source."

The doctor asked me, abruptly: "Could you see them when you were a child?"

I guessed that he had formulated the hypothesis that this was, in essence, some disorder that had overtaken my organism fairly recently.

"Since infancy!" I replied, forcefully. "I can provide you with the necessary proofs."

"Can you see them now?"

"I see them—the garden contains a considerable number of them."

"Where?"

"On the path, on the lawns, on the walls, in the air…for there are aerial as well as terrestrial ones—and also aquatic ones, although those rarely leave the surface of the water."

"Are they numerous everywhere?"

"Yes, and scarcely less numerous in towns than in the fields, and in houses than in the streets. Those that prefer enclosed spaces are smaller, though, doubtless because of the difficulty of moving around—although wooden doors are no obstacle to them."

"What about iron…glass…brick?"

"Impermeable to them."

"Would you care to describe one of them—preferably a large one?"

"I can see one of them near that tree. Its form is extremely elongated, and rather irregular. It is convex on the right, concave on the left, with bulges and indentations; one might imagine it to be a cross-section of a gigantic, thickset caterpillar—but its structure isn't characteristic of the kingdom, for structure is extremely variable between species, if one may use that term in this context. Its infinitesimal thickness is, on the other hand, a universally general quality; it can scarcely be more than a tenth of a millimeter, although it is five feet long and 40 centimeters broad at its greatest width.

"What defines it most obviously, and its entire kingdom, are the lines that cut across it in every direction, terminating in networks that thin out where two systems of lines meet. Each system of lines is equipped with a center, a sort of swollen patch slightly elevated above the mass of the body—or sometimes, by contrast, hollowed out. These centers have no fixed shape, sometimes being almost circular or elliptical, sometimes twisted or spiral, sometimes divided by several constructions. They are astonishingly mobile, and their magnitude varies on an hourly basis. Their borders vibrate very rapidly, by virtue of a sort of horizontal undulation. Generally, the lines emerging from them are broad, even though there are also some very thin ones; they diverge, finishing up as infinitely delicate traces that gradually vanish.

"A few lines, however, much paler than the others, are not engendered by centers; they remain isolated within the system and grow without changing color. These lines have the ability to move around within the body and to vary their curvature, while the centers and the lines connected to them remain stable in their respective situations.

"As for the colors of my Moedig, I must renounce any attempt to describe them to you, none of them being in the register perceptible to your eye, and none of them having any name for you. They are extremely bright in the networks, less so in the centers, and very faint in the independent lines—which, in compensation, are highly polished, with an ultra-violet metallic quality, if I might express it thus.

"I have assembled a few observations on the mode of life, nutrition and autonomy of the Moedigen, but I don't want to show them to you for the moment."

I fell silent. The doctor had the recorded words repeated twice over by our impeccable intermediary, then remained silent for some time. I had never seen him in such a state; his features were rigid, mineralized; his eyes vitreous, cataleptic; an abundant sweat was running down his temples and moistening his hair. He tried to speak, but could not. He made a tremulous circuit of the garden, and when he came back his expression and mouth expressed a violent, fervent, religious passion. One might have thought him a disciple of a new faith rather than a placid hunter of phenomena.

Finally, he murmured: "You've overwhelmed me! Everything you've just told me seems perfectly lucid—and have I any right to doubt it, after all the marvels you've already shown me?"

"Doubt!" I told him, hotly. "Doubt fervently…your experiments will be all the more fecund for it!"

"Ah! He went on, in a dreamy voice. "It's prodigy itself—and so magnificently superior to the vain prodigies of Fable! My poor human intelligence is so small by comparison to such knowledge! My enthusiasm is infinite. Something within me, however, doubts…"

"Let us work to dispel your uncertainty. Our efforts will be rewarded a hundredfold!"

IX

We worked. A few weeks sufficed to dispel all the doctor's doubts. Ingenious experiments, undeniable concordances between each of my affirmations, and two or three fortunate discoveries regarding the influence of the Moedigen on atmospheric phenomena left no room for equivocation. The assistance of Van den Heuvel's eldest son, a young man with the greatest aptitude for science, further increased the fecundity of our labors and the certainty of our discoveries.

Thanks to the methodical mentality of my companions, and their skill in investigation and classification—faculties that I gradually assimilated—it did not take long for my presently-uncoordinated and confused knowledge of the Moedigen to be transformed. The discoveries multiplied, the rigorous experiments gave firm results, in circumstances that would, at most, have suggested a few seductive diversions in ancient times, or even in the last century.

We have now been conducting our researches for five years; they are far—very far—from reaching completion. An initial account of our findings will not be ready for quite some time. We are, in any case, strictly determined not to do anything in haste; our discoveries are too important in kind not to be revealed in the greatest possible detail, with the most sovereign patience and the most careful precision. We do not have to get in ahead of any other researcher, we have no patent for which to apply, nor any ambition to satisfy. We are at a height at which vanity and pride fade away. How can we reconcile the delightful joys of our work with the wretched lure of human renown? Besides, is not the mere accident of my constitution the sole source of these things? How petty it would be, therefore, to glorify ourselves?

We live passionately, always on the verge of marvelous things, and yet we live in an immutable serenity.

I have had an adventure that has added to the profound interest of my life, and which, during my hours of leisure, completes my infinite joy. You know how ugly I am, and stranger still, liable to frighten young women. I have, however, found a companion who can accept my affection to the point of enjoying it.

She is a poor hysteric, neurotic girl, whom we found one day in a hospice in Amsterdam. She is considered to be wretched in appearance, as pallid as plaster with hollow cheeks and wild eyes. To me, she is pleasant to behold, and her company is charming. My presence, far from astonishing her, like everyone else's, seemed from the outset to please her and comfort her. I was touched, and wanted to see her again.

It did not take long to perceive that I had a beneficial effect on her health and well-being. On further investigation, it seemed that I influenced her magnetically; my proximity, and especially the imposition of my hands, communicated a veritably curative gaiety, serenity and mental equilibrium to her. In return, I found pleasure in being with her. Her face seemed pretty to me; her pallor and thinness were merely delicacy; her eyes, capable of seeing the glow of magnets, like those of sufferers from hyperesthesia, did not seem to me to have the quality of wildness of which others disapprove.

In a word, I found her attractive, and she returned the sentiment passionately. Soon, I decided to marry her, and easily attained my goal, thanks to the good will of my friends. The marriage has been a happy one. With my wife's health restored, although she remained extremely sensitive and frail, I tasted the joy of being, in the most important aspect of life, like other men. My destiny has been especially enviable for six months; a child was born to us, and that child reproduces all the characteristics of my constitution. In terms of color, vision, hearing, extreme rapidity of movement and nutrition, he promises to be an exact replica of my physiology.

The doctor is watching him grow with delight; a delightful hope has been born in us: that the study of Moedig life, of the kingdom parallel to ours, which requires so much time and patience, will not come to a stop when I die. My son will doubtless pursue it in his turn. Why should he not find collaborators of genius, capable to take it to further extremes? Why should there not be born, to him also, seers of the invisible world?

May I, too, not expect more children? May I not hope that my dear wife will one day give birth to other offspring of my flesh similar to their father? And as I think about that, my heart quivers, and I am filled with an infinite bliss, feeling myself blessed among men.

125

C. Paulon: *A Message from the Planet Mars*
(Paul Combes - 1897)

In 1889, Louis Figuier began running feuilletons *as a regular feature of* La Science Illustrée *under the rubric of* roman scientifique, *beginning with a short story by Jules Verne and continuing with reprinted works by such authors as Louis Boussenard, Albert Robida and "Charles Epheyre" (Charles Richet), as well as original works by authors who had previously published in the field, such as Alphonse Brown and Albert Bleunard.*

The other leading magazine of the same sort, La Science Française, *soon followed suit. After its editor, Émile Gautier, stopped publishing pseudonymous stories, a batch of them began to appear in* La Science Illustrée *under the signature "C. Paulon." One of them,* Les Mines d'or de Bas-Meudon, *was subsequently reprinted in book form in 1903 under the signature Paul Combes, which was presumably "C. Paulon's" real name.*

Paul Combes (1856-1909) was a relatively well-known writer at that time, having published both poetry and fiction, but it is possible that "C. Paulon" was the pseudonym of his similarly named son, who published several books on geology in the early years of the 20th century. The elder Combes was not uninterested in science, however—the younger one could not possibly have been the author of Le Secret du gouffre *(1888)—so the* Science Illustrée *stories could have been an experimental venture on his part. Paul Combes fils' memoir of his father,* Paul Combes, sa vie, son oeuvre *(1910), presumably clarifies any possible bibliographical confusion, but I have not had the opportunity to consult it.*

A Message from the Planet Mars *is interesting as an illustration of the various ways in which writers of the period were attempting to solve the problem of constructing a* roman scientifique. *Although the handicap suffered by earlier authors of being virtually compelled to write off fantastic material as the substance of dreams, is no longer present, it remains manifest that no adequate substitute has yet been found for the other device that other writers all felt obliged to use: that of embedding material within expository lectures, either delivered directly to the reader or pontificated by a character in the story.*

In this respect, the Paulon story illustrates two horns of a dilemma on which many would-be users of fiction in the popularization of science found themselves painfully stuck; A Message from the Planet Mars *is a relatively anodyne conversation-piece, which merely voices its central idea as a hypothetical possibility.*

There is an interesting contrast between the entire tradition of French stories about the possibility of interplanetary communication leading up to A Message from the Planet Mars *and the English tradition that was founded almost immediately after the publication of that story when H. G. Wells' The War of the Worlds began serialization in an English periodical.*

The French tradition had been primarily inspired by Camille Flammarion, who hosted the salon in which Charles Cros introduced his proposal for inter-planetary communication by optical means (see An Interastral Drama*), which was subsequently repopularized in the 1890s, as fictionalized in the subsequent story,* Proving That The Planet Mars Is Inhabited *by Paul Vibert. Paulon's story illustrates the innocent enthusiasm with which the theme was routinely treated in France, blithely unaware of the fact that the innocence was about to suffer a rude and fatal shock—for innocence can never be regained, even if commitment survives, as the French imaginative commitment to the possibility of fruitful and harmonious communication did.*

B.S.

A MESSAGE FROM THE PLANET MARS

One evening last summer, I was reading the latest news in *Le Temps* when my eyes were attracted by the following paragraph:

STRANGE LIGHT ON THE PLANET MARS
On Monday evening, Dr. Krueger, the director of the Central Astronomical Bureau of Kiel, telegraphed to all his correspondents: Luminous projection in the southern region of the Martian terminator observed by Javelle, 16.00—Perrotin.
The "terminator" is the penumbral zone separating day and night.[24]

This news was doubly interesting for me. For a long time, the study of astronomy had transported me imaginatively into the marvelous universe that gravitates outside our little globe. In the second place, a few years previously, I

---

[24] Adalbert Krüger did indeed send such a telegram (on 30 July 1894), but it is unclear why *Le Temps* would have obtained the news that way rather than from Henri Perrotin's own press release. Perrotin, the first director of Nice observatory, spent a good deal of time from 1892 onwards searching for bright spots on the surface of Mars, and was by no means shy of seeking publicity for his "discoveries"—or those of his assistant, Stéphane Javelle. Krüger's telegram is, however, cited in John Munro's "A Message from Mars," published in *Cassell's Magazine* in 1895 (which became the first chapter of *A Trip to Venus*, 1897); Paulon—who was obviously able to read English—might have borrowed it from there rather than from a more immediate source.

had attempted, with an old astronomer, an unforgettable experiment in interastral communication.

That extraordinary man, who lived as a recluse in his observatory, had—or believed that he had—opened a correspondence with the inhabitants of the planet Mars, but means of powerful beams of electric light, intermittently interrupted like the signals of the optical telegraph. I had often considered him to be a monomaniac, but who knows? Perhaps he was not so crazy after all.

In spite of myself, I opened my books, searching among the earlier observations for some natural explanation of the strange light.

Finding nothing, I resolved to go out to consult my friend, Professor Gazen, the well-known astronomer, who is particularly renowned for a sequence of splendid spectroscopic research regarding the composition of the sun and other celestial bodies.

The night was perfectly clear; not a single cloud veiled the dark blue immensity. The stars were resplendent in the depths of the sky, like diamonds fallen from the silvery belt of the Milky Way. The constellation of Orion was shining with a remarkable brightness in the eastern sky, and Sirius was sparkling in the south like a living gem.

I searched with my eyes for the planet Mars, and soon picked it out, to the north, like a big red star surrounded by white constellations.

I found Professor Gazen at his observatory, plunged in calculations.

"I'm doubtless disturbing you," I said to him, as we shook hands. "Such a beautiful night must be favorable to your astronomical work."

"You're not disturbing me at all," he replied, cordially. "I'm observing a nebula, but it will remain above the horizon for a long time yet."

"Good! What's this mysterious light on the planet Mars? Have you seen it?"

"I've seen nothing!" he said. "And yet, I observed the planet for a long time last night."

"But...do you believe that some sort of light has really been seen?"

"Oh, certainly. Nice Observatory, of which Monsieur Perrotin is the director, has one off the best telescopes in existence, and Monsieur Javelle is well-known for the care he brings to his observations."

"And how do you explain it?"

"The light is not on the disk of the planet itself," Gazen replied, "so I was inclined at first to attribute it to a small comet. Perhaps, also, it might be due to a Martian aurora borealis, as a contributor to *La Science Illustrée* has suggested, or a range of snowy mountains, or even a brilliant cloud, reflecting the rays of the rising sun."

"And which of these various hypotheses appears to you to be the most plausible?"

"The one that attributes the light to elevated mountain peaks reflecting solar rays."

"Could it not be the nocturnal lighting of a city, or a powerful luminous projection—in a word, a signal?"

"Oh no, my dear chap!" the astronomer exclaimed, with an incredulous smile. "The idea of communication germinated in a few minds a couple of years ago, when Mars was in opposition and close to the Earth. Perhaps you recall the plan that was made to dispose the lighting of Paris in such a way as to attract the attention of the Martians?"

"No...but I think I've mentioned to you the singular experiment that I made some five or six years ago, with an old astronomer who thought he had established optical communication with Mars."

"Yes, indeed, I remember. The poor old fellow was mad. Like the astronomer in *Rasselas*, he had nourished his visionary idea in solitude for so long that he had ended up mistaking for a reality."

"But might there not have been an element of truth in his imagination? Perhaps the 'visionary' was only ahead of his time?"

Gazen shook his head. "Mars, you see," he went on, "is a much more ancient planet than ours. In winter, its polar ice extends to the fortieth degree of latitude, and its climate must be very cold. If human beings have ever lived on its surface, they must have disappeared a long time ago, or be living in the same conditions as Eskimos."

"But might not the climate be ameliorated by continental and oceanic conditions unknown to us? Certainly, in spring, one can see Mars's polar ice-cap extending as far as the fortieth degree of latitude. Nevertheless, when summer begins it starts to diminish, band by the first days of autumn only a few fragments remain. In 1894 those even disappeared entirely."

"The Martian atmosphere is as rarefied as that of the mountains of our globe at a height of eight thousand meters, and a warm-blooded organism like a human could not live there."

"Like a human, yes!" I replied. "But humans are adapted to their environment. We're too inclined to relate everything we observe to those we see every day. How can we claim that the potential of life is limited to what is familiar to us on our own planet?"

"Besides," Gazen continued, without taking any notice of my reflection, "Your old astronomer's project, consisting of making signals by means of powerful luminous jets, was completely impracticable. No artificial light exists capable of reaching Mars. Think about the immense distance that separates the two planets, and the two absorbent atmospheres to be traversed. The man was mad!"

"I read the other day that there's an electric searchlight in America that can be perceived a hundred and fifty miles away, through the lowest regions of our atmosphere. Such a light, appropriately directed, could be seen from the planet Mars, and there's no reason to suppose that the Martians haven't invented one even more powerful."

"And if they had," said Gazen, laughing, "the idea that they've had of sending us signals just at the moment that it's possible for us to reply, is simply stupefying."

"I don't see anything extraordinary in the coincidence. Two minds often have the same idea at the same time. Why not those of two different planets, if the propitious moment has arrived? Certainly, there's only one unique Mind that inspires the entire universe. Besides, the Martians might have been sending us signals from time to time for centuries, without our having perceived them. Perhaps, at this very moment, we're losing precious time, while they're striving to attract our attention. Would you care to look?"

"Yes, if it'll give you pleasure. But I doubt that we'll see the slightest luminous projection, human or otherwise."

"At least we'll see the surface of Mars, and that already constitutes an admirable spectacle. It seems to me that the contemplation of celestial bodies through a good telescope ought to be part of a complete liberal education, by the same entitlement as a voyage around the world. And yet, although people who wander around the Earth in search of new locations, with great difficulty and at great expense, are numerous, those who think about the sublime spectacle of the heavens that one can contemplate without leaving home are rare. Gazing at those distant worlds has the power to elevate and purify our souls, like a sacred hymn, a noble painting or the verses of great poets. It always has a good effect."

Silently, Professor Gazen turned his large refractor telescope in the direction of Mars, and observed the planet attentively through the large tube for a few minutes.

"Is there no light?" I asked.

"None," he replied, shaking his head. "See for yourself."

I took his place at the ocular, and could not help shivering on seeing the copper-tinted little star that I had seen half an hour before become seemingly much closer, transformed into a vast globe. It resembled a lunar crescent, for a considerable part of its disk was illuminated by the sun.

A white patch indicated the location of one of its poles, and the rest of the visible surface was divided into alternating red-tinted and green-tinted regions. Fascinated by the spectacle of that living world, full of light and pursuing its perpetual course through the unfathomable ether, I forgot my question, and a religious emotion filled my entire being, as under the dome of a vast cathedral.

"Well? What are you doing?"

That voice recalled me to myself, and I began a minute inspection of the dark fringe of the terminator, trying to discover the slightest ray of light there—but in vain.

"I can't see any luminous projection—but what a magnificent spectacle in the telescope!"

"It certainly is!" the professor agreed. "Although it's not always easy to observe the planet Mars, we know it better than the other planets, and at least as well as the moon. Its topographical features have been drawn with care, like those of the moon, and have been given the names of famous astronomers."

"Including you, I hope."

"No, I don't have that honor. It's true that I know someone, an enthusiastic amateur astronomer, who has baptized a quantity of plains and mountains on the moon with the names of his friends and acquaintances, including mine: the Durand crater, the Dubois gulf, Martin bay and so on—but I regret to say that the scientific authorities have refused to sanction that nomenclature."

"I presume that the bright patch in the southern hemisphere is one of the polar ice-caps," I said, my eyes still fixed on the planet.

"Yes," the professor replied, "and one can see them very distinctly advancing in winter and retreating in summer. The reddish-yellow areas are probably continents with ocher-colored soil, and not, as some have thought, vegetation of the same hue. The greenish-gray areas might be seas and lakes. If so, land and water are more equally distributed on Mars than on Earth—a circumstance that would tend to equalize climates—but another, most ingenious hypothesis has recently been formulated by the American Percival Lowell, who has devoted himself very particularly to the study of Mars, and who has recently published a most remarkable book on the planet."[25]

Keenly interested by this introduction, I quit the ocular momentarily in order to listen to the professor.

"On the third of June 1894, which corresponds to May the first in the Martian calendar, Lowell measured the austral polar cap, which extended to the fifty-fifth degree of latitude or thereabouts and was in the process of melting; hundreds of square kilometers were disappearing every day. Now, wherever the loss of the bright white surface was occurring, a dark band appeared, probably produced by the initial fusion of the polar ice. That band followed the retreat of the polar ice, diminishing in breadth with the dimensions of the cap. By the following August there was no more than a scarcely-perceptible fine line around the portions of the ice cap that still remained. Finally, on the thirteenth of October, when the snow had entirely disappeared, the place that it had finally occupied with its border became unrecognizable, and took on a yellow color.

"This having been established by telescopic observation, what can that dark border be if not water? It has the color of it, it follows the melting of the ice-cap step by step, and it disappears with it. Monsieur Lowell concluded that water, very rare on the surface of Mars, only exists in a liquid state thanks to the melting of the polar ice. The American astronomer linked that hypothesis to an explanation of Schiaparelli's famous channels, of which you have certainly heard mention."

---

[25] *Mars* (1895)—the first of Lowell's three books on the planet that became his abiding obsession.

131

"Oh, certainly—the network of regular lines, some of which reach as far as 4,000 to 4,800 kilometers in length, but whose average length is about 2,400 kilometers."

"Well, Monsieur Lowell is of the opinion that that system of lines, so straight and symmetrical, radiating from particular points, the manner in which they put certain points in communication with others toward which other lines converge in their turn, can only result from artificial endeavor. According to him, the lines correspond to the routes of canals dug with the aim of bringing fertility over long distances to areas deprived of humidity."

"Does he have proof?"

"This is what he claims as proof. Two facts are incontestable, since they can be verified telescopically: that the channels are visible in certain seasons, and that in others—always the same ones—they vanish; which is not a consequence of increased distance, because it's when Mars is closest to us that certain channels are not visible, while they become visible when the planet is further away. Nor can one explain the disappearance of the channels by the hypothesis of clouds or fogs that hide them from our view, because, at the same time, the terminal line of the dark regions is as clearly delineated as when the channels are perfectly visible. The channels thus become visible, augmenting or diminishing, for reasons unique to them.

"Although their appearance is temporary, however, their location never varies. Moreover, patient observation shows that, when they are invisible, they become perceptible gradually. One sees them, as it were, increase and decrease in determined seasons. That visible development follows the melting of the polar ice, and it is noticeable that no channel becomes visible until the melting of the ice has made visible progress. Those closest to the polar cap appear first; they become increasingly distinct thereafter, and take on a darker color over time.

"The explanation that presents itself most naturally to the mind is that there must be a flow of water from the pole to the equator; but that is insufficient. In fact, it is necessary to wait a few months for the channels to become visible at the equator; it should not take that much time for the water to arrive there. Besides, in order to be perceptible, it is necessary that the channels be at least a degree in width, which might seem enormous for artificial canals.

"Thus, Monsieur Lowell attributes the observed appearances to the vegetation that develops along the banks of the channels some time after the irrigation of the soil by the water they have brought, which explains the phenomenon of their progressive appearance and the changes they undergo.

"The change in the appearance of the channels consists, not in their seeming broader but in their becoming increasingly dark, and consequentially distinct. If there were high mountains on the Martian surface, they would interfere with the straightness of the channels, but observation informs us that the planet is relatively uniform. The channels are visible in reddish regions as well as well as greenish ones, because they develop or augment the vegetation there with the moisture they bring. They are, therefore, irrigation canals, which, at their meeting-points, give rise to veritable oases.

"From all of the preceding arguments, Monsieur Lowell concludes that, water having become scarce on the planet Mars, the most important problem for the inhabitants must be procuring it. What increases the probability of an intelligent cause for the channels is that double ones can be perceived—which is to say, forming two parallel lines along their entire course; no designer could trace more perfect parallel lines. Their separation varies between four and a half and six degrees, and the vegetation of each, developed along its length, appears to be about a degree in breadth.

"In this hypothesis, the vast red-tinted areas must be vast arid plains or deserts; the systematic patches formerly considered to be lakes must be regions of vegetation, true oases that form, as their changes in color and dimension demonstrate, at points where several canals intersect."

"But in that case," I exclaimed, "the Martians, capable of constructing such a vast irrigation system, have means of action at their disposal that are unknown to us. Their science is more advanced than ours, no doubt about it."

"Don't be too hasty in your conclusions," said Gazen, smiling. "All that is only a hypothesis—very ingenious, I admit, but still, a hypothesis. The natural environment of the Martian surface differs significantly from ours, and the appearances it presents cannot all be explained according to our terrestrial views. Let's make suppositions and try to verify them, but let's not affirm anything."

While he was speaking, mentally overexcited in spite of myself by Lowell's hypothesis, I had resumed my place at the telescope.

Was it an illusion of my imagination? Was it a reality? My attention was suddenly caught by an extremely bright luminous point that appeared on the dark side of the terminator south of the equator.

"Oh!" I cried, involuntarily. "There's the light!"

"Really?" Gazen replied, in a tone that mingled surprise and doubt. "Are you quite sure?"

"Entirely. There's a very distinct light in one of the reddish areas."

"Let me see!" he said, excitedly.

I surrendered my place to him.

"It's true!" he declared, after a moment's observation. "I assume the light has been hidden from until now by a cloud."

Taking turns, we continued silently observing the strange light.

"That can't be the light that Javelle perceived," Gazen said, finally. "It's in the region named Hellas."

"To make signals," I murmured, returning to my obsession, "the Martians would probably have to employ a whole system of lights. Since they have a network of canals, there's no reason why they shouldn't have a telegraphic network, to coordinate their attempts at different points of the planet."

The professor took his place at the ocular again, and I waited for the result of his observations with keen interest.

"Is as stable as possible," he said.

"That stability is cause for reflection," I said. "If it were variable, it would be more readily interpretable as a signal."

"But there's no indication that the signal is necessarily destined for the inhabitants of the Earth," Gazen said, with mocking seriousness. "It might be a floating lighthouse, or a nocturnal message for the autumnal maneuvers of the Martians, who are undoubtedly exceedingly bellicose."

"Seriously what do you think it is?"

"I confess that it's a mystery to me," he replied, becoming profoundly thoughtful. Then, as if struck by a sudden thought, he added: "I'd be astonished if the spectroscope didn't offer us some enlightenment in that regard."

While he was setting up the instrument, I returned to the telescope and observed the enigmatic light once again, which stood out almost in the center of the disk.

Gazen fixed a magnificent spectroscope to the telescope, which he used for his research on nebulas, and recommenced his observations.

"Truly," he exclaimed, getting up from his seat and advancing toward me "that's the most remarkable thing I've ever seen in my long career as a spectroscopist!"

"What is it?" I asked, looking into the spectroscope in my turn, in which I could distinguish a few feeble streaks of colored light standing out against a black background.

"You know that we can take account of the nature of a substance in the incandescent state by decomposing the light it emits in the prism of a spectroscope. Well, those bright and variously colored lines that you perceive constitute the spectrum of a luminous gas."

"Really! And that gives you some indication regarding the origin of the light we've perceived?"

"It might be electric—an aurora, for example. It might be a volcanic eruption, or a lake of fire similar to the Kilauea crater, the famous volcano in the Sandwich Islands. To tell the truth, I have no idea. Let me see if I can identify the bright lines of the spectrum."

I surrendered the spectroscope to him, and when he had looked attentively he exclaimed: "By Heaven! That's extraordinary! The spectrum has changed. Eureka! I recognize it now. It's the spectrum of thallium. I'd recognize that splendid green line among a thousand."

"Thallium!" I cried, marveling in my turn.

"Yes," Gazen replied, excitedly. "Make a note of the observation, and also the time. You'll find a notebook for that express purpose on my desk."

I did as I was asked, and awaited further observations. The silence was so profound that that I could clearly hear the ticking of my watch, set before me on the desk.

After a few minutes, the professor exclaimed: "It's changed again—make another note."

"What is it now?"

"Sodium. Those two yellow bands can't be confused with any other."

A profound silence reigned, as before.

"Another change!" cried the professor, extremely excited. "I can now see a double blue line. What can that be? I believe it's iridium."

Another long pause followed that indication.

"They've disappeared!" murmured Gazen. "A red line and a yellow line have taken their place. That's lithium. Hold on! Everything's gone black."

"What's happening?"

"Everything has disappeared." As he spoke, he detached the spectroscope from the telescope and observed the planet anxiously.

"The light's no longer there," he added, after a minute or so. "Perhaps another cloud is passing above it. Well, we'll wait. In the meantime, let's examine the situation. It seems that we have some reason to be satisfied with tonight's work. What do you think?" It was with a triumphant expression that he stopped in front of me.

"I believe it's a signal!" I said, with conviction.

"Why?"

"Why else would the changes be so regular? I've measured the duration of each spectrum, and I've found that each one lasts for about five minutes before another takes its place."

The professor remained silent and pensive. I continued: "Isn't it from the light that reaches us from them that we've acquired all our knowledge relative to the constitution of celestial bodies? A ray from the most distant star brings with it a secret message for anyone who can read it" Well, the Martians will naturally have had recourse to the same means of communication, as being the simplest and the most practicable. By producing a powerful light they can hope that our attention will be attracted to their planet, and in making it produce characteristic spectra, easily recognizable and modified at regular intervals, they can distinguish their light from any other, and show us that it has an intelligent origin."

"And in consequence?"

"And in consequence, we know that the Martians have a civilization at least as highly developed as our own. To my mind, that's a great discovery—the greatest since the world has existed."

"But it's of little use, to us as well as the Martians."

"From that point of view, a great many of our discoveries, especially in astronomy, are very little use. Suppose you find the chemical composition of the nebula you were in the process of studying…will it reduce the price of bread?

135

No—but it will interest us and inform us. If the Martians can tell us how Mars is constituted, and we can do the same with regard to the Earth, that will certainly be a mutual service rendered to one another by the two planets."

"But the communication can't go any further."

"I'm not so sure of that."

"My dear friend! How can we, on Earth, understand what the Martians say, and how can they understand what we say? We have no common language."

"That's true—but chemical compounds have certain well-defined properties, don't they?"

"Yes. Each one even possesses some particularity that distinguishes it clearly from all the others. For example, those which resemble one another in color or hardness differ in weight."

"Precisely. Well, can't we employ their spectra to designate precisely those particular qualities—*to express an idea?* In a word, can't the Marians talk to us via spectragrams?"

"I see where you're coming from," said Professor Gazen. "And now that I think about it, all the spectra we've observed this evening belong to the group of alkaline metals and alkaline earths, which have very characteristic properties."

"First of all, I suppose the Martians only wanted to attract our attention with a striking spectrum."

"Lithium is the metal we've discovered most recently."

"Good! We can get from that the idea of enlightenment."

"Sodium," the professor continued, "is a metal that has such an affinity for oxygen that it burns in water. Manganese, which belongs to the same group as iron, is so hard that its scratches glass, and like iron, it's magnetic. Copper is red..."

"Signals relating to colors can be taken directly from spectra."

"Mercury, or quicksilver, is liquid at ordinary temperatures, and can give us the idea of *movement, animation*, or even of *life*."

"Having obtained certain fundamental ideas," I continued, "by combining them, we would arrive at conceptions other than the original ones. We could establish an entire ideographic language by signs—the signs being the luminous spectra of different chemical substances. Numbers can be transmitted by simple occultations of light. Then, spectra can enable us to pass by means of an easy slope to equivalent signals: long and short flashes variously combined, similarly obtained by luminous occultations. With such a code, our communication would become indefinite, and would no longer present any difficulty."

"If the Martians are as advanced as you would like to believe, we'd have a great deal to learn from them."

"I hope that we could, and I'm sure that the world could, at least, obtain superior enlightenment on certain points."

"In any case," said the professor, darting another glance at the telescope, "we'll pursue our observations assiduously." Then he added: "For the moment, the Martian philosophers don't seem to want to take their experiments any further. And as the nebula is still there, I'll work on it for a while before finishing for the day. If tomorrow is a fine night, come to see me again. We'll continue our observations—but believe me, it's best not to say anything about them."

As I went back home, I contemplated the rutilant planet gain, as I had done when I came—but very different sentiments were stirring in my heart. The distance and isolation that separated me from it seemed to have disappeared I the meantime, and is stead of a cold and alien star, I saw a familiar world, a friendly planet, a companion of the Earth in the eternal solitude of the universe.

In my dreams, I found myself transported to the very surface of Mars, where an army of scientists was maneuvering a gigantic reflector with the aid of marvelous machines, projecting fantastic beams of light toward the Earth.

When morning came, I ran to buy the interesting book by Percival Lowell that Professor Gazen had told me about, and until the evening I remained immersed in reading it. Everything confirmed my ideas regarding the Martians.

The planet Mars is older than the Earth. Life must have appeared there much sooner, and, in consequence, have been evolving for a longer period of time. If the canals of Mars are the work of animate beings, the latter must be presently endowed with an intelligence more refined than ours, and perhaps our railways, telegraphs, telephones and economic systems were surpassed there a long time ago. To have been able to establish an irrigation system that embraces the entire planet, they must have a social situation in which political parties no longer tear one another apart and different nations regulate their affairs other than by the right of the strongest.

As for the sudden and ephemeral beams of light that have been observed departing from the place where the polar ice-cap has lost its dazzling whiteness, Percival Lowell believes that it is a mistake to attribute them to signals sent by the inhabitants of Mars. According to him, they are easily explained by the eastward reflection of fragments of glaciers that remain attached to mountain slopes, produced at the moment when the planet's rotation gives those slopes the appropriate angle—like those luminous beams that sometimes dazzle us when the window-panes of some house send the rays of the setting sun back to our eyes.

But the luminous spectra?

That is what Percival Lowell has neither seen nor explained, and what I expect to succeed in elucidating with the aid of Professor Gazen.

Unfortunately for our plans, the sky was cloudy the following day, and it has remained more or less unfavorable since then for the observation of Mars. Given these circumstances, and in the hope that some other astronomer, in a more limpid climate, might be able to continue this research. Professor Gazen and I thought it best to publish our discovery without further delay.

Paul Vibert: *Proving That The Planet Mars Is Inhabited* (1901)

Paul Théodore Vibert (1851-1918)'s Pour lire en automobile, nouvelles fantastiques *[For Reading in an Automobile: Fantastic Stories] (1901)[26] is a book that contains, among other things, some significant contributions to the early development of French speculative fiction. Yet, it is a deeply eccentric work by a man who wore his eccentricities flamboyantly and provocatively, alongside his deeply-felt convictions—and seems, in that respect, to have been consciously and conscientiously carrying forward a tradition initiated by his father, Théodore Vibert (1825-1885)—not to be confused with the printer of the same name (1816-1850). Theodore was educated in law and practiced as an advocate in Paris, but, like many lawyers of the time, also had literary ambitions.*

Paul's first book was La Démocratie impériale *(1874), one of numerous works that he was later to categorize in bibliographies of his work as "social propaganda." His next publications were, however, poetry; he published three sets of* Dizaine de sonnets *[Ten Sonnets] in 1875, 1878 and 1879, then the longer* Sonnets parisiens *[Parisian Sonnets] in 1880. He published* Le Péché de la baronne, idylles normandes *[The Sin of the Baroness; Norman idylls] in 1885, which he placed under the heading* Romans *[Fiction] in his bibliographies, and a collection of reprinted* Poésies, contes et nouvelles *[Poetry, Tales and Short Stories], appeared in 1889, but he appears to have given up on his literary ambitions by then.*

Like many men of his era whose literary ambitions were frustrated, Paul eventually settled for a career in journalism, but he seems to have spent a good deal of time traveling, presumably financing his expeditions with his own money, and his colleagues probably regarded him as an amateur dabbler rather than a dedicated professional throughout the 1880s and early 1890s, although he does seem to have worked very assiduously. He visited both North and South America, and published an account of La République d'Haïti *in 1895, but most of his observations and conclusions were decanted into articles for periodicals. His public profile was, however, dramatically raised when he became embroiled in the Dreyfus affair, as one of the unfortunate captain's staunchest defenders. He became closely associated with Georges Clemenceau's campaigning newspaper* L'Aurore, *which published Émile Zola's famous article headlined "J'Accuse."*

---

[26] Available from Black Coat Press as *The Mysterious Fluid*, ISBN 978-1-61227-020-3.

Many of the books Vibert published in this later period were collections of reprints of newspaper articles, loosely organized according to subject-matter. The first was Silhouettes contemporaines [Contemporary Sketches] (1900), but the most interesting, from a modern viewpoint, are the elements of a series launched with Pour lire en automobile in the following year.

In that collection, Paul deliberately grouped together the majority of his fantastic and scientifically-inspired pieces, those evidently being his first priority. Although his preface to the book is as assertively tongue-in-cheek as the items reprinted therein, there is probably no reason to doubt his assertion that he had conceived the ambition to write fantastic stories in the various veins of E. T. A. Hoffmann, Edgar Allan Poe and Jules Verne back in the 1860s, but had never quite got around to it until he was finally encouraged by a friendly newspaper-editor to re-launch himself as a rival to Alphonse Allais—which gave him the opportunity to make up the deficit somewhat, albeit in a calculatedly clownish fashion.

There is also no reason to doubt the allegation made in one of the items in the book that he often gave public lectures at La Bodinière—the exhibition hall of the Théâtre d'Application in the Rue St. Lazare—in the mid-1890s, and that one of the topics that went down well with the audience was interplanetary communication, with the citation of such fictional precedents as Cyrano de Bergerac and Poe; his interest in such subjects was evidently longstanding.

The other books in the Pour lire sequence are Pour lire en bateau-mouche, nouvelles surprenantes [For Reading in a Motor-Boat; surprising short stories] (1905), Pour lire en ballon, nouvelles sentimentales [For Reading in a Balloon; sentimental short stories] (1907), Pour lire en traîneau, nouvelles entraînantes [For Reading in a Sleigh; stirring short stories] (1908), Pour lire en sous-marin, nouvelles énivrantes [For Reading in a Submarine; intoxicating short stories] (1914) and Pour lire en aéroplane [For Reading in an Airplane] (1915), although the last-named is not really part of the series, being entirely non-fictional and ostensibly offering "bird's eye views" of various parts of France.

Because of their brevity, the imagery in Vibert's stories tends to the surreal, and the obligatory absence of elaborate explanatory support gives them a dreamlike quality, even when the ideas deployed therein are directly derived from scientific theory, like his series about life on Mars involving communication by means of Charles Cros' method, as well as another series speculating about the possibilities of "interastral telegraphy."[27]

B.S.

---

[27] Vibert's fellow humorist Tristan Bernard had also employed the Cros method of interplanetary communication in Qu'est-ce qu'ils peuvent bien nous dire? [What are they trying to say to us?] (1897), in which it turns out that the signaling Martians are not, in fact, trying to say anything to us, but are actually attempting to make contact with Saturn.

PROVING THAT THE PLANET MARS IS INHABITED

Curious demonstrations.
The same origin of language as on Earth.
What conclusion can be drawn?

For some time, the scientific world has known about the famous canals of Mars, so regular and so curious in their almost-geometrical forms in the astral province that has been named Libya, which the well-known hemisphere of the planet presents to us in Observatories.

We know that it also possesses an atmosphere, and that there is probably good weather on the surface when it is a little less confused and ruddy. Astronomers, always a little scatterbrained—hence the verb referring to the aiming of their telescopes[28]—would love to see the canals as immense signals that the inhabitants are sending to those of the Earth, and, in the reddish vapor, the revelation of immense fires, lit in order to speak to us by means of conventional signs, somewhat akin to the Saint-Jean fires[29] on the summits of high mountains, reviewed and corrected by a Martial (or Martial?) Chappe.

So long as we do not possess sufficiently powerful telescopes, we are obliged to leave the matter there and remain in the vague domain of conjecture. However, from the day when one can see the moon at sixty kilometers and other worlds in the same proportions, astronomers will take heart and the project of establishing communication with the inhabitants of Mars taken up and seriously studied by a group of Russian scientists.

They would begin by undertaking an attentive study of the planet, and, on days when there is good weather on the surface, acquiring the conviction that the Martians are definitely signaling to us by means of large fires that form designs between two canals.

That was an important point to establish.[30] Mars was inhabited, and even inhabited by highly civilized people who, in possession of very powerful tele-

---

[28] In French, *braquer*—which has no obvious connection with *braque* [scatterbrained].

[29] Fires traditionally lit in some parts of France in celebration of the saint's day (June 24).

[30] Vibert continues to vacillate between future and past tenses, quite uncertain as to how to frame this conjectural essay; for the sake of tidiness, I shall stick to the past tense from now on.

scopes, could probably see what was happening on Earth as if they were standing at a window looking out into their garden.

Armed with that conviction, the Russian astronomers, with admirable devotion, began by gathering the necessary funds, with the aid of a vast national subscription, and as soon as they had the indispensable sums, left to establish themselves in the middle of the Gobi, or Shamo, desert in northern Tibet and China, in the very heart of Asia. There are plateaux there 3300 kilometers long and 7000 broad, where the air is very cold and pure. That is all they would need to enter into direct communication, if possible with the inhabitants of Mars.

Once installed in double-walled wooden barracks, in order not to suffer from the cold, and with all their instruments in place, the Russian astronomers, ever admirable for courage and determination, had six thousand ones of kerosene sent from Baku, which naturally required a delay of several months.

But they had their plan, fully matured, and during that time they had bands of cheaply-hired Mongol nomads dig trenches several kilometers long in the earth where the frozen ground was hard but watertight—whereas, in the sand, the liquid would have seeped away, and it would have been necessary to render it impermeable with some sort of solid coating. It was a gigantic task, but after seventeen months, everything was finished and the ten thousand tons of kerosene were awaiting deployment.

It was no longer necessary to wait for a day when a serene atmosphere was visible on the surface of Mars to attempt to enter into communication therewith—but would the individuals out there take note of their appeal? A cruel enigma.

As you will already have guessed, our Russian scientists had traced a word with the aid of the trenches, over an extent of more than a hundred kilometers.

Thus, on a lovely clear night, cold and starry, at a given signal, the Mongols immediately filled al the trenches with kerosene, and, at another signal, set fire to it.

The moment was solemn. One could have heard the emotion-stirred heartbeats of the twenty-three astronomers gathered there from a kilometer away.

As every eventuality had been anticipated, three of them rose up into the air to an altitude of six hundred meters in a tethered balloon.

The effect was marvelous, and in large printed letters a hundred kilometers long, an immense, bright, luminous word—HELLO—conveyed the first greeting from the inhabitants of the Earth to those of Mars. It was probably the first attempt of this sort, at least in our own solar system, since the world became a world.[31]

---

[31] Vibert inserts a footnote here to explain that his Russian scientists had chosen a French word (*bonjour*) because it seemed preferable to use the scientific and literary language most familiar throughout the world—but the English would

A magnanimous spectacle, calculated to fill such men with emotion. The fire, cleverly maintained in the trenches by the Mongols under the direction of the astronomers—who multiplied their efforts during the night, racing hither and yon on their bicycles and also giving orders by telephone—lasted until morning, until the dawn; and in order to make it even more visible, filings were thrown into the flaming liquid that gave it all the colors of the rainbow in succession, according to the compound thrown or the by-products of the coal mixed with the kerosene.

The effect was striking, grandiose, superhuman—universal in the most sublime sense of the word—and far outshone the spectacle of the electrical luminous advertisements in the Place de l'Opéra and the great boulevards.

Finally, daylight arrived and the colossal *hello* that the genius of humankind might perhaps have hurled through space, on the invisible wings of the mysterious fluid named electricity, to another world was gradually extinguished.

Then a problem arose. Unless the Martians already had something ready, they would be slow to respond, if they had read and understood us. The delay, of perhaps six months, would be long, cruel and anxious for our scientists.

On the other hand, perhaps, by means of powerful and improved methods, the Martians would be able to reply more rapidly…

II. Further demonstrations.
The same origin of language as on Earth.
Certain proofs.

Needless to say, in spite of the phlegmatic temperament typical of Russian scientists, the little company waited with feverish impatience during the months that followed, their eyes always aimed, during the cruelly cold and harsh nights of Pamir, on Libya, the famous astral province of the grand canals of Mars.

They devoted themselves assiduously to all sorts of sports, reading and work, and completed astronomical calculations that represented a decade's work, but the waiting was no less painful.

The big question was whether the inhabitants of Mars—for them, there was no doubt that Mars was inhabited—had read and understood the word launched across space in luminous form.

Assuming that it had been read and understood, three hypotheses then presented themselves to the complex minds of the Russian scientists. Either they had already tried to send signals themselves, and would be able to resume doing so in a matter of hours or days, or they would simply undertake a few large-scale excavations, like us—in which case it was necessary not to expect a reply for six whole months. Some, however, opined in favor of a shorter interval, making the

---

undoubtedly have contested that claim, so the argument applies just as well to the translation.

observation that they were dealing with very advanced, civilized people possessed of powerful means of execution, as their giant canals seemed to suggest, and that one could therefore hope to have a response before so much time had elapsed.

The time went by, therefore, in feverish anticipation, the days dragging lamentably.

In the end, it was the last group who were right; four months later, almost to the night—O truly marvelous and superhuman prodigy!—the inhabitants of Mars sent a response...but let us proceed in an orderly manner, and not let ourselves be troubled by the profound emotion that still grips us by the throat as we inscribe these lines.

So, one beautiful night, they began to distinguish, vaguely at first and then clearly, a red light and then a huge conflagration on the surface of Mars.

All their telescopes were aimed as if they wanted to rape the sky. The moment was solemn and unforgettable. Finally, one astronomer suddenly shouted; "It's definitely in the province of the grand canals—it's definitely Libya."

Gradually, the light became more precise, and our scientists, more dead than alive, no longer feeling their hearts beating, were able clearly to distinguish signs on the Martian surface that they made haste to copy.

That as all, and the following night, nothing remained. As no one understood them, the mysterious signs were sent to the Academy of Letters in St. Petersburg—which, in its turn, was quick to send them to all the Academies in Europe.

It was our Académie des Inscriptions et Belles-Lettres that had the great honor of finding the key and translating the four previously-mysterious and untranslatable signs. One of its members, a distinguished scientist, remarked very judiciously that it was simply a matter of Hebrew words from which the accents and diacritical signs had been removed, as in primitive Hebrew.

The signs meant:

HEU, HEU

KHEU, KHEU

Which is to say: *thank you, thank you*—which meant that the Martians were thanking us and bidding us welcome—and finally: *yes, yes*, or, if you want it more precisely, *that is so, that is so*—which, to their minds, must signify: "We are people like you and Mars is inhabited, as Earth is."

The conversation continued thus for nearly two years, and to speed things up, the Russian astronomers began conversing on the sands in Hebrew, the words being shorter than in French.

By this means, they asked the Martians whether they had known that the Earth was inhabited for a long time, and they replied, always after four months or so: *Lo*—"no." The diacritical mark that ought to have been at the head of the first letter was still omitted.

When they were asked whether they fought against one another, making war, they very wisely replied: *Shalom*—which is to say, "peace," or "greetings," thus giving an important lesson in civilization and humanity to the still-inferior and half-savage peoples of Earth.

I have no room here to report all the conversations—luminous, it must be said—exchanged between the astronomers of Earth and Mars, but I nevertheless want to extract the two great results obtained in such a striking manner:

Firstly, that Mars in inhabited, like the Earth.

Secondly, that a language is spoken there that is very similar to Hebrew, and, and that, in consequence, a unity of language, with respect to origin, exists not only on Earth, as my father has peremptorily and victoriously demonstrated in his works, but probably also on the surfaces of all other inhabited worlds.

That's something; admit that science gives considerable enjoyment to those who devote themselves to it without afterthought.

When will a marriage take place between an inhabitant of Earth and a pretty Martian, thanks to the intermediary of an electric current?

One should never despair of anything, and in the next chapter I shall explain how I myself have in my possession a very nice photograph, surely a good resemblance, of a young and charming Martian woman!

III. How photography came to be possible
between Mars and Earth.
A portrait of a pretty Martian woman. Curious details.

Thanks to the long and persist campaign of the Russian mission, regular communication between the two planets had already existed for nearly two years, and there was no longer any communication with Mars except by the simplified intermediary of the Hebrew language—without diacritical marks, as I have already remarked—when the hazards of a mission enabled me to meet the Russian scientists on the very field of their endeavors.

They knew that I already had an interest in long-distance photography, and how I had had occasion to inform Edison on the subject. They were also not unaware of my profound conviction that electricity, in its triple form of light, heat and fluid, invisible and imponderable, was really the sole and unique agent of all the forces in the universe.

So, suddenly, very amiably, they asked me point-blank: "Would you like to attempt long-distance photography with Mars?"

"Yes—but it would require a fixed point, clearly determined. How could we inform the inhabitants of Mars?"

"Nothing simpler; it will take some time. But leave it to us; we'll take charge of everything and inform you when you have nothing to do but operate—which is to say, to make the attempt."

What was said as done, and those indefatigable scientists began a conversation on the subject with the Martians. Finally, a few months later, they told me that everything was ready, and that they had made the necessary arrangements with their colleagues on the other planet.

As soon as the latter had a fine night, they inscribed their colossal word:
KHEU
Yes, that's so.

A young Martian woman stood in the exact center of the immense fiery letter, in the location of the diacritical sign marked by a dot in the letter's "belly"— with the result that it was possible to fix and restrict my point of observation. If electricity really reaches us through space in the form of dark light, only becoming visible on contact with our atmosphere, there was no reason why my experiment should not succeed. Sat least they sought by that means to give me a confidence that they certainly did not have themselves—but that did not prevent me from having great anxieties and finding myself in a state of perplexity that is very difficult to describe.

For my part, however, while they were discussing and "negotiating" my procedure with the Martians, I had not been wasting my time. Thanks to some exceedingly rich personal friends in the Ukraine, who put unlimited credit at my disposal, I was able to order the immediate construction in several huge pieces, perfectly cast and welded together by blow-torch, of a giant Crookes tube, according to Röntgen's design, inside which the Arc de Triomphe cold have danced.

In order for it not to break under the pressure of atmospheric weight— although it is less heavy at those high altitudes—I had it surrounded by a powerful iron armature, and eventually, by means of a series of machines representing a force of more than seven thousand five hundred horse-power, I succeeded— after great efforts—in evacuating it completely, or very nearly so.

From then on I was ready, and had nothing more to do but operate it, following the now-well-known Röntgen method, to be able to collect, if possible, the X-rays—which is to say, the invisible fluid—that ought to transmit the images from Mars to me.

That same night, in clear weather, Mars showed us at the end of our telescopes the colossal KHEU without the central point. I took more than ten successive proofs with different lengths of pose, according to rigorous preliminary astronomical measurements, which permitted me, with an extremely exact precision—produced chronometrically, but by means of a powerful steam-engine—to take account of the various motions of the two planets during the procedure and maintain a consistent relationship. My apparatus was thus always on the central axis of the visual ray, maintaining parallax between the center of my apparatus and the center of the luminous letter traced in the immense steppes of Libya— the province of the grand canals of Mars, as you will not have forgotten.

These calculations had taken me months, with the assiduous collaboration of three astronomers that I had summoned from France. I thought, therefore, that I had taken all humanly possible precautions, and had thought of everything—but my anxiety was nevertheless great.

I shall pass over in silence the days of labor and anxiety that followed.

O miracle, O matchless joy, I definitely had an image—but it was a dot, and it was necessary to magnify it several million times.

Two problems arose then, cruel and obsessive:

Would I be able to obtain that insensate magnification; and, in obtaining it, would not all the details of the photograph be spoiled—blurred or obliterated?

I was very familiar with star-charts—quite clear, it's true—but no similar operation had ever been attempted.

Again, I shall pass over in silence the long and delicate successive operations, to which my collaborators and I had to devote ourselves for more than a year. All that I can say is that the success was complete, and that when all the magnifying operations were complete, exactly at the central point of the first of the Hebrew letters, where the diacritical mark should have been, the delightful head of a young Martian appeared, as beautiful as the Venus de Milo and Venus-Aphrodite put together.

That supernatural stellar photograph, that planetary portrait, I will be happy to show to anyone who manifests the desire to see it.

If it should happen one day that someone asks for the hand of that young beauty, however, I shall not take any responsibility for it, and will simply send them to the Russian astronomers who enabled me to realize this marvel!

Author's Note: Since I wrote this succinct and faithful account, scientific discoveries and the progress of science have given me abundant support and helped, in a way, to popularize my initial work.

To cite only the principle examples, in the month of June 1900, Monsieur Mercier[32] has undertaken a dogged campaign to initiate regular communication between Mars and Earth. Again, at the end of the same year, the scientific journals published the following note:

"There is talk of a new instrument, the telephot, which will permit sight at very long distances.[33] A newspaper set on a pedestal-lectern, sat up at a specific

---

[32] The person is question is identified in most contemporary and retrospective reports as "A. Mercier" of the French Astronomical Society; his proposal apparently made news by virtue of its blatant eccentricity, in suggesting the use the Eiffel Tower as a billboard and that signals might be projected on to the Moon.

[33] Image-projection devices were frequently discussed under his label (*telephote* in French) in the late 19th century; there is an elaborate description of a hypothetical telephot in Comte Didier de Chousy's *Ignis* (1883) (available from Black Coat Press, ISBN 9781934543887).

height in Paris, might be read in Tours by an individual finished with the new apparatus. A photograph could be taken at that distance. The distance between Tours and Paris is approximately sixty leagues."

Then again, at the plenary session of the Institut on October 25, 1900, Madame Cognet[34] was solemnly thanked for the 100,000-franc prize that she offered to the inventor of interplanetary communications.

Finally, on December 27 of the same year, Ch. Malato[35] took note of the great scientific movement that had finally taken shape, following my articles, in favor of the research to be carried out in order to institute communication with Mars

Let all these friends, known and unknown, receive my sincere thanks here. I am only too glad and proud to have had the good fortune to be able to provoke this great scientific movement.

That said, here is my excellent colleague's note:

"It was a long time ago that truly scientific minds repudiated the old fable of life solely limited to our infinitesimal globe. It is only poor people irremediably brutalized by belief in the mystery of the holy trinity who still consider the sidereal worlds as poor lamps it for our convenience by Father Sabaoth.

"Since spectral analysis has demonstrated the analogy of constitution of these worlds, with one another and with ours, their habitability is no longer envisaged as a dream. It would be an insult to readers of the Aurore to set out to demonstrate at length that organic life, a product of the combinations of matter, may be manifest everywhere that matter exists.

"We are not unaware that Mars and the other planets of our solar system once drifted, confused with the elements forming our Earth in the state of incandescent dust, through the infinity of space. Thus far, everything has confirmed Laplace's hypothesis. Then these swirling masses of dust separated out, condensing to form the worlds that gradually solidified and cooled, continuing, under the double action of centrifugal and centripetal force, to gravitate around the solar nucleus.

"Mars, being smaller than our globe, consequently cooled more rapidly; life must have appeared there sooner; its humankind must therefore be more advanced than ours. Is it necessary to recall the famous rectilinear canals that seem to be the work of conscious design, with the intention of connecting up the planet's seas?

---

[34] I have left this name as it is given in the original, as it is presumably copied from another source, but the prize in question was actually endowed by Clara Guzman in honor of her son, who had been a great admirer of Camille Flammarion. Interestingly, communication with Mars was excluded from the qualification for the prize, as it was held to be too easy. The prize was eventually awarded in 1969 to the crew of *Apollo 11*.

[35] Charles Malato (1857-1938).

"For more than a quarter of a century, intermittent appearances of lights on the Martian surface have encouraged the thought that we are in the presence of appeals made to the terrestrial world by beings probably more powerful than we are. On December 8, 1900—a date which, if the fact is confirmed, will remain immortal in the annals of science—the astronomer Douglas,[36] who is no novice, recorded a signal at Flagstaff Observatory in the United States, of which there can be no mistake: a series of fiery straight lines several hundred kilometers long. These lights, having been suddenly lit up, shone for about an hour and ten minutes, and then were extinguished as quickly as they had been lit.

"Now, nature never proceeds in this manner; it is therefore not absurd to suppose that we are in the presence of an appeal issued by 'brothers in space.'

"Monsieur Douglas' observation has been announced at the central bureau of Kiel by Monsieur Perkering, the director of Harvard University Observatory, a scientist of the first rank; the astronomical publications Nature, *in* London, *and* Astronomische Nachrichten *have reported it."*

It would seem that, in the presence of this fact, the most important to be produced in the history of humankind, and which ought to be the glory of our concluding century, the entire press ought only to have uttered a cry of enthusiasm. One could have understood the most extreme excitement or scientific reputation. Well, nothing! With a few proximal exceptions, there have only been articles by ignorant jokers: military brigandage, militaresque clownishness and the affectations of renowned whores—that is what is most likely to excite the enthusiasm of our contemporaries.

Brave Martians, you are ahead of time! Try again in a few centuries; perhaps humankind will be capable of understanding you. One argument that I have not seen advertised anywhere in favor of the luminous signal is this: the aforementioned signal lasted one hour ten minutes. Now, taking account of the time taken by the light to reach the Earth, that time represents an exact division of the Martian day, one local hour, if you wish.

Since then, it has been observed that it was simply a matter of the Martian dusk, when the sun setting at its horizon gilds or inflames the summits of its high mountains, but this research is no less interesting and worthy of being encouraged.

It would, however, be unpardonable if I were not also to report here, in spite of the length of this note, the following lines by Tapernoux, of June 15, 1900, which prove that every day, a new discovery arrives to confirm my own works:

---

[36] Soon after making this mistake, Andrew Ellicott Douglas (1867-1962) fell out with his boss, Percival Lowell, and William Henry Pickering (whose name is misrendered here as Perkering) when he called the Martian canals into question. He went on to found the science of dendrochronology.

"*Monsieur and Madame Curie, while studying pitchblende—one of the minerals from which uranium is extracted—at the laboratory of the* École Municipale de Physique et Chimie Industrielle, *have observed that some specimens are more active than uranium itself. From this they conclude, very logically, that a third radioactive substance gave its properties to the studied mineral. They have isolated this substance, by means of a series of procedures, and obtained a new metal, polonium, a near relative of bismuth in its analytical characteristics, but which emits Becquerel rays four hundred times as active as those of uranium.*

"*This was a superb result, but our chemists have not stopped there. Long and patient research has allowed them to discover a fourth metal, nine hundred times more active than uranium, to which they have given the well-merited name of radium.*

"*Radium is very similar to barium from a chemical viewpoint. It emits Becquerel rays that permit the production of good photographic prints after a pose of half a minute, as a result of which it is possible to obtain radiographs—those beautiful images of skeletons—without Crookes tubes.*

"*The rays admitted by radium are powerful enough to render barium platino-cyanide fluorescent—a property associated with the strongest does of X-rays.*

"*For centuries, people imagined that only light perceptible to their eyes existed. Crooke and Röntgen probed to them that in a vacuum, an electrical spark gives birth to luminous rays ungraspable by sight, able to pass through certain reputedly opaque bodies, permitting the projection of the silhouette of a human skeleton in spite of the flesh covering it.*

"*Monsieur and Madame Curie offer the scientific world a substance that possesses these properties in itself and permanently. X-rays have revolutionized optics. To what will the Becquerel rays of radium lead?*"

There is nothing to do but wait, confidently.

3F.95
LES TROIS YEUX
MAURICE LEBLANC
LE POINT D'INTERROGATION
COLLECTION
DE ROMANS D'AVENTURES

Maurice Leblanc: *The Three Eyes*
(1919)

Les Trois Yeux *[The Three Eyes] was first serialized in issues 164 (July 1919) to 167 (October 1919) of the monthly magazine* Je Sais Tout, *then it was released as a book by publisher Pierre Lafitte in 1920.*

It was Lafitte who steered Maurice Leblanc (1864-1941) towards writing detective novels à la Conan Doyle's. After reading a few samples, Leblanc brought Laffite his first Arsène Lupin story for Je Sais Tout, *a magazine, which Lafitte had launched in 1904. Lafitte, a smart publisher, immediately saw the potential in the character and the rest is, as they say, history.*

Leblanc began his literary career as a journalist, contributing to Gil Blas, Le Figaro, Comœdia *and* Le Journal. *He had also written a few novels influenced by Guy de Maupassant and Gustave Flaubert. He was grateful to Lafitte for having helped him find his way, and dedicated his first collection of Lupin stories to him, writing "You put me on a road where I did not believe that I should ever venture."*

Lafitte had christened the imprint in which he published Leblanc's—and later, Gaston Leroux'—books "Extraordinary Adventures." The Three Eyes *is, indeed, an "extraordinary adventure" in all the meanings of the term because it belongs to both the detective story and the* roman scientifique. *Leblanc was still clearly influenced by World War I, first mentioning the execution of Miss Edith Cavell, an English nurse, shot in Belgium in 1915 by the Germans for helping Allied soldiers to escape, then the murder of a French war pilot by the German aviator he has shot down in aerial combat. An entire chapter,* The Basilica, *is also devoted to the bombing of the cathedral of Reims by the Germans.*

The theme of The Three Eyes *is original: communication with the aliens is achieved via a "ray" discovered by an obsessive scientist. The process permits the incarnation of not only the ominous, eponymous alien eye, but also that of other images displaced in time, such as the Montgolfier brothers' first balloon ascent and scenes from the Great War.*

This technology is first exploited as a kind of fantastic cinema, leading to a complicated battle to possess its secret. The images are finally revealed as transmissions from the planet Venus, including visions of an exceedingly strange alien environment populated by geometrical figures, thus opening up further possibilities in what the communication with the aliens might reveal—If it can be secured and a dialogue initiated.

J.-M.L.

THE THREE EYES

I. Bergeronnette

As far as I'm concerned, this strange story began on to that autumn day when my uncle Noël Dorgeroux appeared, staggering and troubled, in the doorway of the room which I occupied in his house at Haut-Meudon, near Paris.

None of us had set eyes on him for a week. The victim of that anxiety always triggered by the final test of any of his inventions, he had been living amongst his furnaces and retorts, keeping every door shut, sleeping on a sofa, eating nothing but fruit and bread. And now, suddenly, he stood before me, livid, wild-eyed, stammering, emaciated, as if he had just recovered from a long illness.

He was truly changed beyond recognition! For the first time, I saw him wear unbuttoned the long, threadbare, stained frock-coat which fitted his figure closely, and which he never discarded, even during his experiments or when arranging the many chemicals he used on the shelves of his laboratory. His white tie, always spotless, was unfastened; and his shirt-front protruded from his waistcoat. As for his kind face, usually grave and placid, and still looking so young beneath his white curls, it now seemed unfamiliar, ravaged by conflicting expressions: terror and anguish, but also, to my surprise, hints of the maddest and most extravagant delight.

I could not get over my astonishment. What had happened during those last few days? What tragedy could have caused the quiet, gentle Noël Dorgeroux to be so utterly beside himself?

"Are you ill, uncle?" I asked, anxiously, for I was exceedingly fond of him.

"No," he murmured. "No, I'm not ill…"

"Then, what's the matter? Please, tell me…"

"Nothing is the matter… nothing, I tell you."

I drew up a chair. He dropped into it and took the glass of water I offered him; but his hand trembled so much that he was unable to lift it to his lips.

"Uncle, speak, for goodness' sake!" I cried. "I have never seen you in such a state. You must have gone through some great excitement."

"The greatest excitement of my life," he said, in a very low and lifeless voice. "Such excitement as nobody can have ever experienced before… nobody… nobody…"

"Then, do explain yourself, I beg you!"

"No, you wouldn't understand… I don't understand either. It's so incredible! It's taking place in the darkness, in a world of darkness!"

There was a pencil and paper on the table. His hand seized the pencil and, mechanically, he began to trace one of those vague sketches that become clearer as they get better defined. It soon assumed a more distinct form, representing three geometrical figures which might have been either badly-drawn circles or triangles with curved lines. In the center of these, he drew a regular circle which he blackened entirely and, in the middle of it, he added an ever darker point, as the pupil is to the iris.

"There, there!" he cried, suddenly agitated again. "Look! That's what's throbbing in the darkness. Isn't it enough to drive one mad? Look!"

He seized another pencil, a red one, and, rushing to the wall, he drew the same three incomprehensible shapes, the same three "triangular circles," in the centre of which he took pains to draw the three irises and their pupils.

"Look! They're alive, aren't they? You can see them moving, and wondering... You can see them, can't you? They're alive!"

I thought that he was going to explain, but he did no such thing. His eyes, which were usually full of life, frank and open as a child's, now bore an expression of distrust. He began to walk up and down and did so for a few minutes. Then, at last, opening the door and turning towards me again, he said, in the same breathless tone as before:

"You will see them, Victorien. You must see them too, and tell me they're alive, just as I have seen them. Come to my laboratory in an hour, or rather when you hear a whistle, and you shall see *the three eyes*—and much, much more. You'll see..."

He left the room.

The house in which we lived, the Lodge as it was called, turned its back upon the street and faced an old, ill-kept garden, at the top of which was a big shed housing the laboratory where my uncle had, for many years, been squandering the remnants of his fortune on a series of useless inventions.

As far back as I could remember, I had always seen that old garden ill-tended, and the long, low house in a constant state of dilapidation, with its yellow plaster front cracked and peeling. I used to live there with my mother, who was my aunt Dorgeroux's sister. After both sisters had passed, I'd moved to Paris to carry on with my studies, but I still returned to spend the holidays with my uncle. He was then mourning the death of his son Dominique, who had been killed by a German fighter pilot after a terrifying battle in the clouds. To some extent, my visits diverted my uncle's thoughts from his grief. Then, I had had to travel, and it was only after a long absence that I'd been able to return to Haut-Meudon, where I had now been spending a few weeks, waiting for the end of my holidays and for my appointment as a professor at Grenoble.

During each of my visits I had found him sharing the same habits, the same regular hours devoted to meals and walks, the same monotonous life, interrupted only for some great experiments by the same hopes and ultimately, the same disappointments. It was a healthy, vigorous life, which suited the tastes and the extravagant dreams of Noël Dorgeroux, whose courage and confidence no failed experiment had been able to defeat or diminish.

I opened my window. The sun shone down upon the walls and buildings of the Lodge. Not a single cloud dotted the azure sky. A scent of late roses quivered on the still air.

"Victorien!" whispered a voice below me, from a hornbeam overgrown with red creeper.

I knew that it was Bérangère, my uncle's goddaughter, reading, as usual, on a stone bench—her favorite seat.

"Have you seen your godfather?" I asked.

"Yes," she replied. "He was going through the garden and back to his Lab. He looked quite strange!"

Bérangère pushed aside the leafy curtain where the trelliswork was broken and her pretty face, crowned with rebellious golden curls, came into view.

"Help!" she said laughing. "My hair's caught. And there are spiders' webs too. Ugh!"

These are childish recollections, insignificant details. Yet why did they remain burned in my memory with such precision? It is as if our mind becomes charged with emotion at the approach of some great event which we are fated to encounter, and our senses thrilled beforehand by the impalpable breath of a distant storm.

I hastened down the garden and ran to the hornbeam. Bérangère was gone. I called her. I heard a merry laugh and saw her a little further away, swinging on a rope which she had stretched between two trees, under an arch of foliage.

She was delicious like that, graceful and light as a bird perched on some swaying bough. At each swoop, all her curls flew now in this direction, now in that, giving her a kind of moving halo, which mingled with the leaves that fell from the shaken trees—red leaves, yellow leaves, leaves of every shade of autumn gold.

Notwithstanding the anxiety with which my uncle's excessive agitation had filled my mind, I lingered before the sight of this incomparable vision and, giving her the pet name made up years ago from her Christian name, I said softly and almost unconsciously:

"Bergeronnette!"

She jumped out of her swing and, planting herself in front of me, said:

"You're not to call me that any longer, Monsieur le Professeur!"

"Why not?"

"It was all right once, when I was a mischievous little tomboy, hopping and skipping all over the place, but now..."

"Well, your godfather still calls you that."

"My godfather has every right to."

"And I?"

"No right at all."

This is not a love story; and I did not mean to speak of Bérangère before coming to the momentous part which, as everybody knows, she played in the adventure of *the Three Eyes*. But her part is so closely interwoven with it, from the very beginning and during all the early period of the adventure, with other episodes of our intimate life, that the clearness of my narrative would suffer if she were not mentioned here, however briefly.

So, twelve years ago, a little girl to whom my uncle was godfather, and from whom he used to receive a greeting card each January 1st, arrived at the Lodge. She'd been living in Toulouse with her parents, who'd once had a shop in Meudon, near my uncle's house. Now the mother had died; and the father, without further ceremony, had sent their daughter to Noël Dorgeroux with a short letter, the words of which I still remember:

The child is bored here... My business (Massignac was a wine-agent) *takes me all over the country, and Bérangère is left alone... I was thinking that, in memory of our friendly relations, you might be willing to keep her with you for a few weeks... The country air will restore the color to her cheeks...*

My uncle was a kind, good-hearted man. The "few weeks" turned into several months, then several years, during which Massignac announced several times his intention of coming to Meudon to fetch the child, but never did. So Bérangère stayed at the Lodge and surrounded my uncle with so much joy and boisterous affection that, despite his apparent indifference, he had felt unable to part with her. She enlivened the silent old house with her laughter and her charm. She was the element of disorder and delightful irresponsibility which gives a value to order, discipline and austerity.

Returning this year after a long absence, I had found, instead of the child whom I had known, a girl of twenty, just as much a child and just as boisterous as ever, but exquisitely pretty, graceful in form and movement, with an ounce of the mystery that surrounds those who live solitary lives in the shadow of an old, lonely man.

From the first, I felt that my presence interfered with her habits of freedom and isolation. At once bold and shy, timid and provocative, she seemed to shun me, and during two months of a life lived in common, despite seeing her at every meal and meeting her at every turn, I failed to tame her. She remained remote and wild, suddenly breaking off our talks and displaying, where I was concerned, the most capricious and inexplicable moods.

Perhaps she had an intuition of the profound disturbance that was awaking within me; perhaps her confusion was due to my own embarrassment. She had often caught my eyes fixed on her or observed the change that came over me at certain times. And she did not like it. My admiration for her disconcerted her.

"Look here," I said, adopting a roundabout method so as not to startle her, "your godfather maintains that human beings—some of them more than others—give forth a kind of emanation. Remember that Noël is first and foremost a chemist, and that he sees and feels things from a chemist's point of view. For him, this emanation is manifested by the emission of certain particles, invisible sparks that form some kind of cloud. This is what happens, for example, in the case of a woman. Her charm surrounds you..."

My heart was beating so violently as I spoke these words that I had to break off. Still, she did not seem to grasp their meaning, and she replied, with a proud little air:

"Your uncle tells me all about his theories. It's true that I don't understand them. However, as regards this one, he has spoken to me of a special ray, which he theorized to explain that release of such invisible particles. And he calls this ray after the first letter of my name, the B-ray."

"Well done, Bérangère! That makes you the godmother of a ray, the ray of seductiveness and charm!"

"Not at all," she cried, impatiently. "It's not a question of seductiveness, but of a material incarnation—a fluid which is able to become visible and to assume a form, like the apparitions produced by the mediums. For instance, the other day..."

She stopped and hesitated. Her face betrayed anxiety. I had to press her before she continued:

"No," she said, "I shouldn't to speak of that. It's not that your uncle forbade me to, but it's left such a painful impression..."

"What do you mean, Bérangère?"

"I mean, an impression of fear and suffering. We both saw, on a wall in your uncle's laboratory, the most frightful images—the pictures of three kinds of eyes. But were they truly eyes? I don't know. The things moved and looked at us. Oh, I shall never forget it as long as I live!"

"What did my uncle say?"

"He was totally taken aback. I had to hold him up and bring him around, for he almost fainted. When he came to himself, the images had vanished."

"Did he say anything?"

"He stood silent, gazing at the wall. Then I asked him, 'What was that, godfather?' And he answered, 'I don't know, Bérangère, I don't know. It may be those rays that I mentioned to you: the B-rays. If so, it must be some kind of materialization...' That was all he said. Soon after, he saw me to the door of the garden. And he has shut himself up inside his laboratory ever since. I haven't seen him again until just now."

She stopped. I felt anxious and greatly puzzled by her revelation:

"Then, according to you," I said, "my uncle's discovery is connected with those three pictures? They're geometrical figures, aren't they? Triangles?"

She formed a triangle with her two forefingers and thumbs:

"Yes, the shape was like that... As for their arrangement..."

She picked up a twig that had fallen from a tree and was beginning to draw lines in the sand when a whistle sounded.

"That's godfather's signal when he wants me at the laboratory," she cried.

"No," I said. "Today, it's meant for me."

"He wants you there?"

"Yes—to tell me about his discovery."

"Then, I'll come too."

"But he doesn't expect you, Bérangère."

"Yes, he does!"

I caught hold of her arm, but she escaped and ran to the top of the garden. I caught up with her outside a small, massive door in a fence of thick planks, connected to a shed and a very high wall.

She opened the door an inch or two. I insisted:

"Don't do it, Bérangère! It will only vex him."

"Do you really think so?" she said, wavering a little.

"I'm positive, because he asked me, and no one else. Come, Bérangère, be sensible."

She hesitated. I went through the door and closed it upon her.

II. The Triangular Circles

Noël Dorgeroux had built his laboratory in a piece of wasteland in which paths disappeared amidst withered grass, nettles and stones, filled with stacks of empty barrels, scrap iron, rabbit-hutches and every kind of disused lumber that rusts and rots or crumbles into dust.

Against the walls and outer fences stood his workshops, joined together by driving-belts and shafts, and the laboratory itself, equipped with a furnace, pneumatic receivers, and filled with innumerable bottles and jars containing the most delicate products of organic chemistry.

The view from up there embraced the loop of the Seine, which lay some three hundred feet below, as well as the hills of Versailles and Sèvres, which formed a wide circle on the horizon towards which a bright autumnal sun was sinking in a pale blue sky.

"Victorien!"

My uncle was beckoning to me from the doorway which he used most often. I crossed the yard.

"Come in," he said. "We must have a talk first. Only for a little while—just a few words."

The laboratory itself was lofty and spacious; a corner of it was reserved for writing and resting, with a desk littered with papers and drawings. There was a couch and some old, upholstered chairs. My uncle drew one of them up for me. He seemed calmer, but his glance retained an unaccustomed brilliance.

157

"Yes," he said, "a few words of explanation beforehand will do no harm… A few words on the wretched past, which is that of every inventor who sees fortune slipping away from him. I have pursued it for so long! I have always pursued it! My brain has always seemed to me like a vat in which a thousand incoherent ideas are fermenting, all contradicting each another, until one finally gains strength and emerges victorious. So far, I have lived for that one idea and sacrificed everything for it. It was like a sink that swallowed up all my money and that of others, and their happiness and peace of mind as well. Think of my poor wife, Victorien. You remember how unhappy she was, and how anxious she was about the future of our son, my poor Dominique! And yet I loved her so devotedly…"

He stopped at this recollection. I seemed to see my aunt's face and hear her telling my mother of her fears and forebodings:

"He will ruin us," she used to say. "He keeps on asking me to sell all our investments. He sees nothing but his research…"

"She did not trust me," Noël Dorgeroux continued. "Oh, I had so many disappointments, so many lamentable failures! Do you remember, Victorien, my experiment on intensive germination by means of electric currents? The one about liquid oxygen? And all the others, not one of which ever succeeded? But I never lost faith for a minute. One idea in particular buoyed me up and I came back to it incessantly, as if I were able to see the future. You know to what I refer, Victorien. It appeared and reappeared a score of times under different forms, but the principle remained the same. It was the idea of utilizing solar heat. It's there, you know, in the sun, in its action upon us, upon our cells, our organisms, our very atoms, upon all the more or less mysterious substances that nature has placed at our disposal. I attacked the problem from every side: plants, fertilizers, diseases of men and animals, photographs… For all these, I wanted to fund a use for solar rays, create special processes which would be my secret and nobody else's…"

My uncle was now talking with renewed eagerness; his eyes shone feverishly.

"I will not deny that there was an element of chance about my discovery," he continued. "Chance plays its part in everything. There never was a discovery that did not exceed our inventive effort, and I can confess to you, Victorien, that I do not even now understand what exactly happened. No, I can't explain it, but I believe in it. All the same, if I had not sought in that direction, the thing would never have occurred. It was due to me that the incomprehensible miracle took place. The picture is outlined in the very frame which I built, on the very canvas I designed, and, as you will perceive, Victorien, it is my will that makes the image which you are about to see emerge from the darkness."

He expressed himself in a tone of pride mingled with some uneasiness, as if he doubted himself and his words overstepped the limits of truth.

"You're referring to those three eyes, aren't you?" I asked.

"What?" he exclaimed with a start. "Who told you? Bérangère, I suppose! She shouldn't have. That's what we must avoid at all costs: indiscretions! One word too much and I am undone; my discovery stolen! Only think, the first man that comes along..."

I had risen from my chair, and he pushed me towards his desk:

"Sit down here, Victorien," he said, "and write. You mustn't mind my taking this precaution. It is essential. You must realize what you are pledging yourself to do if you share in my work. Write, Victorien!"

"Write what, uncle?"

"A declaration in which you acknowledge that... But I'll dictate it to you. That'll be better."

I interrupted him:

"Uncle, you don't trust me?"

"I don't distrust you, my boy, but I fear an imprudence, an indiscretion, and, generally speaking, I have plenty of reasons for being suspicious."

"What reasons?"

"Reasons," he replied in a grave voice, "which make me think I am being spied upon, and that someone is trying to discover the secret of my invention. Yes, someone came in here, the other night, and rummaged among my papers..."

"Did they find anything?"

"No. I always carry the most important notes and formulas on me. Still, can you imagine what would happen if they succeeded? So you do concede, don't you, that I am forced to be careful? Write down that I have told you of my investigations and that you have seen their results on the wall in my laboratory, in the room obscured by a black-serge curtain."

I took a sheet of paper and a pen, but he stopped me quickly.

"No," he said, "it's absurd. It wouldn't stop... Besides, you won't talk, I'm sure of that. Forgive me, Victorien. I am so worried!"

"You needn't fear any indiscretion on my part," I declared. "But I must remind you that Bérangère has also seen what there is to see."

"Oh," he said, "she can't possibly understand..."

"Yet, she wanted to come in with me just now."

"On no account must she be allowed to do this! She's still a child and not to be trusted with a secret of this importance... Now, come along."

But, as we were leaving the workshop, we both saw at the same time Bérangère tiptoeing along one of the walls of the laboratory and stopping in front of a black curtain, which she suddenly pulled aside.

"Bérangère!" shouted my uncle, angrily.

The girl turned around and laughed.

"I won't have it!" shouted my uncle, rushing in her direction. "I won't have it, I tell you! Go away, you mischievous child!"

Bérangère ran away, however, without looking much bothered. She leapt on a pile of bricks, scrambled on to a long plank which formed a bridge between two barrels and began to dance as she liked to do, with her arms outstretched like a balancing pole and her bust thrown slightly backwards.

"You'll lose your balance," I said, while my uncle drew the curtain back.

"Never!" she replied, jumping up and down on her spring-board.

She did not lose her balance, but the plank shifted and she came tumbling down among a heap of old suitcases.

I ran to her help and found her lying on the ground, looking rather pale.

"Have you hurt yourself?" I asked.

"Not really... But I think I might have sprained my ankle..."

I lifted her, almost fainting, in my arms and carried her to a wooden bench a little farther away.

She let me have my way and even put one arm around my neck. Her eyes were closed. Her red lips opened and I inhaled the cool fragrance of her breath.

"Bérangère!" I whispered, trembling with emotion.

When I laid her on the bench, her arm held me more tightly, so I had to bend my head and our faces almost touched. I meant to pull away, but the temptation was too much, and I kissed her on the lips, gently at first, then with a force that brought her to her senses.

She pushed me back indignantly and stammered in a rebellious tone:

"Oh, you're so naughty... Shame!"

Despite the suffering caused by her sprain, she managed to stand up, while I, regretting my thoughtless conduct, stood before her without daring to raise my head.

We remained for some seconds in this attitude, in an embarrassed silence through which I could catch the hurried rhythm of her breathing. I tried gently to take her hands, but she immediately pulled away:

"No," she said. "I'll never forgive you."

"Come, Bérangère, it was nothing."

"So you say. Leave me alone. I want to go home."

"But you can't."

"Here's godfather. He'll take me back."

My reasons for relating this incident will soon become clear. For the moment, notwithstanding the turmoil produced by the kiss I had stolen from Bérangère, my thoughts were fully absorbed by the mysterious drama in which I was to play a part with my uncle.

I heard him asking Bérangère if she was not hurt. I saw her leaning on his arm and, together, make for the door of the garden. While I remained trembling, dazed by the adorable image of the girl whom I loved, it was nevertheless my uncle whom I was impatient to see returning. The great riddle already held me in its thrall.

"Let's make haste," cried Noël Dorgeroux, when he came back. "Else it will be too late and we shall have to wait until tomorrow."

He led the way to the high wall where he had caught Bérangère in the act of yielding to her curiosity. This wall, which divided the laboratory from the garden, and which I had not remarked particularly on my rare visits to, was now daubed with a motley mixture of colors, like a painter's palette. Red ochre, indigo, purple and saffron were spread over it in thick, uneven layers, which whirled around a more thickly-coated center. At the far end, a wide curtain of black serge, like a photographer's cloth, running on an iron rod supported by brackets, hid a rectangular space some three or four yards wide.

"What's that?" I asked my uncle. "Is this the place?"

"Yes," he answered, in a husky voice. "It's behind that curtain."

"There's still time to change your mind," I suggested.

"What do you say that?"

"I feel that you're afraid of sharing your secret. You're upset."

"I'm upset for a different reason."

"What reason?"

"Because I, too, am going to see..."

"But you've already done it."

"One always sees new things, Victorien. That's the terrifying part of it."

I took hold of the curtain.

"Don't touch it!" he cried. "No one has the right to touch it, except me. Who knows what would happen if someone else were to open that door! Stand back, Victorien! Take up your position, two paces from the wall, a little to one side... And now, look!"

His voice was vibrant with energy and implacable determination. His expression was that of a man facing death

Suddenly, with a single movement, he drew the black-serge curtain.

My emotion, I am certain, was just as great as my uncle's, and my heart beat no less violently. My curiosity had reached its utmost limits. I had a formidable intuition that I was about to enter a mystery which nothing, not even my uncle's disconcerting words, would help me fathom. I was experiencing the very same feelings which, in him, had seemed to be a disease. I vainly strove to control my reason. I refused to take the impossible and the incredible for granted.

And yet, I saw nothing at first; and there was, in fact, nothing. This section of the wall was bare. The only detail worthy of note was that it wasn't quite vertical, and that its base had been thickened in order to form a slightly inclined plane which sloped upwards to a height of nine feet. What was the reason for this, I wondered...

A coating of dark grey plaster, about half an inch thick, covered the entire section. When closely examined, however, it was not painted, but was rather a layer of some substance uniformly spread, showing no trace of a brush. Some details indicated that this layer was quite recent, like a varnish newly applied.

I observed nothing else. Heaven knows that I did my utmost to discover any peculiarity!

"Well, uncle?" I asked.

"Wait," he said, in an agonized voice. "Wait! The first signs are beginning to appear..."

"What signs?"

"In the middle...Like a diffused light... Do you see it?"

"Yes, I think I do..."

It was like when a little daylight strives to mingle with the waning darkness. A lighter disk began appearing in the center of the wall and spread towards the edges, while remaining more intense in the middle. So far, there was no manifestation of anything out of the ordinary, however. The chemical reaction of a substance previously hidden behind the curtain and now exposed to sunlight was enough to explain this sort of phenomenon. Yet, something gave me the bizarre and perhaps unreasonable impression that an extraordinary phenomenon was about to take place. That was what I expected, as did my uncle Dorgeroux.

Suddenly, he, who knew the characteristics and shape of the phenomenon, reacted, as if he had received a shock.

At the same moment, the *thing* happened.

It was sudden, instantaneous. It leapt in a flash from the depths of the wall. Yes, I know, an image cannot spring out of a wall, no more than it can out of a layer of dark-grey substance only half an inch thick. But I am setting down here the sensation which I experienced, which is the same that hundreds of other people experienced afterwards, with a similar clearness and certainty. It is no use arguing with the undeniable fact that the *thing* shot out of the depths of an ocean of grey matter and appeared violently, like the rays of a lighthouse flashing from the very womb of darkness. After all, when we step towards a mirror, doesn't our reflection appear to us from the depth of that horizon?

Except that, here, it was not my reflection, or that of my uncle Dorgeroux's. Nothing was reflected, because there was nothing to reflect and no reflecting surface. Instead, what I saw was three geometrical figures which might have been described either as circles or triangles composed of curved circles. In their centers was a regular circle, dotted in the middle with a blacker point, as an iris is dotted with a pupil.

I am deliberately using this terminology to describe the same images which my uncle had drawn on the wall of my room. I had no doubt that he had been trying to reproduce those same figures, which had already upset him.

"That's what you saw, isn't it, uncle?" I asked.

"Oh," he replied, in a low voice, "I saw much more than that, very much more... Wait and look right into them."

I stared wildly at the three "triangular circles," as I have called them. One of them was set above the two others; and these two, which were smaller and less regular, but exactly alike, seemed, instead of looking straight before them, to turn a little to the right and to the left. Where did they come from? And what did they mean?

"Look," repeated my uncle. "Do you see?"

"Yes, yes," I replied, with a shudder. "*The thing's moving...*"

Or perhaps, it was no. The outlines of the three geometrical figures remained stationary; not a line shifted. Yet, from this immobility something emerged which seemed to be like a motion. I now remembered my uncle's words:

"*They're alive, aren't they? You can see them moving, and wondering... They're alive!*"

They *were* alive! And, as soon as I experienced this precise and undeniable feeling, I ceased to regard them as an assemblage of lifeless lines and began to see them like eyes, misshapen, different from ours, but furnished with irises and pupils, and throbbing in some kind of abysmal darkness.

"They are looking at us!" I cried, quite beside myself and as feverish and unnerved as my uncle.

He nodded his head and whispered:

"Yes, that's what they're doing."

The three eyes were looking at us. We were conscious of their scrutiny of those three eyes, without lids or lashes, but full of an intense life due to the expression that animated them, a changing expression, by turns serious, proud, noble, enthusiastic and, above all, sad—grievously sad.

I feel how improbable these observations must appear now. Nevertheless, they correspond strictly with the reality as it was beheld later by the crowds that thronged at Haut-Meudon. Like my uncle, like myself, those crowds shuddered before three combinations of motionless lines which had the most heart-rending expression, just as, at other moments, they laughed at the comical expression they were compelled to read into those same lines.

And on each occasion, the spectacle which I am now describing was repeated in exactly the same order. A brief pause, followed by a series of vibrations. Then, suddenly, three eclipses, after which the combination of the three triangles began to turn upon itself, as a whole, slowly at first, then with increasing rapidity, which gradually became transformed into a rotation so swift that one distinguished nothing but a motionless rose-pattern.

After that, nothing. The wall was bare again.

III. An Execution

It must be understood that, notwithstanding these long-winded explanations, the course of these events took actually very little time: exactly eighteen seconds, as I calculated afterwards. But, during these eighteen seconds—and this, I observed again on numerous occasions—the spectators received the illusion of watching a complete drama, with its preliminary expositions, its plot and its culmination. And when this obscure, illogical drama was over, one questioned what one had just seen, as one puzzles over a nightmare which has awakened one from one's sleep.

It must also be stated that none of this was in any way like those absurd optical illusions which are so easily contrived, or those bizarre notions on which a whole pseudo-scientific theory is sometimes built up. This was a physical phenomenon, an *absolutely natural* phenomenon, the explanation of which, when it came to be revealed, was also *absolutely natural*.

I beg those of you who are not already aware of this explanation to not try to guess it. Do not worry with suppositions or interpretations. Forget all the theories that I myself pondered: B-rays, ectoplasmic materializations, or the effect of solar rays. These are so many roads that lead nowhere. The best plan is to be guided by events, have faith and wait.

"It's finished, uncle, isn't it?" I asked.

"No. It's only the beginning," he replied.

"What do you mean? The beginning of what? What's going to happen?"

"I don't know yet."

I was astounded.

"You don't know? But you already knew about this—those strange eyes!"

"It always starts that way. But other images come afterwards, images which vary and that I know nothing about!"

"How can that be possible?" I asked. "Do you mean to say that you don't know anything about them, even though you prepared for them?"

"I prepared for them, but do not control them. As I told you, I have opened a door which leads into darkness, and from that darkness come unforeseen images."

"But what's coming is of the same nature as the three eyes?"

"No."

"Then what is it, uncle?"

"What's coming will be a series of images in conformity with what we are accustomed to see."

"Things which we shall understand, therefore?"

"Yes, we shall understand them; and yet, they will be all the more incomprehensible."

I often wondered, during the weeks that followed, if my uncle's words were to be fully relied upon, and if he had not uttered them just to mislead me as to the origins of his discovery. How indeed was it possible to believe that the key to this riddle remained unknown to him? But, at that moment, I was entirely under his influence, steeped in the mystery that surrounded us. With a constricted feeling in my heart, and my overstimulated senses, I thought of nothing but gazing into the miraculous wall.

A gesture from my uncle warned me. A new dawn was rising over the grey surface.

First, I saw a cloudy radiance whirling around a central point, towards which all the luminous spirals rushed and in which they were swallowed up while whirling upon themselves. Next, this point expanded into an ever-wider circle, covered with a light, hazy veil, which gradually dissipated, revealing a vague, floating image, not unlike the apparitions raised by spiritualists.

Then, after what seemed to be like a hesitation, followed a phantom image, striving with the diffuse shadow and seeking to attain life. Certain features became more pronounced. Outlines and separate planes took shape. At last, a flood of light issued from the phantom image and turned it into a dazzling picture, bathed in sunlight.

It was a woman's face.

I remember that my mental confusion was such that I felt like darting forward to touch that marvelous wall and lay my hands upon the living material in which the incredible phenomenon was vibrating. But my uncle dug his fingers into my arm:

"Don't move!" he growled. "If you budge even an inch, the whole thing will fade away. Just look!"

I did not move. Indeed, I doubt whether I could have done so. My legs were giving way beneath me.

"Look! Look!" he commanded.

The woman's face approached in our direction until it was twice the size of life. The first thing that struck me was her cap, which was that of a nurse, with the head-band tightly drawn over her forehead, and the veil around her head. Her features, handsome and regular and still young, wore that look of divine dignity which the classic painters used to give to the saints who are about to suffer martyrdom—a nobility compounded of pain and ecstasy, of resignation and hope, of smiles and tears.

Bathed in that light, which seemed to be an inward flame, the woman watched a scene invisible to us with her large dark eyes which, though filled with terror, were nevertheless unafraid. The contrast was remarkable: her resignation was defiant; her fear was full of pride.

"Oh," stammered my uncle. "It looks like the same expression that was in the Three Eyes just before. Do you see it? The same dignity, the same gentleness... but also the same dread?"

"Yes," I replied. "It's the same expression, the same sequence."

While I spoke, and while the woman still remained in the foreground, outside the frame of the picture, I felt a remembrance arise within me, as her features were not altogether unfamiliar... My uncle must have felt the same as he said:

"I remember her..."

But, at that moment, the face withdrew to the plane which it had occupied when it had first appeared. The mists that created a halo around it dissipated. Her shoulders came into view, followed by her whole body. We now saw a woman standing, fastened by bonds that gripped her chest and waist to a post the upper end of which rose a little above her head.

Then all this, which until now had seemed to be relatively still, like a photograph, suddenly became alive, like a picture developing into reality, or a statue coming to life. She moved. Her arms, tied behind, and her imprisoned shoulders, struggled against the ropes hurting them. Her head turned slightly. Her lips spoke. She was no longer an image presented for us to gaze at; it was life, moving and living life. It was a scene taking place somewhere in space and time. A whole background came into being, filled with people moving to and fro. Other figures were writhing, bound to posts. I counted eight of them. A squad of soldiers marched up, with shouldered rifles. They wore spiked helmets.

My uncle observed:

"It's Edith Cavell."

"Yes," I said, with a start. "I recognized her too. We're watching the execution of Edith Cavell."[37]

Once more, and not for the last time, I realize how ridiculous this must sound to anyone who does not know how to grapple with what I am telling, and what is the truth of my reporting. Nevertheless, I declare that the notion that this was somehow absurd and impossible did not occur to me as I was confronted with the phenomenon.

Even though no explanation had as yet suggested itself, I had to accept as irrefutable the evidence of my own eyes. All those who saw the thing later, and whom I questioned, gave me the same answer. *Afterwards*, they would challenge their recollections and question themselves. *Afterwards*, they would wonder if it had not all been a hallucination or a vision provoked by some hypnotic suggestion. But, *at the time*, even though their reason was rebelling, and they refused to accept facts without visible cause, they were nevertheless compelled to bow before these images and follow them as they would the representation of a succession of real events.

It was like watching a theatrical representation, or better yet, a cinematographic representation. This was the impression that emerged most clearly from all the comments I gathered. The minute Miss Cavell's lifelike image appeared, I turned around to look for a projector, hidden in some corner of the laboratory, but I saw nothing, and further, I understood that no projection could be achieved in broad daylight without a shaft of light. Yet, I retained that justifiable impression. There was no projector, but there was a screen—an astonishing screen

---

[37] Edith Louisa Cavell (4 December 1865 – 12 October 1915) was a British nurse. She is celebrated for saving the lives of soldiers from both sides without discrimination and for helping some 200 Allied soldiers escape from German-occupied Belgium during the First World War, for which she was arrested. She was accused of treason, found guilty by a court-martial and sentenced to death. Despite international pressure for mercy, she was shot by a German firing squad.

which received nothing from without, since nothing was being transmitted, but everything from within. And that was the sensation I experienced. The images did not come from the outside; they sprang out from within the surface of the wall. The horizon opened out on the farther side of a solid material. From the darkness came forth the light!

Mere words, I know! Words which I heap upon other words before I venture to write those which will retell what I saw come out of the abyss—the execution of Miss Cavell! Of course, I asked myself, if it is a film, how could one have done it? Was it a film like so many others, faked, fictitious, based upon second-hand reports, set in a conventional studio, with paid performers and a heroine who had thoroughly studied the part... All the same, I watched as if I didn't know all of this. The miracle of the spectacle was so great that one was obliged to believe in it, in the reality of the representation. There was no fake here. No make-believe. No part learned by heart. No performers and no studio. It was the actual scene. The actual victims. The horror which thrilled me during those few minutes was that which I should have felt had I beheld the murderous dawn of the October 12, 1915, rise across the thrice-accursed battlefield.

It was soon over. The firing squad was drawn up in double file, on the right and a little aslant, so that we saw the men's faces between the rifle-barrels. There were a good many of them: thirty, forty perhaps, booted, belted, helmeted, with their straps under their chins. Above them hung a pale sky, streaked with thin red clouds. Opposite them were the eight doomed victims.

There were six men and two women, all belonging to the people or the lower middle-class. They were now standing erect, throwing forward their chests as they tugged at their bonds.

An officer advanced, followed by four *Feldwebel* carrying unfurled handkerchiefs. Not any of the people condemned to death consented to have their eyes bandaged. Nevertheless, their faces were wrung with anguish; and all, with an impulse of their entire being, seemed to rush forward to their doom.

The officer raised his sword. The soldiers took aim.

A supreme effort of emotion seemed to add to the stature of the victims, and a cry issued from their lips. Oh, I *saw* and *heard* that cry, a fanatical and desperate cry in which the martyrs shouted forth their triumphant faith.

The officer's arm fell smartly. The intervening space appeared to tremble as with the rumbling of thunder. I had not the courage to look, and my eyes fixed themselves on the distracted countenance of Edith Cavell.

She also was not looking. Her eyelids were closed. But how she was listening! How her features contracted under the clash of the atrocious sounds, words of command, detonations, cries of the victims, death-rattles, moans of agony. By what refinement of cruelty had her own end been delayed? Why was she condemned to that double torture of seeing others die before dying herself?

After everything was over, one party of soldiers attended to the corpses, while the others formed into a line and, pivoting upon the officer, marched towards Miss Cavell. They thus stepped out of the frame within which we were able to follow their movements, but I was able to perceive, by the gestures of the officer, that they were forming up opposite Nurse Cavell, between her and us.

The officer stepped towards her, accompanied by a military chaplain, who placed a crucifix to her lips. She kissed it fervently and tenderly. The chaplain then gave her his blessing, and she was left alone. A mist once more shrouded the scene, leaving her whole figure full in the light. Her eyelids were still closed, her head erect and her body rigid.

She was, at that moment, wearing a sweet and tranquil expression. Not a trace of fear distorted her noble countenance. She stood awaiting death with saintly serenity.

And this death, as it was revealed to us, was neither very cruel nor very odious. The upper part of her body fell forward. The head drooped a little to one side. But the shame of it lay in what followed. The officer stood close to the victim, revolver in hand. And he was pressing the barrel to his victim's temple, when, suddenly, the mist broke into dense waves and the whole picture disappeared...

IV. Noël Dorgeroux's Late Son

The spectator who has just been watching the most tragic of films finds it easy to escape from the sort of dark prison in which he's been suffocating and, with his return to the light, recovers his balance and his self-possession. I, on the other hand, remained for a long time numb and speechless, with my eyes riveted to the empty wall, as if I expected something else to emerge from it. Even when it was over, the tragedy terrified me, like a nightmare prolonged after waking, and, even more than the tragedy itself, the extraordinary manner in which it had unfolded before my eyes shook me to the core. I did not understand. My disordered brain produced nothing but the most grotesque and incoherent ideas.

A gesture on the part of Noël Dorgeroux drew me from my stupor: he had drawn the curtain across the screen.

At this, I vehemently seized him by his two hands and cried:

"What does all this mean? It's maddening! How do you explain it?"

"I can't," he said, simply.

"But you brought me here..."

"Yes, so that you, too, might see it and make sure that my eyes had not deceived me."

"So you have already witnessed other scenes in that same setting?"

"Yes, three times before."

"What scenes, uncle? Can you tell me?"

"Certainly. What I saw yesterday, for instance..."

"What was it, uncle?"

He pushed me a little and gazed at me, at first without replying. Then, speaking in a very low tone, but with deliberate conviction, he said:

"*I saw the battle of Trafalgar.*"

I wondered if he was making fun of me. But Noël Dorgeroux had never been addicted to banter; and he would not have chosen such a moment to depart from his customary gravity. No, he was speaking seriously; and what he said suddenly struck me as so humorous that I burst out laughing:

"Trafalgar! Don't be offended, uncle, but it's really too bizarre! The battle of Trafalgar—which was fought in 1805?"

He once more looked at me attentively and asked:

"Why are you laughing?"

"Good Heavens, I'm laughing because... Well... You must admit..."

He interrupted me:

"You're laughing for very a simple reason, Victorien, which I shall explain to you in a few words. To begin with, you are nervous and ill at ease; and your merriment is first and foremost a reaction. But, in addition, the spectacle of that horrible scene was so—how shall I put it?—so convincing that you looked upon it, in spite of yourself, not as a reconstruction of the murder, but as the actual murder of Miss Cavell. Is that true?"

"Yes, perhaps it is, uncle."

"In other words, the murder and all the infamous details which accompanied it must have been—let's not hesitate to use that word—*filmed* by some unseen witness from whom I obtained that film. And my invention consists solely in somehow projecting it from inside a gelatinous layer of some kind. A wonderful, but credible discovery. Do you agree?"

"Yes, uncle, quite."

"Very well. But now, I am claiming something very different. I am claiming to have witnessed a film of the battle of Trafalgar, with the French and English frigates fighting before my eyes! I must have seen Nelson die, struck down at the foot of his mainmast! That's quite another matter, is it not? In 1805, there were no cinematographic films. Therefore, this can be only a joke or a fraud. Thereupon, all your emotion vanishes, my reputation fades into thin air, and you laugh! I am nothing more than an old impostor, who, instead of humbly showing you his strange new discovery, tries to pull the wool over your eyes! Is that so?"

We had left the laboratory and were walking towards the door of the garden. The sun was setting behind the distant hills. I stopped and said:

"Forgive me, uncle, and please don't think that I am lacking in the respect I owe you. There is nothing in my amusement that need annoy you, nothing to make you suppose that I suspect your absolute sincerity."

"Then what do you think? What is your conclusion?"

"I don't think anything, uncle. I have arrived at no conclusion and I am not even trying to do so, at present. I am out of my depth, perplexed, at the same time dazed and dissatisfied, as if I felt that this riddle is even stranger than it appears, and that it shall always remain insoluble."

We entered the garden. It was now his turn to stop me:

"Insoluble! That is really your opinion?"

"Yes, for the moment."

"You can't imagine any theory?"

"No."

"Still, you saw? You have no doubts?"

"I certainly saw. First, I saw these three strange eyes that looked at us; then, I witnessed the murder of Miss Cavell. That is what I saw, just as you did, uncle. And I do not for a moment doubt the undeniable evidence of my own eyes."

He held out his hand to me:

"That's what I wanted to know, my boy. And thank you."

I have given a faithful account of what happened that fateful afternoon. That evening, we dined together by ourselves, Bérangère having sent word to say she was indisposed and would not leave her room. My uncle was deeply absorbed in his thoughts, and did not say a word on what had happened earlier.

That night, I hardly slept, haunted by the recollection of what I had seen and tormented by a score of theories, which I need not mention here, for none were of the slightest value.

The following day, Bérangère did not come downstairs. At lunch, my uncle preserved the same silence. I tried many times to talk to him, but received no reply.

My curiosity was too intense to allow my uncle to ignore me in this way. I took up my position in the garden before he left the house. Not until five o'clock did he go up to his laboratory.

"Shall I come with you, uncle?" I suggested, boldly.

He grunted, neither granting my request, nor refusing it. I followed him. He walked across the courtyard, locked himself into the main workshop and did not come out until an hour later:

"Ah, there you are!" he said, as though he had been unaware of my presence.

He went to the wall and briskly drew the curtain. He then asked me to go back to his workshop and fetch something which he had forgotten. When I returned, he said, excitedly:

"It's finished!"

"What is, uncle?"

"The Eyes! The Three Eyes."

"Oh, have you seen them?"

"Yes! And I refuse to believe... no, of course, it's an illusion... How could it be possible, when you think about it? Imagine it, if you can—the Three Eyes wore the expression of my dead son's eyes! Yes, the very expression of my poor Dominique. It's madness, isn't it? And yet I saw it. Yes, I saw Dominique gazing at me... At first, with a sad and sorrowful look, which suddenly became the terrified stare of a man who is looking at death in the face. And then, the Three Eyes began to revolve upon themselves. That was the end."

I asked my uncle to sit down:

"I think it's just as you supposed, uncle—an illusion, a hallucination... Dominique has been dead so many years! It is impossible..."

"Everything is impossible, and nothing is," he said. "There is no room for human logic on that wall."

I tried to reason with him, although my mind was becoming as bewildered as his. But he silenced me:

"That'll do," he said. "It's starting again."

He pointed to the screen, which was showing signs of life and preparing to reveal a new picture.

"But, uncle," I said, already overcome by excitement, "where do these images come from?"

"Don't speak," said Noël Dorgeroux. "Not a word."

At once, I saw that this new 'picture' bore no relation to what I had witnessed the day before. I concluded that the scenes presented occurred without any prearranged order, any chronological or serial connection; in short, like the different films exhibited during a theatrical performance.

Now I saw the picture of a small town, as seen from a relatively close height. A castle and a church steeple stood out above it. The town was built on the slope of several hills and at the intersection of the valleys, which met among clumps of tall, leafy trees.

Suddenly, it came nearer and was seen on a larger scale. The hills surrounding the town disappeared; and the whole screen was filled with a crowd swarming with lively gestures around an open space above which hung a balloon, held captive by ropes. Suspended from the balloon was a receptacle serving probably for the production of hot air. Two men came out of the crowd and climbed a ladder, the top of which was leaning against the side of a cab. All this—the look of the balloon, the shape of the appliances, the use of hot air instead of gas, the dress of the people—struck me as possessing an old-world aspect.

"The brothers Montgolfier,"[38] whispered my uncle.

These few words enlightened me. I remembered those old prints recording man's first ascent towards the sky, which was accomplished in June, 1783. It

---

[38] The Montgolfier brothers, Joseph-Michel (1740-1810) and Jacques-Étienne (1745-1799) were balloonists from the commune Annonay in Ardèche, France. They are best known as inventors of the hot air balloon, which launched the first piloted ascent by man in June 1783.

was this wonderful event which we were witnessing, or, at least, I should say, a reconstruction of the event, accurately based upon those old prints, with a balloon copied from the original, with costumes of the period, and no doubt, the actual setting of the little town of Annonay.

But then, if it were a reconstruction, how was it possible that there were so many townsfolk and peasants? There was no comparison possible between the usual number of actors in a cinema scene and the incredibly tight-packed crowd which I saw moving before my eyes. A crowd like that is found only in pictures where the filmmakers have secured access to a public holiday or a royal procession.

Eventually, the wave-like eddying of the crowd suddenly subsided. I received the impression of a great silence and an anxious period of waiting. Some men quickly severed the ropes with hatchets. Etienne and Joseph Montgolfier lifted their hats.

And the balloon rose up. The people in the crowd raised their arms and filled the air with an immense clamor.

For a moment, the screen showed us the two brothers, by themselves and enlarged. With the upper part of their bodies leaning from the cab, each with one arm round the other's waist and one hand clasping the other's, they seemed to be praying with an air of unspeakable ecstasy and solemn joy.

Slowly the ascent continued. And it was then that something utterly inexplicable occurred: the balloon, as it rose above the little town and the surrounding hills, did not appear to my uncle and me as an object which we were watching from an increasing depth below. No, it was the little town and the hills which were sinking and which, by so doing, proved to us that the balloon was ascending. But there was also this absolutely illogical phenomenon, that we remained on the same level as the balloon, that it retained the same dimensions and that the two brothers stood facing us, *exactly as though the images had been captured from the cab of a second balloon, rising at the same time as the first with an exactly and mathematically identical movement!*

The scene was not completed. Or rather, it was transformed in accordance with the method of the cinematograph, which substitutes one picture for another by first blending them together. Imperceptibly, when it was perhaps some fifteen hundred feet from the ground, the Montgolfiers' balloon became less distinct and its vague and softened outlines gradually mingled with the more and more powerful outlines of another shape which soon occupied the whole space and which was revealed to be that of a military aeroplane.

Several times since then, the mysterious screen has shown us two successive scenes of which the second completed the first, thus forming a diptych which displayed the evident wish to convey a lesson by connecting, across space and time, two events which, in this way, acquired their full significance. This time the moral was clear: the peaceable balloon had culminated in the murderous aeroplane. First, the ascent at Annonay. Then, a fight in mid-air, a fight between the monoplane which I had seen develop from the old-fashioned balloon and the biplane which I beheld, swooping like a bird of prey.

Was it an illusion or a "special effect?" Here again, we saw the two aeroplanes not in the normal fashion, from below, *but as if we were at the same height and moving at the same rate of speed.* In that case, were we to suppose that a camera operator, perched on a third flying machine, was calmly engaged in "filming" the shifting fortunes of the terrible battle? Surely, that was impossible!

But there was no good purpose to be served by dwelling on these suppositions over and over again. Why should I doubt the unimpeachable evidence of my own eyes and deny the undeniable? *Real* aeroplanes were maneuvering before my eyes. A *real* fight was taking place upon that old wall.

It did not last long. The man who was alone was attacking boldly. Time after time, his machine-gun flashed forth flames. Then, to avoid the enemy's bullets, he looped the loop twice, each time throwing his aeroplane in such a position that I was able to distinguish on the canvas the three concentric circles that denoted the Allied machines. Then, coming nearer and attacking his adversaries from behind, he returned to his gun.

The German biplane—I observed the iron cross—dived straight for the ground and recovered itself. The two men seemed to be sitting tight under their furs and masks. There was a third machine-gun attack. The pilot threw up his hands. The biplane capsized and fell.

I saw this fall in the most inexplicable fashion. At first, of course, it seemed swift as lightning. And then it became infinitely slow and even ceased, with the machine overturned and the two bodies *motionless, head downwards and arms outstretched.*

Then the ground shot up with a dizzy speed, devastated, shell-holed fields, swarming with thousands of French *poilus.*[39]

The biplane came down beside a river. From the shapeless fuselage and the shattered wings two legs appeared.

The French plane landed almost immediately, a short way off. The victor stepped out, pushed back the soldiers who had run up from every side and, moving a few yards towards his motionless prey, took off his mask and made the sign of the cross.

"Oh," I whispered, "this is dreadful! And how mysterious!"

Then I saw that Noël Dorgeroux was on his knees, his face distorted with emotion.

"What is it, uncle?" I asked.

Stretching towards the wall his trembling hands, which were clasped together, he stammered:

"Dominique! I recognize my son! It is he! Oh, I'm terrified!"

---

[39] An infantry soldier in the French army, during the First World War.

As I gazed at the victor, I also recovered from my memory the time-effaced image of my poor cousin.

"It is he!" continued my uncle. "I was right... the expression of the Three Eyes... Oh! I can't look!... I'm afraid!"

"Afraid of what, uncle?"

"They are going to kill him... To kill him before my eyes... To kill him as they actually did kill him... Dominique! Dominique! Take care!" he shouted.

I did not shout, for what warning cry could reach a man about to die? But the same terror brought me to my knees and made me wring my hands. In front of us, from underneath the shapeless mass, among the heaped-up wreckage, something rose up, the swaying body of one of the victims. An arm was extended, aiming a revolver. The victor sprang to one side. It was too late. Shot through the head, he spun around upon his heels and fell beside the dead body of his murderer.

The tragedy was over.

My uncle, bent double, was sobbing pitifully a few paces from my side. He had witnessed the actual death of his son, killed in the great war by a German fighter pilot!

V. The Kiss

The following day, Bérangère resumed her place at meals, looking a little pale and wearing a more serious face than usual. My uncle, who had not troubled about her during the last two days, kissed her absentmindedly. We lunched without a word. Not until our lunch had nearly ended that Noël Dorgeroux spoke to his godchild:

"Well, my dear, are you none the worse for your fall?"

"Not a bit, godfather. I'm only sorry that I didn't see... what you saw up there, yesterday and the day before. Are you going there presently, godfather?"

"Yes, but I'm going alone."

This was said in a peremptory tone which broke no contradiction. My uncle looked at me. I did not stir a muscle.

Lunch finished in an awkward silence. As he was about to leave the room, Noël Dorgeroux turned back to me and asked:

"Do you happen to lose anything in my Laboratory?"

"No, uncle. Why do you ask?"

"Because," he answered, with a slight hesitation, "I found this on the ground, just in front of the wall."

He showed me a lens from an eye-glass.

"But you know, uncle," I said, laughing, "that I don't wear spectacles or glasses of any kind."

"Neither do I!" Bérangère declared.

"Yes, that's so," my uncle replied, in a thoughtful tone. "But someone who does was there. You can understand my uneasiness."

In the hope of making him speak, I pursued the subject:

"What are you uneasy about, uncle? At worst, someone may have seen the pictures from the wall, which would not be enough—or at last it seems to me—to enable them to steal the secret of your discovery. Remember that I, myself, who was with you, am hardly any wiser than I was before."

I felt that he did not intend to answer and that he resented my insistence. This irritated me.

"Listen, uncle," I said. "Whatever the reasons for your conduct, you have no right to suspect me. I beg you to give me an explanation. Yes, I beg, because I cannot remain in this uncertainty. Tell me, uncle, was it really your son whom you saw die, or were we shown a fabricated picture of his death? If so, what is the unseen and omnipotent entity which causes these phantom images to follow each other in that incredible cinema? Never was there such a problem; never so many irreconcilable questions. Last night, while I was trying for hours to fall asleep, I remembered—it's an absurd theory, I know, but all the same, one has to wonder—that you had mentioned to Bérangère a certain inner force which radiate from us and emit what you dubbed 'B-rays' after her. If so, might one not suppose that, under these circumstances, this force, emanating from your own brain, haunted by a vague resemblance between the expression of the Three Eyes and that of Dominique, projected on the receptive material of the wall the very scene which you had already conjured up in your own mind? Is it possible that that screen, which you covered with a special substance, is registering your thoughts, just as a photographic plate struck by light registers shapes and out-lines? If so..."

I stopped. As I spoke, the words which I used suddenly seemed to me de-void of meaning. My uncle, however, appeared to be listening with some inter-est, and was even waiting for what I would say next. But I did not know what else to add. I had come to the end of my tether, and, though I made every effort to detain him with fresh arguments, I felt that there was no more to be said be-tween us on that subject.

Indeed, my uncle went away without answering any of my questions. I saw him, through the window, crossing the garden.

I felt some anger and exclaimed to Bérangère:

"I've had enough of this! After all, why should I worry myself to death try-ing to understand a discovery which, when you think of it, is not a discovery at all? For what does it consist of? No one can respect Uncle Noël more than I, but instead of a real discovery, this is rather a stupefying way of deluding one's self, mixing up things that exist with things that do not, and giving an appearance of reality to what has none. Unless... But who knows anything about it? It's not even possible to express an opinion. The whole thing is an ocean of mystery, under stifling clouds of obscurity!"

My bad mood suddenly turned against Bérangère. She had listened to me with an air of disapproval, perhaps upset that I was blaming her godfather. As she slipped towards the door, I stopped her and, in a fit of rancor that was unusual for me, I exclaimed:

"Why are you leaving? Why do you always avoid me? Speak, will you? What do you have against me? Yes, I know, my thoughtless conduct, the other day. But do you think I would have acted like that if you weren't always keeping up that sulky reserve with me? Hang it all, I've known you since you were a little girl! I've held your skipping-rope when you were just a slip of a child! Then why should I now be forced to look at you as a woman... one who stirs me to the very depths of my heart?"

She stood against the door and gazed at me with an indefinable smile, which contained a gleam of mockery, but nothing provocative and without a shade of coquetry. I noticed for the first time that her bright eyes, which I had thought were grey, were streaked with green and flecked with specks of gold. At the same time, their expression struck me as unfathomable. What was passing in those limpid depths? And why did my mind connect the riddle of those eyes with that of the Three Eyes?

However, the recollection of the stolen kiss diverted my glance to her lips. Her face turned red. This was a last, exasperating insult.

"Let me be! Go away!" she commanded, quivering with anger and shame.

She lowered her head and bit her lips to prevent my seeing them. Then, when I tried to take her hands, she thrust her outstretched arms against my chest, pushed me back with all her might, and cried:

"You're a mean bully! Go away! I loathe and hate you!"

Her outburst restored my composure. I was ashamed of what I had done and, making way for her to pass, I opened the door for her and said:

"I beg your pardon, Bérangère. Don't be angry with me. I promise you it won't occur again."

The story of the Three Eyes is closely connected with all the details of my love, not only in my recollection of it, but also in actual fact. While the riddle itself is alien to it, and may be regarded solely as a scientific phenomenon, it is impossible to describe how humanity came to know of it without revealing all the vicissitudes of my sentimental adventure. The riddle and this adventure are integral parts of the same story. The two must be recounted simultaneously.

At the moment, being somewhat disillusionized in both respects, I decided to tear myself away from these twin concerns, leaving my uncle to his inventions and Bérangère to her sullen mood.

It was easy to do so as far as Noël Dorgeroux was concerned. We had a long succession of wet days. The rain kept him to his room or his laboratory, and the pictures from the wall faded from my mind like diabolical visions which

176

the brain refuses to accept. I did not wish to think of them, and so I thought of them hardly at all.

Bérangère's charm, on the other hand, obsessed me, notwithstanding the good faith with which I waged this daily battle. Unaccustomed to the snares of love, I became an easy prey, incapable of defense. Her voice, her laugh, her silence, her daydreams, her way of holding herself, her fragrance, the color of her hair became so many excuses for feeling exalted, joyful, suffering or despairing. Through the breach now opened in my soul, which hitherto had known few joys save those of academic study, came surging all the feelings that make up the delights but also the pangs of love, all the emotions of longing, hatred, fondness, fear, hope... and jealousy.

One bright and peaceful morning, I was strolling in the Meudon woods and caught sight of Bérangère in the company of another man. They stood on a corner, talking with some vivacity. The man was facing me. I saw a dandy, with regular features, a dark, fan-shaped beard, and a broad smile which displayed his teeth. He also wore a double eye-glass...

Bérangère heard my footsteps as I approached and turned around. Her attitude denoted hesitation and confusion. But she pointed down one of the two roads, as if she were giving a direction. The fellow raised his hat and walked away. She then joined me and, without restraint, explained:

"It was somebody asking for directions."

"Do you know him, Bérangère?" I asked.

"I never saw him before in my life," she replied.

"Oh, come on! From the way you were speaking to him... Look here, will you swear to it?"

"What do you mean? Why should I swear anything to you? I'm not accountable to you for my actions."

"In that case, why did you volunteer that he was asking for directions? I didn't ask."

"I do as I please," she replied, curtly.

Nevertheless, when we reached the Lodge, she thought better and said:

"After all, if it gives you any pleasure, I can swear that I was seeing that gentleman for the first time, and that I had never heard of him before. I don't even know his name."

"One more thing," I said. "Did you notice that he wore glasses?"

"So he did!" she said, with some surprise. "Well, what does that prove?"

"Remember, your uncle found a spectacle-lens in front of the wall..."

She stopped to think; then shrugged.

"A mere coincidence! Why should you connect the two?"

Bérangère was right so I did not insist. Nevertheless, despite the fact she had answered me with undeniable candor, the incident left me uneasy and suspicious. I could not believe that such an animated a conversation could take place between her and a perfect stranger merely asking her for directions. Plus, the man was good-looking and well off, so I suffered pangs of jealousy.

That evening, Bérangère was silent. It struck me that she had been crying. My uncle, on the contrary, returning from his laboratory, was talkative and cheerful; and I felt more than once that he was about to tell me something. Had anything thrown fresh light on his discovery?

The next day, he was just as lively.

"Life is very pleasant, at times," he said.

And he left us, rubbing his hands.

Bérangère spent all the early part of the afternoon on a bench in the garden, where I could see her from my room. She sat motionless and thoughtful.

At four o'clock, she came in, walked across the hall of the Lodge and went out by the front door.

I followed her, half a minute later.

The street which led to the house turned left, skirting the garden and the laboratory; to the right, the property was bordered by a narrow lane which led to some fields and abandoned quarries. Bérangère often went this way; and I saw by her slow gait that her only intention was to stroll wherever her dreams might lead her.

She had not put on a hat. The sunlight shone in her hair. She picked the cobble stones on which to place her feet, so as not to dirty her shoes with the mud on the road.

Against the stout plank fence which, at this point, replaced the stone wall enclosure, stood an old street-lamp, no longer in use, fastened with iron clamps. Bérangère stopped there, all of a sudden, evidently following a thought which, I confess, had often occurred to myself and which I had had the courage to re-sist—perhaps because I had not found a means of executing it.

But Bérangère had found such means. One could climb over the fence by using the lamp, get inside my uncle's laboratory without his knowledge, and steal a glimpse of one of those sights which he guarded so jealously.

Bérangère made up her mind without hesitation. When she was on the oth-er side, I had no hesitation in following her. I was in that state of mind when one is not unduly troubled by idle scruples; and there was no more indelicacy in sat-isfying my legitimate curiosity than in spying upon Bérangère's actions. There-fore, I, too, climbed over the fence.

My scruples returned when I found myself on the other side, face to face with Bérangère, who had experienced some difficulty in getting down. I said, a little sheepishly:

"This is not a very nice thing we're doing, Bérangère. Don't you think we should leave?"

She began to laugh:

"You leave if you want. I intend to go on. If godfather chooses to distrust us, it's his problem."

I did not try to stop her. She slipped softly between the nearest two sheds. I followed close upon her heels.

In this way we reached the end of the open floor which occupied the mid-section of the laboratory and we saw Noël Dorgeroux standing by the wall. He had not yet drawn the black-serge curtain.

"Look," Bérangère whispered, "over there, do you see a stack of wood with a tarpaulin over it? We can hide behind that."

"But suppose my uncle looks around while we're crossing?"

"He won't."

She was the first to venture across; I joined her without any mishap. We were no more than a dozen yards from the wall.

"My heart's beating!" said Bérangère. "I've seen nothing, you know; only those sort of eyes. And there's a lot more, isn't there?"

Our refuge consisted of two stacks of small short planks, with bags of sand between them. We sat down, in a position that brought us close together. Nevertheless, Bérangère maintained the same distant attitude as before. But now, I only thought of what my uncle was doing.

He was holding his watch in his hand and consulting it at regular intervals, as if waiting for a pre-set time. And that moment arrived. The curtain rose, grating on its metal rod. The wall was now uncovered.

From where we sat, we could see its bare surface as well as my uncle, for the intervening space fell far short of the length of an ordinary theater. The first shapes to appear were therefore absolutely clear. They were the three geometrical figures which I knew so well: the same proportions, the same arrangement, the same impassiveness, followed by that same palpitation, coming entirely from within, which animated them and made them live.

"Yes, yes," whispered Bérangère, "godfather already said so: the Three Eyes are alive!"

"They are," I replied, "and they gaze at you. Just look at the two lower eyes; think of them as actual eyes; you will see that they have an expression. There—they're smiling now."

"You're right, they are!"

"And see what a soft and gentle look they have now... a little serious, too... Oh, Bérangère, that's impossible!"

"What?"

"They have your expression, Bérangère!"

"What nonsense! That's ridiculous!"

"The very expression of your own eyes. You can't see it yourself, but I do. They have never looked at me like that, but all the same, they are your eyes. I recognize their expression, their charm... I know, because they make me feel... er, as yours do!"

But the end was approaching. The three geometrical figures began to revolve upon themselves with the same dizzy motion which reduced them to a confused disk which soon vanished.

"They were your eyes, Bérangère," I stammered. "I have no doubt about it. It was as if you were looking at me."

Yes, they had the same look, but I didn't remember then that Edith Cavell had also looked in that same way at Noël Dorgeroux and me, through the strange Three Eyes, and also that my uncle similarly had recognized the look from his son's eyes before Dominique had appeared to him... If so, was I to assume that each of the films—there was no other word for them—was preceded *by the fabulous vision of three geometrical figures containing, captive and alive, the very expression from the eyes of one of the persons about to come to life upon the screen?*

It was a mad assumption, as were all those which I had been making! I blush to write it down. But, if so, what were these three geometrical figures? A cinema trademark? The trademark of the Three Eyes? What an absurdity! What madness! And yet...

"Oh," said Bérangère, struggling to rise. "I shouldn't have come! It's suffocating me. Can you explain?"

"No, Bérangère, I can't. It's suffocating me too. Do you want to go?"

"No," she said, leaning forward. "No, I want to see more."

And we saw. And at the very moment when a muffled cry escaped our lips, we saw Noël Dorgeroux slowly making a great sign of the cross.

Opposite him, in the middle of the magic space on the wall, was he, himself, standing not like a frail and shifting phantom, but like a human being full of life. Yes, Noël Dorgeroux went to and fro before us and before himself, wearing his usual skull-cap, dressed in his long frock coat. And the setting in which he moved was none other than his laboratory, with its shed, its workshops, its disorder, its heaps of scrap iron, its stacks of wood, its rows of barrels... and its wall, with its serge curtain!

I noticed that detail immediately: the curtain was still covering the magic wall completely. It was therefore impossible to imagine that this scene could have been recorded, absorbed by the wall, which was then drawing it from its own substance in order to show it to us! It was impossible, because Noël Dorgeroux had his back turned to the wall. It was impossible, because we saw the wall itself, then the door of the garden, which opened, and suddenly, I saw myself entering the laboratory.

"You! It's you!" gasped Bérangère.

"Yes, it's I, but on the day when your uncle first told me to come here," I said, astounded. "The day when I first saw a vision on this very wall!"

At that moment, on the screen, Noël Dorgeroux beckoned to me from the door of his laboratory. We went in together. The scene remained empty. Then, after an eclipse which lasted only a second or two, it reappeared. The little garden door opened again and Bérangère, all smiles, put her head through. She seemed to be saying:

"Nobody here. They're in the lab. Upon my word, I'll risk it!"

And she crept along the wall, towards the serge curtain.

All this happened quickly, without any of the vibration seen in the films shown in the cinemas, so clearly and plainly that I could follow our images not as something that might have been filmed in the past, but more like an actual reflection from a mirror. To tell the truth, I was so confused at seeing myself on the wall and yet knowing where I was now that this doubling of my personality made my brain reel.

"Victorien," said Bérangère, in an almost inaudible voice, "you're going to come out of your uncle's workshop as you did the other day, aren't you?"

"Yes," I said, "we seem to be watching everything that happened then."

And we did. We saw my uncle and I coming out of the laboratory; Bérangère, surprised, running away, laughing; then climbing a plank between two barrels and dancing, ever so gracefully; and then, as before, she fell. I saw myself darting forward, picking her up, and laying her on the bench. We saw her put her arms around me; our faces almost touching... And, as before, gently at first, then roughly, I kissed her on the lips. And, as she had done then, she rose to her feet, while I crouched beside her.

Oh, how well I remember it all! I remember, and I still see myself. I see myself on the wall, bending very low, not daring to lift my head, and I see Bérangère, standing up, covered with shame, trembling with indignation.

Indignation? Did she really seem indignant? But then why did her dear face, the face on the screen, display such indulgence and gentleness? Why did she smile with that expression of unspeakable gladness? Yes, I swear it was gladness. Over there, on that magic wall where that exciting minute was being reenacted, there stood over me a happy creature who was gazing at me with joy and affection, who was gazing at me thus because she knew that I could not see her and because she could not know that one day, I should see her.

"Bérangère! Bérangère!"

But suddenly, while the adorable vision on the wall continued, my eyes were suddenly covered as with a veil. Bérangère had turned towards me and put her two hands over my eyes, whispering:

"Don't look! I won't have you look. Besides, it's not true. That vision is a lie... That woman is not me at all... I never looked at you like that."

Her voice grew fainter. Her hands dropped to her sides. And, with all the strength gone out of her, she let herself fall against my shoulder, gently and silently.

Ten minutes later, I went back alone. Bérangère had left me without a word, after her unexpected movement of surrender.

The next morning I received a telegram from the rector of the university, calling me to Grenoble. Bérangère did not appear as I was leaving. But, when my uncle brought me to the station, I saw her, not far from the Lodge, talking to that confounded dandy whom she had pretended not to know.

VI. Anxieties

"You seem very happy, uncle!" I said as we walked briskly to the station, whistling one tune after another.

"Yes," he replied. "I am happy as a man is who has come to a decision."

"Really?"

"And a very serious one at that. It has cost me a sleepless night; but it's worth it."

"May I ask...?"

"Certainly. In short, it's this: I'm going to pull down the sheds in laboratory and build an theater there."

"What for?"

"To exploit the thing... that thing, you know..."

"What do you mean, to exploit it?"

"Well, it's a tremendous discovery, and, if properly exploited, it will generate the money I need—not for my personal enrichment, mind you, but to continue my research without being hampered by sordid financial considerations. There are millions to be made, Victorien, millions! What shall I not accomplish with millions! This brain of mine," he went on, tapping his forehead, "is simply filled with ideas, theories, which need to be tested, but all this takes money... You know how little I care about money, but I need those millions, if I am to carry out my work. And those millions I shall have!"

Mastering his enthusiasm, he took my arm and explained:

"First of all, the land must be cleared of its rubbish and leveled. After that, we'll build the theater, with five rows of seats facing the wall. Of course, the wall shall remain where it is. It is essential, the lynchpin of the whole enterprise. But I shall heighten and widen it, and when it's quite unobstructed, there will be a clear view from every seat. You follow me, don't you?"

"I do, uncle, but do you think people will come?"

"Will they come? What? You, who have seen it, ask me that question! Why, of course, they will! They will pay gold for the worst seat, a king's ransom just to get in! I'm so sure of it that I'll invest everything I have, the last remnant of my savings, into this business. And within a year, I shall have amassed a fortune!"

"The place is quite small, uncle. You will only have a limited number of seats."

"Balderdash! I can have a thousand seats comfortably! At two hundred francs a seat, to begin with, then a thousand francs..."

182

"Seats in the open air, exposed to the rain, to the cold, to all kinds of weather…"

"I've foreseen that objection. I'll have the roof redone for rainy days, and shutters installed on the windows. Bright daylight, sunshine, and other weather conditions, might decrease the number of séances, so I'll take care of that. But that's a trivial matter. Soon, I'll be able to charge two thousand francs per seat, no, five thousand francs! I tell you, Victorien, the sky is the limit! Everyone will want to have been at Noël Dorgeroux's theater at least once in their lives, you know it as well as I do! When all is said and done, the reality is more extraordinary than anything that you can imagine, even after what you have seen with your own eyes."

I could not help but ask him:

"Then there are new images?"

He replied by nodding his head:

"It's not so much that they're new," he said, "as that they have enabled me, with all that I already knew, to find out the truth."

"Uncle!" I cried. "You mean to say that you know the truth?"

"I know the whole truth, my boy," he declared. "I know how much is my work and how much has nothing to do with me. What was once darkness is now dazzling light."

And he added, in a very serious tone:

"It is beyond imagination, Victorien, beyond the most extravagant dreams; and yet, it remains within the province of facts and certainties. Once humanity knows of it, Earth will pass through a thrill of religious awe; and the people who shall come here as pilgrims will fall upon their knees—as I did—like children who pray and fold their hands and weep!"

His words, which were obviously exaggerated, seemed to come from an unhinged mind. Yet, I felt the force of their exciting and feverish influence.

"Explain yourself, uncle, I beg you."

"Later, my boy, when all the details have been cleared up."

"What are you afraid of?"

"Nothing from you."

"From whom then?"

"Nobody. But I still have a few misgivings… wrongly, perhaps. Still, certain facts lead me to believe that I am being spied upon, and that someone is trying to steal my secret. It's just a few clues… things that have been moved from their place… and, above all, a vague intuition…"

"This all sounds very vague, uncle."

"Yes, I admit it," he said, drawing himself up. "And so, forgive me if my precautions seem excessive… Now, let's talk of something else, of yourself, Victorien, of your plans…"

"I have no plans, uncle."

"Yes, you do. There's one at least that you've been keeping from me."

"What do you mean?"

He stopped in his walk and said:

"You're in love with Bérangère."

I did not think of protesting, knowing that Noël Dorgeroux had stood in front of the wall the day before.

"Yes, uncle, I'm in love with Bérangère—but she doesn't care for me."

"She does, Victorien."

I displayed some slight impatience.

"Uncle, I must ask you not to pursue this. Bérangère is still a child; she does not know what she wants; she is incapable of any serious feeling; and I do not intend to think about her anymore. On my part, it was just a fancy of which I shall soon be cured."

Noël Dorgeroux shrugged.

"Bah! A lovers' quarrel! Now this is what I have to say to you, Victorien. The work at the laboratory will take up all the winter. I plan to open my theater to the public on May 14. The Easter holidays will fall a month earlier; and you shall marry my goddaughter then. Not a word! Leave it to me. And I'm also asking you to entrust your prospects to me. You can well understand, my boy, that, when money is pouring in like water—as it will without a doubt—Victorien Beaugrand will no longer need a job which would not give him enough leisure for his private studies and he will be happier living with me with his wife. Yes, I said 'his wife' and I stick to it. Good-bye, my dear nephew, and not another word!"

I walked on, but he called me back:

"You haven't said good-bye properly to me, Victorien."

He put his arms around me with greater fervor than usual, and I heard him murmur:

"Who can tell if we shall ever meet again? At my age! And threatened as I am, too!"

I protested, but he embraced me yet again.

"You're right. I'm talking nonsense. Think of your marriage. Bérangère is a dear, sweet girl, and she loves you. Good-bye and bless you! I'll write to you soon. Good-bye!"

I confess that my uncle's ambitions, at least in so far as they were related to his discovery, did not strike me as absurd; and what I have said of the things I'd seen will explain the reasons for such confidence. For the moment, therefore, I will leave all this aside and speak no more about the Three Eyes and the amazing scenes I'd watched on the magic wall. But how could I not indulge in the dreams of the future which he had conjured, despite Bérangère's hostile attitude and her ambiguous conduct?

During the months that followed, I often clung to the delightful memory of the vision in which I seen the charming picture of Bérangère bending over me with that soft look in her eyes. But I soon pulled myself back and cried:

"I saw the thing all wrong! What I took for affection and, God forgive me, love, was only the expression of a woman triumphing over a man's shame! Bérangère doesn't care for me. What pushed her against me was nothing more than a nervous spasm, and she felt so ashamed that she immediately pushed me away and ran indoors. Besides, she had an appointment with that man the next day and, in order to keep it, let me go without even saying good-bye."

My months of exile therefore were painful. I wrote to Bérangère, but in vain. I received no reply.

My uncle in his letters spoke of nothing but his laboratory. The work was progressing fast. The theater was being erected; the wall was transformed. The latest news, which I received around the middle of March, told me that the only thing left was to install the thousand seats which had long been on order, and to hang the iron curtain which was to protect the wall.

It was during that time that Noël Dorgeroux's misgivings revived, or at least he mentioned them to me in his letters. Two books he'd bought in Paris and which he read in private—in order to hide clues that might lead to the secret of his discovery—had been taken away, then restored to their proper place. A sheet of paper, covered with notes and chemical formulas, had disappeared. There were footprints in the garden. His desk had been broken open, in the room where he'd worked at the Lodge since the demolition of the sheds.

This last incident, I confess, caused me a certain alarm. My uncle's fears appeared to be based upon serious facts. There was evidently someone prowling around the Lodge in the pursuit of a scheme the nature of which was easy to guess. I thought of the dandyish man with the glasses and his relations with Bérangère...

I made a fresh attempt to persuade the girl to communicate with me:

"*You know what's happening at the Lodge, don't you?*" I wrote. "*How do you explain those facts, which to me seem quite significant? Be sure to send me word if you feel the least uneasiness. And keep a close watch in the meantime.*"

I followed up this letter with two telegrams dispatched in quick succession. But Bérangère's stubborn silence, instead of distressing me, served rather to allay my apprehensions. She would not have failed to send for me had there been any real danger. I thought my uncle was mistaken. He was a victim to the feverish condition into which his discovery had thrown him. As the date approached on which he had decided to make it public, he felt anxious, but there was nothing to justify his apprehensions.

I allowed a few more days to pass. Then I wrote Bérangère a letter of twenty pages, filled with reproaches, which fortunately, I did not post. Her behavior exasperated me. I suffered from a bitter fit of jealousy.

At last, on Saturday, March 29, I received a registered bundle of papers from my uncle, with a very explicit letter, which I kept and which I am copying below:

My Dear Victorien,

Recent events, combined with some recent serious events which I will tell you, prove that I am the object of a devious plot against which I have perhaps delayed defending myself longer than I should have. At any rate, it is my duty, because of the dangers which threaten my very life, to protect the magnificent discovery which mankind will owe to my efforts and take precautionary measures, which you will certainly not think unwarranted.

I have, therefore, drawn up—as I always refused to do before—a detailed report of my discovery, the investigations that led up to it, and the conclusions to which my experiments have led me. However improbable it may seem, however contrary to all the accepted laws of Science, the truth is as I state, and not otherwise.

I have added to my report a complete description of the technical processes which should be employed in the installation and exploitation of my discovery, and also my own views on the financial management of the theater, the advertizing, the running of the business, and the manner in which it might be subsequently expanded later by building a second theater in the garden to face the other side of the wall.

I am sending you this report, sealed and registered, and I will ask you to not open it unless I come to some harm. As an additional precaution, I have not included in it the chemical formula which is the actual basis of my discovery. You will find it engraved on a small, thin steel plate which I always carry inside the lining of my waistcoat. In this way, you, and you alone, will have in your hands all the necessary information for exploiting my discovery. It will require no special qualifications or scientific preparation. The report and the formula are sufficient. With these two in your possession, you will be in control, and no one can ever rob you of the profits of this wonderful secret, which I am hereby bequeathing to you.

Now, my dear boy, let us hope that all my presentiments are unfounded and that we shall soon be celebrating together the happy events which I foresee, including first and foremost your marriage to Bérangère. I have not yet been able to obtain a favorable reply from her, and she has for some time appeared to me to be, as you put it, in a rather fanciful mood; but I have no doubt that your return will make her reconsider a refusal which she does not even attempt to justify.

Ever affectionately yours,

Noël Dorgeroux

This letter reached me too late for me to catch the evening express. Besides, was there any urgency for my departure? Should I not to wait for further news?

A casual observation made short work of my hesitation. As I sat reflecting, mechanically turning the envelope in my hands, I perceived that it had been opened and then closed again; what's more, this had been done rather clumsily, probably by someone who had had only a few seconds at his disposal.

The full gravity of the situation at once flashed across my mind. The man who had opened the letter before it was mailed, and who beyond a doubt was the man whom my uncle accused of plotting against him, now knew that he carried a steel plate bearing the essential formula on his person, in the lining of his waistcoat.

I examined the registered packet and observed that it had not been opened. Despite my uncle's instructions, I undid the string and discovered a pasteboard tube. Inside it was a roll of paper which I eagerly examined. It consisted of nothing but blank pages. The report had been stolen!

Three hours later, I was seated in a night train which did not reach Paris until the afternoon of the next day, Sunday. It was four o'clock when I walked out of the station at Meudon. The enemy had for at least two days known the contents of my uncle's letter, his report, and the dreadful means of procuring the formula.

VII. The Man With Savage Eyes

The staff at the Lodge consisted in its entirety of Valentine, an old maid, a little deaf and very short-sighted, who combined the functions of parlor-maid, cook and gardener. She hardly ever left her kitchen, which was located in an extension built onto the house and opening directly upon the street.

This was where I found her. She did not seem surprised at my return— nothing ever seemed to surprise or perturb her—and I realized at once that she was totally unaware of what was going on and she wouldn't be able to tell me anything useful. I gathered, however, that my uncle and Bérangère had gone out half an hour earlier.

"Together?" I asked.

"Good gracious, no! The master came through the kitchen and said, 'I'm going to post a letter. Then I shall return to my laboratory.' He left a bottle behind him, you know, one of those blue medicine bottles which he uses for his experiments."

"Where did he leave it, Valentine?"

"Over there, on the dresser. He must have forgotten it when he put on his overcoat, for he never parts with those bottles of his."

"But it's not there now!"

"That's a funny thing! As far as I know, Monsieur Dorgeroux hasn't been back."

"Has anyone else been here?"

"No... Yes, there was. A gentleman who came for Mademoiselle Bérangère a little while after."

"Did you go to fetch her?"

"Yes."

"Then, he must have taken the bottle while you were away."

"Oh, how Monsieur Dorgeroux will scold me!"

"Who was this person?"

"Upon my word, I couldn't tell you... My sight isn't so good..."

"Do you know him?"

"No, I didn't recognize his voice."

"And did they both go out, Bérangère and he?"

"Yes, they crossed the road... opposite."

Opposite meant the path in the wood. I thought for a second or two. Then, tearing a sheet of paper from my notebook, I wrote:

My Dear Uncle,

Wait for me when you return. Don't leave the Lodge on any account. The danger is imminent.

Victorien

"Give this to Monsieur Dorgeroux as soon as you see him, Valentine. I shall be back in half an hour."

The path ran in a straight line through dense thickets with tiny leaves burgeoning on the twigs of the bushes. It had rained heavily during the last few days, but a bright spring sun was drying the ground and I could distinguish no trace of footsteps. After walking three hundred yards, however, I met a small boy from the neighborhood, whom I knew by sight, coming back to the village, pushing his bicycle which had burst a tire.

"You don't happen to have seen Mademoiselle Bérangère, have you?" I asked.

"Yes, I did," he replied. "She was with a gentleman."

"A man wearing glasses?"

"Yes, a tall chap, with a big beard."

"Are they far away?"

"When I first saw them, they were about mile and a quarter from here. I returned later...They'd taken the old road..."

I quickened my pace, greatly excited, for I was feeling an increasing dread. I reached the old road, but, a little farther on, it brought me to an open space crossed by a number of paths. Which one was I to take? Feeling more and more anxious, I called out:

"Bérangère! Bérangère!"

Suddenly, I heard the hum of an engine and the sound of a motorcar getting away. It must have been five hundred yards from where I was. I turned down a path and, at once, I saw footsteps in the mud—a man and a woman. These led me to the entrance of a cemetery which had not been used for over twenty years and which, standing on the boundary of two parishes, had become the subject of claims and counterclaims.

I found my way in. The tall grass had been trampled down along two lines which skirted the wall, passed before the remnants of what had once been the keeper's cottage, joined around the kerb of a cistern fitted up as a well and continued to the wall of a half-demolished little mortuary chapel.

Between the cistern and the chapel the soil had been trodden several times over. Beyond the chapel, there was only one set of footsteps—the man's.

I confess that my legs almost gave way, although I still had no definite idea about what might have happened. I examined the inside of the chapel and then walked around it.

Something lying on the ground, at the foot of the only wall left standing, attracted my attention. It was a number of bits of loose plaster which had fallen there and which were of a dark-grey color that at once reminded me of the wash with which the wall in my uncle's laboratory was coated.

I looked up. More pieces of plaster of the same color, placed flat against the wall and held in position by clamp-headed nails, formed another screen, an incomplete, broken screen, upon which I could plainly see that a fresh layer of substance had been spread.

But by whom? Evidently, by one of the two persons whom I had been tracking: the dandy with the glasses, or Bérangère, or perhaps by both. But for what reason? Was it to conjure up more miraculous visions? Was I to believe—this supposition quickly became a certainty—that the fragments of plaster had first been stolen from the rubbish in our garden and then pieced together like a mosaic?

In that case, if the conditions were the same, if the necessary substance was spread precisely in accordance with the details of my uncle's discovery, it was possible that I was standing opposite a screen identical to the wall in my uncle's laboratory...

While this was taking shape in my mind, I received an answer to my question when I saw the Three Eyes emerging from the depths of this new wall. They presently opened their threefold gaze upon me—a fixed and gloomy gaze.

Here, in this abandoned cemetery just as in the laboratory where my uncle had summoned these inexplicable phantoms from the void, the Three Eyes were awakening to life. They looked through the fragments of disjointed plaster, chipped in one place, cracked in another, as they had done through the carefully tended wall. They gazed in this solitude just as if Noël Dorgeroux had been here to kindle and feed their mysterious flame.

The gloomy eyes, however, were changing their expression. They became wicked, cruel, implacable, savage even. Then, they faded away. I waited for the visions which those three geometrical figures generally heralded, and, after a break a kind of pulsating light appeared, but so confused that it was difficult for me to make out any clearly defined scenes.

I could barely distinguish some trees, a river, a low-roofed house and some people, but it was all vague, misty, unfinished, broken up by the cracks in the plaster, impeded by causes of which I was ignorant. One might have fancied a certain hesitation in the will that evoked the image. Moreover, after a few fruitless attempts, and an effort of which I perceived the futility, the image abruptly vanished and everything relapsed into death and emptiness.

"Death and emptiness," I said aloud.

I repeated the words several times. They rang within me like a funeral echo with which Bérangère's memory now mingled. The nightmare of the Three Eyes had become one with the nightmare that drove me in her pursuit. And I remained standing in front of the abandoned chapel, uncertain, not knowing what to do.

Bérangère's footprints brought me back to the well, near which I found the marks of both her slender soles and her pointed heels in four places. The well was covered with a small, tiled dome. In years past, a bucket was lowered by means of a pulley to bring up the rainwater that had been gathered from the roof of the house.

There was, of course, no valid reason to make me believe that a crime had been committed. The footmarks did not constitute a sufficient clue. Nevertheless, I felt myself bathed in perspiration; and, leaning over the opening, from which floated a damp and mildewed breath, I shouted:

"Bérangère!"

I heard not a sound.

I lit a piece of paper, which I'd twisted into a torch, throwing a glimmer of light into the reservoir, but I saw nothing save a sheet of water, black as ink and motionless.

"No," I said in protest. "It's impossible. I have no right to imagine such an atrocity. Why should they have killed her? It was my uncle who was threatened, not her."

I continued my search and followed the man's single track. This led me to the far side of the cemetery, and then to a road lined with of fir-trees, where I came upon some cans of gasoline. The motorcar had started from here. The tire tracks ran through the wood.

I went no farther. It suddenly occurred to me that I first should think of my uncle, defend him, and take joint measures with him.

I therefore turned back, walking towards the post-office. But, remembering that this was Sunday, and that my uncle, after dropping his letter in the box, had likely returned to his laboratory, I ran back to the Lodge and called out to Valentine:

"Has my uncle come back? Has he read my note?"

"No," she replied. "He must have gone directly to his laboratory."

"But you should have seen him?"

"Not necessarily. He might have used the new entrance to the theater."

"I see," I said. "In that case, I'll go through the garden."

I hurried away, but I found the little door locked. Nut even though there was nothing to prove to me that my uncle was in the laboratory, I felt certain that he was—and I also felt that my assistance had come too late.

I called. No one answered. The door remained shut.

Terrified, I went back to the house and out into the street and ran around the Lodge in order to use the new entrance that Valentine had mentioned.

It turned out to be a tall gate, flanked on either side by a ticket office and giving access to a large courtyard in which stood the back of the theater.

This gate also was closed by means of a strong chain which my uncle had padlocked behind him.

What should I do? Remembering how Bérangère and I had climbed over the wall, I went to the other side of the laboratory in order to reach the old lamp-post. The same deserted path skirted the same stout plank fence, the corner of which ran into the fields.

When I came to this corner, I saw the lamp-post. At that moment, a man appeared on the top of the wall, caught hold of the post and let himself down. There was no room for doubt in my mind: that man had just been with my uncle! But what had passed between them?

The distance separating us was too great to allow me to distinguish his features. As soon as he saw me, he turned down the brim of his soft hat and drew the two ends of a muffler over his face. A loose-fitting grey rain-coat concealed his figure. I received the impression, however, that he was shorter and thinner than the dandy with the glasses.

"Stop!" I cried, as he ran away.

My call only hastened his flight. I darted forward in pursuit, shouting insults and threatening him with a revolver I did not have, but in vain. He covered the whole width of the fields, leapt over a hedge and reached the edge of the woods.

I must have been younger than he, for I soon perceived that the interval between us was decreasing. I should have caught him up, if we had been running across open country. But I lost sight of him at the first clump of trees; and I was about to abandon my efforts to catch up with him, when, suddenly, he retraced his steps and seemed to be looking for something.

I made a rush for him. He did not appear to be perturbed by my approach. He merely drew a revolver and pointed it at me, without saying a word or ceasing his investigations.

I now saw what he was looking for. Something lay gleaming in the grass. It was a piece of metal which, I soon realized, was none other than the steel plate on which Noël Dorgeroux had engraved his chemical formula.

We both flung ourselves to the ground at the same time. I was the first to grab the steel plate, but his hand gripped mine; and on it, half-covered by the sleeve of his rain-coat, there was blood!

I was startled and suffered from a moment's faintness. The vision of Noël Dorgeroux dying, possibly dead already, flashed upon me so suddenly that the man succeeded in overpowering me and stretching me underneath him.

As we lay one against the other, our faces almost touching, I only saw part of his, the lower half still being hidden by the muffler. But his two eyes glared at me, under the shadow of his hat, and we stared at each other in silence, while our hands continued to grapple.

Those eyes of his were cruel and implacable, the eyes of a murderer whose entire being is bent upon the supreme effort of killing. Where had I seen them before? For I certainly knew those savage, glittering eyes. Their gaze penetrated my brain which had already been deeply impressed with them. They bore a familiar look, which I had seen before. But when? In what eyes had I seen that savagery? In the eyes looming out of the wall perhaps? The eyes shown on the fabulous screen?

Yes, those were the eyes! I recognized them now! They had shone out of the infinite space that lay within the depths of the plaster! They had lived before my sight, a few minutes ago, on the ruined wall of the mortuary chapel. They were the same cruel, pitiless eyes, the eyes which had perturbed me then even as they were perturbing me now, sapping my last remnant of strength.

I released my hold. The man sprang up, dealt me a blow on the forehead with the butt of his revolver, then ran away, carrying the steel plate with him.

This time, I did not think of chasing after him. Without doing me any great hurt, the blow had stunned me. I was still tottering on my feet when I heard, in the woods, the same sound which I had heard near the cemetery: that of an engine being started and a car getting under way. The motorcar, driven by the dandy with the glasses, had come to fetch my assailant. The two villains, after having probably rid themselves of Bérangère, and certainly rid themselves of my uncle, were making off...

My heart wrung with anguish, I hurried back to the foot of the old lamp-post, hoisted myself to the top of the fence and jumped into the courtyard of the laboratory, between the main building and the wall of the new theater.

This wall, entirely rebuilt, taller and wider than it used to be, now had the size and importance of the outer wall of a Greek or Roman amphitheater. Two square columns and a canopy marked the place of the screen, whose plaster, from the distance at which I stood, did not seem yet to have been coated with its layer of a dark-grey composition, which explained why my uncle had left it uncovered.

Nor could I at first see the lower part, which was concealed by a heap of materials of all kinds. But how certain I felt of what I should see when I came nearer! How well I knew what was there, behind those planks and building materials!

My legs were trembling. I had to seek a support. It cost me an untold effort to take a few steps forward.

Right against the wall, in the very middle of his laboratory, Noël Dorgeroux lay prone, his arms twisted beneath him.

A cursory inspection showed me that he had been murdered with a pick-axe.

VIII. Someone Will Come Out Of The Shadows

Despite my uncle's advanced age, there had been a violent struggle. The murderer, whose footprints I traced along the path which led from the fence to the wall, had flung himself upon his victim and had first tried to strangle him. It was not until later that he had seized a pick-axe with which to strike Noël Dorgeroux.

Nothing of intrinsic value had been stolen. I found my uncle's watch and notebook untouched. But his waistcoat had been opened, and the lining, which formed a pocket, was, of course, empty.

I wasted no time. Passing through the garden and the Lodge, where I told old Valentine in a few words what had happened, I called our nearest neighbors, sent a boy running to the police station, and returned to the abandoned cemetery, accompanied by some men with ropes, a ladder and a lantern. It was growing dark when we arrived.

I had decided to go down the well myself; and I did so without experiencing any great emotions. Notwithstanding the reasons which had led me to fear that Bérangère might have been thrown into it, the crime appeared to me to be quite improbable. And I was right. Nevertheless, at the bottom, which was perforated by cracks and held only a few puddles of stagnant water, I found in the mud, among the stones, brickbats and potsherds, an empty bottle, the neck of which had been knocked off. I was struck by its blue color. This was doubtless the same bottle which had been taken from the dresser at the Lodge. When I brought it back to the Lodge later that evening, Valentine identified it for certain.

What had happened might therefore be reconstructed as follows: the dandy with the glasses, having the bottle in his possession, had gone to the cemetery to meet the motorcar waiting for him and had stopped in front of the chapel, to which were nailed the fragments from the laboratory wall. He had smeared these fragments with the liquid contained in the bottle. Then, when he heard me coming, he had thrown the bottle down the well and, without having time to see the picture which I myself saw ten minutes later, he'd run away and had gone in the car to pick up Noël Dorgeroux's murderer.

Things as they turned out confirmed my theories to a great extent. But what of Bérangère? What part had she played in all this? And what had happened to her?

The criminal investigation, which first began in the laboratory with the local gendarmes, was taken over the next day by an Investigating Magistrate and two detectives, which I assisted. We learned that the car containing the two accomplices had come from Paris on the morning of the day before, and that it had returned there the same night. Both coming and going, it had carried two men whose descriptions tallied exactly with that of the two criminals.

We were then favored by an extraordinary piece of luck. A road worker in the Bois de Boulogne told us, when asked about the motor-car, that he recognized it as having been kept in a garage in a house close to where he lived, and he also recognized the dandy with the glasses as one of the tenants of that same house!

He gave us the address. It was located behind the Jardin des Batignolles. It was an old tenement house swarming with tenants. As soon as we described the dandy to the concierge, she exclaimed:

"You mean, Monsieur Velmot—a tall, good-looking man, don't you? He has had a furnished flat here for over six months, but he only sleeps here now and again. He is out of town a great deal."

"Did he sleep at home last night?"

"Yes. He came back yesterday evening, in his motorcar, with a gentleman whom I had never seen before, and they did not leave until this morning."

"In the motorcar?"

"No. It's still in the garage."

"Have you the key of his flat?"

"Of course! I do the cleaning."

"Show us over, please."

The flat consisted of three small rooms; a dining-room and two bedrooms. It contained no clothes or papers. Velmot had taken everything with him in a portmanteau, as he did each time he went away, said the concierge. But pinned to the wall, amid a number of sketches, was a drawing which represented the Three Eyes so faithfully that it could not have been made, except by someone who had seen the miraculous visions.

"Let's go to the garage," said one of the detectives.

We had to call in a locksmith to gain admittance. In addition to the muffler and a coat stained with blood, we found two more mufflers and three silk handkerchiefs, all twisted and dirty. The license plate of the car had been recently unscrewed. The number, newly repainted, was false. Apart from these details, there was nothing especially worth noting.

I am trying to summarize the phases of the initial investigation as briefly as possible. This narrative is not a detective story anymore than it is a love story. The riddle of the Three Eyes, together with its solution, is the only object of this narrative, and the only interest which the reader can hope to find here. But, at the stage which we have reached, it is easy to understand that all these events were so closely interwoven that it is impossible to separate them from each other. One detail leads to the next, which in its turn affects what came before.

So I must return to my earlier question: what part had Bérangère played in all this? And what had happened to her? She had disappeared, suddenly, somewhere near the chapel. Beyond that point, there was not a trace of her, not a clue. And this inexplicable disappearance marked the conclusion of several weeks during which her behavior might easily have seemed unusual even to the most indulgent eyes.

I felt this so clearly that I declared emphatically to the Magistrate:

"She was captured and taken away."

"Prove it," he replied. "Find some justification for the secret rendezvous she made and kept all through the winter with that fellow Velmot."

The police based their suspicions on a disturbing fact which they had discovered and which I had missed. During his struggle with his assailant, very likely at the moment when the latter, after reducing my uncle to a state of helplessness, had stepped away to fetch the pick-axe, Noël Dorgeroux had managed to scrawl a few words with a broken flint at the foot of the screen. The writing was very faint and almost illegible, for the flint in places had merely scratched the plaster; nevertheless, it was possible to decipher the following:

B-ray... Berge...

The term *B-ray* evidently referred to his invention. My uncle's first thought, when threatened with death, had been to convey in the briefest—but also, unfortunately, the most unintelligible—form the particulars which would save his marvelous discovery from oblivion. *B-ray* was an expression which he himself understood, but which suggested nothing to those who did not know what he meant by it.

The five letters *B.E.R.G.E.*, on the other hand, allowed of only one interpretation. They stood for *Bergeronnette*, the pet name by which Noël Dorgeroux called his goddaughter.

"Very well," I told the Magistrate. "I agree with your interpretation. It relates to Bérangère. But my uncle was simply wishing to express his love for her, and his extreme anxiety on her behalf. In writing his goddaughter's name at the very moment when he was in mortal danger, he showed that he was uneasy about her, that he was recommending her to our care."

"Or that he was accusing her," retorted the Magistrate.

Bérangère accused by my uncle! Bérangère capable of being complicit in the murder of her godfather! I remember shrugging, but there was no reply that I could make beyond protests based upon no actual fact and contradicted by appearances. All that I said was:

"I fail to see what motive she could have had!"

"A very considerable motive: the exploitation of that wonderful scientific secret which you mentioned."

"But she was ignorant of it!"

"How do you know? If she was in league with the two accomplices, she wouldn't have been. The manuscript which Monsieur Dorgeroux sent you has disappeared: who might have been in a better position to steal it? However, I make no accusations. I have my suspicions, but that's all. All I'm trying to discover is the truth."

But the most minute investigations led to no result. Was Bérangère also a victim of the two criminals?

The Magistrate wrote to her father in Toulouse. Massignac replied that he had been in bed for a fortnight with a sharp attack of influenza, and that he would come to Paris as soon as he was well, but that, having received no news from his daughter for the past year, he was unable to provide any particulars about her.

So, when all was said and done, whether kidnapped, as I preferred to believe, or in hiding, as the police suspected, Bérangère was nowhere to be found.

Meanwhile, the public was beginning to grow excited about a case which, before long, turned into a pitch of delirium. No doubt, at first there was merely a question of the crime itself. The murder of Noël Dorgeroux, the abduction of his goddaughter—the police had agreed, at my earnest entreaties, to treat this as the official version—the theft of my uncle's manuscript, the theft of the formula.. All this, at the outset, only puzzled men's minds as a cunningly-devised conspiracy and a cleverly-executed crime. But not many days elapsed before the revelations of my uncle's discovery, which I was constrained to make diverted all the attention of the newspapers and all the curiosity of the public.

Notwithstanding the promise of silence which I had given my uncle, I as forced to speak the truth. I had to answer the Magistrate's questions, to tell all I knew, to explain matters, to give details, to write a report, to protest against ill-formed judgments, to rectify mistakes, to specify, enumerate, classify, in short, to confide to the authorities—and by way of consequence, the eager reporters—all that my uncle had said to me, all his dreams, all the wonders of the wall, and all the phantasmal visions which I had beheld upon it.

Before the week was over, Paris, France, the whole world, knew in every detail, save for a few details which concerned Bérangère and myself alone, what was, at once and spontaneously, described as the mystery of the Three Eyes.

Of course, I was met with irony, sarcasm and uproarious laughter. A miracle finds no believers, except among its astounded witnesses. And what but a miracle could be put forward as the cause of a phenomenon which, I maintained, had no credible cause?

The viewing of the execution of Edith Cavell had been a miracle. So was the representation of the fight between two airmen, and the scene in which Noël Dorgeroux's son had been shot. So, above all, was the looming of those Three Eyes, which throbbed with life, which gazed at the spectator, and which were the eyes of the very people about to figure in the spectacle!

Nevertheless, one by one, voices were raised in my defense. My past was scrutinized, the value of my evidence was weighed, and although some people were still inclined to accuse me of being sick or prone to hallucinations, at least they had to admit my absolute *bona fides*. A party of adherents took up the cudgels for me. There was a noisy battle of opinions. Ah, my poor uncle had asked for wide publicity for his theater! His fondest wishes were now far exceeded by the strident and tremendous clamor which continued like an unbroken peal of thunder.

For the rest, all this uproar was dominated by one idea, which took shape gradually and summed up the thousand theories which everyone had been debating. I am copying it from a newspaper article which I have carefully preserved:

In any case, whatever opinion we may hold of Noël Dorgeroux's alleged discovery, whatever view we may take of Victorien Beaugrand's common sense and mental balance, one thing is certain: we shall sooner or later know the truth. When two such competent people as Velmot and his accomplice join forces to accomplish a definite task, namely the theft of a scientific secret, when they carry out their plot so skillfully, when they succeed beyond all hopes, their purpose is certainly not to enjoy the results of their enterprise in secret.

If they have Noël Dorgeroux's manuscript in their hands, together with the chemical formula that completes it, their intention is assuredly to make all the profits on which Noël Dorgeroux himself was counting. To make these profits, his secret must be exploited. And to exploit such a secret, its possessors must act openly, publicly, in the face of the world. To do this, it will not be advantageous to them to settle down in a remote corner of France or elsewhere and to set up their enterprise there. To do so, also, would be the same as an admission of guilt. No, it will pay them better and do them no more harm to take up their quarters frankly and cynically in the Dorgeroux theater and make use of what has been accomplished there by the great scientist himself.

In summary, therefore, we believe that before long, someone will come out of the shadows, remove the mask from his face, and the conclusion of this unfinished drama will be enacted in the fullness of the day three weeks hence, on the date of May 14, as fixed, during the inauguration of the theater erected by Noël Dorgeroux. And this inauguration will take place under the vigorous management of the man who will be—who already is—the owner of this prodigious secret—a formidable person, we must admit.

The argument was entirely logical. Stolen jewels are sold in secret. Money changes hands anonymously. But an invention yields no profit unless it is exploited publicly.

Meanwhile, the days passed and no one was "coming out of the shadows." The two accomplices betrayed not a sign of life. It was now known that Velmot, the dandy with the glasses, had practiced all sorts of trades. Some Paris manufacturers, for whom he had traveled in the provinces, furnished an exact description of his person. The police learned a number of things about him, but not enough to enable them to lay hands upon him.

Nor did a careful scrutiny of Noël Dorgeroux's other papers supply the least information. All that the authorities found was a sealed, unaddressed envelope, which they opened. The contents surprised me greatly. They consisted of a will, dated five years back, in which my uncle, while naming me as his residuary legatee, gave and bequeathed to his goddaughter, Bérangère Massignac, his laboratory and everything it might contain on the day of his death. With the exception of this document—which was now of no importance, since my uncle, in his last letter to me, had expressed different intentions—the police found nothing but various notes which had no bearing upon the great secret.

Thereupon, they indulged in the wildest conjectures. Not even the greatest chemists whom they called in to examine the wall were able to throw a light on my uncle's secret. Their examination revealed nothing in particular, for the layer of plaster with which it was covered had not received any special glaze, and it was precisely the formula of this glaze that constituted Noël Dorgeroux's secret.

But the glaze existed on the old chapel in the cemetery, where I had seen the Three Eyes appear. They did find something clinging to the surface of the fragments of plaster taken from that spot, but they were not able, even with these, to produce a compound capable of yielding any sort of vision. The right formula was obviously lacking, and so, no doubt, was some other essential ingredient which had already been washed away by the sun or the rain.

At the end of April, there was no reason to believe in the prophecies that had predicted the opening of the theater. The curiosity of the public increased at each fresh disappointment and on each new day spent in waiting. The Lodge had become a place of pilgrimage. Motorcars and carriages arrived in swarms. The people crowded outside the locked gates and the fence, trying to catch a glimpse of the wall. I even received letters containing offers to buy the laboratory at any price that I chose to name.

One day, old Valentine showed into the drawing-room a gentleman who said that he had come on important business. I saw a man of medium height with hair which was turning grey and a face which was wider than it was long, made even wider by a pair of bushy whiskers and a perpetual smile. His threadbare dress and down-at-heel shoes denoted anything but a rich man. However, he expressed himself at once in the language of a person to whom money is no object.

"I have any amount of capital behind me," he declared, cheerfully and before he had even told me his name. "My plans are made. All that remains is for you and me to come to terms."

"I beg your pardon?" I asked.

"I have come to make you a business proposition!"

"I am sorry, sir," I replied, "but I am not interested in any business at the moment."

"That's a pity!" he cried, still more cheerfully and with his mouth spreading even farther across his face. "I should have been glad to take you into partnership. However, since you're not willing, I shall act alone, without, of course, exceeding the rights which I have in your uncle's laboratory."

"Your rights in the laboratory?" I echoed, astounded by his statement.

"Yes," he answered, with a loud laugh. "My rights. That's the exact word."

"I don't follow you."

"I admit that I wasn't very clear. Well, suppose—you'll soon understand why—that I have inherited Monsieur Dorgeroux's property."

I was beginning to lose patience and I took the fellow up sharply:

"I have no time to spare for jesting, sir. My uncle left no relatives except myself."

"I didn't say that I had come into his property as a relative."

"As what, then?"

"As an heir, simply... As the lawful heir, specifically named as such by Noël Dorgeroux."

I was a little taken aback and, after a moment's thought, asked:

"Do you mean to say that my uncle made a will in your favor?"

"I do."

"Show it to me."

"There's no need to show it to you. You've already seen it."

"I have?"

"Yes. You saw it the other day. It must be in the hands of the Investigating Magistrate."

I lost my temper:

"Ah! It's that you're speaking of! Well, to begin with, the will isn't valid. I have a letter from my uncle..."

He interrupted me.

"That letter doesn't affect the validity of the will. Anyone will tell you that."

"So what?" I exclaimed. "Even granting you that it might be valid, my uncle mentions nobody that will it except myself for the Lodge and his goddaughter for the laboratory. The only one who benefits, other than myself, is Bérangère."

"Quite so, quite so," replied the man, without changing countenance. "But nobody knows what has become of Mademoiselle Massignac. Suppose that she were dead..."

I grew indignant.

"She is not dead! She can't be!"

"Very well," he said, calmly. "Then suppose that she's alive, that she's been kidnapped, or that she's in hiding. In any event, one fact is certain: she is under twenty, and consequently she's a minor, and therefore, she cannot administer her own property. From a legal point of view, she exists only in the person of her guardian, who, in this case, happens to be her father."

"And her father?" I asked, anxiously.

"Is myself."

He put on his hat, took it off again with a bow, and said:

"Théodore Massignac, forty-two years of age, a native of Toulouse, a commercial traveler in wines."

It was a violent blow. The truth suddenly appeared to me in all its brutal nakedness. This man, this shady and wily individual, was Bérangère's father; and he had come in the name of the two accomplices, working in their interest and placing at their service the powers with which circumstances had favored him.

"Her father?" I murmured. "Can it be possible? You are her father?"

"Yes, I am," he replied, with a fresh outburst of hilarity. "And, as such, I'm also the beneficiary of Noël Dorgeroux's bequest, with the right to draw all profits from it for the next eighteen months—for eighteen months only! You can imagine that I'm itching to take possession of the laboratory to complete the works and prepare for May 14 an inauguration worthy in every respect of my old friend Noël Dorgeroux."

I felt beads of perspiration trickling down my forehead. He had spoken the words which were expected and had been foretold. He was the man of whom public opinion had said: *When the time comes, someone will come out of the shadows.*

IX. The Man Who Came Out Of The Shadows

When the time comes, the newspapers had said, *someone will come out of the shadows and remove the mask from his face.*

That face now beamed expansively before me. That someone, who was about to play the game of the two accomplices, was Bérangère's father. And the same question continued to suggest itself, each time more painfully than the last:

What part had Bérangère played in this horrible tragedy?

There was a long, heavy silence between us. I began to stride across the room and stopped near the fireplace, where a dying fire was smoldering. From there. I could see Massignac in the mirror, without his perceiving it; and his face, at rest, surprised me by a gloomy expression which was not unknown to me. I had probably seen some photograph of him in Bérangère's possession.

"It's curious," I said, "that your daughter should not have written to you."

I had turned around very briskly; nevertheless, he had had time to expand his mouth and resume his smile:

"Alas," he said, "the dear child hardly ever wrote to me and cared little about her poor daddy. I, on the other hand, am very fond of her. A daughter's always a daughter, you know. So you can imagine how I jumped for joy when I read in the papers that she had come into money. I should at last be able to devote myself to her and use all my strength and my energy for the great and wonderful task of defending her interests and her fortune."

He spoke in a honeyed voice and assumed a false and unctuous air which exasperated me. I questioned him:

"How do you propose to fulfill that task?"

"Quite simply," he replied, "by continuing Noël Dorgeroux's work."

"How so?"

"By opening his theater."

"For what purpose?"

"To show to the public the fantastic images which your uncle used to produce."

"Have you seen them?"

"No. I speak from your evidence and your interviews."

"Do you know how my uncle used to produce them?"

"I do, since yesterday evening."

"Then you have seen the manuscript of which I was robbed and the formula stolen by the murderer?"

"Since yesterday evening, I say."

"But how?" I exclaimed, excitedly.

"How? By a simple trick."

"What do you mean?"

He showed me a bundle of newspapers from the day before and continued, with a smirking air:

"If you had read carefully yesterday's papers, or at least the more important of them, you would have noticed a discreet advertisement. It read, '*Proprietor of the Laboratory wishes to purchase the two documents necessary for working. He can be seen this evening at the Place Vendôme.*' Nothing much in there, right? But to the possessors of the two documents in question, how clear in its meaning... and what a bait! To them, it was the one opportunity of making a profit, because, with all the publicity attaching to this affair, they were unable to benefit from their crime without revealing their identities to the public. My calculation was correct. After I had waited an hour by the Vendôme Column, a luxurious motorcar picked me up, you might almost say without stopping, and, ten minutes afterwards, dropped me at the Place de l'Étoile, with the documents now in my possession. I spent the night reading the manuscript. Oh, my dear sir, what a genius your uncle was! What a revolution his discovery is! And in what a masterly way he expounded it! I never read anything so methodical and so lucid! All that remains for me to do is now mere child's play."

I had listened to Massignac with ever-increasing amazement. Was he assuming that anybody would for a moment credit so ridiculous a tale?

He was laughing, however, with a look of a man who congratulates himself on the events with which he is mixed up, or rather, perhaps, on the very skillful way in which he believes himself to have manipulated them.

With one hand, I pushed in his direction the hat which he had laid on the table. Then I opened the door leading into the hall.

He rose and said:

"I am staying close by, at the Station Hotel. Would you mind having any letters which may come for me here forwarded there? For I suppose you have no room for me at the Lodge?"

I abruptly gripped him by the arm and shouted:

"You do know what you're risking, don't you?"

"In doing what?"

"In pursuing your enterprise."

"Upon my word, I don't quite see..."

"Prison, sir, prison."

"Oh, come on! Prison!"

"Prison, sir. The police will never accept all your stories and all your lies!"

His mouth widened into a new laugh:

"What big words! And how unjust, when addressed to a respectable father who seeks nothing but his daughter's happiness! No, no, sir, believe me, the inauguration will take place on May 14... unless, of course, you oppose the wishes which your uncle expressly stated in his will..."

He gave me a questioning look, which betrayed a certain uneasiness; and I myself wavered as to the answer which I ought to give him. My hesitation yielded to a motive of which I did not weigh the value clearly, but which seemed to me so imperious that I declared:

"I shall raise no opposition; not that I respect a will which does not represent my uncle's real intentions, but because I am bound to sacrifice everything to his fame. If Noël Dorgeroux's discovery depends on you, go ahead. The means which you have employed to get hold of it do not concern me."

With a fresh burst of merry laughter and a low bow, he left the room.

That evening, in the course of a visit to our family's solicitor, and the next day, through the newspapers, he boldly set forth his claims, which, I may say, from a legal point of view, were recognized as absolutely legitimate. But, two days later, he was summoned to appear before the Investigating Magistrate and an inquiry was opened against him.

Against him is the right term. Certainly, there was no fact to be laid to his charge. Certainly, he was able to prove that he had been ill in bed in Toulouse, nursed by a woman who had been looking after him for a month, and that he had left his apartment there only to come straight to Paris. But what had he done in Paris? Whom had he seen? From whom had he obtained the manuscript and the formula? He was unable to furnish explanations in reply to any of these questions.

He did not even try.

"I am pledged to secrecy," he said. "I gave my word of honor not to say anything about those who handed me the documents I needed."

Massignac's word of Honor! Massignac's scruples! Lies, of course! Hypocrisy! Subterfuge! But, all the same, however suspect he might be, it was difficult to know of what exactly to accuse him, or how to proceed with such accusation when made.

And then, there was this suspicion, perhaps even a presumption, that Massignac was nothing but the willing tool of the two criminals. But all this was swept away by the great movement of curiosity that carried people off their feet. Judicial procedure, ordinary precautions, regular adjournments, legal procrastinations which would normally delay the entry into possession of a legatee were one and all neglected and abandoned. The public wanted to see and know, and Théodore Massignac was the man who held the prodigious secret.

He was therefore allowed to have the keys to the laboratory and the theater, and went in alone, or with laborers upon whom he kept a close eye, replacing them often with fresh crews in order to avoid plots and machinations. He often went to Paris, throwing off the scent of the detectives who dogged his every movements, and returned with bottles and cans carefully wrapped up.

On the day before that fixed for the inauguration, the police were no wiser than on the first day in matters concerning Massignac, or Velmot's hiding place, or the murderer's, or Bérangère's. The same ignorance prevailed regarding Noël Dorgeroux's secret, the circumstances of his death, and the ambiguous words which he had scribbled on the plaster of the wall before expiring. As for the miraculous visions which I have described, they were denied or accepted as vigorously and unreasonably by both disputing parties. In short, nobody knew anything.

And this was likely the reason why the thousand seats of the theater were sold out within hours. Priced at a hundred francs apiece, they were bought up by half-a-dozen speculators who resold them at trice and three times their original price. How delighted my poor uncle would have been, had he lived to see this!

The night before May 14, I slept very badly, haunted by nightmares that kept on waking me with a start. At the first glimmer of dawn, I was sitting on the side of my bed when, in the deep silence, which was barely broken by the twittering of a few birds, I seemed to hear the sound of a key in a lock and a door creaking on its hinges.

I must explain that, since my uncle's death, I had been sleeping next to the room that used to be his. Now, the noise came from that room, from which I was separated only by a glazed door covered with a chintz curtain. I listened and heard the sound of a chair moved from its place. There was certainly someone in the next room; and this someone, obviously unaware that I occupied the adjoining chamber, was taking scarcely any precautions. But how had he gotten in?

I sprang from the bed, slipped on my trousers, took up a revolver, and drew aside a corner of the curtain. At first, the shutters were closed and the room was plunged in darkness; I saw only an indistinct shadow. Then the window was opened softly. Somebody lifted the iron bar and pushed back the shutters, thus letting the light in.

I now saw a woman return to the middle of the room. She was draped from head to foot in a brown cloak. Nevertheless, I recognized her at once.

It was Bérangère!

I had a feeling not so much of amazement as of sudden and profound pity at the sight of her emaciated face, her poor face, once so bright and eager, now so sad and wan. I did not even think of rejoicing at the fact of her being alive, nor did I ask myself what clandestine business had brought her back to the Lodge. The one thing that held me captive was the painful spectacle of her pallid face, with its feverish, burning eyes and blue eyelids. Her cloak betrayed the shrunken figure beneath it.

Her heart must have been beating terribly, for she held her two hands to her chest to suppress its throbbing. She even had to lean on the edge of the table. She staggered and nearly fell. Poor Bérangère! I felt anguish-stricken as I watched her.

She pulled herself together, however, and looked around. Then, with a tottering gait, she went to the mantelpiece, where two old engravings, framed in black with a gold beading, hung on either side of the mirror. She climbed on a chair and took down the one on the right, a portrait of d'Alembert.[40]

Stepping down from the chair, she examined the back of the frame, which was closed by a piece of old cardboard, the edges of which were fastened to the sides of the frame by strips of gummed cloth. Bérangère cut these strips with a pen knife, bending back the tacks which held the cardboard in position. It came out of the frame; and I then saw—she had her back turned to me, so no detail escaped me—that there was a large sheet of paper covered with my uncle's writing inserted between the cardboard and the engraving. At the top, in red ink, was a drawing of the three geometrical eyes.

Next came the following words, in bold black capitals:

---

[40] Jean-Baptiste le Rond d'Alembert (1717-1783), French mathematician, physicist and philosopher. Until 1759 he was, together with Denis Diderot, a co-editor of the *Encyclopédie*. D'Alembert's formula for obtaining solutions to the wave equation is named after him.

Instructions for working my discovery, abridged from the manuscript sent to my nephew.

And forty or fifty very closely-written lines followed, in a hand too small to allow me to decipher them from a distance.

Besides, I had not the time. Bérangère merely glanced at the paper. Having found the object of her search and obtained possession of an additional document which my uncle had provided in case the manuscript should be lost, she folded it up, slipped it into her bodice, replaced the cardboard and hung the engraving where she had found it.

Was she going away? If so, she was bound to return as she had come, that is to say through my uncle's dressing-room on the other side of the bedroom, of which she had left the communicating door ajar. I was about to stop her and had already taken hold of the handle, when, suddenly, she moved a few steps towards my uncle's bed and fell on her knees, stretching out her hands in despair.

Her sobs rose in the silence. She stammered words which I was able to catch:

"Godfather! My poor godfather!"

And she passionately kissed the coverlet of the bed beside which she must often have sat up watching my uncle when he was ill.

Her fit of crying lasted a long time and did not cease until as I entered. Then she turned her head, saw me, and stood up slowly, without taking her eyes from my face:

"You!" she murmured.

Seeing her make for the door, I said:

"Don't go, Bérangère."

She stopped, looking paler than ever, with drawn features.

"Give me that sheet of paper," I said, in a voice of command.

She handed it to me, with a quick movement. After a brief pause, I continued:

"Why did you come to fetch it? My uncle told you of its existence, didn't he? And you... you were taking it to my uncle's murderers, so that they might have nothing more to fear and be the only persons to know his secret? Speak, Bérangère, will you?"

I had raised my voice and was advancing towards her. She took another step back.

"You shall not move, do you hear? Stay where you are. Listen to me and answer me!"

She made no further attempt to move. Her eyes were filled with such distress that I adopted a calmer demeanor:

"Answer me," I repeated, very gently. "You know that, whatever you may have done, I am your friend, your indulgent friend, and that I mean to help you and advise you. My feelings for you are proof against everything. It is more than

205

affection; you know what they are, don't you, Bérangère? You know that I love you?"

Her lips quivered, she tried to speak, but could not. I repeated again and again:

"I love you! I love you!"

And, each time, she shuddered, as if these words, which I spoke with infinite emotion, which I had never spoken so seriously or sincerely before, wounded her in the very depths of her soul.

I tried to put my hand on her shoulder, but she avoided my friendly touch.

"What can you see to fear in me?" I asked. "I told you I love you? Why not confess everything? You are not a free agent, are you? You are being forced to act as you do and you hate it?"

Once more, anger was overpowering me. I was exasperated by her silence. I saw no way of compelling her to reply, of overcoming that incomprehensible obstinacy, except by clasping her in my arms and yielding to the instinct of violence which urged me towards some brutal action.

I stepped boldly forward, but she spun around on her heels, so swiftly that I thought that she would drop to the floor in the doorway. I followed her into the other room. She uttered a terrible scream. At the same moment, I was knocked down by a sudden blow. Massignac, who had been hiding in the dressing room and watching us, had leapt at me and was attacking me furiously, while Bérangère fled to the staircase.

"Your daughter," I spluttered, defending myself. "Your daughter!... Stop her!..."

The words were senseless, seeing that Massignac, beyond a doubt, was Bérangère's accomplice, or rather the inspiring force behind her, as indeed he proved by his determination to put me out of action, in order to protect her against my pursuit.

We rolled over the carpet and each of us was trying to master his adversary. Massignac was no longer laughing. He was striking harder blows than ever, but without using any weapon and without any murderous intent. I hit back as lustily and soon discovered that I was getting the better of him.

This gave me additional strength. I succeeded in flattening him beneath me. He stiffened every muscle to no purpose. We lay clutching each other, face to face, eye to eye. I took him by the throat and snarled:

"Ah! I shall get it out of you now, you wretch, and learn at last..."

And suddenly I stopped. My words broke off in a cry of horror and I clapped my hand to his face in such a way as to hide the lower part of it, leaving only the eyes visible. Oh, those eyes riveted on mine! I knew them! Not with their customary expression of smug and hypocritical cheerfulness, but with the other expression, which I was slowly beginning to remember. Yes, I remembered them now, those two savage, implacable eyes, filled with hatred and cruelty, those eyes which I had seen on the wall of the chapel, those eyes which had looked at me on that same day, when I lay gasping in the murderer's grip in the woods.

And again, as on that occasion, my strength forsook me. Those savage eyes, those atrocious eyes, Massignac's real eyes, overpowered me.

He freed himself with a laugh of triumph and, speaking in calm and deliberate accents, said:

"You're no match for me, young fellow! Don't you come meddling in my affairs again!"

Then, pushing me away, he ran off in the same direction as Bérangère.

A few minutes later, I perceived that the sheet of paper which the daughter had found behind the old engraving had been taken from me by her father; and then, but not until then, I understood the true purpose of his attack.

The theater was duly inaugurated on the afternoon of that same day. Seated in the box-office was the manager of the establishment, the possessor of the great secret, Théodore Massignac—Noël Dorgeroux's murderer.

X. The Crowd Sees

Théodore Massignac sat behind the counter at the box-office! Théodore Massignac, when a dispute of any kind arose, left his desk and hastened to settle it! Théodore Massignac walked up and down, checking the tickets, showing people to their seats, speaking a pleasant word here, giving a masterful order there, and doing all these things with his everlasting smile and his obsequious graciousness.

He displayed not the slightest sign of embarrassment. Everybody knew that Massignac was the fellow with the broad face and the wide-cleft mouth who was attracting the police's attention. And everybody was fully aware that Massignac was at the very least the straw man who had carried out the whole business and made away with Noël Dorgeroux's invention. But none of this interfered with Massignac's jovial mood—not the sneers, nor the apparent hostility of the public, nor the more or less discreet supervision of the detectives attached to his person.

He even had had the effrontery to paste on boards, to the right and left of the entrance, two great posters representing Noël Dorgeroux's handsome face, with its grave and candid features!

These posters gave rise to a brief altercation between us. It was pretty lively, though it passed unnoticed by others. Scandalized by the sight of them, I went up to him, a little while before the time set for the opening, and, in a voice trembling with anger, I said:

"Remove those at once! I will not have them displayed. The rest, I don't care about. But this is too much! It's a disgrace and an outrage!"

He feigned an air of amazement.

"An outrage? You call it an outrage to honor your uncle's memory and to display the portrait of the talented inventor whose discovery is on the point of revolutionizing the world? I thought I was paying homage to him."

I was beside myself with rage.

"You shan't do it," I spluttered. "I will not consent, I will not consent to be an accomplice to your infamy."

"Oh, yes, you will!" he said, with a laugh. "You'll consent to this as you'll do to all the rest. It's all part of the game, young fellow. You've got to swallow that bitter pill because Uncle Dorgeroux's fame must be made to soar above all. Of course, I know, a word from you and I may be arrested. But what then? What will become of your uncle's great invention? I'll tell you, my lad! It'll end up in the trash because I'm the sole possessor of all his secrets and his formula. The sole possessor, do you understand? My friend Velmot, the man with the glasses, was only a tool. So was Bérangère. Therefore, if Théodore Massignac is put away, that's an end to the astounding fame of Noël Dorgeroux. No more glory, no more immortality. Is that what you really want, young man?"

Without waiting for my reply, he added:

"And then, there's something else—a word or two which I overheard last night. So you're in love with my daughter, aren't you? Ha! Ha! You're prepared to defend her against all dangers! Well, in that case, be logical, what do I have to fear? If you betray me, you also betray your sweetheart, am I right? Daddy and his little girl were a team, working hand and glove, you might say. If you arrest one, what becomes of the other? Ah, I see you're beginning to understand! You'll be good now, won't you? There! That's much better! We shall see a happy ending yet; you'll have heaps of children crowding around your knees and who will thank me for getting them a nice little earner!"

He stopped and watched me, with a jeering air. Clenching my fists, I shouted, furiously:

"You, villain! Oh, what a scoundrel you are!"

But some people were coming and he turned his back on me, after whispering:

"Hush, Victorien! Don't insult your future father-in-law."

I restrained myself. The horrible brute was right. I was condemned to silence by motives so powerful that Massignac would soon be able to fulfill his plan without having to fear the least revolt of conscience on my part. Noël Dorgeroux and Bérangère were watching over him.

Meanwhile, the theater was filling up fast, and the motorcars continued to arrive in swift succession, pouring forth a torrent of privileged people who, because of their wealth or their position, had paid anywhere from ten to twenty louis for a seat. Financiers, millionaires, famous actresses, newspaper proprietors, artistic and literary celebrities, British and American magnates, secretaries of great labor unions, all flocked feverishly towards that unknown spectacle, of which no program was available, and which they were not even certain of beholding, since it was impossible to say whether Noël Dorgeroux's secret had really been recovered and employed in the right way.

Indeed, no one, among those who believed the story, was in a position to declare that Massignac had not taken advantage of the whole business in order to arrange the most elaborate of hoaxes. The very tickets and posters contained these words, hardly meant to be reassuring:

In the event of unfavorable weather, the tickets will be available for the following day. Should the exhibition be prevented by any other cause, the money paid for the seats will not be refunded; and no claims to that effect shall be entertained.

Yet, nothing had restrained the tremendous outburst of curiosity. Whether confident or suspicious, people insisted on being there. Besides, the weather was fine. The sun shone out of a cloudless sky. Why not indulge in the somewhat anxious gaiety that filled the hearts of the crowd?

Everything was ready. Thanks to his wonderful activity and his remarkable powers of organization, Massignac, assisted by architects and contractors, and acting on the plans drawn by my uncle, had completed Noël Dorgeroux's work. He had recruited a numerous staff, especially a large and stalwart body of men, who, as I heard, were lavishly paid and who were tasked with the duty of keeping order.

As for the theater itself, built of reinforced concrete, it was completely filled up, well laid out, and quite comfortable. Twelve rows of elbowed seats, supplied with movable cushions, surrounded a floor which rose in a gentle slope, divided into twelve tiers arranged in a wide semicircle. Behind these was a series of spacious private boxes, and, at the back, a lounge, the floor of which was not more than ten or twelve feet above ground level.

Opposite all this was the wall itself. It stood well away from the seats, being built on a foundation of masonry and separated from the spectators by an empty orchestra pit. Furthermore, a grating, six feet high, prevented access to it, at least as regards its central portion. When I say a grating, I mean a businesslike grating, with spiked rails and crossbars forming too close a mesh to allow even the passage of a man's arm.

The central part of the wall was the screen, which was raised to about the level of the fourth or fifth tier of seats. Two pilasters, standing at eight or ten yards' distance from each other, marked its boundaries and supported an overhanging canopy. For the moment, all this space was masked by an iron curtain, roughly daubed with gaudy and badly-drawn landscapes.

At half-past three, there was not a vacant seat, nor an unoccupied corner, in the theater. The police had ordered the doors to be closed. The crowd was beginning to grow impatient and give signs of a certain irritability, which betrayed itself in the hum of a thousand voices, nervous laughter and jeers, which were becoming increasingly caustic.

"If the thing goes wrong," said a man by my side, "there will be some fracas."

I had taken up my stand, with some journalists of my acquaintance, in the lounge, amid a noisy multitude which was all the more peevish because they were not as comfortably seated as the audience in the stalls.

Another journalist, who was invariably well-informed and of whom I had seen a good deal lately, replied:

"Yes, there will be a fracas, but that's not our worthy Massignac's main danger. He is risking something far more serious."

"What?" I asked.

"To be arrested."

"Do you mean that?"

"I do. It's the universal curiosity that has kept him free until now. If it's satisfied, he'll be all right, but if not, if he fails, they'll lock him up. The arrest warrant has already been signed."

I shuddered. Massignac's arrest implied the gravest possible peril to Bérangère.

"And you may be sure," my acquaintance continued, "that he is fully aware of this, and that he is feeling anything but cheerful inside."

"Inside, perhaps," replied one of the others, "but he doesn't allow it to appear on the surface. There, look at him: did you ever see such swagger?"

Suddenly, a louder din came from the crowd. Below us, Massignac was walking crossing the empty space of the orchestra pit. He was accompanied by a dozen of those sturdy fellows who composed his staff. He made them sit down on two benches which were evidently reserved for them and, with the most natural air, gave them his instructions. And his gestures so clearly denoted the sense of the orders being imparted—what they would have to do if anyone attempted to approach the wall—that a loud clamor of protest arose.

Massignac turned towards the audience, without appearing in the least put out, and, with a smiling face, gave a careless shrug of the shoulders, as if to say:

"What's the trouble? I'm taking precautions. Surely, I'm entitled to do that!"

And, retaining his bantering geniality, he took a key from his waistcoat pocket, opened a little gate in the railing, and entered the last enclosure before the wall.

This looked so much like a lion-tamer taking refuge behind the bars of his cage, and made such a comic impression that the hisses from the crowd became mingled with bursts of laughter.

"The worthy Massignac is right," said my friend the journalist, in a tone of approval. "In this way, he avoids two perils: if he fails, the malcontents won't be able to break his head; and if he succeeds, the enthusiasts can't make a rush for the wall and learn the secret. He's a smart customer, that one. He has prepared for every eventuality."

There was a stool in the fortified enclosure. Massignac sat down on it, half facing the spectators, some four paces in front of the wall. Then, holding his watch towards us, he tapped it with his other hand to explain that the decisive hour was about to strike.

The extension of time which he thus obtained lasted for some minutes. But then, the uproar began anew and became deafening. People suddenly lost all confidence. The idea of a hoax took possession of every mind, all the more as people were unable to grasp why the spectacle should begin at any particular time rather than another, since it all depended solely on Massignac.

"Curtain! Curtain!" they cried.

After a moment, not so much in obedience as because the hands of his watch seemed to command it, Massignac rose, went to the wall, slipped back a wooden slab which covered two electric buttons, and pressed one with his finger.

The iron curtain descended slowly and sank into the ground.

The screen appeared in its entirety, in broad daylight and of larger proportions than the ordinary.

I shuddered before this flat surface, over which the mysterious coating was spread in a dark-grey layer. The same tremor ran through the crowd, which was also seized with the recollection of my depositions. Was it possible that we were about to behold one of those extraordinary spectacles, the story of which had given rise to so much controversial discussion? How ardently I longed for it! At this solemn minute, I forget all the phases of the drama, all the loathing that I felt for Massignac, all that had to do with Bérangère, the madness of her actions, the anguish of my love, and thought only of the great game that was being played around my uncle's discovery. Would the miracle that I had seen before now vanish in the darkness of the past? Or would the incredible visions arise again to teach the future the name of Noël Dorgeroux? Had I been right in sacrificing vengeance for my uncle's murder on the altar of his posthumous glory? Had I become the accomplice of the murderer in not denouncing his abominable crime?

Yes, I felt I had made myself Massignac's accomplice and even, deep down, his collaborator and his ally. If he had need of me, here was no doubt in my mind that I would have hastened to his side. I would have encouraged him with all my confidence and assisted him to the full extent of my abilities. First and foremost, I would have strived to see him emerge victorious from the struggle he had undertaken, because, above all, I wanted my uncle's secret to come to life again. I wanted light to spring from the shadow. I did not wish for this noble genius' many years of research and his supreme discovery to be flung back into oblivion.

Now, not a sound broke the profound silence. The people's faces were set, their eyes all focused on the wall. They experienced the same anxiety as I, waiting for that which was as yet invisible, but which was preparing to emerge from the depths of the mysterious substance. And the implacable will of a thousand spectators united with that of Massignac, who stood there below, with his back bent and his head thrust forward; wildly questioning the impassive wall.

Massignac was the first to see the first premonitory gleam. A cry escaped his lips, while his two hands frantically beat the air. And, almost at the same time, like sparks crackling on every side, other cries were scattered in the silence, which was instantly restored, heavier and denser than before.

The Three Eyes were there.

The Three Eyes had just appeared inside their three curved triangles on the wall.

In the presence of this inconceivable phenomenon, the spectators did not have to undergo the kind of initiation through which I had passed. To them, from the outset, three geometrical figures, dismal and lifeless though they were, represented three eyes; to them also, they were living eyes even before they became animated. And the excitement became even more intense when those lidless eyes, consisting of hard, symmetrical lines, suddenly became filled with an expression which made them as intelligible to us as the eyes of any human person.

It was a harsh, proud expression, containing flashes of malignant joy. And I knew—as we all knew—that this was not just a random expression, with which the Three Eyes had been arbitrarily endowed, but that of a being who looked upon real life with that same look and who was about to appear to us in real life.

Then, as always, the three figures began to revolve dizzily. The disk turned upon itself. And everything faded to black...

XI. The Cathedral

The crowd could not recover from its stupefaction. It sat and waited. It had heard through me of the Three Eyes, of their significance as a message, a preliminary illustration, something like the title of the forthcoming spectacle. It had read my declarations about Edith Cavell's eyes, Philippe Dorgeroux's eyes, Bérangère's eyes, all those eyes which I had seen, and it sat still in obstinate silence, as if it feared that a word or a movement would scare away the invisible god who lay hidden within the wall.

The crowd was now filled with absolute certainty. This first proof of my sincerity and perspicacity had been enough; there was not a single unbeliever left. The spectators had stepped straight into regions which I had reached only through several painful stages of examination. Not a shadow of protest impaired their sensibility. Not a doubt interfered with their faith. I saw around me nothing but serious attention, restrained enthusiasm, and suppressed exaltation.

All this suddenly found vent in an immense shout that rose to the skies. Before us, on the screen which had until now remained empty and bare, appeared spontaneously, in a flash, hundreds, thousands of men, swarming in unspeakable confusion.

It was obviously the suddenness and complexity of the image which so profoundly stirred the crowd. The sudden emergence of innumerable life out of nothingness galvanized it like an electric shock. In front of it, where there had been nothing, now swarmed another crowd, as dense as itself, whose excitement mingled with theirs and whose uproar, which it was able to guess, was added to its own! For a few seconds, I had the impression that the crowd was losing its mental balance and swaying to and fro in an access of delirium.

However, people soon regained their self-control. The need, not of understanding—they didn't seem to care about that at first—but of seeing and grasping the entire phenomena mastered the force that had been let loose in their midst. The crowd became silent again. It gazed. And it *listened*.

Yonder—I dare not say on the screen, for, in truth, so abnormal were its dimensions that the picture overflowed the frame and was propelled into the space outside—that which had first struck us as being pure disorder and chaos became organized in accordance with a certain rhythm, which eventually grew more perceptible. The movement to and fro was that of artisans performing a well-regulated task; and we could finally see that that task involved the construction of a huge edifice.

The style of these artisans' clothes, so different from ours, the tools which they used, the appearance of their ladders, the shape of their scaffoldings, their manner of carrying loads and of hoisting the necessary materials in wicker baskets to the upper floors, all these things, together with a multitude of other details, indicated that the scene we beheld took place in the thirteenth or fourteenth century.

There were numbers of monks supervising the works, calling out orders from one end of the vast site to the other, setting out measurements and not disdaining to mix the mortar themselves, to push a wheelbarrow, or to saw a stone. Women, shouting at the top of their voices, walked about bearing jars of wine with which they filled cups that were immediately emptied by the thirsty laborers. A beggar went by. Two tattered singers began to roar a ditty, accompanying themselves on a sort of guitar. We saw a troop of acrobats, all lacking an arm, or a leg, or both legs, preparing to give their show. Then, the scene changed without any transition, like a stage setting altered by the mere pressure of a button.

What we now saw was the same picture of an edifice in the process of being built, but this time, we could clearly distinguished what it was. We saw the base of a Gothic cathedral displaying its huge proportions. And stonecutters, masons, sculptors, carpenters, apprentices and monks swarmed everywhere on the scaffolding, which had reached the lower level of the towers, as well as along the fronts, before the niches, and on the steps of the porch.

Then, we noticed that the clothes were no longer the same. A century or two had passed.

Next came a series of images which succeeded one another without our being able to separate them from each other, or ascribe a beginning and an end to each sequence. By a method no doubt similar to that which the cinematograph uses to show us the growth of a plant, we saw the cathedral rising imperceptibly, blossoming like a flower whose exquisitely molded petals open one by one and, lastly, being completed before our eyes, without any human intervention.

Thus came a moment when it stood out against the sky in all its glory and harmonious strength. I recognized it as the Cathedral of Reims, with its three recessed doorways, its host of statues, its magnificent rose windows, its wonderful towers flanked by airy turrets, its flying buttresses, and the lacework of its carvings and balconies.[41]

A long shudder passed through the crowd. It understood what those who were not present could not easily be made to understand, by means of insignificant words. It understood that, in front of it, stood something other than the photographic representation of a building. With a profound and accurate intuition, it understood that it was not the victim of an unthinkable hoax. And so, it became imbued and overwhelmed by the utterly disturbing sense of having witnessed the most prodigious of spectacles: the *actual* erection of a church in the Middle Ages, the *actual* work of the thirteenth-century builders, the *actual* life of the monks and artists who had erected the Cathedral of Reims.

Enlightened by their subtle instinct, not for a second did the spectators doubt the evidence of their own eyes. What I had denied, or at least what I had questioned, with reservations and flashes of incredulity, the crowd accepted with a certainty against which it would have been madness to rebel. It had faith. It believed with religious fervor. What it saw was not an artificial recreation of the past, but that past itself, revived in all its living reality.

Equally real was the gradual transformation which continued to take place, no longer in the actual lines of the building, but, as one might say, in its substance, and which was revealed by progressive changes that could not be attributed to any other cause than that of the passage of time. The great white mass grew darker. The grain of the stones became worn and weathered, and they assumed that appearance of rugged bark which the patient gnawing of the years is apt to give them. It is true, the cathedral did grow old, yet it lived, for age is the beauty by which man gives shape to his dreams.

It lived and breathed through the centuries, seeming all the fresher as it faded, and more beautiful as its legions of saints and angels became mutilated. It

---

[41] Construction of the present Reims Cathedral began in the 13th century and concluded in the 15th century. A prominent example of High Gothic architecture, it was built to replace an earlier church destroyed by fire in 1210. Although little damaged during the French Revolution, the present cathedral saw extensive restoration in the 19th century. It was severely damaged during World War I and again restored in the 20th century.

sung its solemn hymn into the open sky over the houses which had gradually surrounded its aisles, over the town above whose crowded roofs it towered, over the plains and hills which formed the dim horizon.

At different times, people came and leaned against the balustrade of some lofty balcony, or appeared in the frame of the tall windows; and the costume of these people enabled us to note their successive periods. Thus, we saw pre-Revolutionary citizens, followed by soldiers of the Empire, who in turn were replaced by other nineteenth-century civilians and by laborers building new scaffoldings, and by yet more laborers, engaged in the work of restoration.

Then, a final vision appeared before our eyes: a group of French officers in service uniform. They hurriedly reached the top of the tower, looked through their field-glasses and went down again. Here and there, over the town and the country, hovered those small, woolly clouds which mark the bursting of a shell.

The silence of the crowd became anguished. Their eyes stared apprehensively. We all felt what was coming and we were all judging a spectacle which had shown us the gradual birth and marvelous growth of the cathedral, only to lead us to its dramatic climax. We expected this climax. It followed from the dominant idea which gave the film its unity and its *raison d'être*. It was as logical as the last act of a Greek tragedy. But how could we foresee all the savage grandeur and all the horror contained in that climax? How could we foresee that the bombardment of the Cathedral itself formed part of the climax only as a preparation and that, beyond the violent and sensational scene which was about to rack our nerves and shock our minds, there would follow yet another scene of the most terrible nature, a scene which was strictly accurate in every detail?

The first shell fell on the north-east part of the Cathedral, at a spot which we could not see, because the building, though we were looking down upon it from a slight elevation, presented only its west front to our eyes. But a flame shot up, like a flash of lightning, and a pillar of smoke whirled into the cloudless sky.

Then, almost simultaneously, three more shells followed, three more explosives, mingling their puffs of smoke. A fifth shell fell a little more forward, in the middle of the roof. A mighty flame arose. The Cathedral was on fire.

Another phenomenon followed, which was really inexplicable in the present state of our cinematographic resources. I say cinematographic, although the term is not perhaps strictly accurate, but I do not know how else to describe these miraculous visions, nor do I know of any comparison to employ when speaking of the visible parabola of the sixth shell, which we followed with our eyes through space, and which even stopped for a moment, before resuming its leisurely course and stopping again a few inches from the statue which it was about to strike.

This was a charming and ingenuous statue of a saint lifting her arms to God, with the sweetest, happiest, and most trusting expression on her face; a masterpiece of grace and beauty; a divine creature who had stood for centuries, cloistered in her shelter, among the nests of the swallows, living her humble life of prayer and adoration, and who now smiled at the death that threatened her.

There was a flash, a puff of smoke, and, in the place of the little saint in her daintily carved niche, a yawning gap appeared!

It was at this moment that I felt that anger and hatred were awakening all around me. The murder of the little saint had roused the indignation of the crowd; and it so happened that this indignation found an occasion to express itself. Before us, the cathedral grew smaller, while, at the same time, it got closer. It seemed to be leaving its frame, while the distant landscape came nearer and nearer. A hill, bristling with barbed wire, dug with trenches and strewn with corpses, rose and fell away; and we saw its top, which was fortified with bastions and cupolas of reinforced concrete.

Enormous guns displayed their long barrels. A multitude of German soldiers were moving swiftly to and fro. It was the battery which had been shelling the Cathedral.

In the center stood a group of officers, field-glasses in hand, sword-belts unbuckled. After each shot, they watched the effect through their binoculars and then nodded with an air of satisfaction.

But suddenly, a great commotion took place among them. They drew up in single rank, assuming a stiff posture, while the soldiers continued to serve the guns. From behind the fortress, a motorcar appeared, accompanied by a cavalry escort. It stopped on the esplanade and a man wearing a helmet and a long fur cloak, which was lifted at the side by the scabbard of a sword of which he held the hilt, stepped briskly to the foreground. We recognized the Kaiser.[42]

He shook hands with one of the officers. The others saluted more stiffly than ever and then, at a sign from their master, extended and formed a semicircle around him and the officer whose hand he had shaken.

A conversation ensued. The officer, after an explanation accompanied by gestures that pointed towards the town, called for a telescope and had it correctly pointed. The Kaiser put his eye to it.

One of the guns was ready. The order to fire was given.

Two pictures followed each other on the screen in quick succession: that of a carved stone balustrade smashed to pieces by the shell, and that of the German

---

[42] Wilhelm II (Friedrich Wilhelm Viktor Albert; 1859-1941), last German Emperor (Kaiser) and King of Prussia, reigning from 15 June 1888 until his abdication on 9 November 1918. Despite strengthening the German Empire's position as a great power by building a powerful navy, his erratic foreign policy greatly antagonized the international community and are considered by many to be one of the underlying causes for World War I. When the German war effort collapsed after a series of crushing defeats on the Western Front in 1918, he was forced to abdicate, thereby bringing an end to the House of Hohenzollern's 300-year reign.

Emperor drawing himself up immediately afterwards. He had seen! He had seen the blow, and his face, which appeared to us suddenly enlarged and alone upon the screen, beamed with intense delight!

He began to talk volubly. His sensual lips, his upturned moustache, his wrinkled and fleshy cheeks were all moving at the same time. But, when another gun was obviously on the point of firing, he held his peace and looked in the direction of the town. Just then, he raised his hand to a level just below his eyes, so that we saw them by themselves, between the hand and the peak of the helmet. They were hard, evil, proud, implacable. They wore the expression of the miraculous Three Eyes that had throbbed before us on the screen.

They lit up, glittering with an evil smile. They saw what we saw at the same time, a whole chunk of cornices falling to the ground and more flames rising in angry pillars of fire. Then the Kaiser burst out laughing. One picture showed him doubled up in two and holding his sides amid the group of generals all seized with the same uncontrollable laughter. He was laughing! It was so amusing! Reims Cathedral was ablaze! This venerable monument to which the Kings of France used to come for their coronation was falling into ruins! The might of Germany was striking the enemy in his very heart! The German heavy guns were things that were noble and beautiful! And it was he who had ordained it, he, the Kaiser, the King of Prussia, master of the world, William of Hohenzollern! Oh, the joy of laughing his fill, laughing to his heart's content, laughing the frank, honest laughter of a jolly German!

A storm of hoots and hisses broke loose in the theater. The crowd had risen as one, shaking their fists and bellowing forth insults. The attendants had to struggle with a troop of angry men who had invaded the orchestra.

Massignac, behind the bars of his cage, stooped and pressed the button.

The iron curtain rose.

XII. The Shapes

On the morning of the day following this memorable spectacle, I woke late, after a feverish night during which I twice seemed to hear the sound of a shot.

A nightmare! I thought, when I got up. I was haunted by the pictures of the bombardment, and I thought that what I'd heard was the bursting of the shells.

The explanation was plausible enough: the powerful emotions I'd felt in the wake of watching the latest "film," coming after my meeting with Bérangère the previous night, and my struggle with Théodore Massignac, had thrown me into a state of nervous excitement.

But, when I entered the room in which my coffee was served, Massignac came running in, carrying a heap of newspapers which he threw on the table. I saw under his hat a bandage which hid his forehead. Had he been wounded? Was I to believe that there had really been shots fired outside?

217

"Pay no attention to this," he said, having caught my eye. "It's a mere scratch. I've bruised myself." And, pointing to the newspapers, he added: "Read that, rather. It's all about the Master's triumph."

I made no protest against the loathsome brute's intrusion. "The Master's triumph," as he had said, and Bérangère's safety, compelled me to observe a silence by which he was to benefit until the completion of his plans. He had made himself at home in Noël Dorgeroux's house; and his attitude showed that he was aware of my helplessness. Nevertheless, despite his arrogance, he seemed to me anxious and preoccupied. He no longer laughed; and, without that fake, cheery laugh, he disconcerted me more than ever.

"Yes," he continued, drawing himself up, "it's a victory, a victory acknowledged by everyone! Not a single article strikes a false note. Surprise and enthusiasm, stupefaction and heaps of praise, all running together. On the other hand, no one has any plausible explanation for what they saw. They're all mystified, befuddled, like blind men walking without a stick. Well, it's a thick-headed world out there!"

He stood in front of me and bluntly continued:

"What's next, then?" he said. "Can't you guess? It's really too funny! Now that I understand the entire business, I'm petrified by the idea that people can't see through it. This is an unprecedented discovery, I agree, and yet so simple! In fact, you can hardly call it a discovery, for when all is said and done... Look, the whole business is totally within the capacity of anyone to figure out. Tomorrow or the next day, someone will say, 'I know the trick!' I'm sure of it. You don't have to be a man of science for that, believe me. Quite the contrary!"

He shrugged and continued:

"But, I don't care. Let them find out the truth. They'll still need the formula, and that's kept inside my head and nowhere else. Nobody knows it, not even my friend Velmot. Dorgeroux's steel plate? Melted down. The instructions which he left at the back of D'Alembert's portrait? Burned to ashes. So there's no danger of any competition any time soon. And, as the seats in the theater are selling like hot cakes, I shall have pocketed a million in less than a fortnight, two millions in less than three weeks. After that, good-bye, gentlemen, I'm off! By Jove! It won't do to tempt Providence—or the police!"

He took me by the lapels of my jacket and, standing straight in front of me, his eyes fixed on mine, said, in a more serious voice:

"There's only one thing that would bother me: to think that all these beautiful images would no longer appear upon the screen after I'm gone. It shouldn't be! No more miraculous visions? No more fairy tales to make people talk? That would never do, would it? Dorgeroux's secret must not be lost. So I thought of you. After all, you're his nephew! And you love my dear Bérangère. Some day or other you'll be married. And as I'm working for her, it doesn't matter whether the money comes to her through you or through me, does it? Listen to me, Monsieur Beaugrand, and remember every word I say. Listen! You've observed that the base of the wall below the screen stands out a little. Dorgeroux contrived some kind of recess there, containing several containers filled with different substances, and a copper vat. In this vat, one mixes certain quantities of those ingredients in predetermined proportions; then one adds a solution from a little bottle prepared on the morning of the performance, according to your uncle's formula. Then, an hour or two before sunset, one dips a big brush in the wash thus obtained and daubs the surface of the screen evenly with it. You do that for each performance, if you want the pictures to be clear, and, of course, only on days when there are no clouds between the sun and the screen. As for the formula, it is not very long: it's fifteen letters and twelve figures, like this..."

Massignac repeated slowly, in a less decisive tone:

"Fifteen letters and twelve figures... Once you know them by heart, you can rest easy. And so can I. What do I risk in giving you the formula? You swear you won't tell, eh? Besides, I hold you through Bérangère. Well, those fifteen letters..."

He was obviously still hesitating. His words seemed to cost him an increasing effort. Suddenly, he pushed me back, struck the table angrily with his fist and cried:

"No, no, no! I shall not speak. It would be too stupid! I should keep this thing to myself! Should I let go of this business for two mere millions? No! Not even for ten millions! For twenty! I can mount guard for months, if necessary, as I did last night, with my gun on my shoulder... and thief dares enter the laboratory, I'll shoot him like a dog. The secret belongs to me, Théodore Massignac, and no one else! Let no one dare to steal it from me! It's my formula! I risked my neck to get it, and I'll defend it to my last breath. And if I kick the bucket, well, then, too bad! I'll carry it with me to the grave!"

He shook his fist at invisible enemies. Then suddenly, he caught hold of me again:

"That's what things have come to. I don't care about the police... They'll never dare arrest me as long as I have Dorgeroux's secret. But a thief lurking in the darkness, a would be murderer who fires at me as he did last night, while I was mounting guard... For you must have heard, Victorien? Oh, a mere scratch! And I missed him, too. But the next time, the swine will aim better and.... Oh, the filthy swine!"

He began to shake me violently.

"But he's your enemy too, Victorien! Don't you understand? It's the man with the glasses—that scoundrel, Velmot! He wants to steal my secret, and also rob you of the girl you love. Sooner or later, you'll have your hands full with him, just as I have. Won't you defend yourself, you damned milksop, and attack him when you get the chance? Suppose I told you that Bérangère's in love with him? Ah-ha! That makes you jump! You're not blind surely? Can't you see for yourself that it was for him she was working all winter long, and that, if I hadn't put a stop to it, I, too, should have been cheated? He's handsome. She's in love with him—his obedient slave. Why don't you punch his fancy mug? He's here. He's prowling about. I saw him last night. Blast it, if only I could put a bullet in him!"

Massignac spat out a few more oaths, mingled with offensive epithets which were aimed at myself as much as at Velmot. He described his daughter as a lunatic, threatened to kill me if I committed the least indiscretion, and finally, with his mouth full of insults and his fists clenched, walked out backwards, like a man who fears a final desperate assault from his adversary.

He had nothing to be afraid of. I remained impassive under the storm of abuse. The only things that had roused me were his accusation against Bérangère and his blunt assertion of her love for Velmot. But I had long since resolved not to let my feelings for her affect my behavior, to ignore them entirely, not even to defend her, condemn her or judge her, and to refuse to take anything about her for granted until I obtained undeniable proofs.

At the bottom of my heart, I felt a profound pity for her. The horrible tragedy in which she was mixed up was only increasing in violence. Massignac and his accomplice were now shooting at each other. Once again, my uncle's secret was causing an outburst of passion; and everything seemed to indicate that Bérangère would soon be swept away in that storm.

What I read in the newspapers confirmed what Massignac had just told me. The articles lie before me as I write this memoir. They all expressed the same combative enthusiasm; but none of them predicted the truth, which was about to be discovered. While some ignorant and superficial journalists engaged in wild and preposterous speculations, the better writers maintained some reserve and appeared to be mainly concerned in fighting off the notion of a miracle, to which a section of the public was all too ready to believe.

This is no miracle, they wrote. *We are in the presence of a scientific riddle which will be solved purely by scientific means. In the meantime, let us confess our total ignorance.*

In any event, the comments of the press could not fail to increase the public's excitement. At six o'clock the next evening, the theater was almost taken by assault. The wholly inadequate security staff vainly attempted to stop the crowd. A numbers of seats were seized by force by people who had no right to be there. The night's performance began in tumult and confusion, amid hostile clamors. Mad applause greeted Massignac when he passed through the bars of his cage.

True, the crowd lapsed into silence as soon as the Three Eyes appeared, but it remained nervous and irritable; and the spectacle that followed was not one to alleviate those symptoms. It was a strange spectacle, the most difficult to understand of all those which I had seen so far. In those cases, the mystery lay solely in the fact of their presentation. We beheld normal, natural scenes. But this one showed us *things that were the opposite of reality*, things that might happen in the nightmare of a madman, or in the hallucinations of a man victim of an attack of delirium.

I hardly know how to describe these *things* without sounding myself as if I had lost my sanity; and I would not dare to do so if a thousand others had not witnessed the same grotesque phantasmagoria, and, above all, if this crazy vision—there is no other word for it!—had not happened to be the determining factor which set the public on the track of the truth.

A thousand witnesses, I said, but I admit, a thousand witnesses who subsequently differed in their descriptions, thanks to the inconsistency of the impressions they had received, and also the rapidity with which they succeeded each other.

So what did I see? Animated shapes. Yes—that and nothing more. Living shapes. Every visible thing has a shape. A rock, a pyramid, a scaffolding around a house has a shape; but you cannot say that they are alive. Now *this* thing was alive. *This* thing bore perhaps no more relation to the shape of a living being than to the shape of a rock, a pyramid, or a scaffolding. Nevertheless, there was no doubt that *this* thing acted in the manner of a being who lives, moves, follows this or that direction, obeys individual motives, and attains a chosen goal.

I will not attempt to describe these shapes. How indeed could I do so, considering that they all differed from each other, *and that they even differed from themselves* within the space of a second! Imagine a sack of coal—the comparison was forced upon me because of the black, lumpy appearance of one of the Shapes—swelling into the body of an ox, only to shrink immediately to the proportions of a dog, and next, to grow thicker or to draw itself out lengthwise. Imagine this mass, which has no more consistency than a jellyfish, putting forth three little tentacles, resembling hands. Lastly, imagine the picture of a town, not a horizontal town but a perpendicular one, with streets standing up like ladders; and along these avenues, the Shapes rising like balloons. This was the first vision. Then, right at the top of the town, the Shapes came crowding from every side, gathering upon a vast horizontal space, where they swarmed like ants...

I felt—and it was the general impression—that this space was like a public square. A mound marked its center. The Shapes stood there, motionless. Others approached by means of successive dilations and contractions, which appeared to constitute their method of advancing. Then, on the passage of a group of no great dimensions, which seemed to be carrying a lifeless Shape, the multitude of the living Shapes fell back.

What happened next? However clear my sensations may have been, however precise the memory I retained of them, I hesitate to write this down in so many words. I repeat, that vision transcended the limits of absurdity, while provoking a shudder of horror of which one was conscious, yet without understanding why. Because what did it all mean? Two powerful Shapes protruded their three tentacles, which wound themselves around the lifeless Shape that had been brought up, crushed it, compressed it, and, rising in the air, waved to and fro a small mass which they had separated from the original Shape, like a severed head, and which contained the geometrical Three Eyes, staring, lidless, void of any expression.

It meant nothing. It was a series of disconnected, unreal visions. And yet, our hearts were wrung with anguish, as if we had been present at a murder—or an execution. And yet, those incoherent visions were perhaps what contributed most to the discovery of the truth. Their absence of logic brought about a logical explanation of the phenomena. The excessive darkness kindled a first glimmer of light.

Today, those things from the past which I describe as incoherent and dark seem to me quite orderly and absolutely clear. But on that late afternoon, with a storm brewing in the distant sky, the crowd, recovering from its painful emotion, became noisier and more aggressive. The exhibition had disappointed the spectators. They had not found what they expected and they manifested their dissatisfaction by threatening Massignac. The incidents that were to mark the sudden close of the performance were brewing.

"Mas-si-gnac! Mas-si-gnac!" they shouted, in chorus.

Standing in the middle of his cage, with his head turned towards the screen, he was watching for possible early signs of a new picture. And, as a matter of fact, if one looked carefully, the signs were there. One might say that, rather than pictures, there were reflections of pictures skimming over the surface of the wall like faint clouds.

Suddenly Massignac extended one arm. The faint clouds were assuming definite outlines; and we saw that, under this mist, the spectacle had begun anew.

But it continued as if with difficulties, with intervals of total suspension and others of semi-darkness during which the visions were covered by a mist. At such moments, we saw almost deserted streets in which most of the shops were closed. There was no one at the doors or windows.

A cart, of which we caught sight now and again, moved along these streets. It contained, in front, two gendarmes dressed as in the days of the Revolution and, at the back, a priest and a man in a full-skirted coat, dark breeches and white stockings.

An isolated picture showed us the man's head and shoulders. I recognized and, generally speaking, the whole audience recognized, the heavy-jowled face of King Louis XVI. His expression was hard and proud.

We saw him again, after a few interruptions, in a great square surrounded by artillery and black with soldiers. He climbed the steep steps of a scaffold. His coat and neck-tie had been removed. The priest was supporting him. Four executioners tried to lay hold of him.

I am obliged to interrupt my narrative of these fleeting images, which I am deliberately wording as dryly as possible, in order to make it quite clear that they did not produce then the terror which my readers might suppose. They were too short, too desultory, and so poor from a strict cinematographic standpoint—one that the public had adopted in spite of itself—that they excited irritation and annoyance rather than dread.

The spectators had suddenly lost all confidence. They laughed, they sang, they booed Massignac. The storm of invective increased when, on the screen, one of the executioners held up the head of the king and faded away in the mist, together with the scaffold, the soldiers and the guns.

There were a few more timid attempts at more images, in which several persons say they recognized Queen Marie Antoinette, attempts which sustained the patience of the onlookers who were anxious to see the end of a spectacle for which they had paid so heavily to attend, but, in the end, the violence could no longer be contained.

Who started it? Who was the first to rush forward and cause the ensuing disorder and the resultant panic? Subsequent inquiries failed to identify the culprit. There is no doubt that the whole crowd obeyed its impulse to express its dissatisfaction, and that its more turbulent members seized the opportunity to attack Massignac and even try to take down the fabulous screen. This last attempt failed before the impenetrable rampart formed by the security guards, who, armed with knuckledusters and truncheons, repelled the attackers. As for Massignac, who, after raising the curtain, had had the unfortunate idea of leaving his cage and running to one of the exits, he was struck as he ran and swallowed up in the angry swirl of rioters.

After that, everybody attacked his neighbor, with a frantic urge for strife and violence which brought into conflict not only the enemies of Massignac and the partisans of order, but also those who were angry, and those who had no desire other than escaping from the turmoil. Sticks and umbrellas were brandished on high. Women seized one another by the hair. Blood flowed. People fell to the ground, injured.

I myself did my best to get out and shouldered my way through this indescribable fray. It was no easy work, for a number of policemen and many people who had not been able to gain entrance were now pushing towards the doors of the theater. At last, I succeeded in reaching the exit through an opening in the crowd.

"Make room for a wounded man!" a tall, clean-shaven fellow was shouting, in a stentorian voice.

Two others followed, carrying in their arms a person wrapped in overcoats.

The crowd fell back. The little procession moved out. I seized my opportunity.

The tall fellow pointed to a private motorcar waiting outside:

"Driver, I'm requisitioning you! By order of the Prefect of Police. Come along, you two, and get a move on!"

The two men put the victim into the car and took their places inside. The tall fellow sat down beside the driver and the car drove off.

It was not until the very second when it turned the corner that I guessed in a flash, and without any cause whatsoever, the identities of the "tall fellow" and the "wounded man" who had been carried off so assiduously. Notwithstanding his change of face, since he no longer wore either beard or glasses, I knew the tall man was Velmot, and the man whose identity had been so carefully hidden was Massignac.

I rushed back inside and informed the Police Commissioner who was in charge of the Dorgeroux case. He whistled up his men. They leapt into taxi cabs and cars, but they were too late. The roads were already filled with such traffic that they were unable to move.

And thus, in the very midst of the crowd, by means of the most daring stratagem, taking advantage of a crush which he had undoubtedly created, Velmot had succeeded in carrying off his accomplice and sworn enemy, Massignac!

XIII. The Veil Is Lifted

I will not linger over the two films of this second performance and the obvious connection between them. At the present time, we are too close to the resolution of this extraordinary story to waste time over minute, tedious, and unimportant details. However, one must note that, on the following morning, a newspaper printed the first part, and, a few hours later, the second part of the famous Prévotelle report, in which the problem was attacked in such a masterly fashion, and solved with such an impressive display of logic that I shall never forget it.

I shall also never forget that, during that night, while I sat in my bedroom reflecting upon the manner in which Massignac had been spirited away, while the long-expected storm burst over Paris, Benjamin Prévotelle was writing his report, and that I was about to hear it all from his open lips!

At ten p.m., in fact, one of our neighbors, whose telephone my uncle and Bérangère had been in the habit of using, sent word to say that someone from Paris wanted to talk to me most urgently.

I went around in a very bad temper. I was worn out with fatigue. It was raining cats and dogs, and the night was so dark that I bumped into things as I walked.

When I arrived, I took up the receiver. Someone at the other end addressed me in a trembling voice:

"Monsieur Beaugrand, excuse me for calling at such an hour... But I have discovered..."

I did not understand at first and asked who was speaking.

"My name will mean nothing to you," was his answer. "I'm Benjamin Prévotelle. I'm not anyone of particular importance. I am an engineer by profession, a graduate from the École Centrale..."

I interrupted him.

"One moment, please... Benjamin Prévotelle, you say? But I know your name! Yes, I remember it now… I saw it mentioned in my uncle's papers."

"Really? You've seen my name in Monsieur Dorgeroux's papers?"

"Yes—but without any comments or notes."

The speaker's excitement increased:

"Oh," he said, "can it be true? If Monsieur Dorgeroux made a note of my name, it means he read a paper of mine, which I wrote a year ago, and that he believed in the explanation of which I am beginning to catch a glimpse today."

"What explanation?" I asked, somewhat impatiently.

"You'll understand, Monsieur, you'll understand when you read my report."

"Your report?"

"A report which I am just writing now. Listen, I was present at both screenings and I have discovered..."

"Discovered what?"

"The answer, Monsieur! The solution of the problem!"

"What!" I exclaimed. "You've discovered it?"

"Yes, Monsieur. I should tell you that it was a very simple problem, so simple, in fact, that I am anxious to be the first to publish it. So I rang you up Meudon on the chance of getting you... Oh, do listen to me, Monsieur! You must believe me and help me..."

"Of course, of course," I replied, "but I don't quite see..."

"Yes, yes," Benjamin Prévotelle implored, appealing to me in a despairing tone of voice. "You can do a great deal. I only want a few particulars..."

I confess that his statements left me a little doubtful. However, I answered:

"If they can be of any use to you, I'll be happy to oblige."

"Perhaps one alone will do," he said. "It's this. The wall with the screen was entirely rebuilt by your uncle, Monsieur Dorgeroux, was it not?"

"Yes."

"And this wall, as you have said, and as everyone had observed, stands at a given angle with its lower part."

"Yes."

"Is it also true that Monsieur Dorgeroux intended, as you have said, to have a second theater built in his garden and use the back of the same wall as a screen, is it not?"

"Yes."

"Well then, this is the particular which I'd like you to give me. Have you noticed if the back of the wall stands at the same angle with its lower part?"

"Yes, I've noticed that."

"In that case," said Prévotelle, with a note of increasing triumph, "the evidence is incontrovertible. Monsieur Dorgeroux and I are in agreement. The pictures do not come from the wall. The cause lies elsewhere. I will prove it, and, if Monsieur Massignac were to oblige..."

"Monsieur Massignac was kidnapped this evening," I informed him.

"Kidnapped? What do you mean?"

I repeated:

"Yes, kidnapped. And I presume that the theater will be closed until further notice by the Police."

"But this is terrible! Awful!" Prévotelle gasped. "Why, in that case, I couldn't check my theory! There would never be any more pictures! No, that won't do at all! Because I don't know the formula! Nobody does, except Massignac. It's absolutely necessary that... Hello? Don't cut me off, Mademoiselle! One moment more, Monsieur Beaugrand! I'll tell you the whole truth about the pictures. Three or four words will be enough... Hello? Hello?..."

Prévotelle's voice suddenly died away. I was clearly aware of the physical distance that separated him from me just as I was about to learn the miraculous truth which he claimed to have discovered.

I waited anxiously. A few minutes passed. Twice the telephone rang, but there was no one on the line. I decided to leave and had reached the bottom of the stairs when I was summoned back in a hurry. Someone was asking for me again.

"Someone!" I said, going upstairs again. "But surely, it must be Prévotelle."

I took up the receiver and asked:

"Monsieur Prévotelle, are you there?"

But at first, I only heard my name, uttered in a very faint, indistinct voice—a woman's voice:

"Victorien... Victorien..."

"Who is it?" I asked, very excitedly, though I did not yet understand. "Hello? Yes, it's I, Victorien Beaugrand... Who is speaking?"

For a few seconds, the voice sounded nearer and then seemed to fall away. After that came total silence. But I had caught these few words:

"Help, Victorien! My father's life is in danger! Come to the Blue Inn in Bougival..."

I stood dumbfounded for I had recognized Bérangère's voice!

"Bérangère," I muttered, "calling on me for help..."

Without even pausing to think, I rushed to the station.

A train took me to Saint-Cloud and another two stations further. Wading through the mud, under the pelting rain, and losing my way in the dark, I covered the mile or two to Bougival on foot, arriving in the middle of the night.

The Blue Inn was closed, but a small boy dozing under the porch asked me if I was Victorien Beaugrand. When I answered affirmatively, he said that a lady, by the name of Bérangère, had told him to wait for me and take me to her, at whatever time I might arrive.

I trudged beside the boy through the empty streets of the little town, to the banks of the Seine, which we followed for a while. The rain had stopped, but the darkness was still impenetrable.

"The boat is here," said the boy.

"Oh! Are we crossing?"

"Yes, the young lady is hiding on the other side. Be very careful not to make a noise."

We landed soon after. Then a stony path took us to a house where the boy knocked on the door three times.

Someone opened the door. Still following my guide, I went up a few steps, crossed a corridor lit by a candle, and was shown into a dark room where some-one was waiting. Instantly the light of an electric lamp struck me in the face.

The barrel of a revolver was pointed at me and a man's voice said:

"Silence, do you understand? The least sound, the least attempt at escap-ing, and you're done for. Otherwise, you have nothing to fear; and the best thing you can do is to go to sleep."

The door was closed behind me. Two bolts were shot.

I had fallen into the trap which Velmot—I did not hesitate to accuse him—had laid for me through Bérangère.

This unaccountable adventure, like all those in which Bérangère was in-volved, did not alarm me unduly. I was probably too weary to seek reasons for her conduct and worry about the man whose instructions she followed. But why had she betrayed me? Why had I incurred Velmot's ill will? And what had com-pelled him to capture me, if I had nothing to fear from him as he had claimed?

These were all idle questions. After groping through the room and finding that a bed—or rather a mattress—and some blankets, I took off my boots and coat, wrapped myself in the blankets, and, a few minutes later, I was fast asleep.

I slept well into the following day. Meanwhile, someone must have entered the room during the night, for I discovered a chunk of new bread and a bottle of water on the table. The cell which I occupied was small. There was enough light coming through the slats of a wooden shutter, firmly barricaded outside, to ena-ble me to see. After opened the narrow window, I saw that one of the slats was half-broken and, through the gap, I perceived that my prison overlooked from a height of three or four feet a strip of ground at the edge of which little waves lapped among the reeds. Realizing that, after crossing one river, I was facing an-other, I concluded that Velmot had brought me to an island in the Seine. Was this not the island which I had beheld, in a fleeting vision, on the chapel in the cemetery? And was it not here that Velmot and Massignac had established their headquarters last winter?

Most of the day passed in silence. At about 5 p.m., I heard voices and a loud argument. This happened under my room and, therefore, in a cellar, the grating of which opened just beneath my window. I listened attentively and on several occasions, thought I recognized Massignac's voice.

The discussion lasted a full hour. Then someone made his appearance outside my window and called out:

"Hey, you fellas, come on and help me! He's a stubborn beast and won't talk unless we force him."

It was the same tall fellow who, the day before, had forced his way through the crowd by making an outcry about a wounded man. I recognized Velmot, the dandy who'd been the object of Bérangère's affections, but a leaner Velmot, without his beard or glasses.

Two men, accomplices with sinister figures, joined him.

"I'll make him talk, the brute!" repeated Velmot. "I've got him here, at my mercy. It'll be the Devil if I don't succeed in making him spill the beans! We must finish by nightfall. You're still with me?"

He received two dubious-sounding grunts in reply. He sneered:

"You're not too wild about it, eh? All right, I'll proceed without you. Just lend me a hand."

He stepped into a boat fastened to a ring on the bank. One of the men pushed it with a hook between two stakes planted in the mud and standing out well above the reeds. Velmot knotted one end of a thick rope to the top of each stake and, in the middle, fastened an iron hook, which hung four or five feet above the water.

"That's it," he said. "I shan't need you anymore. Take the other boat and go and wait for me in the hangar. I'll join you there in three or four hours, after Massignac has blabbed his little story and after I've had some plain speaking with our new prisoner. Then we'll be off."

He walked away with his two assistants. When I saw him again, twenty minutes later, he had a newspaper in his hand. He laid it on a little table which stood just outside my window. Then he sat down and lit a cigar. He turned his back to me, hiding the table from my view. But as he moved, I caught sight of his paper, the *Journal du Soir*, which was folded across the page and which bore a sensational headline running right across the top:

THE TRUTH ABOUT THE MEUDON APPARITIONS REVEALED!

I was shaken to the very depths of my being. So Prévotelle had not lied! He had discovered the truth and managed, in the space of a few hours, to publish the report which he had mentioned to me.

Glued to the shutter, I strove to read the article! But these were the only lines that met my eyes, because of the manner in which the paper was folded. And how great was my excitement at each word that I made out!

I have carefully preserved a copy of that paper, by which at least a part of the great mystery was revealed to me. I am reprinting below that famous article, which Benjamin Prévotelle had had published that very morning:

Yes, the fantastic problem of Meudon has been solved! A young engineer published this morning, in the form of 'An Open Letter to the Academy of Sciences,' the most sober, clear and convincing report conceivable. We do not know whether the official experts will agree with his conclusions, but we doubt if any objections, which are frankly stated by the author at the onset of his report, will be powerful enough—however momentous they may be—to disprove the theory which he propounds. His arguments seem unanswerable. His proofs are such as to compel belief. And what doubles the value of this admirable report is that it does not merely appear to be unassailable, but it opens up to us the widest and most marvelous horizons.

In fact, Noël Dorgeroux's marvelous discovery is no longer limited to what it is, or what it seems to be. It implies consequences which as yet cannot be foretold. It is calculated to upset all our ideas of man's past and all our conceptions of his future. Not since the beginning of the world has there been an event to compare with this. It is, at the same time, the most incomprehensible event and the most natural, the most complex and the simplest.

A great scientist might have announced it to the world as the result of a long and arduous research. Yet, he who, thanks to his prodigious intuition and intelligent observation, has achieved this inestimable glory is little more than a lad in years.

We are excerpting below a few particulars gleaned during an interview which Benjamin Prévotelle was kind enough to grant us. We apologize for not being able to give more details about him personally, except to state that he is twenty-three years of age and a former student of...

That day, I had to stop reading there, because the subsequent lines escaped my eyes. I wondered if I would ever learn more?

Velmot had risen from his chair and was walking to and fro. After a brief disappearance, he returned with a bottle of some liqueur, of which he drank two glasses in quick succession. Then, he unfolded the newspaper and began to peruse the article, or rather to reperuse it, for I had no doubt that he had read it before. His chair was right against my shutter. He sat leaning back, so I was able to see, not the end of the introductory article, but the report itself, which he read rather slowly.

The sky was cloudy and daylight was diminishing, which made reading even harder.

I read simultaneously with Velmot:

An Open Letter to the Academy of Sciences

I will beg you, gentlemen, to regard this memorandum as only the briefest possible introduction to the more important essay, which I propose to write later, and to the innumerable volumes to which it is almost certain to give rise in every country, and to which it will serve as a modest introduction.

I am writing hurriedly, allowing my pen to run away with me, improvising hastily as I go along. You will find omissions and defects, which I do not attempt to conceal, and which are due in equal proportions to the restricted number of observations which I was able to make at Meudon and the obstinate refusal with which M. Théodore Massignac has rejected my every request for additional information. But the remarkable feelings created by the miraculous pictures makes it my duty to offer the results, as yet extremely incomplete, of my investigation, for which I have the legitimate ambition of claiming the right of first publication. I thus hope, by confining my hypotheses to a limited scope, to assist towards establishing the truth and satisfying public curiosity.

My investigations commenced immediately after the first revelations made by M. Victorien Beaugrand. I collated all his statements and analyzed all his impressions. I collected all that M. Noël Dorgeroux had said and went over the details of all his experiments. As a consequence of carefully weighing and examining all these things, I did not attend the first performance at Meudon as a casual thrill-seeker or dabbler in mysteries. On the contrary, I went there with a well-considered plan and a few working implements, deliberately selected and concealed under my own clothing and that of a few friends who were kind enough to assist me.

First of all, I had a camera. This was a matter of some difficulty. M. Massignac had his misgivings and had prohibited the introduction of so much as the smallest Kodak. Nevertheless, I succeeded. I had to. I had to provide a definite answer to the first question, which might be called the critical question: were the Meudon images due to individual or collective suggestions, possessing no objective reality outside those who experienced them, or were they real and did they have an external cause? The answer to that question may certainly be deduced from the absolutely identical impressions received by all the spectators. But today I am adding a direct proof which I consider to be unassailable. The camera refuses any sort of suggestion. It is not a brain in which a picture can be created, or an hallucination formed out of inner images. It is a witness that does not lie and is not mistaken. Well, this witness has now spoken. The photographs I took certify that the phenomenon is real. I hold at the disposal of the Academy seven negatives of the screen obtained by instantaneous exposures. Two of them, representing the Reims Cathedral on fire, are remarkably clear.

Our first item is therefore settled: the screen is the seat of an emanation of light rays.

While I was obtaining the proofs of this emanation, I submitted it to various means of investigation which physics places at our disposal. I was not, unfortunately, able to make as many or as accurate experiments as I would have wished. The distance of the wall, the local arrangements and the inadequacy of the light emitted by the screen worked against me. Nevertheless, by using the spectroscope and the polarimeter, I ascertained that this light did not appear to differ perceptibly from any natural light diffused by a white surface.

But a more tangible result—and one to which I attach the greatest importance—was obtained by examining the screen by means of a revolving mirror. It is well known that, if our ordinary cinematographic pictures projected on a screen are viewed in a mirror to which we impart a rapid rotary movement, the successive pictures are dislocated and yield images in the field of the mirror. A similar effect can be obtained, though less distinctly, by turning one's head quickly so as to project the successive pictures upon different points of the retina. I thought that I should apply this method of analysis to the animated projections produced at Meudon. I was thus able to prove positively that these projections, like those of the ordinary cinematograph, break up into separate and successive images, but with a rapidity which is notably greater than those in the operations to which we are accustomed. I found that they averaged 28 images per second.[43] On the other hand, these images are not emitted at regular intervals. I observed rhythmic alterations, in both acceleration and slowing down, and I am inclined to believe that these are somehow connected to the extraordinary impression of steroscopic relief which all the spectators at Meudon received.

The foregoing observations led up to a scientific certainty and naturally guided my investigations into a definite direction: the Meudon pictures were genuine cinematographic projections upon a screen, perceived by the spectators in the ordinary manner. But where, then, was the projecting apparatus? How did it work? This is where the gravest difficulty lies, for hitherto, no trace of such a device has been discovered—not even the least clue to its very existence.

Is it possible to suppose, as I did, that the projections may be created from within the screen itself by means of an underground device, even though it is difficult to imagine such a device? This theory would obviously greatly relieve our minds, by attributing the pictures to some clever trick of engineering. But it was with good reasons that, first M. Victorien Beaugrand, and afterwards the audience itself, refused to validate such a theory. The visions bore a stamp of authenticity and unexpectedness which struck all who saw them, without any exception. Moreover, specialists in cinematographic "special effects," when questioned, candidly admitted that, despite their expert knowledge, they could not explain how these images might have been created.

---

[43] In the cinema, the number of images per second was initially 16. During the transition to sound, it was normalized to 24.

Further, it may be noted that the exhibitor of these images possesses no power beyond that of receiving them on a suitable screen, and that he himself does not know what is about to appear next on that screen.

Lastly, it may be added that the making of such films—even if it were possible—would be a long and arduous operation, necessitating extensive equipment and a numerous staff of actors, and it is really impossible that these preparations could have been effected in absolute secrecy.

This was exactly the point to which my inquiries had led me on the night before the second performance. I will not presume to say that I knew more than any random member of the public about the fundamental nature of the problem. Nevertheless, when I took my seat, I was in a better condition mentally than any of the other spectators. I was standing on solid ground. I was self-controlled, free of feverish excitement, or any other factor that might have impacted my attention. I was hampered by no preconceived ideas, and no new ideas, no new facts, could come within my reach without my immediately noticing them.

This, in fact, is what happened. The new fact was the bewildering and mystifying spectacle of the grotesque "Shapes." I did not immediately draw the conclusions that I should have, or at least, I was not aware of doing so, but my perceptions were aroused. Those entities with three arms became connected in my mind with the initial riddle of the Three Eyes. If I did not yet understand, at least I had an intuition of the truth. If I did not know, at least, I suspected. A door was opening. The light was beginning to dawn.

A few minutes later, as will be remembered, came the gruesome picture of a cart conveying two gendarmes, a priest and a king who was being led to his death. It was a confused, fragmentary, mutilated picture, continually broken up and pieced together again. Why such an anomaly?. Until then, as we know and as M. Victorien Beaugrand had told us, the pictures had always been admirably clear. Now, we beheld a flickering, defective image, dim and at times almost invisible. Why?

At that critical instant, this was my only train of thought. The horror and strangeness of the spectacle no longer counted. Why was this, technically speaking, a defective picture? Why was the faultless mechanism, which until now had worked with perfect smoothness, suddenly performing poorly? What was the grain of sand in the gears?

The answer came to me with a simplicity that confounded me. The problem was familiar to everyone. We had before us cinematographic pictures. These pictures did not come from the wall itself. They did not come from any part of the theater. Then, whence were they projected? And what obstacle was now preventing such projection?

Instinctively, I made the only movement that could be made, the movement which a child would have made if that elementary question had been put to it: I raised my eyes to the sky.

It was absolutely clear—an immense, empty sky.

Clear and empty, yes, but only in the part which my eyes were able to scru-
tinize. Was it the same in the part hidden from my view by the upper wall of the
theater?

The mere silent utterance of these words was enough to make me almost
swoon. They bore the tremendous truth within themselves. I had only to speak
them for the great mystery to vanish utterly.

With trembling limbs and a heart that almost ceased to beat, I climbed to
the top of the theater and gazed at the horizon. Yonder, towards the west, I saw
light clouds floating...

XIV. Massignac and Velmot

Clouds floating... Clouds floating...

I repeated these words mechanically while trying to decipher what followed, but they were the last I was able to read. Night was falling rapidly. My
eyes, tired by the strain and difficulty of reading the article, strove in vain
against the increasing darkness, and suddenly refused to obey any further effort.

Besides, Velmot rose soon after and walked to the bank of the river. The
time had come for action.

What that action was to be, I did not know. Since the beginning of my cap-
tivity, I had entertained no personal fears, even though Velmot had mentioned
that he intended to have "some plain speaking" with me. My uncle's great secret
continued to occupy my mind so much that nothing that happened elsewhere had
any effect upon me, except to the extent that it was useful or injurious to his
reputation. There was now someone who knew the truth, and the world was
about to learn it. How could I think of anything else? How could anything interest me, except Benjamin Prévotelle's arguments, the ingenuity of his investigation, and the important results which he had achieved?

Oh, how I, too, longed to know the truth! What could his new theory be?
Did it fit in with all that we knew to be real? And would it fully satisfy me? After all, I was the one who had penetrated farther than any other into the heart of
the mystery, and reaped the largest harvest of observations.

What astonished me was that I still did not understand. And I am even
more astonished now. Though standing on the very threshold of the truth, the
door of which was opened to me, I was still unable to see. No light flashed upon
me. What had Benjamin Prévotelle meant to say? What was the significance of
those clouds drifting in a corner of the sky? If they tempered the light of the sunset, and thus exerted an influence over the pictures, why had he asked me about
the surface of the wall which faced precisely the opposite quarter of the Heavens—that is to say, the east? And why had he accepted my answer as a confirmation of his theory?

Velmot's voice drew me from my dreams and brought me back to the window, which I had left a few minutes earlier. He was stooped over the grating.

"Well, Massignac," he said, sneering, "are you ready to talk? I'll get you out this way; that'll save my dragging you up the stairs..."

Velmot went down the stairs, and I soon heard beneath me the loud outburst of a renewed argument, ending in howls and then, suddenly, in a silence that was the most impressive of all. I now got my first impression of what Velmot was plotting, and, without wasting my pity on the wretched Massignac, I shuddered at the thought that my turn might be next.

The thing was done as Velmot had said. Massignac, bandaged like a swathed mummy, rigid and gagged, rose slowly from the cellar. Velmot then returned, dragged him by the shoulders to the bank of the river and tipped him into the boat.

Then, standing on the bank, he addressed him as follows:

"Now, Massignac, my lad, this is the third time that I'm appealing to your common sense, and since you're forcing me, I'll do it again now for the fourth time. But you're going to give in, I fancy. Come, think for a moment. Think what you would do if you were in my place. You'd act just as I'm doing, wouldn't you? Then, what are you waiting for? Why don't you talk? Does your gag bother you? Just nod and I'll remove it. Do you agree? No? In that case, you won't be surprised if we start upon the fourth and last phase of our conversation. My apologies if it strikes you as even more unpleasant."

Velmot sat down beside his victim, wielded the boat-hook and pushed the boat between the two stakes projecting above the water.

These two stakes marked the boundaries of my field of vision through the gap in the shutters. The water played around them, spangled with sparks of light. The Moon had appeared from behind the clouds. I distinctly saw every detail of Velmot's "conversation."

"Don't resist, Massignac," he said, "it won't do you any good. Eh? What? You think I'm being too rough with you? But you're not made of glass, are you? So stop whining! Are we there yet...? Perfect!"

Velmot had stood Massignac up and placed his left arm around him. With his right hand, he took hold of the iron hook fastened to the rope between the two stakes, pulled it down and inserted the point under the bonds with which Massignac was swathed, at the height of the shoulders.

"Perfect!" he repeated. "You see, now I don't trouble to hold you anymore. You're standing up all by yourself, like a dummy at the fair..."

He took the boat-hook again, hooked it into a stone on the bank, and pulled, this making the boat glide from under Massignac's body, which promptly sank into the water. The rope between the stakes was sagging, so only half of the villain's body emerged above the water.

Then Velmot said to his former partner in crime, in a low voice, which I nevertheless could hear without straining my ears. I have always believed that he spoke that day with the intention that I should hear what he said:

"This is what I have in mind, old chap. We haven't much more to say to each other. In an hour from now, possibly sooner, the tide will come in and the water will rise—above your mouth, which won't make it easy for you to talk. And out of that hour, in all decency, I'll give you fifty minutes to consider your predicament and change your mind..."

He splashed a little water over Massignac's head with the boat-hook. Then he continued, with a laugh:

"You do grasp your position, don't you? The rope by which you're fastened, like an ox in a stall, is attached to these two stakes by a couple of slip-knots, nothing more... So, at the least movement, the knots may slip down an inch or so. You will have noticed it just now, when I let you go. Splash! You went down a half a head lower! Besides that, the weight of your body alone might be enough to cause you to slip, and nothing can stop it... unless, of course, you talk. So, are you ready to talk?"

The moonbeams shifted to and fro, casting light and shade upon this dreadful scene. I could see the dark shape of Massignac, who himself remained plunged in semi-darkness. The water came half-way up his chest.

Velmot continued:

"Logically, old fellow, you should choose to talk. Our respective positions are clear. Between us, we set up a nice little business which succeeded thanks to our joint efforts; but you pocketed all the profits, thanks to your trickery. I want my share, that's all. And for this, you only need to tell me Dorgeroux's famous formula and supply me with the means of making the experiment. If you do that, I'll release you, and I'm sure that you will give me my share of the profits for fear that I might be competing with you if you don't. Is that a bargain or not?"

Massignac must have made a gesture of denial or uttered a grunt of refusal, for he received a smack across the face which resounded through the silence.

"I'm sure you'll excuse me, old chap," said Velmot, "but you'd try the patience of a saint! Do you really mean to say that you'd rather croak? Or perhaps you think I'm going to give in? Or that someone will come and rescue you? You, dummy! You chose this place yourself last winter! No boats come this way. Opposite, there's nothing but fields. So any rescue is out of the question. As for me feeling any mercy towards you, forget it! Damn it! Why don't you realize the position you're in? I showed you that article this morning. With the exception of the formula, it's all out there—Dorgeroux's secret and yours! So who's to say that this clever engineer won't find the formula next? Who's to say that, in a week, in a month perhaps, the whole thing won't worth a centime, and that I could have had my hands on a million, and like a fool, I didn't grab the opportunity? Oh, no, that won't do at all!"

There was a pause. A ray of light gave me another glimpse of Massignac. The water had now risen above his shoulders.

"OK! I've nothing more to say to you," said Velmot. "Let's wrap this up. Do you still refuse?"

He waited for a moment, then continued:

"In that case, I won't insist. What would be the point? You've decided your own fate and would rather take the final plunge. Good-bye, old chap! I'll drink a glass and smoke a pipe in your memory."

He bent towards his victim and added:

"Still, it's a fellow's duty to provide for everything. If, by any chance, you change your mind at the last moment, you have only to call me... There, I'm loosening your gag... Good-bye, Théodore!"

Velmot pushed the boat back and landed, grumbling:

"It's a dog's life! What a fool the brute is!"

As he'd planned, after bringing the chair and table to the water's edge, he sat down and poured himself a glass of liqueur and lit his pipe.

"Here's to your health, Massignac!" he said. "At the present rate, I can see that, in twenty minutes, you'll be having a drink too. Whatever you do, don't forget to call me. I'm listening for all I'm worth, old chap."

The Moon had become veiled with clouds, which must have been very thick, for the bank grew so dark that I could hardly distinguish Velmot's figure. I was persuaded that this implacable contest of will would end in some compromise, that Velmot would give up, or Massignac talk. Nevertheless, ten, then fifteen minutes passed, which seemed interminable. Velmot smoked quietly and Massignac whimpered a little, but did not call out. Five minutes later, Velmot rose angrily.

"It's no use whining, you damned fool! I've had enough of you! Will you talk? No? Then die, you rat!"

And I heard him snarling between his teeth:

"Perhaps I'll do better with the other one."

Whom did he mean by "the other one"? Me?

In point of fact, he turned to the left, towards the part of the house where the door was.

"Damn it!" he swore, almost immediately.

Then, I heard nothing more from that direction. What had happened? Had Velmot knocked himself against the wall in the dark, or against an open shutter?

I could not see him from where I stood. The table and chair were faintly outlined in the gloom. Beyond that was the pitchy darkness from which came Massignac's muffled whimpers.

Velmot is on his way, I thought. *A few seconds more and he'll be here.*

I didn't understand the reason for his coming after me, anymore than the reason for torturing me. Did he think that I knew the formula? That I had refrained from turning Massignac in to the police because we had an understanding? If so, did he mean to compel me to talk by using the same methods? Or was it about Bérangère—whom we both loved and whose name, to my surprise, he had not even mentioned to Massignac? There were so many questions to which I hoped he would provide answers.

236

If he comes, I thought.

Because Velmot still wasn't there! There was not a sound in the house. What was he doing? For a little while, I stood with my ear glued to the door, ready to defend myself, even though I was unarmed.

But still, he didn't come.

I went back to the window. There was no sound on that side either.

The silence was terrible; it only seemed to increase and spread all over the river and into space, not even broken by Massignac's stifled moaning anymore.

I tried to force my eyes to see, but in vain. The water remained invisible. I no longer saw, nor heard Massignac.

It was a terrifying moment! Had he slipped down? Had the deadly, suffocating water risen to his mouth and nostrils?

I struck the shutter with a mighty blow of my fist. The thought that Massignac was either dead or about to die, which until then, I had not truly accepted, filled me with distress. His death would mean the definite and irreparable loss of my uncle's secret. It was as if Noël Dorgeroux was dying for a second time!

I redoubled my efforts. There was no doubt in my mind that Velmot was somewhere about and that I would have to fight him, but I didn't care. Nothing would stop me. I had to rush out to save not Massignac, but, as it seemed to me, Noël Dorgeroux, whose wonderful work was about to be destroyed. All that I had done hitherto in protecting him and his criminal enterprise with my silence, I was bound to continue to do by saving from death the only man who knew the indispensable formula.

As my fists were not enough, I broke a chair and used it to hammer one of the bars. The shutters were not very strong, as some of the slats were already missing. Another split, and yet another, until I was finally able to slip my arm through and lift the iron cross-bar hinged outside. The shutter gave way. Now I only had to step through the window sill and drop to the ground below.

Velmot was certainly leaving the field clear for me.

Without losing an instant, I ran past the chair, threw over the table, and easily found the boat.

"I'm here!" I shouted to Massignac. "Hold on!"

With a strong push, I reached one of the stakes, repeating:

"Hold on! I'm here!"

I seized the rope at the level of the water and felt for the hook, expecting to bump against Massignac's head. But I touched nothing. The rope had slipped down; the hook was in the water and carried no weight.

The body must have gone to the bottom and the current had swept it away, I thought.

Nevertheless, on the off-chance I was wrong, I dipped my hand as far as I could into the water. But suddenly, a shot pulled me up. A bullet had just whistled past my ear.

At the same time, I saw Velmot, whom I could barely make out, crouching on the bank, like a man dragging himself on all fours. He stuttered, in a choking voice:

"Oh, you creep, you seized your opportunity, didn't you? And you think you're going to save Massignac? Just you wait a bit, you stinker!"

He fired two more shots, guessing at my whereabouts, for I was sculling away rapidly. Neither of them hit me. Soon, I was out of range.

XV. The Splendid Theory

It is not just today, as I am relating that tragic scene, that it seems to me nothing but a minor appendix to my story. I already had that impression at the time when it was taking place. My reason for not putting more emphasis on it is that, to me, it was all some kind of interlude. Massignac's sufferings, his subsequent disappearance, and Velmot's strange behavior—seemingly abandoning a matter to which he had, until then, applied himself with such diabolical eagerness—were just so many details which became trivial when compared to the Benjamin Prévotelle's revelations.

That event remained the center of all my preoccupations and, as I rushed to Massignac's assistance, I had the forethought of grabbing the newspaper in which I had read the first half of the young engineer's essay from the chair! To me at that moment, to be free meant above all things—even above saving Massignac and, through him, the formula—the opportunity of reading the rest of the article and learning what the whole world had already found out!

I used the boat to circle the island, and, using city lights to guide me, ran it ashore on the main bank. A tramway went by. Some of the shops were still open. I was between Bougival and Port-Marly.

At 10 p.m., I was in a comfortable hotel with the newspaper. But I had not had the patience to wait so long. On the way, by the feeble lights of the tram-car, I glanced at a few lines of the article. One word told me everything I need to know. Now, I, too, was acquainted with Prévotelle's marvelous theory. I knew and, knowing, I believed.

The reader will recall the place which I had reached in my uncomfortable perusal of the article. Prévotelle's experiments had led him to conclude, first, that the pictures were real cinematographic projections, and, second, that these projections, since they didn't come from inside the theatre, had to originate from outside. The last projection, that portraying events from the French Revolution, had been interfered with by some obstacle. What obstacle? His mental condition being what it was, what could Prévotelle do other than raise his eyes to the sky?

The sky was clear. But was it also clear beyond the part that could be observed from the lower benches of the theater? Prévotelle had climbed to the top and looked at the horizon.

Yonder, towards the west, clouds were floating.

238

And Prévotelle had continued, repeating this same phrase:

Clouds were floating on the horizon! And, because of that fact, the pictures on the screen had grown less distinct, or even had vanished altogether. One could say that this might be a mere coincidence. On three separate occasions, when the film lost its brilliancy, I turned towards the horizon, and on each occasion, I saw clouds passing. Could three coincidences of this kind be due to chance? Could any scientific mind fail to see herein a relation of cause and effect, and admit that, in this instance, as in that of many images previously observed which had been disturbed by an unknown cause, the interposition of the clouds acted as a veil by intercepting the projection on its way?

I haven't been able to make a fourth test, but that does not matter. By then, my thoughts had advanced so far that I was able to work and think without being stopped by any obstacle. There is no such thing as being checked midway in our pursuit of truth. Once we catch a glimpse of it, it becomes revealed in its entirety.

At first, certainly, instead of subordinating the explanation I so eagerly sought to the body of human sciences, scientific logic propelled me into an ever more mysterious region, almost despite myself. And when I returned home after this second projection—about three hours ago—I asked myself whether it would not be better to confess my ignorance rather than elaborating after wild theories beyond the confines of human science. But how could I have done so? Despite myself, I continued to work on the problem. Induction fitted into deduction. Proofs were accumulating. Even as I was hesitating to follow a path whose direction confounded me, I reached my goal and found myself sitting down at my desk, pen in hand, ready to write this report, dictated as much by my reason as my imagination.

I had the first step: following the imperious diktats of reality, I had admitted the theory of extra-terrestrial communication, *or at least of communications coming from beyond the clouds.*

Was I to suppose that they emanated from some airship hovering in the sky, beyond the cloud belt? Leaving aside the fact that no such airship was ever observed, one must note that luminous projections powerful enough to light the screen at Meudon from a distance of several miles away would have left a trail of diffused light in the air which could not have escaped notice. Furthermore, in the present condition of science, we can state unambiguously that such projections could not be achieved.

What then? Should we cast our eyes farther, traverse space in one bound and assume that the projections have an origin which is not only extra-terrestrial but alien?

Now that I have written that *word, the idea is no longer mine. How will it be received by those who will read this report tomorrow? Will they welcome it* with the same fervor and the same awe that thrilled me, with the distrust at the beginning and the same enthusiasm at the end?

Let us, if you will, recover our composure. The examination of the phenomena has led us to a definite conclusion. However startling this conclusion may be, let us examine it with perfect objectivity and subject it to all the tests we can apply to it.

Extra-terrestrial projection: what does that mean exactly? The expression seems vague, and our thoughts wander, so let us look into it more closely. First of all, let us establish as an impassable boundary the frontiers of our solar system and, within that immense circle, focus on the more accessible and, consequently, the nearer points. For, when all is said, if there are really extra-terrestrial projections, they must necessarily emanate from fixed points in space, preferably from those celestial bodies within sight of the Earth. Therefore, we might attribute the origin of those projections to one of these five fixed points: the Moon, the Sun, Jupiter, Mars and Venus.

If, furthermore, we suppose—as it is more likely—that these projections follow a rectilinear direction, then the unknown point from which they emanate will have to satisfy two conditions: first, it must be in such a position that photographs can be taken from it; secondly, it must be in such a position that the images obtained can be transmitted back to us.

Let us consider a projection for which it was possible to determine a place and a date. The first Montgolfier balloon, filled with hot air, was sent up from Annonay at 4 p.m. on June 5, 1783. It is easy, by referring to the contemporary calendars, to learn which celestial bodies were at that moment above the horizon, and at what height. We thus find that Mars, Jupiter and the Moon were invisible, whereas the Sun and Venus were at 50 and 23 degrees respectively above the horizon of Annonay and, of course, towards the west.

These two points alone were therefore in a position to witness the Montgolfier brothers' experiment. But they did not witness it from the same altitude: a picture taken from the Sun would have shown things as seen from above, whereas, at the same hour, Venus would have shown them from an angle very nearly approaching the horizontal.

This is our first clue. Are we able to check it? Yes, by looking at the dates of the projections observed by M. Victorien Beaugrand and by determining whether, on such dates, the projecting point would have been able to light up the screen at Meudon. On those days, at the hours which M. Beaugrand reported, Mars and the Moon were invisible, Jupiter was in the east, the Sun close to the horizon, and Venus a little way above it. Projections emanating from the latter could therefore have fallen upon the screen, which, as we know, faced westwards.

This example shows us that, however dubious my theory may appear, we are now able, and shall be even better able in the future, to subject it to a strict verification. I did not fail to use this method with respect to the other projections, and will attach a special table to this essay to offer all the data which I have verified, although in some haste. In all the cases which I examined, the projections were achieved under such conditions that they can logically be attributed to the planet Venus and to that planet alone.

Two of these projections, the one which showed the execution of Miss Cavell to MM. Beaugrand and Dorgeroux, and that which enabled us to witness the bombardment of the Reims Cathedral, appear to have been taken, the first in the morning, because of the time of Miss Cavell's execution, and the second from the east, because it showed a shell fired at a statue which stood on the east front of the Cathedral. This proves that the images could be taken indifferently in the morning or the evening, from the west or the east. That is a powerful argument in favor of my theory, because Venus, which is both the Evening and the Morning Star, faces the Earth at daybreak from the east, and at sunset from the west.

This is also why M. Dorgeroux, who was a prodigious visionary, had his wall constructed with two surfaces having an identical inclination towards the sky, one facing west, the other east, and each in turn exposed to the rays of Venus the Evening Star and Venus the Morning Star—as M. Beaugrand himself has just confirmed to me by telephone.

These are all the proofs which I am able to furnish at the moment. There will be others. There is, for instance, the time of the apparitions. Venus is sinking towards the horizon; on Earth, twilight reigns; and the pictures can appear regardless of the sunlight.

We should also note that M. Dorgeroux, deferring all his experiments, last winter rearranged his entire Laboratory and demolished the old garden. Now this interruption coincides exactly with a period during which the position of Venus on the farther side of the Sun prevented it from communicating with Earth.

All these proofs will be supplemented by a more exhaustive essay and an analytical examination of the pictures that have been, or will be, shown to us.

Although I have written this report without stopping to answer the objections and difficulties which arise at every line, although I have been content only with setting forth the logical and almost inevitable sequence of the deductions which led up to my theory. I should be failing the Academy and the public if I allowed them to believe that I am not fully aware of the weight of those objections and difficulties. I did not, however, consider it a valid reason for abandoning my task.

It is our duty to bow when science utters a formal veto; but the same duty also compels us to persist when science merely confesses its ignorance. These are the two principles I observed in seeking not just the source of the projections, but rather the manner in which they were made—for that is where the whole problem lies.

It is easy to declare that they emanate from Venus; it is not easy to explain how they travel through space and how they exercise their action, at a distance of many millions of miles, on an imperceptible screen with a surface of only three or four hundred square feet. There are physical laws which I am not entitled to transgress. I am at most entitled to advance where science is obliged to be mute.

Therefore, and without any discussion, I will admit that we cannot suppose that light is the agent behind these projections. The laws of diffraction are absolutely opposed to the strictly rectilinear propagation of luminous rays, and hence to the formation and reception of pictures at such exceptional distances. Besides, the laws of geometrical optics, even at a rough approximation, and the complicated refractions which would inevitably occur in the respective atmospheres of Earth and Venus, would scatter optical images. The veto of science is therefore peremptory with respect to the possibility of these transmissions being optical in nature.

I would be quite willing to believe that the inhabitants of Venus may have already tried to communicate with us through the means of light signals and that, if they abandoned their efforts, it was precisely because the imperfection of our human science made them useless. We know for a fact that Lowell and Schiaparelli saw brilliant specks and a transient gleam on the face of Venus, which they themselves attributed either to volcanic eruptions or, as is more probable, to the attempts at communication of which I have spoken.[44]

But science does not stop us from asking ourselves whether, after the failure of these attempts, the inhabitants of Venus did not resort to another method of communication. How can we avoid thinking, for instance, of the X-rays, whose strictly rectilinear path would allow for the formation of pictures so clear that one couldn't wish for anything better? In fact, it is not impossible that these rays were used for the transmission of the Meudon images, although the quality of the light when analyzed by a spectroscope makes this supposition highly improbable. Also, how are we to explain by means of X-rays the taking of the terrestrial scenes which we saw moving on the screen? We know, of course, if we refer back to the specific example of the Montgolfier brothers, that neither them nor the surrounding landscape emitted X-rays. It is, therefore, not through these rays that the Venusians could have obtained the instantaneous images which they later transmitted back to us.

This exhausts all the possibilities for an explanation which might be considered in light of our current scientific knowledge. In fact, I would not have dared to venture into the domains of such theories and suggest a solution in this essay if M. Dorgeroux had not authorized me to do so. The fact is that, a year ago, I published an article entitled An Essay on Universal Gravitation, which was not particularly well received, but which must have attracted M.

---

[44] The so-called "Spokes of Venus" recorded in 1877 by Schiaparelli and 1896 by Lowell. It now appears that the structures Lowell witnessed may have been reflections of blood vessels in his eye.

Dorgeroux's attention, because his nephew, Victorien Beaugrand, found my name written among his papers, and M. Dorgeroux cannot have known my name except through this article. Nor would he have taken the trouble to write it down, if the theory of gravitational rays which I developed in said article had not seemed to him well suited to explain the problem raised by his discovery?

I will therefore ask the reader to refer to this article. There, he will find experimental results, still vague but by no means negligible, which I used to formulate my theory of gravitational rays. He will see that such rays are propagated in a strictly rectilinear direction at a speed which is three times that of light, so that they would take approximately 46 seconds to reach Venus when she is nearest to Earth. Finally, my reader will see that, although the existence of these rays, thanks to which universal attraction is exercised according to the Newtonian laws, is not yet accepted, and although I have not yet succeeded in making them visible by means of suitable receivers, I nevertheless give proofs of their existence which must be taken into consideration. And M. Dorgeroux's approval is also a proof that they must not be neglected.

It is not unreasonable to believe that, while our poor rudimentary science, after centuries of efforts, has remained ignorant of these essential factor in the equilibrium of planets, the Venusian scientists have long since passed this inferior stage of knowledge, and that they possess photographic receivers which allow images to be taken by means of said gravitational rays with truly wonderful perfection. Looking down upon our planet, knowing all that happened here, witnessing our helplessness, they were therefore waiting to communicate with us by the only means that seemed possible to them. They were waiting, patiently and persistently, formidably equipped, sweeping our land with their invisible rays, searching and prying into every nook and corner, gathering images in their receivers and projectors.

And one day, a wonderful thing happened. Their beam struck the layer of the substance on the screen where alone the spontaneous work of chemical decomposition and immediate reconstitution could be performed. On that day, thanks to Noël Dorgeroux—and thanks to luck, since he was admittedly pursuing an entirely different series of experiments—the Venusians established the connection between our two worlds.

The greatest fact in the history of mankind had been accomplished!

There is evidence even that the Venusians knew of M. Dorgeroux's earlier experiments, that they realized their importance, that they were interested in his labors, and that they followed the events of his life, for it is now many years since they took the pictures showing how his son, Dominique, was killed in the war. But I will not recapitulate here the details of each of the films displayed at Meudon. This is a work which anybody can now perform thanks to the theory I am setting forth here. However, we must consider attentively the process by which the Venusians tried to give those films a sort of uniformity. It has been rightly said that the sign of the Three Eyes is a trademark, like the mark of any of our great film producers, a trademark which also strikingly proves the Venusians' superhuman resources, since they succeeded in giving to those Three Eyes, which have no relation to our human eyes, not only the expression of our own eyes, but something even more impressive: the expression of the eyes of the person destined to be the main character in each film.

But why was this particular mark chosen? Why eyes and why three? At the stage which we have now reached, do we need to answer this question? The Venusians themselves have provided us with an answer by showing us that apparently absurd film in which strange shapes *assuredly lived and moved before our eyes, likely in accordance with the principles of Venusian life. Were we not the breathless spectators of a picture taken among them and by them? Did we not behold, as a companion picture to the death of Louis XVI, an incident representing the martyrdom of some great personage whom the executioners tore to pieces with their* three hands, *severing from his body a shapeless head with* three eyes?

Three Hands! Three Eyes! Dare I, on the strength of this fragile comparison, go beyond what we saw and declare that the Venusians possess the symmetry of the triangle, just as man, with our two eyes, two ears and two arms, possesses bilateral symmetry? Shall I try to explain their method of progressing by successive distentions and moving vertically along vertical streets, in towns built perpendicularly? Shall I have the courage to state, as I believe, that Venusians have organs which give them a magnetic sense, a sense of space, an electric sense, and so on—organs numbered by threes? No. These are details with which the Venusian scientists will supply us when it pleases them to enter into further communication with us.

And, trust me, they will not fail to do so. All their efforts for centuries past have been directed towards this end. Let us talk, *they will say to us as they must have said to M. Dorgeroux, and as they undoubtedly succeeded with him. It must have been a stirring conversation, from which this great scientist derived such power and certainty that it is to him that I shall now defer. Before concluding, I would like to add two further proofs based on what he himself tried to write at the foot of the screen during the last few seconds of his life—a twofold declaration made by* the man who knew:

B-ray... B E R G E...

When thus expressing his supreme belief in the so-called "B-rays," M. Dorgeroux no longer meant those mysterious rays which he had once imagined to explain the phenomena, and which would have consisted of the materialization of pictures born within and projected by ourselves. Now better informed and mire far seeing with respect to the result of his experiments, he meant the gravitational rays, the existence of which he had learned through my article, and perhaps also through his communications with the Venusians, who use them in the same manner as that ordinary light rays are used by our humblest photographers.

As for the five letters B E R G E, they are not the first two syllables of the word "Bergeronnette"—a fatal error of which Bérangère Massignac was the victim—but the word Berger, *complete but for its last letter. At the moment of his death, in his already clouded brain, M. Dorgeroux, in order to identify Venus as the source of the projections, could find no better expression than* L'Etoile du Berger—*the Shepherd's Star. The proof is therefore absolute. The man who knew had time to tell us the essential part of what he knew: by means of gravitational rays, the Shepherd's Star is sending its messages to Earth!*

If we accept the successive deductions enumerated in this preliminary essay, which I trust will someday prove to be a replica of the report stolen from M. Dorgeroux, there still remain a number of points about which we do not possess any element of truth.

What is the form of the recording and projecting apparatus employed by the Venusians? By what prodigious machinery do they obtain such a perfect fixity in their projections between two celestial bodies, each animated with such complicated movements in space? And, to consider only what is close at hand, what is the nature of the screen employed for the Meudon projections? What is that dark-grey substance with which it is coated? How is that substance composed? How is it able to reconstruct the pictures?

These are still many questions which our scientific research is incapable of answering. But at least, we do not have to declare them insoluble. I shall even go farther and declare that it is our duty to study them by all the means which the public authorities are bound to place at our disposal.

M. Massignac is said to have disappeared. Let the opportunity be seized. Let the Meudon theater be declared national property! It is out of the question that a single individual should, to the detriment of all mankind, remain the sole possessor of such tremendous secrets, and have it in his power, if he so pleases and according to his whims, to destroy them for all time. This cannot be allowed!

Soon, we must enter into new, unbroken communication with Venus. They will tell us the age-old history of our past, reveal to us the great scientific problems which they have solved, and help us to benefit from their advanced civilization, compared to which our own seems filled with nothing but confusion, ignorance, the lisping of babes and the stammering of savages...

XVI. The Kiss

We have but to read the newspapers of the time to realize that the excitement caused by the Meudon pictures reached its apex with Benjamin Prévotelle's article. I have four of those newspapers, dated the following day, on my table as I write. Not one of them contains a single page that does not refer to what had become known as "Prévotelle's Splendid Theory."

For the rest, the chorus of approval and enthusiasm was general, or very nearly so. There were barely a few cries of protest uttered by experts who felt exasperated by the boldness of his essay even more than by its flaws. The public saw not a theory, but a fact, and accepted it with the faith of true believer confronted with the divine truth. Everyone contributed his own proof as yet one more stone added to the edifice. The objections, however strong they might be— and they were set forth without compromise—seemed temporary and capable of being removed by closer study and a more careful confirmation of the phenomenon.

And all the articles, the interviews and the letters that appeared supported Prévotelle's own conclusions and recommended the very same measures he had proposed. Action had to be taken without delay and a series of experiments had to be conducted at the Meudon theater.

Amidst this effervescence, Massignac's kidnapping didn't seem to matter much. He had disappeared? There was nothing to enable one to tell who had taken him or where he was confined? So what? It made very little difference. As Prévotelle had said, the opportunity was too good to miss. The doors of the theater had been sealed on the first morning. What were the authorities waiting for? Why not begin the experiments at once?

As for me, I did not breathe a word of my Bougival adventure, for fear of implicating Bérangère, who was directly involved in it. Nevertheless, I returned to the banks of the Seine. A speedy investigation showed that Massignac and Velmot had lived on the island during a part of the winter in the company of a small boy who, when they were away, looked after the house which one of the two villains had rented under a false name. I explored the island and the house. No one was living there now. I found a few pieces of furniture, a few household items, but nothing more.

On the fourth day, a provisional *ad hoc* committee was appointed and met at the theater in the middle of the afternoon. As the sky was cloudy, they contented themselves with examining the containers discovered in the basement of the wall, and, after lowering the curtain, cutting off strips of the dark-grey substance at different points of the screen along the edges.

The subsequent analysis revealed absolutely nothing out of the ordinary. They found an amalgam of organic materials and acids, which it would be tedious to enumerate here, and which provided no explanation at all for the phenomenon.

On the sixth day, the sky became clear again, and the committee returned, together with a number of officials and a few sightseers who had succeeded in joining them.

The wait in front of the screen was fruitless and just a little ridiculous. All those people looking out for something that did not happen, standing with wide-open eyes and distorted faces, in front of a wall that had nothing on it, wore an air of solemnity which was delightfully comical.

An hour was spent in anxious expectation. The wall remained bare.

The disappointment was all the greater since the public had been waiting for this test as the expected climax of this sensational tragedy. Were we to give up all hope of knowing the truth and admit that Noël Dorgeroux's formula alone was capable of producing the pictures? I, for one, was convinced of it. In addition to the substances removed and analyzed, there was a solution, manufactured by Massignac from my uncle's formula, which he kept carefully, as my uncle used to do, in blue phials or bottles, and which was spread over the screen before each projection in order to give it the mysterious power of receiving the images.

A thorough search was conducted, but no phials, no blue bottles, were found.

There was no doubt about it: people were starting to regret the disappearance—perhaps the death—of Massignac. Was the great secret to be lost just as Benjamin Prévotelle's theory had proved its importance?

On the morning of the eleventh day after the date of Prévotelle's article, that is to say, on May 27, the newspapers printed a note signed by Théodore Massignac in which he announced that, in the late afternoon of that same day, a third exhibition would take place under his own direction.

He actually showed up at about noon. However, the doors were closed and guarded by four policemen and he was unable to obtain admission. But at 3 p.m., an official from the Prefecture of Police arrived, with the powers to strike a deal with the villain.

Massignac laid down his conditions: he was once more to become the absolute master of the theater, which could be surrounded by police, but would be closed between the performances to everybody but himself. None of the spectators was to carry a camera or any other scientific instrument.

Everything was agreed in order to continue the interrupted series of miraculous exhibitions and resume communication with Venus. This capitulation from the authorities before the boldness of a man whose crime was known to all showed that Prévotelle's theory had been adopted by the government.

The fact is—and no one failed to realize it—that those in power were giving way in the hope of turning the tables later and, by some subterfuge, laying their hands on the screen when it would be in working order. Massignac felt this so clearly that, when the doors opened, he had the effrontery to distribute a pamphlet reading:

WARNING!

The audience is hereby warned that any attack on the management will have as its immediate consequence the destruction of the screen and the irreparable loss of Noël Dorgeroux's secret.

For my part, as I had had no proof of Massignac's death, I was not surprised by his return. But the change in his features and attitude astounded me. He looked ten years older; his figure was bent; and the everlasting smile, which used to be his natural expression, no longer lit up his face, which had become emaciated, yellow and anxious.

He caught sight of me and drew me to one side:

"That scoundrel Velmot has behaved very badly towards me! First, he beat me black and blue, down in that cellar. Then, he lowered me into the water to make me talk. I spent ten days in bed before I got over it! By Jove, it's a miracle I'm here now! What a villain! But he hasn't got away with it altogether. He's got his share of trouble too—worse than I did!—at least I hope so. The hand that struck him was steady enough and showed no sign of trembling."

I did not ask him what hand he meant, or how the tragedy had ended on the island. There was only one thing that mattered:

"Massignac, have you read Prévotelle's report?"

"Yes."

"Does it agree with the facts? Does it agree with my uncle's account, the one which you stole?"

He shrugged.

"What business is that of yours? What business is it of anybody's? Do I keep the pictures to myself? You know I don't. On the contrary, I'm trying to show them to everybody and honestly to earn the money which they pay me. What more do they want?"

"They want to protect the discovery..."

"Never! Never!" he exclaimed, angrily. "Tell them to shut up and stop all that nonsense! I've bought Noël Dorgeroux's secret, yes, bought and paid for it. I mean to keep it for myself, and for myself alone, against everybody else and despite any threat. I shan't talk now anymore than I did when Velmot had me in his grip and I was on the point of croaking. I tell you, Monsieur Beaugrand, Noël Dorgeroux's secret will perish with me. If I die, it dies. I've sworn an oath on it."

When, a few minutes later, Massignac moved towards his seat, he no longer wore his former air of a lion-tamer entering a cage, but rather looked like a hunted animal startled by the least sound and trembling at the approach of the man with the whip. His security guards were there, wearing their ushers' chains and looking as fierce and aggressive as ever. I'd been told that their wages had been doubled.

But there seemed to be no need for such a precaution. The danger that threatened Massignac did not come from the crowd, which preserved a religious silence, as though it were preparing to celebrate some solemn ritual. He was received with neither applause, nor invective. The spectators waited gravely for what was about to happen, though no one guessed what would be happening.

Those seated on the upper rows of seats—of whom I was one—often turned their heads upwards. In the clear sky, shimmering with gold, shone Venus, the Evening Star.

What a moment! For the first time in the history of the world, men felt certain that they were being observed by alien eyes and watched by minds which differed from their own. For the first time, they were connected in a tangible fashion with that great beyond, once inhabited only by their dreams and aspirations, but from which the friendly gaze of their new brothers now fell upon them. These were not legends and phantoms cast into the empty Heavens by our thirsting imaginations, but living beings who were addressing us in the natural language of the pictures, until the hour, now near at hand, when we would be able to communicate like friends who had lost and found one another.

Their eyes, their Three Eyes, were infinitely gentle that day, filled with a tenderness which seemed born of love and which thrilled us with an equal tenderness, with the same love. What were they prefigurating, those women's eyes that quivered before us so attractively and with such smiles and delightful promise? Of what happy and charming scenes of our past were we to be the astonished witnesses?

I watched my neighbors. All, like myself, were leaning towards the screen. The sight affected their faces before it occurred. I noticed the pallor of two young men beside me. A woman, whose face was hidden from me by a thick veil, sat with her handkerchief in her hand, ready to shed tears.

The first scene represented a landscape full of glaring light, which looked like the Italian countryside, with a dusty road along which cavalry men, wearing the uniform of the French Revolutionary armies, were galloping around a coach drawn by four horses. Then, immediately afterwards, we saw in a shady garden, at the end of an avenue of dark cypresses, a house with closed shutters standing on a flower-decked terrace.

The carriage stopped at the foot of the terrace and drove off again after setting down an officer who ran up to the door and knocked with the pommel of his sword.

The door opened almost at once. A tall young woman rushed out of the house, with her arms outstretched towards the officer. But, at the moment when they were about to embrace, they both took a few steps backwards, as though to delay their happiness and, in so doing, to taste its delights more fully.

Then the screen showed us the woman's face; and words cannot depict the expression of joy and love that turned this face, which was neither very beautiful nor very young, into something more alive with youth and beauty than anything else in this world.

After that, the lovers flung themselves into each others' arms, as if their lives, too long kept apart, were being reunited. They kissed.

We saw nothing more of the French officer and his Italian lover. A new picture followed, less bright but equally clear, that of a long, battlemented rampart, marked with a series of round, machicolated towers. Below and in the center, among the ruins of a bastion, were trees growing in a semicircle around an ancient oak.

Gradually, from the shade of the trees, there stepped into the sunlight a young girl, clad in the style of the fifteenth century with a full-skirted gown trailing behind her. She stopped with her hands open. She saw something that we were unable to see. She wore a bewitching smile. Her eyes were half-closed; and her slender figure seemed to sway as she waited.

What she was awaiting was the arrival of a young page, who came to her and kissed her on the lips while she flung herself at him.

This enamored couple certainly moved us, as the first couple had done, not just because of the passion that possessed them, but because we knew we were seeing an actual couple who had been alive, really alive, a long time ago. Our feelings were no longer those we had experienced during the earlier exhibitions. Gone were our skepticism and ignorance. We now knew that we were beholding the lives of real human beings from our past. They were not play-acting for our entertainment actions which they had rehearsed before; they were performing them for the first time. It was their first kiss!

This feeling of reality surpassed everything that could be imagined! To see a fifteenth century page and damsel kissing each other!

After that, we saw the Greek Acropolis, standing against the sky of two thousand years ago, surrounded by houses and gardens, with palm trees, well tendered roads, temples... The Parthenon, not in ruins, but in all its splendor and perfection! A host of statues surrounded it. Men and women climbed its stairways, and they were Athenians from the time of Pericles or Demosthenes![45]

They came and went in all directions. They talked together. Then they drifted apart. A little empty street ran down between two white walls. A group passed and moved away, leaving behind a man and woman who stopped suddenly, glanced around them, and kissed each other fervently. And we saw, underneath the veil behind which the woman's forehead was shrouded, two great, dark eyes whose lids fluttered like wings, eyes which opened, closed, laughed and wept.

Thus we traveled back through time and understood that those who, gazing down upon the Earth, had taken these pictures wished, in showing them to us, to remind us of the forever youthful and eternally renewed, act of universal love. Through this, they proclaimed themselves to be like us, governed and exalted by the same sentiments, though perhaps not expressed in the same fashion. The same impulses may sweep them along, but they couldn't know the adorable union of the lips.

---

[45] Greek statesmen from the Golden Age of Athens, from respectively 495-429 and 384-322 BC.

Other couples passed. Other times were displayed. Other civilizations appeared. We saw the kiss of an Egyptian peasant and a young girl; and that exchanged up in a hanging garden of Babylon between a princess and a priest; and that which transfigured to such a degree as to make them almost human two brutish beings squatting at the door of a prehistoric cave; and more kisses, and yet more.

They were brief visions, some of which were indistinct and faded, like an ancient fresco, yet penetrating and potent, because of the meaning which they conveyed, full at the same time of poetry and brutal reality, of violence and serene loveliness.

And always the woman's eyes were the center, the purpose, and the justification of the pictures. Oh, the smiles and the tears, the gladness and the despair, and the exquisite rapture of all those eyes! How our friends up there must also have felt all the charm of them, in order to dedicate them to us! How they must have felt, and perhaps regretted, the difference between those enchanted eyes and their own, so gloomy and devoid of expression! There was such sweetness in those women's eyes, such grace, such ingenuousness, such adorable perfidy, such distress, such seductiveness, such triumphant joy, such grateful humility... and such love, when they offered their lips to their lovers!

I was unable to see the end of those pictures. There was a movement about me in the midst of the crowd, which was beside itself with excitement, and I found myself next to the woman in mourning, whose face was hidden beneath a veil.

She thrust these aside. I recognized Bérangère. She raised her passionate eyes to mine, flung her arms around my neck, and gave me her lips, while she stammered words of love. And in this way, I learned, without any need for explanation, that Massignac's insinuations against his daughter were false, that she was the terror-stricken victim of the two scoundrels and she never ceased to love me.

XVII. Supreme Visions

The exhibition of the following day was preceded by two important pieces of news which appeared in the evening papers. A group of financiers had offered Théodore Massignac the sum of ten million francs for Noël Dorgeroux's secret and the right to operate the theater. Massignac was supposed to give them his answer next day.

But, at the last moment, the authorities received a telegram from Toulouse from the maid who had claimed to have nursed Massignac in his house a few weeks before. She now declared that her master's illness had been feigned, and that he had left the house on several occasions, each time carefully concealing his absence from his neighbors. And one of these absences matched the day and time of Noël Dorgeroux's murder. The woman's testimony therefore forced the authorities to reopen an investigation that had already elicited much presumptive evidence of Massignac's guilt.

The upshot of these two bits of news was that the fate of my uncle's secret now depended on chance, that is, it could be saved by an immediate purchase, or lost forever by Massignac's arrest. This alternative added to the anxious curiosity of the spectators, many of whom correctly believed that they may have witnessed the last of the Meudon exhibitions. They argued about the most recent news and for or against Prévotelle's theory. Some claimed that the young engineer, to whom Massignac had refused admission, was preparing a whole series of new experiments with the intention of proving the truth of his theory, the simplest of which consisted in erecting a scaffolding outside the theater and setting up an intervening obstacle to block the projections from Venus.

I, myself, had thought of nothing since the previous day but Bérangère, whom I had pursued through the crowd, but who had succeeded in escaping me. I was smitten with love; I had held her against me, trembling, happy to abandon herself for a few moments to a kiss upon which she bestowed all the fervor of her incomprehensible soul. Yet, she had fled, easily losing me among the closely packed tiers of seats. Eventually, I abandoned any attempt at finding her. I tried forgetting her. I set my mind to focus only on my uncle's secret. My life was swallowed up again by that great riddle which those astonishing events had set in motion before us.

The new projection began, after the most sorrowful and heart-rending look that had yet animated the miraculous Three Eyes, with that singular phantasmagoria of creatures which Benjamin Prévotelle had proposed that we should regard as the inhabitants of Venus, and which, for that matter, it was impossible for us not to regard as such. I will not try to define them with greater precision, nor to describe the setting in which they moved. One's confusion in the presence of those grotesque Shapes, those absurd movements, and those startling landscapes was so great that one hardly had time to receive exact impressions, or to deduce the slightest theory from them. All that I can say is that we were the observers, as we had been on the first occasion, of a manifestation of public order.

There were a number of spectators and a connected sequence of actions tending towards a clearly defined end, which seemed to us to be of the same nature as the first execution we had beheld. Everything, in fact—the grouping of certain Shapes in the middle of an empty space and around a motionless Shape, the actions performed, the cutting up of that lone Shape—suggested that this was an execution in progress—the taking of a life.

In any event, we were perfectly aware, through the previous instance, that its real significance would come only with the second part of the film. Since nearly all the pictures were two-fold, assembled around an analogy or an antithesis, we had to wait before we could figure out the general idea behind this projection.

This soon became apparent; and the mere narrative of what we saw showed how right my uncle Dorgeroux's prophecy was when he had said:

"*Men will come here as pilgrims and will fall upon their knees and weep like children!*"

We saw a winding road, rough with cobbles and cut into steps, climbing a steep, arid, shadowless hill under a burning sun. It almost seemed we could see the eddies rising, like a scorching breath, from the parched soil.

A mob of excited people was scaling the abrupt slope. On their backs hung tattered robes, that of the beggars, or artisans of middle-eastern origins.

The road disappeared and reappeared at a higher level, where we saw that this mob was preceding and following a company consisting of soldiers clad like Roman legionaries. There were perhaps sixty or eighty of them. They were marching slowly, raggedly, carrying their spears over their shoulders, while some were swinging their helmets in their hands. Now and again, one stopped to drink.

From time to time, we became aware that these soldiers were but an escort to a smaller group consisting of a few officers and civilians clad in long robes, like priests. A little apart from them stood four women, the lower halves of whose faces were hidden by veils. Then, suddenly at a turn in the road, where the group had become slightly disorganized, we saw a heavy cross outspread, jolting its way upwards. A man was underneath, almost crushed by that intolerable burden which he was condemned to bear to the place of his martyrdom.

He stumbled at every step, made an effort to stand up, fell again, dragged himself yet a little farther, crawling, clutching at the stones on the road, and then moved no more. A blow from a staff, administered by one of the soldiers, made no difference. His strength was exhausted.

At that moment, another man came down the stony path. He was stopped and ordered to carry the cross. He could not and quickly made his escape. But, as the soldiers with their spears turned back towards the man lying on the ground, three of the women intervened and offered to carry the burden. One of them took the end, the two others the two arms, and thus they climbed the rugged hill, while the fourth woman raised the condemned man and supported his hesitating steps.

At two further points, we were able to follow the painful ascent of him who was going to his death. And, on each occasion, his face was shown upon the screen. We did not recognize it. It was unlike the face which we expected to see, according to the usual representations. But how much more fully satisfied the profound conception which it evoked in us by its actual presence!

It was *He*; we could not doubt it for a moment. *He* lived before us. *He* was suffering. *He* was about to die before us. Each of us would have liked to avert the menace of that horrible death; and each of us prayed with all our might for some peaceful vision in which we could have see *Him* surrounded by *His* Disciples and gentle womenfolk.

The soldiers, as they reached the place of torture, assumed a harsher aspect. The priests with ritual gestures cursed the stones amid which the tree was to be raised and retired, with hanging heads.

Now came the cross, with the women bending under it. The condemned man followed them. There were two of them now supporting *Him*. *He* stopped. Nothing could save *Him* now. When we saw *Him* again, after a short interruption of the picture, the cross was set up and the agony had begun.

I do not believe that any assembly of men could ever be thrilled by a more violent and noble emotion than that which held us in its grip at this moment, which—let it be clearly understood—was the very hour at which the world's destiny was settled for centuries and centuries.

We were not guessing at its nature through legends and distorted narratives. We did not have to reconstruct it from ancient documents or conceive it according to our own feelings and imagination. *It was there*, that unparalleled hour. It lived before us, in a setting devoid of grandeur, which seemed to us lowly and poverty-stricken. The bulk of the sightseers had gone. A dozen soldiers were playing dice on a flat stone and drinking. Four women stood in the shadow of the crucified man, whose feet they bathed with their tears. At the summit of two other hillocks hard by, two other figures were writhing on their crosses. That was all.

But what a meaning we read into this gloomy spectacle! What a frightful tragedy was enacted before our eyes! The beating of our hearts wrung with love and distress was the very beating of that Sacred Heart. Those weary eyes looked down upon the same things that we beheld, the same dry soil, the same savage faces of the soldiers, the same countenances of the grief-stricken women.

When a last vision showed us *His* rigid and emaciated body and *His* sweet ravaged head in which the dilated eyes seemed to us abnormally large, the whole crowd rose to its feet, men and women fell upon their knees, and, in a profound silence that trembled with prayer, all arms were despairingly outstretched towards the dying God.

Such scenes cannot be understood by those who did not witness them. You will find their description in these pages no better than in the newspapers of the time. They piled up adjectives, exclamations and apostrophes, but gave no idea of what the vivid reality had been like. On the other hand, all the articles stressed the essential truth which emerged from the two films of that day, and rightly declared that the second explained and completed the first.

Yonder too, among our distant brethren, a God had been delivered to the horrors of martyrdom; and, by connecting the two events, they intended to convey to us that they, like us, possessed a religious belief and ideal aspirations.

In the same way, they had shown us by the death of one of their rulers and the death of one of our kings that they had known the same political upheavals. In the same way, they had shown us by visions of lovers that they, like us, yielded to the power of love. Therefore, the same stages of civilizations, the same efforts of belief, the same instincts, the same sentiments, existed on both worlds.

How could messages so positive, so stimulating, have failed to increase our longing to know more about it all and to communicate more closely? How could we anything else but think of the questions which it was possible to ask, or the mysteries which could now be solved, problems of the future and the past, problems of civilization, problems of destiny?

But the same uncertainty lingered in us, keener than the day before. What would become of Noël Dorgeroux's secret? Massignac had now accepted the ten millions which he had been offered, but on condition that he would be paid the money immediately after the next performance, and receive a safe-conduct for America. Although the investigation in Toulouse had confirmed the accusations brought against him by his maid, the deal was about to be authorized, so greatly did the importance of Noël Dorgeroux's secret outweigh all ordinary consideration of justice and punishment.

Finding itself confronted with a state of things which could not be prolonged, the government yielded, but obligated Massignac to sell the secret under penalty of immediate arrest. Further, they surrounded him with agents who were instructed to arrest at the first sign of any trickery.

When the iron curtain rose before the next exhibition, twelve policemen took the place of the usual guards.

And then began a presentation to which these special circumstances imparted a great deal of gravity and which was both poignant and implacable.

As on the other occasions, we did not at first grasp the significance which the scenes projected on the screen were intended to convey. These scenes passed before our eyes as swiftly as the love scenes displayed two days before.

There was no initial vision of the Three Eyes. Instead, we plunged straight into reality. In the middle of a garden sat a woman, young and beautiful, dressed in the fashion of 1830. She was working at a tapestry stretched on a frame and, from time to time, raised her eyes to cast a fond look at a little girl playing by her side. The mother and child smiled at each other. The child left her sand castles and came and kissed her mother.

For a few minutes, there was merely this placid picture of ordinary human life.

Then, a dozen paces behind the mother, a tall, close-trimmed screen of foliage was gently thrust aside and, with a series of imperceptible movements, a man came out of the shadows, young and well-dressed like the woman.

His face was hard; his jaws were set. He had a knife in his hand.

He took three or four steps forward. The woman had not hears him; her little girl could not see him. He came still farther forward, with infinite precautions, so that the gravel did not crunch under his feet, nor any branch touch him.

He stood over the woman. His face displayed a terrible cruelty and an inflexible will. The woman, unknowing, was still smiling and happy.

Slowly the man's arm was raised above that smile, above that happiness. Then it descended with equal slowness, and, suddenly, it struck a sharp blow to the heart, beneath the woman's left shoulder.

There was no sound; that is certain. At most, a sigh, like the single sigh emitted, in the awful silence, by the crowd.

The man withdrew his bloody weapon. He listened for a moment, bent over the lifeless body that had huddled into the chair, felt her pulse, and then walked back with measured steps to the screen of foliage, which closed behind him.

The child had not ceased playing. She continued to laugh and talk.

The picture faded away.

The next film showed us two men walking along a deserted path, beside which ran a narrow river. They were talking without animation; they might have been discussing the weather.

When they turned around and retraced their steps, we saw that one of them, the one who hitherto had been hidden behind his companion, carried a revolver.

They both stopped and continued to talk quietly. But the face of the armed man suddenly became distorted and assumed the same criminal expression which we had beheld in the first picture. And suddenly, he pointed the gun and fired. The other man fell. The murderer flung himself upon him and snatched his wallet.

We saw four more murders, none of which had as its perpetrator or its victim anyone who was known to us. They were sensational, very short, restricted only to their essential facts—the peaceful representation of a scene in daily life followed by the sudden explosion of crime in all its bestial horror.

The spectacle was dreadful, especially because of the expression of confidence and serenity maintained by the victims, while we, in the audience, saw the phantom of death rise over them. The waiting for the final blow, which we were unable to avert, left us all breathless and terrified.

And then, one last picture of a man appeared to us. A stifled exclamation rose from the crowd. It was Noël Dorgeroux!

XVIII. The Château de Pré-Bony

The exclamation of the crowd proved to me that, at the sight of the great scientist, who was known to all by his portraits and by the posters exhibited at the doors, the same thought had instantaneously struck us all. We all understood from the start. After the series of criminal pictures, we knew the meaning of Noël Dorgeroux's appearance on the screen, and knew the inexorable climax of the story which we were being told. There had been six victims. My uncle would be the seventh. We were going to witness his death and see the face of his murderer! All this was planned with the most disconcerting skill and with a logic whose implacable rigor wrung our very souls. We were caught in a horribly painful

256

track which we were bound to follow to the end, notwithstanding the unspeakable passion of our feelings. I sometimes ask myself, in all sincerity, whether the series of miraculous visions could have continued much longer, since the nervous tension which they demanded seemed to exceed our human resistance.

A succession of pictures showed us several episodes, the first dating back to a time when my uncle had not yet discovered the great secret, since his son was still alive. It took place during the Great War. Dominique, in uniform, was embracing his father, who was weeping and trying to hold him back. After Dominique went, Noël Dorgeroux watched him go with all the distress of a father who shall not see his son again.

Next, we have my uncle in his laboratory, with its sheds and workshops, just as it used to be. Bérangère, still a child, was running to and fro. She must have been thirteen or fourteen at most.

We then followed their existence in pictures which showed us with what hourly attention my uncle's labors had been watched *from up there*. We saw him become older and a little more bent. Bérangère grew up, which did not deter her from playing and running about.

We then saw her as I had found her the previous summer, and, at the same time, we saw my uncle standing on a ladder, daubing the wall with a long brush which he kept dipping into a can. He stepped back and looked at the wall with a questioning gaze; the screen was now marked out. There was nothing; yet something vague and confused must have already appeared in the substance, because he seemed to be waiting...

There was a click and, suddenly, everything changed. The theater arose, unfinished in parts, as it was on that Sunday in March when I had discovered my uncle's dead body. The new wall was there, surrounded by its canopy. My uncle has opened the recess contained in its basement and was arranging his containers. But, now, beyond the theater, which grew smaller, we saw the woods and the undulations of the adjoining meadow.

A man came up and moved towards the path which skirted the fence of the property. I recognized him at once: it was the same man with whom I was to struggle half an hour later, in the wood through which he had just come. It was the murderer!

He was wrapped in a raincoat whose upturned collar touched the lowered brim of his hat. He walked uneasily. He went up to the lamp post, looked around, climbed up slowly and made his way into the Laboratory. He followed the same path which I had taken myself that day after him and thrusted forward his head as I had done.

Noël Dorgeroux was standing before the screen. He has closed the recess and jotted down some notes in a book. The victim suspected nothing.

Then the man threw off his hat. He turned his face in our direction. It was Massignac!

The crowd was expecting him so much that there was no demonstration of surprise. Besides, the pictures were of a nature that left no room for impressions or interpretations. The consequences which might ensue from the public proof of Massignac's guilt were not yet apparent to us. We were not living through the minutes which were elapsing *in the past*, but through those which were elapsing *in the present*; and until the last moment, we thought only of knowing *whether Noël Dorgeroux, whom we already knew to be dead, was still going to be murdered*!

The anticipated scene did not last very long. In truth, my uncle had not been aware for a minute of the danger that threatened him. Contrary to what was elicited at the inquiry, there was no trace of that struggle of which the traces appeared to have been discovered. This struggle occurred *afterwards*, after my uncle had been struck down and was lying on the ground, motionless. It took place between a murderer seized with insensate fury and the corpse which he seemed bent upon killing anew.

In fact, it was this act of savage brutality that let loose the rage of the crowd. Held back until then by some kind of unreasoning hope, petrified in terror by the sight of the loathsome act they had just beheld on the screen, the spectators were stirred with anger and hatred against the very visible murderer whose existence suddenly provoked it beyond endurance. They experienced a sense of revolt and a need for immediate justice, which no considerations were able to stay. The crowd underwent an immediate change of attitude. It withdrew itself abruptly from the evocation of the past, and flung itself into the reality of the present. Obeying an unanimous impulse, they poured helter-skelter down the theater and, flowing like a torrent through every gangway, rushed to assault the iron cage in which Massignac was sheltering.

I cannot describe accurately what happened next. Massignac, who attempted to flee at the first moment of the accusation, found in front of him the twelve policemen, who next turned against the crowd when it came dashing against the grille. But what resistance could those twelve men offer?

The grille fell. The police were flattened in the crush. In a flash, I saw Massignac, braced against the wall, taking aim with two revolvers held in his outstretched hands. A number of shots rang out. Some of the attackers fell. Then Massignac, taking advantage of the others' hesitation, stooped swiftly towards the electric battery in the foundation. He pressed a button.

Right at the top of the wall, the canopy overhanging the two pillars opened like a sluice and sent forth streams of a bluish liquid, which seethed and bubbled in a cascade over the whole surface of the screen.

I then remembered his terrible prophecy:

"*Noël Dorgeroux's secret will perish with me. If I die, it dies!*"

In the anguish of peril, at the very bottom of the abyss, he had conceived the abominable idea and had had the courage to carry out his threat. My uncle's work had just been utterly destroyed.

Nevertheless, I darted forward, as if I could still avert the disaster by saving the scoundrel's life. But the crowd had grabbed its prey and was passing it from hand to hand, like a howling pack worrying and rending the animal which it had hunted down.

I succeeded in pushing my way through with the aid of two policemen, and then only because Massignac's body had ended by falling into the hands of a group of less infuriated assailants, who were embarrassed by the sight of the dying man.

They gathered around him to watch his agony, and one of them, raising his voice above the din, called to me:

"Quick, quick!" he said, when I came near. "He is speaking your name."

At the first glance at the mass of bleeding flesh that lay on one of the tiers, between two rows of seats, I perceived that there was no hope, and that it was a miracle that this corpse was still breathing. Still, it was uttering my name. I caught the syllables as I stooped over the face mauled beyond recognition and, speaking slowly and distinctly, I said:

"It's I, Massignac—Victorien Beaugrand. What do you have to say to me?"

He managed to open his eyes, looked at me with dimly, then closed then again immediately while stammering:

"A letter... a letter... sewn in the lining..."

I felt the rags which remained of his jacket. He had done well to sew it inside, for his pockets were empty. I read my name on the envelope.

"Open it... open it," he said, in a whisper.

I tore open the envelope. There were only a few lines scribbled in a large hand across a sheet of paper, a few lines of which I took the time to read only the first, which said:

Bérangère knows the formula.

"Bérangère!" I exclaimed. "But where is she? Do you know?"

At once, I understood the imprudence of which I had been guilty in mentioning the girl's name aloud. Bending lower down, I put my ear to Massignac's mouth to catch his last words.

He repeated the name of Bérangère time after time, in an effort to give me the answer which I had been asking, and which his memory perhaps refused to provide. His lips moved convulsively and he stammered forth some hoarse sounds which were more like a death-rattle, but which enabled me to distinguish the words:

"Bérangère... Château... Château de Pré-Bony..."

However great the tension of the mind may be when concentrating on an idea which entirely absorbs it, we still remain subject to the thousand sensations that assail us. Thus, at the very moment when I rose and, in a whisper, repeated, "Château de Pré-Bony... de Pré-Bony," the vague impression that another had heard the address which Massignac had given began to take shape. In fact, I perceived, *when it was already too late*, that this other man, thanks to his position at my side, must have also been able to read the opening line of Massignac's letter. And that other man's make-up suddenly dropped away before my eyes to reveal the pallid features of Velmot!

I turned around. He had just made his way out of the group of onlookers who stood gathered around and was already slipping through the shifting masses of the crowd. I called out. I shouted his name. I dragged detectives in his wake. But I was too late!

And so, Velmot, the implacable enemy who had not hesitated to torture Massignac in order to extract my uncle's formula, now knew that Bérangère knew that formula! And he had, at the same time, learned where she was hiding!

The Château de Pré-Bony!

Where was it? In what corner of France had she taken refuge after her god-father's murder? It couldn't be very far from Paris, seeing that she had asked for my assistance, and that, two days ago, she had come to Meudon. But whatever the distance, how was I to find it? There were a thousand châteaux within a radius of twenty-five miles from Paris.

Yet, I thought, *the solution to this mystery lies there, in that château. All is not lost and all may still be saved, but I have to get there at once. Though the miraculous screen has been destroyed, Massignac has given me the means of reconstructing it. I have to get there by daybreak, or Velmot will have Bérangère at his mercy.*

I spent the whole evening in inquiries. I consulted maps, newspapers, directories. I asked everywhere; I telephoned. No one was able to supply the least information as to the whereabouts of the Château de Pré-Bony.

It was not until the morning, after an agitated night, that a more methodical scrutiny of recent events gave me the idea of starting my investigation in the very district where I knew Bérangère had stayed. I hired a motorcar and had my-self driven to Bougival. Frankly, I had no great hope, but my fear that Velmot might discover her retreat before I did caused me such suffering that I kept telling myself:

That's it... I'm on the right track... I'm sure to find Bérangère. That villain shall not touch a hair of her head...

My love for Bérangère had suddenly became purged of all the doubts and suspicions that had poisoned it. I no longer troubled myself to explain her conduct, nor to establish the least proof for or against her. Even if her kiss had not already wiped out every disagreeable recollection, the danger which she was incurring was enough to restore all my faith in her and all my affection.

My first inquiries at Ville d'Avray, Marnes and Vaucresson told me nothing. The Château de Pré-Bony was unknown. At La Celle-Saint-Cloud I finally found a clue. There, in a local inn, thanks to a casual question, I located Velmot. A tall, pale-faced gentleman, I was told, often motored along the Bougival road and had been seen prowling outside the village that very morning.

I questioned my informant more closely. It really was Velmot! He had a four hours' start on me. And he knew where to go! Also, he was in love with Bérangère! Four hours' start, for that clever and daring scoundrel, who was staking everything on this last throw of the die, was a lot! Who could stop him? What scruples could he have? To seize upon Bérangère, to hold her in his power, to compel her to speak: all this would be child's play. And he was in love with Bérangère, too!

I remember striking the table with my fist and exclaiming, angrily:

"No, no, it's not possible! That château is bound to be somewhere near here! I must find it!"

Thereafter, I did not experience a moment's hesitation. On the one hand, I hadn't not mistaken in coming here. On the other hand, I knew that Velmot, having heard Massignac's last words and knowing the region had begun his campaign at dawn.

There was a crowd of people outside the inn. Feverishly, I asked them about the château. Finally, someone mentioned a crossroad sometimes known as "Pré-Bony" on the road to Saint-Cucufa, some two or three miles away. One of the roads which branched from it led to a new house, of not very imposing appearance, which was inhabited by a young married couple, the Comte and Comtesse de Roncherolles.

I felt that it was only because of sheer will power that I had managed to find a possible location which it now behooved me to investigate at once.

I made my way there hurriedly. As I was walking across the garden, a young man alighted from horseback at the foot of the steps.

"Is this the Château de Pré-Bony?" I asked.

He flung the reins of his horse to a groom and replied, with a smile:

"At least, that's what they call it, rather pompously, in Bougival."

"Ah!" I murmured, taken aback by this piece of good news. "So it's here... and I'm in time!"

The young man introduced himself. He was the Comte de Roncherolles.

"May I ask to whom I have the honor...?" he inquired.

"My name is Victorien Beaugrand," I replied.

And, without further preamble, trusting the man's looks, which were frank and friendly, I added:

"I have come about Bérangère. She's here, isn't she? She found shelter here?"

The Comte flushed slightly and eyed me with some suspicion. I took his hand and said:

"If you please, Monsieur, my request is very serious. Bérangère is being hunted down by an extremely dangerous man."

"Who?"

"Velmot."

"Velmot?"

The Comte threw off all further pretense and repeated:

"Velmot! The man whom she loathes! Yes, she has everything to fear from him. Fortunately, he does not know where she is."

"But he does... since yesterday," I exclaimed.

"Ah! But he will still need time to make his preparations, to plan his move..."

"He was seen not far from here, yesterday, by the locals."

I began to tell him what I knew, but he did not let me finish. Obviously as anxious as myself, he drew me towards a lodge, standing some distance from the main house, which Bérangère occupied.

He knocked. There was no answer, but the door was open. He entered and went upstairs to check Bérangère's room. She was not there.

He did not seem greatly surprised.

"She often goes out early," he said.

"Perhaps she is at the house?" I suggested.

"With my wife? No, my wife is not very well and would not be up yet."

"What then?"

"I presume she has gone for her usual walk in the ruins of the old castle. She likes the view from there, which embraces Bougival and the whole river."

"Is it far?"

"No, just at the end of the park."

Still the park stretched some way back, and it took us a good five minutes to reach a circular clearing from which we could see a few lengths of broken wall perched on the top of a ridge among some fallen heaps of stone work.

"There!" said the Comte. "Bérangère has sat on this bench. Look—she has left the book which she was reading."

"And her scarf, too," I added, anxiously. "But it's rumpled and the grass around shows signs of having been trampled... My God! I hope nothing happened to her!"

I had barely finished speaking when we heard cries from the direction of the ruins—cries for help or of pain, we could not tell which. At once, we darted along the narrow path which ran up the hill, cutting across the winding forest road. When we were halfway up, the cries broke out again. We then saw a woman's figure among the crumbling stones of the old castle.

"Bérangère!" I cried, increasing my pace.

She did not see me. She was running, as if someone was in pursuit of her, and taking advantage of every bit of shelter that the ruins offered.

Then, a man appeared, looking for her, threatening her with a revolver which he carried in his hand.

"It's he!" I stammered. "Velmot!"

One after the other they entered the ruins, from which we were now separated by at most forty yards. We covered the distance in a few seconds and I rushed ahead towards the spot through which she had slipped.

As I arrived, a shot rang out, some little way off, and I heard moans. Despite my efforts, I could get no farther because the passage was blocked by brambles and ivy. My companion and I struggled desperately against the branches which were cutting our faces.

At last, we emerged on a large platform, where, at first, we saw no one among the tall grass and the moss-encrusted rocks. Still, we had heard a shot and cries of pain coming from where we now stood...

Suddenly, the Comte, who was searching a short distance in front of me, exclaimed:

"There she is! Bérangère! Are you hurt?"

I rushed forward and saw Bérangère lying outstretched in a tangle of leaves. She was so pale that I thought that she had died. I felt very clearly then that I would not survive her. I completed my thought by saying, aloud:

"I will avenge her first. The murderer shall die by my hand, I swear it."

But the Comte, after a hurried inspection, declared:

"She's not dead; she's breathing."

And I saw Bérangère open her eyes.

I fell on my knees besides her and, lifting her fair and sorrow-stricken face in my hands, asked her:

"Are you hurt, Bérangère? Tell me, my darling."

"I'm not hurt," she whispered. "It's just the exertion—the excitement."

"But surely," I insisted, "he fired at you?"

"No, no," she said, "it was I who fired."

"Do you mean it? *You* fired?"

"Yes, with his revolver."

"You must have missed him. He must have escaped..."

"No, I did not miss. I saw him fall... quite close to the edge of this ravine."

She pointed to a deep ravine to our right. The Comte went to check it and called me immediately. When I stood beside him, he showed me the body of a man lying, head downwards, his face covered with blood. I approached and recognized Velmot. He was dead.

XIX. The Formula

Velmot dead! Bérangère alive! What joy! What new sense of security! This time, the evil adventure was over, and the girl whom I loved had nothing more to fear.

My thoughts then harked back to Noël Dorgeroux and his formula, in which his great secret was summed up. With the clues and the means in our possession, mankind was now in a position to continue my uncle's work.

Bérangère called me back:

"He's dead, isn't he?"

I felt intuitively that I should not tell her a truth which might be too heavy for her to bear, and which she was perhaps even afraid of hearing. So I replied:

"No. We haven't found him... He must have ran away..."

My answer seemed to relieve her, and she whispered:

"In any case, he is wounded... I know I hit him."

"Rest, my darling," I said, "and don't worry anymore about anything."

She did as she was told; and she was so weary that she soon fell asleep.

Before taking her home, the Comte and I went back to Velmot's body and lowered it down the slope of the ravine, which we followed to the wall that surrounded the estate.

As there was a breach at this spot, the Comte said that Velmot could not have entered the property anywhere else but here. And, in fact, a little lower down, at the entrance of a lonely forest road, we found his car. We deposited the body into it, placed the revolver on the seat, drove it to a distance of half a mile and left it at the entrance to a clearing. We met nobody on the road. The death would very likely be attributed to suicide.

An hour later, Bérangère, now back to the lodge and lying on her bed, gave me her hand, which I covered with kisses. We were alone, with no more villains around. There was no hideous shape prowling in the dark. No one was able to thwart our rightful happiness anymore.

"The nightmare is over," I said. "There is no obstacle left between you and I. You won't try to run away, will you?"

I watched her with some anxiety. She was still, to me, a creature full of mystery; and I felt there were still many secrets hidden in the shadowy places of her soul. I told her as much. She, in turn, looked at me for a long time, with her tired and fevered eyes, so different from the careless, laughing eyes which I had loved long ago, and she whispered:

"Secrets? My secrets? No. I have only one secret; and that secret was the cause of everything."

"May I hear it then?"

"Yes, because I love you."

I felt a thrill of joy. Often I had experienced a profound intuition of her love, but it had been spoiled by much distrust, suspicion and resentment in the past. But now, Bérangère was confessing it to me, gravely and frankly.

"So you do love me," I repeated. "Why did you not tell me earlier? How many misfortunes could have been avoided! Why didn't you?"

"I couldn't."

"But now you can, because there's no longer any obstacle between us?"

"There is still the same obstacle as ever."

"Which one?"

"My father."

I said in a lower voice:

"You do know that Théodore Massignac is dead?"

264

"Yes," she said, softly.

"What then?"

"But I am his daughter."

I cried eagerly:

"Bérangère, there is something I want to tell you; and I assure you before-hand..."

She interrupted me:

"Please, don't say anymore. There will always be *that* between us. It is a gulf which we cannot hope to bridge with words."

She seemed so exhausted that I made a movement to leave her, but she stopped me:

"No," she said, "don't go. I'm not ill... I want everything to be quite clear between us. I want you to understand every single thing that I have done. Listen to me..."

"We can do this tomorrow, Bérangère..."

"No, it must be done today," she insisted. "I must tell you what I have to say. Nothing will do more to restore my peace of mind. Listen to me..."

She did not have to entreat me long. How could I have wearied of looking at her and listening to her? We had been through such trials when separated from each other that I was now afraid of being parted from her.

She put her arm around my neck. Her beautiful lips were quivering beneath my eyes. Seeing my gaze fixed upon them, she smiled:

"You remember... Outside the Laboratory... The first time... That day, I hated you... and adored you... I was your enemy... and your slave... Yes, all my independent and rather wild nature was up in arms at not being able to shake off a recollection which gave me so much pain... and yet, so much pleasure!... I was conquered. I ran away from you, but I also kept coming back to you... and I would have come back if that man—you know whom I mean—had not spoken to me one morning..."

"Velmot! What did say? What did he want?"

"He'd been sent by my father. What he wanted, as I perceived later, was to use me to enter into Noël Dorgeroux's life and rob him of the secret of his invention."

"Why did you not warn me?"

"From the start, Velmot asked me to be silent. Later, he ordered it."

"You should have disobeyed him..."

"But had I committed the least indiscretion, he would have killed you. I loved you. And I was afraid because Velmot harassed me with his passion which my hatred for him only stimulated. How could I doubt that his threat was serious? From that time onward, I was trapped. With one lie and another, I became his accomplice... or rather *their* accomplice, for my father joined him in the course of the winter. Oh, what torture! That man loved me... and yet, he was so contemptible! I lived a life of terror, always hoping that they would grow tired of their schemes that were leading nowhere..."

"What about my letters from Grenoble? And my uncle's fears?"

"Yes, I know, my uncle often mentioned them to me. Without revealing my father's plot to him, I put him on his guard. It was at my request that he sent you that report which was stolen. Of course, he never anticipated they would go as far as killing him. Notwithstanding my watch, I could see that my father had found a way into the Laboratory at night... He had at his disposal methods of which I knew nothing... But between theft and murder... No, a daughter cannot believe such things..."

"So, on that Sunday when Velmot came to fetch you at the Lodge while my uncle was out...?"

"Yes. that Sunday, he told me that my father had given up his plan and wanted to say good-bye to me, and that he was waiting for me at the chapel in the old cemetery, where the two of them had been experimenting with the fragments removed from the old wall in the Laboratory. As it happened, Velmot had taken advantage of his call at the Lodge to steal one of the blue phials which my uncle used. I did not notice this before, but he had already poured part of the liquid on the improvised screen at that chapel. I was able to get hold of the phial and throw it into the well. Just then, I heard you calling me. Velmot rushed at me and carried me to his car, where, after stunning me with his fist and binding me, he hid me under a rug.

"When I recovered, I was in his garage at Batignolles. It was night. I was able to free myself and find a window which opened onto the street. I jumped out. A gentleman and a lady who were passing by picked me up, for I had sprained my ankle as I fell to the ground. They took me home with them. Next morning, I read in the papers that Noël Dorgeroux had been murdered."

Bérangère hid her face in her hands:

"Oh, how I suffered! Was I not responsible for his death? And I would have given myself up, if Monsieur and Madame de Roncherolles, who were the kindest of friends to me, had not prevented me. To give myself up meant ruining my father and, as a consequence, destroying Noël Dorgeroux's secret. This last consideration convinced me. I had to repair the wrong which I had unwittingly caused, and fight against those whom I had helped.

"As soon as I was well again, I set to work. Knowing of the existence of the written instructions which your uncle had hidden behind the portrait of D'Alembert, I had myself driven to the Lodge on the evening before the inauguration. My intention was to see you and tell you everything, but it so happened that the kitchen entrance was open and I was able to go upstairs without attracting anybody's attention. It was then that you surprised me, in your uncle's bedroom..."

"But why did you run away, Bérangère?"

"You had the documents; and that was enough."

"No, you should have stayed and explained yourself."

"Then you shouldn't have spoken to me of love," she replied, sadly. "No one should love Massignac's daughter—a murderer's daughter!"

"But the result, my poor darling," I said, with a smile, "was that Massignac, who was in the house, of which he had a key, and who overheard our conversation, took the document and, through your fault, remained the sole possessor of the secret. Not to mention that you left me face to face with a formidable adversary!"

She shook her head: "You had nothing to fear from my father. Your danger came from Velmot, and him I watched."

"How?"

"I had accepted the Roncherolles' invitation to stay at their château at Pré-Bony, because I knew that my father and Velmot had stayed in that region during the past winter. Indeed, one day I recognized Velmot's car coming down the hill at Bougival. After some searching, I discovered the shed in which he kept his car. On May 15, I was watching there when he went in, accompanied by two men. From what they said, I gathered that they had kidnapped my father at the end of the performance and taken him to an island where Velmot was hiding, and that the next day, he would be using every possible method to make my father speak. I did not know what to do. To denounce Velmot to the police meant supplying them with evidence against my father. My friends the Roncherolles were temporarily away. Longing for assistance, I telephoned you to make an appointment with you."

"I kept the appointment that same night, Bérangère."

"You came that night?" she asked, surprised.

"Of course, I did. But at the door of the inn, I was met by a boy who claimed to have been sent by you. He took me to that same island where Velmot locked me up. The following day, I witnessed him torture Massignac. My dear Bérangère, it wasn't a very clever plan!"

She seemed stupefied and said: "I sent no boy. I never left the inn and waited for you all night. Somebody must have given us away, but I can't think who."

"It's simple enough," I said, laughing. "Velmot must have a crony of his at the inn, who told him of your -call. Then he must have sent that boy to intercept me."

"But why lay a trap for you and not for me?"

"Very likely, he was waiting until the next day to capture you. But he was more afraid of me and wanted to seize the opportunity to keep me under lock and key until your father had spoken. Also he was probably obeying motives which we shall never fully elucidate, and do not really matter. The fact remains, Bérangère, that, the next day..."

"The next day," she resumed, "I managed to find a boat and, in the evening, to row to the island to the place where my father was dying. I was able to rescue him."

I was bewildered and said:

"What! It was you who saved him? You succeeded in landing your boat, finding Velmot in the dark, and hitting him just as he was turning on me? It was you who stopped him? It was you who set Massignac free?"

I took her little hand and kissed it with emotion. The dear girl! She had done all she could to protect Noël Dorgeroux's secret; and all with courage, undaunted pluck, risking death twenty times over and not recoiling, at the great hour of danger, from the terrible act of taking a life!

"You must tell me all this in detail, Bérangère. Go on with your story. Where did you take your father to?"

"To the other side of river and from there, using a gardener's cart, to the Château de Pré-Bony, where I nursed him back to health."

"And Velmot?"

She gave a shudder.

"I did not see him again for days—in fact, not until this morning. I was sitting on the bench by the ruins, reading. Suddenly, he appeared before me. I tried to run away. He stopped me and said:

" 'Your father is dead. I have come from him. Listen!'

"I distrusted him but he went on to say:

" 'I swear I come from him. To prove it, he told me that you knew the formula. He confided it to you during his illness.'

"This was true. While I was nursing my father, in this very lodge, he said to me one day:

" 'I can't predict what may happen, Bérangère. It is possible that I shall destroy the screen at Meudon, out of revenge. It will be a mistake. In any case, I want to undo that act of madness beforehand...'

"He then made me learn the formula by heart. And this was a thing which no one except my father and myself could know, because I was alone with him and kept that secret. Velmot, consequently, was telling the truth."

"What did you say?"

"I just said: 'Well?'

"Velmot said:

" 'His last wish was that you should give me the formula.'

" 'Never!' I replied. 'You lie! My father made me swear never to reveal it to anyone, whatever happens, except to one person.'

"He shrugged his shoulders:

" 'Victorien Beaugrand, I suppose?'

" 'Yes.'

" 'Victorien Beaugrand heard Massignac's last words. And he agrees with me, or at least is on the point of doing so.'

" 'I refuse to believe it!'

" 'Ask him for yourself. He's up there, in the ruins...'"

"I was in the ruins?"

"Let me finish. That's what he said next:

" 'In the ruins—fastened to the foot of a tree. His life depends on you. I offer it to you in exchange for the formula. If not, he's a dead man.'

"I did not suspect the trap which he was laying for me. I ran towards the ruins as fast as I could. This was what Velmot wanted. It was a deserted spot, which gave him an opportunity to attack me. He seized it at once, without even trying to conceal his falsehood.

" 'Ah-ha! I caught you, my dove!' he cried, throwing me to the ground. 'I knew you! You'd be sure to swallow the bait! He's your lover, after all! For you do love him, don't you?'

"Obviously, his initial purpose had been to obtain the secret from me by threats and blows. But what happened was that his jealous rage against you and my hatred for him made him lose his head. Now, he wanted his revenge. He had me in his arms. Oh, the monster!"

She hid her face in her hands. She felt very feverish; and I heard her stammering:

"The monster! I don't know how I got away from him. I was worn out. Still, I managed to bite him and escape. He ran after me, brandishing his revolver; but just as he caught me, he tripped and dropped it. I picked it up and, when he came after me again, I fired..."

She fell silent. The painful story had exhausted her. Her face retained an expression of bewilderment and fright.

"My poor Bérangère," I said, "I have done you a great wrong. I have often—too often—accused you in my heart, without guessing what a wonderful and plucky creature you were."

"You could not be expected to understand me."

"Why not?"

She murmured sadly:

"Because I am Massignac's daughter."

"No more of that!" I cried. "You are the one who always sacrificed herself and who always took the risk. And you are also the girl I love, Bérangère, the girl who gave me all her life and soul in a kiss. Remember Bérangère... the other day I found you again and when the sight of all those visions of love threw you into my arms..."

"I have forgotten nothing," she said, "and I never shall forget."

"Then you consent?"

Once again she repeated:

"I am Massignac's daughter."

"Is that the only reason why you refuse me?"

"Can you doubt it?"

I allowed a moment to pass and said:

"So if fate had willed it that you were not Massignac's daughter, you would consent to becoming my wife?"

"Yes," she said, gravely.

The hour had come to speak; and how happy I was to be able to do so. I repeated my sentence:

"If fate had willed it that you were not Massignac's daughter... Bérangère, did it ever occur to you to wonder why there was so little affection between Massignac and you? Why, on the contrary, there was so much indifference? When you were a child, the thought of going back to him and living with him used to upset you terribly... All your life was wrapped up in Meudon. All your love went to my uncle—your godfather. Don't you think that we are entitled to interpret these feelings and instincts as a special instinct?"

She looked at me in surprise:

"I don't understand," she said.

"You don't understand, because you have never thought about these things. For instance, is it natural that the death of the man whom you called your father should give you such an impression of deliverance and relief?"

She seemed dazed:

"Why do you say, *the man whom I called my father*?"

"Well," I replied, smiling, "I have never seen your birth certificate, and, as I have no proof of a fact which seems to me improbable..."

"But," she said, in a changed voice, "you have not the least proof either that it is not so..."

"Perhaps I do," I replied.

"Oh," said Bérangère, "it would be too terrible to say that and not let me learn the truth!"

"Do you know Massignac's writing?" I took a letter from my pocket and handed it to her. "Read this, my darling. It is a letter which Massignac wrote to me and which he gave me as he lay dying. I read only the first few words to begin with and went at once in search of you. Read it, Bérangère, and have no doubts: it is the evidence of a dead man."

She took the letter and read aloud:

Bérangère knows the formula and must not communicate it to anyone except you alone, Victorien. You will marry her, will you not? She is not my daughter, but Noël Dorgeroux's. She was born five months after my marriage, as you can confirm by consulting the public records. Forgive me, both of you, and pray for me.

A long pause followed. Bérangère was weeping tears of joy. A radiant light was being thrown on her whole life. The awful weight that had bowed her down in shame and despair no longer bore upon her shoulders. She was at last able to breathe, hold her head high, look straight before her and accept her share of happiness and love. She whispered:

"Is it possible? I—Noël Dorgeroux's daughter?"

"It is possible," I said, "and it is certain. After his struggle with Velmot and the care which you bestowed upon him, Massignac repented. Thinking of the day of his death, he tried to atone for his crimes and wrote that letter... which evidently possesses no legal value, but which you and I will accept as the truth. You are the daughter of Noël Dorgeroux, Bérangère, of the man whom you always loved as a father... and who wanted us to be married. Will you dream of disobeying his wishes, Bérangère? Do you not think that it is our duty to join forces and, together, complete his great enterprise? You know the indispensable formula. By publishing it, we shall make Noël Dorgeroux's wonderful life work endure forever. Do you consent, Bérangère?"

She did not reply and, when I again tried to convince her, I saw that she was listening with an absent expression, in which I was surprised to find a certain anxiety:

"What is it, darling? You accept, do you not?"

"Yes, yes," she said, "but, before everything else, I must try to jog my memory. Only think! How careless of me not to have written the formula down! Certainly, I know it by heart. But, still..."

She thought for a long time, screwing up her forehead and moving her lips. Suddenly she said:

"A paper and pencil... quick!"

I handed her a notebook. Swiftly, with a trembling hand, she jotted down a few figures. Then she stopped and looked at me with eyes full of anguish.

I understood the effort which she was making and, to calm her, said:

"Don't rack your brains now... It'll all come back later... What you need today is rest. Go back to sleep, my darling."

"I must remember it... at all costs... I must..."

"You will—some other time. You are tired now and excited. Rest yourself."

She did as I said and ended by falling asleep. But an hour later, she woke up, took the sheet of paper again and, after a minute or two, stammered:

"This is dreadful! My brain refuses to work! Oh, but it hurts..."

The night was spent in these vain attempts. Her fever increased. The next day, she was delirious and kept on muttering letters and figures which were never the same.

For a week, her life was despaired of. She suffered horribly with her head and wore herself out scribbling lines on her bed clothes.

When she became convalescent and had recovered her consciousness, we avoided the subject and did not refer to it for some time. But I felt that she never ceased to think of it and that she continued to seek the formula. At last, one day, she said with tears in her eyes:

"I have given up all hopes, my dear. I repeated that formula a hundred times after I had learned it; and I felt sure of my memory. But not a single recollection of it remains. It must have disappeared when Velmot was clutching my throat. Everything grew dark, suddenly. I know now that I shall never remember it."

She never did remember. The exhibitions were not resumed. The miraculous visions did not reappear.

And yet, what investigations were pursued! How many businesses were created which attempted to exploit the lost secret! But all in vain: the screen remained lifeless and empty, like a blind man's eyes.

To Bérangère and me it would have meant a sorrow incessantly renewed, if love had not brought us peace and consolation. The authorities, who showed themselves to be fairly easy going in this case, never found any traces of the woman whom they thought was Massignac's daughter. I was dispatched on a mission to the Far East. I sent out for her; and we were married there without attracting attention.

We often speak of Noël Dorgeroux's great secret; and Bérangère's lovely eyes then become clouded with sadness.

"Certainly," I say, "the lost secret was a wonderful thing. There was never anything more thrilling than the Meudon pictures; and those which we had a right to expect might have opened up horizons which we are not able to conceive. But are you quite sure that we should regret them? Would knowledge of the past and the future have spelled happiness for mankind? Is it not rather an essential law of nature that we should be obliged to live within the narrow confines of the present and see before or behind us no more than lights which are still just glimmering, or lights which are being faintly kindled? Our knowledge is adjusted to our strength; and it is not good to learn and to decipher too quickly truths to which we have not had time to adapt and riddles which we do not yet deserve to elucidate."

Benjamin Prévotelle made no attempt to conceal his disappointment. I keep up a regular correspondence with him. In every letter that I receive from this great scientist I anticipate his anxious questions:

"Does she remember? May we hope?"

Alas, my answers leave him no illusions:

"Bérangère remembers nothing. You must not hope."

He consoles himself by waging a fierce contest with those who still deny any value to his theory; and now that the screen has been destroyed, and it has become impossible to support his theory with material proofs, the number of his adversaries has increased and they propound objections which he must find extremely difficult to refute. But he has every sincere and unprejudiced person on his side.

He likewise has conquered the public. We all know, by our reasoned conviction, and we all believe, out of our ardent faith, that, although we now receive no more communications from our brethren on Venus, they—those strange beings with Three Eyes—are still interesting in us with the same fervor, the same watchfulness, the same impassioned curiosity.

Looking down upon us, they follow our every action; they observe us, study us, and pity us; they count our misfortunes and our wounds, and perhaps also envy us, when they witness our joys and when, in some secret place, they surprise a man and a woman, with love in their eyes, join their lips in a kiss.

José Moselli: *The Planetary Messenger*
(1924)

The Great War inevitably changed everything for French writers in general, and—as it turned out—for writers of romans scientifiques *in particular. Several writers who had begun to build highly promising careers in the genre, including Maurice Renard and J.-H.* Rosny Aîné, *found the marketplace much more hostile thereafter, as publishers began to feel, rightly or wrongly, that the technological weaponry deployed in the war had created a general hostility to technology, and that works of fiction featuring scientific advancement now could not help being bleakly pessimistic—not a good selling-point for popular fiction.*

The upmarket periodicals that had dipped a toe in speculative fiction after the end of the Great War soon stopped dabbling in it, confining the genre to the arena of action-adventure fiction, but even that arena had itself shifted markedly in the direction of lowbrow and juvenile fiction, in parallel with American "pulp fiction." One of the most prolific writers in that sector of the field was José Moselli (1882-1941), who frequently dabbled in speculative technology for the purpose of hyping up the melodramatic component of his thrillers, going to a remarkable extreme in the gory futuristic extravaganza La Fin d'Illa *(1925).[46]*

Moselli did make a brief attempt to write romans scientifiques *of a more dedicated stripe for the* Almanach scientifique *[Scientific Annual], an experiment in more earnest popularization briefly published as an accessory to the long-running periodical* Sciences et Voyages. Le Messager de la planète, *which first appeared in the 1925 issue of the* Almanach Scientifique *(published in 1924), provide an interesting example of the way in which some popular examples of* roman scientifique *had begun to mirror, probably not entirely coincidentally, the kind of speculative fiction that was beginning to appear in the American pulp magazines, and would eventually obtain its own generic niche there, initially as "scientifiction," and then as "science fiction."*

It also provides a kind of elegy for the French tradition that had culminated in Paulon's Un Message de la planète Mars, *addressing the same question in the same hopeful manner—but adding a tragic twist, which transcends its admitted awkwardness to achieve a certain bleak poignancy, in a fashion akin to one of the most famous and effective early pulp sf stories, Raymond Z. Gallun's* Old Faithful *(1934).*

Le Messager de la planète *not only illustrates a watershed in the unsteady evolution of French* roman scientifique, *but also, by re-voicing a particular philosophical cynicism that runs through the entire tradition, a cynicism that is*

---

[46] Available from Black Coat Press as *Illa's End*, ISBN 978-1-61227-031-9.

subtly different from its parallels in British and American scientific romance, but is not absent even from the most vulgar pulp sf, it reflects an essential element of the speculative imagination: that thinking about what we might become inevitably encourages a dissatisfaction with what we are.

B.S.

THE PLANETARY MESSENGER

Muffled in thick furs from top to toe, Ottar Wallens, the geologist, and Olaf Densmold, the astronomer, advanced slowly over the ice-field.

Fifty meters ahead of them, the sled guided by Lobyak, an Alaskan Indian, was gliding over the white plain. Then there was the wilderness: frozen snow, blocks of ice, grey sky, devoid of reflections. Not a breath of air, but a temperature of twenty-eight degrees below zero.

The three men—the geologist, the astronomer and the native—had left their ship, the three-master *Sirius*, eleven days before, which had brought them from Bergen as far as Wilkes Land. The *Sirius* had advanced as far as the seventieth parallel before being stopped by the ice-sheet.

The expedition's objective was not, strictly speaking, to reach the South Pole, but to get as close to it as possible and to complete the observations of Amundsen and Shackleton, from the meteorological, astronomical and geological viewpoint. As the *Sirius* could go no further, the two leaders of the expedition had decided to advance across the ice-sheet.

In addition to numerous scientific instruments, including a small wireless telegraph apparatus, they were carrying provisions of all kinds for six weeks, light and improved camping equipment and weapons all securely stowed on a sled pulled by twelve Alaskan dogs steered by Kobyak, a gigantic native hired in Nome in western Alaska.

Ottar Wallens, the geologist, was about forty-two years old. He was a strong fellow, slightly round-shouldered, with a round face and a snub nose supporting a pair of spectacles with horn frames. He was brusque, and quick to lose his temper. A member of the Royal Academy of Christiania and numerous scientific societies, he had published several works on the composition of the polar continents, which made him an authority.

His companion, Olaf Densmold, had just turned fifty-one. He was thin and bony, with a face like the prow of a ship furnished with little round eyes, dark and piercing. Taciturn by nature, he remained mute for entire days. His notable work on the satellites of Jupiter had caused a considerable stir; he was cited as one of the foremost living mathematicians.

In the course of the long crossing undertaken by the *Sirius* between Bergen and Wilkes Land, which had taken more than two months, the scientists, who were already acquainted, had become friends—or, rather, got used to one another. Both, at any rate, were equally interested in the success of the expedition that bore their name…and now, side by side, they were advancing over the bleak ice-sheet.

They did not say much. Since their departure they had had time to tell one another everything, about their past, their projects, their ambitions and their disappointments, and there were no incidents to discuss.

It was the end of September, the Antarctic spring. A pale sun appeared for a few hours every day.

Olaf Densmold made a few astronomical observations of no great interest; then they set off again. March, camp, meal, sleep—life was monotonous.

Kobyak was as taciturn as Densmold; if he talked, it was to his dogs, to encourage or threaten them. The crack of his whip's thong constituted the bulk of his speech.

The sled had already left behind the region attained by previous explorers. It was now advancing into the unknown—an unknown as bleak as it was monotonous. No plants. No trees. Nothing. The ice. In places, it was a uniform plain; further away, gigantic blocks in extraordinary, tormented forms: perfect cubes, veritable frozen waves, dunes, pyramids, the whole cut by precipices, cliffs with neat edges, as if carved by a machine. Some of these precipices were several meters wide; it was necessary to go around them. Their depth varied between ten and a hundred meters. Gurgling sounds sometimes rose up from them, revealing the labor of melt-water. Elsewhere the ice gave way under the weight of the explorers, who had to devote all their attention to following the tracks of the sled closely—for the dogs' instinct did not deceive them.

That day, they had already been on the move for four hours, and they appeared to be making satisfactory progress, not very tiring. The stillness of the air rendered the cold quite tolerable, and the surface of the ice was sufficiently smooth.

For a few moments, however, Kobyak, who usually marched head down, raised his face toward the pale sky, turning is head from right to left, like someone sniffing the wind.

"He has an odd expression, the guide," Ottar Wallens suddenly muttered to his companion.

By way of response, Densmold shrugged his shoulders fatalistically, as if too indicate that Kobyak's countenance was of no importance to him.

"The barometer's high, though," Wallens went on. "I don't think any storm's threatening us."

A further shrug from Densmold.

At that exact moment, Kobyak heard a kind of whistling, which stopped the dogs in their tracks—and the Indian, turning round, waited for the two scientists to catch up with him. Which they did.

"Well?" demanded Wallens, curtly.

"Camp," said Kobyak. "Shelter. Big storm. Big storm coming. Not good."

Without saying a word, the two Norwegians approached the sled and consulted the barometer that was attached to it. It indicated SET FAIR—but the alcohol, in its glass tube, was lowering with terrifying rapidity.

It was definitely necessary to camp.

The three men busied themselves with that.

Within a few minutes, the dogs were unhitched and tied up, the sled placed in a hollow in the ground. Then, with the aid of their knives, the explorers carved blocks of ice, with which they built a sort of conical hut that would serve them as a shelter.

Meanwhile, the sky had darkened somewhat. The dogs, which had just finished their ration of smoked salmon, distributed by Kobyak, were growling dully.

In the hut, the alcohol stove had been lit. A kettle set on top was singing softly.

Suddenly, the storm burst with unexpected violence. Within a few seconds, swirls of thick snow were falling from the blackened sky, while the sinister howling of the dogs mingled with the whistling of the squalls.

The hut, well constructed, did not budge.

A long hour went by. Their meal concluded, the three men had lit their pipes and were smoking in silence.

Kobyak suddenly got up. In response to Wallens' mute interrogation, he pointed to the hole, hollowed out at ground level, that had permitted the explorers to enter the ice-hut; the snow had blocked it completely.

It was necessary to clear the opening; if not, they would be asphyxiated before very long. The Indian had understood that before the scientists.

Armed with his snow-knife, he slowly cleared a path through the icy wall. In a few minutes, he had dug a kind of tunnel into which he disappeared.

Enveloped in their thick sleeping-bags, Ottar Wallens and Olaf Densmold lay side by side, having not exchanged a single word. They could not do anything except wait.

The formidable growl of the tempest reached their ears, no longer muffled but distinct, very close.

Amid the whistling gusts, frightful detonations resounded, drowning out the barking of the miserable dogs, which were howling desperately.

"Kobyak must have cleared the opening completely," said Wallens. The tumult of the storm blotted out his voice.

An icy blast, penetrating through the hole into which the Indian had disappeared, caused the flame of the stove to flicker. A brief but very obvious quiver shook the hut—and the detonations ceased.

The dogs barked more loudly.

A few minutes went by. Kobyak did not reappear.

277

The two scientists were still mute. They assumed that the Indian must be working to clear the entrance to the hut within a wide perimeter, in order not to be obliged to do it again.

But an hour went by, then two...

Otto Wallens saw that Densmold was asleep. He was snoring. The geologist consulted his watch and saw that it had stopped. He felt his throat gripped by a strange anguish, so violent that he turned to his companion and shook him awake.

"Well?" demanded Densmold, sitting up and frowning.

"It's been more than three hours since Kobyak went out, and he hasn't come back."

"Three hours?"

"At least. My watch has stopped."

Instinctively, Densmold took out his own. "So has mine," he observed, astonished. At eleven minutes past two."

"Eleven minutes past two—mine too!" said Wallens sliding out of his sleeping-bag as quickly as he could.

The stove, almost out of fuel, was no longer producing anything but a flame without warmth.

Ottar Wallens shivered, and drank a few sips of the stewed tea contained in the saucepan suspended over the stove. Then, having taken an electric torch that had been set on a box, he moved to the barometer.

He started in alarm. The column of alcohol seething in the glass tube was moving up and down, marking 800, 750 and 700 millimeters within a minute.

"Come and look at this, Densmold!" he exclaimed, in a tone of voice that caused the astronomer to think, momentarily, that he was mad.

When the latter, too, had seen the strange agitation of the alcohol, he was transfixed by amazement. "Phenomenon...telluric...aurora...astonishing!" he murmured.

"We need to find out what happened to Kobyak," Wallens observed.

The astronomer made no reply. Plunged as he was in profound reflection.

Without insisting, Wallens slid into the tunnel hollowed out by the Indian through the wall of ice. Crawling on his hands and knees, he went around an abrupt bend to his left and emerged, two meters further on, beneath columns of fine but densely-aggregated snowflakes that the squalls were whirling around diabolically.

The darkness was complete, but toward the southeast—an approximate direction—Ottar Wallens thought he could make out a diffuse glow with a greenish tint, which seemed to be coming from the ground.

Was it an illusion? A mirage? Some new phenomenon of refraction? Head bowed beneath the violence of the wind, the geologist wondered.

The thought of Kobyak wrenched him from his hypotheses. At the top of his voice, he called out to the Indian. He did not see anything move, and heard nothing.

The dogs were no longer barking. Only one noise persisted: the formidable whistling of the wind.

"Kobyak! Kobyak!"

Nothing.

Ottar Wallens' disquiet gradually turned to anxiety—an anxiety close to terror, all the more so because he felt himself gripped by a bizarre feeling of sickness. It seemed to him that a powerful vibration was agitating the ground beneath his feet and the air he was breathing.

He stiffened himself, and called out again—with no more success.

In the darkness, he headed toward the sled, which formed an enormous white mound a few paces from the hut. He soon reached it. As he passed close to the dogs, he heard a few feeble whimpers, which reassured him slightly.

Stopping beside the sled, he renewed his appeals; they were as vain as the others.

The vibrations he could feel were becoming increasingly intense. It seemed to him, now, that a veritable tremor was agitating his body, the ground and the snow.

I'm going mad! he thought.

Having closed his eyes, he opened them again, and saw nothing abnormal—except for that greenish light toward the south-east, which seemed to emanate from the ground itself.

"Kobyak! Kobyak!" he shouted, again. Only the gusts of wind replied. The dogs had fallen silent.

Suddenly, Ottar Wallens was afraid—a terrible, panicky fear; the fear of going mad in the snow-veiled darkness.

It seemed to him that frightful perils were lying in wait for him. He summoned up all his self-composure, and slowly made his way back to the hut.

Not without difficulty, he found the opening, which the snow was already beginning to obstruct. He unblocked it, and, sliding into the conduit, cleared a path all the way to the interior of the hut.

Sitting on a box, with is elbows on his knees, Olaf Densmold was looking at something that he was holding in his hand.

"Kobyak hasn't come back?" asked the geologist, stupidly, although he could see perfectly well that his colleague was alone in the hut.

"No," said Densmold, curtly, raising his head. "But my compass is completely crazy. The needle is no longer pointing in any direction. It's pointing toward the ground, as if we were on top of the magnetic pole."

"Yes, yes..." Wallens murmured, preoccupied.

"What? Are you trying to say something?"

"Um...no...but I felt an odd vibration just now, and I saw...something green...a green glow, close by..."

"Ah!"

"Yes...not far from the sled," Wallens specified.

"And Kobyak?" asked Densmold, after a moment's silence.

"No trace. I called several times. I went as far as the sled. I went past the dogs. He's not there."

"Fallen in the snow, no doubt, and been covered over," Densmold muttered. "That compass worries me...after the barometer...which is increasingly unsteady. Strange!"

"And our stopped watches. You didn't feel that vibration? It was as if I were drunk, just now."

"Perhaps," the astronomer murmured. "I can't be sure..."

The wind must have lost strength, for its roaring could scarcely be heard.

Ottar Wallens sat down next to the stove. "Best to wait for daylight," he concluded. "It won't be long."

Densmold remained mute. He continued staring at the large compass he was holding in his hand. "I wonder what it means!" he murmured, eventually. "One might think that the compass were displacing alternately to either side of the magnetic equator. Look, Wallens! The needle...it sometimes points east, sometimes west. Curious!"

"Curious," the geologist repeated. "But...Kobyak? Do you think he's dead?"

Making no reply, Densmold gave a slight shrug.

Ottar Wallens shivered. "It's cold," he murmured. "If Kobyak's dead, we'll be in a difficult situation...with regard to the sled...and the dogs to look after."

"The compass worries me more. How are we going to steer?"

"We have reserve compasses..."

"Which must be as crazy as this one..."

"The stars..."

"Oh, we can take direction from them—but what if it's foggy? Anyway, perhaps the phenomenon is only temporary. It would be interesting to know the cause and write it up!"

"Let's wait for daylight," Wallens concluded. "It won't be long." So saying, the geologist got into his sleeping-bag and tried to go to sleep, without succeeding.

Densmold, still sitting on the box, continued staring at his compass. Wallens saw him suddenly get down on to his knees, introduce himself into the tunnel connecting the hut to the outside and disappear. He came back less than ten minutes later.

"It's daylight," he muttered. "I've found Kobyak."

"You...where is he?"

"Dead. Eaten by the dogs. I killed two of the beasts, trying to make them let go of his remains. I got carried away. It was a mistake. Come and see. The storm's over."

Alarmed, and still prey to a dull anxiety. Ottar Wallens slid out of his sleeping-bad, readjusted his fur garments, and went out behind the astronomer.

Outside, there was absolute calm. Nothing any longer recalled the formidable nocturnal storm. A lugubrious grayish-yellow daylight illuminated the icefield. In a few strides, the two men were beside the dogs. On the ground, amid the blood-stained snow, the shapeless remains of Kobyak were visible. The digs, sitting motionless on their haunches, ears pricked, eyes bloodshot and muzzles panting, seemed anxious. They did not budge when they saw the scientists approaching.

"The...the *thing*! Did you see it?" Wallens demanded, extending his arm toward the south-east. He had just remembered the greenish light that he had seen during the night.

It had disappeared.

Olaf Densmold turned round. He was still holding his compass. "The thing?" he repeated. "Yes! It repels the compass needle! Come on!"

Leaving the dogs behind, the two men went around the white mound formed by the snow-covered sled and, guided by the magnetized needle, advanced at a rapid pace. They covered about a kilometer without discovering anything.

The "thing," whatever it was, was further away than they had thought.

They were beginning to doubt its existence when, having climbed a rise in the icy surface, they made out a cavity a few meters away, with the approximate form of a funnel about fifteen meters in diameter, and double that in depth.

They drew nearer to it. Having reached the edge, they recoiled, dazzled. At the bottom of the cavity lay something that looked like an enormous emerald: a polyhedral emerald with multiple facets, about seven meters in diameter. The facets, hexagonal in shape, appeared to be a little less than ten centimeters in diameter. A diffuse greenish light sprang forth from them.

Olaf Densmold shook his head and looked at his companion, who looked back at him.

At the risk of sliding into the icy funnel, they both moved a little closer to the rim. Wallens almost overbalanced; the astronomer only just had time to hold him back. A fragment of ice, dislodged by Wallens' boot, rolled into the funnel and collided with the polyhedral emerald.

A kind of hum was heard, increasing in pitch, becoming a dry whistle, which gradually intensified, modulating a series of very soft but very intense sounds one by one.

In the meantime the polyhedron changed shape.

Unable to believe their eyes, the two scientists watched the facets disappear, the walls of the *thing* becoming as smooth as those of a block of crystal, and the thing itself took on the form of a perfect sphere—a sphere of emerald!

"I'm going mad!" said Ottar Wallens, rubbing his eyes.

"*I'm going mad!*" repeated an echo from the depths of the funnel.

"Shut up," muttered Densmold, who was staring with wide open eyes, his lips pinched.

Slowly, the sphere was changing shape.

It became a cone, a cube, and then, successively, a rectangular parallelepiped, a pyramid and a cylinder: the principal figures of three-dimensional geometry.

The sounds continued to emerge. They were chromatic scales of an infinite softness, with short or long-drawn-out notes.

As motionless as statues of stupor, the two scientists watched without finding a word to say.

Suddenly, the sounds ceased. The *thing* resumed the form of a polyhedron—the one it had had originally—with glittering facets.

"Either we're crazy, or we have before us the most marvelous thing that has ever existed," said Ottar Wallens. "The men who have invented this, and who..."

"*They aren't human!*"

"They aren't human?"

"No! This...apparatus can't have been transported here. It must weigh several tons, and..."

"Oh!" Wallens exclaimed. "You think it's come...from another planet?"

"I think so. It's apparently made of a substance that doesn't exist on Earth, a magnetic metal—my compass is the proof of that—which is as malleable as mercury. That's what permits it to change shape. It doesn't flow, doubtless being attracted toward the center of the thing by apparatus we know nothing about. Magnetic or gyroscopic? And the *thing*'s inhabited. The...people inside wanted to prove their science to us by setting the principal figures of geometry before our eyes..."

"Anything's possible," Ottar Wallens admitted, who was gradually recovering from his stupor. "Although there's no reason to believe that the inhabitants of other planets make use of the same geometry as us. Henri Poincaré has demonstrated that Euclidean geometry is the most appropriate, but he also proved that others exist!"

"I know. But you're not unaware that the other planets are spherical, like the Earth...that they're composed of the same elements as our globe. Why not think that science on other planets has followed the same path as on ours?"

"We need to go down into the funnel and enter into communication with these people," Wallens murmured. "They must have means at their disposal that we don't know. It was them who, just now, reproduced my voice when I said that I was going mad. They must be able to hear us. Oh, Densmold, we've made a discovery that's a thousand, a million times more important than that of a pole! Just think that we're going to be the first humans to communicate with our brethren of other planets, and..."

"Are you sure that they're beings like us, Wallens?" the astronomer cut in, staring at his colleague.

Wallens felt a slight shiver. "I think so!" he said.

"If they are, it's necessary to be very wary, my dear chap! Man is a wolf to man! What if they intend to murder us?"

"They've come as ambassadors, and aren't stupid enough to massacre the first creatures they see! And we should be honored to be the people who welcome them..."

"Gently, Wallens! These beings, whatever they are, have come to explore the Earth. How can they know, on seeing us, that we're humans—which is to say, that we're the most civilized, and the only rational, beings on the planet? Suppose that they themselves have the form of dogs? They might think that dogs were the kings of the Earth, and that we're..."

"My dear Densmold, the best way of finding out is to go and see!" Wallens observed. "You're wasting time."

"Let's go," said the astronomer, briefly.

The sides of the funnel, carpeted with a thick layer of snow, were fairly easy to descend, all things considered.

Lying on their bellies, the two men let themselves slide over the white surface, slowing themselves down with their hands and knees. Within a few seconds they were at the bottom, their feet touching the surface of the *thing*.

They got to their feet, and realized almost immediately that the polyhedron was giving off a mild heat that had melted the ice around it, and was continuing to melt it. Thus, the *thing* was slowly descending, while hollowing out in the mass of the ice what mariners call a "bed."

Olaf Densmold knelt down beside the polyhedron and took off his gloves. With his bare hands, he felt one of the facets. The surface was as soft and smooth as the finest satin. A soft warmth emanated from it.

"Oh!" exclaimed Wallens, who was still standing up, looking into the polyhedron. "There's someone...I saw...a silhouette, like that of a human...a biped. They're human...it was a man, Densmold. I had..."

A brief whistle-blast rang out, followed by eight more.

Instinctively, the two scientists stepped back. They had felt the *thing* vibrate beneath them. Backed up against the ice, they saw the polyhedron resume a spherical form.

In its upper part a cap about seventy centimeters in diameter rose up, pushed by four rounded stalks. The lid stopped a little more than a meter above the sphere. Through the opening, an unimaginable being appeared.

It bore some resemblance to a human of short stature, but not a man possessed of true skin and bone. A sort of sheath, made of a gray substance reminiscent of lead, was molded to its torso and limbs. Of facial features, there were none to be seen. Instead of eyes, large goggles garnished with faceted lenses. Nose and mouth hidden beneath a mask bristling with hairs seemingly made of red gold. Hemispheres of gray metal, about half the size of an orange, covered the ears. The sheath enveloped the feet and hands, which—like the rest of the body—seemed to be coated with a thin layer of lead.

The extraordinary creature stood upright and leaned on the emerald lid, with slow, awkward, maladroit, almost grotesque gestures, and remained there for a few seconds, considering the two scientists—who, for their part, never took their eyes off it.

The being was undoubtedly reassured, for it walked slowly toward them. One might have thought that the soles of its feet were fitted with suckers, like the feet of flies, for it did not slip once on the uniform and sloping surface of the sphere.

"It's a Martian!" said Ottar Wallens.

"Or a Venusian," observed Densmold.

Whatever it was, the being came to meet them.

Having arrived in front of them, it extended its arm, touched them, and palpated them. They shuddered; the strange individual's hands were veritably scorching. On contact with them, the scientists felt a bizarre sensation of wellbeing and lightness. One might have thought that the hands were producing a beneficent current that gave strength and vigor.

Turning round, the being bent down, and drew several geometrical figures on the funnel's wall of ice—simple ones first, then more complicated ones: helices, ellipses and sinusoidal curves. Finally, it stopped and waited.

With the aid of his ice-axe, Olaf Densmold traced in his turn other figures of transcendent geometry.

The being must have understood their meaning very well; it immediately demonstrated relationships by means of the new symbols. And, doubtless content to have thus entered into communication with the two Terrans, it made a sign for them to follow it, climbed the side of its strange apparatus and disappeared inside.

Ottar Wallens and Olaf Densmold, with increasing alarm, observed that the surface of the sphere was now becoming uneven—which permitted them to climb up it relatively easily.

The astronomer introduced himself into the opening first. He fell about four meters on to an elastic floor, which deadened his fall, and was immediately joined by Wallens.

The two men saw that they were in a spherical compartment about four meters in diameter, whose walls produced a greenish phosphorescent light—the same shade that Wallens had perceived the night before. By means of gestures, the bizarre being drew the attention of its guests to a motionless globe floating like a balloon, equidistant from the floor and the ceiling. It was made of a shiny black substance somewhat reminiscent of agate, and measured less than a meter in diameter.

The being touched it. Luminous dots appeared on its surface, irregularly disposed.

"Oh!" Densmold exclaimed, in a strangled voice. "But that's a map of the sky...seen...seen from Mercury!"

"From Mercury?"

"Yes, from the planet nearest to the Sun, which completes its orbit in twenty-eight days, and where the ambient temperature must be frightful! Look—there's the Sun...and then, on the other side, Venus, Earth, Mars... Marvelous! Satellites unknown to us... Oh!"

The luminous dots had abruptly disappeared. The entire sphere was suddenly nothing but a block of light.

Shadows appeared on it.

Gradually, the two scientists recognized the terrestrial continents: the two Americas, the Old World, Australia...

But a kind of fog erased everything, and, as if they were stationed at the ocular of a colossal telescope, the two men saw passing before them plains, oceans and cities—cities whose houses appeared, one after another, in their natural dimensions.

"New York!" said Densmold, who had traveled a great deal. "Can you see Long Island? The Singer Building? Ah! There's a tropical island...an archipelago...doubtless the Bermudas..."

Europe... London...

Everything disappeared. The black sphere lit up inside again.

Breathlessly, Densmold and his companion made out a planet where everything was red, covered by banks of clouds.

"Mars! That's Mars!" Densmold explained.

Was it Mars? Who could say? Strange cities appeared, complicated architectures, among which were beings resembling humans equipped with crabs' pincers and protruding eyes, circulating and jumping about, accompanied by other nightmare creatures.

And again, the sphere went black.

Not far away, a kind of large funnel made of gray material, filled with a liquid that resembled molten gold, as suspended above a tripod. The strange being took the knife that Densmold was carrying in his belt and threw it into the funnel.

The wooden handle disappeared immediately, as if eaten away by an acid. The steel blade bubbled, lost its form, became a sort of sponge, and changed color.

The being took the metal fragment out of the vat and handed it to the astronomer.

"Oh! But…it's silver!" exclaimed Densmold, after examining it.

Ottar Wallens took it from his hands and ascertained, with no possible doubt, that the steel blade had been changed into a silvery mineral.

The metal fragment having been handed back to the extraordinary being, it was successively transformed into lead, gold, platinum…

"The unity of matter! They've mastered the unity of matter!" murmured Densmold, almost wild-eyed.

But the being took his hands and made him touch two balls, reminiscent of diamonds, embedded in the wall.

Immediately, the astronomer felt his fatigue disappear. Blood flowed to his brain. Everything seemed clear to him, natural and ordered. It seemed to him that he was now capable of solving the most transcendental problems.

Ottar Wallens, having touched the two balls felt the same impression of physical contentment in his turn.

They had not yet seen everything.

By means of an invisible mechanism, the uncanny creature caused a trapdoor framed in the floor to rise up. Through the opening, the two scientists made out pistons, crank-shafts and complicated cog-wheels.

"It's all broken in there!" Wallens suddenly exclaimed, leaning over the hole. "That's why he had to land!"

The geologist straightened up. He felt rejuvenated. He had recovered the vigor he had had at twenty. A large smile had spread across his sullen face, and the austere and taciturn Densmold was in the same state of mind.

With its hand, the being showed the scientists a box set on the floor. It pressed lightly on one of its corners, and a dull hum became audible.

By means of gestures, the being tried to explain something that must have been very important. Densmold and Wallens racked their brains, looking at one another, but they did not understand—no, they did not understand.

Tirelessly, the being repeated its demonstration, its explanation.

A gentle music resounded, in different keys, divided into three parts, its chords as marvelous as any terrestrial musician had ever contrived.

The ball on which the map of the sky, terrestrial cities and those of another planet had appeared lit up. Fleshless faces appeared, their skulls scarcely covered by thin parchment-like pellicle, with toothless mouths and piercing little round eyes like balls of emerald. Those eyes were gazing with curiosity and anguish; the features vibrated, grimacing.

They were doubtless inhabitants of Venus or Mercury, who could see their fellow—the one they had sent to Earth and for whom they could do nothing—by means of the mysterious sphere.

Ottar Wallens and Olaf Densmold, their hearts gripped by anxiety of a dolorous sympathy, saw the being turn back to them and, doubtless, stare at them through its thick goggles. They thought they saw the lenses of the goggles dulled by a slight mist.

"He's weeping!" murmured Wallens.

The agate ball became black again.

For ten seconds or so, the scientists and their host remained motionless. The green light emanating from the walls enveloped them with a livid halo that gave them a phantasmal appearance.

The being continued to stare at the two men.

Finally, it seemed to come to a decision, and leaned over the box that had produced the extraordinary music and few minutes earlier. Crackling vibrations were coming from it, separated by silences. These vibrations were sometimes brief and sometimes prolonged. Each series differed from the preceding one, as much by its sonorous intensity as the rapidity with which the sounds were emitted.

"Those vibrations," Densmold murmured, listening to them, "doubtless represent the relationship of things—of everything. The world is nothing but an ensemble of vibrations, Wallens, as you know; the slowest are sonorous, then luminous. Sound, light and matter are merely vibrations differing only in intensity. Those we can hear—I sense it—represent all the states of matter: solid, liquid, gaseous, sonorous, luminous, electrical. The great secret is in front of us and this man...this being...knows it. Look!"

Shadows appeared on the black ball. A dazzling violet light appeared.

"Luminous vibrations," murmured the astronomer.

A sort of hemispherical gong appeared in silhouette; the two scientists saw it vibrate, while the sonorous waves emitted by the box resounded more slowly...

There was no mistake about it; the mysterious being was trying to communicate the different wavelengths of luminous and sonorous waves to the humans. It was doubtless watching their faces for the effect of his demonstration. But did it understand human expressions? Who could ever know?

It suddenly stopped its fantastic experiment and, as if seized by a new idea, bent down. Through the trapdoor opened in the floor it pointed out to its guests the displaced cogwheels and the bent crank-shafts of the mysterious mechanism that they had already seen.

"The engine that permitted this machine to get here has broken down," Wallens murmured, shaking his head, "and the poor Mercurian—if he is a Mercurian—takes us for miserable savages from whom he can't get any sense. Our science is nothing by comparison with his. We need to take him back to the *Sirius*, and then come to fetch his apparatus...or, at least, to take it apart.

"Enclosed in this hull are the solutions to the principal scientific problems that have been studied since the world began. If we can succeed in understanding the Mercurian and making ourselves understood, human science might gain ten centuries. Think that this being is familiar with vision at a distance, through the ether, that he can communicate with other planets that he..."

"Yes, but if he dies, or we die, all that is lost," Densmold interjected.

A faint whistle was heard.

The being, who was standing under the opening of the sphere, rose up slowly, vertically, as if drawn by a balloon. Beneath him, the two men thought they could make out a shadow—the shadow of a cylinder on which he was standing.

Having reached the rim of the opening, the being climbed on to it, awkwardly, and disappeared outside. His arms showed through the hole and made the two men understand that they should place themselves under the opening, as he had done.

Wallens, whose mind was a little quicker than his companion's, was the first to divine what was being asked of him. He immediately felt himself lifted up, as if by the floor of a elevator—and yet his feet were not resting on anything visible.

Having climbed over the rim of the opening, he stood upright on the sphere beside the mysterious being. Densmold joined him shortly afterwards.

With its extended arm, the being immediately indicated the four cardinal points. It pointed to the Sun, around which its hand described a kind of orbit. Then, still moving awkwardly, it descended from the sphere and stepped on to the bottom of the funnel of ice, the slope of which it began to climb.

The two scientists followed it without saying a word, wondering what it intended to do.

The being reached the surface of the ice-field and stood up. Densmold and Wallens saw it suddenly shiver and recoil, in the grip of a terrible fear.

Two of the dogs forming part of the sled-team had just appeared.

"Get back, filthy beasts!" growled Densmold.

Too late! The two dogs, in unison, had leapt at the being's throat. It closed its hands upon them.

A whistling sound drowned out the barking of the dogs; a puff of green smoke sprang forth, and the group—the being and the dogs—collapsed on the ice, as if thunderstruck.

Rooted to the spot, the two scientists watched. They no longer understood, no longer knew...

The dogs already had vitreous eyes. They were quite dead...but what about the mysterious being?

Densmold was the first to recover. He went to the inert body of the extraordinary individual and touched its arm. A feeble shock, like that produced by an electric current, made him jump.

He stepped back, livid.

The being still did not move.

"But...it's *burning*!" Wallens exclaimed, hoarsely.

It was true. A mist was rising from the body lying on the ice.

The two scientists, who thought that they were going mad, saw the sheath of grey metal curl up, open and burst, revealing red parchment-like skin; they heard crackling: the ear-covers, the goggles and the mask melted under the action of a heat whose source remained invisible. And around the body, the ice liquefied, forming little rivulets of muddy water that congealed again a few meters further away under the effect of the rigorous ambient temperature. The hair of the two dogs turned red, mingling its characteristic odor with the acrid and metallic scent emitted by the cadaver of the nameless being.

In less than five minutes, it was all over. Nothing more remained on the ice but the bodies of the two dogs, half-consumed by fire, and a few blackened strands similar to tin-plate debris.

"I'm wondering if I might be mad," said Wallens, gravely.

"We aren't mad," Densmold affirmed. "But we might yet go mad, irrespective of all this. We have to set a course and make a forced march back to the *Sirius*. We can get there in ten days..."

"What about the compass?"

"Oh—yes! Well, if we can't make use of our compasses, we'll use the wireless telegraph to call for help, giving them our position."

"That might be better."

Without saying any more, the two men headed back to the sled. In the hours that followed they cleared away the thick layer of snow that had covered it—a rude and thankless task; the intense cold had hardened the snow, and made it difficult to scrape away.

Finally, the sled was free. The scientists reached the wireless telegraph apparatus.

With pausing for a moment's rest, without even eating anything, they set up the collapsible antenna they had brought, made of tubes of duralumin that slid into one another, and stabilized it by means of stays.

It was dark—a pale and foggy night—by the time they had finished. They rapidly heated up a little tea and pemmican in the hut where they had spent the preceding night, swallowed it all and went back to work, by the light of little electric torches.

All the efforts they had just made were in vain. Olaf Densmold realized that the apparatus was no longer working. The accumulators were flat. Guaranteed accumulators, tested extensively before their departure! It was impossible to send any message at all.

"Nothing to be done!" murmured the astronomer, having re-examined the accumulators. "The *thing* must have caused our accumulators to lose their charge. We have no option but to go back to the *Sirius*."

Ottar Wallens made no reply. He looked at his colleague, and they both understood. They were thinking about the crazed compasses. It would be necessary to navigate by the stars. If it had not been for the fog, that might have been possible, albeit difficult—but for want of precision in their calculations, the two men risked wandering for a long time on the ice before rejoining their ship—and their provisions would not last forever.

"We'll get our bearings as often as possible," Densmold declared. "We'll rectify our direction as many times as necessary, but we'll get there. It's the destiny of humankind that we're holding in our hands!"

"Yes," the geologist murmured, "that's true..."

They distributed a ration of smoked salmon to the dogs, checked their ropes—for only the two dogs that had perished with the being had escaped—and went back into their ice-hut.

All night long they talked, feeling neither cold nor fatigue; the marvelous possibilities opened to science by the extraordinary apparatus fallen from the sky kept their minds occupied. Innumerable problems, biological, astronomical and geological, were about to be elucidated. Mathematics would make progress. They would know what electricity was, what matter was, what life itself was!

And while human beings still existed on Earth, or even on the neighboring planets, the names of Ottar Wallens and Olaf Densmold would never die! What glory! A superhuman glory, above all others!

At daybreak, the two men rapidly swallowed a little tea and dried powdered eggs. They went out. The weather was good.

The two scientists, not without a certain awkwardness, repacked the equipment of the camp. They loaded it on to the sled, to which they hitched the dogs. And headed northwards, toward the *Sirius*.

They soon realized that they were not going as fast as they had hoped. The dogs, reduced in number by four, and instinctively divining the inexperience of their guides, only went forward slowly, stopping whenever they liked and only starting off again when they wanted to.

All the compasses remained crazy, and it was necessary to navigate by means of the sun.

At midday, Densmold called a halt and took a bearing. He calculated that the sled had drawn thirteen kilometers nearer to the *Sirius*. Only half a stage! More than four hundred kilometers remained to be traversed before reaching the ship—four hundred kilometers in a straight line, which meant more than six hundred in reality.

"We'll have to ration ourselves," Wallens declared.

"Yes."

The two men ate, and set off again, still as slowly.

They covered twelve stages: less than a hundred kilometers, for several times, enveloped by the fog, the explorers went astray and lost ground.

The compasses were no longer crazy now—they were no longer functioning at all, the needles having lost their magnetic properties due to some unknown cause.

But the supplies might last two months with careful rationing...

Alas, one night, while the two exhausted scientists were asleep, the dogs, having detached their insecurely-fixed ropes, had a feast. Pemmican, flour, smoked salmon, dried eggs—they spoiled what they did not devour.

When they awoke, Densmold and his companion saw the disaster at first glance. The dogs had fled, and of their provisions, nothing to speak of remained.

"It was you who tied up the dogs yesterday!" Densmold remarked, fixing is colleague with a cold stare.

"I tied them up solidly—I don't know what's happened!" the geologist protested, in all good faith.

"Let's gather up what can be saved," said Densmold, without persisting. "It's not much, but we couldn't carry any more, and the sled's too heavy for us to think of taking it."

What remained? Enough for them to live on half-rations for a week, perhaps, and then...

Without saying a word, the two men collected the debris of every sort that was scattered over the ice.

The appetite of the big dogs of Alaska is formidable. The beasts had not left much.

In an hour, they had finished.

The scientists, bent beneath the weight of their sleeping-bags and their meager provisions, set off over the interminable ice-field.

Wallens was carrying the stove and the supply of alcohol, Densmold had taken charged of the sextant, the chronometer and the books necessary to calculate a bearing.

Fortunately, the weather was good.

Six stages were crossed.

The food supplies diminished rapidly. In order to be able to march, the unfortunates had to eat.

No more fog. They were now advancing in the right direction.

"No more than 101 kilometers," Densmold declared, one day, having taken a bearing. "The ice is flat here; we can do that in three days..."

"Yes, but we only have a pound of pemmican left."

That day, the two men each ate fifty grams of food, and made one final cup of tea with the last of their alcohol.

Densmold, although he was the older, still had some strength, but Wallens seemed reduced to the utmost limit of weakness. They decided to rest for a few hours before setting out again.

With empty stomachs, and their temples beating anemically, they lay down side by side in their sleeping-bags.

Toward the middle of the night, Wallens, who was not asleep, caught sight of his companion slip out of his sleeping-bag, stick the little bag containing the last of the pemmican in his belt, roll up his pack and put it on his shoulders.

He understood. Densmold, who had reproached him several times for slowness, was about to abandon him, in order to travel more rapidly and keep for himself the scraps of provisions that constituted their last resource.

"Densmold!" he called out, involuntarily.

The astronomer turned round. "Oh, you're awake," he said, coldly. "Well, yes, I'm leaving you. We'll both perish if I wait for you, that that won't do anyone any good. I'm going to try to reach the *Sirius* by a forced march. Someone will come to look for you. *Au revoir!*"

"Densmold! You can't do that! You can't abandon me..."

"I can," declared the astronomer, who had paused. "It's my duty. Science before all! You'll slow me down. If I stayed with you, we'd both perish. Adieu!"

And he drew away at a rapid pace.

Ottar Wallens groped at his belt. In spite of his weakness, he had kept an automatic pistol, in order to make use of it if some prey appeared. He armed it, raised his hand, took aim and pressed the trigger.

A detonation. A scream.

His skull shattered, Olaf Densmold collapsed on the ice, and did not move again.

Exactly two weeks later, the little expedition sent out by the Sirius in search of the two scientists who had not come back discovered Olaf Densmold's corpse lying on the ice, with a bullet in his head.

And Ottar Wallens? Had he died of hunger? Of cold? Had he been swallowed by a crevasse, in a snowstorm? He was never found.

And somewhere, toward the austral pole, the nameless engine, come from who knows where, continues, under the action of its weight—if it is subject thereto—to sink into the ice, taking with it the secrets for which humans have been searching for hundreds of millennia, and will find...when?

Paul Gsell: *Wireless Communication with the Stars* (1930)

T.S.F. avec les étoiles *(1930) hammers its message home in no uncertain terms in a final chapter whose argument deliberately echoes, albeit in a light-hearted manner, one of Plato's best-known dialogues. The story is, in essence, a boisterous comedy, but the tone of its satire varies markedly as the angst-ridden protagonist, the aptly-named Jacques Lagité, seeks an answer to his own self-defined existential predicament by examining a series of exemplary societies.*

The narrative swings from amiable absurdity to scathing caricature with a casual ease, but also produces a sharp poignancy in several places where its slippery velvet glove is removed, in order to issue a challenge to the reader's thinking, and the iron fist beneath is revealed in all its intellectual and emotional brutality.

Paul Gsell (1870-1947) is remembered today primarily as a critic, whose book L'Art *(1911), recording his discussions with the sculptor Auguste Rodin, remains in print. He also made copious records of his conversations with another of his friends, the writer Anatole France. The literary influence of France's satirical novels is important, in terms of the novella's cavalier narrative strategy and skeptical rhetorical standpoint. Gsell had written at least one previous work of* roman scientifique, *the similarly satirical* L'Homme qui lit dans les âmes *(1928)[47], but there is no detailed bibliographical account of his copious writings, so he too might have produced further ventures.*

Gsell's invention of "astral wireless" is not without precedent. The invention and employment of such a technology is featured in some of the stories of Paul Vibert, whose satirical tone and attitude has something in common with Gsell's, but Vibert merely sketches the notion and a few of its corollaries while Gsell's elaborately organizes extrapolations of it and provides a far more satisfactory analysis, the comedy of which does not detract from its intellectual discipline and underlying seriousness.

In several respects, T.S.F. avec les étoiles *is a story very much of its time, not only because it is an imaginative product of a particular phrase in the development of radio broadcasting, but also because of its constant preoccupation with the threat of a more destructive repetition of the Great War. In the latter regard the story echoes the macabre tenor of a great deal of interbellum futuristic fiction, and the black humor of the account of the planet of the Forgetful is*

---

[47] Available from Black Coat Press as *The Man Who Could Read Minds*, ISBN 978-1-61227-860-5.

only unusual in its conciseness, as is the cynical account of the collapse of civilization on the doomed planet Grul.

The novella does, however, make a serious attempt to transcend the preoccupations of its day in order to address eternal questions, and the breath of its imagistic spectrum enables it to do that, while it relative coherency supports the rare conviction of its conclusion. Characters who set out to find the secret of happiness in contes philosophiques *usually fail to find it, merely learning resignation, and Jacques Lagité is privileged in that regard, although not all readers will be able to sympathize with his ultimate acquisition, for a variety of reasons.*

B.S.

WIRELESS COMMUNICATION WITH THE STARS

I. Folly or Genius?

Toward the end of 194*, a strange emotion began to stir humankind.

A physicist, Barnabé Letord claimed to have communicated by wireless with the planets.

He was an aged professor. At first it was thought that the fellow had gone senile. His first experiments before friends confirmed them in that opinion.

Having created darkness in his laboratory at the Collège de France, he showed them vague shadows on a luminous screen, which passed back and forth, becoming more evident and vanishing without it being possible to grasp their true nature.

"Divine that enigma," he said, with a luminous smile. As everyone held their tongue he declared, triumphantly: "They're beings from beyond the sky." And he added: "Yes, inhabitants of distant planets. Soon, I'll be able to make them less indistinct."

Behind his back, his listeners tapped their foreheads with their index fingers.

In the press, discreet allusions circulated regarding Professor Letord's "daydreams." For some time, it was a theme for delicate mockery. Was the old man "out to lunch" or was he the victim of tricksters?

A few weeks later, in a session to which he had invited the highest competences of the scientific world, he spent a good hour searching, he said, for the wavelength. The dazzling circle of the projector remained ironically virginal. The operator gave the excuse of the great delicacy of the operation and the manipulations, but sniggers were springing forth from the perfidious shadows, when a proud exclamation resounded: "Look!"

Suddenly, on the screen, with a perfect clarity, a troop of gnomes appeared, who resembled humans, but whose fantastic appearance was disturbing. Their enormous skull, which measured at least half their height, was mounted on a very stocky body with thin arms and legs. They resembled the caricatures with big heads that represent contemporary celebrities in humorous magazines.

Those apes were not walking. They were sitting on little wheeled platforms that transported them very rapidly wherever they wanted to go. With a muted sound of continuous rolling, they moved around for some thirty seconds.

Suddenly, the screen became immaculate again.

"Oh! Cut off already!" exclaimed the professor, with some disappointment. "But you know enough now to take account of the facts."

And, switching on the lights in the room, he explained that the hallucinatory race lived on a very distant planet, probably a satellite of Vega.

"Those were," he affirmed, "images that an unknown astral correspondent has just transmitted to Earth by wireless."

Then the scientist explained his discovery. He had succeeded in isolating special vibrations that were propagated throughout the universe with a speed infinitely greater than that of Hertzian waves. He had constructed apparatus to capture them. One day, he thought he had discerned mysterious signals. Suspecting that they emanated from other planets, he had worked hard to test that hypothesis. After countless fruitless attempts and many alternations of enthusiasm and dejection, he had finally collected, by means of a kind of television, precise projections like the one that had just been offered to the audience, and which, without a doubt, reproduced astral scenes. And he had found a means of recording the sounds that accompanied them synchronically.

Naturally, that speech left the entire audience incredulous. "But what authorizes you to suppose," said one, in a mocking tone, "that people from beyond the sky deliver themselves to this intersidereal correspondence?"

"I'm obliged to believe it," said Letord, "since I receive their messages. I suppose that, on many planets, civilization is very advanced and they have already been making use of the astral wireless communication that I've just invented for a long time."

"And these operators send you their radio signal through the immensity?"

"They aren't destined for me; but they're expedited through all regions of space, and I've intercepted a few of them. Soon, I hope to be able to address myself to them in my turn."

The members of the audience shook their heads and exchanged furtive winks. Barnabé Letord had begun to adjust his tubes, cross wires, turn screws and illuminate intermittent light-sources. Then he switched off the lights again and almost immediately, an improbable animal appeared on the screen, the forms of which surpassed in extravagance the most audacious fantasies of Greek mythology and Oriental theogonies, harpies, centaurs, chimeras, hippogriffs and winged dragons. It was a centipede, for it had at least a hundred feet or tentacles, which it was agitating in all directions. Over its body and its limbs a quantity of eyes opened, the furious pupils of which were rolling incessantly. A mouth provided with three rows of teeth in each jaw was hissing with rage and gaping frightfully, as if to grasp an invisible prey.

At that moment, another monster bounded into view, which began to fight with the first. The newcomer was bristling with pincers, spikes and saws, which were not mechanical engines but living instruments like those that certain fish possess—swordfish and narwhals—or certain insects. Whereas those weapons are minuscule in the coleopteran and hymenoptera, however, they were gigantic in the combatant from beyond the sky. Furthermore, like electric eels, it launched electric discharges; but they were much more redoubtable, because they burst forth noisily, attaining the enemy's tentacles at a distance, and the contractions and writhing of those appendages proved the efficacy of the fulminating sparks.

That duel between two apocalyptic beasts, one of which was seeking to envelop and the other in order to pierce it, evoked in some ways the encounters of a retiarius and a swordsman in the Roman arena. It was both impassioning and burlesque, for the whirling of the fleshy arms and the blades, the rolling of the flamboyant eyes and the threats of the distended mouths resembled a delirious parody of hatred—to such an extent that when the scene was abruptly effaced before the denouement of the drama, loud laughter broke out in the room.

"A fine trick!" someone shouted

At first, Barnabé Letord did not seem to understand that remark.

"Come on, what do you take us for?" growled one of the luminaries of the Académie des Sciences

"Confess," then, said another pontiff, "that you're serving us doctored films."

Red with shame, Barnabé Letord protested his good faith in vain.

"Old joker!" sniped one of his oldest friends.

Then the professor got annoyed, seethed with rage, and ended up delivering a magisterial back-handed slap in the face of one of the most jovial jesters.

The slap brought a riposte. There was a fine brawl, in which Letord came off worst, for everyone was against him.

He called his colleagues imbeciles. He shouted them down. Many of them, draping themselves in their importance, declared gravely that high science had just been insulted. Others broke the machines in the laboratory with blows of their canes.

The next day, the quarrel was set before public opinion. In numerous articles, the representatives of official knowledge pronounced against the inventor of astral wireless. They demanded vengeance for his indecent deceit, his insults and his conduct. Charging him with insanity, they demanded that he be retired without delay from his chair at the Collège de France and locked up in Sainte-Anne.

The unanimity of those eminent persons impressed the public powers so much that Letord was immediately interned in the asylum.

Very rapidly, however, a counter-current formed in the camp of free science. There were Letordists and Antiletordists. As always, politics and religion got mixed up in it. The Freemasons, the Zionists and the Republican Left were for Letord, the center and the right against him. In the Latin Quarter, the students, divided into two factions, delivered themselves to pitched battles when they encountered one another at the street corners on the descent from the Montagne Sainte-Geneviève, and there was a hailstorm of jeers, punches and blows with sticks.

Among the newspapers, *L'Espérance, L'Horizon, Le Progrès, Le Mieux-Etre, Tous nos droits, La Torche, Le Brandon* and *Sans dessus-dessous* were Letordist; *La Nation, Cocorico, Rataplan, L'Ordre, L'Intérêt Public, Fructidor* and *Sursum Corda* were Antiletordist.

Each party defended its convictions furiously, without a shadow of proof—for people only fight about what is not demonstrated, and indisputable truths, such as two and two make four, have never excited anyone. In any case, it was not about the sequestered scientist at all, but the advantage each person found in enrolling himself under one banner or the other. That is generally the basis of all the great quarrels that agitate society from time to time.

One of the principal editors of *Tous nos droits*, Jacques Lagité, after having demanded the liberation of the prisoner with extreme violence, had the belated scruple of verifying whether Letord was actually of sound mind and whether he had really made the discovery of which he boasted. He went to visit him in Sainte-Anne, talked to him for a long time, and wrote a luminous article about astral wireless that was reprinted by all the Letordist periodicals.

Two days later, the inventor was released—not because of the article, but because the political party that supported him had just overturned the ministry. Jacques Lagité nevertheless claimed all the credit for the action taken in the scientist's favor.

Barnabé Letord hastened to bring his labors to a successful conclusion, and was served in his final trials by a marvelous stroke of luck. He improved the emissions, which still left much to be desired and succeeded in regulating meticulously the sending of messages to the most distant stars. Even better, responses from certain planets began to reach him.

He also perfected the polychromy of the images that he received, for it is worthy of remark that they were colored like the reality itself.

Those prodigious results were registered by scientific committees that surrounded them with all the requisite guarantees. At first, Letord's adversaries had systematically denied the facts. Then, enabled to participate in the verification, they were obliged to consent to yield to the evidence.

Jacques Lagité, having become the great scientist's best friend, was his spokesman in the press, and signaled each progress accomplished in dithyrambic terms.

France, always belated in recognizing the genius of her children, was forced to admit that of Barnabé Letord when all the other nations had proclaimed it, and no doubt subsisted for anyone. Astral wireless had been definitively invented, disciplined and rendered practical. The ancient dream of all poets and all the inspired had been realized. The appeal of intellect had been perceived beyond the abyss, and the silence of limitless space was finally broken, thanks to a few mechanisms composed of mirrors, cassettes, levers, dials, needles and metal wires.

Intelligence exulted vertiginously toward the infinite. It was about to fathom countless mysteries previously triply sealed. A formidable expectation held the human race breathless.

II. Lagité Seeks Happiness

Everyone was talking about astral wireless. Everyone was dreaming about it. But Jacques Lagité was talking and dreaming about it more than anyone else. His name—which, by a curious coincidence, had always depicted his character marvelously—had never been as fully justified.

It is necessary to admit that he now had reason to be impassioned. A specialist in the new invention, he wrote paper after paper, gave numerous lectures, responded to ten telephone calls a minute, and maintained a written correspondence with all the countries on Earth. Six shorthand typists he had hired were insufficient for that purpose.

That trepidation on Jacques' part extracted him from his customary reflections, and that was a great advantage, for every time he returned to himself he fell into the deepest melancholy. He had tried everything to satisfy or to distract himself. He had educated himself avidly, but, although he was very versatile, his knowledge had little depth. In fits and starts he dipped into Letters, Sciences and Arts, and lost his taste for them just as rapidly. Nothing satisfied him.

He had tried to enrich himself, but in vain. In particular, a company that he had founded to render horse-chestnuts comestible had volatilized a considerable fraction of his capital.

He searched continually for happiness; he was, in consequence, very unhappy.

One Sunday in spring, Jacques was finishing lunch on a terrace in his small property in Bois-le-Roi, in the company of his young wife Viviane and a friend, Doctor Jean Placide. Young foliage of a delicately acidulated green, cobaea flowers and wisteria decked the arbor where the meal was concluding. The view through a bay overlooked a barrage on the Seine, the waterfall of which, in limpid sheets and foamy eddies, sparkled with a thousand gold and silver reflections.

The air was very mild and the light divinely amorous.

Naturally, the three were chatting about sidereal wireless.

Jacques said that the velocity of Letordian waves had just been measured by a method similar to the one that had allowed the velocity of light to be calculated. It had arrived at numbers that far surpassed all known evaluations. The vibrations were transmitted almost instantaneously to the astronomical limits attained by the most powerful telescopes. Thus, the distances that luminous rays would have taken centuries to travel were traversed in the blink of an eye by the new radiations. It was to be anticipated that conversations would soon be established easily with all the inhabited worlds.

And Jacques sighed, in a sort of ecstasy. "Then, we shall finally discover the happiness that always flees us!"

Viviane and Jean Placide looked at one another in surprise. The young physician declared that he was, of course, as intoxicated as all scientists by the limitless possibilities of the new wireless, but he confessed that he could not see how it would ensure human beings of happiness.

"Blindness!" riposted Jacques. "Among the myriads of planets, many must be older than ours, and progress presently unimaginable here must already have been realized there. The inhabitants of those worlds therefore enjoy a perfect felicity. And by communicating with them, we shall discover their secrets and we shall only have to borrow their experience to become supremely happy."

Those words had been spoken with a spasmodic ardor.

Jean Placide raised a Havana that he was in the process of enjoying to his lips, chewed it, inhaled the smoke, blew it out in a long blue spiral, and then looked intently at Jacques. "You don't have it, then—happiness?"

"No," said Jacques.

"There are people," Jean remarked, "who don't merit their good fortune. Come on, old chap...happiness? Look around you. It's the exquisite fare that has just been offered to us; it's the mocha worthy of houris, the five-year-old brandy, this cigar, which would make the nostrils of the Eternal fare with delight; it's the pleasure of our conversation; it's the paradisal landscape; it's..."

"I hate rustic meals," Jacques cut in, "but I forgive my wife her whim."

"Oh!" cried Viviane. "I thought I was giving you pleasure!"

"Risking eating caterpillars in the sauce, fearing being stung by a bee!"

"What ideas!"

Jean said, calmly: "Happiness, my dear Jacques, is an adorable woman."

Viviane smiled palely. Jacques was beginning to hate her, because he had ceased to love her.

Stendhal has talked about the crystallization of desire around the little irregularities of a cherished face and body. There is also a crystallization of hatred around the very perfections of a person who has become indifferent. Jacques was now acquiring a distaste for Viviane's delicate complexion, her ash-blonde hair, her violet eyes and her delicate hands. Those attractions were antipathetic to him, because he was sated by them. At that moment he was imagining an amber cleavage, sharp teeth, tapering and combative fingers, everything that delighted him about his brunette mistress of the moment.

Viviane murmured: "He hasn't even noticed my new hairstyle."

"Fluffed up like a Pekinese!" sniggered Jacques.

"It's you who recommended this fashion to me!"

That was true; but it was sufficient for her to accomplish one of Jacques' wishes for him to change his caprice.

He turned toward his friend. "A sad happiness, the one of which you speak! A few poor pleasures for a mediocre sensuality."

"Thank you!" said Viviane.

"Seriously," Jacques went on, bitterly, "How can you expect me to be happy? Our present existence is so flat, so paltry. We experience so many needs, without being able to content them. How many times I have dreamed about the people of the future! I tell myself that they will truly know the joy of living, because they will collect all the fruits of our pains, and the future will have brought them a host of sensual pleasure unknown to us. Exactly what I expect of astral wireless is to procure us immediately the plenitude of satisfactions that I only glimpsed previously for our distant descendants."

"Oh," said Jean, "you truly are Jacques Lagité, always unquiet; you don't repose for a moment in the possession of what you have. Fundamentally, you personify an entire modern generation who, struck by a universal giddiness, flutter incessantly, perpetually running after chimeras and never stop to 'seize the day,' as the old poet puts it. A stupid and macabre jazz-band!"

"Jean is right," ventured Viviane.

"How stupid you are!" snapped Jacques. In his bad mood, he had not measured the harshness of the remark.

Viviane shuddered, closed her eyes momentarily, and seemed to retreat dolorously into herself.

Jacques, who felt guilty, tried to justify himself by means of a worse offense. "You only say things to displease me," he growled.

"Listen, my friend," said Viviane, tremulously, in a low voice, "If I thought that I could render you any happier by leaving you..."

"That's it—you've had enough of me!" he exclaimed, hypocritically.

"Jacques!" she moaned.

"Well, so be it," he said, completely unhinged. "Let's separate."

And as he noticed a tiny spider on the edge of a water-jug, he said: "Look at that!" And he took hold of the crystal and smashed it into a thousand pieces on the ground.

Then, without bidding adieu to Jean, who continued smoking philosophically, he fled. A minute later, they heard the automobile emerge from the garage, and the vehicle carried Jacques toward Paris.

Viviane, her elbows on her knees and her face in her hands, was shaken by endless sobs. She continued shedding tears, and repeating: "The bad man! The bad man!"

Jean stroked her like a child, and with compassionate caresses her ended up saying: "Come on, come on; don't worry. If Jacques abandons you, you won't lack adorers."

She recoiled abruptly and looked at him maliciously through her tears. "I thought you were more delicate," she said.

"But..."

"You're prompt to betray amity. Personally, I'm more faithful to amour."

"How can you love that madman?"

"He's better than you! Yes, Monsieur Epicurean, you savor your pleasures egotistically. That's not enough to seduce me. Jacques gets carried away, but his perpetual anxiety is a rarer quality than your bliss. It attaches me to him. I'd like to soothe it, to calm it. He no longer loves me, it's true, but none of his passions lasts, because he's always animated by a more ardent desire. Perhaps he'll come back to me. Anyway, I love him..."

"I love you too," Jean implored.

She smiled silently. He asked her the reason for that.

"It's a wicked thought," she said. "I'm annoyed by being loved by you, but I experience some consolation in it"

He drew closer to her eagerly.

"La la!" she said. "I tell myself that I'm still lovable, and that Jacques will doubtless perceive it one day..."

He grimaced with chagrin. "He makes you so unhappy!"

"Yes, but I'm glad at the same time."

"What do you mean?"

"I love my suffering, and I wouldn't give it up for anything in the world."

"Viviane!"

"Jean, never talk to me again about your love. Never, you understand! Otherwise, I won't be able to see you any longer. And I'd regret that, for I need your friendship."

With that, she gave him his leave, holding out her hand, which he brushed with his lips.

III. The Planet Venus

Jacques had gone to live with the pretty Cora, his mistress, who painted fans.

Immediately, he had an astral wireless set installed in her home. Barnabé Letord supervised the installation personally, and wanted Jacques to begin a correspondence with the planet Venus, where he had just made some curious observations.

"Venus," he told his friend, "is populated by humans very similar to us. I was astonished by that, because I didn't think that two similar races could exist on two different worlds. But I recalled what Newton wrote: *Natura est ubique sibi consona*. Nature repeats herself everywhere. And since, by the study of spectral rays, science had already demonstrated that the chemical elements of which the Earth is composed are identical in all the stars, I judged it less singular, on reflection, that life should reproduce exactly the same forms on several planets.

"In addition, although astral wireless is in its infancy on our world, we can now make a prediction. We will only ever be able to communicate with sidereal beings who resemble us, more or less, for they alone are in a position to exchange ideas with Earth. Evidently, many species are living in the universe that are not similar to us in any fashion, but it's obvious that we can never know them. Having said that, I'll get back to Venus, and draw your attention to a surprising coincidence. By virtue of a miraculous divination, our astronomers have given Venus the name precisely suited to it, for it really is the planet of Amour."

As soon as the illustrious scientist had got his apparatus working, the public square of a great city appeared on the screen. The houses only differed from ours in their style. The motifs of the sculpture were mostly borrowed from general anatomy. Lingams were employed everywhere, from sideboards to balconies, and from gutters alongside pavements to gutters on roofs.

The men and women of Venus were clad in floral garments of a rather smart appearance.

At a crossroads in the foreground, a young woman prey to an extraordinary excitement was rummaging in her handbag. As at the cinema, the vision was replaced momentarily by the little bag, greatly magnified and held open. It had several pockets, and the main compartment was provided with a small mirror, lipstick and a powder-puff. There was a special compartment for a dainty revolver. It was presumably the current model of all handbags in that country.

A very large feminine hand took possession of the weapon.

Suddenly, the scene reverted to the public square, where the young woman was pursuing a man, firing all the bullets contained in the loading mechanism at him. Her aim was so poor that the bystanders hit by the errant projectiles were falling before her like cardboard figures.

The drama had scarcely finished when a second madwoman fired at point-blank range at another female inhabitant of Venus. The victim had not yet hit the ground when a ephebe, addressing a mute adjuration to the heavens, blew his brains out. Alongside him, a young woman threw herself under the wheels of a heavy truck. And at the same moment, a frenetic couple precipitated themselves from the top of a tower, and the two were crushed on the ground.

"Oh!" said Jacques horrified. "You're mistaken, my dear professor. That is surely not the planet of Amour but the planet of Hatred and Madness."

"Not at all! I've observed it carefully. All those people are in love. That's why they kill and detest one another. There's nothing more usual on the planet Venus. And it's doubtless by virtue of idleness that one of the witnesses of such banal scenes are transmitting them through the heavens. The exasperation of physical desire produces those frightful deregulations. But continue watching. I'll leave you to it."

Jacques saw a huge hall in which a jury of grave individuals was sitting. By the dignity of their features, they were recognizable as wily tradesmen, prudent manufacturers and experienced rentiers. Before them were arranged objects of all sorts that had served to kill: revolvers, knives, hammers, smoothing irons, razors, nails, chipped pairs of scissors, forceps, and even a handkerchief twisted into a strangling cord.

The members of the jury were examining that apparatus in the manner of connoisseurs. They waxed ecstatic over the rare pieces that were not designed for killing, and which only an unbridled passion had been able to transform into deadly weapons.

Then they had the men and women who had employed those instruments enter, one by one.

The president, an old man with a snowy beard, clasped in his arms the first of the murderesses, who had apparently committed the finest crime of passion, and pinned to her breast a golden insignia in the form of a heart in flames.

He shook the hands of the other assassins, congratulated them warmly, and distributed the same decoration to them, but in silver or bronze.

After that, everything vanished.

"My word!" said Jacques. "Some of our juries at the assizes operate in much the same fashion. But if that's the radiant land of Amour, I'd prefer not to live there."

He observed other natives of Venus. They were proud of the wounds they had received from their lovers and showed off their crippled limbs of blinded eyes. They were just as proud of having lost noses in less violent but no less deadly encounters.

It is necessary to add that on that planet, the slightest mark of courtesy that a husband might give to his wife, or lover to her admirer is to offer the other a gallant weapon that cuts through flesh and bone. No wedding-basket is devoid of that durable gift, and no polite liaison without that present of amity.

Lagité had many occasions in the following days to communicate with the planet Venus. He learned to speak with the inhabitants; Letord, who returned, helped him to do that. In fact, the great scientist had just made a new discovery of capital importance. He had noticed that the sidereal beings made use in their interplanetary conversations of the same language, a kind of Esperanto, which had been adopted long before by all the stars linked by wireless.

Barnabé Letord had compiled a grammar and a vocabulary of that language and he had lent them to Jacques, who was soon in a position to interrogate benevolent correspondents on Venus. They gave Lagité a thousand details of the greatest interest regarding their mores.

Naturally, on that world consecrated to Cythera, the women are sovereign. They hold almost all the public employments and only leave a tiny fraction to their male companions. Their conception of social functions is, moreover, very personal. They only install themselves in their offices in order to take care of their beauty.

When taxpayers present themselves at a window in order to acquit some civic duty—to bring money to pay their taxes for instance—the pretty functionaries do not seem to perceive that they are in a hurry. They inspect their pretty faces attentively, in a hand mirror, pout in order to be better able to apply a stick of rouge to their lips, and place the crimson substance with the decision of great pastel-painters.

In the meantime, they slyly address a smile to the waiting citizens; they authorize them thus to be witnesses to their toilet and take pleasure in it—for they have no doubt that they have come solely to admire them, and that the other reasons they invoke are merely futile pretexts. In consequence, they take out their powder puffs and cover up the luster of their noses with the powder. Then they put blue kohl under their eyelids, and unctuous mascara on their lashes. They make use, in fact, of compounds almost the same as the women on Earth, although the names of the products are different.

After heightening their beauty in that fashion they write their amorous correspondence, searching the ceiling with ecstatic gazes for the tender epithets with which it pleases them to gratify their lovers.

When they have finished, they tell the taxpayers politely that the closing bell has just sounded, that they will have to come back the following day in order to hand over their money—and, with a dry click, the close the little copper plate.

Who could complain? They are so delightful?

The women on Venus are not content to be bureaucrats. They fill the most elevated positions and direct all the ministries.

When a jurist, an administrate or an officer or merit wants to deploy his talents he must, above all, please Madame la Ministress; and there is no other means available to him than to frequent that lady's salon assiduously. It is necessary that he spends entire afternoons and evenings here, lying or sprawling on cushions, sipping infusions, digesting cocktails, nibbling ginger-flavored petit fours and praising his hostess on the color of her dress and the excellence of her hair-style.

Those representations of the charming sex have only one design: to make intelligent people waste as much time as they can. The proud refuse to lend themselves to that convention, but they only spoil their existence more surely, since, without the support of women, they vegetate perpetually.

It is appropriate to point out that influential ladies only accord their protection to handsome and passionate mortals. To those, they even permit judicious speech, and while they speak, they observe that they have gleaming eyes. They willingly accept them as lovers, or they seek to procure friends for them in their entourage, for they obtain almost as much pleasure from the amours of others as they own. They tire rapidly of the males they love, and pay no more attention to them thereafter than to the peel of an orange or a laddered stocking. Deprived of the benevolence that they inspired, they naturally lose all their qualities and are no longer good for anything.

The Parliament, it goes without saying, is composed entirely of women, for they have supplanted men in all circumscriptions. One of Lagité's correspondents was kind enough to enable him to witness, thanks to wireless, a session of the Chamber of Lady Delegates.

In the bosom of that assembly, there is gossip, vociferations, lies, slander, strutting and the hurling of insults, exactly as in our terrestrial parliaments, and that it not where their singularity lies. At the very most, one can remark that the adversaries, instead of punching one another with their fists, as they do here, grab them by their hair and rake them with fingernails. What gives a particular character to the Parliament of Venus, however, is the subjects that are treated there.

Jacques witnessed a debate that appeared to be very serious. Should women shave their armpits or not?

Some delegates opined in favor of liberty, but the majority, always tyrannical, turned a deaf ear to that, and in order to attest its power, pronounced in favor of shaved armpits.

After that, they debated the color of stockings for the following month. It was decided that they would be a bright rose color, lightly tinted with tea.

An important debate was sparked on another issue, the solution of which, Jacques was told, would have a profound influence on the forthcoming elections. It was a matter of knowing whether to preserve "combinations," which, in spite of their charm and decency, offered inconveniences, and whether there should not be a reversion to good old bloomers.[48]

---

[48] Although this usage exists in English as well as in French it has fallen somewhat out of fashion, so it might be worth noting that the *combinaisons* [combinations] of the Belle Epoque, which first appeared in the late 1870s and reached the peak of their popularity in the 1890s, were underwear garments that combined the chemise and the drawers into a single garment. They are now rare on the High Street but can still be purchased on line, with the aid of catalogue illustrations that exhibit their peculiar appeal flamboyantly. The fact that the Venusian Parliament voted in favor of them in 1930 might have suggested to contemporary readers, in spite of the briefly-renewed fashionability in 1920s America of camiknickers, that, notwithstanding the sophistication of their wireless appa-

305

The Cabinet tabled a vote of confidence in declaring itself in favor of combinations, and obtained a large majority.

At one moment, a report by Madame the Ministress of War with regard to a frontier incident nearly took a tragic tone. That was because Her Gracious Excellence with responsibility for Armaments had a wart on her nose the made her ugly and rendered her bellicose. They succeeded in calming her down by indicating an ointment that would cure her defect, and the war was avoided.

All the parties agreed nevertheless that it was necessary to be careful of national security, and the Ministress was warmly applauded when she announced that she had just entrusted the direction of the General Staff to an individual of universally recognized valor, the famous inventor of a permanent wave.

Jacques conserved some doubts regarding the advantages that would result for humankind of such a progress of feminism. He was certainly wrong, for one or several failed experiments prove nothing, and the flaws they reveal can always be amended.

One day, when he had put himself in communication with Venus, a very beautiful naked woman, with large dark and insolent eyes, shiny and sinewy brown hair, lips demanding amour and a vigorously and supply braced torso, suddenly appeared in the luminous circle.

She nibbled the white flesh of her arms, paraded her gaze complaisantly over her milky shoulders, her firm breasts, her smooth and shadowy abdomen, her divinely pulp, firm and satined thighs, caressed those priceless treasures with her soft and dainty hands, and invited the entire universe, by way of wireless, to contemplate her.

Jacques, enfevered, uttered exclamations of wonder.

The woman's chamber resembled an immense corolla. The floor was strewn with soft cushions that invited the most attractive games. In the center stood a golden tall pistil crowned with a large fleuron that distributed a soft light. Stamens, also in gold, curved back against the walls, terminating in luminescent incense-containers.

Jacques learned subsequently that flowers, some of which are, among us—contrary to all reason—symbols of candid virginity, rightly symbolize on that world the paroxysms of sensuality. Are they not, in fact, the heady alcoves in which Nature shelters the mysteries of fecundation?

The occupant of the amorous calyx caused the enticing profiles of her loins to veer toward contrasted mirrors; she stood up, lay down and left no one ignorant of her most confidential graces. Then she concealed them, in order to render them irresistible. One might have thought that the she-devil, knowing that she was being watched by millions of desires scattered in infinite space, was striving to stimulate them to the point of fury.

---

ratus and their enmity to armpit hair, the Venusians were a little behind the times.

306

Fascinated and hypnotized, Jacques could no longer take his eyes off her. He had lost all notion of current life. From the first moment, that woman from beyond the sky had taken entire possession of his senses, his reason and his will.

He was on his knees before the idol.

"What does this extravagance signify?" growled Cora, his mistress, behind him.

He did not know that she was there. She had gone to deliver some fans and he had not heard her come back in, so absorbed was he by the plant of Amour.

Surprised, he cut off the communication abruptly.

Ha!" said Cora. "You're feasting on obscenities. You surely have a guilty conscience, since you're not admitting me to your pleasure. This wireless communication with the stars doesn't tell me anything worthwhile, I warn you."

He coaxed her in order to soothe her, but he could not see anything except the other woman. He could scarcely discern the fan-maker before him, and in what she said to him he only perceived an importunate buzz.

From then on, he waited for Cora to go out, and he immediately took advantage of it to invoke his astral divinity. Glad to subjugate him, she had the whim of chatting with him. Jacques knew that she had the poetic name of Gilniz, which, in the Venusian language, means Promise.

Frightfully coquettish, she talked to him about her lovers. An adolescent had committed murder in order to steal a diamond, which he had offered to her. The father of a family, in order to pay for magical garments for her, had gambled his fortune and, having lost, killed himself. In a rivalry that she had provoked, a young captain had challenged his best friend to a duel.

While relaying these tragic proofs of her power, she simpered, smiled and burst into laughter.

Jacques was henceforth bewitched by her, for precisely the same reason that enabled her to reign over so many hearts in the land where she lived. She enslaved whomever she wished because she did not love anyone. Setting her lovers ablaze without burning herself, she refused herself out of cruelty or, if she delivered herself, only did so out of egotism, and was never as distant as when one thought that one possessed her. In sum, she was no closer to those who embraced her than to Jacques, from whom she was separated by an incalculable distance—and she appeared all the more attractive because she was inaccessible.

Lagité no longer maintained any reserve in the expression of his sentiments, and, as it amused her, she responded to him without restraint. At that distance, modesty was not an issue, since no effect could result from the most violent covetousness or the least dissimulated advances.

Naturally, he was careful to cease the conversation when he heard Cora come back.

At present, Promise was playing with Jacques like a cat with a mouse. She blew him impetuous kisses, and with expiring expressions she held out her arms to him recklessly.

"Come on, make a little effort," she mocked, "You'll never reach me, alas!"

He stuck his lips to the places on the screen where his correspondent's suggestions were displayed, and followed in vain the moving reflection of her mouth and her splendid nudity.

Cora surged forth one day while he was delivering himself to that unrestrained pursuit, and howling with chagrin and jealousy, she rushed at the screen, smashed it into a hundred pieces, broke the mechanism and, stamping her feet in rage, crushed them underfoot.

It would not have taken as much for Jacques, who had had enough, to break up with the young woman.

In need then of a domicile, he thought that, in sum, perhaps it would be wise to return to his hearth. He was sure of finding there the independence that the quarrelsome humor of his mistress had compromised. Certainly, he no longer loved his wife, but he appreciated her mildness and her proud reserve. So he went back home.

Viviane, who had been thinking about her husband incessantly, was bathed in tears when she saw him coming back through the window. She mopped her eyes quickly, put carmine on her cheeks to hide her pallor, and arranged her hair with a charming artistry. Then, forcing herself to smile in order that he would not read too much criticism in her gaze and would not be put off by her chagrin, she welcomed him as if he had only been away momentarily.

Well, Jacques said to himself, *she scarcely holds anything against me, and doesn't seem to have experienced any pain because of my absence. And I thought she'd be so unhappy! She's quite indifferent, and has only ever had affection for me.*

That is the way that we interpret, unjustly, the sentiments of people we no longer love.

He reinstalled his astral wireless equipment.

He wanted to become a painter in order to reproduce the features of Promise when she appeared in the screen. He bought canvases, paints and brushes, and became a dauber. At first, he found in that new hobby an appeasement of his eternal fever. Painting was now the sole joy for him. A pox on ink and words, which described so poorly! He no longer touched a pen.

He had wanted to frequent the studio of a professional, but he was told that the less he learned of paining, the more he would succeed in it. Such was the fashionable doctrine; he conformed to it, and painted a portrait of Promise in the nude.

In order to be surer of the resemblance, he strove to paint it on the screen itself, and to superimpose his lines and colors of those to the living image. He had asked Promise not to move, and she had consented to that. But as she was the most skittish creature she could not keep still, and the unfortunate Jacques drew six arms, three abdomens and five thighs. By that sign, the esthetes of

Montparnasse recognized genius; but their eulogies did not content him, and he persisted stubbornly in continually recommencing the portrait of his lover.

He scarcely hid anything from Viviane, whom he now believed to be insensible. She learned thus about Jacques' chimerical amour, and that redoubled her sadness, for she understood that such a passion could only lead her husband to despair. And although she judged, rightly, that she was prettier than Promise, she knew that she could never compete with that rival, since she had belonged to Jacques, whereas the other was unrealizable Desire.

IV. The Planet Mechania[49]

Almost at the same time, Letord conversed with his friend regarding the observations he had made of another planet, a satellite of the star Epsilon belonging to the constellation Cygnus

You will doubtless remember that is the course of the stormy demonstration given to his colleagues by the inventor of sidereal wireless, a strange species of gnomes had appeared on the screen.

Since then, Letord had studied the star they inhabited and had baptized it Mechania

That was the new world he designated to Jacques.

"Technology," he told him, "is taken to an extreme there."

"Bravo!" exclaimed Lagité. "I'm sure that the natives of Mechania are friends of veritable progress and do not allow themselves to be distracted, like those of Venus, by the folly of their senses. It's evidently among them that I'll discover happiness."

He therefore put himself in continuous communication with the Mechanians. Their immense skulls remained a cause of stupor for him, and even of repulsion, for some time. He questioned them regarding the origin of that singularity.

The memory was conserved on the planet of a very remote era in which the heads of the Mechanians had almost the same proportions as that of humans, but by virtue of calculating, solving equations, imagining plans for apparatus and determining components and resultants, they had developed their mental capacities to such an extent that their brains had been hypertrophied. Their swelling encephalum had exerted pressure on the walls of their cerebral container had gradually forced it to an enormous distention.

By way of compensation, as the Mechanians only made use of machines henceforth for action and locomotion, they had allowed their arms and legs to atrophy, which had become extraordinarily thin. They were constantly seated on the little platforms previously mentioned in regard to the projections at the Collège de France.

Thos vehicles, provided with propulsive organs of great complexity, can move over the ground, in the air, and over water, even diving beneath the surface. When the Mechanians want to launch themselves into the sky, under the

---

[49] The name of the planet is rendered as Mécante rather than Mécanie [Mechania] at this point in the original, although it is given in the contents page and in the body of the text as Mécanie; I have assumed that the variant is a misprint, but it is not impossible that the author was establishing a momentary confusion between the mechanization of the society and an echo of *méchante* [wicked].

action of a spring wings opened above their apparatus. When they want to dive into the sea, two halves of a hull envelop them and form a kind of submarine cortex. Those machines attain prodigious velocities; it is banal among the Mechanians to accomplish a tour of the world in six hours, although the diameter of their globe is three times that of Earth. It is a little pleasure trip to go in the afternoon from the temperate zone to the pole or the equator and come back before nightfall.

Nothing is done except by machines. In apartments, along the walls, innumerable buttons are aligned, which it is sufficient to push in order to enter into communication with all points on the globe. From their offices, the chiefs of enterprises can direct exploitations situated at enormous distances. By means of a simple pressure of a finger, they launch irresistible fluids that light blast-furnaces at the antipodes, transport formidable loads, dig canals and tunnel through mountains—for the Mechanians have domesticated the most monstrous forces for their service: hurricanes, tidal waves, avalanches, volcanic eruptions, colossal molecular energy and even the rotation of their plant.

They are however, far from savoring a universal felicity, and the coin has its other side.

The very aspect of Gronovoc, their principal city, is scarcely engaging. The smallest houses there have two hundred and fifty stories, for materials have been invented that permit very elevated constructions. At the foot of those gigantic dwellings, the widest thoroughfares, impenetrable to daylight and incessantly illuminated artificially, seem subterranean. The rich are lodged at the top of the buildings and benefit from terraces open to the sky. The poor huddle at the bottom.

In that great city the din is stupefying. It is an infernal and perpetual cacophony composed of the roar of engines, the howl of trumpets, the roar of sirens, and the thunder of wheels and crazy helices. And at the base of the cliff, the Babelesque skyscrapers are shaken by a storm of vibrations, trepidations and violent shocks, as if a terrible seismic disturbance were continually overturning the country.

Even when they are at repose in their apartments, the Mechanians are thrown about incessantly, as if on the back of an untamed horse. It is, moreover not rare for those monumental buildings, long undermined and cracked by the universal tremor, suddenly to collapse, crushing thousands of inhabitants.

The air stinks with the fumes of all the factories that surround Gronovoc. A disgusting soot rains down in the streets and, insinuating itself into the most beautiful apartments, soils the precious furniture. Acrid and mephitic emanations catch the throat and provoke tearing coughing fits. The vapors are so pernicious that they even attack stone and steel, and corrode them rapidly. How can the Mechanians resist them? A mystery.

In truth, they are furnished with the wherewithal to breathe. A flourishing industry consists of seeking almost-virginal air in countries that are still nearly

311

new. It is sealed in vast containers and divided into sown and sealed bladders, which are sold very dear to those as rich as Croesus. Pure air is the rarest of goods on Mechania, and is reputed to be the greatest delight because it is beyond price, but the poor cannot enjoy it, and for them, that is the gravest reason for them to execrate the rich.

Another scourge on Gronovoc, and perhaps the most intolerable, is the difficulty of circulation there. The streets and the sky are so cluttered with machines that it is almost impossible to fray a path through them. Mechanians who want to use the public highways or launch themselves into the air on their flying platform have to wait for an opening for hours. The Prefect of Police, Chiappac, has lost his renown as a skillful man for that reason.

At every moment, Mechanians are smashed to pulp in the inevitable collisions. The resulting bottleneck is so complete that vehicles crashing on the ground and gyroplanes blown to pieces on the spot form an indescribable magma in which no vehicle can any longer move.

Thus, the very excess of technology renders machines completely useless.

Outside the cities, the spectacle is just as desolating. Nowhere are woods, meadows, rocks and rivers to be seen. Everywhere, forests have been razed in order to make way for factories, quarries and mines. Everywhere, running water is imprisoned in mill-races, pipes and turbines, from which it only escapes filthy and noxious. From chimneys, forage wells, hideous slag-heaps, suspended chaplets of blackened skips, antennae, gigantic gangling cranes and inextricable tangles of steel beams and metallic cables, the whirlwinds of humming engines dishonor the earth and the sky.

In a few places, Mechanian engineers, in order to ward off the regrets of poets, have substituted for trees, which could only perish in the midst of that chaos, masts bearing zinc leaves painted green.

As he collected that information, Jacques felt his enthusiasm cooling. He followed a great sporting event, that of the Eight Days. For a week, the Mechanians circled their planet indefatigably in ultra-rapid aircraft. Some of them effectuated as many as fifty complete tours in twenty-four hours. By night, the fulgurant headlights pursued one another through the sky, transmitting, so to speak, an incessant illumination.

Loudspeakers continually promised a bonus offered by a manufacturer of a vaseline or a laxative to the fastest execution of the next two or three circuits of the world. The lure of recompense provoked momentary vertiginous rivalries of speed. It was then that crashes between competing airplanes occurred, and mortal falls. But no one attached any importance to those futile incidents. With the aid of a sort of large spoon, the formless debris of the victims was scooped into an *ad hoc* receptacle and the fantastic round dance did not pause for such trivia.

The person who was proclaimed the winner of the Eight Days had completed the tour of Mechania four hundred and thirty times during the ordeal. His record was saluted by a universal delirium of joy on the planet.

Jacques searched in vain for a rationale for that crazy performance.

"It authorizes all hopes," a Mechanian told him, "for it allows the imminent time to be glimpsed when the world can be circled in five minutes."

"But again," said Jacques, "what would be the purpose of that?"

"To beat the record."

"But why beat the record?"

"How can you ask?"

Jacques could not get anything more out of his interlocutor.

He understood then that the machine, after having been the servant of the Mechanians, had enslaved them despotically in its turn.

Caught up by the frenzy of machines, the people no longer had any other ideal than delivering themselves to the omnipotence of their engines. They were no longer acting in order to arrive at a goal or to accomplish a task, but in order to savor a pleasure. Their unique concern was to obey the crazy rhythm of the apparatus that they had invented. The Machine was their divinity, their devouring idol. They enjoyed the bloody dangers with which it threatened them, and like fanatical Hindus having themselves crushed under an enormous rolling pagoda, they continually confronted, joyfully, the horrible death that Machinism reserved for them.

"What lunatics!" Lagité repeated, privately.

It was certain that the Mechanians were unaware of any veritable joy. Not only had they unlearned the most exquisite relaxation, walking on foot, but they had lost the pleasant habit of sitting down together around a table in order to have a meal seasoned with amiable words. They no longer ate, they only swallowed hastily chemical pills exactly dosed to maintain their strength.

They no longer slept either. Thanks to an electrical apparatus applied to the nape of the neck, they eliminated the toxins that accumulated there and procured immediately the vigor that sleep gives us. Like Macbeth, they had "murdered sleep." Of the bath in forgetfulness, the voyage in the lands of the impossible that, after every day, delivers us without annihilating us, the Mechanians had deprived themselves forever, by their own fault.

They had suppressed the night. An artificial sun that lit up above the city every evening and sources of light springing forth everywhere maintained an eternal daylight; but the harsh light of that radiation rendered their large eyes opaque, just as the perpetual tintinnabulation had ruined their eardrums.

And under the pretext of never wasting a moment in sleep, they spoiled their entire lives in disorderly running around.

Their sad existence was darkened even further by a secret terror. The Mechanians were fearful of a sudden catastrophe that would cause multitudinous deaths among them, which might perhaps scythe them all down at a single stroke. They expected incessantly to be swept away in the frightful cyclone of a universal war.

Already, ten years before, that curse had fallen upon Mechania, and the ravages committed by science had surpassed all the horrors of old.

In a matter of hours, asphyxiating vapors, mortal rays and epidemics deliberately spread had destroyed immense populations. A few scientists in the laboratories had sufficed to prepare bacterial cultures, to rotate pegs and to mix venomous substances for entire races of Mechanians to be exterminated.

And as, in ten years, science had made incredible progress, it had its disposal, for evil even more than for good, a few levers whose manipulation would unleash cataclysmic forces, the immediate consequence of which would be to send three quarters of the Mechanians to the other world.

It might be, therefore, that one morning, the leaders of one nation, in order to ensure world sovereignty, would order several other nations to be sacrificed, without warning. That unprecedented crime would be carried out in less time than it takes to dance a foxtrot.

Jacques was not astonished that that lugubrious prospect tormented the devotees of Machinism excessively, and he began to think that almost all the advantages conquered by intelligence had very heavy tributes for a ransom.

He heard mention of a new invention. It was an automatic woman whose author called her the Synthetic Eve. Made in chrome steel and vulcanized rubber, the young woman imitated nature rather faithfully. She was painted pink and dressed in the same way as the most elegant Mechanian women.

Jacques saw her functioning.

By means of a little phonograph that she had in her throat, she repeated, while admiring herself: "I'm beautiful. Oh, how beautiful I am?" Microphones lodged in her delightful nacreous ears corresponded with all the fibers of her body and, depending on what was said to her, she turned her head, talked, fluttered, moved her arms, legs and the rest. If anyone asked her whether she would like rings, bracelets, or lace, she immediately replied: "Yes, yes!" If she were offered a five-string pearl necklace, a dress in the latest fashion, or a racing avionette, her face lit up with a very gracious smile, and she lay down immediately.

Other phrases, on the contrary, such as "Love me," "Have pity," and "Be good," did not produce any effect on her whatsoever. She seemed not to hear them, and did not flinch. That was because she had a platinum heart. Apart from that insignificant detail she resembled the majority of Mechanian women well enough to pass for one. However, those ladies and damsels did not agree, and in order not to disoblige them, the Mechanians told the inventor that his Synthetic Eve would be incomplete as long as she had no soul.

Jacques was witness to another episode that rendered him pensive.

A Mechanian child who was returning with his father from a short excursion of seven thousand kilometers had descended in a public square in Gronovoc. He was gazing at, and sniffing with a keen pleasure, a fragile blue thing that he was holding in his fingers.

At the sight of that fragile object, Mechanians flocked around the little boy. "Where did you find that?" they asked him.

"Out there."

"How pretty it is! How pretty it is! No jewel offers such variegated hues. And those lines, so softly flexible! And those gentle dwellings! And the perfume of that marvel! One might think that one is inhaling the air of paradise. We've never seen or smelled anything similar. What can it be?"

A white-haired old man who had approached said: "Hang on! Nearly ninety years ago I saw those jewels. They were sometimes discovered then in the vicinity of Gronovoc. But what was it called...? Oh, my wretched memory...no, I can no longer remember."

And Jacques, who was observing that scene attentively, murmured pensively: "The unfortunates! They no longer know flowers."

V. The Danaïde

At no time had Lagité stopped thinking about Gilniz, the divine Gilniz whose name meant Promise and who had set his desires ablaze, but who had been quite unable to satisfy them.

Excruciated by his passion for her, he continued to address incendiary litanies of amour to her, and his obligatorily platonic erethism caused him an unspeakable torture.

In order to staunch his intolerable thirst he was obliged to have recourse to the complaisance of more accessible lovers. He thought that only Venusian prostitution could offer him the intoxication that he intended to demand of it, so he wandered in the little streets that the Faubourg Saint-Antoine confines. Breathless, his temples buzzing, he frequented the popular dance-halls where the girls charge twenty-five centimeters to "sweat one" with their protector.

Although he disguised himself for those adventures, the strange torment of his gaze and his gait denounced him as a stranger to the depths, and the prostitutes, whom he troubled, did not allow him to approach them voluntarily, until he succeeded in making them laugh by executing the black bottom with a parodic rascality. The majority of those who accompanied him into nearby dives, however, disappointed him. None of them realized the kind of frantic ghoul that had been forged in his imagination. The poor creatures lacked all lyricism in their decadence. Not attaching to it any stupor or dishonor, nor any pleasure, they delivered themselves to it as to a monotonous chore; and in the middle of the liveliest frolics they begged, somnolently: "You'll give me forty bullets, my darling."

Jacques quit them without his fever having calmed down.

He ended up, however, discovering one who responded better to his ardors. She called herself La Crépue.[50] Having welcomed many lovers, she had never known amour. Suddenly she was "smitten," and no longer dreamed about anything night or day but Jacques. He instructed her in the sensualities he desired, and they both savored them frantically.

Lagité strove thus to deceive himself, for in the paroxysm of his transports, it was the woman from beyond the sky who offered herself to his transports. He had even warned La Crépue that he would call her Gilniz at such moments, and she had accepted that whim passively, without understanding it.

But she had a pimp, Grêlé of La Bastoche,[51] and that gentleman thought it very bad that his lady found so much charm in someone other than himself. He did not criticize her for abandoning herself to him, but for enjoying it, and, above all, for tiring herself out. He reproached her for "working poorly" and no longer bringing him sufficient profit. Seeing that neither his objurgations nor his brutalities would bring her back to her duty, he hid one night in the vicinity of the cheap hotel in which the two lovers had gone upstairs. When they came down again, and Jacques had arranged a rendezvous with La Crépue for the next day, Grêlé, who followed him treacherously, suddenly planted a "shiv" in his back. Lagité uttered a loud scream; that saved him, for people came running and his attacker ran away without finishing him off.

After being patched up in a pharmacy, Jacques returned home in an auto.

Viviane had conceived some suspicions regarding her husband's absences, but she had feared knowing too much because, always tremulous with amour, she dreaded that by making protestations she might see Jacques desert the hearth again. When he came back covered in blood she felt, at the same time as a bitter anxiety, the dolor of being cruelly enlightened regarding his crapulous frequentations.

But what could she say?

It was necessary, above all, to help the wounded man.

In truth, he was not gravely injured. She cared for him and watched over him. He believed that he had become indifferent to her, and was surprised by so much attention. He explained it as the mechanical solicitude that one shows to a habitual companion.

As a challenge, Grêlé had boasted before La Crépue of having "bloodied the bloke." Panicked, she had first asked for news of Jacques from the concierge of the house where he lived; then, reassured, she had written to her lover to tell him that she would wait for him henceforth in another quarter, in order to put the jealous individual off the track.

---

[50] i.e, "the Hairy one."
[51] La Bastoche is a slang term for the area surrounding the site of the Bastille. The literal meaning of Grêlé would refer to the victim of a hailstorm, but in thin instance it presumably refers to smallpox scars.

As Jacques, without precaution, had left the letter lying around, his wife had found the piece of paper and she had deciphered, disgustedly, the naively ignominious babble:

I miss you, my little man. I've left Grêlé. Come, my Jesus. I'll be very nice. I'll do anything, Your Crêpue for life.

How many tears Viviane shed in secret!

Sometimes, she had surges of indignation; she told herself that her honor demanded that she revolt and make violent reproaches to her husband. Then she understood that it would compromise forever the hope of winning him back. She also thought that a delicate individual like him could not wallow for long in that mud, that he would weary of it, and that she would then reap the benefit of his repentance.

In the end, she could not help loving Jacques all the more because he was in peril. And, pretending not to know anything, she drained her chalice while closing her eyes, as children swallow a bitter remedy.

Quickly reestablished, thanks to the cares she lavished upon him, Jacques had returned in all haste to his whore in order to try again to tame his howling desire and forget the woman from the stars. The two lovers testified a new fury of sensuality to one another. But every time Jacques separated from La Crêpue, far from experiencing an appeasement, he was, on the contrary, more enfevered.

A profound enigma! Nature, which permits the assuagement of hunger and thirst, does not permit lust ever to be sated. The more humans seek to content their genesic appetite, the more they sense it increasing. And if they cease to obey it, it is not because they cease to desire, but only because they cease to be able to satisfy that desire.

The sculptor Auguste Rodin, one of the great philosophers of modern times, has carved in marble a *Danaïde* that depicts that verity.[52] In vain she strives to capture the ironic wave in her bottomless urn, Breathless, harassed and prostrate, she folds herself up in her martyrdom. In her flesh, the nape of her neck and her spine clenches and twists, her loins stretch as if to burst, her entire body is arched, writhing to implore mercy. But she will draw the deceptive water in vain eternally; the gods will never set a term to her suffering, for their ferocious law wants Desire to be an infinite abyss, which no Ocean can ever fill.

Jacques was now being consumed by the fire he had sought to extinguish, and one might have thought that he had killed the gaiety of his heart.

Viviane, who saw him constantly wasting away, was invaded by a poignant anguish. One evening, he was gripped by weakness, and she thought he was

---

[52] *La Danaïde* (1889), now preserved in the Musée Rodin, was originally intended to figure in a portal depicting the Gates of Hell, but was omitted therefrom and completed independently. The statue is sometimes known as "La Source," translated into English as "The Spring," all that translation does not capture the whole meaning.

going to die. She summoned Jean. In order to save her husband, she had the cruelty of invoking the amour that she inspired in the young physician. The best of women are ever ready, for the benefit to the man they cherish, to make those they do not love suffer atrociously.

As soon as he had come running, Jean addressed a gaze of comical despair to her, and, with heroic disinterest, he studied means of snatching Jacques from death. After having examined the invalid, he retained an impassivity so constrained, and avoid so carefully meeting Viviane's gaze, that she divined a fatal verdict and could not suppress a cry of dolor.

Jean's opinion was that it was necessary to carry out a blood transfusion.

The joy of devotion illuminated Viviane. She would have liked to die for Jacques. Jean was determined to spare her. She reproached him for his scruple as a proof of hatred for the moribund, and the unfortunate physician found it very difficult to resolve such a complicated case of conscience.

After a few days, during which Viviane did not take any repose, Jacques seemed reborn. He had woken up and pronounced inconsequential words. She brushed his forehead with a kiss.

"My darling!" he murmured.

Exultant with happiness, she kissed his lips.

"Is that you, Crépue?" he said, as if in a dream.

She felt a cruel pinch in the heart, and wiped her mouth involuntarily with the back of her hand.

Jacques recovered more rapidly than Jean had thought.

"Are there any letters?" he had asked Viviane as soon as he had recovered consciousness.

She knew very well what letters he meant. With a passably hypocritical air of innocence, she deposited all the correspondence on the bed on which Jacques was lying. He searched feverishly, in vain, for the handwriting of the girl of the gutter. As he scanned the newspapers he had not read, he learned that she had been murdered by Grêlé, who had been caught by the police.

He sighed profoundly, but he did not know himself whether he was experiencing the relief of a liberation or the chagrin of a mourning. We are the last to know our own hearts.

VI. The Planet of the Eighty Senses

Barnabé Letord came to visit the convalescent, and when Jacques admitted the cause of his malady to him, the great scientist told him in a mocking tone: "Such a misadventure wouldn't happen on a certain planet that I've just studied. People there abandon themselves freely to all desires without ever being inconvenienced by fatigue."

"Tel me about that country right away!" cried Lagité.

Still mocking, Barnabé Letord confided to him the necessary indications, the wavelength and the astronomical precisions. Jacques had no greater urgency than to communicate with the new star.

The inhabitants he saw there differed from humans above all by virtue of strange structures they bore on the head. A forest of singular apparatus was planted around their forehead and over the surface of their skull. They were large antennae that resembled those of cockchafers, wasps, amts and butterflies. They made up a dense and high spray of plumes of various dimensions, which affected all forms and all colors, and vaguely resembled the horrific plumage with which Red Indian chiefs adorn themselves.

At first, Jacques mistook those diadems for artificial ornaments. He made allusion to that in a conversation with one named Jozibal, whose amity he had rapidly gained in that planet.

"Are you not inconvenienced," he asked him, "by all those appendices swaying over your head?"

"Not at all. They're as light as air. In any case, we're accustomed to them, for we possess them from birth. They're part of us, and they're indispensable to us for sensation.

"For sensation, you say? Do you not, like us, have sufficient sensations with your eyes, your touch, your ears, your smell and your taste?"

"No, certainly not, my dear Terran, and we're surprised that you can content yourself with so few."

"How many senses do you have, then?"

"Eighty."

"Good God!" aid Jacques. He broached the question that piqued his curiosity most of all: "I'm assured that you never weary of pleasures."

"Rather say that we never exhaust them, for when one of our organs is fatigued or worn out we can replace it with another."

"Oh!" said Jacques, supremely interested. "Explain that to me."

"It's quite simple. When we're at table, for instance, and we feel our stomach getting heavy, it's permissible for us to continue eating for as long as we wish. It's sufficient to substitute a new stomach for the one that is no longer functioning. We unhook one and fit another, and the trick is worked."

"Marvelous! And tell me, is it the same for the other organs from which we derive so much pleasure?"

"Of course."

"What? You dispose of spare parts in your effusions of tenderness and you can prolong your ecstasies indefinitely?"

"Assuredly."

Lagité was jubilant.

As he was methodical and wanted to proceed in an orderly fashion, he first asked Jozibal to enable him to witness a sumptuous feast.

"Nothing easier," said the Multisensitive. "I'll take you via the wireless to the palace of a man named Grimalik. Poor for a long time, he has just been enriched by an unexpected inheritance. He has invited a lot of friends to celebrate his recent good fortune and they're occupied in banqueting."

Jacques was delighted to be admitted to such a joyful spectacle.

The guests had gone to table at midday, and it was evening. The dwelling, of splendid magnificence, appeared to have been edified on the model of the sumptuous porticoes that shelter the patricians of Venice feasting around Christ in the masterpiece of Paolo Caliari.[53] Svelte columns sprang lightly from the ground, seemed to send one another elegant arches, and delighted to mind by virtue of the fine harmony of their blue, green and pink marble. Along the walls, luminous mosaics representing rural scenes spread a suave radiance, and large bays opened to the vertiginously violet night.

Grimalik had not yet had the leisure to form his taste, but he had addressed himself sagely to excellent artists, who had served him well. Majordomos, virtuosos of gastronomy, had given notice for a week ahead of the menus that were to succeed one another. Immeasurable lists mentioned innumerable victuals, the least of which were so enticing that saints would have damned themselves in order to taste them.

It was agreed that before the end of the first period, the dishes would be announced for the following week, and only the repose that the guests procured in neighboring chambers would interrupt, at the end of the night, the joys of gluttony. According to the regular program, however, the feasting would recommence as soon as the host and his guests were out of bed.

Grimalik, who had suffered from hunger in his youth, intended to take his revenge in that fashion. Having reached maturity, he had decided to remain constantly at table henceforth, and to devote all the minutes of his existence to an immense and unique feast that would only end with his death.

Maîtres d'hôtel incessantly brought extraordinarily delicate dishes that were reminiscent of our shads in the snowy whiteness of their flesh, our gilded pullets, the pink slices of our roast meats, our translucent jellies, our most unctuous compotes, our foamiest brioches and our most brittle marzipans, Winewaiters incessantly poured Edenic wines and divine liqueurs into the cups.

An exquisite music, with rose up at intervals, maintained mild and cheerful thoughts in the audience.

When the guests had taken pleasure in the thousand treats of the dessert and the repast seemed ready to conclude, the orchestra, which had just been

---

[53] The reference is to the Biblical feasts, most famously *The Wedding Feast at Cana* (1563) and *The Feast in the House of Levi*—originally titled *The Last Supper*—(1573), painted in elaborate and sumptuous fashion by Paolo Caliari, better known as Veronese.

playing languorous airs, suddenly burst forth with resounding fanfares to announce the beginning of a new banquet,

Then the maîtres d'hôtel made a tour of the tables, presenting the guests with a basket of empty stomachs, as we are offered the bread-basket. The exchange of organs was operated instantly, beneath the waistcoat; and everyone resumed eating, with a hearty appetite

There was a second round of dorados, pheasants, ortolans, roast lamb, puddings, marmalades and, once again, triumphant poultry, succulent meats, ineffable salads, prodigious crusty pâtés, and more miraculous creams, paradisal fruits, fabulous cakes, and so on, without respite or pause.

A few vagabonds whom Grimalik counted among his friends and whom he had been careful not to forget—for wealth had not stunned him—were immediately drunk. For from being offended by them, the amphitryon was moved by hearing them launch coarse sallies and lewd refrains.

"Hey," he cried, "get a grip on yourself, Tobobol, Eat and drink. And you, my old Ralabak, you don't have such a feast when you carry your merchandise on the docks. Don't stint yourself."

The more refined guests savored every dish. They came back to them, delighting in them again, and making signs to the lackeys from time to time to bring the basket of stomachs. Then they plied the fork and raised their cups with a revitalized ardor.

Grimalik was with the angels. His friends were no less happy.

That night, when the sky was tinted pink by the approach of dawn, the company, after eighteen hours spent at table, went to bed entirely satisfied.

And Jacques said to himself: *After all, perhaps that's happiness!*

The next day he found the *bon vivants* almost as radiant as the day before. He noticed, nevertheless, than some of them were attaching themselves less devotedly to eating well and drinking well. By the fourth day, several of them seemed to be bored. They were nibbling. They were not weary, because they could renew their hunger indefinitely, but as they were presented with the same aliments or very similar ones, they could no longer feel an equal contentment.

On Grimalik's orders, the master chefs applied themselves to inventing increasingly impressive dishes. Processionally, to the sound of thunderous marches, they brought monstrous animals on the platforms of gigantic platters with raised arms—a red deer, for example, whose pieces, expertly marinated and cooked, were sown back into its skin, reposed, with its feet tucked under its abdomen, on florid grass, but displayed its antlers nevertheless, resplendent with fine gold. Huge birds that had been stuffed with flavorsome mincemeat and then reclad in their sparkling plumage, displayed their tails and seemed to be preparing to take flight.

At first the guests had applauded those victorious entrances and their appetites had been reanimated by them, but gradually, indifference gained them. They were beginning to lose interest in the interminable guzzling, and with the backs of their hands, almost all of them waved away what was offered to them. After a week, there were defections around the tables.

Bitterly, Grimalik ordered his chefs to diversify their recipes further. He stamped his feet; he howled; he now judged the rarest sauces and the most ingenious sorbets execrable. The principal majordomo protested firmly that no one could do any better. With that, the host threw a truffle purée, which was a masterpiece, at his head. The juice ran over the variegated waistcoat of the officer, who wiped it away in a dignified fashion and resigned. He was replaced by his deputy.

A week later, there was only a small group of faithful adherents around Grimalik, who was holding firm solely as a matter of honor. Soon, he remained alone, bleak and infinitely discouraged. He had changed stomachs frequently, but his servants, in spite of their skill, had proved to be incapable of varying the nourishment sufficiently. And Grimalik, having exhausted all experiments in gastronomy in a matter of days, dismissed his army of cooks. He only kept an insignificant little scullion, and no longer ate anything but very simple foods, like boiled eggs, boiled potatoes and white cheese, because any culinary preparation made him feel sick.

Lagité interrogated his correspondent regarding that adventure, who smiled and told him that it was commonplace on the planet of the eighty senses. That was, for Jacques, a great subject for reflection.

Then, giving another direction to his thoughts, he said: "But what about Amour, Amour?" he cried. "Instruct me, then, as to what it is on your world. After all, if your strength is repaired at will, you're certainly the most fortunate of mortals."

"Oh," replied Jozibal, "you can judge that better for yourself. I'll introduce you to an adolescent and a young woman who are among my friends. They love one another, and it's their first romance. Know that we never raise any obstacle to the testimonies of passion. In that regard, our mores are less hypocritical than yours. You can converse with those tender lovers as much as you please."

Lagité saw the turtle-doves emerging from a boscage.

There was the enchantment of the cheerful season in which, on that world as on Earth, the trees bear more flowers than leaves, and the buds resemble jewels of gold and coral, bursting in order to allow the passage of their underwear, still frayed, the green tips of which powder all the twigs of the bushes joyfully. The little birds indulge in singing competitions. The silver dragonflies cling together in pairs, amusing themselves by firming gallant airplanes with eight wings. The butterflies describe crazy histories in the crystal sky by means of their eccentric zigzags; and on the grass, which the tearful dawn had enriched with diamonds, roe deer and their hinds were bounding, with the odd little white behinds.

Perhaps you will be astonished that the countryside on that star was almost identical to our own, but it only seemed so to the eyes of a human like Jacques.

It appeared quite different to the eyes of the Multisensitives, whose sight is very different from ours. We shall explain that in due course.

The lovers who were introduced to Jacques were charming. There was no need to ask them whether they were happy. They never ceased taking one another's cheeks between their ten fingers in order to kiss one another.

Lagité talked to them, but they scarcely had the leisure to reply to him. Getting up at cock-crow, after having spent all night cooing, each of them carried a wicker basket bound with brightly colored ribbons, which contained the jewels they had exchanged.

"Excuse us," they said, laughing, and went back into the boscage.

Jacques told Jozibal that they reminded him of the poetry of Catullus.

"My Lesbia, give me a thousand kisses, and then another thousand, and then a hundred more; afterwards, we'll lose count, in order that no one will any longer be able to know the number of our kisses."

"Well, yes," said the Multisensitive, "that's it, exactly. But your Catullus, with all his prowess, was a braggart, while our couple don't nourish themselves on imagination."

"Oh, the rogues. You'll give me news of them?"

"I won't fail to do so."

The next day, Jacques learned from his informant that, without distinguishing noon from midnight, the young people had embraced continuously.

Other days went by in the same fashion. And Lagité said to Jozibal: "I think that they've surpassed the figure of a thousand."

"I think so too, because, for a week, they've been devoting twenty-two hours out of twenty-four to amour."

On the ninth day they were as fresh as on the first. But they were sulking, turning their backs on one another, and no longer going into the wood. They did not take long to separate.

Surprised by that discord, Jacques asked the reason for it.

"Everything encourages the belief," Jozibal replied, "that the lovers were dissatisfied with one another."

"Did they think that they hadn't given one another enough kisses?"

"If they'd given one another a hundred times as many, they wouldn't have been any happier. It's a fatality of Nature that our desire always surpasses our joys immensely."

"That the fatality in question rules on Earth," said Jacques, "I can understand, for our human joys are brief, but yours...!"

"They are nothing in comparison with our wishes."

Jacques was very disconcerted.

"The disillusionment of that couple," Jozibal went on, "is common to almost all Multisensitives. After a few trials, which demonstrate to us the impossibility of ever being sated, we end up considering physical lust as a lure, and from then on we make the decision only to indulge in it with extreme moderation. We scarcely sacrifice to amour as much as human do, and more often than not we're content to exchange tender words. So when our villagers encounter young people who are impatient, they shout to them, jovially: "That will pass before we meet again!"

Lagité continued to inform himself. He wanted to know what the multitude of sensations were experienced by the inhabitants of the privileged planet.

"First of all," said his correspondent, "the five senses with which you're provided are present to us with an incomparable delicacy."

"Oh," said Jacques, vexed, "I can read without spectacles."

"Pooh! What's that? Our sight surpasses in penetration your most magnifying microscopes. In order to look at minuscule objects, it's sufficient for us to adapt our vision by means of a very slight effort. For instance, at this moment, there's a fly on my table. I can see it as large as an elephant. I'm admiring its eyes with a hundred facets polished like mirrors, in which my window and the sky are reflected a hundred times. Its enormous trunk is extending toward a droplet of water that appears to me as a voluminous and resplendent crystal sphere. And in that droplet, I perceive fish of all the colors of the rainbow. They're innumerable microbes that are floating, swimming, or agitating around them bright tresses of multicolored filaments, iridescent and gilded."

"What enchantment!" said Jacques.

"Even better, with a little more attention, we discover the ultimate mysteries of the infinitely small."

"Truly?"

"Thus, for instance, I can discern quite clearly the smallest molecules of that liquid."

"Bah!" sad Jacques.

"Here's a molecule of water. It's composed of atoms of oxygen and hydrogen, which I can see gravitating continuously like words in the immensity. For me, a multitude of stellar systems are rotating in that droplet."

"You're giving me vertigo."

"We're accustomed to these spectacles. The colors that seem to you to be uniform are decomposed for us at every second into their trillions of vibrations, for we have the gift of noting infinitely fugitive impressions. And as soon as we desire it, Nature entire is to our eyes an endless quivering of prodigiously rapid undulations, which intersect in all directions like the cerulean waves of an opal ocean."

"That's unusual!"

"We can also see a long way."

"I've heard it said that eagles in the Alps soaring a thousand meters in the air can perceive a rat in a furrow."

"Your eagles make me laugh," said Jozibal. "With a little application we can see everything—yes, everything. Our sight, like your Roentgen rays, pierces obstacles that are opaque for you. When I sail on the sea, my gaze plunges without difficulty into the most fearful abysses. I see the blinding phosphorescence spread in the supreme depths by masses of plastic jelly, the prototypes of all life. I see the fulgurations of luminous monsters that pursue one another and devour one another. I see the algae that form impenetrable flexible forests in which supple embroideries, diaphanous fringes and incandescent lace move endlessly."

"How beautiful that must be!"

"My sight traverses the soil of our planet and focuses wherever I wish. Here, innumerable leagues below my feet, is a grotto in which, under fantastic pressures and temperatures, an infinite number of marvelous substances are in the process of creation. It's a crucible greater than all your cathedrals, in which golden lava is bubbling, where sparkling swirls of rubies, torsades of topazes and spirals of beryls are unrolling and stretching out, where arrows of turquoise and sprays of sapphire are fusing, where a single diamond as dazzling as a sun and so colossal that it couldn't be contained in any of your public squares is crystallizing in a formidable furnace of myriads of spurting flames."

"What magical visions!" cried Jacques.

"In the same way, our ears perceive harmonies ungraspable for you."

"One of our ancient philosophers, Plato, said that the Just, after life, will be lulled by the music of the celestial spheres."

"We enjoy it. It's a grave, rather sad melody, sometimes as strident as a burst of ironic gaiety, often as imperious and harsh as the voice of an implacable master, at other times sweet and nostalgic, like an immaterial harp."

"Ah, how I'd like to hear it!"

"Oh, one wearies of it at length, you know."

"But my dear friend, tell me about your other senses."

"Look, for example, at these two little violet plumes that stand up above my ears. Can you see them?"

"Perfectly."

"Thanks to these organs, I can exchange thoughts with the other inhabitants of our plan, no matter what distance separates me from them."

"A sort of natural wireless, in sum?"

"That's exactly it. Instantaneously, it's possible for me to chat with a friend who is at the Antipodes."

"That's very agreeable. You're unaware, then, of the chagrin of absence."

"Hmm. Absence isn't always regrettable. In many cases, one would be very glad to be liberated from certain bores. And you can't imagine how we're sometimes exasperated by feeling our little violet plumes vibrate, agitated by incessant appeals."

"Exactly like our telephone, which renders us enraged."

"There isn't any means of avoiding that tyranny, except to have the two antennae excised. Some of us arrive at that extreme by virtue of aggravation. What else shall I tell you? Other antennae allow us to communicate with animals and permit us to know everything that is happening in their brains."

"That's exciting."

"Not as much as you might think. If you could read the mind of a monkey, a pig or a wolf, you'd probably find it very similar to that of a human."

"Ah!"

"I'd like to describe all our senses to you, but how? The words that designate them in our language are untranslatable into yours."

"At least describe your joys to me."

"They're paltry."

"Truly, it seems to me that you don't appreciate appropriately the marvelous favors with which Destiny has heaped you."

"What do you call marvelous favors?"

"Your eighty senses!"

"Alas, that's a derisory figure."

"If only we had them!"

"You'd lament them, like us. Oh, yes, we deplore every day not being able to grasp anything of the innumerable effluvia with which we're brushed by Universal Life."

"You're very ungrateful."

"Not at all. Think about all the secret forces traveling through space. Can you imagine the fabulous quantity of energies analogous to light, to heat, to sound, that are seething everywhere and from which none of us can profit because the pitiful infirmity of our organism forbids them to us. Try to imagine the inexhaustible sources of mysterious currents that are completely lost to us; and recognize with me that our unfortunate eighty senses are ridiculously insufficient. It's at least a million that we'd need in order to begin to communicate with immense Nature."

"That's true!" said Jacques, struck by Jozibal's remarks. "You're not happy, then?" he added.

"We're very unhappy. Have you not observed the despair of Grimalik and the two young lovers after their vain experiments?"

"Yes, but, to tell the truth, I don't really understand why you don't obtain mire benefit from your precious gifts."

"Think about it. As soon as we make use of them, we want to make more use of them, even more, always more. Well, although those excesses are not fatal to us, as in your case, although we don't risk falling ill or dying of them, they nevertheless fill us with an atrocious affliction. We can multiply the return of sensuality, but our indomitable desire rebounds indefinitely toward higher summits. That is why, as soon as we understand the deceptiveness of that absurd pursuit, we abstain from desire."

You judge yourselves as unfortunate as humans, then?"

"More, because out richer senses allow us to measure more accurately the impossibility of being happy."

Lagité meditated for several days on the planet of the eighty senses. He compared the Multisensitives to humans, his contemporaries, so avid for known or unknown enjoyments, and concluded quite naturally that the frantic search for pleasures could not procure happiness in any fashion—in which he was in accord with all moralists, past, present and future.

While he was thinking, he happened to turn his eyes toward the astral wireless screen, and uttered a cry.

He had just seen Gilniz, his Gilniz, his beloved from beyond the sky, in the arms of an inhabitant of Venus.

The scene was certainly worthy of a great painter or a great sculptor, for the two lovers were young and beautiful, and their couple presented all the charm of a pagan masterpiece. But Jacques had his reasons for not liking that spectacle, and jealousy drew roars from him.

It was certainly by design that Gilniz was showing herself to him in her amorous diversions, for she continually disengaged slightly from an embrace in order to look furtively to the side or over the shoulder of her accomplice, to observe the effect that it was producing on Lagité.

She pushed effrontery so far as to call out to him: "Jacques, I present to you my young friend Varluz."

"Curse you!" howled Jacques.

"Poor Jacquot!" she mocked.

"If only," he added, "you had chosen your partner better."

"For what are you reproaching him?"

"For being ugly. He's a fop with insignificant features, an androgyne with forms devoid of vigor."

Jacques was unjust, but sincere, for we never fail to accuse of bad taste the woman who prefers another man to us.

Gilniz continued laughing.

"But after all," he said, "Why are you imposing this odious vision on me?"

"It's my caprice," she said. "And what use can you be to me, except to spice my pleasure with your impotent anger?"

"I'll die of it!"

"What an intoxication to be loved to the point of death!"

Then Jacques insulted without interruption the woman from beyond the sky, who laughed, and kept laughing.

Planted in front of the screen, he vomited invectives. His fists clenched, his face forward, his eyes bulging, the veins in his neck swollen as if to burst, he launched volleys of insults at the two lovers.

Suddenly, he felt a hand on his shoulder. It was his friend Barnabé Letord.

The professor, who often visited Letord, had knocked on the door in vain, and had come in without further ado. At a glance, he had understood. He began by sagely cutting the communication and advising the journalist to calm down.

Jacques was haggard. It took him a long time to recover his breath and his voice.

"Those," said Letord, "are very deadly emotions. I'm aware of your adventure; you've already told me about it—and I think I might have the remedy for your despair."

"You can cure me?" said Lagité, eagerly.

"Why not? I'll put you in contact with a star whose inhabitants forget everything that inconveniences or disobliges them. In watching them live, you might perhaps lose the memory of your deplorable amour. Then the wireless will have repaired the harm that it has done."

That same day, Jacques entered into relations with the race that the scientist had just indicated to him.

VII. Dancing Planet

The Forgetful do not know any of our troubles.

A great misfortune, in striking us, afflicts us, and we fear its return. They immediately start whistling, singing and dancing, and it no longer appears to them.

Lagité envied them.

To tell the truth, he remarked in the Forgetful strange intermittences of memory. For instance, they recall very clearly the money they have lent, but never the money that they owe. If it is their mistress who is waiting for them at a rendezvous they remember it, but not if it is their legitimate wife. They always recognize their friends who have become rich, but never those who have fallen into poverty. These mental defects are, in sum, rather awkward, because they can generate suspicions as to the quality of their soul.

Dancing, which they practice with so much passion, is for them the great means of procuring forgetfulness. Their choreography, however, is neither amiable nor tender, and Lagité remarked, not without astonishment, that it resembled greatly the kind that is fashionable among us. Away with gentle cadences that lull and enchant! The Forgetful want violent and brutal dances that extract them from reality.

They borrow them from the most abject peoples, for instance, from oxherds who, in their world, correspond to coarse Argentine gauchos. Or they reproduce the vulgar and sinister frolics of pimps and prostitutes. Or again, it is from their most backward tribes, their cannibal peoples, that they request lessons in rhythm. Thus, when they deliver themselves to their favorite pleasure they give the impression of lunatics escaped from their guardians. They shiver, slap their thighs and buttocks, and leap on all fours, or with their legs in the air and heads downwards.

As for their music, it is in keeping. There are no melodious and charming chords, but raucous sounds, the appeals of rutting beasts, the trumpeting, growling, bellowing and gasps of avid instincts, a racket of a menagerie in revolt.

"Exactly like our jazz," Jacques noted, amazed. "In the depths of the heavens, jazz is triumphant, as it is here! How small the world is!"

So, from dawn to dusk, and from dusk to dawn, on that planet, people leap and twirl. It is not only young people who are drawn away by that vertigo but mature people, old men and pregnant women. And it is asserted that some precocious infants even start dancing in their mother's womb. People dance at home, they dance in the street, they dance everywhere. Judges taunting the accused, as is their custom, physicians killing their patients, merchants ribbing their clientele, whores plucking popinjays, and functionaries twiddling their thumbs all dance competitively. Some gamblers wager that they can dance for an entire week, night and day, without sleeping.

Dancing Planet was the name that Letord gave that star.

In order to abolish their memory more completely, the Forgetful also have recourse to drugs. One of them, named the Philosopher, whose acquaintance Jacques made, furnished him with precise information regarding those poisons; and that was a further opportunity for Lagité to observe troubling analogies between Dancing Planet and Earth.

Thus, the Forgetful make incessant use of a white powder called chichi, exactly similar to our cocaine. They snort it, the way we take coke, and then sense a vivid current of air, which, penetrating into their head, empties it of all thought. The pleasure of losing the brain seems prodigious to them, and once they have enjoyed it they can no longer do without it. Chichi takes away from its fanatics appetite, reason, health and life, exactly like our coke. But from the moment that it plunges them into a stupid ataraxia, they ask for nothing more, and they march lightly to the tomb.

Jacques' correspondent cited many other stupefying agents of which the inhabitants of Dancing Planet make continual abuse, and which procure them along with stupidity, a more or less rapid death. Lagité commenced from then on seriously to doubt whether that race was a model to follow.

The Philosopher told him that in reality, forgetfulness was not a sovereign remedy for all evils, and in that regard he told him the instructive story of a young Forgetful woman.

Her name was Riri. She had large forget-me-not blue eyes, a slightly turned-up nose and fleshy lips like twin cherries; and she smiled incessantly.

Her mother, named Valnou, had died tragically a few weeks after bringing her into the world, and Riri had been brought up by an aunt. When Riri had grown up, that aunt took her into a charming little wood near the city and said to her:

"Try to remember what I'm going to tell you. You see that rural dance-hall. It's there that your mother met your father. They danced together, after which, the good Valnou, whose head was spinning a little, came to repose with him on their flowery bank of grass. She told me that herself. As she was tired, she went to sleep and she had an enchanting dream.

"She thought that the god of Amour took her in his arms and that, flying away with her, he took her on a beautiful excursion above these woods, ponds and hills. When she woke up, it was your father who was holding her in an embrace; I owe it to the truth to recognize that she took great pleasure in it.

"Until you were born, your father remained your mother's good friend, but when you were born, he left her, without anyone being able to discover what had become of him. And Valnou came back here to shed burning tears. One day, on that little bridge over there, she threw herself into the river and drowned there."

"Oh, Aunt," said Riri, "how right you were to bring me to this fatal place. I'll come back here often, in order to preserve the memory of my mother's sad example, in order not to fall into the same error."

Ad she did, in fact, come back.

She met a young man there, who complimented her on her beauty and offered to take her to the nearby dance-hall.

"No," she said. And, by telling him the whole story of Valnou's disgrace, she made him understand that it was futile to persist.

"On the contrary," he said. "You can dance with me, since the dire fate of your mother will retain you on the slope of error."

That reflection seemed luminous to Riri, so she danced; and then her head spun, and then she went to rest on the grassy bank, and then she had an exquisite dream, and then she gave birth to a little girl named Titi, and then her lover abandoned her, and then she drowned herself.

"And that," said the Philosopher, is where forgetfulness leads.

"Is that adventure true," Jacques asked, "or have you invented it?"

"It's scrupulously exact," replied the other.

"It seems marvelously symbolic. Fundamentally, your story of Riri is the story of all the generations that succeeded one another on Earth as well as on the planet, for the Forgetful."

A few days later, the Philosopher said to Jacques: "You know that a terrible war ravaged our planet only a few years ago..."

"What! You too!" said Jacques. Is it necessary that from one end of the immensity to the other, the same horrible catastrophes are renewed? But go on..."

"In one of our capitals," said the Philosopher, "An Unknown Soldier was buried under a majestic triumphal arch..."

"Ah!" said Jacques. "Exactly like us!"

"And this is what has just happened. The other morning, near that arch, passers-by gathered around a former combatant dressed as if he had returned from the trenches, with his cape torn, stained and dirty, his cap staved in, and his boots and trousers caked in mud. His face was the color of ash, with a short beard pricklier than the shell of a horse-chestnut. His eyes were burning with fever in their sunken orbits.

"In a hoarse voice he said to the people surrounding him: 'I've risen from my tomb.'

"They decided that he was mad. He went on: 'I'm the Unknown Soldier.'

"They shrugged their shoulders and left him, going on their way. But now, people are talking about him. I've just met him, wandering over one of our battlefields, where there was the greatest massacre. I want to show him to you, and for you to hear him via wireless, with the aid of an apparatus I take with me when traveling. And in order for you to understand what he says, I'll translate it for you into interastral language."

"I'm obliged to you," said Jacques.

On his screen, a mountainside was projected. Venerable fir-trees had once shaded that landscape, but the hurricane of shells had striped them all of their branches, sliced, shattered, and uprooted them, turning them upside down.

A tavern served as a rendezvous for the tourists that had been attracted, at first, by the history, and who continued to come out of habit, but who could hardly remember the recent tragedy.

Some young women were talking a walk while waiting for poultry that was being prepared with their intention to finish roasting.

"From this viewpoint," a guide said to them, "you can see an area where at least two million soldiers were killed." He pointed out a nearby clearing. "In that narrow space alone, at least two hundred thousand combatants died."

"Why tell us that?" murmured the darlings. "It isn't cheerful."

And their companions added: "It's necessary not to talk about the war any longer; it's boring. Let's have lunch."

Thy feasted, therefore, in the open air, and the champagne corks popped joyfully.

Then, to the sound of a vielle[54] and a bagpipe, they organized a hop on the very spot that the cicerone had pointed out to them. They needed to stretch their limbs, agitated by the wine. One dancer stumbled over a bone that was sticking out of the ground, and nearly fell, but her dancing-partner caught her, and no one took any notice of the negligible incident.

Suddenly, parting the bushy branches of two decapitated fir-trees, the Unknown Soldier loomed up on a rock. He stood there for a long time, impassively, his arms folded, and no one paid any attention to him. He was emaciated and cadaverous; his gas-mask surmounted the long thinness of his face like a monstrous dome. His waxy skin was stuck so closely to his cheekbones that he might have been mistaken for a death's-head.

---

[54] The elastic term *vielle* was originally applied to a kind of lute, and then to a hurdy-gurdy. It seems to be used here to refer to an accordion.

On the height of his stone pedestal he seemed enormous. A phantom of all those whose bones blistered the soil, he lowered the heavy gaze of the past upon the present.

He cried: "Are you not ashamed?"

Through the fol-de-rol of the music, a young woman heard him. She perceived him, and stopped instantaneously as if changed into a statue of salt, her arm extended toward the apparition.

Those who were around her followed the direction of her hand with their eyes, and were immediately petrified. Communicated from one to another, the immobilization rapidly gained the whole assembly, including the musicians, who interrupted their tune at the measure they had commenced.

All of the stared at the Revenant, and stood there, his eyes dilated and his mouth open.

Suddenly, as one of the witnesses of the scene fled, howling with fear, all the others, seized by panic, dispersed in the blink of an eye. They ran all the way to the horizon without looking back. Even the tavern-keeper and the dishwasher, one throwing away his white cap and the other her dish-rag, ran downhill recklessly to the plain.

As for the Unknown Soldier, grim and not deigning to say a word to the Philosopher, who had been left alone with him, he resumed his way of the cross through the folds of the terrain fertilized by the blood of his brothers.

The newspapers of Dancing Planet related that episode in a few words. The journalists were only astonished that a lunatic had been left at liberty.

Jacques asked his correspondent to continue to give him news of the Unknown Soldier, and the Philosopher promised Lagité to attach himself to the specter's footsteps.

Two days later, immense forges appeared on the screen, filled with a volcanic rumble of machines. In an enormous hall, axles were rotating relentlessly, which activated innumerable transmission belts, connecting-roads, levers, pistons and endless chains.

On aerial rails, carts were moving rapidly. Gigantic steel cylinders were suspended from metallic cables, which, having been brought thus to powerful machines, were subject to a quantity of transformations. Borers hollowed them out, emptied them and turned them into tubes. Under the bite of irresistible scrapers, steel chips were detached and twisted regularly into long, glittering spirals, reminiscent of strange curls of hair.

The tubes were fitted into one another, engaged in thick hoops that circled them, bound them and gave them a formidable solidity.

At the end of that cyclopean manufacture, which required the efforts of an army of workers and the expense of incalculable treasures, cannons of ten, twenty and thirty meters with terrifying mouths were lined up, their interior mathematically rifled: artillery capable of hurling enormous shells extraordinary distances, the explosion of which would disembowel the most massive ramparts, sink marine leviathans instantaneously, raze towns and asphyxiate entire peoples.

Under hangars with infinite and desolating perspectives, projectiles, interminably arranged, were classified in accordance with their height, their width and their destructive properties.

Before those frightful threats of massacre was a group of important individuals, who were strutting, leaping and frolicking. They were the directors of the factory, flanked by military men, governors and diplomats belonging to several nations of Dancing Planet.

One statesman, speaking to his foreign colleagues, said to them flippantly: "Dear allies, thanks to these toys, of which we're making such an abundant provision for you and for ourselves, I think that we're in a position to pulverize all our enemies."

The Philosopher was listening to them, and spoke to them with authority. By what entitlement was he there? A mystery—but as each member of the audience thought himself to be alone in not knowing who he was, he was allowed to say whatever he wished.

"It seems to me," he observed, "that we might have employed our time better since the last war."

"What war?" asked the Forgetful.

"The one that left twelve million dead ten years ago."

"Oh, yes…," they said.

"Consider that it was with toys exactly like these that the admirable result in question was obtained."

"Indeed," conceded a diplomat.

"Are you not of the opinion that it's necessary henceforth to find another way to regulate relations between peoples?"

"Another way?"

"Yes. For example, an unshakable agreement of all nations, a decisive resolution no longer to deceive one another, to associate equitably in all their enterprises, to submit without reserve to a jurisdiction agreed by them in advance to resolve all their disputes. Would that sage organization and that reciprocal confidence require much more intelligence, effort and sacrifice than the unlimited accumulation of all these diabolical engines?"

"Aha!" said the Forgetful. "You're a pacifist."

"Is it not our primary duty to want peace?"

"Undoubtedly, undoubtedly," replied the diplomat. "And we ourselves, in a large number of debates, conferences, congresses, committees, consultations, conventions, sessions, meetings, commissions, colloquia, determinations, deliberations, communiqués, motions, memoirs, conclusions, communications, suggestions, leagues, societies and international groups, are gradually elaborating the code of the peace."

"Well, is that code ready?"

"Not yet, but we've signed a pact."

"Ah! Will it suppress war."

"It puts it outside the law."

"Words! Does it let it live?"

"Evidently."

"You haven't accomplished anything, then?."

"Such is certainly our opinion. And that is why our governments continue to arm themselves to the teeth."

With that, a general cried: "Universal fraternity—what a chimera!"

And everyone agreed: "War is a necessity."

"Beneficent!"

"No progress without war!"

"Blood is the fecundating dew of all civilization!"

Chatting animatedly, the Forgetful had turned their backs on the rows of shells.

One of the diplomats concluded: "This will always be the ultimate reckoning." He turned round abruptly in order to indicate the munitions.

But his arms fell back, and his companions were as petrified as he was.

As if he had emerged from the ground between the nearest projectiles, the Unknown Soldier was standing there, sinister and hallucinatory, as he had appeared on the accursed mountain.

Again, he cried: "Are you not ashamed?"

The amazement of the official personages did not last long.

"Oh, it's the madman," said one of them, "the famous madman that the newspapers have mentioned. Inoffensive, after all."

And they drew away, laughing...

The next day, Jacques saw a pretty house in the suburbs of a great city on Dancing Planet. A low fence surrounded the little garden appended to it. Sitting on a bench, a robust woman was knitting. She had scarcely passed thirty, and, plump and insouciant, she seemed happy.

In a pathway, the master of the house, red-faced with large bulging eyes, a thick neck and a pot belly, was making two young boys of twelve or thirteen, provided with model weapons, perform military exercises.

"Present arms...! Quicker! Mark time...! Present arms! At the double! Up! Up...! At ease! I ordered: 'At ease!' Good God, what dawdlers you are! If you don't shape up, you'll never be able to kill anyone. What good will you be if you don't even know how to use a rifle? Have you no courage? Don't you love your fatherland? If you love it, it's necessary to hate all foreigners, it's necessary to learn to kill, to kill quickly, and to kill abundantly. That way, your nation will be able to crush other peoples and enslave the world."

The Unknown Soldier had just come to lean on the fence.

He listened, he looked and he condemned with the concentrated anger of a judge confronted with a nameless infamy.

Addressing the woman, he said: "Wife, do you recognize me?"

She raised her head instantly and was shocked to perceive him.

"Who are you?" she said.

"The dead man."

"The dead man?"

"Yes, your husband."

"What?"

"I've risen from the tomb in order to see what's happening."

She sat there, open-mouthed.

"This is your lover, then. I remember. He was our neighbor, While I was in the trenches, he was under cover. I remember. When I was on leave, I noticed something shady between you. Yes, already, while I was with the martyrs out there, you were cheating on me..."

Incapable of turning her eyes away or articulating a word, she wondered whether she was dreaming while awake.

He went on: "Now he's eating your widow's pension, and, being a chauvinist, like all those under cover, he's stuffing the heads of my kids, training them for slaughter. That's how our death has served!"

The lover questioned the woman, dully: "Who is he? Do you know him?"

"No," she said. "It isn't him, since he's dead—at least, they said so; but no one ever knew what became of him."

Suddenly, an old cat that was curled up on a bench near his mistress, warming himself in the sun, stretched himself, saw the phantom and leapt on to his shoulder with a single bound, rubbing himself tenderly against his bushy beard.

"Ronronni!" said the Soldier. "My old Ronronni! Animals have better memories than people."

"It's him! It's him!" cried the woman. "A ghost! A ghost!"

And she fainted.

The lover had run into the house. He came back with a revolver, which he aimed at the Soldier. "Get away!" he howled

The other did not budge.

Two detonations rang out.

The Specter did not shudder.

"I hit him, though!" growled the shooter.

"One can't kill the dead," said the Specter.

The lover threw away the revolver and fled.

"Adieu, lads!" said the Soldier to the children, who were bewildered and nailed to the spot. Then, slowly and heavily, at a pace that scraped the road, he resumed the route to the city. Blood was flowing from one of his sleeves and tracing a thin continuous red line on the ground.

Behind him trooped poor people who were already mature, or even old. An irresistible power was impelling them. They had made war and, alone among the Forgetful, they retained a vague memory of it.

They murmured: "It's the Unknown Soldier. He said so and it's true. Let's follow him. He'll speak to us."

The Phantom went all the way to the triumphal arch. As he drew closer to it, his march became more leaden. He appeared to be climbing Calvary. His companions matched his dolorous tread religiously, advancing with extreme slowness. They were all as distressed as he was. And that ascension was so poignant that no one thought of impeding it. The police limited themselves to channeling the fantastic cortege and containing the curious on the sidewalks.

When the Soldier arrived under the arch he saw the Memorial Flame dancing ironically, and by pressing a spring, he extinguished it.

"Lie!" he growled. Then he cried, furiously: "Forgetfulness is a crime!"

And, lying down on the slab, with his hands joined, as if he were a recumbent stone figure on a Medieval sepulcher, he expired.

In the crowd, some said: "He's gone back to sleep. It's necessary to lift the slab in order to lay him in his coffin again." But when night fell, the cadaver was taken away. When he was undressed, it was perceived that he bore two fresh wounds, in one shoulder and the arm.

Lagité interrogated the Philosopher: "Can you explain that enigma to me?"

"It's not my responsibility."

"Do you believe in ghosts?"

"No. I can imagine several keys to the mystery—but so can you, I imagine. Choose the explanation that pleases you most."

"Have you not remarked the extreme resemblance of your planet to the Earth?"

"In fact, people forget there almost as quickly there as they do here, and it's for that reason, without a doubt, that among all the worlds, ours are the most backward."

"I thought for a moment," said Lagité, "that Forgetfulness might procure happiness."

"Do you still think so?"

"Certainly not—for, although Forgetfulness effaces painful memories, it perpetually brings back misfortune and deprives us of the divine benefits of experience. Au revoir, Philosopher."

"Au revoir, Lagité."

VIII. The Star

Jacques was thinking again, somberly, about his ferocious lover from beyond the sky when he saw the face of an inhabitant of Venus appear on the screen.

He recognized him immediately. It was Varluz, the lover he had seen with Gilniz.

"What do you want with me?" he cried, angrily. "I hate you. I don't want to see you. What evil joy leads you to torment me? Disappear! Disappear!"

"Monsieur," replied Varluz, who knew that Frenchmen address one another thus, "I don't mean you any harm. On the contrary, I feel sorry for you."

"Keep your pity. I don't want it."

However, the other spoke so softly that Lagité ended up consenting to listen to him.

"Gilniz," said Varluz, "has wagered that she can drive you to suicide within a week."

"I'll enable her to win her bet."

"You're mad!"

"She's so beautiful that she's worth the sacrifice of my life."

"No, she's a rather vulgar woman, and there are many among us more beautiful."

"Why do you love her?"

"I did love her, I don't know why; but I no longer love her, and, having possessed her until the point of distaste, I see her now as she is."

"Youth, charm and intelligence," said Jacques, "she has all the graces; she's incomparable."

"What an error!" said Varluz. "Out of compassion, I'll tell you the truth. At a distance, Gilniz seems exquisite to you, and it's true that she was once quite pretty. But at close range one sees the commencement of goose-feet, wrinkles in the forehead and creases in the neck, an unfortunate down on the chin and hollows in the shoulders. She fights those defects with an arsenal of unguents and incessant massages, but she has to do a great deal to dissimulate the erosions of time."

"You're calumniating her!"

"I'll call upon one of my friends, who is here, and who was Gilniz's lover before me. For you must suspect that, at her age, she has had several"

"Gilniz is a ruin," the friend affirmed. And they both continued, speaking alternately:

"Gilniz is ugly."

"Ignorant."

"Stupid."

"Nasty."

"Hateful."

"I believe you're sincere," said Jacques, "but that's because Heaven has overloaded you and rendered you very difficult by giving you the most adorable women in the universe."

"Not at all," exclaimed Varluz. "Your women on Earth are infinitely more beautiful than ours."

"Oh, nonsense!"

"I swear to you. Very recently, my friend and I have chanced to see on your Earth a marvelous woman whom we've named the Perfect."

"Bah! Describe her, then."

"Impossible!"

"Try, though."

"We'll certainly remain far below the model," said Varluz. "But since you beg us, here it goes: her eyes launch lightning flashes."

"They're very soft," said the friend.

"She's robust," added Varluz

"As light as a butterfly," the friend contributed.

"Melancholy."

"Very jovial."

"Can't you agree, damn it?" said Lagité.

"We are," said Varluz. "It's because the most opposed merits are conciliated in her. She's sometimes this and sometimes that. I love her for certain qualities, my friend for others, for we're both madly smitten. Oh, how we envy you for respiring the air that bathes her and treading the ground that bears her!"

Lagité was beginning to love her too, so communicative was their ardor. "You assure me that she's more desirable than Gilniz?"

"A thousand times!"

"I beg you to make your portrait more precise," he insisted.

They told him that the terrestrial woman was blonde, of medium height, that her voice and her laughter were enchantments, and that, without any doubt, a host of mortals must kiss the traces of her footfalls.

That final hyperbole orientated Jacques' imagination.

"She's a film star," he said.

"We don't know, but it's possible."

"Where have you seen her?"

As they were about to respond, the communication was suddenly interrupted.

Lagité swore like a Templar.

He made countless attempts to resume the conversation, but he did not succeed; the apparatus his correspondents were using was probably defective.

It was necessary for him to make a decision.

Surely she's a film star, he thought.

By dint of repeating that, he eventually put a name to the conviction: "It's Ellis K. Pittsworth. I'll wager that it's her. Doesn't she respond in every way to the description? More beautiful than Gilniz? In truth, they ought to know, since they live near Gilniz. But in that case, that's the cure for my folly. I love Ellis K. Pittsworth, I adore her, and I want her."

Such was the soliloquy to which he delivered himself.

He had never encountered the celebrated American star, but he had seen enough of her in the films in which she appeared to place himself in the number of her fans.

One of those cinematic romances, above all, had triggered the delirium of crowds. It was a weepie entitled *The Vengeance of Amour*. Ellis K. Pittsworth played the role of a certain Miss Rosalind, a completely insensible young woman. Rosalind was triumphantly seductive, but she remained deaf to all the pleas of her adorers. It seemed to her that amour was degrading; she did not intend to submit to it at any price, and wanted her heart to remain proudly free.

A quantity of suitors filed through her home. Rosalind's parents welcomed them sadly, for they were only too well aware of their daughter's arrogant humor. Sometimes, they risked intervening with her in favor of some suitor provided with great merits, whose success they desired keenly, but she always blocked her ears. The number of desperate actions caused by her disdain was uncountable.

One young millionaire had laid all his wealth at Rosalind's feet. He had offered her a marble palace full of fabulous marvels, statues by Phidias and Praxiteles, paintings by Raphael, Titian, Rembrandt and Watteau, priceless jewels, books and manuscripts calculated to drive the most ostentatious bibliophile mad. Rosalind had declared: 'I don't care about your palace, or you.'

To which the amorous fellow had replied: "If you don't accept it, I'll burn it."

She had contented herself with shrugging her shoulders. Immediately, he had set fire to the sardanapalesque accumulation of treasures and had hurled himself into the blaze. Naturally, the film reproduced all the phases of the tragic holocaust. Many other lovers similarly dismissed by Rosalind had sought and found death. It was their espousal with death that gave the film an irresistible attraction and kept the public breathless.

Before the eyes of the impassive Rosalind, a champion racing driver who adored her took part in a contest and drove his machine at such a fantastic speed that his intention to kill himself gave rise to an intolerable anguish. In his bolide he overtook the vehicles of his competitors with a temerity that wrenched exclamations from the spectators. Suddenly, the inevitable accident occurred; the demented auto escaped from the track, bounded into the air, fell back at an enormous distance and turned a dozen horrifying somersaults before immobilizing definitively. Then, by a tragic hazard, the stretcher carrying the frightfully mangled body of the champion passed in front of Rosalind, whose face did not betray the slightest emotion.

Two aviators who loved one another like brothers and who had had the misfortune to fall in love with Rosalind at the same time had decided, after having endured her refusals, to die together. At an altitude of five thousand meters the two heroes of the air smashed their apparatus voluntarily in a frightful collision, which left a long wake of flames as they fell.

The description of the other catastrophes with which the reel of film was packed would be tedious. Let us limit ourselves to noting that Rosalind's scorn put a frightful end to a mountain-climber who scaled perpendicular walls vertiginously and then fell into a bottomless precipice, a navigator who launched himself on to a furious sea in a frail boat, and an animal tamer who excited his wild beasts to the point of devouring him.

Those suicides were so well imitated that nothing revealed the trickery, and the public had gooseflesh. Finally, the tearful mother of a young man came to beg Rosalind not to refuse her child: a vain intercession; the young man killed himself, and his mother after him. But, in order not to belie the title of the film, Amour avenged himself, and Rosalind expired under the revolver of a final lover, who then turned the weapon against himself.

That deplorable tissue of ineptitudes had enjoyed a success with stupid crowds all over the world to which masterpieces of thought and fantasy had never been able to aspire. And it was thus that Miss Ellis K. Pittsworth had conquered star status among the most dazzling stars of the United States.

Lagité had no doubt that she was the extraordinary woman designated by the two inhabitants of Venus. The penchant that she already inspired in him suddenly increased, and he did not attempt to put a brake on it, since he hoped that it might be a distraction for his unfortunate passion.

Giving Viviane the pretext of a journalistic investigation, he therefore set forth for Hollywood.

There, he succeeded fairly rapidly in being introduced into the little group who frequented Miss Ellis K. Pittsworth, and had himself introduced to her.

To tell the truth, the star was a creature as puerile and mediocre as she was vain. She had commenced by selling flowers in the city of Cinema; a director had noticed her, made her his mistress and had confided the principal role in the famous *Vengeance of Amour* to her, and the star had been launched in order to launch the film. An incredible debauchery of publicity had been unleashed in favor of Miss Ellis. Surprising stories had been told about her. Her dresses were woven from the feathers of hummingbirds. The water of her baths was made up of dew collected by a multitude of servants from odorous plants. Her favorite dish was the tongues of nightingales. She had had a barman to whom she was attached invent a cocktail that bore her name, and in which all know species of alcohol—which is to say, exactly three thousand six hundred and fifty four—were expertly mixed.

These items of information, trumpeted at great expense by all the newspapers in the world, had created a prestigious popularity for Miss Ellis. From that moment on she had become an idol drunk on incense. She no longer listened to any but the most absurd caprices; and by virtue of a phenomenon often observed among cinema artistes, she identified with her role, even in real life. She affected with regard to her fervent admirers the indifference of Miss Rosalind, and pushed indifference as far as barbarity.

One of her fantasies, above all, had produced an effect of terror on public opinion.

She had invited an amorous young man who had pursued her with entreaties that would have moved any other woman to comparison to come to contemplate her at her home. "But before then," she specified, "prove the sincerity of your passion send me your oath in writing to look me full in the face and not to turn your eyes away from me for at least a minute."

The other had sworn something that seemed to him to be so simple and had hastened to the nocturnal rendezvous she has assigned to him.

He had passed through rooms in which a profound obscurity reigned, through which he had been directed by invisible guides.

Then, suddenly, he had been pushed into a room of which Miss Ellis K, Pittsworth, standing on a pedestal, occupied the center. She was constellated by an infinite number of jewels, which were electric lamps of a prodigious intensity. Above her forehead was a resplendent diadem formed by several juxtaposed suns. It was an apparatus as powerful as the maritime lighthouses with the moist distant range.

Miss Ellis closed her eyes. When she was told that the adorer had entered, she commanded him: "Look at me for a minute, an entire minute; I order that it should be verified.

He was so madly in love that he agreed to submit to that extravagant demand. He believed that he could support the glare of the fulgurant light. Operators equipped with dark glasses followed the second hand of the clock. Half a minute had not gone by when the amorous young man cried: "Blind! I'm blind!"

Then she cried, sniggering: "He hasn't kept his oath, since he can no longer look at me. Throw him out."

Such was the woman, the perverse child, that Jacques Lagité proposed to conquer.

She, of course, allowed him to sigh without taking any pity on him. She only seemed to be more desirable. Every day he discovered new seductions and found more grace in the attractions she refused to him. But he remarked, dolorously, that she showed herself more merciful with regard to a very rich man, Arthur W. Ricklin, the Chewing-gum King.

Ricklin seemed to have at his service a genie from the *Arabian Nights*. All that Miss Ellis desired, everything that she seemed to covet with a glance, everything that she wished for idly while yawning, was instantaneously granted to her: jewels, twelve-cylinder autos, luxury animals, palaces, estates and insensate fêtes.

Lagité nourished a furious jealousy with regard to the Chewing-gum King. He was afflicted by not being as rich.

When he expressed his regrets in that regard to a young American named William J. Burkle, who practiced astral wireless as ardently as he did, that confidant sketched a smile and said: "My dear Monsieur Lagité, I've been in communication for a few days with the Planet of Gold. Come and see me at my home. You'll see what sort of happiness the inhabitants of that star have.

"Oh," said Lagité, "if I had their good fortune, I'd be immensely happy!"

So saying, he went to Burkle's house.

IX. The Planet of Gold

Scarcely was he there than the apparatus, tuned in advance, projected the image of a city whose appearance struck Jacques Lagité with surprise. The houses, the passers-by, the pavements, the vehicles and the trees were so shiny that one could not look at them without blinking. Reflections sprang from all sides, intersecting, filing the air with myriads of flashes.

"You're in the land of Gold," the American said to Jacques.

"What a strange spectacle!" Lagité murmured. He added, in a low voice: "It's terrifying!"

An instant later, he was talking to an Orian to whom Burkle had introduced him, whose name was Bassadec.

"I can see," said that person to Lagité, "that you're eager to know about our way of life."

"Indeed," said Jacques.

"Many of your peers," said Bassadec, "Are ecstatic about the substance of which we're made. I can assure you, however, that it isn't pleasant to be made of gold."

At that moment, Burkle manipulated his wireless apparatus so that Bassadec's face occupied the entire screen. It was a repulsive vision. Bassadec looked like one of those men coated in metallic powder who pretend to be statues at fairs. He was sticky with gold. But what caused a frisson was the sight of his gold gums and tongue when he opened his mouth, and, above all, his eyes. Instead of being limpid, like ours, they were both opaque and radiant, like the back of a golden spoon. The golden pupil, marked by a slight round bump, moved from side to side without letting and thought or sentiment filter through.

Bassadec continued: "In truth, there are on our planet, as on your Earth, things and being who are not made of gold, mortals on veritable flesh, animals, plants and fruits that are natural; but they're only found far from our cities. A certain number of us, known as 'gold-handlers' possess from birth the deadly gift of transforming everything they touch, and even approach, into the resplendent metal."

"That's quite bizarre," said Jacques. "Our ancient Greeks imagined a fable of which your words remind me. They related that King Midas had received from a divinity the favor of turning everything into gold."

"Well," said Bassadec, "in our country that power is a reality. Here there are many King Midases. I'm one of them myself."

He was interrupted by a golden domestic who came to announce a visitor. Bassadec said to Jacques: "It's a young cousin that I'm about to welcome. She has always lived in the country. She often writes me exquisite letters, and I know that she's adorably pretty. I asked her to come. It's my dream to marry her, for I'd like to found a family. I authorize you to witness our first conversation."

The young woman came in. She was not made of gold; she resembled the most charming women on Earth: pale blue eyes, a complexion of almost diaphanous freshness; her lips were not thickened by rouge like those of our elegant women, but their soft crimson revealed the attractive purity of her blood and her tenderness.

On seeing her, Bassadec seemed transfigured.

For an instant, his hard gaze seemed to become profound, and translucent.

Then something frightful happened.

As Bassadec contemplated her, the azure of the young woman's eyes changed progressively into an opaque yellow color. It was a sort of leucoma that, born in the center of the pupil, expanded to invade the entire eyeball. Soon, the entire surface of what had been the celestial liquid of tears and laughter solidified like a lake frozen in the course of a harsh winter.

Bassadec's features expressed a poignant dolor. He moved his face very close to the young woman, as if he wanted to capture there a living light that was withdrawing forever. And his own gaze, momentarily softened, was covered with a new gleaming armor.

"The golden leprosy!" he cried.

Now the golden tint was spreading from the woman's eyelids to her cheeks, and all of her face. Her smile, initially as caressant and as aerial as a dancing ray of sunlight, mutated into a hypocritical and fixed grace.

"A golden smile!" murmured Bassadec, sobbing.

"What's the matter, cousin?" she asked him.

"Oh," he said, hiding his face in his hands. "I love you…and I'm very unhappy."

"I don't see what's so sad about that. I love you too, my cousin, and if you wish, my happiness will be yours."

Raising his head again, he put his arm round his cousin's waist and tried to give her a kiss; but the young woman's lips had just acquired a splendor of newly-minted coin.

He sighed: "A golden kiss!" And, relaxing his embrace, he said, bitterly: "Forgive me, I'm suffering…"

"I can see that, and without being able to explain your chagrin, I share it."

She thought that she ought to express compassion, and addressed soothing words to him, as if to an invalid. He remained silent.

Then she said: "Look; you're making me cry."

He looked again. In his cousin's eyes, two metallic pearls condensed, grew, slid over the edges of the eyelids, and swelled into thick, sparkling, heavy, droplets that rolled down the cheeks.

"Golden tears!" said Bassadec. He added: "I need to be alone."

When she had left him, he said to Jacques: "Now you know what the golden leprosy is, the terrible contagion of our planet."

Jacques was still anguished.

Bassadec went on: "Our scientists affirm that it commences with the hardening of the heart. From there it reaches the eyes, and then the entire body."

"It's certain that I no longer envy you," said Lagité.

"You've just seen what becomes of the women we love: golden statues. Even those who say that they are our friends have a heart of metal As soon as they frequent us our gold flows over them, their gaze is veiled and we can no longer read their souls. The most envied possessions—houses, châteaux, domains—as soon as they fall into our hands, lose all the charms with which art or nature has adorned them and no longer reflect anything but the glacial radiation of gold. No sooner have we admired a beautiful painting than it is converted into a uniform sheet of gold. Our greedy majordomos only serve us extremely rare and complicated dishes, which are transformed as soon as they appear on our table. Oh, the indigestible nourishment! How fortunate you are, you who can regale yourselves with salads and good vulgar wine!"

Jacques felt sorry for him, and asked: "What are your occupations?"

"To a host of worthy fellows we offer wind, fog or smoke, and they come running in a host to give us their petty savings of golden coin in exchange."

"That's a simple métier."

"Not as much as you think. It's not always easy to see smoke. It's necessary to shout very loudly, to run out of breath and become hoarse on the steps of the Temple, where that merchandise is offered. Between gold-handlers, we fight rude battles. Bold competitors succeeded in depreciating our stock. Then the clientele demand their money back. If we can't return it we're dishonored and we have to blow our brains out." Bassadec took a pretty little golden revolver out of a drawer. "You see this plaything. It's loaded. I always have it within arm's reach."

"What a frightful threat! It's paying very dearly for the privilege of piling up a lot of gold coins."

"I ought to admit that a number of my colleagues abstain today from shooting themselves in the head. They prefer to live, and the judges send them to nurse their sick honor in an establishment called the Santé."[55]

"Very good. But what do you do with your gold coin?"

"We fill strongboxes buried in our cellars."

---

[55] In the early twentieth century La Santé Prison, built on a site where there was once a sanitarium, was the principal place of criminal detention in Paris.

"A singular happiness!"

"We count our wealth repeatedly. We congratulate ourselves when we observe that it surpasses that of our rivals."

"Good. But there are always people richer than you."

"Indeed," Bassadec admitted. "That's our continual torment. But the richest among us dreams lamentably about becoming even richer."

"Are you never happy, then?"

Bassadec reflected for a few seconds. "No," he said, "never, since we lack amour. And when I die on my treasures, my despair, you see, will be to search all my memories in vain for a single gaze of a sincere lover."

"Poor rich man!" sighed Lagité. But he added within himself: *Which doesn't alter the fact that if I had so much gold, it would be easy for me to conquer Ellis K. Pittsworth.*

At the same moment, someone came to announce that the Chewing-gum King had hanged himself from a tree in one of the estates that he had given to Miss Ellis. He had committed suicide because he had learned that the star was cheating on him outrageously with a boxer names Elias Mokololo.

Lagité welcomed that news with chagrin. He deplored the fact that Miss Ellis had not chosen him as an accomplice to betray Arthur W. Ricklin. *Why*, he wondered, *is she smitten with that pugilist? Is he worth more than me? Am I not infinitely more seductive? To prefer a negro to me!*

That thought no longer quit him.

His friend Burkle, whom he saw again a few days later, was struck by his sadness and asked him the cause.

Jacques told him, and exclaimed: "If only I were a boxer! If only I were an athlete!"

To which Burkle replied mysteriously: "I want to offer you a spectacle that might perhaps distract you." And taking him home with him, he placed him in front of the sidereal screen again.

X. Sporting Planet

Jacques saw a crowd at a crossroads.

In the foreground, a strange being was standing. He had a small head, a low brow, immense legs, strong thighs and powerful calves; he was cleaved all the way to the chin. He was the inhabitant of that star who had entered into correspondence with Burkle. His name was All-legs. Very obliging, he willingly translated into sidereal Esperanto the conversations going on around him. Lagité understood without difficulty what the members of the crowd he was observing on the screen were saying.

There were many individuals there just as extraordinary as All-legs, although very different. Some of them were remarkable by virtue of enormous fists much more voluminous than their head—fists that could stun an ox with a single blow. Others possessed massive biceps, like stout oak branches, which knotted as they flexed, rounding out and selling into formidable globes.

All of them, however, had a skull as flat as those of reptiles and fish.

Jacques widened his eyes as he looked at them.

A number of the natives of the planet had neither biceps, nor fists, nor thighs, nor calves, and were scarcely visible, so paltry were they. But they were neither the least active not the least strident. They were running in all directions, shouting and vociferating, apparently prey to a delirious excitement.

"Tomorrow is the great day," they howled. "Thanks to Bruto, we're sure of winning. To our nation, victory over all the others! Hurrah for Bruto! Bruto is our pride, Bruto is our glory. What science in the attack! What artistry on the defensive! What a glance! What energy! What valor! Bruto is the thunder and the lightning! He's a hero! He's our savior! He's the flower of our blood, the supreme effort of our race! We put all our hopes in him. All our destinies repose on him. Oh, Bruto, Bruto, our noble, our prodigious, our divine Bruto!"

"Who are they talking about?" Jacques asked "This celestial Bruto they adore is doubtless a great general? I think they must fear an invasion, and are expecting the salvation of the fatherland from him. My word, I'm dying of the desire to make his acquaintance."

"Nothing easier," replied All-legs.

And following that amiable correspondent, who was equipped with a portable wireless apparatus, Jacques penetrated into a vast and luminous hangar.

Important people were running around there as feverishly as the crowd in the public square.

The attention of all was magnetized by a central point toward which All-Legs slipped, with some difficulty, through the close ranks of the audience.

Suddenly, he said to Jacques; "Well, here's the individual you want to see."

Lagité found himself confronted by a large ape, a frightful gorilla: jaws ignobly heavy and jutting, a broad snub-nose which seemed to have been indefatigably and implacably hammered; prominent eyebrows bearing the traces of terrible blows that that broken them in several places. The eyes, in the depths of hollow orbits, were blinking like dying flames. The bestial muzzle was ornamented by a forest of russet hairs that rendered him even more hideous.

Lagité looked at the ape with some impatience.

Where, then, is the magnanimous Bruto?" he asked

"In front of you," said All-legs.

"What! This gorilla..."

"...is Bruto, our great boxing champion."

"I don't understand."

"Your friend Burkle hasn't told you what our planet is, then?"

Burkle intervened. "My dear Lagité," he said, "I wanted to let you discover the planet of sports—Sporting Planet, where athletes are kings—for yourself.

Bruto, the gorilla you're contemplating, is the object of general fanaticism in this country because he's fighting tomorrow, according to what All-legs tells me, a gorilla no less massive and no less ugly than himself, named Poussah, the champion of another people.[56] They're disputing the royalty of boxing. Over the entire planet, you won't find a beggar, a toothless old crone or a street-urchin with a shit-stained shirt who isn't impassioned by that fight. The people whose gorilla triumphs will be proclaimed the foremost of all, and the one whose gorilla is beaten will suffer a mortal humiliation. Now you're informed."

Stupefied, Jacques continued to observe the gorilla, especially his hairy fists, which were as large as valises.

Bruto seemed anxious. Furtively, he reached out toward a flask, but before he could grasp it, his trainer had snatched it away, crying: "You know very well that a champion doesn't have the right to be thirsty without the authorization of his manager."

A moment later, Bruto dropped his paw on a basket of fruits that happened to be within his reach. The trainer pulled it away rudely.

"You know very well that a champion doesn't have the right to be hungry without the authorization of his manager."

"Truly," said Jacques, "That's a king less free than a slave."

Suddenly, Bruto gave signs of the most intense delight. He had just perceived, in the midst of the people present, a little she-monkey who, opening her mouth all the way to her ears, addressed the most provocative of smiles to him. He ran toward her, jostling everyone in his passage, and there were hectic caresses, ardent clashes of muzzles and passionate purrs of tenderness.

The trainer spat out an oath. "Who let that female in? I've strictly forbidden the door to her."

And, calling acolytes to his aid, he bounded forward to snatch the gorillette away from Bruto.

They had a great deal of difficulty doing so. The gorilla held firm. Sometimes, a wild anger was legible in his eyes, sometimes a poignant supplication. He would rather have died than be separated from the little she-monkey. But nothing could soften his torturers. They loosened his arms by force and, in spite of his desperate groans, they expelled the object of his amours.

"You know very well, though, Bruto," the despot concluded, severely, "that a champion doesn't have the right to without the permission of his manager." With that, he ordered: "Let's get to work!"

Then an imposing fellow came to plant himself in front of Bruto and landed a volley of punches methodically on his muzzle. The gorilla submitted to that martyrdom almost without a peep.

---

[56] A poussah, in French, is the name of a figurine with a rounded base, which rights itself automatically if tipped over, like an American "Bobo doll."

That's called *soaking it up*,"[57] All-legs specified.

The huge ape's muzzle was tumefied. From time to time he uttered a muted plaint, and moved backwards

"Bruto!" cried the manager, furiously.

And the gorilla repented, offering himself again to the avalanche of blows; his poor face was swollen with bruises.

That barbaric exercise lasted a full quarter of an hour.

"How much compassion Bruto's face inspires in me!" said Jacques.

The next day was that of the Bruto-Poussah match.

In the eighteenth round, after a ferocious combat, Bruto reckoned with his adversary.

Each of them was in a state as bad as the other. Bruto's head, shoulders and chest were nothing but a crimson mass. His shredded muzzle left his broken teeth visible. One of his eyes was buried beneath a swelling over his cheekbone; the other, having been torn out, was hanging from the orbit like a huge bloody billiard-ball.

"Victory! Victory!" howled the unbridled crowd. They scarcely had time to wipe Bruto's face. His adorers seized him in haste and perched him on their shoulders. All-legs followed them with agility.

From all the crossroads, all the streets and all the houses the multitude rushed toward the victor. Living whirlwinds incessantly unfurled around him, and his escort had a great deal to do to prevent him from being crushed. The city, the nation and the world were seething with an overflowing joy.

Four hundred inhabitants of the capital perished, stifled. One of them, who emerged from his swelling dazedly and seemed not to understand anything, was snatched up by the turbulence, knocked down, trampled flattened and reduced to pulp. It was learned that he was a great scientist who had discovered a short while before the unique formula to which all the laws of nature were obedient. At the very moment when he had been torn apart, his mind was doubtless concentrated on an equation that would have opened up new and infinite horizons to science.

The people, informed of that loss, consoled themselves immediately, considering it as the utterly negligible ransom for the immense delight caused by the victory of the national ape.

Bruto's bearers continued to swing him around through the tumultuous popular effervescence. Suddenly, the gorilla escaped them. In spite of the lamentable state of his eyes, he had discerned his gorillette in the midst of the crowd, on the arm of a puny little fellow, who was kissing her without restraint.

---

[57] The French *encaisser*, employed at this point in the text, has several meanings, but with regard to punches it means taking a beating or handing one out. It could, however, also be construed to mean "boxing" in the straightforward sense of putting something in a box; the covert *double entendre* is probably intended.

Bruto had reached the couple rapidly. The panicked gorillette tried to flee; the champion tried to grab hold of her. At that moment, the little lover, so pitiful, of whom it seemed that Bruto ought only to make a mouthful, rapidly opened a long, sharp cutlass, which he plunged into the champion's side all the way to the hilt. And the emperor of all past, present and future boxers fell, stone dead.

"What good did it do him to be so strong?" concluded Jacques, philosophically.

All-legs, detaching himself from the crowd, resumed the conversation with his terrestrial friends.

Jacques asked him whether Bruto would be regretted for a long time on Sporting Planet.

"Oh," said All-legs, "nothing is forgotten as promptly as a champion. I was once the champion runner. Who remembers?"

"At least," said Jacques, "in the epoch of their glory, the aces of sport savor the ineffable joy of deploying their physical strength magnificently."

"Not at all; for instead of building our muscles in order to render our life more agreeable and more useful, we waste our entire life building muscles." He went on: "We're never happy, you see. A frightful anxiety eats us away incessantly. We run fast, but we always want to run faster, and we tremble constantly that a rival will snatch our record away from us. But what annoys us most of all is the abandonment in which we're left when our vigor declines. I, All-legs, once so acclaimed, counts for no more today than an old wheezy horse. And it's the same for all the old kings of the stadium or the ring. If they dared, they'd sent us to the abattoir."

Jacques shook his head in a melancholy fashion. "It's certain," he said to Burkle, "that I wouldn't want to live on Sporting Planet. However," he added, "I know a boxer on Earth who is happy. That's Elias Makalolo."

At that moment, someone came in to announce that Elias Makalolo had just been beaten in five seconds in San Francisco. Apparently, his little fêtes with Miss Ellis had harmed his fitness considerably.

The next morning, when the defeated boxer presented himself guilelessly at the star's residence, she had him thrown out.

Who was delighted? Lagité.

He recommended putting forward his amorous candidacy obstinately. No less obstinately, Miss Ellis dismissed him, but always with teasing remarks that retained Jacques rather than putting him off.

While he was agape with idolatry before the star, she became madly smitten with a certain John La Blague, a cinema actor, an utter imbecile who ordinarily had the employment of a buffoon.

"My God!" lamented Lagité. "Why am I not a cinema artiste, then?"

He exposed that ambition to the star herself, who suggested treacherously that he present himself to a director in order to assume the most reckless roles—

for example, leaping from a moving express train, entering into a burning building, or going over Niagara Falls.

Convinced that he would amaze the beauty thus, he did not hesitate to follow her advice, and was accepted.

Miss Ellis became increasingly cheerful, and promised herself a rare delectation in watching him kill himself before her eyes.

It was at that moment when Viviane arrived on America. For several months she had not received any letter from Jacques. Suspecting that a new danger was menacing him, she resolved to fly to his aid. Without warning him, therefore, she came to Hollywood and, adopting a false name, she carefully avoided meeting him.

She learned that he was courting Miss Ellis with an unfortunate perseverance, and that the star was amusing herself with him as with a marionette.

She understood that her husband's life was at the mercy of a caprice of the scatterbrain in question, and she was even more convinced when she was informed of the audacious exploits that he had promised to accomplish on signing his contract as an artiste.

As she was very good herself, she could not imagine fundamental malevolence, and thought that he simply desired to move Miss Ellis. She therefore paid her a visit and spoke to her naively as a sister. She told her how much she loved Jacques, how much she was suffering, and begged her to cease her inhumane games with him.

The star let her finish, and then, with the closed face of a disdainful doll, she said: "Madame, your husband is only one of the most obscure of my millions of admirers, and I scarcely discern him at my feet. Play with him? He's too indifferent to me. If you value him so much, you ought to take better care of him. Take him back, please. It's the greatest service you could do me."

Viviane asked her to excuse her, and above all not to reveal the step she had taken to her husband. The star made no response. And when she saw Lagité again she hastened to say to him in a honeyed tone: "I've had a visit from your wife, my little Jacques."

"My wife?"

"Yes, your wife, Viviane. She's in Hollywood. She came to confide her subjects of complaint to me. How can you render such a sweet creature unhappy? It's necessary to take pity on her, my little Jacques, and not to see me anymore. I promised her formally to detach you from me, and I no longer want your homage. I'm sacrificing it to the tranquility of your charming wife. Go find her, my little Jacques. Go on. And make her happy. She deserves it. Forget me. Adieu, my little Jacques. I authorize you to kiss my foot."

Lagité had gone pale with rage, and remained nonplussed. He asked where his wife was. Miss Ellis possessed that information, and gave it to him.

Lagité ran to the hotel indicated. Scarcely was he in his wife's presence than he said: "Why have you been to see Miss Pittsworth? What need do you have to interfere in my sentimental life? You had proved sufficiently that you didn't care about me. The separation scarcely cost you. We had each organized our existence apart. It was a tacit convention with which you seemed comfortable. And suddenly, out of idleness or malfeasance, you come to trouble an amity that is very dear to me."

Viviane tried to interrupt him.

"Jacques, Jacques, my dear Jacques, don't you know that I still love you, that I never stopped loving you? Jacques, Jacques, my dear Jacques, I've only ever acted for your benefit. I no longer even think about myself. I've acquired the habitude of suffering! But I don't want anyone to cause you to die. You're letting yourself be led astray. Don't you know where you're being led? I wanted to save you from yourself."

"If I've gone astray," said Jacques, "that doesn't concern anyone but me, and I beg you not to occupy yourself with me any longer. Return to Europe. I no longer want to see you here."

Viviane went on: "Jacques, Jacques, I love you. Jacques, surely you'll thank me some day for having warned you. Surely you'll recognize that I'm obeying an immense tenderness. Jacques, my Jacques, look at me. Jacques, try to reflect for a moment. Try to get a grip on yourself..."

He turned his gaze away from her willfully, clenched his fists, ground his teeth, and growled impatiently: "Will this last long?"

"Look at me one last time," she said, "since you can no longer tolerate me."

He consented to make her that gift.

He saw Viviane's eyes bathed pitifully with tears; he saw her lips trembling and extended toward him, against all hope.

This wife's expression was so dramatic that, without him being conscious of it, a sort of revelation of amour took place in his mind. But that did not last for more than a second. He remained immobile and harsh.

Quickly, in a low voice and a heart-rending tone, she said: "Adieu, Jacques.

"Adieu," he said, dryly.

She left.

A few days later, in New York, Jacques was shooting his first big film with Miss Ellis K. Pittsworth.

The principal episode was to bring the emotion of the spectators to its paroxysm. In the scenario, the hero followed a ledge a few centimeters wide along the façade of a skyscraper at the height of the forty-fourth floor. Then he made an enormous leap through the void in order to launch himself into a bedroom whose window was open. He rejoined his lover thus, without anyone being able to suspect the vertiginous route he had taken.

That role had been reserved for Jacques, and that of the lover for Miss Ellis.

351

It would not have been difficult to fake the scene, but the star, by means of her promising smiles, piqued Lagité's boldness. She succeeded in making him request himself that the terrifying prowess be accomplished veritably. By means of plunging views, they would impose on the public the certainty of witnessing an acrobatic extravagance, implausible and yet real. And that conviction would give the film an inestimable price.

Jacques signed a paper in which he took full responsibility for his crazy stunt.

An extraordinarily high building was found in New York, which fulfilled exactly the conditions of the film. The narrow ledge and the window separated from the neighboring wall by a distance that only a champion long-jumper was capable of crossing seemed to have been designed expressly to respond to the intentions of the scenario.

At the appointed date the artistes and cinematographers were projected by the elevator to the forty-fourth floor. The operators posted themselves above, below and on all sides.

Then Jacques steppe over a sill and placed both feet one in front of the other on a thin projection. He stuck his back against the concrete wall that descended vertically all the way to the causeway a hundred meters below. In the sudden silence of all other sounds, the *tac-tac-tac* of the recording apparatus was unleashed. In the depths of the abyss, Jacques could see large streetcars, autobuses and vehicles without number reduced to Lilliputian proportions. The passers-by were no more than busy ants and the drama that was beginning to unfold up above could not even attract their attention, so distant were they from it.

Fifty meters below Lagité doves were circling, and their flight caused him to experience an impression of vacillation. He noticed a group of children at the very foot of the wall and wanted to shout to them to move away, for he feared that he might fall on them, but his voice choked.

A cinematographer began to chide him without mildness: "Get on with it, then! Play your role, damn it! Think about what you're doing."

Jacques stiffened, and began to walk mechanically, easing along the façade. He reached the angle from which he had to jump. It was absolutely necessary that he make a leap, because there was no room to turn around to return to his departure point.

He could never understand why, at that moment, his memory evoked the infinitely sad face of Viviane. Directly opposite him, but at a distance that seemed insurmountable, he perceived Miss Ellis, who was addressing a strange smile to him. The star's eyes were shining with a strange joy, and fascinated him. Her hands extended toward him and her fingers were trembling, as if to attract a prey.

The cinematographer who had admonished Jacques shouted again: "Go on, then! Jump!"

Jacques could no longer detach his gaze from Miss Ellis's eyes

And suddenly without him understanding how it happened, he found himself launched into space.

The extremity of his feet came down on the sill of the window he had to attain, and one of his soles slipped on the stone corner, but the other held. He had a frightful sensation. Miss Ellis who, according to the scenario, was supposed to help him, made use of her extended arms not to help him regain his equilibrium but to push him back into the void. Jacques' knees received the shock of those perfidious little hands, which, while appearing to help him, tried, on the contrary, to throw him to his death.

Making a supreme effort to lean forward, he remained for a quarter of a second—which is to say, an eternity—wondering whether he was about to fall into the room or outwards into the gaping void.

Then his will-power, perhaps violating the law of gravity, pushed him into the room where the star was.

He rolled on the parquet, but got to his feet immediately. And, closing the window abruptly, he took Miss Elis by the arms and held them tightly against her body.

"Slut!" he shouted, in her face.

She laughed spasmodically.

Then like a boor, for he had lost control of himself, he rained a magisterial volley of blows over the shoulders and back of the American woman. She protected herself as best she could with her hands and arms. Jacques seemed to relieve his quivering nervous tension thus. As for Miss Ellis, she did not seem overly upset by the adventure. Letting the storm pass, she limited herself to moaning: "Sorry, sorry, Jacques, Jacques, my little Jacques."

It even seemed that the rain of blows had produced the beneficent effect of a cold shower

When he had duly corrected her he took her, with no further ceremony, on the carpet. To tell the truth, she scarcely resisted, and started to sigh ecstatically: "My dear Jack, my love, my little Jacky!"

Then, at the first relay, she looked at him tenderly, as if to beg for further caresses, and she repeated: "Jacky, Jacky, little Jacky."

Lagité thought: *What, then? That's all it was? And it's for that that I was breathless with desire for so long? I thought she was so attractive, but she's insipid! I thought she was so beautiful, but she's vulgar! I thought she was so intelligent, but she's stupid!*

And without saying a word, he left.

He returned to Europe.

Viviane, who had preceded him there, had taken literally recommendation that Jacques had made to her no longer to appear in his presence. She had rented lodgings. of which she had not sent him the address.

As soon as he was in Paris, Lagité received a communication from the star Venus.

It was Varluz and his friend who were telephoning.

"Aha! There you are!" Jacques said to them. "I congratulate you for having informed me so well. I found her, your unequaled woman. She was the most repulsive creature of whom one could dream."

"Who are you talking about?"

"The woman you indicated to me, the American star Miss Ellis K. Pittsworth."

"We never signified her to you. We know her well, for so much renown surrounds her that we wanted to see her on our screen. But we judged her insignificant. No, no, dear Monsieur, the Earthwoman who seemed to us so beautiful, and who certainly is..."

"You've seen her again?"

"Yes, very recently."

"Where is she?"

"In Paris."

"In Paris you say?"

"Yes."

"Where?"

"Rue..."

Once again, the apparatus ceased functioning.

"Thunder!" howled Jacques. "Always cut off when I'm expecting a capital revelation. One might think that Destiny is playing with me."

He grumbled and raged, and tried every means to renew the conversation, but in vain.

Once again, he was prey to a frightful pessimism.

In the course of the conversation he had with Professor Letord he exhaled his irremediable bitterness.

"The happiness I seek," he said, "flees me incessantly. Recently, I thought I'd discovered amour down here. What a disappointment awaited me! All our dreams of felicity, when I see them realized in the planets, appear to me to be ridiculous. And since our wishes, even when they're fulfilled, can't bring us any contentment, there's no doubt that the universe is very badly made. I'm beginning to believe that nothing is as it should be, that everything is topsy-turvy, and that it would be necessary to change the world radically to render existence acceptable."

"In that case," said Letord, smiling, "I have what you need."

"How?"

"I'll introduce you to the Topsy-Turvy Planet."

"What star is that?"

"A world in which everything works in the opposite fashion to this one. Perhaps it will please you."

XI. The Topsy-Turvy Planet

Jacques saw then the most bewildering spectacle that astral wireless had yet contrived for him.

On a road he saw a horse harnessed to a cabriolet, identical to those of our countries. The horse was trotting and the cabriolet was rolling; but it was not the animal that was drawing the vehicle—it was the other way around. The vehicle was going backwards and pulling the horse at a good speed. The occupants of the carriage had their backs turned to the direction in which they were going. One of them, who was holding the reins, reached out from time to time to deliver strokes of the whip to the animal, which was lifting its legs alternately and running backwards with extreme celerity.

Recovering from his stupor slightly, Jacques asked: "Where are they going?"

"Apparently, where they desire to go," replied Letord. "What is certain is that they're going briskly."

Lagité agreed.

He saw an express train that was traversing the countryside. The train was similar to outs, except that, like the cabriolet, it was going backwards. To be sure, that happens among us when a locomotive is hitched behind wagons and pushes them, but in the topsy-turvy world certain details indicated that the locomotive was functioning in a fashion exactly opposite to ours.

Thus, the smoke, which on our world escapes in thick clouds and dissipates in the air, after having floated for a few moments in a long trail, was flowing in an inverse direction. It gradually formed in the air, became a gray cloud above the train, then caught up with the engine, amassed in thick swirls and was suddenly engulfed in the funnel with a tumultuous violence.

When the train came very close, in the brief moment in which he was able to observe the platform of the engine, Jacques saw, not without amazement, that the stoker was drawing pieces of coal out of the furnace, which were extinguished, and which he threw into the tender in the aspect of large black lumps.

"Where is that train going?" Lagité asked.

"It's going," said Letord, "to the station that, here, would be that of departure, and on that planet is that of arrival."

Jacques took his head in his hands in order to prevent it from bursting.

"It's necessary to do that," said Letord. "Fundamentally, the trains on that world depart and arrive as they do here, more or less regularly. What is backwards on Earth is forwards there. And that's the only difference; perhaps it's not very sensible."

The professor had naturally given the natives of the planet in reverse the name of Retrogrades. For some time already he had linked himself in amity with one of them, named Edaramac, and they had frequent conversations.

355

Let us note that when the Retrogrades want to translate their ideas into sidereal Esperanto they always begin their words at the end. It is on that condition alone that they render them comprehensible to their correspondents on other worlds.

Edaramac kindly offered to allow Jacques to witness via wireless the birth of an old man.

Lagité and Letord then found themselves in a cemetery in the land of the Retrogrades. A large audience was stationed around a crypt occupied by a coffin covered with a great many sheaves of roses and lilies.

The undertakers moved aside the heap of flowers, lifted the heavy bier on to their shoulders, and walked backwards to a hearse, on to which they loaded their burden. After that, the crowd formed a long procession behind the plumed vehicle and started walking backwards toward the dead man's domicile.

The hearse followed them, slowly and solemnly, still going backwards, in the fashion of the land.

The body was taken up to the mortuary chamber. The undertakers unscrewed the coffin, took the dead man out and laid him in his bed.

Then he uttered a profound sigh. He started crying like a new-born baby, opened his eyes to the light, with difficulty, closed them again, and then opened them again.

Jacques thought aloud: "In truth, whether one starts life at one end or the other, birth and death have no more difference than an entrance door and an exit door."

Edaramac told him that the resemblances were, in fact, considerable. And for Jacques' instruction, he indicated many others.

"Isn't that old man who has just come into the world similar to your babies? No hair, no teeth. He can only eat pap. He doesn't talk; he babbles. His intelligence is unsteady. He's a child. He has no more sex than a baby. Women serve him, while caressing him, according him an indulgent and protective solicitude. They rebuke him when he's dirty and when he's demanding; they repress his tantrums.

"In accordance with the natural laws of our planet, he'll rejuvenate as he gets older. He'll take several years to become a vigorous individual, an active and enlightened person, important in the State. He'll maintain himself for some time in that fortunate situation, Women will address engaging smiles to him and treat him as a conqueror. He'll make them suffer and take pride in being tortured by them. Then he'll rejuvenate further. He'll become a veritable child; his consciousness will weaken; he'll no longer be able to talk; he'll eat pap again, and women will spank his bottom. One day, in a warm bedroom, he'll enter his mother's womb, and nine months later, he'll return to the nothingness from which he emerged."

"I can see," said Jacques, "that on your world, as on ours, one goes from impotence to impotence and from oblivion to oblivion, savoring few brief and feeble joys in the interim."

"That's it exactly," replied Edaramac. He went on: "Our public life is also very similar to yours. We go from one war to another, passing through a peace that is always too short. Or, if you prefer, we go from one bad peace to another bad one, passing though atrocious and impious wars."

"Absolutely as we do," sighed Jacques.

"Our civilization," said Edaramac, "of which we are proud follows almost the same curve as yours. We depart from a profound darkness that you all decadence and we shall end up, I believe, in another night no less black, which you call primitive barbarity. Your progress, by an exactly opposite route, borrows the same trajectory and goes, like ours from nothing to nothing."

"That's true," said Jacques.

"However," said Edaramac, "on observing you closely, I'm obliged to think that we are more favored than you are."

"Why?"

"I've learned that among you, life becomes harder from day to day. Your produce gets incessantly dearer. In order to eat, drink, sleep and pay for the smiles of courtesans, you constantly spend more; and you always have to furnish more labor, always make more effort, in order to procure what is indispensable to you."

"That's only too true," said Jacques, afflicted.

"Here, on the contrary, everything is better arranged, and our products are less sophisticated than before. I've also heard it said that in your cities, it has become very difficult to find lodgings. There are not enough apartments there, except for the rich, who don't flinch at paying extravagant sums to proprietors. We once suffered from that nasty encumbrance, but it has ceased now; there are few among us who don't possess their dwelling, and the others pay modest rents for the habitation of their choice.

"From one year to the next, our existence is less feverish and less unsteady. We no longer know the bustle that once rendered the streets of our capitals impracticable. We are getting rid of inventions that were very dangerous, like the airplane and the automobile. We are giving ourselves the charming pleasure of traveling in carriages throughout peaceful countryside and savoring exquisite cuisine in our village inns, and excellent vintage wines."

"Alas," said Lagité, "how far that time is from us!"

"I also know that morality is declining in your countries, that criminals are incessantly becoming more audacious, that even your children are committing murders, the accounts of which in your newspapers make the hair stand on end"

"You're well-informed," said Jacques.

"Here," said Edaramac, "those horrors were once frequent, but they are becoming rarer, and we observe with pleasure that our society is heading toward the reign of Virtue."

"So much the better for you," said Jacques. "In sum, it would be in our interests to imitate you sometimes—which is to say, to live backwards."

"Pardon me," said Edaramac, "but it's you who live backwards and we who live forwards.

"Perhaps you're right," said Jacques, "and I'm too courteous to contradict you."

The conversation was left there, and Jacques said to Letord: "Fundamentally, in spite of certain temporary superiorities, the existence of the Retrogrades is too similar to ours for me to desire it. Backwards or forwards, life is as detestable in one direction as the other."

After that session, therefore, Lagité returned home more desolate than before. A bell rang on his wireless apparatus. It was the inhabits of Venus, Varluz and his friend, once again.

"Ah! Finally!" cried Jacques. "You can say that you've damned me. Lord God, may your apparatus function! Repair it once and for all! Now, quickly, quickly, the name of the woman whom you consider to be the most accomplished creature in the universe, and whom you have nicknamed the Perfect."

"Her name?" said Varluz. "She hasn't revealed it to us. She consents to talk to us in order to distract herself, but she's so reserved and so discreet that she hides her name from us."

"Her address too, it goes without saying?"

"Yes," said Varluz, "but we possess it, for we were in communication with the person who occupied the same apartment before her. It's in Paris, forty-four Rue de Rennes, on the fourth floor.

"Very good," said Jacques. But in order for me to recognize the Perfect reliably, repeat to me what she looks like."

"Adorable! Adorable!"

"That's understood, but tall or petite?"

"Tall," said Varluz.

"Petite," said his friend.

"Ah!" said Jacques. "Always this discord! Are you talking about the same woman?"

"Certainly," said Varluz. "Only, for myself, I like tall women and he likes petite ones. At such a distance, everyone sees his divinity in the aspect that seduces him the most."

"You told me that she's blonde?"

"Yes, like gold," said Varluz.

"Like ripe wheat," said his friend.

"She's blonde, that point is established. The color of her eyes?"

"Blue," said Varluz.

"Maroon," said his friend.

"Damn it!" said Jacques. "You're odious, with your contradictions. Anyway I'll run to the address you've given me."

"Be careful," said Varluz. "There's another woman with her constantly, a friend that she cherishes with all her soul, and who lives with her."

"Damn!" said Jacques. "I don't want to make a mistake. Give me a portrait of the friend...but you're going to tell me black and white again. I'll compare the two women myself, and I'll quickly discern the more beautiful."

"There's no mistaking her," said Varluz.

Jacques thanked them and set forth at a rapid stride. He climbed four floors of the indicated house, and without seeking a pretext under which he could present himself to the mistress of the apartment, he rang the doorbell.

The door opens.

Who does he see?

His wife.

Very surprised, she allows the radiance of a boundless joy to appear on her face. She is on the point of saying to him: "Oh, my dear husband, you've searched for me and you've found me!"

For an instant, he is struck by the extraordinary transfiguration of his wife; then he says: "What! You live here?"

Immediately, the flame that has just illuminated Viviane is extinguished. "Didn't you know?"

"No," says Jacques, and remains nonplussed.

"Why have you come, then?""

He looks at her with increasing embarrassment. "Don't you share this apartment with a friend?" he stammers.

"Yes, with a young Englishwoman, Miss Pearson."

"Oh! Can you describe her to me?"

"Certainly. Thick golden blonde hair..."

"That's it. And the color of her eyes?"

"Maroon."

"I was sure of it. Can I see her?"

"No, she's in London at the moment."

"Can you give me here address in England."

She noted it down on a piece of paper and asked him: "Do you know Miss Pearson?"

"Someone has told me about her."

"Would you like me to write to her?"

"No thank you. Common friends will take charge of introducing me."

"So be it."

"Au revoir, Viviane. Excuse me for having disturbed you..."

"Jacques, Jacques, it's not..."

He had taken her hand and, without thinking about it, had retained it in his own. There is sometimes a secret will within us better than our own.

Suddenly, he got a grip on himself again, and, releasing Viviane's hand, he retreated toward the door. He was not very proud of himself. On tiptoe, like a thief, he escaped.

He resembled a somnambulist who follows a path between obstacles without seeing them.

The following day he was in London, outside the house in which he expected to find Miss Pearson.

He asked the porter for her.

"Miss Pearson?" said the man. "Don't you know?"

"No..."

"She was run over by a tram yesterday."

There we go, thought Jacques. *It was written that I would never know the most beautiful woman in the universe.*

He returned to Paris.

"Still as dark?" Letord asked him, when he saw him again.

"In truth, your topsy-turvy planet wasn't of a nature to cheer me up. And since that sorry experience, nothing has reconciled me with life. Well, I've ended up suspecting that it's me who is incapable of savoring the pleasures of existence. I suppose I don't have enough intelligence to discover the beauties of creation. Perhaps if I were more intelligent..."

"You think, then, that intelligence procures happiness?" Letord interjected.

"How do I know?"

"Well, my dear friend, I'll conduct you via wireless to a land inhabited by beings whose brains are the most luminous and the best constructed. They know everything at birth. They foresee everything and forget nothing. It's sufficient for them to see a cause to divine its most distant results. They're the Sages."

As usual, he turned screws and handles, and said: "Here's the planet of the Sages."

XII. The Planet of the Sages

Jacques saw two lovers in a park from a tale of enchantment.

It was dusk. Light breezes swayed clusters of roses the festooned an arbor like cassolettes of incense. For the crown of an elm, a nightingale launched its plaint into the golden sky, which seemed to be weeping diamond tears. The long, thick grass, from which hundreds of downy moths were rising, enchained the footfalls of the couple and invited them insidiously to lie down. The male retained his companion, drew her against him, implored her, and sought passionately the sensuality of the chalice of her lips.

360

But she turned her head away sadly. "No," she said to him, "no. It would be folly to make the voyage to the land of blue dreams tonight..."

"But..."

"Oh, my beloved, don't you know what the fatal effects of our amour would be? Can't you foresee them, as I can?"

"I love you. I love you and I don't know anything else. Every note the nightingale sings is a kiss fluttering toward you; every frisson of the nocturnal breeze is a caress that envelops you; every star, every rose is a counsel of amour. Don't refuse so much joy!"

"Is it necessary that desire blinds you? The woe of which I'm apprehensive is doubtless distant, but I can see it; I can see it with the bitter certainly that the privilege of being able to read the future clearly gives us. If you testify your amour to me here, I shall have a son who will be our joy to begin with. He will grow up, he will be handsome, he will have as much courage as intelligence. At twenty-five he will marry a young woman worthy of him. But alas, it's in this very park that the cruelty of Fate will be attested. Our son, conceived in the ecstasy of this evening, will be as sensible as we are to the enchantment of this exquisite location. At the end of a heavy summer day, he will stroll on this lawn with his wife. They will come to sit down in the shade of that elm, already so majestic, and which, in twenty-five years, will be immense. While they are intoxicating themselves with kisses, all their sagacity will vanish for an instant. They will not pay attention to the rapid approach of a storm. And lightning, striking the tree, will kill them instantly."

The lover looked at her with terror.

"What despair we will experience," she said, "on learning of the death of those cherished children, scythed down in their radiant beauty, snatched from our infinite tenderness! What frightful regrets for our old age! Oh, my beloved, do you still want a pleasure for which we will pay later with such suffering?"

"No, certainly not," he said, sadly.

Then, sagely, close to one another but carefully avoiding any contact between them, they returned home and put off until another day the effusions of their amour.

At that moment, Sufar appeared; he was Letord's correspondent on the planet of the Sages. He was the one who had hidden a recording apparatus in the grass in order to permit Letord and Jacques to follow the conversation of the lovers.

"What do you think of that couple?" he asked Lagité.

"The lover is a mere fool," said Jacques, "unless he's lost his taste for such an annoyingly far-sighted woman."

"Don't think that she was talking nonsense," said Sufar. "All that is strictly accurate."

"Well, it's a great calamity to perceive such distant disasters; and I believe that one would never sacrifice to amour if one calculated its consequences in that way."

That same evening, Sufar took our two friends through the streets of the capital of the Sages. Many natives of the land were standing with one foot in the air, like storks sleeping with one leg raised. Lagité asked what that signified.

"To satisfy your curiosity," said Sufar, "you're going to hear one of those whose attitude astonishes you. Here is one of my relatives, who is standing outside his mistress's house."

He approached the individual in question, who was talking to himself out loud.

"Ought I to go up to see my little friend No, because she'll ask me for a pearl necklace, and if I give it to her, she'll have other demands, which will end up putting me on my uppers.

"Should I go home? No, for if I break it off with my mistress, chagrin will trouble my head, I'll administer my affairs badly and I'll run to disaster."

Sufar left him to his irresolution and said to Lagité: "All the other Sages that you see here on one foot are stopped in the same way by insoluble alternatives."

They went to see one of his friends, a great industrialist. He was at his work-table, pen in hand, his arm in suspense. And, much like the other, he was talking to himself:

"Should I sign this letter to accept a larger metallurgical order? Yes, or else a competitor will supplant me, and won't take long to ruin my enterprises. But no, because, worn out by excessive labor. I'll neglect my wife, who will cuckold me, and her treason will overwhelm me with dolor and drive me to suicide."

Sufar extracted him from his reverence and said to Jacques: "In all our dwellings, Sages remain thus, with a hand or a foot in the air."

"What a people!" said Jacques.

The next day, Sufar enabled Jacques and Letord to witness a Council of Ministers. He had greased the palm of one of his cousins, an usher at the palace of the Presidency, who had dissimulated an apparatus in a corner of the room.

Against the wall, on a platform, they perceived a beautiful statue of a naked woman whose gaze was meditative and forehead high but whose legs and arms had been cut off at the level of the torso. Lagité put off until after the session asking Sufar what the image represented.

The Ministers examined several important matters

Should a new city be built at the mouth of a certain river?

"Yes," said Their Excellencies, "for that port is indispensable to our national commerce."

"No," they said, a moment later, "for in fifty years, to the day, according to ineluctable previsions, there will be an earthquake in that region, and the city will be entirely destroyed."

Conclusion: nothing was decided.

Another question: should they found a colony in a certain territory rich in future promise?

"Yes," said the Ministers, "for it's necessary to direct out there the surplus of the metropolitan population."

"No," said the same Ministers, "for that colony, in sixty years and six months, will excite the jealousy of a neighboring nation by its prosperity, which will take possession of it after a murderous war."

Conclusion: nothing was decided.

A third question: the great coquette of the National Theater had broken her contract and was performing on another stage. That caused some scandal, for among Sages as among fools, the actions and gestures of the princesses of the comedic gambling-den impassion everyone.

Ought the capricious individual be constrained to respect her contract?

"Yes," said the Ministers, "for the example of her rebellion is fatal."

"No," they said, immediately thereafter, "for the sly fox is very well in with several members of the opposition, who will bring down the government."

Conclusion: nothing was decided.

After which, the session was concluded and Their Excellencies retired, very satisfied with themselves.

Jacques did not know what to think He interrogated Sufar about the statue devoid of arms and legs.

"Oh," said his correspondent, "she presides over all our meetings and assemblies. She's the image of our wisdom: a head to reflect, but no legs with which to walk or arms with which to act. A long time ago, we recognized that extreme meditation is the sworn enemy of action."

"Possibly," said Jacques. Then, addressing Letord, he added: "I think that among the Sages, the only joys are those of intelligence. They're doubtless so intoxicating that they must console people for any affliction."

"I believe as you do," said Letord.

"It's necessary to question Sufar, who knows everything, on that subject. He'll be able to reveal to us the radiant perspectives of wisdom, and we'll be content."

"That's right," said Letord.

Sufar told them that he was ready to respond to them regarding the most arduous questions, and Lagité began by asking his opinion regarding the principal theories of terrestrial philosophy. "Our Greek Sages," he told him, "are famous. Plato affirms the God, who is infinitely rich, has espoused the extreme poverty of the world, and that all appearances are born from their marriage."

"Pooh!" said Sufar.

"Aristotle declares that Divine thought is the idea of a thought, and that that is sufficient to make the world turn."

"Bah!"

"Plotinus believes that God allows all creation to tumble from his loins and then to climb back toward him."

"Your Greeks were terrible quibblers," said Sufar, "with a great deal of impertinence."

"The English," said Jacques, have excelled in morality. Bacon, Hobbes, Locke, David Hume, Berkeley, Bentham, Stuart Mill and Spencer esteem that individual interest is confounded with the general interest, and that it's necessary to work for the public good, because that is what returns the most to the individual."

"Your English are accountants," said Sufar.

"Spinoza," said Jacques, "has reduced God to being nothing but a gigantic theorem in geometry."

"That's not so stupid," said Sufar

"Leibniz has declared that God has created an imperfect world because, if creation had been prefect, it would not have been distinguished from the creator."

"Your Leibniz absolves Providence very lightly of all the evil that one observes in the world."

"Kant says that Necessity rules the world but that humans are nevertheless free, because they choose their character themselves before birth."

"Bizarre!"

"His disciples, the Germans Fichte, Hegel and Schelling, seek the first principle of all things. Fichte believes that he has found it in the Self, to which the Non-Self is opposed, Hegel in Being, which is opposed to Non-Being, Schelling in the Subject, as opposed to the Object. And each of them extracts the entire Universe from his formula, as a consequence. As for their compatriot Einstein, he enslaves the world to a single force: inertia."

"Your Germans want the great All to behave in a Prussian manner."

"The Frenchman Descartes opines that our will can manipulate as it pleases within our brains the little pineal gland, and thus direct the animal spirits that accomplish all our actions. Maine de Biran claims to prove our liberty by means of our sentiment of effort. According to Bergson, the material universe descends a slope, Life climbs up it again and, thanks to their liberty, humans climb that slope faster than other living beings."

"Your turbulent Frenchmen," said Sufar, "are insurgent even against the discipline of Nature."

"Meyerson, another French philosopher,[58] proclaims that nature is essentially unintelligible. In order to understand it, it would be necessary to return it to unity, but that is impossible, for it is frightfully diverse and changing."

"Ha ha! Your Meyerson isn't an idiot."

---

[58] Émile Meyerson (1859-1933), born in Poland and educated in Germany, was naturalized as a French citizen after World War I.

"The American pragmatist William James recommends Christian belief as the one that has the best usage in contemporary life."

"The American, if he could, would put God in a tin can," said Sufar.

"But what do you think of those systems?" Lagité said.

"Almost all of them are full of falsity. How do you expect your feeble reasoning to adapt to the infinite complexity of the world? The Universe, in its progress, doesn't care what you think and won't yield in the slightest to the petty rules of your understanding.

"Even we, in spite of our sagacity, only see a little more clearly than you. In all probability, the word is ruled by a capricious and extravagant will, which seems to amuse itself with the games you call hide-and-seek and blind-man's-buff. Hiding from the creature, it cries; 'Cuckoo!' It imposes on us the law of seeking it with eyes blindfolded, groping at hazard. What is disconcerting is that it takes pleasure in that puerile amusement.

"Dear inhabitants of little Earth, take it from the Sage who is talking to you: life is just a trick of a mocking Demiurge. It would be much better if nothing existed."

"In that case," said Jacques, "why don't the Sages seek to destroy themselves?"

"That's because destruction is still action," said Sufar. "That desperate resolution would have many repercussions. Our abolished race would probably be replaced by others that would be worse. That's why we continue to live. But we reduce out existence almost to negligibility. We only eat, drink and procreate just enough to perpetuate our species, and no more. We act as minimally as possible; we think. On which note, I wish you much pleasure."

And he took his leave of them.

"They're not light-hearted on that world," Jacques murmured. "Truly, the philosophy of that Sufar has given me a chill in my spine. Anything rather than such a wisdom! I prefer to be poor in spirit.[59] I'd have more chance of being happy."

"Perhaps," replied Letord, smiling, "and I can even enable you to make the judgment. Come back tomorrow and I'll show you the planet of the Poor in Spirit."

"Decidedly," said Jacques, "one can never catch you at a loss."

---

[59] The original has *pauvres d'esprit*. Because the word *esprit* can mean "mind" or "intelligence" in French, as well as "spirit" what Jacques is implying by contrasting his desire with the intelligence of the Sages is that he would rather be unintelligent, but the French phrase, like its English equivalent, is famous by virtue of its use in vernacular versions of the gospel according to Saint Matthew, in which Jesus says that the poor in spirit are blessed because theirs is the kingdom of Heaven. The author also seems to have in mind during the next chapter Christ's assertion, via Matthew, that the pure in heart will see God.

XIII. The Planet of the Poor in Spirit

The following day, Jacques, punctual at the rendezvous, saw people in the streets of a city whose faces were radiant.

Gross jowls, double and triple chins, florid complexions, large red ears, wide mouths, ecstatic gazes and comfortable paunches: in sum, they had all the attributes of perfect contentment. Even those who chanced to be thin seemed rapturous. They were laughing angelically, singing, and dancing rather than waking.

"Good!" exclaimed Jacques. "These people aren't downcast."

Letord introduced him to one of the Poor in Spirit, bursting with delight and obesity. "This is my friend Nirup," he said. "He's going to tell us the secret of the universal felicity distributed over this planet.

"It is," said Nirup, with a sigh, "that we possess certainty."

"Certainty, you say?" said Jacques, eagerly.

Nirup shaped a profound affirmative nod of the head.

"Doubtless you've searched for that certainty for a long time?"

"Searched?"

"Yes. I imagine that your scholars have worked hard and studied a great deal before discovering it?"

"Don't talk to me about scholars!" said Nirup. "We despise them. We glory in being as ignorant as carps."

"But then..."

"We draw the truth from a big book that fell from the sky thousands of years ago."

"What?" said Jacques. "What is written in such an ancient book can still be applied to all present circumstances? Does it contain solutions to all the new difficulties that emerge, and all the questions that modern science poses?"

"I've already told you that science is of no importance to us," said Nirup. "But everything is in the big book. Everything!"

"I'd have more confidence in a new book," Jacques opined, "in which the concerns of the present time are reflected."

"You don't understand anything," said Nirup. "The older a book is, the more confidence one can have in it."

At that moment, the enthusiastic songs resounded of a cortege that was passing in a neighboring street.

"Ah!" said Nirup, with a manifest sympathy, "those are worshipers who are going to see Him."

"Who is Him?" Jacques asked.

"Him, Him! He has no other name. Him! Oh, Him!" Nirup rolled the whites of his eyes and seemed inundated by an ineffable voluptuousness.

"But in sum," Jacques said, "tell me about this Him that you idolize."

"He's our benefactor," said Nirup, "and our king. And he only shows himself to him, the Poor in Spirit. The mortals of other planets would like very much to see him. It's their dearest ambition. But he's obstinate in hiding from them. At least, he only permits them to see him via astral wireless. We alone enjoy the signal privilege of possessing him in our midst."

"Can you enable us to know him?" asked Letord.

"I consent to that," said Nirup. "Let's go to his palace."

A few minutes later, Letord and Lagité saw a dense crowd that filled an immense room sustained by high columns. In that nave, which resembled a sanctuary a fabulous luxury reigned, but in dubious taste: sky-blue vaults strewn with stars, statues that were gilded or painted in loud colors, garish paintings, stained glass with the insipid translucency of syrups and candied fruits.

The audience was waiting silently at the foot of a triumphal golden throne, which was unoccupied.

Suddenly, a brightly-clad chamberlain appeared. Organs launched forth squalls of harmony. And on the royal throne, the individual summoned by all the prayers of the crowd took his place. It was the Him of whom Nirup had spoken.

Letord and Lagité had not imagined him as he was.

The sovereign of the planet of the Poor in Spirit. had the appearance of a fat well-to-do bourgeois. Like the majority of his subjects, he was red-faced and stout, with a long white beard: a debonair aspect that was nevertheless belied by false gleams that traversed his eyes, of different colors.

With a single movement, the members of the crowd had prostrated themselves, face down, and they maintained that attitude for some time. Then they put themselves on their knees and modulated hymns to the glory of their monarch.

"How beautiful he is! How beautiful he is!" they repeated. "How good he is! How wise he is! Happy, happy, a hundred times happy are those he governs with so much mildness! Long live Him! Long live Him!"

And the songs alternated with ovations.

"They're really treating him like a God," said Jacques to Letord. "And yet there's nothing divine about him. Don't you find him rather vulgar?"

"Yes, indeed," murmured Letord.

Him quit his throne, and with a generous condescension he passed through the ranks of the multitude in order that they could contemplate him at closer rage. Jacques thus had the opportunity to observe him more closely, and he found him even more disquieting. Beneath the feigned bonhomie of that powerful individual he discerned a sort of knavery, a perfidious cruelty.

He questioned Nirup about the monarch's habits.

"Very simple, even rustic," Nirup replied. "He's passionate about horticulture and possesses a splendid orchard. Of course, he doesn't like people stealing his fruits, That's a trait of his character. He's a good father, but he prefers his apples to his children, and condemns marauders to death pitilessly."

"That's frightful," said Jacques.

"What do you expect?" said Nirup. "One takes that for granted. Otherwise, an excellent heart."

Him had emerged from his palace and, as was his custom, he wandered through the streets of his capital.

As he passed by, everyone cheered and bent their knees.

He went into a dwelling of poor appearance, which he had already visited on previous days. It was his pleasure to visit thus, unexpectedly, his most modest subjects as well as his highest dignitaries.

He climbed a humble stairway and headed straight for the small bedroom where a child was lying. The parents followed him to the bed. They fixed Him with the suppliant gaze of a whipped dog.

"Our darling is a little better," they said, in a whisper.

Him smiled benevolently and, as he had done the day before and the day before that. He put his forefinger on the head of the poor child, sternly.

The child woke up then. His eyelids opened immeasurably. His eyes fluttered with a panicky rapidity. His lips trembled. His hands were continually agitated under the covers. His eyes, tipped backward, seemed to want to flee torturing visions, and he uttered a long hoarse plaint.

The sovereign lifted his finger.

The pain immediately ceased, as if by a miracle, and the child sighed, appeased.

The king, still paternal, replaced his index finger on the forehead of the invalid. The signs of an atrocious suffering reappeared immediately. The infant howled. The modulations of his scream had the effect of his parents of a red-hot iron turning back and forth in their bosom. The paltry body stiffened, braced, and contracted.

Something infernal was happening in the brain of that unfortunate little being, that no living being would have been able to imagine, because such an exasperation of dolor was the very entrance to annihilation.

And with a last savage cry, the supreme breath was liberated. In an ultimate convulsion, the child slumped on his side; the index finger of the sovereign accompanied the head inexorably in that displacement. Finally, the body was immobilized.

The parents sobbed, with great heaves of their curbed shoulders.

Him said to them: "That's done it!" And he smiled again.

Then, an insensate scene unfolded. The parents knelt down, took the hand of the sovereign, covered it with kisses and stammered: "Thank you! Thank you! How good you are to have killed our child! You're too good!"

Now, they too were smiling through their tears, and repeating: "Thank you, thank you."

Other witnesses who had come into the room with the king made a chorus with the parents: "Glory to Him! Glory to Him!" they clamored. "Everything that he decides is perfect! If he had cured that child, we would have blessed him. But since he didn't want to, we bless him all the same. He's always right. The suffering that he distributes so abundantly is much preferable to joy. Suffering is the supreme felicity. Glory to Him! Glory to Him!"

They went out with the sovereign, toward whom the actions of grace of his subjects rose up without discontinuity through the streets.

Lagité and Letord looked at one another without saying a word.

The king, continuing his march, went into a second house. A young mother was in the course of giving birth to a child there. Around her there was a joyful expectation, nuanced nevertheless with some apprehension. The husband was proud of having created life. He was already puncturing his dear wife offering her breast to the nursling and forgetting her dolors in the rapture of maternity. He saw her in advance appealing by means of gentle baby-talk to the intelligence and tenderness in two little flowers of light.

However, she was lamenting, and breathing heavily, and the midwife was striving to encourage her with comforting words.

The sovereign appeared.

Among the people present there was the same blaze of confidence as there had been in the house of the little invalid previously.

Him approached the body agitated by a cruel swell and placed his broad hand thereon. Instantly, it was as if the young mother froze. She uttered a feeble groan and became inert,

"There!" said the king. He added, speaking to the husband: "Your son will live."

"Oh, thank you, thank you!" said the father. "How good you are! How good you are!"

And again the noisy demonstrations of gratitude erupted.

"That woman has ceased to suffer," they said. "Glory to Him! He wanted the life of the mother to serve as ransom for that of the child. Blessed is he! Blessed is he!"

Lagité leaned toward Letord's ear and said to him, with alarm: "But what is this sadistic madman? He scares me. And what is this people who magnify him for such sins?"

The sovereign, nodding his head, went on his way.

He made a third halt and went up to another dwelling. There, a young mathematician was gasping. He was in an armchair near the window, enveloped in blankets. Within arm's reach, on a table, were sheets of paper covered in formulas. An old man, his professor, was standing beside him.

On that planet, where study was disdained, the two scholars loved one another all the more because their mutual affection compensated them for the general indifference.

The invalid had taken the old man's hand and was looking at him sadly. He was desperate to complete a great discovery toward which his precocious genius was guiding him.

"I would have needed another week," he said.

"But you're going to live," said his friend, turning away in order to hide his tears.

The king, who had remained on the threshold momentarily, advanced toward them.

"Save him!" said the professor. "Save that prodigious intelligence!"

"You believe in my power, then, scholar?"

"I will believe in it."

Without responding, Him placed his hand on the breast of the moribund genius, whose head inclined over his shoulder.

"It's over!" said the sovereign, challenging the dead man's friend with an ironic glance.

Overwhelmed, the old scholar remained silent,

As for the worshipers of the king, they resumed their dithyrambs: "Long live Him! Long live Him! That young mathematician was a genius, it seems. Our king has condemned him. He has done well. Perish all scholars, all geniuses, provided that Him is triumphant! From Him, we accept everything with joy! Let him test us, let him torment us, let him inflict upon us and ours the most refined tortures, let him crush us! So much the better! Glory to Him alone!"

And they sang until they ran out of breath.

"They're happy, it's undeniable," exclaimed Lagité. "They are even the only happy mortals that we've observed thus far in the planets. But away with such a happiness! They're truly too poor in spirit!

So saying, he cut the communication, without even saluting the bloated and blissful Nirup.

XIV. A Celestial Crash

After that further disappointment, Jacques had fallen back into his hypochondria.

He was dreaming more than ever about his Gilniz.

He forgot about everything the inhabitants of Venus might have said against her. And since it was impossible for him to love the terrestrial woman whom his correspondents claimed to be marvelous, it was toward Gilniz that his exacerbated desires were redirected.

He had, however, sworn not to think any more about his mistress beyond the sky, and he had kept that oath for a long time.

Suddenly, though, after a brief internal struggle, he evoked the apparition that haunted him on the screen, and Gilniz smiled at him.

"Ingrate lover," she said, "why have you neglected me? I'm so stupid, that I think about you incessantly. Oh, my beloved, what an unspeakable dolor it is not to be able to respond to your desire!"

Strangely enough, she seemed sincere. Was she? Perhaps by caprice, during the moment when she was speaking.

And the bewitchment immediately recommenced. Jacques now saw Gilniz every day; he seemed irresistible condemned to that folly.

The astral wireless itself, however procured him a diversion of sorts from his amorous torment; for that invention, the prodigies of which were enfevering the entire world, suddenly brought its devotees the most anguishing surprise that it had yet contrived for them.

From a distant star, a prolonged, persistent, painful signal reached all the receiving posts, which was translated by sonorous appeals of an unusual timbre and by extraordinarily sinuous flashes.

It soon became clear that it was an immense cry of distress launched into infinite space: a sort of intersidereal S.O.S.

Letord was the first to identify the planet from which the heart-rending request for help was coming, it was Phi in the constellation Canis Major. Without delay, he invited Lagité to witness his observations.

The astronomers of Phi had just acquired the certainty that in a short time their globe was about to collide with satellite number three of the star Omega. The pulverization of the two spheres would be the infallible result.

As soon as Barnabé Letord had put that news into circulation, all the wireless enthusiasts of the Old and New Worlds adjusted their apparatus, in order to witness the imminent tragedy.

The catastrophe was no more distant than thirty-five days. The astronomers of the threatened planet had indicated by means of calculations of an unchallengeable precision the exact minute and second at which the collision would occur.

It goes without saying that the inhabitants of Phi gave their globe another name. They designated it by the word Grul, and for them, the satellite of Omega was the star Lap. That is what we shall call the two heavenly bodies in our story.

The prediction of the scientists of Grul had initially been greeted with skepticism, but the ruling class had not taken long to believe it, and the masses had soon sensed that it was a matter of an irremediable condemnation. In any case, Lap, which had previously had a small diameter, was growing continually. Now, everyone could take account of that increase with the naked eye, without any recourse to astronomical telescopes.

The race in peril found itself almost in the situation of a paralytic who, placed on a railway track, can see an express train growing in magnitude on the horizon. The scientists of Grul addressed themselves fearfully to their colleagues on other worlds and asked them whether anything could be attempted—but they only obtained, as you can imagine, evasive responses or nonsense.

371

Barnabé Letord had wanted to make contact with the inhabitants of the other star that was about to perish. He had succeeded, not without difficulty.

In fact, while the inhabitants of Grul resembled humans closely, the population of Lap was composed of veritable monsters, only a few of which were capable of employing wireless.

The professor of the Collège de France remembered perfectly that during his earliest experiments he had chanced to communicate with Lap. He had even collected the famous apocalyptic image that his colleagues had accused him of having composed by trickery.

In pursuing his investigations, he also learned that the monsters of Lap were the products of hybridizations unknown anywhere else. Any species coupled with any other, and fabulous types were born in consequence: fish with human heads, like the Oannes of Babylonian legend, winged lions like that of Saint Mark, sirens, harpies—in sum. all imaginable fantasies of genesic power. Some of those creatures enjoyed a highly developed intelligence, but they were rare.

The interest awakened throughout the universe in the frightful adventure, therefore, generally turned away from that pandemonium in order to concentrate on Grul.

That was a world of very advanced civilization. The greatest geniuses in the various orders of knowledge had realized innumerable inventions there, which had suppressed all physical servitudes. High Science reigned uncontested, and life was an enchantment.

As soon as the conviction of an imminent end was imposed, however, all activity stopped. Merchants closed their shops. The population, soon hungry, broke down the doors, and the majority of the merchants who defended their property were massacred.

If the consumption of products assembled on the planet and ready to be utilized had been methodical, it would have far surpassed needs until the fatal hour. But a frenzy had taken hold of all the inhabitants, and they stimulated one another mutually to stuff themselves with victuals. Like filthy rodents that, with a single bite, poison the most precious products, they delved at hazard into crates and barrels, and after the few extractions they made, they abandoned the remainder to putrescence.

The very spectacle of that plunder gave them the idea that everything would soon run out, and like insensates they hurled themselves upon one another to dispute the booty, murdered one another, stuffed themselves, and then, stuffed again and dead drunk, snored in the wine and the blood.

Famine became rife about a fortnight before the denouement, and battles around the almost-exhausted aliments became increasingly ferocious.

Jacques, at Letord's house, followed those lamentable scenes, thanks to the scientists of Grul, who continued relentlessly to solicit the illusory aid of all the thinking brains in the entire universe.

"What desolation," cried Jacques, "to think that a few weeks ago, that people was perhaps the wisest and most fortunate in infinite space! With what incredible rapidity the varnish of civilization that covers the primitive savagery of the most polite society cracks!"

The attention of the two friends was attracted by episodes of another sort. The approach of the end suppressed all restraint of instinctive impulses. Young people of both sexes contented one another mutually at crossroads, like animals, without anyone raising any obstacle. Mature women cajoled schoolboys brazenly. Incests were committed before the eyes of everyone, and the sight of those aberrations, far from scandalizing the witnesses, suggested to them the firm design to imitate them.

Only ten days remained. Lap, which appeared in the nocturnal sky like an enormous bomb enveloped by a metallic gleam, was visible even by day, and exercised a frightful obsession upon those who raised their eyes.

Rich people who, at the first news of the catastrophe, had amassed choice food supplies, gathered in the domain of one of them. It was an area as large as a small province and renowned for the enchantment of its landscapes. A magical palace stood in the midst of age-old forests. The master of the abode invited his friends to continual rejoicing there. And at first, the fêtes were rather well ordered. An orchestra executed passionate tunes that procured an aphrodisiac ecstasy. Couples spread outside the sumptuous dwelling beneath the opaque foliage and sought the numbing of the senses there.

On the sixth day before the deadline, however, the musicians, besieged by the common haunting, produced so many false notes and discords that they could not continue playing. And the lovers whose gallant conversations had been interrupted by frightful silences ceased to madrigalize. As they headed for the thickets they forgot that they were together and went back separately to the château.

It had been forbidden ever to make allusion to the horrible terminus, but no one succeeded in being distracted from it. Repeatedly, one of the condemned pronounced in a loud voice the number of days that separated them from death. Growls of anger greeted that reminder, and the importunate individual was thrown out of the gates of the estate.

In spite of that severity, a young poet started to howl: "Five days! Five days!"

He climbed on to a platform on the golden balustrades and repeated his cry from there. He was told to shut up, bombarded with cups and crystal vases, from which he took refuge behind columns, and which fell back and shattered into a thousand pieces on the mosaics, in the midst of the oaths of those they struck. And he, driven by a Dionysian delirium, resumed his refrain:

"Five days! Five days! That's all that remains to you. Employ them well. Into those few hours concentrate all that the years of your life promised you. Intoxicate yourselves with so much amour, wear yourselves out with so many enjoyments, that in five days your vigor will turn into decrepitude, your blond hair will turn white, your eyes will tarnish, your heart and your blood will finish blazing, and Death, thinking to surprise you in the spring of your youth will only scythe down ice-cold old men."

Then he put his arms around two young dancing girls and they staggered away in their embrace.

Suddenly, his orgiastic excitement took possession of the entre audience. And as, in the kennels, the first bark unleashes a furious din, a colossal roar of salacity resounded. It was a gigantic exhalation of desire, with which spasmodic laughter, songs, hiccups and demented clamors were mingled.

That little society, which, among the elite of the land, had once represented the rarest distinction, was precipitated without restraint into an unspeakable debauchery. Madmen and madwomen bowed their heads together over large alabaster vases filed with wine and drank avidly, like animals from a pond; then, all garments torn away, they appeared in a furious saraband of nudity that undulated through the enormous palace, over the pavements of the halls, along the marble stairways, the thresholds of doors and the steps of perrons. Masters, musicians and servants were now confounded, and the baseness of certain valets set the tone for the bacchanal.

When no more than two and a half days remained, many of the guests were dead of excess. Others were so sated by lust that they remained inert. Only a few got up, staggering, in order to drink more, to eat scraps steeped in wine and fall back among the sprawling nudities, scattered pell-mell.

Very few of them were conscious of what was happening when a barbaric rumor filled the surrounding park and a mob of vagabonds irrupted into the château with the violence of a muddy inundation.

The intruders were innumerable and sordid, faces leaden with fatigue and striped by scars, with meager and blackened flesh that their tattered rags rendered visible. It was the populace, who, having dilapidated the provision of the towns, had spread out into the country, where they exterminated the peasants in order to feast on their flocks. The rumor had run around those bandits that fabulous provisions had been heaped up in the château where the orgy had been unleashed.

Armed with billhooks, pikes, pitchforks, clubs, cutlasses and axes, they had formed a compact column in order to head for the goal of their brigandage. The first to enter the palace hurled themselves upon the women, murdered the guests and rushed upon the food and the drink. The rich scarcely defended themselves, so exhausted were they. In any case, any struggle was vain against the multitude of the invaders. Other vagabonds followed incessantly. They continued to kill, to guzzle and to swill; they choked the unconscious women under constantly renewed assaults; then they massacred one another in order to snatch shreds of victuals; they paddled, slipped and rolled in the blood that streamed in cascades over the steps, over the flagstones, along the walls and all the way to the distant pathways of the park.

Finally, they set fire to the edifice, and the flames devoured, in a matter of seconds, the accumulation of marvels that the greatest artists had created.

None of those sinister visions escaped Letord and Lagité. For, in the same way that in our most treble battles, reporters are always to be found of an inconceivable temerity, heroic transmitters on Grul never ceased to circulate and collect for the wireless testimonies of the lugubrious destiny of the unfortunate planet.

"Frightful! Frightful!" repeated Jacques. And again he meditated on the short time that had been required for barbarity to efface so many centuries devoted to the triumph of intelligence.

Other information, however, proved to the two friends that all thought was not dead on the star in question. Among several scientists of Grul a supreme preoccupation had been born. Since they could not save themselves, they wanted to transmit everything that they had discovered. They communicated their latest endeavors feverishly to their colleagues on other worlds. As in conflagration one hastily wraps the most precious objects in blankets in order to throw them out of the windows, they launched into the sky all of their magnificent knowledge. They dictated word for word certain treatises in which their noblest doctrines were condensed, and adjured the worlds not to allow any of it to be lost.

In their principal city, Professor Gasbi, the director of the Central Institute, had organized a service informed the universe hour by hour. It was a matter of consigning for future science a rigorously objective aspect of events. The messages were numbered carefully.

No. 34839, second day of the third week of the twelfth month, midday. The collision will take place, as everyone knows, tomorrow at eleven hours, ten minutes and twenty-three seconds. Presently, we are only separated from it by twenty-three hours, forty-nine minutes and thirty-seven seconds.

Lap is clearly visible in broad daylight. Its apparent diameter is one meter thirty.[60] The contours of its shores can easily be discerned. That observation permits us to resolve a question that has divided our scientists. The ridiculous thesis of Professor Bono on the form of the continents of Lap was completely erroneous. It is that of Professor Gasbi that is correct.

No. 234840, thirteen hours. A few details regarding the activity of our Institute. We have to deplore the dejection of many of our collaborators, who, dominated by an anxiety otherwise excusable, are no longer interested in our studies.

---

[60] Author's note: "To minimize complication, we are translating into terrestrial units the measurements of length and time employed by the inhabitants of Grul."

Young Doctor Rilu is pursuing his magisterial research on immortality. He believes that he has found henceforth the principle that will assure living beings of a perpetual existence. In order to bring the discovery definitively to a conclusion, he will devote himself to one last experiment.

Other various items of information were accompanied by live pictures. All the wireless enthusiasts on Earth, like the populations of Grul, saw Lap increasing in size from moment to moment. They remained amazed by the calm physiognomy of Professor Gasbi and the ardent labor of Doctor Rilu.

On the morning of the last day the following message was received:

No, 34897, third day of the third week of the twelfth month, eight o'clock in the morning. The gravitational effects of the approach of Lap are beginning to make themselves felt. On Grul, the weight of objects and living beings is diminishing. Plates thrown into the air with a moderate force rise easily to a hundred meters and fall back slowly, without breaking

Professor Gasbi, wanting to verify the new conditions of weight personally, has just made, in spite of his age, a leap of thirty meters in height in the courtyard of the Institute.

A short time afterwards a communication was sent from Lap by one of the rare intelligent creatures inhabiting it. It was a disconcerting vision.

The monsters of that planet, tormented by an apprehension that even overtook the unconscious beings, were agitating desperately. Long serpents with multiple feet were delivering themselves to strange contortions. Enormous fish, with a thrust of their caudal fin, were springing out of the sea and launching themselves into the air through the liquid mountains that they lifted up with themselves. Beasts bristling with spikes, like gigantic porcupines, were making disorderly leaps, colliding with one another, howling and fleeing in all directions. A panic terror had taken possession of that entire hideous race, whose violent and futile efforts to escape destruction rendered them pitiable nevertheless,

And the dispatch of coded messages from Grul continued:

No. 34940. An indescribable panic is observable in all living beings. The inhabitants of the city are running around at random in the streets, colliding and resuming their route without following any direction.

Animals are giving evidence of the same disarray. Little birds are flying into walls and falling in front of cats, which neglect to seize them. Reptiles, rats, dogs and wolves, meet at crossroads without the enemy species seeking to harm one another.

No. 34941. Five past eleven. The panic of intelligent beings and animals has suddenly turned into a kind of torpor. All of them are still, lying down flat on the ground, seemingly paralyzed.

No. 34942. Six minutes past eleven. Remarkable instance of the persistence of the genesic instinct.

At the same time as that announcement was formulated, visible on the screen, in the midst of the mortal torpor of nature entire, was a young couple perfectly indifferent to everything that was happening. The two lovers, sitting on a bench, were exchanging ecstatic gazes.

No. 34943. Seven minutes past eleven. The hindrance of breathing is becoming intolerable. Lap is invading the entire sky. One can distinguish forests, rivers and lakes.

No. 34944. Eight minutes past eleven. Monsters recalling species long extinct on Grul are falling from Lap on to our planet.

No. 34945. Nine minutes past eleven. Darkness is falling progressively with great rapidity. Our city will be at the exact point of impact of the two globes.

At that moment, one saw again, in the gloom, the couple of young lovers. They were saying to one another: "Forever!"

And they took one another in a frenetic embrace.

No. 34946. Ten past eleven. Doctor Rilu will make a communication to all his colleagues in the universe.

Then, by the light of a lamp, the face of the young scientist appeared, transfigured by joy, and he was heard to say: "I have just discovered the secret of immorta..."

The phrase remained incomplete. Everything was eclipsed.

Jacques and Letord looked at one another. A frightful anguish prevented them from speaking for a long moment.

"When three hundred years have gone by," said Letord, finally, "our astronomers will observe in that part of the sky a sudden and colossal conflagration. The formidable impact of the two planets has certainly developed so much heat that the two spheres have immediately been converted into flaming gas. A prodigious blaze must now be illuminating that region of space."

"And that's what has become of the admirable civilization of Grul," said Jacques. "That cataclysm is, of all our astral experiences, the one that discourages me the most. Until now I had conserved a vague hope of finding happiness on the planets. I haven't discovered it anywhere, but it seems to me that the inhabitants of Grul were close to it. And behold the atrocious irony! In the blink of an eye, by virtue of a stupid whim of fate, all the long efforts of one of the most intelligent races have attempted in order to be happy have been annihilated."

"Oh, my dear friend," said Letord, "such stellar encounters are very rare."

"Agreed," said Jacques, "But whatever the delay accorded to planets might be, all of them must perish."

"That's possible."

"At least, all of them will cool. And on all of them, life will end up being extinguished, along with its chimerical promises of happiness."

"That's certain," Letord agreed.

"That, then, is the condemnation of all faith in the future," said Jacques. "Oh, I don't know why I'm avid to see one of those worlds where life is agonizing. There must be a bitter need in me for suffering, for the vision does me harm. But I'm avid to learn, and perhaps the satisfaction of my desire will compensate me for my dolor. Have you discovered one of those planets, my friend?"

Letord did not reply.

Then Jacques said, with an extreme vehemence: "My friend, my friend, I want you to give me that spectacle."

"I hesitated to propose it to you," said Letord, "But I am of the opinion that Science bears within itself the appeasement of all our sadness, and you have always been so passionate for the Truth that you will be able to support yet again looking it in the face."

XV. The Last Couple

At a further rendezvous at Professor Letord's house, Jacques saw on the screen a country whose aspect caused him a constriction of the heart.

A snowy mountain dominated an immense icy extent: there was winter everywhere, but not, as for us, a cold season in which the pulsation of life continues to beat, when rivers flow beneath the ice and when the sap remains moist in the heartwood of trees. On the planet that Lagité was looking at, the land and the water were definitively as hard as marble, and death reigned implacably. It gave the evident impression that henceforth, no effluvium of spring would ever soften that rigidity.

There was a torrent there that was precipitating from the heights, but its disheveled cascades were forever immobile. They hung down in weighty sheets, in heavy vitrified draperies, and the foam no longer swirled in the gulf, but had been solidified for centuries to come.

From the summits, the sea was visible in the distance, but its great angry waves no longer stirred; it was nothing but an infinite disorder of enormous pieces of ice. It was deducible that before being fixed in that hard eternal chaos, the liquid masses of the Ocean, still free, had risen from the most profound of its abysms in many revolts against the crystal cope whose ice had ended up oppressing them. And in the configuration of those colossal and bizarre asperities, the prolonged struggles of movement against an endless slumber were recounted.

Now, even in its deepest declivities, the Ocean no longer formed anything but a single block, as dense as granite.

A perpetually livid, although very pure, sky covered that desolate landscape. The sun of that aged universe no longer had the strength to illuminate its planets. It rose redly in space, and its surface was striped by the moving shadows that pass over a semi-consumed hearth.

At the first glance, no inhabitants could be seen.

However, on the indications of Letord, who had already explored that land by wireless, Jacques distinguished, in a rocky fissure in the flank of the mountain, two torpid beings next to a dying fire.

They had a vaguely human appearance, except that their spine was curved toward the ground and their emaciated faces revealed a mortal lassitude. They were clad in the skins of polar bears, the snowy color of which was confounded with the general hue of the region; that is why it had been difficult to discern them.

They were two old people. They only moved with difficulty. The husband had a long white beard; his hands were resting on his knees and he had difficulty breathing. The wife, almost as old, consulted the slightest desires of her companion, and busied herself around him slowly.

She presented the meat that she had cooked to him. She had doubtless taken it from some long-dead animal conserved by the ice with which the cold was dressed. She also offered him the marrow that she had extracted from the broken bone, and insisted that he nourish himself with it. But he refused the food stubbornly. Then he fixed his large dull eyes, in which his imminent end was written, upon his wife.

Sitting next to him against the rocky wall that protected them from the wind, she covered her face with her hands and sobbed.

"I imagine," said Letord, "that they're the last two representatives of a race that, I have reason to believe, was possessed of a superior intelligence."

"But how can these images be reaching our screen?" Jacques asked. "It's not, I assume, that old couple who are transmitting them?"

"Certainly not," said Letord. "But what I suppose is that there is extremely improved transmission apparatus nearby, which was created in the most flourishing epoch of the planet. Those instruments have continued to function, unknown to the degenerate descendants of those who invented them. What confirms my hypothesis is that I've received other images, originating from locations where there was no being endowed with reason. In any case, save for this troglodyte couple, I haven't discovered any trace of life on the globe we're observing. There are neither animals nor plants there. The ice has killed everything.

"Anthropomorphs of the species we can see here must have been the last to resist because they possessed fore to warm them, and also to convert ice into the water indispensable to their existence. But now the fatal hour has come in which they too must disappear, and perhaps we're witnessing their supreme day."

Jacques remained silent, sunk in a profound reverie.

By means of an unexpected effort, the old man had straightened his torso; then, vacillating on his legs, he had clung on to projections in the rock in order to stand up.

His wife, frightened by that caprice, extended her arms toward him to prevent him from falling.

Now, almost upright, he contemplated the plain where his ancestors had reigned in an immemorial past. He allowed his already-vitreous eyes to wander over that empire. His gaze paused and lingered for a long time over the evidence of a very remote epoch.

For centuries, a machine, very reminiscent of our most powerful locomotives had been overturned alongside an embankment. Overturned and corroded by rust, it lifted toward the sky two enormous wheels, the only ones that remained. Doubtless pillagers had often come to borrow pieces of metal from it, for the mantle of snow that extended everywhere had not covered it completely. The rails on the embankment were also visible over a long extent, because the sleepers had been disinterred in many places in order to serve as combustible fuel.

A very ancient seaport displayed its pensive ruins. Disjointed moles, dismantled walls and a crumbling citadel still spoke of a splendor forever defunct.

In one of the basins, the prow of a gigantic ship rose above the ice. That arrogant wreck had triumphed over time and protested against the fate that had enchained it after so much vagabondage through the tempests.

On a crest, something extended that evoked the monstrous skeletons of certain fossils conserved in the glazed halls of our museums. It was the metallic framework of what had once been an immense dirigible.

The old man no longer detached his eyes from it. In the solemnity of his expression, the astonishment was translated that those vestiges had always caused him. He considered them as sacred monuments, and addressed a mute prayer to them.

While he was turned toward the plain, his wife tried to decipher in his physiognomy the ideas that were haunting him. Then, remarking that he was shivering, she tried to reanimate the fire. She picked up a shard of wood; but before throwing it into the flame she kept it in her hands for a moment, and as it was wood with a very hard grain and highly polished, she passed it gently over her cheek in order to feel the caress.

Her husband, who glimpsed that gesture, asked her what she was holding.

So far as Lagité could discern, it was the rounded extremity of an airplane propeller.

"That's surely what it is," said Letord. "Tell me, isn't it strange that intelligence throughout the universe has flowed almost exactly the same stages? It's a verity that I have now registered many times in the course of my research."

Having considered the blade of the propeller, the old man approached it to his lips and kissed it, as a savage testifies his piety to a fetish. All kinds of unconscious reminiscences doubtless remounted in his brain with regard to that relic of such a savant industry.

Then he returned the debris to his wife, which she threw on to the fire without any further respect. And the wing that had transported mortals intoxicated by audacity through the sky served to prolong for a few moments the shivering existence of the last survivors of their once-sublime race.

The old man had directed his bleak gaze toward the plain again. He was seized by a great frisson, which made his teeth chatter. His wife hastily removed the fur by which she was covered and threw it over her husband's. She tried to make him sit down, but he would not consent to it. An obstinacy of grim pride kept him upright. And, as he confronted the great dead city, his almost-opaque eyes were suddenly traversed by a radiant gleam.

The memory of his ancestors, of their power, of their ambitions, of the impetus that had driven them for such a long time to assault the impossible ignited his obscure soul with a single surge.

The flamboyant folly of a species that had shaken violently the doors of all mystery in order to attempt to become divine was concentrated within him for one final time. He raised his arms convulsively toward the somber zenith as if to demand infinite space; and then, exhaling a great cry of distress, he fell to the ground.

His wife, who had leapt forward in vain in order to sustain him, knelt down beside him, lifted his inert head, took his face between her hands, kissed his eyes and called out to him in a heart-rending voice. Then she lay down on his breast and remained there, quivering with dolor.

Letord and Lagité could not hold back their tears.

"She won't take long to follow him," said Letord, "and the planet, depopulated henceforth, will continue to drag in its ironic waltz the ruins of what intelligence once dared, in vain."

"I don't know what effect that vision produced on you, my dear friend," said Jacques, "but it put me to the torture. It seems to me that in contemplating that phantom globe today I've just launched myself in a single bound all the way to the last hours of humankind on Earth, and now I can see with a blinding clarity that the pursuit of happiness, the dream of all mortals, is a delusion. It's a mirage to make humans advance on the harsh road of existence.

"They go on and on toward felicity, the thirst for which consumes them. If they don't have it yet they console themselves with the thought that they're continually getting closer and that, thanks to their hard efforts, their descendants will enjoy it in a distant future. But Nature mocks them so cruelly that it is preparing today the suppression of all consciousness and all life. What good, then, are all the fabulous conquests of thought and its boundless hopes, if all of that must inevitably perish and be buried in icy slumber?"

Letord put a hand gently on his shoulder and said: "My friend, can it really be that, among so many image that have unfurled before your eyes, you've never recognized happiness?"

"Where, then, would I have seen it?"

"Every time a great amour is revealed to you. You've seen it, for instance, when the two lovers of the planet Grul cried: 'Forever!' You've seen it a moment ago when, under the mortal wind, the last woman of the dying planet took off her garment for her companion, who was dying. Believe me; all our hopes and all our dreams might be deceptive, but not Amour, because it finds its joy immediately in itself. Sincere amour is the infinite happiness."

"That's false!" cried Jacques. "That's false! Amour is a damnation! I've tried to love, recklessly. I still love, with an extreme passion, and I'm atrociously unhappy."

"My dear friend," said Letord, "that's because you don't know how to love."

Lagité shrugged his shoulders and, cut to the quick, he quit Letord abruptly.

XVI. The Crimes of Astral Wireless

The astral wireless that was causing Jacques to make such cruel miscalculations was, as you can easily imagine, provoking an extreme agitation all over the world, and no one could yet foresee whether it was bringing our species more profit than harm.

Among the innumerable ideas transmitted by the distant stars, it was the deadliest that humans welcomed with the greatest ardor. They were avid, above all, for inventions applicable to the art of war.

They were of all kinds: for example, extraordinarily improved cannon that sent formidable projectiles incredible distances and annihilated an army in a moment; explosives that, dropped from an airplane, hollowed out enormous craters; liquids that, spread like rain over a great city, disengaged deleterious vapors capable of depopulating it entirely in three minutes...

The governments of our sphere, put in possession of these formulas and plans, judged that the first people to make use of them would exercise a universal hegemony, and strove to procure without the slightest delay the most powerful means of combat. But as means of extermination that seemed superior to previous ones were arriving every day from the depths of infinite space, all the nations continually threw their new materiel on the scrap-heap in order to replace it relentlessly, and everywhere, arsenals filed up with machines that provoked in advance a general terror almost as desolating as war itself.

In addition, the wireless furnished a quantity of recipes for alcohols and stupefying agents previously unknown, which our race set about preparing feverishly, although it had no need of them to brutalize itself.

Were these scourges at least compensated by notable advantages?

In truth, the revelation of very useful prodigies reached our planet continually. People learned, for instance, how to manufacture cheaply an artificial flour better than that of wheat, and splendid fabrics produced by rapid methods that cost next to nothing, Diseases long reputed to be incurable were cured. In brief, every hour lengthened the interminable list of the benefits of astral wireless. But that downpour of miracles did not engender the enthusiasm that might have been imagined.

It is worthy of remark, in fact, that human beings, when they await a discovery, attach much more importance to it than when they enjoy it. Thus, flying through the air was the divine ambition of humans since their origin, but from the moment when aircraft began to traverse the atmosphere, children scarcely bothered to look up in order to gaze at them. It was the same for the marvelous presents of astral wireless. What people yearn to have before possessing it becomes almost indifferent once they have it at their disposal.

It is necessary to add that the majority of these inventions caused intolerable upheavals. People had not had time to adapt their tastes to one innovation when they were already being asked to renounce it and accept other changes. Every social organization was shaken without respite. In the blink of an eye, large groups of laborers became unnecessary, and chemists replaced them. Or, for armies of laborers, builders and weavers, a few technicians were substituted, who obtained the same results by directing ingenious machines.

Attempts were made to train redundant workers for new tasks, but that reeducation required time, and the instability of every profession, with incessant crises of unemployment, provoked a furious exasperation among those who experienced them. They gathered in meetings and formed menacing processions, which the police tried in vain to disperse. Bloody brawls followed, one after another.

And while revolt was rumbling on all sides, war suddenly broke out.

Two countries whose relations had already been delicate for some time, Japan and the United States, delivered themselves more than all the others to a vertiginous arms race. On indications that came directly from beyond the sky, they had constructed many dreadnoughts, torpedo-boats and submarines, of every kind and all dimensions.

One day, a Japanese fleet set forth for the Philippines in order to annex them, and American vessels hastened to find them. A gigantic and frightful naval battle had the Pacific as its theater, the name of which seemed a poignant irony. The incomparable equipment of which the adversaries made us proved its excellence only too well. In less than a quarter of a hour, the two armadas were annihilated.

Riddled like colanders by a hurricane of projectiles, the immense ships sank. Some of those vessels, hit by torpedoes of "the latest model," were reduced to impalpable debris.

In addition, the battle remained indecisive, for it had been equally fatal to both nations. The small numbers of vessels that were still afloat were so badly damaged that their crews could not even think of continuing the combat.

In that infernal encounter, the United States and Japan had just deployed, in order to destroy one another, all the magnificent qualities that they might have used in common for the good of humanity. When their rage had dissipated, the sailors of the two heroic peoples were suddenly seized by an immense respect for one another, and, adding the finest of virtues to those they had dilapidated so sadly, they rivaled one another in generosity in order to save without distinction of origin those shipwreck victims who could be rescued.

The news that spread through the world on the subject of that massacre and the scenes of devotion that followed it excited universal pity. That carnage was judged unanimously to be so stupid and so hideous that diplomatic steps were immediately attempted by the most important neutral nations to put an end to the war.

From that moment on a general conspiracy of minds was formed against astral wireless, held responsible for the slaughter. Moralists, in books, journalists, in their newspapers, politicians at the podium and the populace, in meetings, demanded its prohibition. Only a few scientists demanded its maintenance in the name of their studies—but governments began to wonder whether the interests of science ought to hold in check those of society entire. It seemed that from then on, astral wireless was threatened with an irrevocable suppression.

XVII. The Most Adorable Woman in the Universe

Let us return to Jacques Lagité.

One day, while he was seeking a wavelength in order to communicate with Gilniz, he chanced to perceive the speech of some inhabitants of Venus, and although he did not know them, they entered into conversation with him.

"How fortunate you are," they said to him, "to inhabit the Earth."

"Oh yes," said Jacques, "it's your mania on your planet to envy our lot. If you had any suspicion, however, of the chaos in which we're struggling..."

"It's not a matter of your chaos! You're more than compensated for all your miseries, since the Perfect lives among you."

"That story again! It's already been told to me by two of your compatriots. But the Englishwoman they designated to me under the title of the Perfect died in London, run over by a tram."

"We've never heard any mention of your Englishwoman; what we're attesting is that a daughter of your race surpasses in seduction all the women in the universe."

"Even yours?" said Jacques

"Naturally," replied the Venusian.

Damn, thought Jacques, *here's a new trail to follow in order to break the spell of Gilniz. Perhaps it's finally salvation...*

"You interest me greatly," he said "Tell me everything you know about this mortal woman nicknamed the Perfect, like the other that I couldn't succeed in meeting. In what does her charm consist? Is it in the regularity of her physiognomy, the just proportions of her body or the sovereign harmony of her attitudes?"

"She possesses all those merits," said the Venusian, "but they're the least of her attractions. Her ineffable grace comes, above all, from her heart. Can you imagine a feminine face in which a painter of genius wanted to symbolize the joy of devoting oneself until death to a beloved individual? That's precisely the supernatural light that the Perfect radiates."

"Truly," said Jacques, "you're giving me an extreme desire to seek out this marvel."

"We'll guide you with pleasure," said the Venusian, "although it will be quite difficult. The Perfect is in fact, very mysterious, and has never revealed her name."

Just like the other one, thought Lagité.

"Certain indications," the inhabitant of Venus continued, "lead us to believe that at the moment, she's residing in the south of France."

While describing the landscape in which she was habitually framed he mentioned a large ruined bridge of several stages of arcades.

"Undoubtedly the Pont du Gard!" exclaimed Jacques. And by the details that his informer added, he recognized the Roman aqueduct with certainty.

Immediately making the decision to undertake the journey, he went to beg Barnabé Letord to accompany him. The professor consented to that; and the following day, they arrived at the Pont du Gard by auto.

Jacques was equipped with a portable wireless apparatus.

"What road is it necessary to follow?" he asked the inhabitants of Venus.

"The one that runs alongside the river, upstream of the bridge, on the right bank."

Letord and Lagité took that road, and a few minutes later, they interrogated their correspondents again.

"Are we on the right track?" asked Jacques.

"You're getting warmer," said the Venusian. "A short distance away, there's a small rustic manor. That's where it's necessary to go."

The two friends stopped at the gate of the Château de Saint-Privas.[61]

"Is it really here that we're going to discover the Perfect?" Jacques asked Venus.

"Yes, you're getting hotter and hotter."

Lagité rang the bell. A maidservant appeared.

"Will you please tell your mistress that the great scientist Barnabé Letord and the journalist Jacques Lagité, passing by the Pont du Gard, would be glad to be admitted to visit the château?" said Jacques.

The maidservant let them into the courtyard, where they sat down on a garden bench. And almost immediately, Jacques perceived Viviane before him, very blonde, gilded by the sun, refreshed by the pure air, quivering with the joy of seeing him again.

"Ah! Jacques, it's really you!"

He could not repress his surprise He was merely careful to translate it with the rudeness that he had testified when he had rediscovered his wife for the first time in Paris. He kissed her coldly, out of simple courtesy.

"Have you been here for a long time?" he asked her.

"About a month. Friends who own this dwelling were kind enough to put it at my disposal for a few weeks."

"Is there no one else with you?"

"At the moment, I'm alone with my domestic."

Then Jacques communicated with the planet Venus again.

"You assured me," he said, "that the Perfect lived in this château."

"Well, yes," said the inhabitant of Venus, "since she's standing in front of you."

"What!" said Jacques. "The woman that is before me..."

"...Is the Adorable, the Unique, the Perfect. Were we wrong to designate her to you as the sum total of all seductions? Oh, the divine woman! We can't weary of contemplating her. What an incredible happiness we experience merely in being able to gaze at her celestial features on the screen! Have you ever seen a woman more exquisite? Anyway, you can confirm our judgment yourself, for as soon as you were in her presence, you embraced her invincibly."

"But she's my wife, imbecile that you are!"

"Oh, that's not very polite!" said the Venusian.

Jacques cut the communication.

Professor Letord covered his lips with his hand in order not to burst out laughing.

Viviane, who had understood, did not allow her thoughts to show.

---

[61] The author has altered the spelling slightly of the Château de Saint-Privat, two kilometers upstream from the Pont du Gard, which was in private hands when the story was written but is now on the official list of historic monuments and open to the public.

At that moment a peremptory voice was heard. It came from an apparatus situated in a room whose widow was open:

"Users of astral wireless are required to obey the following summons, by order of all the governments of Earth, interpreting the will of all peoples. By reason of the innumerable scourges provoked by astral wireless, all apparatus consecrated to that means of correspondence is to be destroyed within two days. Contravention of this proscription will incur a penalty consisting of an imprisonment of one year and a fine of ten thousand francs."

"Lord God!" said Jacques, looking at Letord. "That's your invention condemned without appeal."

"I've been expecting it," said the professor. "And the recent calamities that have been unleashed justify the measure all too well. I have no recriminations, therefore."

In spite of her intention to dissimulate her malicious joy, Viviane allowed it to burst forth in the tone of her voice, her bright gaze and the gracious impetus of her gestures as she proposed to the two friends a walk along the banks of the Gardon. They would have all the requisite leisure that evening or the next day to visit the property.

XVIII. A Dialogue in the Socratic Manner on Amour and Happiness

The weather was adorably autumnal.

Under the somber vault of foliage, the crystalline cascades of the river bounded with noisy delight. The strollers, intoxicated by the purity of the air, had the impression of gliding through space rather than walking.

A troop of grape-pickers—a *colle*, to use the regional expression—went past singing a song in the Provençal language greeting the autumn and the grape harvest, and looking forward to drinking the produce. Long carts were transporting the barrels full of opulent grapes, which trembled heavily at every jolt of the wheels.

Viviane took Jacques and Letord to a group of noble plane-trees that shade the Gardon a few hundred meters beyond the Roman bridge. They sat down on the bank.

At that spot, sand forms a golden carpet under the shallow river, and allows its resplendent blondeness to emerge into the sunlight in places. The water, which launches a thousand silver gleams, is so transparent that all the polished shiny pebbles on its bed can be distinguished. The various streams of the Gardon seem to be separating playfully in order to reunite again. Sometimes they hasten in a narrow passage and hollow out a well in which the swirling current takes on topaz hues. Sometimes they spread out lazily and no longer seem to want to leave such an enchanting landscape.

Fishermen were hauling out nets in which numerous carp were wriggling. Naked children were getting muddy joyfully, heaping through the waves.

Viviane said that it made her want to walk barefoot over the sand. And, taking off her shoes and stockings, she amused herself like a little girl refreshing her legs.

Her two companions amused themselves in joining her, rolling to their trousers to their thighs. They laughed when they chanced to slip on a flat stone and the water wet their garments—and Viviane rejoiced in having rejuvenated those masculine souls so laden with cares.

They came back to lie down under the great trees.

Jacques considered Viviane and thought: *So it's her that the inhabitants of Venus judge to be the most seductive of women, the one they name the Perfect. It's true that she's very pretty, in fact; and if it were impossible for me to possess her, how I'd adore her myself!*

Then, looking at the scenery, he admired the bell-tower of a distant village. He remarked on the vaporous blue color of the village.

"My dear friend," said Barnabé Letord, "that shade is indeed delightful. But you never change. It's always necessary for you to turn your gaze toward the horizon. It's that alone that attracts and delights you. However, that azure village, if we went there, would seem much less beautiful to you than the place where we are."

Jacques stated laughing.

"For myself," Letord went on, "I can't imagine that we could find a more vivid pleasure anywhere than here. I could believe myself transported into the famous landscape by Nicolas Poussin in which shepherds are gathered around a tomb, deciphering the inscription that summarizes all terrestrial joy: *Et in Arcadia ego.*"[62]

"I understand the lesson," said Jacques. "You're criticizing me for never collecting the happiness that is offered to me. But how can I? My fantasy always seeks superior joys further on."

"Well," said Letord, "if you've never encountered happiness, it's precisely because you've always looked for it too far away."

"Bah!"

"Well, yes. You've pursued it all the way to the moon and the stars."

"Alas!" Jacques murmured.

"To tell the truth," said Letord, "your misadventure is that of the majority of men. One could believe that they set out expressly to be unhappy, for they only ever desire what it's impossible for them to obtain. Take note that even if they realized their dreams, they wouldn't be happy. Every wish, as soon as it's

---

[62] The painting in question, one of two with the same subject, also known as *Les Bergers d'Arcadie* (1637-38) has become much more famous since the present story was written, because of its association with modern myths of Templar treasure and the Holy Grail. The significance of the epitaph [roughly, I also exist in Arcadia] has been much debated.

granted, loses the prestige that caused it to be confused with happiness, and it's replaced by others, even more painful and torturing."

"Oh, how right you are!" said Lagité. "But what can one do, then? What can one do to be happy?"

"Love," said Letord.

"Yes, that's your anthem," said Lagité, laughing. "Love! But you, my dear professor, who talk so well, what are your amours?"

"Science!" said Letord, proudly. "I love her with a fervent amour. It's the passion that counts. I also love my fellows, and for them, I would gladly give my life."

"I know that," said Jacques, suddenly becoming serious again. "It doesn't alter the fact that you did them a bad turn by offering them astral wireless."

"Oh, my friend," said Letord, "every discovery is very good or very bad, depending on whether it is employed for good or for evil. If humans have made poor use of my invention, I can't do anything about it!"

Lagité shook his hand silently.

With new force, Letord affirmed: "It's necessary to love."

"So be it!" said Jacques. "But what proof is there that amour procures happiness?"

"It is happiness itself. Amour—by which I mean disinterested amour, that of true lovers in whom all egotism is abolished, the amour of the scientist and the thinker for their mission, the amour of the humblest mortal for his quotidian task, draws its intoxication from its own ardor. And all of life is only made to furnish us with pretexts for loving! Our destiny has no other meaning.

"If we ought to labor relentlessly for our brethren, if we ought to aid them incessantly, to render their existence less harsh, if we ought to struggle against their suffering, relieve and suppress it, it's in order to show them our love. And from that we extract immediately an immense happiness, because amour, once again, experiences all its joy in giving itself.

"What does it matter, then, if we fall into the grave one after another? What does it matter that nations pass, that our very planet is condemned to perish? At every moment, humans are free to love and to be infinitely happy. At every moment they are free to enjoy a sublime melody in the concert directed by Amour. You know full well, my friend, that good musicians, when playing a beautiful symphony, put all their artistic sensuality into every note that they cause to vibrate. In the same way, in life, when it is Amour that orchestrates its chords, every minute is immediately filled with a limitless felicity.

"But I'm losing myself in the clouds. I'm only talking about devotion to science and love of humanity. I'm forgetting that I have a listener who certainly represents amour under a less solemn and more tender aspect."

"Well, my dear Monsieur," said Viviane, ever jovial, "evoke for us now the pleasures of lovers."

"You're making fun of me," said Letord. "That isn't the affair of an old professor. However, I accept the challenge. These benevolent trees and this merry water are listening to me favorably, as the plane-tree of the Ilissus inspired the words of Socrates and young Phaedrus. Or rather, it's you, my dear Madame, who are going to instruct us, for I want to interrogate you. Isn't it true that people name amour sentiments very different from one another, and even opposite?"

"Oh, certainly," said Viviane. "There are vile and filthy amours, and others that are celestially blue."[63]

"Isn't it true that amour shouldn't be confused with desire?"

"You're going to make me blush. Desire, naturally, accompanies veritable amour, but amour doesn't always accompany desire, which is often—how shall I put it—that of a bitch on heat."

"Isn't it true that, without amour, physical desire is incapable of procuring happiness?"

"I don't know," said Viviane.

"I can guarantee it," said Letord, "and I'll tell you why. It's because desire occupies the entire soul, which is infinite, violently, and the satisfactions that it seeks are always finite; they are, therefore, only ever a very small contentment for insatiable demands."

"That seems just," said Viviane.

"Veritable amour, on the contrary, already finding all its happiness in itself, enjoys an infinite plenitude."

"I'm sure of it," said Viviane, ardently.

Letord darted a sideways glance at Jacques, whose gaze was following the fleeting water, and he concluded: "The happiness that so many of us seek so far away is very close to us. It's within us. In order to discover it, we have only to love the beings who need our love."

"It's beautiful, what you say," murmured Viviane.

"My dear Madame," said Letord, "it's even more beautiful to feel it. And what is entirely admirable, what is sublime, is the heart of a noble woman who continues to devote herself in secret when she is repaid with ingratitude and neglect."

Viviane stiffened momentarily. Suddenly, she hid her face in her hands and burst into tears.

And Lagité, leaping toward her, clasped her in his arms. He was weeping too. He hugged her, and gave her endless kisses.

"Excuse my rambling," said Barnabé Letord, flippantly.

---

[63] Socrates makes this argument in the *Phaedrus*, but Letord, in setting out to elicit it from Viviane, understandably leaves out other aspects of the Platonic dialogue, including its homosexuality and the fact that Socrates characterizes love as a species of madness.

Through her tears, Viviane addressed a smile of gratitude to him.

They stood up.

It was now evening. Passing over the river again on the monumental bridge, the eternal witness of so many ephemeral existences, they took the road of return. And as the air was cool, Viviane took off her scarf, involuntarily, to cover Jacques' shoulders.

Lagité remembered the frozen planet where the last woman had made the same loving gesture in favor of the last man.

Barnabé Letord preceded the lovers, and repeated in a cracked voice a line from the grape-pickers song: "Cut the grape, and have a good time!"

They went back inside.

Jacques, a disciplined citizen, smashed his astral wireless apparatus.

"It is, however," he cried, "the instrument that enabled me to discover the Perfect." And he underlined those words by giving Viviane further kisses.

Maurice Renard: *On The Planet Mars*
(1939)

*Fantasies of alien interaction of the "inverted" kind popularized by The
War of the Worlds—in which the aliens come to us rather than our going to
them—took a great leap forward in France when the most outspoken propagan-
dist for a new literature of the* merveilleux scientifique, *Maurice Renard (1875-
1939) produced the novel that can be regarded as his masterpiece, and as one of
the classics of that genre,* Le Péril bleu *(1911).*

*Renard's conception of the nascent genre, of which he nominated Wells as
the central exemplar and J.-H. Rosny* Aîné *the principal domestic practitioner,
was inherently various and wide-ranging, to a much greater extent than the
Vernian fiction with which he contrasted it in his 1909 "manifesto" for the genre,* Du Roman merveilleux-scientifique et de son action sur l'intelligence du
progrès. *The straightforwardly melodramatic twists of Renard's stories are en-
gineered with appropriate flamboyance, allowing them to work at the same
"middlebrow" level as Wells' classic scientific romances, an obvious cut above
the downmarket works of Jean de La Hire, and Gustave Le Rouge. In terms of
winning a large audience for the genre it exemplified, however, Renard's works
were no more successful in the longer term than the others were, and like them,
he eventually found himself lacking the kind the encouragement that would have
enabled him to produce more work of a similar kind, let alone to attempt to su-
persede it within its presumed framework.*

*By 1925, the deeply disillusioned Renard had come to the conclusion that
"scientific marvel fiction" had no commercial future in the respectable sectors
of the French marketplace, and had abandoned his attempts to develop it, although he still had a few finished works which he reformulated in order to make
them saleable.* On the Planet Mars *was his last published story.*

B.S.

ON THE PLANET MARS

"Monsieur le Directeur," said the inhabitant of the planet Mars, manifesting a great agitation, "the Earth is inhabited! I'm now certain of it!"

"Really?" said the other Martian, with the utmost calm.

We are able to transcribe in these terms, for the usage of human brains, this
commencement of an extraterrestrial dialogue—but will the reader please accept

that the reality did not correspond in the slightest to the images that the preceding sentences will have suggested to him?

First of all, did this exchange of ideas produce any vibration of sound in the planet's atmosphere? No words had emerged from the mouths of the two Martians; they were conversing by means of silent waves of which we can give no better definition. Did they, in fact, possess mouths? One could not see any trace of them. To our human eyes, they presented themselves in the form of two lenses[64] about two meters in diameter, standing upright on the ground thanks to the temporary flattening of their bases. These lenses, of which one was reddish and the other bluish, were very thick and perfectly opaque in the middle, but that thickness decreased toward a periphery which, so to speak, did not exist, for the lentil was not delimited by a sharp and precise border; they faded gradually into space like a nebula.

Imagine two lenticular nuclei, variously colored, each fading away into a peripheral fog, and you will have an approximate idea of the two superior Martians in question. No faces, meaning no physiognomy; and if we have permitted ourselves to say that one of them manifested a great agitation, it is because that is what its color indicated, by way of an unaccustomed glare.

"Yes," it continued. "Inhabited! I haven't left my observation apparatus for several days, and I've clearly perceived intermittent lights that can only be signals produced by intelligent beings with an awareness of mathematics."

"You're young, my friend!" said the blue Martian, whose body took on a lovely moiré effect of green-tinted concentric ripples.

"I assure you, Monsieur le Directeur, that I'm not the victim of an optical illusion. This is a matter of *signals*, which are being sent from there *to us*, and to which we can reply without difficulty, given the advanced state of our Martian science."

"Ta ta ta!" said the director. "Chimeras and foolishness!"

His interlocutor's red tint suddenly paled, only to become, a moment later, deeper than before. "In spite of the respect I owe you," he said, "in spite of your age and your scientific knowledge, Maître, I cannot admit your skepticism and I stand my ground. I don't have the right. The question is more important than us—you as well as me. Just think! The plurality of inhabited worlds! The problem of communication between the people of the universe! Maître, we have brothers on the Earth—I can prove it to you. Are we to remain indifferent to their efforts, deaf to their appeals?"

As it expressed itself thus, the young Martian—who was undoubtedly some astronomer attached to an observatory—became increasingly animated,

---

[64] The original referent of the French term for a glass lens, *lentille,* is a lentil. Although it makes little difference merely as a specification of shape, the choice of translation is bound to have a considerable effect on the reader's conceptualization of the Martians, and the other possibility needs to be noted.

moving back and forth by rotating itself as if it were a wheel, which is the fashion in which such individuals progress.

"Do you think you're the first to discover that the Earth is inhabited?" the old Martian replied, softly.

"Pardon?" said the young one, nonplussed, suddenly ceasing to rotate.

"These lights have already been noticed by others. Others have drawn the necessary conclusions from those manifestations. Let me tell you, furthermore, that we did not have to wait for them to be produced to discover what you have just discovered. For many years, we have known that the Earth is inhabited by a great quantity of diverse creatures, one species of which has dominated the others for thousands of years by virtue of the power of the mind. That is humankind. It is, down there, what we are here. Certain instruments of observation, of a range that you cannot imagine, allow us to know with great precision what is happening on Earth."

"What do you mean? What instruments? Are they kept secret, then?"

"Oh yes. Only our elders, of which I am one, know the whole truth concerning the Earth. There is nothing we don't know about the mores of humankind and its history."

"Is it possible?" exclaimed the neophyte, utterly flabbergasted.

"You need, my young friend, to forget these signals that you've glimpsed. Swear to me that you will never mention them to anyone—for the Grand Council had decided that it will not reply, under any pretext, to Earth's solicitations."

"But why?" asked the other, desperately.

After a pause, the old Martian continued, in his mute language. "If you were a human on Earth, you would have some difficulty in believing that the inhabitants of our Mars are peaceful, and that they live wisely and quietly—for the Terrans have given our globe the name of their god of war, and they are convinced that we are bellicose. You will agree with me, however, that life is pleasant here and that nothing ever happens to trouble the harmony that reigns among us. Alas, my son, I cannot say as much for the Earth. Everything is certainly not perfect on Mars—but down there! If you only knew!"

"All the more reason, Maître, to communicate the benefits of our civilization to the Terrans!"

"Hmmm! It's just that, you see, the Grand Council decided otherwise—and it would be only prudent, my young friend, for you to conform to their decisions! Believe me, we have nothing to gain from commerce with humans, but everything to lose! Come on, let's repeat it together: the Earth is uninhabited!" Perceiving the hesitation that he had provoked, the blue Martian went on, paternally: "Give in. It's a matter of orders that one does not debate. We are no longer in the domain of science, but that of public safety. Humans equal danger! Danger! It's necessary that they don't exist, so far as we're concerned."

For a moment, the young Martian contemplated the Earth-star shining in the sky with a lovely blue light. And as he revered the wisdom of the elders, he said: "Very well. The Earth is uninhabited."

OTHER ANTHOLOGIES OF FRENCH SCIENCE FICTION
introduced & annotated by Brian STABLEFORD

The Aerial Valley: Five utopian fantasies by Jacques Fabien, Victor Hugo, Gustave Marx, Jean-Baptiste Mosneron de Launay and Turrault de Rochecorbon.

Automata: The Imaginative Legacy of Jacques de Vaucanson; Fourteen scientific romances by Charles Barbara, Jacques Boucher de Perthes, Frédéric Boutet, Didier de Chousy, Léon Daudet, Emile Goudeau, Arnold Mortier, Henri Ner, François-Félix Nogaret, Jean Rameau, Romain Rolland, Ralph Schropp, Marcel Schwob and Edmond Thiaudière.

The Bald Giants: Thirty-Nine scientific romances by Alfred Capus, Louis Champeaux, Gustave Geffroy, Edmond Haraucourt, Albert Keim, Pierre Mille, André Monselet, Maurice Montegut, Joseph Montet, René Morot, Maurice Renard, Gabriel Tarde, Louis Ulbach and Adrien Vély. (*forthcoming*)

The Conqueror of Death: Eight scientific romances by Alphonse Brown, Paul Combes, Camille Debans, Emile Gautier and Georges Price.

The Germans on Venus: Thirteen scientific romances by Alphonse Allais, Rémy de Gourmont, Jules Lermina, André Mas, Eugène Mouton, Louis Mullem, Charles Nodier, Nicolas-Esmé Restif de la Bretonne, Adrien Robert, X.B. Saintine, Marcel Schwob, Louis Ulbach and Théo Varlet.

The Humanisphere: Four utopian fantasies by Paul Adam, Victor Considérant, Joseph Déjacque and Fernand Giraudeau.

The Incredible Adventure: Three interstellar excursions by Louis ForestPaul Gsell and François Léonard.

Investigations of the Future: Seven scientific romances by Pierre-Simon Ballanche, Victor Fournel, Alfred Franklin, Théophile Gautier, Arsène Houssaye, Jean Jullien and Maurice Spronck.

Journey to the Isles of Atlantis: Seven scientific romances by Pierre Billaume, Félix Bodin, Gaston Derys, Pierre Grasset, Gustave Guitton, Pierre Hégine, Julie Lavergne and Louis Lemercier de Neuville.

The Man With the Blue Face: Eight scientific romances by Alfred Assolant, Camille Debans, Arnould Galopin, Charles Guyon, Ernest d'Hervilly, E.M. Laumann, Bernard Lazare and Gaston de Pawlowski.

The Mirror of Present Events: Ten scientific romances by Georges de La Fouchardière, Henri Lanos, E.M. Laumann, François-Félix Nogaret, Jean Rameau and Régis Vombal.

Nemoville: Twelve scientific romances by G. Bethuys, Alfred Bonnardot, Alphonse Brown, Emma-Adele Lacerte, Claude Manceau, René du Mesnil de Maricourt, Pierre Mille,José Mosellli, C. Paulon and Emerich de Vattel.

The New Moon: Four fantastic voyages by Henri Delmotte, Alexis-Jean Le Bret and Edmé Rousseau.

News from the Moon: Nine scientific romances by Georges Eekhoud, Stéphane Mallarmé, Guy de Maupassant, Louis-Sébastien Mercier, Eugène Mouton, Fernand Noat, Jean Richepin, Adrien Robert and Albert Robida.

The Nickel Man: Eleven scientific romances by Jacques Boucher de Perthes, Pierre Bremond, Léon Daudet, Georges Espitallier, Louis Gallet, Pierre de Nolhac and Ralph Schropp.

On the Brink of the World's End: Seven scientific romances by Raoul Bigot, Jacques-Antoine Dulaure, Charles Epheyre, Jules Hoche, Joseph Méry and Colonel Royet.

The Revolt of the Machines: Eight scientific romances by Michel Epuy, Emile Goudeau, X. Nagrien, Gaston de Pawlowski, Jules Perrin, Edouard Rod, Jules Sageret and Louis Valona.

The Supreme Progress: Eighteen scientific romances by Paul Adam, Charles Cros, Charles Epheyre, Eugène Mouton, Louis Mullem, X.B. Saintine and Victorien Sardou.

The World Above the World: Nine scientific romances by S. Henry Berthoud, Michel Corday, Alphonse Daudet, Camille Flammarion, Henri Lanos, André Mas, Jules Perrin, René de Pont-Jest and Charles Recolin.